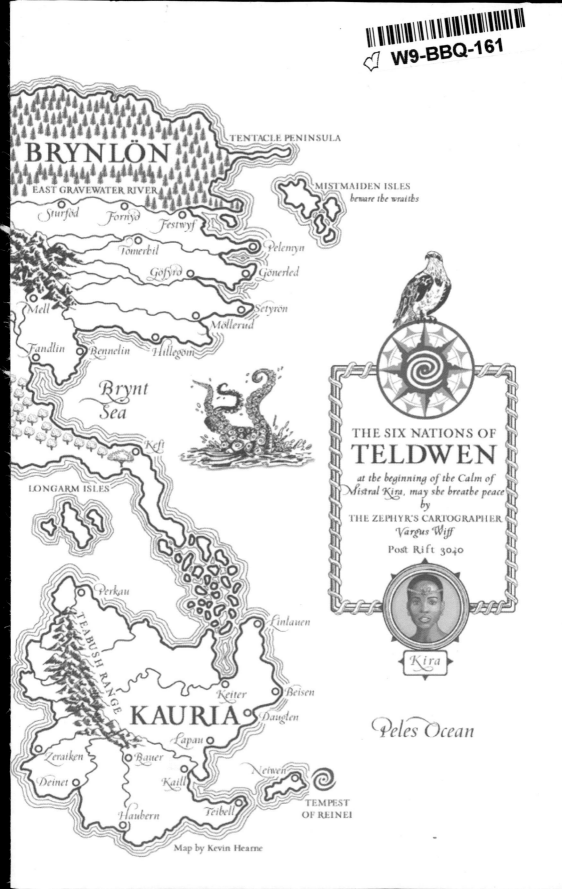

BRYNLÖN

TENTACLE PENINSULA

EAST GRAVEWATER RIVER

MISTMAIDEN ISLES
beware the wraiths

Sturföd Fornyd
Festwyf

Tomerhil Pelemyn

Göfyrd Gönerled

Mell Setyrön

Möllerud

Fandlin Bennelin Hillegöm

Brynt
Sea

Keft

LONGARM ISLES

THE SIX NATIONS OF

TELDWEN

at the beginning of the Calm of
Mistral Kira, may she breathe peace
by
THE ZEPHYR'S CARTOGRAPHER
Vargus Wiff

Post Rift 3040

Kira

Perkau

TEABUSH RANGE

Linlauen

Keiter Beisen

Dauglen

KAURIA

Lapau

Zeraiken Bauer

Deinet Kaill

Neiwen

Teibell

Haubern

Peles Ocean

TEMPEST
OF REINEI

Map by Kevin Hearne

BY KEVIN HEARNE

THE SEVEN KENNINGS

A Plague of Giants

A Blight of Blackwings

THE IRON DRUID CHRONICLES

Hounded

Hexed

Hammered

Tricked

Trapped

Hunted

Shattered

Staked

Besieged

Scourged

THE IRON DRUID CHRONICLES NOVELLAS

Two Ravens and One Crow

Grimoire of the Lamb

A Prelude to War

OBERON'S MEATY MYSTERIES

The Purloined Poodle

The Squirrel on the Train

The Buzz Kill (in the anthology Death & Honey)

A BLIGHT OF BLACKWINGS

A BLIGHT OF BLACKWINGS

BOOK TWO OF THE SEVEN KENNINGS

KEVIN HEARNE

DEL REY

NEW YORK

Published in the United States by Del Rey, an imprint of Random House, a division of Penguin Random House LLC, New York.

DEL REY and the HOUSE colophon are registered trademarks of Penguin Random House LLC.

Endpaper map drawn by the author

LIBRARY OF CONGRESS CATALOGING-IN-PUBLICATION DATA
Names: Hearne, Kevin, author.
Title: A blight of blackwings / Kevin Hearne.
Description: First Edition. | New York : Del Rey, [2020] | Series: The seven kennings ; 2 |
Sequel to: A Plague of Giants.
Identifiers: LCCN 2019038082 (print) | LCCN 2019038083 (ebook) |
ISBN 9780345548573 (hardcover) | ISBN 9780345548580 (ebook)
Subjects: GSAFD: Fantasy fiction.
Classification: LCC PS3608.E264 B65 2020 (print) | LCC PS3608.E264 (ebook) |
DDC 813/.6—dc23
LC record available at https://lccn.loc.gov/2019038082
LC ebook record available at https://lccn.loc.gov/2019038083

Printed in the United States of America on acid-free paper

randomhousebooks.com

2 4 6 8 9 7 5 3 1

First Edition

Book design by Caroline Cunningham

For bards and storytellers and people

who dream of a better world

Dramatis Personae

FINTAN, BARD OF THE POET GODDESS KAELIN: Raelech bard assigned to perform daily for the people of Pelemyn, telling the story of the Giants' War.

DERVAN DU ALÖBAR: Brynt historian tasked to write down the Raelech bard's tale, but increasingly drawn into spycraft against his will.

OLET KANEK: Daughter of Hathrim hearthfire Winthir Kanek and determined to live a life outside of his rule. A firelord of the First Kenning.

ABHINAVA KHOSE: The first person to discover the Sixth Kenning, on the run from the Nentian government with his animal companions, Murr and Eep.

TALLYND DU BÖLL: Brynt tidal mariner and second könstad of Pelemyn. Widowed mother of two boys.

HANIMA BHANDURY: Known as the Hivemistress, she is one of the blessed Nentian children leading the resistance in Khul Bashab.

KOESHA GANSU: Joabeian captain of an exploratory vessel searching for a passage through the Northern Yawn— and also for her missing sister.

MAI BET KEN: Fornish ambassador to Ghurana Nent, assigned to Melishev Lohmet. Seeks to ally Forn with the blessed of the Sixth Kenning.

BHAMET SENESH: Viceroy of Khul Bashab, determined to stamp out the threat to monarchist rule that the Sixth Kenning represents.

TUALA, COURIER OF THE HUNTRESS RAENA: Raelech courier who lives an ascetic life and pines for a childhood love.

GONDEL VEDD: Kaurian scholar of languages. Married, fond of mustard and Mugg's Chowder House.

DARYCK DU LÖNGREN: Brynt gerstad of a mercenary ranger corps employed by the city of Grynek, and later, Fornyd.

A BLIGHT OF BLACKWINGS

Day 20

THE HEARTHFIRE'S FURY

Few revelations light up a gathering more than the intelligence that there's a traitor somewhere nearby. The tension sparks and pops like fresh pine logs in the hearth. If extra fuel for the fire is needed, just make it clear that said traitor is most likely responsible for the deaths of the friends and family of the gathered. Chances of enjoying a quiet evening after that are close to zero.

The Raelech bard's assertion that a traitor had worked with the Bone Giants hit the crowd like a pat of butter thrown in the skillet, sizzling and steaming and spreading angrily. It was not just the shock of betrayal that got people talking but a matter of wrestling with the timeline. We were now in the month of Thaw and he'd been speaking of events that occurred late in the previous summer, so that meant the pelenaut had known about this traitor for at least half a year.

"Wait," a mariner nearby us on the wall said. "Who's this Vjeko, then? You've found him already, right? Or you wouldn't have said anything. The pelenaut let you say that because he's already got him."

"More tomorrow, friends," Fintan called out to Survivor Field, his kenning allowing his voice to be heard far out into the peninsula and all through the city of Pelemyn. Then he stepped down from his stage and headed for the stairs descending into the city, rumbles of protest trailing him.

"Come on, Dervan," he said, waving at me to follow. "I need a word."

"You might want to slow up," I replied. "My knee won't get me down those stairs that quickly."

"Oh, right. Sorry. We should try to hurry, though."

"Because everyone wants some answers from you?"

"Yes. And I don't have them."

I hobbled gingerly down the stairs behind him, putting weight on my cane, and considered what that meant. He must have been told by someone to include mention of Vjeko in Gondel's latest story. Most likely Föstyr, the pelenaut's lung, had relayed information from Röllend himself. In the streets, Fintan smiled at everyone who asked him about the traitor and he kept moving, saying only, "Tomorrow," and I grew certain that he knew nothing at all about this. Which meant the traitor wasn't caught yet. Revealing his existence was intended to flush him out, despite the unrest it would cause.

"You mentioned me in your tale today," I said.

"Glad you caught that."

"No one ever asked me about this Krakens' Nest, or Nest of Man-Eaters, or anything like it."

"There was no need. That part of the story, at least, I already know, and I'll be sharing it in coming days. But I was told to mention it now on purpose."

"Why?"

"I'm sure you can guess. You're part of the puzzle somehow. Just like everyone else, I'm being given pieces and fitting them together with some pieces I already have."

"But you have many more pieces than I do," I said, to which he shrugged.

"Maybe."

Fintan led us to Master Yöndyr's establishment, the Siren's Call, where a single mariner assigned to him provided protection and a modicum of privacy. There was little to fear from Nentian assassins anymore since the expulsion of Ambassador Jasindur Torghala, but in such a busy place we did need someone to fend off those who just wanted a "quick word" with the bard. It was not uncommon for him to be recognized now, and a truly quick greeting was always welcome, but Master Yöndyr made a point of telling everyone in his pub that Fintan was there, and he served us himself—honored guests indeed— so we were watched and drinks were bought for us and I began to wonder if we should not have tried to find someplace quieter.

"How's Numa?" I asked him once we had giant schooners of Mist-maiden Ale placed before us. Fintan's lifebond, a courier for the Triune Council of Rael, had arrived only the day before.

"Running back home as we speak," he said. "Our time together was too short, but she's well, and I'm happier for seeing her."

I made a noise of approval as I drank from my monstrous vessel. It may have echoed a tiny bit.

"We could practically drown in these things," Fintan observed, and grabbed his with both hands. "I am fairly certain this container is larger than a human stomach."

"It is the most agreeable of challenges," I said, smacking my lips.

The bard's voice bounced off the interior of his schooner as he raised it to his mouth. "Yes, it is." When he put it down with satisfaction, he flashed a grin that was partially obscured from view by his large nose, but then a thought chased it away. "I have a different challenge that may not be so agreeable now, but I might as well get it out of the way before Master Yöndyr brings over something to eat."

"Oh, yes, you said you needed a word."

He nodded and sighed. "I have a strange, vague message to deliver specifically to you, via Numa, from the Triune Council."

"The Triune knows of my existence?"

Fintan chuckled. "Yes, they heard about this project of ours almost immediately—Numa let them know about it weeks ago, after leaving me here. They don't know anything about the Nentian attempts on my life yet, I don't think, but they have the idea that you have the ear of the pelenaut and represent a different channel, I guess, than the customary diplomatic ones."

I snorted. "The customary channel is to have Numa talk to the pelenaut directly. Your couriers can speak to Rölly whenever they arrive. Involving me makes no sense. That's adding a middleman."

The Raelech bard spread his palms in a gesture of surrender. "I understand, believe me. But there's a feeling that this message might be better heard by someone besides the pelenaut—his lung, perhaps, or someone else you may know of—and they want to leave it up to you to decide."

Blinking and shrugging, I said, "Okay."

"This is going to be word for word from the mouth of Clodagh, recorded by Numa and then by me."

"So . . . not the Triune Council, then, but a single member of it," I said, mentally preparing myself. Fintan nodded once.

"Message reads: 'Someone in the employ of the Brynt government has stolen a personal item from me. Do not attempt to deny it: I know that you have it. If this item is used against me or Rael, there will be terrible consequences.'"

And there it was. She knew we had taken her journal, knew it compromised her, and threw in a threat to forestall acting on the information inside. Fintan had even hinted that they knew the Wraith existed, or some shadowy spymaster figure like him, and this message was clearly intended for him rather than for Pelenaut Röllend. And by delivering it to me she implied that she knew, or at least suspected, that I had some kind of connection to the Wraith. But I had to act as if I knew nothing about it. "That's all? What personal item?"

Fintan shrugged helplessly. "I don't know. I only have that message."

"Does she want this item returned, or an official investigation, or reparations, or what?"

"I don't know that either."

"So I'm just supposed to walk up to the pelenaut and accuse him of stealing whatever it is and warn him against using it? You're giving me week-old fish guts, Fintan, and telling me to make them smell like fresh flowers. That's not my job. You can forget it."

"Fair enough," he said with a nod, and then held up his hands again. "You'll get no argument from me. I've delivered the message and was told I could leave it entirely to your discretion, so it's done. We can forget it like you said and enjoy whatever Master Yöndyr is bringing over." His eyes flicked toward the kitchen, and I followed his gaze to find a jolly proprietor heading our way, carrying a tray laden with meats and cheeses. That he still had any when the city was suffering shortages was impressive.

"Fine," I said before Master Yöndyr arrived, "but please let the Triune know the next time you can that I am not a channel of any sort. I'm an old soldier with a bad knee who writes down histories. They should talk to the lung or to our diplomats or whoever, and just leave me out of everything."

"I will," he said, and then beamed as our food arrived. It was excellent fare and gave me time to think about what to do. The Wraith needed to be informed, but apparently I was being watched by someone who didn't mind reporting my movements to Rael. Should I inform Rölly too—or instead? Did my old friend even know about the theft or the fact that Clodagh had ordered my wife's death? I wasn't sure the Wraith told him everything, and he might be quite surprised and annoyed to find out all this had been done without his knowledge or consent, though Mynstad du Möcher *had* said Gerstad du Fesset had been sent by the pelenaut to Rael on a special mission. That meant Rölly knew about the journal, at least, if not its full contents.

The entire exercise may have been designed to see where I would run first. I hated this game—worrying about what to do, who was watching me, and letting it ruin the joy of the moment. Abruptly I remembered that I wasn't required to play the game and had in fact told Fintan in so many words that I wouldn't. Simply forgetting about it seemed the best option and brightened my attitude considerably, since it would require almost no effort. Taking a large draught from the giant schooner of ale might even help the process along, so I grasped it with both hands and tipped it back, guzzling it until I could drink no more. The long, loud belch that followed shortly afterward was the sum total of effort I would put into doing Clodagh's bidding, and it also drew a round of wry applause from the pub.

When I stumbled drunk into my home hours later, trying not to wake Elynea and her kids, I thought something felt off but didn't want to investigate and try to light candles with such degraded motor skills. I'd wind up burning down my house. So I crashed into my bed, woke up with a hangover on what was to be the twentieth day of the bard's tales, and discovered what had felt off.

The house was empty. Elynea had once again moved out and left me a note on top of a gift basket of assorted marmalades, my favorite.

> *Dear Dervan,*
>
> *With Bel Tes Wey's help, we have found accommodation near the furniture workshop—a place for just the three of us— and won't need to trouble you for hospitality anymore. You have been the kindest and most generous of hosts.*
>
> *Thank you always,*
>
> *Elynea*

I checked their bedroom. The bed was made, all their belongings absent. Well. Good for them. That was the best possible news.

But I was alone again.

It was a rare morning of late in that no one disturbed me during the making of my toast and tea, but I didn't feel the sense of victory that should have accompanied it. It sounded like my chewing echoed off the walls of my empty house. Since I couldn't do much to help myself feel any better, I spent some time chatting with Dame du Marröd across the street and helping her get her spring garden planted, before it was time to meet Fintan and get the day's writing done. He was bleary-eyed like me, recovering from last night's carousing, and had little to say apart from an inquiry.

"I don't suppose anyone's told you how I'm supposed to answer the inevitable questions I'm going to receive about the traitor? Something I'm supposed to work into today's tale?"

"No, I've not been told anything. You don't know already?"

"No, they gave me the information about Gondel Vedd but neglected to tell me what happened next."

"That's odd."

"It's fine for now. I have plenty of other tales to tell in the meantime."

We kept working and guzzling tea and felt restored by the end of the session.

"I think I used to recover faster from nights like that when I was younger," Fintan said.

"You and me both."

The massive sea of humanity on Survivor Field churned and seemed especially excited for the bard's tale to begin. I worried a little that they might be upset about him shouting "Traitor!" and then never pointing the finger at anyone. But faces turned and voices quieted when he strummed his harp, and his voice was carried throughout the city and the peninsula, thanks to his kenning.

"Hello, fine people of Pelemyn," Fintan said. "Today I'm going to play for you a Hathrim smoke song. The people of the First Kenning assign a lot of meaning to smoke, as you might imagine, and though smoke can take many forms, the songs are very structured and were invented long ago, shortly after the discovery of the Fifth Kenning, so there are five lines to a traditional smoke song, and they are often meditative." Fintan began to pluck at his harp with a series of rolling notes that swelled and then fell again until they steadied into a gentle rhythm. "Some of the Hathrim are more meditative in the practice of their faith than others. People often assume sometimes that the nature of fire is to destroy a thing, but look deeper and it is really fire's nature to change a thing, whether by forging or baking or glassmaking or what have you. We are going to hear of some destruction in today's tales, but I would not want anyone to assume that the work of some individuals is the nature of their people or their faith. In fact, I would like to share with you all that I greatly admire and esteem Hollit and Orden Panevik, a couple of wonderful people over eleven feet tall who live and work here in Pelemyn. They own and operate a restaurant down by the docks called the Roasted Sunchuck. Hollit is the chef and Orden is a master mixologist behind the bar, and they've been here for many years. They love Brynlön. And I love Hollit's bladefin steaks." He paused for polite laughter. "I need to try the sunchuck next. I hear it's very good. Anyway, this is for you, and for my friends Hollit and Orden."

He sang just one line at a time, and in between there were extended musical breaks that bridged into another key, scaling up to the third line, and then back down to the original key for the last line.

> *One Puff: I feel in my core the need to stop and ponder.*
> *Two Draws: I am beset by problems I am helpless to solve as I am.*
> *Three Drags: To be well again I must change, yet change is painful.*
> *Four Breaths: To remain the same is also painful, so I welcome*
>   *change.*
> *Five Pulls: May this fire transform me and light my way to a better*
>   *future.*

After the customary break he gave everyone to get seated, he pulled out one of his black seeming spheres—his supply replenished by Numa's visit—and grinned at Survivor Field.

"I have a new story to begin with you today. There will be more regarding the traitor Vjeko, never fear. The pelenaut will have much to share. But it is not yet the time."

That earned a dismayed response from more than one throat, including mine, but Fintan pressed on.

"We met our new narrator earlier on the periphery of events, and you just heard of her surrender to the Nentians at the Godsteeth, but now she will get to speak to you in her own words. Friends, I give you Olet Kanek."

He threw down his fragile egg of a stone, and when it shattered, the gas billowed up, covered him, and then revealed a much taller new form. Olet Kanek was eleven feet tall or more and armored, save a helmet. Her red hair spilled free about her head and rested on her steel shoulders. I thought her simultaneously attractive and fearsome, for she clearly knew how to use the weapon sheathed at her side. Her lips were drawn down in worry, or perhaps it was just solemnity.

let

I sparked up a bowl of leaves and inhaled, the gases searing the lining of my throat, a fiery salve for my scorched heart. The gulls and black-wings circling overhead keened with hunger, the slosh and slap of the tide against the hull an unsteady rhythm to their arias, but I focused on breathing in and then breathing out a plume of smoke, willing not just the toxins but poisonous thoughts to exit my body.

My plume met and mixed with one from the mouth of La Mastik, priestess of the Flame, who had sparked her own pipe. We were the last two lavaborn among the Hathrim who had escaped the eruption of Mount Thayil, and we had much to burn away and transform in the purity of fire. We also needed to forge new steel in our minds for the trials ahead, and fire was necessary for that. La Mastik was thinking much the same, and she gave voice to it, eyelids half closed and her voice a reverent prayer.

"May our lungs ever prove the bellows to forging new fires, new paths, and new creations," she intoned.

"May our purpose burn pure and blue," I responded, in tandem with those who watched us.

Her eyes snapped fully open and locked on mine, held them as we drew deeply on our pipes. This was going to hurt, but it needed to be done. The other passengers on the boat listened raptly, on their knees, hands clasped in front of them. In the ritual of a funeral smoke, there is comfort, even if it is only witnessed rather than performed: It is a drape of order over a whirlpool of chaos, a refuge from wind and water. We all needed it now. The customary rites for the dead could not be observed in this case, and we needed to resort to this secondary ceremony as we sailed north to Talala Fouz, the capital of Ghurana Nent.

"Thurik witness our love and respect for those who fell at Baghra Khek," La Mastik said. "Their memories will burn in our minds until we ourselves are ashes."

I have always appreciated that sentiment. It is good for the lavaborn to be reminded that we are not invincible. It is true that Gorin Mogen inflicted terrible casualties all by himself, but he was ultimately defeated by a Fornish greensleeve. Their bantil plants destroyed some houndsmen, and their spore pods slew more that inhaled too deeply; thornhands removed the spines and organs of many who ventured outside the walls. But the bulk of the other lavaborn were trampled by a stampede of kherns that were supposedly summoned by a Nentian boy who'd found the Sixth Kenning.

We learned that the Fifth and Sixth Kennings were more than a match for the First, and should they continue to work in tandem, the world will change.

That was hot popping logs to me: I had wanted it to change for a long time anyway.

"The Mogens," I began after exhaling a new puff of smoke. "Gorin, Sefir, and Jerin, whose fire saved us and birthed a new city."

Shedding tears at this point was not only allowed but encouraged by social convention. It was no hardship to summon them; they rose and spilled down my cheeks without effort for Jerin, if not for his parents.

The challenge would be to make them stop, for I regretted Jerin's death so deeply and until now had not been free to show it. I had felt such surprise to find him a kindred spirit who wished to be free of his father, like me. Surprised and somewhat chagrined that I liked him, since our fathers wanted precisely that and had arranged our marriage without our consent. He was supposed to be agreeably awful and easy to despise. But he'd impressed me so that I felt I might actually grow to love him. And then he was gone.

I had some hope left: I could still pursue the dream we had of a city born of goodwill instead of blood and fire.

The funeral smoke was good for us. The other boats sailing along-side and behind had no lavaborn, but they had firebowls and people willing to lead and list the names of the dead, and we did right by our fallen. We left the carrion birds behind, and the sun sank below the surface of the Larik Ocean before we were through giving voice to our grief, but I spoke into the quiet afterward, hoping my words would carry across the water to other boats.

"Hathrim, hear me! I do not know what this Nentian king will ask of us when we arrive in Talala Fouz. I do not know if he will agree to our proposal. But I want you to know that you are all free. Free to come with me if we are given leave, and free to return to Hathrir at any time. I am not your hearthfire; I make no claims of leadership. I am just one of the lavaborn who want to live a new life in a new place, in a new way with new friends, and you are welcome to join me if you choose. May Thurik's flame burn brightly within you all."

It was not a speech my father would have made, nor would Gorin Mogen. It did not stoke fire here or fuel passion there, urging some specific answer or course of action. It burdened them with choice, and some, I think, were displeased. Most were simply confused: They had never not been ruled by a firelord. But the result was silence and heads in motion: turning to either side to see how others were reacting, some shaking their heads in condemnation, others nodding in approval.

I was satisfied with that. If I preached freedom on one hand and burned hot at disagreement, then I was no better than a sand badger snapping at his own ass. No better than my father, the Hearthfire Winthir Kanek, who told me one day I could forge my own future and told me the next I must forge a marriage with a stranger.

After the funeral smoke, I kept careful watch of my feelings. I worried that I would lead people to their ruin. I worried that I would die without ever knowing love. I worried about what my father would do when he heard I wasn't coming home. But I smiled in the sun and took my turn at the oars and kept my worries hidden until night, when I huddled under ice-howler furs, my cheek pressed against the bottom of the glass hull, and wondered how peoples of all kennings or no kennings could live together in peace.

When we finally landed in Talala Fouz, most of our people were shunted to the northern banks of the West Gravewater, in a poorly developed area, while La Mastik and I were led to the palace to deliver our petition.

I had a letter signed by Tactician Diyoghu Hennedigha and Viceroy Melishev Lohmet, but I did not know what it said: It might contain instructions that we be executed immediately. But we represented thousands of Hathrim. Killing us all would not be easy, and we had not come for any sort of conflict. They might decide simply to kill La Mastik and me and tell the remainder of our people to go home or be destroyed.

Talala Fouz was my first experience of a Nentian city—Baghra Khek, I felt, did not qualify, even though Gorin Mogen gave it a Nentian name.

It was a place of startling industry, deplorable poverty, and immense wealth, the economic conditions capable of taking dizzying climbs or dives when one crossed a street. The king's palace was a white-walled cake with swooping slate rooftops, surrounded by manicured gardens and ebullient bronze fountains. The lintels above the doors were high enough to admit us without ducking, and the skylight room with the king's throne at the back was likewise roomy for us.

The current king of Ghurana Nent had been crowned before my birth, so his given name had been forgotten by the common folk long ago. Once seated upon the throne, every king was supposed to be an avatar of Kalaad's will beneath the sky, so they were all known as King Kalaad, followed by an ordinal number and often a disparaging or humbling epithet like "the Unwashed" or "the Unmannerly." This one was King Kalaad the Unaware, forty-fourth monarch of Ghurana Nent.

I wondered if that epithet was supposed to be his excuse for having done nothing of significance for twenty years. Perhaps he was simply unaware that anything needed to be improved? Except that he didn't look unaware when we arrived. He was showing his age, his once-black hair now a long white mane, but there wasn't the slightest hint of senility in his bearing or expression. He was sharp-eyed and quick. And it became clear to me that he *had* been doing something significant for twenty years: He'd been keeping himself in power and keeping the kingdom exactly the way he wanted it—profitable for those who supported him.

King Kalaad didn't speak to us directly—at least, not at first. He relayed instructions through a chamberlain, even though we could hear and see him perfectly well. The chamberlain presented our letter to him and he glanced up at us. We towered above him, even though his throne was elevated several steps above our feet. I could tell it annoyed him, because his mouth turned down at the corners. He rubbed at his naked chin as he examined the seal, then waved the envelope and said, "Have them wait over to one side." He apparently did not want us looming in his peripheral vision as he read. He frowned and pursed his lips as he broke the seal and scanned the contents, raised his eyebrows once, then grunted. Again within our hearing, he told his chamberlain, "Have them return. I have questions." Only when we stood before him this time did he deign to acknowledge we were capable of hearing him speak and could reply without the chamberlain's prompting.

"Ignoring all this nonsense about the Sixth Kenning and defeating Gorin Mogen with fewer than five Nentian casualties, it says here you do not want to return to Hathrir but instead establish a city in the north under my control?"

"Yes, King Kalaad."

"How will you do that?"

"We'll build a rudimentary road as we go. That road can be improved over time and timber harvested. We will send taxes once a year to you, provided we survive, then more frequently as the road improves."

"That's what I truly want to know. How will you survive, heading into the Gravewood with winter coming on?"

I gestured to La Mastik. "We are both lavaborn. The Gravewood has no shortage of fuel. We will hunt and fish and forage and live on what supplies you might grant us."

"So all you want is permission and supplies?"

"That's correct."

King Kalaad the Unaware sniffed. "I don't see the benefit to me. Giving you food and sundries to take into the Gravewood amounts to little more than supporting an extended mass suicide."

"You stand to gain much! A path through the Gravewood, access to the northern shore and the timber of the north, and a new city site suitable for expansion, where every citizen will be paying taxes into your government coffers. Already you have a similar opportunity in Baghra Khek, which can now be settled and flourish. That city's development cost you nothing," which I realized was untrue after I said it. It cost Hashan Khek about two thousand men, all slain by Gorin Mogen's lavaborn and houndsmen. I'm not sure the king would count that as a cost, however. Melishev Lohmet's pet tactician, Ghuyedai, had spent their lives like puffballs in the wind, so they must have held no value to him. "Think of this as developing two cities, then, for the price of one."

The king snorted. "A sales pitch. Unexpected."

I took it from his expression that he didn't like sales pitches and was inclined to refuse. I jumped in with a hint at what he'd have to deal with if he said no. "And, of course, this will ensure you won't have thousands of Hathrim trying to find work in your river cities. Our people can't go back, so we must seek a way forward."

His eyes slid over to his chamberlain and he raised a single eyebrow, which was a signal for his chief courtier to weigh in.

"New revenue streams will please everyone," the chamberlain ventured, confirming what I thought: This government was all about money. Money for a few, anyway. All the various moral and logistical issues we faced were of no consequence except that they might provide a new source of revenue.

The king slumped back in his chair and sighed. "All right. You'll strike north from Ghuli Rakhan. You can sail your boats upriver?"

"Yes."

"Do that. The boats will become property of the viceroy there upon your arrival, which he will use for the river trade. In return, he will supply you with what you need out of his own resources. I will write a letter to that effect and give it to you shortly. But I want you out of Talala Fouz today, is that clear?"

"It is, but may we have some food for the journey?"

"You may purchase some from the royal victualer at the same discount we receive from merchants. I will see to that as well." He turned to his chamberlain. "Take them to the victualer and insist on the discount. Then return here for the letter I'm writing to the viceroy." He rose from his throne and padded to his writing desk, off to one side, idly flicking his wrist our way. "That is all," he said, the sum of his grace delivered. Our royal audience ended without ceremony, and we dutifully followed the chamberlain to purchase some food and potable water, since the Gravewater itself did not qualify. Getting that delivered to our landing site on the northern shore and organizing a hasty departure burned most of the remaining daylight hours, but the Nentians were helpful. They wanted us to be someone else's problem as quickly as possible so that they could return to squeezing profits out of their people and natural resources.

Privately, while the boats were being loaded and the sun hung low in the sky, La Mastik and I drew off to one side and had another smoke, this time a celebratory remembrance of the occasion. I waggled the king's letter to the viceroy in front of her.

"We are going to start a new city founded on principles of equality," I said. "No hearthfire. No viceroy. Leaders elected among the people, like they do in Rael. We are forging something new for Nentians and Hathrim. And my body will be no man's prize."

La Mastik nodded and smiled a thin-lipped smile as she expelled a breath of smoke from the side of her mouth, the colored-glass chain leading from her nose to her ear gleaming in the firelight. "Have you considered what you will do if your father comes looking for you? He has probably heard what happened at Baghra Khek already."

I shrugged. "All the more reason to leave sooner rather than later. He'll move more slowly than us, and he can't simply invade to chase us down. The Nentians are going to notice."

"And what will you do when that white-haired king eventually sends a viceroy to rule this city we're starting?"

I shrugged and puffed idly at my pipe. "The Gravewood is dangerous. The road to our city will remain perilous for many years to come."

La Mastik smirked and blew a ring of smoke into the starlit night. "Thurik protect us and burn our enemies."

I returned her wry smile as I gave the ritual answer. "May his fire warm our hearths."

Fintan dispelled his seeming, shrinking down to his much smaller Raelech size, and withdrew another sphere, upon which to imprint the new form he would take momentarily.

"You'll recall that while Olet and her people sailed north from the Battle of the Godsteeth, Abhinava Khose and I were riding north on stolen horses, trying to arrive ahead of any message from Viceroy Melishev Lohmet that might suggest that we were horse thieves or worse. We got there a bit after Olet, so the king *had* heard of us, but during the ride I may have been a tad excited to be riding with the world's first plaguebringer."

He chuckled and threw down his seeming sphere, the oily gases

forming around him in the shape of the handsome young man from
Khul Bashab.

Abbinava

I don't know what to think of this Raelech bard who's decided to travel
with me. He smiles easily and laughs a lot and has wonderful stories to
share. He speaks Nentian and even knows a few Nentian songs. But he
also thinks I'm somebody important, someone good for the world,
and that makes me nervous. Or ashamed. A whole suite of emotions,
really, because I don't think I'm very good.

I've killed people who may or may not have deserved it. My actions
have caused others—among them my family—to be killed by creatures of the plains. Two viceroys—Melishev Lohmet and Bhamet
Senesh—would like to see me dead. And maybe the king would like
the same, even though we are riding directly to him to find out. Riding
on horses we stole from the Nentian cavalry.

Fintan dismisses my worries as "growing pains." Mere misunderstandings.

"The Sixth Kenning is going to change the world. Not just Ghurana
Nent. It's going to be great for everyone, the way Brynt hygienists are
great for everyone."

"You're thinking about how pests will leave your crops alone and
how safe your chickens will be from foxes, right?"

"Well, sure."

"We're a long way from bringing peace to the henhouses of Rael,"
I told him. "Before we get to that point, a lot needs to change in this

country, which is organized around the fact that the animals of the plains are incredibly dangerous. So much of our freedom is circumscribed by concern for our safety. Our oppression is for our own safety. We must endure the taxes and rule of a corrupt nobility for our own safety. It is the primary justification for their actions, their favorite lever of power. So when the beast callers come along and say, *Hey, we don't have to be afraid of the beasts anymore,* how do you think our noble rulers are going to react?"

"I think I see."

"Yes. They'd like us to disappear if possible. Or, failing that, they're going to make people distrust us and say that *we* are the new threat to their safety, casting us as the bad guys."

"You've thought a lot about this already."

"Yes," I replied, leaving out the fact that I'd thought through much of it with the help of Tamhan, who was back in Khul Bashab. I wondered how he was; whether Hanima, Sudhi, and Adithi were all well and making progress on starting the beast callers clave. "I know a little of the world's history. The people who discovered the kennings never lived long."

"They were the fulcrums of history."

I greeted that sentence with a few moments of silence before responding. "Okay, sure, that's one way to look at it. Another way is that they were consumed by the people they wanted to help. And the thing is, Fintan, I do want to help. But I don't want to be some tragic figure people learn about ages hence from bards."

"Oh. *Oh!* You don't think I'm just waiting around for you to die, do you?"

"No. I mean . . . *are* you?"

"No! I'm certainly interested in what you do next, but I very much want to witness your victories."

"Well, thanks. But victories imply battles, and I'd rather avoid those."

"Understood, but change won't happen without conflict. Anytime someone wants to try something new, some ancient sack of bones starts talking about tradition and how it's worked great so far, and inertia therefore keeps terrible situations terrible. If you don't want to encounter conflict, what would you rather do?"

"I think I'd like to explore. See the world with Murr and Eep." My friends, a bloodcat and a stalk hawk, paced beside us in the grass. "And figure out a way to change things for the better without hurting people."

"You sound a bit like Olet Kanek."

"I do? Wait, who's that?"

"You do sound like her, in general. She's the daughter of Hearthfire Winthir Kanek, who rules Tharsif and Narvik. Didn't you see her at Baghra Khek? Tall redhead in armor."

"Oh, yeah, I remember. We didn't talk much."

"Well, I was stuck on a boat once with her and Jerin Mogen, and they dreamt of starting a new city somewhere that wasn't beholden to the ways of their fathers."

That did sound a bit like me. I didn't want to be beholden to the ways of my father either. "Do you think it is ridiculous to dream such things? Are such changes even possible?"

"Of course they are! Were you taught about what the Fornish were like before the Fifth Kenning was discovered? The clans warred constantly. The First Tree made them stop all that and put the Canopy first. Now some of the clans still bicker, but they don't shed blood."

"Okay, yeah, but that's the First Tree imposing order. I can't impose anything."

"You could."

"By throwing my power around and growing old so fast that I die young? No thanks."

"It's not desirable, no."

"Not at all. Let's hope the king will be receptive to change without blood. I mean, if he'll even agree to see us. Kings don't typically talk to hunters."

"He'll see us. We have information he wants."

When we presented ourselves at the palace, we were able to get an audience by saying we had news of the Battle of the Godsteeth, as the bard decided to call it. The king already knew the result, since Olet Kanek had arrived some days ago, but he wanted to hear Fintan's account, because he couldn't quite believe what he'd heard.

King Kalaad the Unaware was an elderly man whose hair had gone from glossy black to glossy white, and his eyes were piercing. He appeared hyperaware to me. I wondered if the epithets attached to kings made them strive to be the opposite of whatever theirs was.

"Welcome, bard," he said, and then the eyes fell on me. "And you, citizen. I'm told you're a hunter who also witnessed the battle?"

"Yes, sir. I participated in it."

"Participated? So you're in the army?"

"No, sir, I was more of a mercenary, employed by Viceroy Lohmet. I stampeded a boil of kherns into the lavaborn as they emerged from their walls to wipe out the Fornish catapults, effectively ending the battle. The rest of the Hathrim surrendered after that."

The king leaned forward in his throne, his eyes searching me up and down. "So you're the boy who supposedly found the Sixth Kenning?"

"I did find it, yes, sir."

"You can control animals?"

"I don't wish to control anyone. But I can speak to them, and they often do as I ask. And I can sleep on the plains without fear of flesh eels or any other creature."

As I had done with the viceroy's chamberlain, I proved that animals would listen to me by requesting the palace vermin to show themselves briefly before being dismissed to return to their hiding places. It would have been better to demonstrate with Murr and Eep, but I'd had to leave them outside the city, since I couldn't guarantee their safety. The king leaned back, considering the small tide of bugs and rodents fleeing his throne room. "This is suddenly the most interesting audience I've ever had. Arguably the most interesting audience ever for a king of Ghurana Nent. Evidence of a new kenning doesn't happen every day. I'm told you wish to start a clave, with the right to refuse commissions."

"Yes, sir. As I dislike controlling others, I wish not to be controlled."

"You would refuse to aid your country?"

"I did not refuse to fight the Hathrim at the Godsteeth. Viceroy Lohmet engaged me to eliminate the lavaborn and I did, resulting in their surrender and preserving the lives of your army. My willingness to aid the country against invasion should not be in question, sir."

"So, tell me, Abhinava Khose, what should I question?"

"I will not use the Sixth Kenning against our own people to compel their obedience, to punish them, or to be used in any way as a lever of power. The Sixth Kenning should be a boon to all Nentians and not a hammer wielded against them."

The king's mouth turned upward on one side. "Does that courtesy extend to me? To my viceroys, officials, and soldiers?"

"It does. So long as they do not try to compel my service with threats. There will no doubt be great demand for the clave's services, and the clave, not the government, gets to choose which projects will receive priority."

The king laughed and clapped his hands, rubbing them together. "Ah, negotiating already! Well, we should. We certainly should. There is much to think about, and when we get more of the blessed—there must be more already, am I right?"

"Yes, sir."

"Well, the more there are, the more we'll need a framework for their employ, or we'll have chaos. I confess I haven't taken time to read the draft agreement Lohmet sent me; it only just arrived. I am glad you've come to me here so that we can speak directly and not have to worry about delays or the reliability of intermediaries. It will take some time, regardless, to think things through. Can you stay for a while so that I can clear my schedule and be involved in the talks?"

"Yes, sir." His willingness to even discuss a clave, much less accept one, surprised me immensely, and I wasn't sure I could trust it. The viceroys had given me the impression that the king would never permit a clave outside the government's control. Which suggested they were lying shitsnakes. Or maybe the king was, and this was all a ruse to lower my guard so he could hit me with a fatal "accident" later. It would be easy for him to arrange something and I'd have to be wary. But he seemed eager to proceed at the moment.

"Excellent. Do mornings or afternoons work better for you?"

"I prefer mornings, sir."

"Discuss the dawn of a new era at dawn! I like it." The king immediately told the chamberlain to clear or reschedule his commitments in the mornings for the next week, and then he asked Fintan to recount what he'd seen at the Battle of the Godsteeth, just to compare it to the reports he'd received from others.

I could not believe this was going so well. King Kalaad was infinitely more patient and open than I'd been led to believe; he was a far better leader than his viceroys. Was he unaware of how terrible Melishev Lohmet was? Were all of his viceroys awful humans and he simply didn't know? Or did he know and approve, a poisonous serpent on the throne that was bright and beautiful and yet incredibly deadly? Fintan had barely started his narrative of the battle when a breathless page burst in, all apologies, to interrupt.

"Sir, Hearthfire Winthir Kanek is here, and he demands an audience most urgently."

King Kalaad blinked several times, trying to process the revelation. "Winthir Kanek is here? Now?"

"He's in the foyer with one other giant."

"No army behind him?"

"I'm told there are more giants on his ship, but it appears to be a normal crew."

The king looked to his chamberlain. "His daughter left the city days ago, correct? Rowing upriver?"

"Yes, sir."

"Did any choose to return to Hathrir?"

"No, sir. They all went with her."

"All right, let him approach. You two, however," he said to Fintan and me, "need to get out. If he's angry about the defeat of Gorin Mogen, he'd better not see you here."

"Is there any way we might hear his audience but remain unseen, sir?" Fintan asked.

The king paused, then hooked a thumb over his right shoulder. "The rearmost guard space is empty. I wouldn't mind a perfect recall of this audience, so you can listen there, but remain quiet and do not reveal yourselves until he has exited."

I didn't know what he meant at first, but evidently Fintan did. While the king ordered more guards to be brought in for a visual show of force, the bard led me to the indicated wall, which was covered in a remarkable tapestry of plains animals. Upon closer inspection, I saw that there were doors on hinges that swung both ways, leading to small rooms in which a bodyguard could wait and watch. A view slot of mesh fabric allowed us to see and not be seen, and these corresponded to areas of shadow in the tapestry.

It was a tight squeeze in there for the two of us, but we made it work and were both able to watch through the view slot as Winthir Kanek stormed into the skylight room.

His hair very nearly brushed the ceiling, and I saw why he was feared among the Hathrim. He was powerfully built, even for a giant, perhaps even more muscled than Gorin Mogen. His braided blond hair and beard fell over his lava dragon leathers, and he did not look like he had come for a pleasant chat. His jaw was set in a grim line, and I could tell he was clenching his teeth so he wouldn't bellow at someone. He was unarmed in the conventional sense, but a firelord like him could set the room aflame with little effort, and the giant with him was blessed with the First Kenning as well, since he was also wearing the lava dragon leathers.

"King Kalaad," Winthir growled in broken Nentian, "thank you for seeing me on short notice. This is the famous fury Pinter Stuken."

"Stones and bones," Fintan whispered. "Olet told me about him."

"Welcome, Hearthfire Kanek," the king said. "I was told the matter was urgent."

"It is. But first I must congratulate you on your victory at the Gods-teeth. Gorin Mogen behaved rashly and paid for it."

"Thank you. You must have heard about it very quickly to have gotten here in advance of my own army's return."

"I did, and I hired a Kaurian cyclone to speed my journey here, because my daughter was with Mogen and I heard that she sailed here instead of home."

"That she did."

The hearthfire's eyes flickered with blue flames. "Where is she?"

King Kalaad said, "Somewhere upriver. She wants to settle down in the Gravewood."

"Do not jest with me. I am not in the mood. I want my daughter now."

"I do not jest. She and her party left here immediately after stopping to take on supplies."

"You just let her go?"

"Why would I stop her? She wants to build a city in exchange for food and then pay me taxes."

Winthir Kanek pointed a finger at the ground and then at himself. His face was red, and the finger was too, the tip almost incandescent with heat. "She has obligations to her country," he ground out. "Obligations to me."

"She did not mention them. And even if she did, it's not my place to get involved with her family duties. She did say she didn't want to return to Hathrir, and obviously neither did anyone else in her party."

"So she's made herself hearthfire of Mogen's people?"

"I don't know. She never used that title and I never heard anyone call her that."

"I want her back."

The king threw up his hands. "And I want a pet beaver. Look, I can send any message you like upriver, but obviously I can't produce her now."

"That's not good enough. She can simply say she never got the message. I'll catch up to her myself."

"I'm afraid I can't allow that, Hearthfire."

"What? Didn't you just say it's not your place to get involved in family matters?"

"It's not, and I promise to do whatever I can to help. But I just can't have you wandering around with a fury in tow. The last hearthfire who was allowed to stay in Ghurana Nent did not behave well."

"I am not Gorin Mogen."

"I'm aware."

"I'm much more dangerous."

"I'll take your word as gold."

"You really shouldn't patronize me. Let me go find my daughter, King Kalaad, or I will burn your city to the ground."

That was an outrageous bluff. The guardsmen shifted at that and a few raised their crossbows. The king held out a hand to stay them and called him on it.

"That is a ridiculous ultimatum, sir."

"I've already sailed all the way up here. That should hint at my commitment to bringing her home myself. I will not be stopped. You defy me at your peril."

Maybe he wasn't bluffing.

"You'd start a war. The Fornish, the Raelechs, even the Brynts and Kaurians would get involved."

"Only if anyone survives to tell them I'm responsible. Otherwise it's a tragic accident, isn't it? Fires happen all the time. Final warning: Let me go."

"I don't imagine you'd take kindly to anyone showing up at your hall and issuing commands. Let me draft a message with you and affix my seal and send it upriver with my fastest courier."

"Enough." The hearthfire turned to his fury. "Pinter, the guards. Now."

The fury turned into pure fire. Flames licked out to the hands and faces of all the guards at once, so that they couldn't bring their crossbows to bear; their nerves forced them to drop the weapons instead, but then they just kept burning. The lava dragon armor fell to the floor, and Winthir Kanek dropped with it, flattening himself in a push-up to reduce his silhouette if any guards were fortunate enough to take a shot. The hearthfire stretched out a hand and sent a gout of flame to kill King Kalaad—an act of such impetuousness and sheer evil that I could scarce believe it. No wonder Olet wanted to get away from him. He casually murdered people who didn't give him what he wanted.

Guards popped out of the secret compartments like ours, two on either side of the throne, and Fintan placed an arm against my chest to ensure I didn't do the same and make myself a target. One guard did get a shot off at the hearthfire, and the bolt sank into the meat of his left biceps, but he and the others were soon human candles. The tapestry on the wall caught fire near the throne, and the flames began to work their way across the wall toward us. There was no one left alive in the skylight room but the Hathrim and us.

Pinter Stuken coalesced into human form again and bent to pick up his lava dragon hide.

"I'll get it," the hearthfire said, levering himself up on one hand. "Burn the city down, like I said."

"The people too?"

"I don't really care. I just want them too busy to worry about stopping us. We're going to find Olet and burn anyone who gets in my way."

They exited, leaving us in an inferno with a very hot door to burst through. Fintan rammed his shoulder against it and we tumbled into some open space. We had to get out before the ceiling collapsed, but where could we go if they were going to burn the whole city down?

"The kitchen," Fintan said, coughing.

"What?"

"It's stone and has a back exit."

"How do you know?"

"Perfect recall. I've seen plans for the palace and grounds. Follow me."

We scurried past the cooking corpses of the king and his guard and peeked out of the exit. The Hathrim were nowhere in sight. Fintan took us around a corner and down a few halls, where people were quite rightly panicking as smoke and flames roiled along the ceilings.

The kitchen was already in the process of being evacuated when we got there. The roof was on fire. When we stepped outside, coughing and eyes streaming from smoke, we saw that other buildings were likewise burning from the roof down. Pinter Stuken had set them all alight.

There had to be something I could do to stop them, but there wasn't a handy boil of kherns nearby. Not that they would do any good against a fury anyway.

But I remembered how a hive of moss hornets had been surprisingly effective against a firelord, and I wondered if something similar might work here. I searched with my kenning for creatures with poison bites, but there were very few within city limits. There was one, however, lurking in the dungeon, feeding on rats there. A face jumper.

Spiders with bodies the size of a fully extended hand, they were deadly to humans but thankfully didn't find us terribly delicious. Still, a goodly number of people died from their bites every year.

I encouraged the spider to exit the dungeon via one of the many ventilation shafts that ended topside and went to meet it, dragging Fintan along.

"Where do you think we can find Winthir Kanek?" I asked.

"Down by the docks, probably, going to board his ship. Why?"

"The Hathrim need to know that Nentians are not defenseless anymore. These hearthfires look at us as easy pickings now that the other nations are worried about that invasion on the east coast. That needs to stop."

"What, are you fireproof all of a— Gyaaah, is that a face jumper? Stay back!"

"It's okay." I invited the spider to perch on my right hand. It neatly leapt up and rested in my palm, about the weight of an orange, its six eyes looking at me. Fintan backed a couple of lengths away.

"I don't know if you've heard, Abhi, but those things have a habit of *jumping.* On your *face.*"

"She won't bite us," I said, sensing that she was female. "Will you? Little cutie."

"Cutie?"

"Don't hurt her feelings, now. Let's go."

We set off into the chaos. Some folks were trying to fight the fire and others were running for their lives, heading to the river. Pinter Stuken wasn't purposely targeting people, just the buildings, but plenty of folks got trapped. It was impossible to tell where the fury was; he could be any ball of flame on the rooftops.

Winthir Kanek was easy enough to spot once we rounded the corner leading down to the docks. He towered over everyone, clutching his left arm as he walked, and people streamed around him, paying him no mind. Hathrim weren't that uncommon in this port city. No one but us knew what he had done, and few people, if any, had figured out that the fires were due to the work of a fury. When there's a fire, figuring out who started it always runs far behind escaping it and putting it out.

I wasn't sure it was my place to avenge the king, but I couldn't let this hearthfire treat us like kindling and go upriver to do the same to others.

"Jump away as soon as you're done," I told Cutie as we caught up to the hearthfire. "I'll take you back to the dungeon."

I extended my hand toward the hearthfire's backside—which was about my head height—and Cutie leapt from my fingers onto the giant's lava dragon armor. She scrambled silently up his back, none of the sensation ever getting through to his skin, and he didn't seem to notice the extra bit of weight. When she got to his shoulder, she perched for a moment, positioning herself for the strike, then pounced.

Face jumpers inject a massive amount of venom in a fraction of a second and leap away. The head or face is their primary target because the venom works quicker that way, and the pain is such that their prey will be too busy pawing at it to look around for a spider to squash.

Cutie landed neatly on the ground to Winthir Kanek's right and scurried back to me, leaping up to my outstretched hand. The hearthfire clutched the bite with his right hand and screamed, fire shooting out of his face, since his instinct was to solve all his problems by burning them. But the venom was in the blood, and he couldn't let go of his flesh the way a fury could. He lasted a good deal longer than many creatures would, being a giant, but inside of a minute he succumbed in much the same way the king had: taken by surprise, unable to defend himself, and in agony.

"One down," I said.

"One down?" Fintan's eyebrows performed some impressive acrobatics as he goggled at me. "You think you can take on a fury the same way?"

"Nope. But I don't want to be here when he discovers his hearthfire is dead. Back to the dungeon vent for us! I promised Cutie."

"Is that the best place for her now?"

"The dungeon probably won't burn, and it'll still be full of rats. So, yeah, perfect place. Whatever prisoners are down there are going to be safer than everyone else."

"How are you going to fight a fury?" he asked as we wove through the panicked masses. We were definitely moving against the tide at this point, but the appearance of Cutie had some power to make people swerve out of our way.

"I don't know. I'm making this up as I go along."

Pinter Stuken must have found Winthir Kanek's body just as I returned Cutie to safety at her vent, with my thanks. A fireball bloomed in the sky in a show of emotion that I thought was a little outsize to commemorate the death of such a man. What affection could the fury have truly had for someone who used him to terrorize people? Who had asked him to spend years of his life on burning down a city? For to burn so steadily as he had, Pinter had to be feeling poorly right now.

And in a moment he might think he should take over and rule in Winthir's stead. He might already be thinking along those lines. I had no confidence that he would be a model of restraint and diplomacy after he had so readily agreed to raze the city.

"We need to return to the docks," I said, a plan forming in my mind. "I need to see the Hathrim ship but not be seen."

That was easier said than done. Everyone wanted to go to the river right then; running out onto the plains wasn't an attractive alternative. Which reminded me to communicate with Murr and Eep and tell them not to worry about me and to stay away from the city.

When we finally did make it down to the docks—via a route that did not take us past the body of Winthir Kanek—we saw that someone had wisely decided to start ferrying people across to the camp area on the northern shore. Plenty of others were simply heading upriver or out to sea, cramming the hired boats to the rims, having made the calculation that all was lost and there was no use lingering.

We were perhaps ten berths away from the Hathrim ship and Pinter Stuken was there, dressed again in his lava dragon armor, shouting and gesticulating at the giants on the boat and, once, pointing back into the city, where Winthir Kanek lay dead. Delivering the news, no doubt. He looked angry and visibly older, crags on his face that were not there before.

That gave me pause. Was it worth it, going after him? It would cost me some time, no doubt, to defeat him as I planned. How much, I had no way of knowing in advance.

But I looked behind me at the clouds of black smoke rising from a city on fire, at the parents clutching crying children, all with soot-stained faces like mine, everything lost at Pinter Stuken's willingness to destroy on another man's whim.

Yes. It would be worth it to prevent him from doing this to others. It was not only criminal; it was an act of war.

"Face me," I told Fintan. "Pretend we're in conversation. We can't be seen staring at them."

"Why would they notice?"

"They might start looking around soon."

"What are you going to do?"

"Just move your lips meaninglessly, gesture once in a while, and watch from the corner of your eye."

I reached out with my kenning to locate pests in the city—there were still plenty—and directed them to pester Pinter Stuken in waves.

First, a cloud of flies descended upon him, which he tried to swat at but eventually burned. Then mosquitoes. Then hornets, which managed to sting him a few times before he went all flames again, expending energy at the task. I waited until he'd dressed again and then hit him with the wasps. Grasshoppers flew in from the plains. A swarm of roaches followed, which he could easily avoid and burn but which unmistakably let him know that he was not welcome here. That's when he figured out that someone must be behind all this and started looking around. Fintan said as much. I never made eye contact.

He was also scanning the ground for more approaching vermin, so that's when I had a blackwing dive at his head from behind and give him a good peck in the ear. He cursed and cooked the bird, but then he looked up and saw a cheek raptor circling high above and pretty clearly targeting him. It was too high for him to blast, but now he couldn't let his guard down. Give a cheek raptor the same chance as he gave that blackwing, and it would tear his face off.

Pinter thought it best to go home at that point and leave Winthir Kanek's body behind. He shouted orders and his crew cast off and rowed to midstream before heading out to sea. The cyclone that the hearthfire mentioned filled their sails with wind and sped them on their way. I made sure the cheek raptor kept following, and then I dropped off the side of the dock into the river, much to Fintan's surprise. This was going to be the hard part, because I couldn't count on anything being especially close by. Just searching for something to help me was going to take plenty of energy.

I found what I needed, but they were leagues away. A stabbing pain grew behind my eyes as I relayed my requests, and then I fell backward into the water, exhausted.

I rose, spluttering, trying to walk a bit closer in to shore, and Fintan was there to help me. He was trying to pull me fully out, but I resisted.

"No, I need to stay in the water to see if it works."

"If what works?"

"Right now Pinter Stuken is worried about that cheek raptor following him. He's probably climbing up to the crow's nest to get closer to it, thinking he'll be able to blast it. So he won't see what's coming. Not that he could do anything about it, heh heh."

I made Fintan wait for the report as it happened and then told him: "A Larik whale just rammed their ship from below and toppled Pinter Stuken, along with some others, into the sea. He was too tired from his exertions here to take his flame form before he dropped in, and once in, he couldn't. A bladefin followed up, grabbing him by the leg and dragging him down to make sure he'd never surface again. That's how you kill a fury: Drown him. A pod of dolphins is now rescuing all of the other sailors, bringing them back to the ship. That was a measured response to what they did here today. I'm hoping that will teach the folk of the First Kenning that the Sixth Kenning is real and they won't last long with the world's wildlife after them."

"Well," Fintan said, and then, after a pause: "Well."

That made me laugh. "I've struck a bard speechless?"

"Savor the moment, because it won't happen again. What now?"

"Now you tell me how old I look."

"I wouldn't say you look older. Maybe . . . more mature."

"That's older. I'm supposed to be a youth."

"Looking a bit older isn't so bad. It gives you gravitas. That can go a long way sometimes."

"Will gravitas get me upriver?"

"No, but is that what you want?"

"I don't want to stay here." I gestured to the burning city, the oily clouds of smoke spreading in the sky. "There's going to be a fight over who gets to be king of these ashes, and I don't want to be caught in the middle. But exploring the Gravewood sounds like a great time."

"It does?"

"If you don't have to worry about the animals eating you, yeah. I could help Olet Kanek start this new city. You think she'll be mad that I killed her dad with a dungeon spider named Cutie?"

"I don't know. On the one hand, she is clearly not anxious to do what her father wants and has made plans to get as far away from him as possible. On the other, he's her dad."

"Maybe you could ask her for me first."

"Maybe. So you want to go?"

"I do. You have a boat?"

"The Raelech embassy has one twenty or so berths down. We can catch a ride with them."

"Will they let me bring Murr and Eep with me?"

"I'm sure they will."

I didn't have a lot of good choices in front of me. I was a wanted man in Khul Bashab, so going home was out. Viceroy Melishev Lohmet had put my death on his to-do list. The king might have been truly willing to work something out with me, but we'd never know now. Going upriver was the only way forward I could think of.

I wished I could talk things through with Tamhan. I hoped he was doing okay in Khul Bashab.

THE MISTMAIDEN
ISLES

Fintan and I were informed after his tale that Pelenaut Röllend would like to meet us for breakfast in the morning, and when the sun crawled out of the ocean, a mariner arrived at my door and escorted me to the home of Tallynd du Böll, Pelemyn's tidal mariner. Rölly and his lung, Föstyr, soon joined us.

We had a mess of peppered eggs and some sliced sausage from Tallynd's seemingly never-ending supply of gift baskets.

"Enjoy this last bit of luxury," she said. "I'm donating the remainder today to the refugee kitchen in Survivor Field. It's starting to get dire out there. Found out from a hygienist that some kids haven't had protein in a week. That's unacceptable. After this I'm going to escort some fishing boats out to the Mistmaiden reefs and bring in a haul just for the people in the field."

Fintan and I thanked her for that, and I was seized by the overwhelming desire to give her a gift basket for giving away all her gift baskets. Our cultural mandates can tie us up in knots sometimes.

Rölly frowned as he spoke to Föstyr. "I know food supplies were already on our list of things to revisit soon, but perhaps you could move that to the top of the list? I hadn't heard about the protein shortages among the refugees, and I'd like to know why not but also make sure it doesn't continue or happen again."

We ate somewhat guiltily after that, and I wondered if I was pulling my weight; next to the crisis of basic needs some people were facing, I didn't feel that my duties were more important than, say, joining a fishing-boat crew.

"Forgive me for not spending longer on pleasantries," Rölly said after a few moments, "but I have plenty to do and I just wanted to speak to you, Fintan, about your story last night. I believe it made clear what's to come, as you promised; the Nentian throne was not overthrown so much as suddenly left vacant and Melishev was able to seat himself?"

"That is correct, Pelenaut. More details to come, of course, but you have the essential drift."

"So that was months ago, and we hadn't heard because the Granite Tunnel collapsed and their capital was burned down. With all that going on, it's little wonder they didn't try to reach out to us on the other side of the continent. Melishev was ill when he took the throne, and I'm given to understand he must be even worse now?"

"He's well-nigh buried."

"Sending a hygienist will take weeks. He might be dead by the time they get there—or he might be dead already."

"That is true."

"Still, those Nentian merchants pulled at my heart. I wouldn't want the families of Subodh, Ghurang, and Poudresh punished because I failed to act. Or Jahm's family, for that matter. But I don't like rewarding hostage taking, so I'm going to release one hygienist to each country—one to Rael, Forn, and so on—to deal with any dire needs as the leaders of each country see fit. I believe we have stabilized our situation here and are making excellent progress in the river cities, so I feel I can let a few return abroad."

"I am sure everyone will be grateful."

"What I'm wondering is if there is some other information in the stories ahead that I should know now. Any other new leaders in the west I should know about? Who took over for Winthir Kanek, for example, in Narvik and Tharsif?"

Fintan chewed thoughtfully and swallowed before answering. "I have no idea who the new hearthfires are. Numa hasn't reported it to me, and so I assume for the moment that the Hathrim are occupied with internal affairs rather than making noise abroad. There are some surprises ahead—developments in both the north and the south—that I think will bear the stamp of revelation for many people, but nothing that affects your day-to-day business right now. We have spoken privately about some events in the north that we agreed can wait their turn, and what little else has happened you already know, as you've been getting reports from your quartermaster up there. What I'm going to share about the north came from people I was with, and the rest came from Numa, who reported extensive goings-on in Ghurana Nent before she presented me here to you."

Rölly simply stared at the bard for a long while, holding his gaze, making it clear he didn't truly believe there was nothing else he should know at the moment. I had no idea what they might be referring to, and it took a supreme effort of will not to break in and say, *Hey, what are you talking about?*

"Very well," Rölly finally said. "If you think of anything later, Master Bard, that I might not know but might find relevant, please make sure you get word to me through Dervan or a mariner. I don't wish to be surprised again. I'll be quite displeased, in fact, if I discover you're holding something back right now that can help my people."

"Some of what's to come will no doubt help your people, and mine," Fintan said. "But not right now. It will only be helpful once the Raelech army arrives—plus the Fornish reinforcements and the Kaurian fleet—and we are still weeks away from that."

"Yes, we are."

"Then you can cease to worry, Pelenaut. The past cannot change and it won't affect the present, and the future it will inform is still some distance away."

Föstyr grunted. "The past always affects the present." He waggled a fork at Tallynd. "The second könstad here has some information to share with you now that will have an effect, I promise you."

I noticed that Tallynd's eyes locked with Rölly's at that point, and he gave her the barest of nods. Something was up, and I couldn't wait to discover what it was. But Rölly placed his napkin over his unfinished breakfast and excused himself. "I have much to do—hygienists to assign and food shortages to address—so I hope you'll excuse me. Dervan, if you'd accompany me, I'd like a word."

My gaze dropped down to my unfinished plate. There was still plenty to be enjoyed, luxuries from Tallynd's gift baskets, but that butter and jam spread deliciously on crunchy perfection almost sang to me that it could not bear to be left behind. "Can I . . . bring my toast?"

"Yes, bring your toast. I know how important that is to you."

I salvaged it, grateful that it wouldn't go to waste, and bid Fintan farewell, promising to meet him that afternoon for our daily recording session. We left him with Tallynd and Föstyr, and I supposed I'd hear about whatever they discussed later.

Once outside, the pelenaut waited for me to devour my toast and matched his pace to my slow one. Mariners preceded and followed us at a discreet distance.

"How's the bard been of late, Dervan?"

"He's been plagued by nightmares of the Hathrim."

"That's it? I know Numa just visited him. Did he behave differently afterward, say anything strange, ask you anything?"

I thought of sharing the intelligence that Clodagh knew we'd stolen her journal but remembered that I didn't want to be a go-between or play their spy games. I didn't want to lie either. "Apparently the Triune Council is aware that we're writing the bard's tales down. They relayed a brief message to me, but it's nothing that concerns you."

"Let me know if anything changes."

"What are you looking for?"

"I'll know it when I see it. Or rather when you tell me about it."

That made me wrangle somewhat with my decision to keep quiet. What if the message from Clodagh was what he was looking for?

Clearly he was expecting something from the Raelechs, or he wouldn't be checking in with me. But, no, I firmly wished to keep myself and the world of espionage at a distance, and sharing that would only draw me closer to that world.

Rölly made excuses—the very good excuses that he had a country to see to—and left me alone soon after that, and I found myself abruptly with nothing to do. I no longer had any classes to teach at the university. I'd have no work to do with Fintan until that afternoon. It was time to find an occupation, for I'd be presented with more such moments in the future.

Thinking of Tallynd's promise, I took myself down to the refugee kitchen on Survivor Field and volunteered to work however they could use me. I was chopping vegetables soon enough and a bit later was slicing up sausages and cheeses from Tallynd's gift baskets into portions for children.

Noon arrived all too soon and I promised I'd return as often as I could. There was plenty of work for volunteers there.

Fintan was beaming when I met him for lunch. "Tallynd told me the most amazing story," he said. "People are going to learn a lot today."

I asked what he meant by that, but he told me I'd have to wait.

"Today you'll see a familiar face and two new ones," he said hours later from atop the wall. "But first, an original song for you all today based on a true story: This is 'The Tragical, Lamentable, Entirely Preventable Swamp Duck Death of Jahm Joumeloh Jeikhs.'"

> *I want to tell you a story of a bootmonger*
> *Who isn't with us any longer;*
> *He was rude at the table and ate too fast*
> *So now we must speak of him in the past.*
>
> *It wasn't just a case of bad luck*
> *That made him choke on a glazed swamp duck;*

It was his poor manners alone
That made him inhale that fatal bone.

So please slow down and chew your food
Or you'll be short of breath, my dude;
You'll turn blue and asphyxiate
And fall facedown into your plate.

(Chorus)
For safety and propriety
Please tell your little tykes
Of the tragical, lamentable, entirely preventable
Swamp duck death of Jahm Joumeloh Jeikhs.

Jahm grabbed a breast and a leg and and thigh
And crammed them in, I don't know why;
Perhaps it was the rich fire glaze
That tempted him to end his days.

But there hasn't ever been a sauce
Rich enough to justify such a loss;
The extreme high speed at which he fed
Caused him to choke and then drop dead.

The proper thing to do at table
Is to enjoy each bite as long as you're able;
You sure don't want a glazed swamp duck
To be the end of all your good luck.

(Chorus)

"I can't believe you did that," I said during the break.

"I told you it was too good to pass up," the bard said. "Jahm will serve as a warning to generations. And I wanted those Nentian merchants to hear it before they left town with their hygienist."

After the break, Fintan pleased everyone by taking the form of our national heroine, Second Könstad Tallynd du Böll, and I grinned with anticipation. I couldn't wait to hear what she'd shared with him that morning.

When your time is running out, that which you normally view as mundane can become a treasure. A flowering weed in the garden, a thing to be despised on most days, can become a beauty of the world—a miracle of life!—if only you believe that such a flower might never be seen again. Noting what may be the last time for everything infuses every moment with poignance and sentiment. And even the sentiment gets its chance to be cherished, because when might one have the luxury to feel that again?

The pelenaut's orders had me feeling that way. I was to scout the Mistmaiden Isles up close, a deed not undertaken for many years. In fact, I could find no records that they had ever been truly scouted at all. Delving into the archives, I found no records but maps, and even those were suspect, since no one could tell me when last they were surveyed. I was privately informed by the pelenaut's master of charts that cartographers just copied what had already been done years ago, and accuracy was not a priority. After all, why worry about charting coastlines accurately when no one would dare to sail there?

"How long since the isles were last surveyed?" I asked the master of charts.

She shrugged. "I don't know when the last survey was completed, Second Könstad."

"Ten years? Twenty?"

"Oh, much more than that. Long before you or I were born. It might have been our great-grandparents' time."

My jaw dropped, and she waggled a finger at me.

"That's being optimistic, mind. If someone who knew the answer for sure told me it was three hundred years or more, I wouldn't be surprised."

"Three hundred? Do you know what three hundred years of tide does to a coast? The coastlines are going to be entirely different now!"

"I understand, Second Könstad, believe me. But no one wants to sail near the wraiths. Those islands are left alone for good reason. I do have a record of a survey ordered by the pelenaut from one hundred twenty-seven years ago, and the quartermaster of Festwyf was supposed to recruit a company for the task and outfit a ship for that purpose."

"Oh? And did the quartermaster follow through on that?"

"I have no record of it—perhaps some records in Festwyf's archives can break through this dam we find ourselves up against. But since we have no completed survey from that time, we may deduce that the quartermaster either failed to send out a crew or did send one out but they never returned."

I closed my eyes and sighed, trying to let my frustration hiss out of me. I have often envied the Kaurians for their ability to breathe peace. I usually find my own peace in the currents of the ocean, in keeping pace with whales migrating through our coastal waters, but those seasonal moments of bliss were far away from me right then. The master of charts had an excellent point: I, too, would leave the islands alone if I had a choice. But now it was clear these islands were a huge blind spot for the Brynts—one we all knew was there and had willfully avoided, as if nothing in the isles could ever harm us so long as we left them alone.

I hugged my boys tightly before I left and told them I loved them and always would and that they should never ever forget that. Which of course scared them. My own fears were flowing into them, the tears in my eyes telling them that I was about to do something dangerous.

They didn't want me to go. Neither did anyone else, especially me. But I knew that I *needed* to go.

So I set out from the Lung's Locks with a waterproof carisak full of paper and ink, just in case I found a safe place to take down some notes, along with an oilskin and a bedroll. I sleeved myself through the waves to the Mistmaiden Isles at the fastest pace I could comfortably maintain. My plan was to never set foot on any of the isles—a reef, a crag, maybe, but never where I might come face-to-mist with a wraith. All we really knew about them was that they didn't like the living and couldn't swim.

But though they couldn't inhabit or cross the water, I didn't know what my kenning could do against them. Certainly no weapon could harm them, since they lacked substance, but would a squirt in the eye do them any damage? If I walked on the isles wreathed in a swirling shield of water, would they be able to penetrate it to do me harm? It sounded like it might work in theory, but I wasn't willing to experiment.

In the old tales, wraiths were said to have some power to lure people to their doom. If the tales held a droplet of truth, it would be better for me to remain unseen. If I didn't return, the likelihood of anyone ever coming after me, much less finding me, was incredibly small. It had taken a hundred twenty-seven years after the last expedition to send me out, after all. If that expedition had ever actually been sent.

What few reliable records the master of charts could find indicated that perhaps not all four of the islands were inhabited by wraiths, but there was no solid information on which ones were safe and which were not. I must therefore treat all of them with the same excess of caution. And the wraiths were not the sole danger: I was going there to locate a Bone Giant fleet, after all, and perhaps something that could conceivably be called the Seven-Year Ship, possibly crewed by men with pale skin, if the information we had from the Kaurian scholar was correct. And, of course, there were krakens. Always krakens, once you got away from the coasts and into open ocean, preventing us from finding out what might lie beyond the edges of our maps.

It occurred to me that the Bone Giants might have had some secret colony hidden in the Mistmaiden Isles for centuries and we obviously had never figured it out because we had never explored them. Or, more implausibly but still inescapable to my paranoid mind, perhaps the infamous ship was in fact crewed by wraiths, a sort of ghost ship. That possibility chilled me.

The churning of my mind was not echoed by the sea, thankfully. It was a calm day, and as I traversed the deep channel between the continent and the islands, I sensed nothing large moving beneath me. The krakens, if they were out there, were still for the time being, or perhaps not interested in something as tiny as me.

The southernmost island, according to our out-of-date maps, was a smallish one, shaped like a kidney bean with the inner curve facing north. When I found the island, it proved to be both bean-shaped and empty of wraiths, so far as I could tell, as well as unoccupied by a fleet of ships. It did have fantastic fishing; its populations had never been touched by a net.

I moved on to the neighboring island located to the northwest, which was also uninhabited and its shoals also blessed with extraordinary schools of fish. I found some rough rocks offshore on which to set up my bedroll and an oilskin for the night. I could technically sleep in the ocean, since I'd never drown, but that was an outstanding way to get caught and slowly digested by a nocturnal bloom of stalking jellyfish.

I slept poorly but did appreciate waking with the dawn and witnessing seabirds dive for their breakfast. I dove for mine as well, spearing a sandy flounder with my glass knife and returning to the rock to cut off some fresh fillets and eat them raw. It was a clear, sunny day, even finer than the last. An auspicious morning on which to encounter wraiths, if such a thing had to be done.

Taking the time to write down a report of seeing nothing on the southernmost islands was an exercise in procrastination. I wanted to do my duty but didn't especially want to find anything either.

Of the two islands left, the one to the northeast of where I'd slept was the smaller, so I went there first. The big island was so large I doubted I'd be able to complete a circuit of it in a day. It then occurred to me that it might be convenient to name the islands. Bean for the smallest one. Bolt for the second, since it was a bit of a zigzag shape. And the drawings I'd seen of this third one looked like the silhouette of my boys' least favorite vegetable—it had a small stalk and floret, anyway—so I named it Broccoli. No doubt the master of charts would disapprove, but it gave me some comfort to exert this small measure of control.

The big island looked like a mess on the map and I toyed with the idea of calling it Barf, just to really outrage the master, but decided to reserve judgment on that until I'd scouted it.

Broccoli, like Bean and Bolt, was free of habitation but lush with wildlife on its shores and in its depths. Living in the reefs on the eastern side were fish I'd never seen before—many new species, in fact—and if I'd had the leisure to watch and document them, I would have gladly taken it. But I kept circling Broccoli until sometime in the late morning, when I was in a strait between it and the big island.

I was traveling south at that point and periodically looking west, to my right, to see if I could spy the big island at all across the strait, and I could. A low, gently undulating ridge of dark green. And then, suddenly, patches of white.

Were those sails?

I stopped, treading water and squinting to be sure. There was just enough distance and glare that I couldn't be certain, so I first pushed water beneath me and then pulled it up underneath, shooting myself high into the air as if I'd been ejected from a whale's blowhole. At that height I could confirm that, yes, those were sails, quite a lot of them, and that I'd most likely found the fleet I'd been sent to find. When I dove back into the ocean, I immediately abandoned my circuit of Broccoli and sleeved myself toward the fleet, taking note of the currents and vibrations in the water.

I found quite a bit of activity underneath those boats. The vibrations might be normal, because these waters were full of creatures whose purpose was to consume and be consumed. But it also might be a feeding frenzy of bladefins and other creatures reacting to a new abundant food source.

The flat bottoms of the boats, when I reached them, were familiar to me. These were definitely Bone Giant vessels, the same barely seaworthy craft they'd employed for the invasion. What were they invading here?

I surfaced cautiously near one of the boats and checked to make sure there were no sentries with spears guarding them. Satisfied that the boat in front of me, at least, was anchored and abandoned, I hauled myself aboard to search for intelligence. I found nothing of significance on board—no convenient letter announcing what they were planning to do there—allowing me to depart without further ado. But I did stand up in the boat and count all the rest of the ships that I could see.

The fleets that had attacked our cities comprised one hundred boats carrying one hundred giants each. Ten thousand. These boats were the same size as those in the invasion fleet, but there were only thirty-five of them anchored in the inlet. It was a sizable inlet and could have held a full hundred boats easily. But either this force was a fraction of the fleet sent to the islands and the other sixty-five boats were anchored elsewhere, or it hadn't been the same size as the other fleets to begin with.

Why had these boats come here? I squinted at the shore, covered in thick forest, and saw no buildings. But I did see a ship of a different design moored at a weather-beaten dock extending from a small sandy beach. Perhaps there was a path leading into the forest and then to some settlement or habitation hidden in the trees, but I could not see any details from where I was. I'd have to swim to the shore for a closer look.

But all that feeding activity I had sensed was right underneath that boat at the dock. My kenning kept me safe from the water but not from the creatures in it; I could of course kill anything quickly by pulling water through its nervous tissues, and I could move quicker than most anything that might want to eat me, but I had to see them coming first. My ability to scramble brains would do me little good if a bladefin managed to chomp me in half.

I dove off the edge of the boat and sought the bottom of the inlet, letting my eyes adjust to the gloom of the deep water. It was clouded with the sediment being thrown up underneath the ship.

Slowly, my senses alert for vibrations in the water that would warn me of danger far in advance of sight or sound or smell, and keeping low and searching for threats from above, I advanced toward the dock.

There were at least two bladefins, some smaller scavenger fish, and a whole army of blue crabs crowded around a churning mess of blood and sand underneath the keel of the strange boat. The crabs were responsible for most of the suspended debris in the water, for they were tearing at a buffet of bodies. Bone Giant bodies—or Eculans, as the scholar Gondel Vedd told us they call themselves. In a strange moment that echoed the night the Bone Giants attacked Pelemyn, I saw a crab sidestep across the bottom of the sea with a severed hand grasped in its claws.

I moved forward until the water was so cloudy I couldn't see a length in front of me. Going in there blind would be unwise, and it was unlikely I'd find anything beyond what I already knew: The bodies of a whole lot of dead Eculans were being eaten. I could feel that there were plenty of teeth and claws in there. I rose to the surface, slowly, so as not to alert any creatures of my presence. Whatever they felt of my passage in the water, it wasn't the cavitation or flailing of prey. I moved inside the currents of the water itself.

Upon breach, I saw that I was only ten lengths or so from the ship. It was not like the Eculan ships at all, nor like any ship I'd ever seen. It possessed elements of Brynt design in that it had a finely carved bowsprit and a deep-keeled hull, but it also had fine carvings along the deck rails and the main cabin in the Fornish style. Its sails and rigs looked as if a Kaurian had advised the shipwrights. But the lower boards of the hull were smeared with a black substance that was unfamiliar; it wasn't pitch or tar, precisely, which was occasionally used as a water repellent, but something like a varnish. The black substance came about halfway up the hull, and then it transitioned to a different varnish, which brought out the green in the wood and gave the whole thing a wet sheen even though I was sure the boards were perfectly dry.

And there were bodies on deck. Eculan ones. There were more on the dock and the beach, which I hadn't seen from a distance. But these few didn't account for the whereabouts of three and a half thousand troops on those ships. There might be something close to that number underneath the ships, however, and scattered about the lagoon now, albeit in pieces. They would have died weeks ago if they died at the same time as the ones on the shore, and the crabs would have plenty to eat for a while.

What had killed them? They weren't riddled with arrows, and I saw no obvious wounds from spears or swords. Were they bitten by poisonous insects, perhaps? Or was the boat itself cursed?

The boat had to have something to do with it, or else their corpses wouldn't be grouped underneath it and the dock.

I scooted a little closer to the shore, circling around the churn of the feeding grounds to get a better view of the trees. Something about them looked strange to me. The canopies were fine, leaves gently undulating in the sea breeze, but something bothered me about the trunks. They were blurred or indistinct somehow, which was strange considering that it was such a clear day. I blinked and wiped my eyes to make sure there wasn't salt or something impairing my vision, and I looked again. The trunks were still hazy.

It wasn't until I was five lengths from the beach that I understood what was happening. The trees were perfectly normal. But their outlines were blurred because underneath their canopies, taking shelter from the sun, was a haunting of wraiths, just waiting for me to set foot on dry land.

Once I knew what I was looking at, I could make out some individual shapes. The wraiths were gaunt, translucent creatures with mouths yawning in an eternal scream—and I wanted to scream myself, they were so horrifically twisted from anything human. As one of Bryn's blessed, I'm not affected by the temperature of the ocean, but I

shivered nonetheless. How the wraiths could ever be considered allur-
ing, as the old Drowning Songs taught us, I could not fathom. Unless
their allure was actually some kind of magic they worked across the
land, and the water was protecting me. Or perhaps they simply hadn't
seen me yet.

I ducked underneath the waves and sleeved out to the Eculan ships,
protecting my ears from any songs of temptation they might sing to
get me to come ashore. Once I surfaced behind the stern of a flatboat
in the middle of the fleet, I peered back at the strange ship moored at
the dock and tried to make sense of it.

The wraiths certainly could have killed the Eculans without weapons. But there weren't any wraiths on the dock or on the boat—
a strange boat that was, in all likelihood, the Seven-Year Ship for which
the Eculans had been searching. There would be no reason for their
bodies to be on it, around it, and mostly underneath it unless they had
tried to board it and perhaps sail it away. Someone or something had
methodically slain them all.

But who? The wraiths? Possible. Even probable. But who owned the
ship, and where were they? Why was the ship docked here? Had it been
here all along? And what, if anything, did this island have to do with
the Seventh Kenning?

That Kaurian scholar had said the faithful would be taken on the
Seven-Year Ship and shown the truth of the Seventh Kenning. Did that
mean the Mistmaiden Isles were the source of that kenning?

Was this inlet, in fact, the source of it? And all those dead Eculans on
the boat and underneath it were seekers who hadn't been blessed? If
so . . . where were the people who *did* get blessed?

There were too many questions and not enough answers. But I did
have a few important facts to take back with me.

The Eculans had found their Seven-Year Ship. But none of them
survived finding it, so the rest of the Eculans weren't aware that it had
been found. That meant the Bone Giants would continue with whatever they had planned.

I stopped and reconsidered: unless sixty-five boatloads *had* survived finding it and moved on. All the other Eculan fleets had been a hundred ships.

But that theory didn't make a lot of sense to me; I couldn't believe the Eculans would just leave the Seven-Year Ship behind after they'd mobilized such huge resources to find it. Greater minds than mine would need to solve the puzzle once I gave them the few pieces of information I had.

To be thorough, I searched the island's circumference to ensure that there weren't sixty-five more boats anchored somewhere. I didn't find any, but I saw plenty of wraiths. Once I knew where to look for them, I saw them everywhere, waiting among the trees.

And then, on the northern coast of the island, when I surfaced to check the shore, one of them saw me. I did not realize it at first. I heard no irresistible call, felt no yearning in my chest for some ethereal beauty. But I was sleeving closer to the shore anyway, a casual, unthinking detour, and a wraith was emerging from the trees, its form shimmering and wobbling in the sunlight, to meet me where the water lapped at the sand.

And I wondered why I was moving forward, why in the wide deep blue I would ever think it might be a good idea to swim up to one of these nightmares, a ghastly spectre that clearly intended to consume me or my spirit, its mouth yawning ever wider for me to step in, yet I could not stop my progress, could not even slow down.

Panic rose within me as it became clear that I *had* been snared, not with any song or beckoning gesture but by some invisible, unheard magic, and if I did not figure out a way to turn or reverse course, I would crawl dripping onto the beach and into the wraith's ravenous embrace.

I tried to use my kenning to spray water at it, but that didn't work. I could do nothing but propel myself closer. I tried to blink and that didn't work either: My gaze was locked upon my target, my eyelids glued open.

Could I move my arms, I wondered? Yes! But only in certain ways—not, I discovered, to swim backward or tread water. But I could move them forward and accelerate toward my doom. Not that it made much difference, since I was moving well under the propulsion of my kenning.

Desperate as I entered the shallows—I'd hit the sand soon and have to stand up—I shot my arms forward as if to perform a breast-stroke, then flipped my hands palm up and convulsed my fingers, thereby splashing some water into my face, directly into my unblinking eyes.

Freedom! My eyes closed and I kept them shut, ducking my face down into the water and feeling my kenning return to my full control just as my hands ran into the ocean floor, the wraith only a length or two away at the water's edge, silent and hungry. I turned and sleeved myself away from there, remaining underwater and safe from any further enchantment.

I shook and shivered, my physical revulsion coming late. The legendary power of wraiths to lure people was *real*. Terrifyingly real. But water's ability to defy their powers was also real.

I paused and floated in place once I'd achieved some distance, my heart hammering against my ribs. I remained there for a while, taking deep breaths, until I calmed down and felt safe again. Then I resumed my circuit of the island, peeking up from the surface only briefly to check for ships before dipping underwater. I did not want to be snared again, even if I knew how to break their enchantment.

When the sun sank in the west, I was too exhausted to travel all the way back to Pelemyn. I spent another fitful night on the crag off the coast of Bolt. I didn't see wraiths among Bolt's forest—I looked—but I couldn't be sure they weren't there somewhere.

When I headed home on the third day to report, I knew what I'd name the big island: That one would be called Blight, and I'd argue with the master of charts until she accepted it. She could call the other islands what she wished, and the pelenaut might want to fully explore them and establish a small seasonal fishing camp on one of them someday, but that big island should be named after its nature.

The murmurs and conversation at the end of that tale continued for a while, and Fintan let people talk a bit before he moved on to the next. The Mistmaiden Isles have always been spooky for Brynts; as Tallynd suggested, we tried not to think about them, and if we did by accident, then we'd actively try to think of something else infinitely more pleasant, even if that was damp underwear, creeping mold, or reading aloud an entertaining story to one's parents and suddenly running into a steamy sex scene. But now we had actual names for the islands and knew about the prospect of plentiful fishing and maybe even settlement on three of the islands. And we had the possibility that the Seven-Year Ship had been found, which might prove pivotal to securing our safety. There was more than a little wondering aloud at why we were learning about Tallynd's discovery only months later. Obviously the pelenaut had seen fit to keep that information close, just as he now saw fit to release it.

"Next I have a new narrator for you," Fintan said. "You have met her before, briefly, in some of Abhi's tales. But now you'll get to hear her story in her own voice. This the hivemistress, Hanima Bhandury."

The young woman who took shape in the smoke looked a little bit different from many Nentians—frail and malnourished, I suppose, with well-defined cheekbones. Her clothes didn't fit her and didn't even seem like they were hers; she was practically swimming in a hooded tunic, and her boots were too big and looked like a men's style. Her hair, while straight and black like that of all Nentians, was cut short about her head and something of a tangle, which I was fairly certain meant she was the poorest of the poor, because she couldn't afford to keep it long; when one lived outdoors and the next meal was uncertain, baths and brushes and shampoos would be luxuries. Still, her eyes were alive with light and she smiled easily, her voice musical. With apologies to Fintan, I am not sure I've met anyone with more personal charisma.

Hanima

The city blats before me, rude and smelly like old Khamen Chorous soon after he gulps down his borchatta soup, and if you wrinkle your nose and curl your lip in disgust, he laughs hoarsely, showing you his three brown teeth, amused that you have no choice but to smell the fruits of his ass. Yes: That is the city of Khul Bashab.

The city has always been this way, but only recently have I begun to suspect it doesn't always have to be. That certainly seems to be the opinion of foreigners who visit Khul Bashab; they comment on its smell as if cities should be fragrant. They look at the desperate people living by the docks and wonder aloud how the government can let it happen. I never thought much about how Khul Bashab got this way, or what could or should be done about it, until I left the city to seek a kenning. Now that I've been blessed by the Sixth Kenning, I'm experiencing the world much differently and imagining how it *can* be better, and you know what that feeling is like? It's the best!

I mean, apart from making me a hunted fugitive, it's the best. Hiding from the viceroy's muscle-y military guys gives me plenty of time to think about how to get rid of the city's stench, I suppose, among many other problems I need to solve.

What does the viceroy do all day up in his tower, I wonder, instead of solving the city's problems? I bet he shouts at people for things to be done and then slips marinated eels down his jiggly throat.

That thing! Do it now! Om nom nom! Shout and chomp. Shout and chomp. Except he never shouts about how many of his people are going hungry or makes sure that they have something to chomp on. He works to keep us down, not lift us up. That is, if he works at all;

mostly he's letting people with money exploit the people without it and directing his soldiers to protect the money.

I am probably being unkind, and I should stop. But I'm forced to think of him up in that tower since I have to hide from him in the daylight.

Adithi is feeling sorry for herself because she didn't do anything wrong and yet she has no choice but to ride in our wagon now. Sudhi has left us, horrified and guilty and thinking he's somehow unfit to be around other people. And I get it, I do, especially the horror if not the guilt.

All right, all right, I guess I have to face it, but here's the thing: Killing the guards at the gate was an accident! Though I doubt anyone will believe that. We are in a churning pond of poo, and Tamhan had warned us we'd probably be in one no matter what once our kennings became known, but we didn't think it would get so skyboned so fast.

When I arrived at the Hunter Gate with Sudhi, Adithi, and Tamhan, the guards acted like we were criminals, because we were riding horses no one was using anymore. *We* hadn't killed the cavalry guys—that was Abhinava who did that, and he wasn't with us. What were we supposed to do, just leave their horses out on the plains to be eaten by wheat dogs? I think if we had left the horses behind and simply lied, saying we'd never seen any cavalry or anything, no, sir, we could have entered without incident—or at least without more than the normal level of harassment. But Adithi wanted to make sure those horses were taken somewhere safe, which was fine, except the guards fixated on what had happened to the men riding them. We did lie about that—or, rather, Tamhan did. He told the guards we'd just found those horses on the plains and didn't want them to die. We dismounted and held out the reins and I even smiled at them, which is something I'd never done to someone working for the viceroy.

Maybe my smile wasn't very convincing. Or maybe they didn't believe us because we were covered in blood. It was our own blood, from the seeking where the bloodcats had bitten us, and I had lost a nipple to one of them, but the guards weren't concerned for our welfare or grateful that we'd been thoughtful enough to save those horses and return them. Instead, they came out of the gates with spears pointed at our bodies and threatened us with angry voices, and I thought maybe I was going to die, because I'd seen soldiers kill folks like me before. And my hive, which had followed me the whole way from the seeking in a sort of dispersed swarm, just . . . acted. I didn't tell them to fly into the face of the guard coming at me and sting him until he died screaming, but they did it anyway. And Sudhi didn't tell his khole-shar viper to strike out and bite the face of the guard coming after him either, but that's what happened, and we were left standing at the open gate with five cavalry horses and two dead guards and a growing crowd of ogling spectators.

I am glad Tamhan was with us. He's not blessed with a kenning but instead with a keen mind and a treasury. His father is a crony of the viceroy's, so Tamhan knows something of how their games are played.

"Inside," he told us, and we entered, stepping over the bodies. He asked Adithi to tell the horses to return to the garrison stables on their own, and then we had to go into hiding while Tamhan went home to his protection and privilege and a bed made out of fine soft cheeses, probably, I don't know. I would totally sleep on cheese if I were him.

Tamhan said he was going to clear our names and help us get a beast callers clave established. I'm not sure that those things are possible now, but I'm hanging on to that hope like a cheek raptor with two fresh scoops of someone's face. Hope that tomorrow will be better is how I survive each day.

Sudhi took off after that, very upset, his face scrunched into lines of distress. He said he had a place to go and he'd contact Tamhan as soon as he could. And once he was gone, Tamhan led us down a six-brick street—an alley, really—and said we'd need to disappear. And I'd need to keep my hive dispersed or someone would use the swarm to find me. Adithi was not supposed to do anything with the horses from that point on; Tamhan wanted to cast some doubt about her abilities and spread different rumors.

"I'm going to be watched and won't be able to get messages to you for a while," he said. "So I need you to find someone you trust—someone who can't be bought—to contact me."

Adithi and I exchanged a glance.

"How? We're poor and we only know other poor people, who can easily be bought or threatened. Plus, no one we know would ever make it to your door. *We* would never make it to your door."

Tamhan stopped. "Good point. That's a truth, isn't it? Something we need to change."

I snorted. "Add it to the list."

He grinned at me. "It's getting long, isn't it? Well, how about this: My father has a stall at the River Market. Khatri Meats. You know it?"

"Yes."

"I'll go down there early every morning when it opens, then browse the market afterward before leaving. That should give your messenger opportunity to find me. Just tell them to be careful—they might get questioned afterward."

"We'll use a beggar," I said, thinking quickly.

"There are lots of beggars."

"He or she will ask for money to buy bread and honey. Then you'll know that they can speak to us."

More than a week passed, and we heard nothing in all that time. We recruited old Khamen Chorous to look for Tamhan in the River Market, but he didn't show up. Adithi and I worried but got by with a little help from my hive.

The bees spread out over the city, looking for little gardens and window boxes and so on, but I also had them note dwellings where humans didn't seem to be currently living. That told us where we could steal some clothes that weren't caked in blood, and where we might find some food from the pantries or root cellars. After a couple of days living on rooftops, we found a place that had been closed up for an extended leave and we were able to break in, quietly, and become silent residents, safe from the searches being conducted by the city watch. It was comfortable and cozy and ridiculously luxurious for me. Whoever owned the house probably thought it wasn't good enough; that's why they weren't there. But it had a roof and the floor wasn't muddy. They did not understand how precious those very simple things were to someone in my circumstances. I slept well for the first time in years.

The property was near the Fornish enclave, which was full of flowering plants, and it had a huge old tree in the backyard, and I told the queen if she built her hive up high, no one would probably even know she was there.

She and the girls got to work right away. They needed to start making honey for the winter. Planning ahead for lean times.

I was sitting outside in the twilight of dusk, my head thrown back with a serene smile on my face, watching my hive come home with loads of nectar, when Adithi emerged from the house to join me. She'd brushed her hair out and looked like a proper swell.

"Hey," I said.

"Hey," she replied through a yawn, folding her legs underneath her and grunting.

"Sleep well?"

"Yeah. Those bed things sure are better than rooftop shingles or alleyway bricks."

"So true. Beds are the best. You know what else is the best?"

Adithi sighed and covered her face with her hands, then spread a couple of fingers and peered at me between them. "You're going to say bees, aren't you."

"That's right! Bees are the best. I've been thinking about how they do things and how we do things and I think we can learn from them."

"We're not insects, though, Hanima."

"I know. We're not horses either, but I imagine you'd say we could learn things from them, right?"

"Well, yeah. We should all probably get more fiber. Oats are really good for you."

"Granted. So hang with me on this: Look at how bees organize themselves. Everybody works, including the queen. And everybody is taken care of until they die. And you know what you don't have? Poor bees!"

"Well, no, but they don't have an economy or currency or a political system—"

"Aha! But they do have a system! And that system is organized so that all bees are valued. Same goes for termites and ants. If you want evidence of some kind of natural law, I'd say that's it. If you're alive, you're worth something. The system we have says you and I have no reason to exist, because we don't have jobs or husbands or children, and for some reason—a reason they just made up, not a real reason— that's not natural. That's the way somebody decided it should be, and it's the worst."

My new friend blinked. "Your blanket statements always surprise me. How do you know it's the worst?"

"Because we're miserable—or we were, until very recently. Desperate enough to walk into the plains and let some bloodcats bite us, right? The people we know down by the river are all still miserable. And it's not because it's Kalaad's will or mere chance. It's because that's the system we have. It was created by folks at the top and it's enforced with muscle they pay for, and there's nothing about it that's natural. They are actively choosing not to help those who need it. Letting people starve and die of exposure? Abusing poor folk for daring to exist? How is that natural? Or right?"

Adithi shrugged. "You're not going to get any argument here. But you are going to get a question about what you think we should do about it."

"I don't know yet. But I agree with Tamhan that things have to change. If we don't hear from him soon, we should start thinking of what we can do on our own."

Another shrug. "There's nothing."

"I don't believe that. We can do something."

"Hanima, look, I love your optimism. It keeps me going, you know? But do you think Viceroy Senesh is going to change how he does things because we ask him? No. As soon as we reveal ourselves, he's going to throw us in a dungeon and let the rats nibble on us."

"Rats won't bother us anymore. We're blessed."

"You know what I mean. We can still starve and get chills and things. Swords still cause ouchies. If they didn't, we wouldn't have to sleep during the day and skulk around at night."

"True enough."

Once the sun was down and the temperature started to cool, Adithi and I dressed in new hooded tunics we had bought with some money Tamhan had given us. We pulled them over our heads, effectively hiding much that would make us recognizable to others. They obscured our hair and faces, and we had found some used men's boots, so we passed for men in the darkness. We weren't the filthy, bloodstained urchins everyone was looking for. We were men doing manly things.

We stayed out of the swell neighborhoods and took the alleys and back roads to the River District. They were unpatrolled and therefore dangerous in one sense but safe from being discovered by the city watch, which was more important. Besides, thanks to our blessing, we were both stronger and faster than we used to be, and we knew enough about the streets to recognize when someone had chosen us as a mark. So we sneaked, but with confidence.

Confident sneaking is the best.

We found Khamen Chorous in an alley near the riverside wall, sitting on an upturned crate outside his tent, nursing a tin cup of weak tea he'd made from thrice-used leaves. He'd boiled it over a grate stretched across a garbage fire in a metal pail. When we caught his eye—unlike on the previous days, where he'd shaken his head and we moved on—he waved us over. He flashed his three brown teeth at us in welcome and spoke in a low voice. There were a few other people in the alley, but they were spaced apart, their territory agreed upon in advance and privacy guaranteed, except for what one spoke aloud and bounced off the walls.

"Saw your boy today, I did, I did. Much hair, very shiny, super swell he is. And look at you, all cleaned up and looking like you've been sleeping indoors."

I kept my voice low as well. "We are, for now. What did he say?"

"Two whole words! He said, 'For Hanima,' and dropped some coins and a triangle of paper in my bowl."

"Keep the coins," I said, and Khamen laughed until he coughed up something and spat to the side.

"Already spent them. Bought bread and honey with it, just like I said. That was the best I've eaten in weeks." His fingers fished into a pants pocket and reappeared with a curious wedge of folded paper shaped like a hunk of cheese. Maybe Tamhan had slept on it.

"Did the city watch give you any trouble?" I said as I took it from him.

He shook his head. "No more than usual. I got told to move along before lunchtime, as always. But after I pocketed what he gave me, some other swell comes over and asks what was in there. I showed him two coins and left the note in my pocket. He gave me another coin! Then he asks if your boy said anything, and I told him he said, 'For Kalaad,' and then he says I can earn more coin if I let him know if I see either of you or that other kid with the stripe of yellow hair."

He meant Sudhi. "Have you seen him?" I asked.

"No."

"If you do, will you let him know he can stay with us?"

"Of course."

Adithi said, "Did this man give you a name?"

"No. Said he'd be back to check with me later."

I shook my head. "He works for the viceroy, Khamen. Be careful."

"I know, girl, I know. Anything you want me to say to the kid if I see him again?"

I scanned the alley in either direction. No faces looking our way. "Maybe we should read this first."

"Sure, sure." He regarded his garbage fire doubtfully. "You probably want a candle for that, though. Think I have one in my tent."

"All right." As Khamen lumbered to his feet, I backed away and gestured to Adithi that she should do the same. She looked confused but moved with me and soon knew the reason for it. A minor explosion of flatus from Khamen's backside detonated as he dropped to all fours and crawled into his tent. He giggled until he coughed again, but eventually he emerged triumphant, holding a small taper.

"Sorry about that!" he said, though he clearly was not. He lit the candle over his garbage fire before handing it to Adithi. I unfolded the note, which said "Burn after reading!" at the top in a neat hand.

"What's it say?" Adithi demanded. I glanced at her—she was close enough to see if she wished.

Softly, I asked, "Can you read?"

She pressed her lips together and gave the barest shake of her head. "Only a little. Some shop signs. Not fancy handwriting like that."

"I'll teach you, then." To Khamen I said, "Excuse us a moment," and pulled Adithi a little way down the alley, halfway to the next garbage fire, where someone was boiling borchatta soup. I read aloud, quietly:

> Hanima & Adithi—
>
> I am being watched constantly, so do not attempt to see me. Also stay away from Abhinava's family home; they are watching that too.
>
> The viceroy wants you very badly but is trying to keep your existence a secret. We need you to be known but unseen and safe. The city needs to know the Sixth Kenning is real and that you are not doing the viceroy's bidding. Do what you can for the river folk and they will protect you, but beware of new faces— they may be spies.
>
> I have a group of friends who will post broadsides about the beast callers clave and your vision for a life outside the walls. This will provoke Senesh. He will search openly for you and not be gentle and it will be dangerous. But it will stoke resentment as well as demonstrate that you are not on his side. I will not do this until you are ready, however. Are you safe? Let me know.

It was unsigned, which was smart, in case we didn't actually burn it. "I don't think we should write back. It will put Khamen at risk. Too much can go wrong."

"I agree."

I lit the note with the candle and hurried back over to Khamen to throw it on his garbage fire. He grunted at the brief flare of illumination.

"What should I tell the swell lad if he comes back?" he asked.

"Tell him, 'Message received. Proceed.' That should be enough. Thanks, Khamen."

"Glad to do it. Good to hear you talking."

"Thanks." Of the many benefits to being blessed, I prize the return of my speech above all else.

"Say. If I got blessed, you think I'd get my teeth back?"

I winced and sucked my teeth. "I don't think so, and here's why. During the seeking, we were bitten by many bloodcats. One of them actually bit off my nipple. Everything that could heal is healed now, but that didn't grow back. I'm permanently disfigured. So I think the blessing is a repair-but-not-replace kind of thing."

"I see. I'm not anxious to try it, you understand. Just curious."

"Khamen, if you had a safe place to squat, would you go there? Nothing fancy, but basic shelter and a bed?"

"Beds are pretty fancy for someone like me."

"Me too."

"Well, sure, I wouldn't mind if I knew of such a place."

"Good. Maybe we can arrange something. We'll see you soon, all right?"

"All right, Hanima."

Once we are out of earshot, Adithi asked me, "What do you think we can arrange?"

"I have a plan, Adithi, and it's the best. All these people without a roof over their heads?"

"Yeah?"

"We're going to put a roof over their heads."

The last line of that tale made Hanima an instant favorite out on Survivor Field. They openly applauded when the bard dispelled her seeming. Many of the refugees had tents and whatever few belongings they had managed to accumulate since arriving, but little else. Fintan promised them more soon.

"We'll be back to Hanima in three days' time," he said.

I wondered how Rölly and the city's powerful and well-off had received the tale. The pelenaut is nothing like the Nentian viceroys—he truly cares, and I know he's working to help as much as he can—but I can't imagine anyone with power is ever comfortable hearing an open discussion of systemic change.

"And now I introduce you to not only a new person but a new people. I had the great privilege and honor to meet Koesha Gansu myself. How and when and where—I'll let that develop naturally. But I hope we all may see more of her people in the future. From what I understand, they live on some islands across the ocean, albeit a bit north of here, parallel with the Mistmaiden Isles. They are a seafaring people who have been seeking to cross the Northern Yawn for many years. So I take you back now to the beginning of her journey to our lands."

The seeming that Fintan took was definitely of a different people. Koesha Gansu might look at least somewhat like the Nentians, but she didn't dress like them. She was in a navy-blue uniform trimmed in maroon. Her hair was black and piled or braided underneath an interesting hat like a two-tiered cake embroidered with some gold thread. The hat was perched high up on her head, perhaps pinned to her hair, allowing us to see that Koesha had expressive arched eyebrows and a forehead as yet unwrinkled by age. She wore polished leather boots that nearly reached her knees, and they matched her belt, into the front of which she had tucked two long knife scabbards, their hilts crossing so that she could draw them at the same time to either side. Her skin tone was close to that of a Nentian, sort of a sunbaked sand but with cooler undertones than the coppery hues of the Nentians.

Fintan had her speaking Brynt with an accent that must provide hints at her native language, using shortened vowels and chopping off consonants sometimes.

Koesha

I paused a moment before giving the order to sail and beamed a smile at my crew. We might return someday to glory, having circumnavigated the globe with our reputations cemented in history, and we might die far from home and wind up food for some dark beast of the deep, but regardless of what happened in the days ahead, we would most likely never be so well scrubbed again. Ocean voyages were not conducive to personal hygiene, and I just wanted to fix the image of spotlessness in my mind.

"I want you all to look around and lock this in your memory," I called out, "so that when weeks from now one of you inevitably asks, 'Remember when we were clean?' you can all say, 'Yes!'" The women laughed, musical and light, like wind chimes in a soft summer breeze. It was truly good, a moment of pure hope.

"Ready to set sail, Zephyr Gansu," my first mate reported after hearing the same words from the bosun.

"Take us out of the harbor and tack around the island," I ordered. "May Shoawei bless our journey."

The bosun ordered lines cast off, sails rigged, and reeled off the myriad other commands necessary to get a ship under way. The women jumped to it with glee. In that moment we were breathing the fresh air of adventure and anticipation, an intoxicating cocktail like no other.

Friends and family of the sailors waved and blew kisses from the quay, and we all had opportunity to wave back at least once.

My little brother was there, weeping, and my parents were putting on a good show of looking unconcerned and happy for me because they knew it was what I needed, and they were nothing if not the best parents. They looked the same when they bade farewell to my sister, Maesi, two years ago. My sister who never returned, and whom I was determined to find.

I was also determined to find the elusive passage across the Northern Yawn. To have the keel slice through ice melt, navigate the globe, and come back to safe harbor. To sail into the unknown and return to the known: That is a journey few have accomplished.

Once we cleared the northern shore of Joabei, the full force of the westerly wind smacked into us as we tacked into it. Then I engaged my kenning, asking those prevailing winds to swerve around my ship, curl back on themselves like a whirlwind, and billow my sails east, so that we were at once sailing against the wind and with it.

This decision was a bit fraught, and one could argue it had not ended well for Maesi and I was blowing ill wind over a grave—in fact, it *had* been so argued. By my cousins, by the relatives of the women on my crew—by most everyone who heard about my plan to sail east against the prevailing winds of Shoawei. Sailing with the wind— heading west—was the pious and righteous direction to explore, even though far more people had died going that way than going east. The krakens must think of our shipping lanes as a buffet.

There were some distant uninhabited islands that way—great fishing, supposedly—and once, long ago, someone had tried establishing a village there, but it didn't take hold. When the resupply ship arrived the next year, the villagers had all vanished. It was safer and more profitable to focus our trade with Omesh to the south during the summer months than reach for more-distant shores.

I was leaving exactly two years after Maesi had left. Systematic record-keeping of courses, time of year, and disappearances had revealed that fewer ships got lost in the hottest summer months—almost none; the krakens retreated somewhere during that season, most likely to some unholy spawning grounds, and thus it was the best time for exploration. We knew that there was a landmass—a large island or a continent—to the east. That had been confirmed in the past few years by a number of cautious explorers who sailed out and back. But the more adventurous—those who had tried to map its coastline, perhaps, or set foot there—never returned.

My crew didn't know I wanted to map the coastline or find my way through the Northern Yawn to come home again from the west. They thought we were going to reconfirm the eastern continent, maybe map a tiny bit of it, and return before the krakens stirred in the deep again. That made for a very tight schedule.

It took us most of a month to cross the ocean, to get utterly filthy, and for the lookout in the crow's nest to shout that she spied land ahead. We'd have to turn around soon to avoid the krakens.

My first mate, Haesha Laejeong, reminded me of this fact. She was a friend of mine from school days, who'd not been jealous when I had sought a kenning and found it. A true friend happy for the happiness of others. She admired what she called my "graceful eyebrows," and I admired her gifts: high cheekbones and perfect skin and a voice to either beguile or command.

"Some of the crew have asked when we're going to turn back," she informed me over a glass of wine in my cabin. That was the acceptable way for the crew to question me: Approach the bosun or the first mate with their concerns, and they would then play go-between. My officers acted as both bubble and test audience for me.

"Not yet," I said.

"Aye, that's fine to say right now, but still: when? They're going to keep asking, Koesha, and forcing me to ask you." When we were alone, she dropped my title, and it was a relief to us both. "So if you can name the date of our return, that would be wise."

"I can't put a date on it. I'm looking for something, and when I've found it, we'll return."

Haesha blinked. "All right. Can I share with the crew whatever it is you're looking for?"

I circled the rim of my wineglass with a finger, considering. It was a sweet white vintage, because if I'd wanted early-stage red vinegar, I'd have just bought some.

"I'm looking for my sister," I admitted.

"You think she's alive?"

"No. I mean . . . I hope she is, of course. But that is not what I expect or what I seek. What I'd like is to chart some of the coast and travel inland a bit, see if we can determine whether it's this mysterious land that's responsible for missing crews. If it seems safe, then it was the sea. One or the other had to have killed her, so which was it? If we find something on land, then . . . we can report that. If not, then . . ."

"It was the krakens."

"Yes."

"But taking time to investigate might only ensure that the sea takes us before we can make it home."

"We won't stay long. And I'll add my kenning to the western winds to speed our journey back. That should give us a couple of weeks to explore."

"Two weeks? You've done the math on this?"

I pursed my lips. "You're right. Fifteen days instead of sixteen. Play it safe and stay ahead of the tentacles, as they say."

"Timeless advice."

I paid painstaking attention to the stars and the time and made copious notes of the coast but directed the helm to skirt the northern shore rather than drop anchor. It was all cliffs and rocks anyway; we would need to find a more hospitable stretch for a landing party.

On top of the cliffs, a dense forest of trees stretching for leagues north and south brushed the sky and swayed in the wind. There were also some soft hills carpeted in evergreens, but no true mountains that I could see. We saw no evidence of settlements, likely because we saw no fresh water. We'd need to find some for ourselves soon and stock up for our journey back.

Once we found a river or a stream emptying into the sea, I'd go ashore personally to investigate. And because Maesi would have needed fresh water too, I also hoped to find some sign that she had been there.

If I found nothing, I might let Haesha convince me to turn around. If I found evidence that Maesi had survived the crossing and was somewhere in this new land, however . . . I'd sail on by myself if I had to.

Fintan enjoyed his cup at Master Yöndyr's that evening, listening to people talk about his tales and noting whether they seemed most excited about Tallynd's discovery, the Sixth Kenning in Ghurana Nent, or Koesha Gansu obviously sailing toward the Nentian coast with more knowledge of krakens than we had. We had never heard that the krakens retreated in the summers before.

But we both limited ourselves to a single drink before heading home. It had been a long day and our minds were exhausted.

"I'm so tired I doubt I'll dream at all tonight," Fintan said as we parted. "Which would be perfect."

Day 22

THE SEVEN-YEAR SHIP

All I want in the morning is a peaceful time for toast. Give me that first, and then throw life at me. But it was not to be. Knuckles rapped on my door after I'd buttered my bread but before I'd managed to apply marmalade.

Gerstad Nara du Fesset greeted me at the threshold, her arm still in a sling, and I invited her in.

"Thanks, Dervan, but I can't. I'm here to deliver a message and then I have other duties."

"Oh. What is it?"

Instead of giving me a verbal message, she presented me with a sealed envelope. "This."

"What's it about?"

"No idea. I'm just running errands. But I was told to do this first, so I guess it must be important. Better read it sooner rather than later."

"Do you need a reply?"

"They didn't say I did, so I think we're done here."

"Oh." She waved and took a step away and I said, "Nara? Are you all right? We haven't spoken in a while and I've been worried."

"I'm fine, Dervan. Just keeping busy. I'm sure you are too."

She gave me a small smile that didn't reach her eyes and I knew something was bothering her, but if I kept prying I'd only be bothering her more. It was enough that she knew I cared.

Taking the note to the kitchen, I placed it on the counter next to my toast and paid attention to my breakfast, letting the envelope know that however important its contents might be, they were not more important than the proper slathering of marmalade on a buttered slab of rye. I took toast, tea, and envelope to my kitchen table, enjoyed a bite and a sip, then broke the seal.

Inside was a note for me in a crabbed script and another sealed envelope with no addressee, just an illustrated pair of eyes.

The note read:

> *Master du Alöbar,*
>
> *I require your services this morning on an urgent matter. The enclosed envelope is intended for a Brynt agent who cannot be seen near the palace. I need you to simply leave it at a dead drop, which is underneath a refuse bin in the alley behind the Kraken Good Time Inn outside the city walls. The proper bin is marked with a yellow star. I need this small favor done as soon as possible, please, in return for the many services I have done you. Please burn this note before proceeding, but proceed with all haste.*
>
>

Yours in wretched darkness,
Master Butternuts

"Drown me!" I shouted. "No. Drown him! I don't want to do any of his spy shit!"

But I didn't know how to refuse. He had done me quite a few favors, from refurnishing my home to finding out who'd ordered my wife to be poisoned to promising vengeance upon the perpetrator. All I had to do was take a walk outside the walls and place this letter underneath a bin. As far as skulduggery was concerned, that didn't sound so bad. I might even find the exercise invigorating.

Muttering curses all the while, I burned the note with a candle and then stepped outside with my cane and the sealed letter. I waved at Constable du Bartylyn, who was passing by and had absolutely no updates on my stolen furniture, save for a speculation that someone else must have farted on it by now, and if I thought about that long enough, it might make me feel a little bit better about never seeing it again.

He walked away, whistling, and I thought he was a singularly strange individual for trying to comfort me with thoughts of thieves tooting their foghorns on my property. But perhaps I should give him full marks for innovative community policing.

The walk to the city gates and then outside them was the opposite of relaxing. Anytime someone's eyes flickered in my direction, I was positive they could see that I was up to something dastardly. Yet they walked on and raised no alarms.

The Kraken Good Time Inn might have actually been a good time, but I would not know since I never set foot inside. I circled around to the back, saw six stinking bins of trash, and noted that the fourth one from the left had a small gold star painted on one side. I tipped it up slightly and slid the envelope underneath, even though it was crawling with insects. I let the bin rest and wiped my hands on my pants. The alley smelled foul, and I felt like I needed a bath after that.

I never made it out of the alley. Four mariners—two in front, and two behind—appeared with halberds pointed in my direction and demanded my immediate surrender.

"Okay," I said, raising my hands. "You got me."

"Damn right we do," one snarled. "Traitor."

"What? Who are you looking for? Because it isn't me."

"It's you, all right. You're the one who just put a letter underneath that bin."

"So?"

"So you're a traitor, fish head."

"Sir, I'm a patriot. Pelenaut Röllend is my friend."

An impact on the back of my head ended that conversation before I could receive any reply. I woke up someplace dank and dark, nursing a headache far worse than the previous day's hangover. It was not the sort that tea would fix very quickly.

There was a light source coming from a hallway, dimly seen through a grille of bars. I was in a dungeon.

"Huhhrr. Gleh. Huh. Hey!" I felt that last word was the correct one, so I said it again. "Hey!"

A voice from the hallway said, "He's awake," and another replied, "I'll let them know," before the tap of bootheels receded on stone.

"Can I—"

"Shut up, traitor," the first voice said. "You can talk all you want when they ask you questions. Nothing's happening until then."

Considering how much pain I was in and the spinning of my senses, I was content to remain silent. I held myself still and patiently waited for my skull to cease punishing me. It might be a long while.

The pain might have receded the tiniest smidgen when, after some inderminate time, they moved me to a different room, with some better lighting and significantly less mold. They sat me down at a table and chained me to it. There were two chairs on the other side, and after a few minutes Pelenaut Röllend and his lung, Föstyr du Bertrum, entered and took the seats. There was no flash of welcome or friendship in their eyes.

"Rölly, what—"

"Let us ask the questions, Dervan." My old friend held up the envelope with the eyes on it. "Did you write this?"

"No! You've seen my handwriting. I was given it and told to drop it under that bin outside the walls."

"Who gave it to you?" Föstyr asked.

"Gerstad Nara du Fesset."

Neither of them showed any surprise at this. "And she told you to drop it under the bin?" the lung asked.

"No, she just gave me an envelope. Inside that envelope was a note plus that envelope you have there. The instructions told me where to drop it."

"Do you still have the instructions?" Rölly said.

"No, it said I should burn them after reading, and I did."

Föstyr pinched the bridge of his nose as if a headache was coming on. He could have mine if he wanted.

Rölly sighed in frustration. He fished out three sheets of paper with various things written on them and arranged them in front of me, each obviously written by a different person.

"Were the instructions you burned written in the handwriting of any of these notes you see here?"

I scanned them quickly and picked out the crabbed script of the Wraith immediately. I chucked my chin at it.

"Yes. The middle one. That's it. Master Butternuts."

Rölly and Föstyr exchanged a dour glance. "You're sure?"

"Positive."

"Do you know what's in this letter you dropped off?" Rölly said, waggling it in front of me briefly before unfolding it. The seal had already been broken.

"No."

"Do you know what language it's written in?"

"Brynt, I assume."

"No, Dervan. It's Eculan. And it's signed by Vjeko, the traitor we've been looking for."

"Ohhhhhhh, shiiiiit." My poor treatment by the mariners suddenly made sense.

"Yes, Dervan. Infinite fields of dire, malodorous shit. Because Gondel Vedd, the only man who can read it, isn't here."

I blinked. "He's not? But we just heard about this Vjeko character a couple days ago."

"True, but the bard was sharing events that happened months ago. Gondel left us shortly after that time, and we've been looking for this Vjeko character ever since. We sure could use Gondel to read this to us now. Unless this Master Butternuts can do it for us. Who is that, by the way?"

"Oh, that's just my nickname for him. You know who it is. The Wraith."

"You're not jesting with me right now, are you? It's not the time."

"I'm not, Rölly. I swear to you as both a subject and as a friend. Master Butternuts is the Wraith."

Rölly put the unsealed letter in Eculan down on the table next to the middle note I'd picked out. They were written in different languages, but it was without doubt the same handwriting.

"The instructions you were given were in this handwriting, which you've accurately identified as the Wraith's. And he sent you to drop off a letter signed by Vjeko. A letter that he wrote. So you see our problem."

I took a deep breath before replying and saying the words aloud, realizing the horrific truth. "Yes. The Wraith is the traitor Vjeko."

"Yes. Our own master of spies betrayed us and attempted to erase our people from the face of Teldwen. And you're working for him."

"What? No! I mean, yes, I did this one thing for him, but I didn't know he was a traitor! The instructions said it was intended for a Brynt agent."

Föstyr cleared his throat and said, "That's one of many problems we face. Who is this letter actually intended for, and where are they? As for the Wraith being the traitor, we've suspected that for a good while. We saw the teeth a long time ago and now we see the bladefin behind them, thanks to this confirmation. The tale the bard told about Gondel's intelligence and Tallynd's tale about finding the Seven-Year Ship were precisely to provoke this kind of response. We knew where the dead drop was, and we just needed to wait for him to use it again."

"Okay. So what are the other problems?"

The lung snorted. "Who else is working for him? And are they unwitting accomplices or are they traitors with full knowledge of their complicity? And how do we deal with the Wraith himself?"

"I don't understand," I said. "Are you unable to arrest him or pull the water out of his brain, or what?"

"It's easier said than done," Rölly said. "We're fairly certain he's not a normal person."

"How so? I mean, he's sick and he sits in the dark. If you listen to him breathe, it doesn't sound like he can beat a bowl of pudding to death."

Rölly quirked an eyebrow at Föstyr. "Shall I tell him?"

The lung nodded. "Might as well."

Rölly leaned forward and lowered his voice, even though it was only the three of us in the room. "Tallynd saw something else about the wraiths on Blight. Just as we made sure the bard included some of Gondel's information in his tale, we made sure that a very important detail was left out when Tallynd recounted her story to the bard. We didn't want it to be public knowledge."

"But you're okay with telling me now?"

The pelenaut shrugged. "Sure. We're going to take care of this today one way or the other. Here's the thing: The wraiths had twisted faces—you heard Tallynd's report correctly there—but the rest of their bodies were recognizably *not* from here. They were tall, thin Eculans. Every single one of them."

"You mean the wraiths are Bone Giants?"

"Yes. And that song the bard sang a while back about mistmaidens and mistmen and how attractive they are? That was a barrel of fish heads. There is no way you'd ever think kissing them was a good idea."

"So what are you saying, Rölly? The Wraith is somehow allied with the Bone Giant wraiths on the Mistmaiden Isles?"

"No, Dervan. I'm saying he *is* a wraith. He *is* a Bone Giant. He's the one who sold us out, who coordinated the attack, who gave the Bone Giants everything they needed to know to wipe us out."

It was too huge for my mind to grasp. "I don't get it. How did we not figure out that he's a Bone Giant before now?"

"Because he's in a Brynt body. One that the Wraith possessed long ago. It's why he's been sick for decades but somehow never dies."

A cold tremor shuddered through my body. I remembered that candlelit portrait on the wall in the Wraith's dark room, of a ghostly wraith standing among the trees of some nameless island, and thinking at the time it was a heavy-handed scare tactic. It was far scarier now that I knew the Wraith probably viewed it as a self-portrait. And it was also infuriating—the arrogance of it, I mean—to realize he was laughing at me the whole time while I thought "the Wraith" was just a name he'd adopted rather than his actual nature.

"Never dies?" I said. "How long have you known this?"

"We didn't know for sure he was the traitor until just now, when you identified his handwriting. We've only suspected. His reports are always written by someone else. And it's taken a long time to confirm things and investigate in a way that didn't alert him. He has people everywhere."

"Okay . . . wow. Walk me through how you got there?"

Röllend leaned back and gestured to his lung, and Föstyr took his cue.

"After the first attacks on our cities, we knew there had to be a traitor, because the strikes were too well timed and executed not to have been made based on inside information. We began with the hope that the traitor couldn't be a Brynt who agreed to plan their own people's genocide. That code name for a contact that Tallynd found—Vjeko—seemed to confirm this, since it wasn't a Brynt name. That meant the traitor had to be either a Bone Giant or some other foreign national. We were pursuing the foreign-national idea, obviously, until Tallynd reported that the wraiths were Bone Giants. We talked a lot about what that might mean, but Könstad du Lallend—our top military adviser, in case you haven't heard of him—pointed out that maybe a wraith could escape the island if it had a body to ride along in. And if that happened, then . . . it could potentially live among us and we'd never know."

"That sounded improbable to me at first," Rölly interjected. "I didn't think possession could be so subtle as to escape notice. But I didn't want to dismiss anything. I wanted everything investigated. So we went back to that master of charts Tallynd mentioned in her story and asked her if she would mind running up to Festwyf and seeing if they had anything in their archives."

"You sent the master of charts to a dead city all by herself?"

"No. With Tallynd. The archives were untouched; the Bone Giants just killed everyone and moved on. So she found a record of the pelenaut's request to survey the Mistmaiden Isles from a hundred twenty-seven years ago. The quartermaster at the time *did* send out a crew of ten volunteers. But only two returned—a man and a woman, both mariners—and the report said they were raving mad, speaking words that made no sense, and they had not completed a survey of any kind."

"Holy turtle balls," I said, my horror growing.

"It gets more interesting," Föstyr said. "Because I did a little digging. A lot of digging, really, in our archives here. Turns out that a man named Ursen du Mylseböck and a woman named Ysabel du Köpen came to Pelemyn from Festwyf one hundred twenty-five years ago and made themselves very useful to the government. They were former mariners. That man is now known only as the Wraith."

"Kraken cocks! And the woman?"

"Still using the same name. You've met her."

"I have? I don't recall meeting her."

"She's his assistant. Surely you've met. Acts like she's heard of emotions but can't seem to imitate them properly."

"Oh, drown me! Approval Smile!"

"What?"

"That's what I call her. She smiles only when you do what she wants."

"That's the one." He waggled a finger at me. "That's an astute observation."

"So they're both possessed by wraiths?"

"We think so," the lung affirmed. "It would fit with the description of them speaking a strange language upon their return to Festwyf. And it would account for the fact that they've been working in Pelemyn for a hundred twenty-five years. We have records to prove it. Scattered and fragmented, and some records that should be there are missing, which we find suspicious, but if they did try to purge records, they missed some. They're probably one hundred fifty years old, or else very close to it."

"And the wraiths that possessed them are keeping their bodies alive?"

"It would seem so."

I rattled my chains on the table as I attempted to throw up my hands in frustration and failed. "How have you two not soiled your pants yet? Because I'm experiencing both a fight *and* flight response right now. This is the most horrifying thing I've ever heard. Are the original Brynts even still alive, or are the wraiths fully in charge of their minds?"

"We don't know."

It made me wonder what else they did or didn't know. I'd assumed that the Wraith was sharing everything with Rölly and Föstyr, but if he was a traitor, that might have been a foolish assumption.

"Rölly . . . were you aware of a recent operation in Rael in which Nara du Fesset managed to steal the journal of Clodagh of the Triune Council?"

"Yes. I've read it."

"The whole thing?"

"Yes."

"Then you know she ordered the death of my wife, Sarena."

The pelenaut blinked. "What? No, I don't recall reading that."

My jaw dropped, and another cold shiver racked my spine. "There wasn't a passage in there about a poison crafted in Aelinmech for a Brynt spy?"

"No. It was almost uniformly boring. Clodagh is mired up to her neck in Raelech internal squabbles, railing against the other members of the Triune."

"There was nothing about Sarena in there? Nothing that could remotely be attributed to her?"

"No. Why would there be?"

"Because the Wraith—that bloody bastard Wraith—said there was!

And whatever is in there, Clodagh thinks it's embarrassing. Because she told me as much through Fintan."

Rölly frowned. "Are you saying she sent a message to you through Fintan?"

"Yes. Numa was here recently, right?" The pelenaut nodded and I continued. "She relayed a message from Clodagh to Fintan, and he relayed it to me: She knows the journal was stolen and she threatens retribution if we try to use it against her."

Rölly blew a raspberry. "Well, I can understand that. It's seedy. Unseemly. Even gross, maybe. Not sure what the right word is. But it's all Raelech drama and none of our concern. I don't have any interest in sharing its contents. I only wanted to know if she planned on using the Raelech reinforcements on their way here to overthrow our rule, but if that's the case, she didn't write it down."

"So she's not plotting the murders of our spies?"

"No."

"You're positive you read the whole thing?"

"Yes."

I thought of that convenient Brynt translation the Wraith had inserted in the journal. He had already known I couldn't read Raelech very well. He'd made it all up. "The Wraith lied to me."

Rölly nodded. "It would seem so."

"That means I still don't know who poisoned Sarena. He just used me. Why? To buy my loyalty?"

Föstyr nodded. "To put you in his debt. So you'd do something for him later, like drop a traitorous letter. And maybe you'd try to do something rash to Clodagh, thinking you were getting revenge, but really you'd be starting a war between Rael and Brynlön."

I clenched my fists and flicked my eyes at Rölly. "Bryn's balls, I really hate this spy shit. This kind of thing is exactly why I told you I wasn't prepared for this. Are you going to kill him? And if so, can I help?"

My friend shook his head. "I don't know. Consider, Dervan: If wraiths are already dead, can we really kill them? I mean, sure, as a tidal mariner I can rip the water out of the body's blood, but will the wraith possessing that body be destroyed at the same time? Or will that wraith simply be free to possess someone else? What if that someone else is *me*, Dervan? What if I go to kill the Wraith and, as a result, a wraith becomes the pelenaut of Brynlön?"

"Oh, drown me. I take it back, Rölly. Do not try to kill the Wraith."

"I've never met him in person, you know. We've always used go-betweens. I'm worried that a face-to-face is what he's waiting for."

"Oh, yeah. That makes a very scary sort of sense. Definitely stay away."

"I will. Or I will until we have him secured. But I worry about our people getting hurt. I don't think he'll go quietly. Okay, listen. We are going to move as quickly as we can, but I need to keep you here until this is over. I am sorry you got roped into this."

"I am too." I ducked my head. "I don't know if I'll ever get over disappointing you."

"No. It's not you. It's not any of us, really. It's him. Or them. It's the unreasoning hatred of someone who has decided against all evidence that we do not deserve to exist because we are not the same as him. We're going to try to contain him now, and some of Föstyr's people will have some additional questions for you. I can't say when you'll be out but hopefully soon."

"So I won't be meeting with the bard anymore?"

"Well . . . not for now. We will make excuses and apologies on your behalf."

I nodded dumbly, but as they got up to leave, I remembered something. "My account of the Wraith—my meetings with him and the lies he told me about Sarena—it's in my manuscript."

"Thank you," Föstyr said.

They exited, and the clang of the cell door closing only made the subsequent silence more pronounced. I didn't even know what they meant when they said they would try to "contain him" but figured I would learn later. Maybe.

In that cold metal pool of silence, I wallowed in the knowledge that I had been legendarily gulled by the Wraith, though I suppose that didn't separate me from the rest of the government very much; he'd apparently been playing a very long game and had safely operated against us under the noses of multiple pelenauts for more than a century.

With hindsight, it was appalling. Any work he had done to weaken Rael or other countries was as much in service to Ecula as it was to Brynlön. And, of course, he had been learning everything he could about Brynlön for decades and passing that information on to the invaders so that they moved through our country with confidence about where and how to strike.

I worried about Gerstad Nara du Fesset. Had she been duped like me? Or was she somehow complicit in the Wraith's schemes? I would not believe it without proof and would not have had cause to wonder, but when one is so masterfully fooled, one begins to doubt even bedrock beliefs, questioning everything that had previously been believed on faith.

There was no way to judge the passing of time until I heard the bard's magical voice reach me in the cell, and while I knew I was going to miss being on the wall and seeing the forms he took, I was relieved that I wouldn't miss any of the tales. He sang a song and took a break, and I wondered if the Wraith and Approval Smile were listening now in some other cell somewhere, frustrated and justly worried about their fates. I hadn't heard anyone clanking around in the dungeon, but they might have them imprisoned elsewhere. Or else they hadn't managed to catch the Wraith after all.

Fintan's voice reached me again. "I'm going to begin today's tales with Fornish ambassador Mai Bet Ken—perhaps you remember her from earlier, when Melishev Lohmet described her strong scent of floral perfume."

There was a pause, no doubt while he took the form of her seeming, and I wished I could see it but did my best to picture a green-robed, diminutive Fornish woman, pale skinned and . . . brunette? I couldn't recall if he had mentioned it before.

Mai

When walking among the weeds, which one do you pull up first? Begin anywhere at random, since they all must be plucked eventually? At the periphery of the infestation, methodically progressing in a certain direction? The biggest first? Start in the middle and work out in a spiral?

In truth it does not matter. What matters is persistence. Determination to prevail. Cultivation of a garden does not require a blessing so much as sweat. Growing up in the Red Pheasant Clan taught me that. I worked in the fields and greenhouses like everyone else, looking after Sif Tel tea bushes and the various herbs we grow for medicinal purposes. I always preferred the tea; it smelled more pleasant than the medicinal plants and didn't make me think about disease.

I do not live in the Canopy anymore, and while I do miss it, I am proud of the garden I've built here in Hashan Khek—a literal one on the Fornish grounds and a metaphorical one of contacts in the Nentian government. A garden of relationships, I suppose, that I'm nurturing as the Fornish ambassador to Viceroy Melishev Lohmet. Tending to him requires quite a bit of work and a lot of floral spritzes applied to my person. If I give off a strong odor, it usually repels advances and shortens my meetings; it's both convenient and efficient, if pungent. Unfortunately, he makes me think of disease rather often, since he's visibly afflicted with something.

This posting has proven to be anything but the sentence to boredom I thought it was going to be. I'd hoped my study of languages and cultures would earn me a posting in Kauria, where I could revel in their universities and libraries and still enjoy fantastic teas, but I got assigned to Ghurana Nent instead, where until recently nothing of import ever happened. We have only three posts in the entire country.

And then Mount Thayil erupted, Gorin Mogen invaded down by the Godsteeth, and suddenly I'm in a hot spot—though only a metaphorical one, thank sun and rain. And my colleague in Khul Bashab, Jes Dan Kuf, is in another. While Melishev marched south with the king's tactician, Diyoghu Hennedigha, in front of a huge army sent from Talala Fouz, I received word from Jes that there are credible reports of some kids finding the Sixth Kenning!

If true, then Ghurana Nent will be changing profoundly. It might change for the better—we can only hope—or it might change for the worse. Forn must be prepared for either eventuality. And I am improbably, terrifyingly, thrillingly, one of the people who can make sure Forn is prepared. I can almost see the elders of my clan reaching for emergency mango juice at the thought of that grimy, sunburnt girl from the fields being in charge of anything. I sometimes wonder if their buds have ever blossomed: The assumption that manual laborers cannot lead rich intellectual lives is offensive. My best thinking usually occurs while working outdoors—so much so that my office is a solarium with the windows open as much as possible.

While Viceroy Lohmet was absent at the Godsteeth, I wrote letters to colleagues throughout Forn, explaining my thinking and arguing that we needed Fornish ambassadors in all Nentian cities to gently push for policies that will not only protect the Canopy but help it thrive with the advent of the Sixth Kenning. We cannot bear to have an inimical neighbor to the south in Hathrir and another in the north.

I sent another batch of letters to the leaders of my clan, specifically arguing that expanding our tea interests would be good for both the Canopy and the Red Pheasants. I haven't heard back yet, but Lohmet has returned, victorious, and summoned me to an audience.

When I enter and see him sitting on his throne, he is as triumphant as a corpse flower, which takes years to bloom and, when it does, smells of death no matter how beautiful the blossom. He smirks while the muscle underneath one eye twitches. He is sweating a little, even though it is cool, a late-summer prelude to autumn. He is still very ill and in need of a Brynt hygienist to cleanse him of contagion. To his left, behind him, looms the tactician, Hennedigha, at parade rest, his face unreadable.

"Ambassador Ken," he says, then coughs a couple of times. "How lovely to smell you again."

"Welcome back, Viceroy. How may I serve?"

"You've no doubt heard of our victory against Gorin Mogen."

"I have. Congratulations."

"It is truly I who should be congratulating you. The Fornish forces led by your greensleeves did most of the work. One of them was personally responsible for slaying Mogen."

"Yes. Nel Kit ben Sah of the White Gossamer Clan. She will be honored for generations."

"Tell me, have you heard from your contacts in Pont about the Brynt hygienist stationed there?"

"I have. They tell me that the hygienist has returned home to Brynlön, called back by the pelenaut himself. I'm sorry to deliver such disappointing news. We are all bereft."

Melishev Lohmet's fingers clutch at the arms of his throne, the knuckles turning ghastly white, and his jaw clenches hard to contain some stream of rotted curses. I drop my eyes and wait, because I know there's more.

"No matter," Lohmet eventually grinds out. "I have extraordinary news to share. Hearthfire Winthir Kanek has burned the capital of Talala Fouz and slain King Kalaad the Unaware. We have this news from the Raelechs. Apparently he was seeking his daughter, who was with Mogen at the Godsteeth but surrendered to me there and begged my indulgence to travel to the capital. She wanted to build a city in the Gravewood, and the king granted her leave."

"I am . . . astounded. You wouldn't jest with me?"

"No. I would not."

"So Winthir Kanek has sacked the capital?"

"No, he is dead. Slain in the street by a face jumper. His fury and crew abandoned his body and escaped while the city burned. Or so they thought. Their ship was rammed by a Larik whale, and Kanek's pet fury, who burned the city down, was lost. We have this too from the Raelechs."

"How would they know all this?"

"Because the Nentian boy with the Sixth Kenning made it happen, and he is with them now, traveling upriver."

"So the Sixth Kenning is real? I've heard only rumors."

"It's real. That same boy was at the Battle of the Godsteeth, and he took out most of the lavaborn—except for Mogen—with a stampede of kherns. We are very grateful for the aid Forn gave us in repelling Mogen, but henceforth such aid shouldn't be necessary."

"This truly is extraordinary news."

"Indeed! And now Ghurana Nent needs a new king." He turns his head to look over his shoulder at Hennedigha. A sly smile spreads on his face, like mold on bread. "What do you think, Hennedigha? Have we not proven our merit? Shall we travel north, fresh victory under our boots, and build a new capital from the ashes of the old?"

The tactician smiles on one side of his face, gives a single nod and a grunt of assent.

"Ha! He speaks eloquently, does he not? Such a lofty lexicon. So that is why I have called you here. We leave in three days' time for the capital with our army to restore order and rebuild Talala Fouz. You may accompany us or remain here in Hashan Khek; it is your decision. Either way, I imagine you have preparations to make, letters to write, and so on."

"I will of course follow you, Viceroy, but perhaps a day or two behind to make sure we have made all necessary preparations. Thank you for letting me know. Is there anything else?"

"Not for now. I have no idea what situation your embassy might be in up there, but you have permission to build or rebuild as needed when you arrive."

I bow and hurry back to our embassy. Rot and wilt the giants for burning us again! Is my colleague in Talala Fouz dead? If not and I've simply not received word, I'll still go. The viceroy invited me, and someone needs to look out for the Canopy's interests. Melishev Lohmet thinks to make himself king, and I have little doubt that, behind Hennedigha's army, he can do it, even if other viceroys covet the throne. There will be unrest, however, in the short term—perhaps even a civil war, if Lohmet's popularity is as polarized as I think it is.

Forn definitely needs eyes and ears in every Nentian city now—not to take sides, but simply to have a better idea which shoots might grow to full flower.

Sometimes, when gardening, it's difficult to know which plants are weeds and which are desired. And some weeds, when allowed to grow, become so entrenched and troublesome that we wish we had the foresight to yank them out when they were seedlings.

Fintan's voice returned to its accustomed timbre as he dispelled Mai Bet Ken and told everyone it was time to find out what Second Könstad Tallynd du Böll found out next in the Mistmaiden Isles.

Tallynd

The pelenaut was almost as interested in the fecund fishing waters as he was in the discovery of the Seven-Year Ship, and he assigned Föstyr, the lung, the task of putting together a group that could build and sustain a fishing camp on either Bean or Bolt.

"Are we in such dire straits already?" I asked, and he shook his head.

"Not yet. But we will be. That's the way the river's flowing. We'll need the sea to sustain us until we can get our agriculture functioning again."

I was granted a few days' rest while Pelenaut Röllend conferred and planned, and when I reported back, I was to return to the Seven-Year Ship, as I suspected. Gerstad Nara du Fesset would be going with me, and together we were to steal the ship and take it to Dead Man's Point, where it could be studied in safety away from the wraiths and kept out of the hands of the Bone Giants. Föstyr would meet us there.

Nara's lifebond, Mynstad du Möcher, stopped by to say farewell at the entrance to the Lung's Locks in the Wellspring. Nara flicked her eyes to me and begged my pardon.

"Of course," I said, and I turned my back and heard their embrace—the creak of the mynstad's leather armor squeezed in her lifebond's arms—then a kiss and soft murmurs of love. I grinned because they were so adorable. But then, following so hard I had to stifle a gasp, a sharp pang of grief seized my heart. I felt myself welling at the memory of such moments with my husband. Squalls of grief can surprise me sometimes, though it's been years. I miss him so much.

"Ready, Second Könstad," Nara said, suddenly beside me at the pool's edge.

"Oh. Good."

"Are you all right?"

"Fine," I said, dashing a tear away from my eye. "Let's go."

The churn of the feeding grounds around Blight was not so severe as it had been a week ago. There were no bladefins in the area anymore, but the crabs and smaller scavengers were still at it, ensuring that the Bone Giants were no more than bones, and even those would eventually be broken down by small creatures that would take a longer time to get the work done.

"Bryn preserve us, this is horrible," Nara said, treading water next to me at the edge of the Eculan fleet.

"Wait until you see the wraiths. That's the true horror."

"What's the plan?"

"We have to enter into that cloud of guts and blood and surface next to the hull of the ship. We need to be stealthy about it so the wraiths don't spot us. Then we cut the lines mooring the ship to the dock and use our kenning to float that ship out of there."

"Are we going to get on board?"

"I have no ambitions of that nature. I'd feel safer in the sea. We don't know if there are wraiths on board or not."

"Oh, squid shit! I didn't even think of that."

"We're safe in the water, even if they are on board. They're going to be someone else's problem, not ours. It's cutting the ropes that will place us in closest proximity to their reach. So silently we go."

I reached out my hand to Nara and she clasped it in hers. Together we ducked underneath the waves and sleeved ourselves through the water a handsbreadth below the surface, probably creating a small ripple as we moved but unlikely to be noticed.

The cloud of sediment—really a diffused suspension of Eculan body fluids and tissue mixed with crab shit—was spectacularly unpleasant. The water felt unclean and greasy, and we could see little chunks of flesh and organs floating past our eyes. Some of it was no doubt getting trapped in our hair, and I would be giving mine a vigorous wash as soon as possible.

A dark slice of the keel appeared eventually, and we descended to surface on the other side of it.

"I never want to do that again," Nara whispered to me, her eyes wide in horror, and I nearly laughed out loud. I clamped my lips together and shook my head in agreement. Nara had little pieces of skin and who knew what in her hair, which meant it was in mine too.

We looked up at the situation. There was a padded fender on the dock to prevent the hull from scraping against the planks and taking damage. There were four hawsers tying the ship to the dock, but we quickly realized that these were too far above the water level for us to reach. There was also a gangplank lowered, so there might indeed be wraiths on board, but the ship wasn't anchored.

That itself was curious to me: This was rigged in such fashion as to indicate a stay of a few days or weeks. It wasn't an ideal situation for an extended period of dormancy, such as seven years. The ship didn't appear to have languished here long either; up close, I could see that the varnish on the hull was new. I didn't see seven years or more of weathering on the boards.

Nara and I pointed to the gangplank at the same time and said in low tones, "That's a problem." There was no way for us to get rid of it without getting up on the dock.

"Hawsers first," I said, pulling out the large serrated glass knife we'd brought with us for the purpose. Hathrim glass knives like these were rare; they were made exclusively for us at enormous expense by one particular firelord in Narvik, shipped overland across the breadth of Forn from Pont to Keft, and then up the coast to us in Pelemyn. No one else had use for such tools; steel was the preferred material for everyone who didn't have to spend most of their working hours in the water. Bryn's blessed, however, preferred tools that wouldn't rust. I had sent the firelord a thank-you note for his skill in my best approximation of calligraphy, using the ink of a great Peles longarm. I liked to think he envied my kenning even as I envied his.

I took the fore and Nara took the stern. On a nodded signal, we both gushed out of the sea just enough to wrap an arm around the hawser and dangle from it while the other arm sawed away at its braided strength.

My eyes darted to the shore and the dock, looking for any signs of approaching wraiths. The splashing noises we'd made might have been heard but might also be the sort of thing that occurred frequently as the feeding went on below. We weren't visually obvious, presenting only a forearm and head above the level of the dock. All I could see in turn was the telltale blurring of the tree trunks, indicating that the wraiths were still milling about the island.

Nara sawed through her hawser first, and I heard her splash back into the water. I followed soon after and then glided over to confer with her.

"Let's wait and watch before taking the next two," I said.

"Okay," she agreed. "My arm could use the rest anyway."

We treaded water, watching the beach for any indication that the wraiths had heard us and listening for any activity on board the boat. It had rocked a little bit at the release of tension and would no doubt do so even more violently once the last two hawsers were severed. At that point only the hooks of the gangplank attached to the dock would keep it moored there, and it would be unsteady.

"When the next two go, we'll need to move fast," I thought aloud. "The ship will visibly move, and I don't think they can miss it. And to get the gangplank unhooked, I'll have to get up on the dock itself."

"Why you? I can do it."

"You have a wife."

She raised an eyebrow. "And you have kids."

"But I bet you promised you'd be back."

Her eyes broke contact with mine. "I did."

"I didn't. It breaks my heart, but the kids know I can't promise them anything anymore, except to love them. And I don't think you can shield yourself from them as well as I can—I can maintain a bubble of water around myself as I walk, and that's the best defense I can think of. So I will do this. Once the gangplank is free, pull a wave to push the boat away."

She nodded acknowledgment of the order, and we separated to attack the last two hawsers. I was hyperconscious of the fact that when these snapped, the release of tension might well whip us toward the ship. My head could be in danger of cracking against the hull.

As before, Nara sawed through hers first. She was thrown against the hull with a thud and grunted in pain as she fell back into the water.

I unhooked my arm and gripped the hawser with just my hand as I sawed through the final braid. The eventual snap was violent, the fibers burning my palm and lashing my left wrist and also whipping my right, causing me to fumble the expensive blade. But I dropped straight into the water rather than suffering a crash against the hull. I hoped Nara was okay, but I didn't have time to check on her. The gangplank needed to be done right now.

I fountained myself out of the water to land on the dock, understanding that stealth wasn't a part of the equation anymore, and I maintained a sheath of water a knuckle deep all around my body as a defense against the lure of the wraiths and perhaps even against their touch. The horrors had already either spotted or heard us. They were no doubt en route to my position, silent and deadly, but looking up and wetting myself in fear wasn't going to get the job done. I focused on the gangplank and nothing else.

The boat was straining hard against the hooks, so taut that I couldn't unfasten them. I pulled the water underneath the hull toward me, to give me the slack to unhook the plank and cast it off so that it would hang uselessly off the side once Nara summoned it away. Once done, I shouted, "Clear!" to Nara, even though I couldn't see her. That's when I realized there was no space for me to drop back into the water. I turned my head to the left and saw that the wraiths were in fact bearing down on me, coming to fetch me since I couldn't be lured to them. Their eyes were blackened pits, pools of night floating in the sun; likewise, their mouths were gaping maws, lined with spectral teeth—for what purpose, I wondered? Would I feel them tear into me, like a bladefin's teeth? The rest of their forms were insubstantial, but the eyes and mouths appeared all too real. I spun to sprint to the other side of the dock and promptly fell flat on my face, as my left foot—speared by an Eculan not so long ago—refused to support such an athletic move. The water sheath I'd been keeping in place splashed away with the impact and my surprise, and I was therefore vulnerable. I kept my eyes shut.

Getting back to my feet would take too long. I threw myself into a roll until I dropped off the dock, opening my eyes only as gravity took me and I couldn't stop my fall. The wispy fingers of the lead wraith clutched at my feet, missing by only a hair; a gust of freezing wind on my toes was the only hint of what fate I'd suffer if they actually touched me. The nasty water welcomed me back with a floating eyeball, and I had never felt so relieved. I shot as quickly as I could underneath the dock and the Seven-Year Ship to the other side, already pushing the waters of the inlet to buffet the hull of the ship and guide it away. I surfaced, facing the ship, and looked around for Nara. She was off to my left, and she cried out when she saw me.

"Tallynd! Thank Bryn! I thought you might be lost!"

We laughed in relief, the way people do when they realize they're still alive and perhaps shouldn't be. The silent milling of the wraiths held no terror for us now that we were safe in the ocean. Or at least it was a reduced terror.

"What say we get ourselves to clearer waters and steer the ship to us from out there?" I said, and she readily agreed. We sped out to the edge of the inlet and spent a while vigorously washing the chum out of our hair. Then we linked hands and worked together to guide the ship on carefully controlled swells out of the inlet and into the open waters of the strait.

We kept a close eye on the deck as it moved in our direction, shepherded by waves of our own making. I saw no telltale wobble in the air that would indicate a wraith was on board, and no one emerged from belowdecks in bewilderment that the ship had become unmoored. It eased out into the strait, and soon enough we were able to leave the wraiths behind.

It was a beautiful ship, it could not be denied. But I couldn't see how it was worth all the effort of the Bone Giants to find it or how it was worth so many lives on all sides.

Without ever boarding it or unfurling the sails, using our kenning only, we tugged it along with us to Dead Man's Point, a clublike peninsula north of Festwyf, due west of the island I call Blight.

There's a dock and a lighthouse there, and when we reached it,

Föstyr and a crew of picked mariners were waiting. We tied it up, secured the dangling gangplank, and a brave volunteer boarded to see
if the ship was truly free of wraiths or other murderous creatures.
When he reported that nothing lived on board, we all followed Föstyr
onto the ship. He headed straight for the ornate cabin and strode
through the unlocked door, and I followed while Nara and the others
went belowdecks.

It was a well-appointed cabin. Luxurious, even. There was a small
bookcase of volumes written in the Eculan language, which should
please that Kaurian scholar no end. Rolled up in a cubbyholed box
were maps and charts in the same language, many of which bore details of the coastline of the Northern Yawn; that pleased Föstyr, but
not as much as the map that showed us where Ecula's five islands were
located in relationship to our eastern coast. That was the true prize
for us.

"Ahh, there it is," Föstyr cooed as he tapped the outline of our enemy's islands. "We know where you are now, you bastards."

There was also a log with a list of dates, seven years apart, but nothing listed for this year. There was nothing of material value in the
cabin, apart from some gold- and silver-lined instruments.

I emerged from the cabin to find Nara climbing up the steps from
below, shaking her head.

"This doesn't make any sense," she said. "No vast treasure in the
holds. There are only lots of bunks—more than you'd need to crew
this vessel—and a few barrels of some vile goop in the cargo hold."

"Nothing else?"

She shrugged. "Kind of a weird-looking cloak down there. But
nothing says to me, 'This ship is worth dying by the thousands for.'"

"Then something else is, and they thought this ship would take
them there."

There were some tools in the bilge, and with Föstyr's permission I
pried off a piece of the outer hull near the hawser port that was stained
with the strange dark resin. We left him there with his mariners and
returned to Pelemyn, to report and to deliver that piece of the hull to

a hygienist I trusted. Her name was Feryn du Landyn, and she lived conveniently close to the docks.

"I found this on a strange ship," I told her when she answered the door, leaving out that it was most likely the one that had prompted the invasion, "and I'd like you to examine its properties with your kenning to see if you can identify what the stain is made of."

"Well, hi, Tallynd," she replied, reminding me that I'd completely forgotten my manners. After I made apologies, she took the hunk of wood from my hands and scowled at it doubtfully. "Might be all I'll pick up is the seawater. The stain is impregnated into the wood."

"I understand. But I'd like you to try. Please."

She sighed and closed her eyes, spreading her palm flat against the wood and seeing . . . I don't know what. Hygienists perceive so much that is unseen, and how they know what's diseased and what's healthful, what's poisonous and what's hearty, is truly beyond my vision. She tried to explain it to me once, that there are tiny structures that make up all substances, and after a while the patterns of those structures become recognizable and can be used to identify components of poisons and so on.

Feryn stood in her open doorway, her expression nonplussed at first, but after half a minute of silence, a furrow developed between her brows and the corners of her mouth pulled down. A flash of teeth followed, and her eyes flew open and she spoke in a sharp tone: "Where did you get this?"

"I told you—"

"Yes, yes, a strange ship, I know, but where? Not on this continent, am I correct?"

"Well, no. I mean, yes, you're correct. What is it?"

She walked toward me, voice pitched low and urgent. "Was this from a Bone Giant ship?"

"Well, not exactly. I mean, there were dead Bone Giants aboard."

"So this is not from their flat-bottomed ships that they used for the invasion?"

"No, why?"

She whirled away from me, her eyes wide. "Bryn preserve us." She put the hull scrap on her desk and immediately grasped for a piece of paper. She scrawled a quick note and address on it, talking as she wrote.

"Meet me at this address as soon as you can with a piece from one of the invasion hulls. A piece from the bottom! I'll explain everything there. I need to confirm something before I say more, because I could be wrong, but if I'm right this explains everything."

"Everything?"

"Well, it explains exactly one thing. A rather important detail we've all been wondering about, like how the Bone Giants crossed the ocean."

I gasped and stared at her for a few seconds to see if she was joking with me, but her expression never wavered. She merely nodded once.

"I'll meet you there as soon as possible."

Fintan's laugh echoed in my cell. Presumably he was chuckling at the crowd's reaction for ending there.

"Don't worry, I'll return to Tallynd and you'll have your answer. For now, let's see what happened when Abhi and I caught up with Olet Kanek in Ghurana Nent."

*let

There were trees on either shore as we left Tel Ghanaz behind us, but the trees to the north were ancient, primeval, never cut, while the trees on the southern shore had been periodically thinned, harvested, and replanted over many years. Regardless, it was a lot of fuel and represented uncountable riches to us. We were rowing our glass boats through a land of treasure. Leagues and leagues of prosperity. My people were smiling, flush with hope, and I was ready to join them, for every stroke of the oars took me farther away from Hathrir.

But word traveled up from the rear of the fleet that there was a Raelech bard and a Nentian boy who dearly wished to speak with me regarding my father. I instructed our boat to land on the southern shore to allow them to catch up and meet with us. La Mastik and I debarked and quickly built a makeshift hearth to welcome them properly. When they arrived, the Nentian boy walked down with a stalk hawk on his shoulder and a bloodcat by his side. The Raelech bard I'd met before. Jerin Mogen and I had taken him up the coast once to Hashan Khek, and he was there at the Battle of the Godsteeth too, when we surrendered. The Nentian boy introduced himself as Abhinava Khose, a plaguebringer of the Sixth Kenning, and I thought I remembered seeing him at the surrender too, though we hadn't spoken.

"This is Murr and Eep," he said, pointing to his animal companions. He looked to be in his early twenties, very handsome for a tiny Nentian person, and he wore khernhide boots. That told me he was either rich or a hunter. I was betting on the latter. He was very polite and begged us to excuse him as he gave his animal friends some time to hunt on the shore while we spoke with the bard.

"We arrived at Talala Fouz a few days after you," the bard began, "and we were in the skylight room with the king when your father arrived with his fury, Pinter Stuken, demanding that you be rendered unto him."

"What? Is he coming after me?"

"No. Not anymore."

"What happened?"

"Please keep in mind I'm only the messenger, all right? Your father demanded permission to pursue you, and the king refused. So your father ordered Pinter Stuken to burn down the city, and he did. But King Kalaad was slain by your own father's hand: I witnessed this with my own eyes. At that point it was war, because Winthir Kanek

killed the king of Ghurana Nent and ordered the razing of the capital. Both your father and Pinter Stuken were slain in the aftermath.
I'm sorry."

My eyes slid to La Mastik, and I pointed a finger at the bard. "Did he
just say my father is dead?"

"Yes. And Pinter Stuken too. I'd like to know how a bunch of Nentians took down a firelord and a fury."

"I would too."

"You're not upset?" the bard asked.

I couldn't stop blinking and shaking my head with tiny little movements. "I can't be. This is not even real to me yet."

"Will you be upset when you think it's real?"

"I . . . I guess not. Well, maybe? I'm not sure. I think I'd be relieved,
more than anything else. That's a terrible thing to say, isn't it?" I knew,
intellectually, that it was. I was supposed to be upset. Some sort of sadness and grief would be appropriate now. But all I felt was wonder—
and hope—at how such a thing could be possible.

"It's understandable, considering what you've been through," La
Mastik said. "You'll hear no judgment from me."

"Thank you." I turned back to the bard. "Will you tell me how they
died?"

"They died from the Sixth Kenning."

"The Sixth Kenning," I repeated, letting the words hang in the air,
searching wistfully for some meaning or context.

It took a moment for them to latch on to something, and then I
whirled to look behind me. "You mean that kid with the bloodcat? He
did it?"

"He did. And Abhi hopes you'll forgive him. It was war. He was trying to save the people of Talala Fouz and beyond, because your father
planned on burning everyone in his way to get to you. We heard him
say it. The way Abhi saw it, he had no choice."

"But I . . . I don't get it. Why is he here? Does he want to kill me
too?"

"No, no, no! He wants to join you. Help you, if he can."

"Help me?"

"The Gravewood is a very dangerous place, which is why there are no settlements. But Abhi can make sure you aren't eaten on the way. He will use the Sixth Kenning to protect your party from predators, which means you're practically guaranteed to arrive at your destination safely."

"Why would he want to do that?"

"He wants to see the Gravewood. And, honestly, he wants to remove himself from the power of politicians in Ghurana Nent. He's not particularly fond of people telling him what to do with his kenning."

"Huh. Well, I can relate to that."

"So would you be okay with him—with us—joining you? No hard feelings?"

"I, uh, I don't know. I need to have a smoke and think it over."

"Understood. I'll withdraw some distance over there and wait for you to call me back."

"Thanks."

When he'd left, I tumbled to the ground and got out my pipe. I shook some leaves into it with trembling fingers. My father was dead. The kid who'd killed him was close enough for me to have my revenge if I wished it. Was that bravery to come to me? Stupidity? An unbelievable arrogance? La Mastik sat beside me and got out her pipe as well; she said nothing about my shaking.

"Where are my tears, Mirana?" I said in a low voice. "I can't keep my hands steady, but I can't cry either. Not even tears of relief. I'm dry as the Glass Desert."

"They might come later. You're shocked, more than anything."

"You think? I tell you, Mirana, I didn't think he could die. I thought he'd just burn forever. Terrorize people. Threaten them, bully them, and send Pinter to incinerate them if that didn't work. I thought it would never end."

"But it has. You have that boy to thank."

"He deserves my gratitude, doesn't he? And my vengeance too."

"That's a problem."

"It is. Let's smoke it out."

We sparked up our bowls and inhaled deeply. After we exhaled, tendrils of smoke wafting skyward, La Mastik said, "You could go home now. You could be hearthfire of Narvik or Tharsif or both."

I shook my head. "No. I'd have to fight someone eventually for it, maybe even right away. And I don't want to risk my life for power. I'd risk it for peace, though."

"You want to continue with this when you don't have to? Never return to Hathrir?"

"That's right. I want to be free of it. And now I guess I am. No one else will come looking for me." Mother had died when I was ten. There were no invisible strings tying me to Hathrir anymore. Laughter bubbled up from my throat, and tears, absent until now and still unexpected, sprang to the corners of my eyes. They were happy ones.

"Here on the banks of the Gravewater, surrounded by riches, I lay my burden down."

"So is that your answer? Let the kid who killed your father join us?"

I puffed on the pipe for a while before answering, and La Mastik joined me, content to wait. We had much to think about, and the ritual of smoking helped. The smoke became a metaphor for whatever problem we faced: The problem is first acknowledged and internalized by breathing in the smoke, then externalized and solved with its exhalation. Or it isn't solved at all and you need to smoke some more.

"I suppose I don't think of it that way, Mirana," I said. "He didn't kill my father so much as save my life—and many other lives besides. I have no doubt that my father was the aggressor, and as the bard said, he would have burned anything to get to me."

"No doubt."

"And so he was justly killed. But you know what that means?"

"What?"

"Our letter to the viceroy of Ghuli Rakhan is from a king who's now dead. Will he still honor it?"

La Mastik shrugged. "I don't know. We should hurry in case he won't."

"I think you're right. We need to get there before word reaches them." I clambered to my feet and opened my mouth to summon the bard, but then I sat back down again. La Mastik looked at me, exasperated.

"What are you doing?"

"Not ready yet. Nope. Need another smoke."

"You just said we should get going."

My fingers were shaking again as I refilled the bowl of my pipe. "It's hitting me now. I'm angry now."

Mirana got out her tobacco for a refill. "That's okay, Olet. It's natural to feel that way. What are you angry about? It's probably more than one thing."

"It is." I sparked up my bowl and inhaled. Mirana did the same. We exhaled in tandem.

"Anger is a fire and you are a firelord," she said. "Name your anger and then you can control it."

"I'm angry at my father for being such a terrible person that his only daughter feels relief at his death. I'm angry at myself for not having the courage or the strength to tell him no or to face him in any meaningful way. And I'm angry at that kid for doing what I should have done. Angry that he thinks he can admit to me he did it and I'll be fine with it because my father really was that terrible. Objectively terrible. I mean, he could have left out that part."

"Which part? Sorry."

"The part where he's the one who killed him. The bard could have just said, 'Hey, your father's dead. Somebody finally got him.' And I wouldn't have known any better."

"But then you might feel compelled to find out who did it. You'd wonder."

"True."

"And this kid might want to be honest with you. His confession can't be anything but contrition. If you want to punish him, he's probably ready for it."

I waggled my pipe stem at her. "And that makes me angry too. Because if I do punish him, then I'd be just like my father. Everyone knows I'm *his* daughter. I'm angry that I'll always be his daughter. I can't burn anything down, even if it deserves to be burnt down, or I'll be just another tyrannical Kanek."

"Some people wouldn't mind that."

"I know. But I would mind it very much. Father surrounded me with stones, like some hearth, and now I can only burn in a prescribed space. It's infuriating."

"I can only imagine."

"Not that the kid deserves to burn. He probably deserves a medal."

"Or at least a slice of cake."

"Ha ha ha! Cake. 'Hey, kid, thanks for killing my dad. Here's some baked goods.' Sure." I grinned at her for another second and then my face fell. "Scorch it, Mirana, why'd you have to say that? Now I want cake."

She laughed, but I really did want cake to celebrate. And knowing that filled me with guilt and shame, and because of that the anger came back too, so much worse than before. I dropped my pipe, stood, and thrust my hands toward the tiny fire we'd built. I poured my rage into it and it burned hotter and hotter, consuming the logs quickly, the flames building and climbing according to my will, a pillar of flame rising to the sky so everyone for miles around could see just how angry I was. The Hathrim traveling with me would see it and understand that something had made me very upset. It was proper for me to do this—if I didn't, then they would question my heart, my devotion to family. That thought made me rage all the more, and the flames grew higher and higher, and when the fuel was nothing but ash, I sent the fire up until it dissipated for lack of oxygen and the pillar winked out of existence.

"Nuhh," I groaned, weariness washing over me as I squatted, suddenly dizzy from the effort.

"Feel better?"

"Sort of. I guess?"

La Mastik picked up my pipe and held it out in front of me. "We should go."

"You're right." I rose and hollered at the bard. While we waited for him to return, I used the time to stow my pipe and compose myself.

"Is it safe?" he asked.

"Perfectly."

I made a point of inviting the bard and the plaguebringer onto my boat. The Nentian boy thanked me and was quick to apologize once he boarded.

"It is I who should be thanking you," I told him. "You've given me my freedom, and I bear you no ill will. Well . . . not enough to do anything. Emotions are messy."

"I understand," he said, and his look of chagrin and empathy was touching. I liked him and wanted to destroy him at the same time. Which only proved my point about emotions.

"Look, kid: I don't want to know how you did it. But I do want to know why you want to join us."

"I have a heart to see new creatures and make new friends in a new place."

"That's all?"

"No," he admitted. "Two viceroys want me dead. And I have no idea how the new king, whenever we have one, will feel about the Sixth Kenning. I don't want to be within their reach."

That was frank enough. His interests were aligned with mine, and his kenning would be invaluable, no doubt.

"We're going to need to do a funeral smoke for my father and Pinter Stuken. These people all knew of them by reputation, but they're Gorin Mogen's people. Still, I'll leave you out of it, and you don't have to admit to it if asked. As far as I'm concerned, they don't need to know."

He thanked me for being so gracious, and we held the smoke that night. And as I'd done before, I gave everyone the opportunity to leave. The bard was kind enough to lend his kenning to my speech so I could be sure that everyone heard me.

"Winthir Kanek and Pinter Stuken are gone. That means there will be new hearthfires in Narvik and Tharsif. You may wish to return and live under a new hearthfire, and I invite you to do so if that desire burns in your heart. Your lives might be better there. They might be worse. There is no way to know, and we must each forge our own future. You may also stay in any Nentian city you wish or move on to Rael or beyond. But if you continue on with me to build a new city, know this: I am not your hearthfire. That position will not exist. I will not fight for it, but I will fight to make sure we are never dominated by such a person. Our leaders will be elected on the strength of their ideas, not on the strength of their sword arm or their kenning. If you have ideas you wish to share with the group or wish to put yourself forward as a candidate for leadership, the Raelech bard will accommodate you. We welcome him and the young Nentian man of the Sixth Kenning, who has joined us. All kennings, all people, are welcome among us."

No one cheered my speech. But no one chose to leave either, and no one volunteered to lead. Perhaps they did not want to seem too eager. Perhaps they didn't know how to live any other way and had never thought of living differently. No matter; there would be plenty of time for those coals to blaze up. I was sure they would eventually.

For my part, a new hope kindled in my breast—not of mere escape, but that a dream might actually come true.

Fintan introduced yet another new character, and I moaned that I was missing it. It was the viceroy of Khul Bashab, Bhamet Senesh, whom I'd never heard described before. I remembered that Lohmet had seemed contemptuous of him and that his cousin was also the viceroy of Batana Mar Din, downriver from him. Beyond that, all I knew was that he hadn't seemed receptive to the idea of the Sixth Kenning being present in his city.

Bhamet

People think I walk around and present my ass to be kissed all day by merchants and river barons and clergy. But that only happens at fancy dinners. They stroke my ego then and smooch away—metaphorically, at least. That is not the reality of leadership, however. The reality is that I must field complaints all day, every day, and settle squabbles. Every settlement inevitably creates one of three kinds of people: enemies I must crush later, nobodies I can safely ignore, and friends I can rely on for support when needed.

I keep lists of all three—yes, even the ones I think I can ignore. Just to know where to look for trouble and where to look for help, and if one of the people I thought I could ignore turns up in either of the other camps later, I want to know that I got it wrong and figure out why. My father taught me that. He said suffering setbacks and encountering obstacles were inevitable in life, but being surprised by someone you should have known would cause trouble? That was inexcusable. And true. Because when he finally got surprised, it was fatal.

This surprising situation with the Sixth Kenning is the sort of thing he'd grudgingly excuse, however. No way to see that one coming. But now that I know these kids calling themselves "beast callers" are out there, I need to find them and ruthlessly remove their ability to undermine my rule, before they can surprise me again. That, my father said, was the key to keeping power. And it's worth doing most anything to keep it, because not having it is always, always worse. One need only look at the dregs living down by the river to see the truth of it.

My cousin has sent me some of his reserves from Batana Mar Din to find these kids, but Kalaad damn Melishev Lohmet for not sending me any help. He's a shitsnake sitting on vast reserves of disposable muscle but refuses to send me any of it.

Well, I will do something about these kids on my own. Khul Bashab isn't the size of Hashan Khek, so they can't hide forever. Eventually we will shine a light into whatever hole they're cringing in and this threat will end.

For they are a threat. I don't need the river barons and church men to tell me they are, because I've already lost cavalry and guards to them, but they're telling me anyway. Almost daily.

"You get taxes with every river fare," a river baron says to me. "But it's the animals of the plains that make that all possible. How are you going to tax people walking in and out of the city if they don't have to fear for their giblets?"

"Our religion is based on Kalaad," splutters Dhanush Bursenan, the patriarch of the church perspiring in such profusion that I had to have someone mop the floor after his audience, for fear of causing the next person to slip in his sweat puddle and fall to their doom. "If the Sixth Kenning is real, then where does Kalaad fit in this?"

"Why are you talking to me?" I ask him. "I'm not a member of the church hierarchy. You're obviously going to need to make some shit up, and isn't that your business?"

He gets the angry sweats after that and points a moist round finger at me. "Our business is pacifying the populace so your regime can continue without rebellion. If there's no need for Kalaad, then you don't have a pacified populace of exploited laborers willing to suffer the enormous piles of khern shit you heap upon their backs every day. You need to get rid of this problem before it spreads, or face the consequences!"

"Are you threatening me?"

"No, I'm not. I'm merely pointing out that these kids *are*. Deal with the threat."

In my mind, Dhanush Bursenan will forever be known as Threat Sweat. He may be repulsive, but he is not wrong. He is an oozing call to action.

All the people on my friends list want the kids removed, and some on the enemies list are clamoring for their clave to be approved; that settles it in my mind. These kids need to run onto the sharp end of a spear so we can all get back to business.

But they're not easy to find. I don't even know all their names. There's some kid with a yellow stripe of hair, who killed a gate guard with a kholeshar viper, and a girl named Hanima, who killed another with bees. There's a second girl, whose name and talents are unknown but might have something to do with horses; the fourth, Tamhan Khatri, claims to have no talent at all and so far has exhibited none. But he went out with all the seekers, and I'd have him in a dungeon and his fingernails in pincers if his father wasn't supplying all my chaktu meat.

He's been somewhat forthcoming, at least under pressure from his father. He says the boy who discovered the Sixth Kenning is a hunter named Abhinava Khose and he's the one who killed my cavalry. That's an easy morsel to give up since this Khose kid is gone and his family is dead, which leaves me no leverage. I think he knows more—like the names of the other blessed kids—but I can't force it from him. I must rely on what scraps his father's frowns can elicit from him. He only got his boy to confirm, reluctantly, that one of the girls is named Hanima, since we supplied it. We heard it in the rumor mill; she had been a well-known mute beggar, but now she can talk to bees and humans alike.

The city watch is looking for them. Spies—both ours and the church's—are on the lookout. I think they're hiding in the shadows with the river folk, since Tamhan recruited the seekers from their ranks. This Hanima person was certainly one of them. She's most likely the leader. Find her—squeeze the wastrels until they give her up—and we'll find the others. We'll snuff them before they become anything more than an inconvenience.

Then we can have a nice dinner and Threat Sweat can dry himself off and pucker up. I'm going to reestablish control, damn it. With knives and clamps and blunt force trauma. Complaints and squabbles might be tiresome, but being in control is far preferable to being told what to do. And having one's ass kissed, metaphorically or otherwise, isn't so bad.

OUR LOVES AND DUTIES

I spent a cold and largely sleepless night in the dungeon, and in the morning they gave me toast. Dry, unbuttered dungeon toast. But I got to enjoy it, if such a thing could be enjoyed, without interruption. I thought it a rather cruel way for the world to give me what I wanted.

And then two longshoremen came to ask me questions. I welcomed them, as Föstyr had led me to believe that I wouldn't be getting out of there without being questioned first.

"Master du Alöbar," one began. He was probably my age, more than a bit jowly, deep lines around the sides of his mouth. Were he to grin, it would be heavy lifting to part the curtains of his cheeks. "The quicker you answer our questions, the quicker you can leave."

"Or not," the other said, a rake-thin man with an even thinner smile. I disliked him immediately.

"Fine. I'm ready."

We sat across from one another at the table.

"Have you ever done any work for another government?"

"No."

"Has your wife ever worked for another government?"

"What?" I almost commented that the question was offensive but then remembered Sarena talking to me about interrogations and confined myself to answering "No."

She'd been exhausted after a trip to Forn, during which she endured a tedious grilling by Blue Moth Clan security, and I asked her how she coped. She demanded that I fix her a cocktail first, and I gladly did so. Once she'd taken a sip, she beamed at me and said, "Plenty of questions in an interrogation are asked merely to see your reaction. If you splutter, question the question, do anything but answer, that still tells them something. If you know what they're looking for, you can try giving it to them. But usually you don't know what they're after, and reacting to provocative questions will only prolong the interview and might give them the wrong idea. The best thing is to answer the questions as quickly and as freely of emotion as you can."

"Won't they think that suspicious too?"

"Of course. But they're going to think everything is suspicious anyway. You're under suspicion or they wouldn't be interrogating you in the first place, right?"

"I see. So answering quickly speeds things up?"

"Maybe. Sometimes. They might also ask you everything again and again until you snap. They look for inconsistencies and then pounce. Don't lie if you can help it. Answer with the truth and they can't trip you up. Answer without emotion and they can't use those emotions against you and ask why you seemed excited or distressed or whatever earlier."

I kept that in mind as Jowls and Rake spent at least an hour asking me more about Sarena's missions than about recent events. When they did get to current events, they asked about the stolen journal and what I'd written about it, what I'd shared with Fintan about it, and whether I'd communicated anything to the Wraith about Clodagh's threats. And then they asked me about Gerstad Nara du Fesset, rapid-fire questions regarding her loyalties and her missions and whether I had ever seen her do this shady thing or exhibit that suspicious behavior.

I was getting powerfully thirsty but didn't want to ask for water, because whenever I did, they would think it significant. *When we asked him about the gerstad, he asked for water instead of answering,* they would say, and instead of considering that I might be genuinely thirsty, they would think I was stalling and hiding something.

"Right," Rake said after what felt like another hour, standing up abruptly and waiting for Jowls to join him. The bigger man lumbered to his feet and turned to the door without saying anything more. "Wait here."

"You say that like I have a choice," I said to his departing back. The door clanged and the cold metal silence settled over me once again, and I shivered. I wasn't sure I was ever getting out. The shuffling steps and creaking of other doors, the jangling of keys, and the squeaking of rats all rattled my nerves and played on my insecurities. I wondered how many prisoners Rölly had down here and whether they were all suspected spies. How much spying was going on, anyway? Especially in countries that were supposed to be our allies? I used to think it was just Sarena and a couple of her acquaintances involved in it, but I was beginning to feel that Brynlön's primary occupation was spying rather than fishing or anything else.

The keys eventually jangled at my door again, and when it swung open, Föstyr du Bertrum stood in the hallway with Gerstad Nara du Fesset. She looked as rough as I felt.

"Come on, Dervan. You get to see the sun again."

I didn't waste my breath asking if it was really true. I just rose and moved as quickly as my knee would allow to get out of that cell.

"You have the pelenaut's deepest apologies for the necessity of keeping you here and enduring those interrogations," the lung said as he led us out of the dungeon. "And mine as well. But we needed to be sure. We thought we could trust the Wraith, and he showed us how foolish that was. In any case, beyond our apologies, you have our thanks for your loyalty. But we're not going to just say that." He handed us each a pouch of coins. "Material proof of our gratitude for your service to Brynlön."

None of that mattered to me. "What of the Wraith?" I asked. "Did you get him?"

"Oh, yes. He is most definitely got. And his accomplice—what did you call her?"

"Approval Smile."

"Yes. They were invited to visit the pelenaut—the sort of invitation they couldn't refuse—and led into a darkened room that, once lit, proved to be made entirely of thick glass and surrounded on all sides—floor and ceiling too—with water. A sort of reverse aquarium. The wraiths cannot escape those bodies now and possess anyone else. They're locked in there, and the door through which they entered is an actively maintained wall of water."

"You just imprisoned them? Why not drown them?" Nara said, and since that was exactly what I'd been thinking, I added, "Yeah!"

"We have questions first."

"You can't trust anything they say," Nara pointed out.

"No, that is true. But we can attempt to verify."

"I want to see them," I said.

"Impossible, I'm afraid." The lung shook his head for emphasis.

"But I have questions too."

"Perhaps at a later date. Right now they are testing their prison and will not submit to any questioning. When they are ready to talk, our questions are going to take precedence."

"How do you question them if they're surrounded by water?"

Föstyr grinned. "Astute! Either the pelenaut or the second könstad relays written questions on a tray through the water wall. They create an air pocket and float it through. At no point is there an avenue for them to escape."

"Won't they run out of oxygen eventually?"

"We refresh the air while they sleep. We have a Kaurian cyclone available who's helping us with that."

"But then that's an avenue of escape," the gerstad said. "They're going to figure it out eventually and wait for that air recycling to occur, however you're doing it. Then one of the wraiths escapes, possesses someone, and we're boned, so to speak."

"We've thought of that too, I promise. We had months to plan this prison and figure out the logistics. But here are the conditions of your release—fully revocable should you violate them." The lung paused in front of the dungeon exit and turned to face us to make sure we were paying attention. We were.

"Not a word to anyone about your absence yesterday. Not to the mynstad," he said to Nara, referring to Mynstad du Möcher, "and not to Fintan. The existence of the Wraith—and his treason— must remain a secret for the short term. The pelenaut will make it public eventually, and when he does, you will be free to share anything you wish with anyone. For now, make what excuses you can live with that keeps our country's secrets. Are we clear on that and on what will happen if you talk about this?"

We both nodded.

"Then I thank you again and I promise to contact you as soon as possible if we can get you to see the Wraith in captivity." He opened the door and allowed us to precede him into the sunlight. It looked to be near noon.

"Dervan, if you wish to meet the Raelech bard and catch up on your tales, you can meet him at the Kaurian restaurant you've visited together before."

"Thank you." I nodded a farewell to Nara and she returned it. We couldn't say anything we might have wished at that point, but I had no doubt we'd find time to speak later.

I returned home and looked carefully at the manuscript. It was all where I'd stored it, but it had clearly been reviewed. Someone had removed it, read it, and put it back. Due diligence, I suppose.

I took my materials and limped, scowling, to the Kaurian restaurant. Fintan's face was a mask of relief and concern when he saw me enter.

"Dervan! You're here! Thank the goddess. Please, sit. Are you well?"

"Yes, I'm well."

"I was worried."

"Sorry about that. Nothing to be done."

"What kept you, may I ask?"

"It's personal, sorry."

"Oh, well, that's fine. Totally fine. But you look unhappy and that distresses me." That only cemented my belief that I am ill-suited for espionage, since I cannot even begin to hide inner turmoil.

"Rough morning," I explained. "There was a problem with my toast. Puts me off my mood."

"Oh. Yeah, I get that way about almond pastries sometimes."

"I beg your pardon?"

"When you love a thing and you anticipate how wonderful it's going to be when you get to enjoy it and then something ruins it—that's what I mean. I get it. Your thing is toast. Mine is almond pastries."

"I didn't know that."

"Your city has absolutely zero almond pastries, Dervan. I checked."

"We're starting to zero out on a lot of foods. I imagine even toast is endangered."

"As is sanity and civilization. And swamp duck aficionados."

"Ah, poor Jahm!"

"Indeed." We placed our order after that from a much-reduced menu and got to work. There was quite a lot, since I was trying to catch up on two days of tales. We didn't quite make it through everything before it was time to go to the wall, but Fintan promised we'd be able to catch up entirely the next day.

When he took his stage, he let everyone know he was going to share another Kaurian wind chime, because he was going to tell us what happened next with Gondel Vedd. That perked me up, not only because Gondel was one of my favorites but because Rölly had told me he'd left Brynlön months ago and we needed him right now. If Fintan was going to share something new from him, how'd he hear of it? I shelved that question for later and enjoyed the song.

When I walk abroad in the world
I am moved to awe and wonder
Grateful for such precious time

For at home I rarely wonder
And worry about the passing time
Cloistered from the precious world

So now it is once again time
For me to embrace the wide world
And renew my sense of precious wonder

After the break Fintan announced we'd meet another new character and I practically pumped my fist, because I'd be able to see them this time. He told us he'd be speaking as Tuala, the Raelech courier who'd accompanied Meara to Brynlön and helped fight the Bone Giants at Göfyrd and witnessed the cleansing by Culland du Raffert. He threw down his sphere, and the seeming that emerged was of a tall Raelech woman, lean and wiry and armored in the dark-red leather pieces that the Raelech military favored. Her black hair was drawn into a simple queue behind her head, and a pair of goggles rested around her neck, where they could easily be drawn up to protect her eyes. I noticed that her Jereh band was the bronze of a single person rather than gold.

I don't trust people who say that you can have it all. It's glib and obviously untrue. And whatever you think "it all" is, you can't have that without also having the fear of losing it. Unless, of course, you are wrapped up so snugly in a cocoon of wealth and privilege that the concept of losing isn't even a thing that's real anymore. Folks like that tell themselves a story where they worked really hard for what they were given, so that anyone who isn't rolling in luxuries and benefiting from cronyism and nepotism simply isn't working hard enough. If they lie to themselves like that, they'll lie to you without blinking.

I ran into one such after a week of rest.

The rest was sorely needed. After the collapse of the Granite Tunnel, I was assigned to escort a stonecutter named Meara to Brynlön. She lost her fiancé, and I think maybe a good part of herself, in that tunnel. If you asked her before that day if she could have it all, she might have said yes, because she was young and in love and could not conceive of a future in which she did not have everything she wanted. Then she made a mistake and destroyed an army of Bone Giants, three-hundred-plus soldiers from the Baseld garrison, including her fiancé, and closed off the major trade route to Brynlön, which had taken years of the blessed working together to build. Ask her if she can have it all now and she will say absolutely not. You often can't even have the one thing you want most.

But she's going to be a polished gem, that one.

We ran into some more Bone Giants outside Göfyrd and watched a tidal mariner drown the entire city. And when it was done, Meara realized that what she can have now is a long path to redemption, a lifetime of building after one afternoon in which she destroyed so much. She will always mourn what she lost, of course, but I think she truly values her blessing now and knows why Dinae chose her. I think she will go down in history as one of the greatest Raelech stonecutters to ever live.

That was the conclusion I came to after a week of fishing on the shores of Goddess Lake near Bechlan, and by "fishing," I mean lying immobile on a beach in close proximity to a fishing pole that I ignored completely because I hadn't even baited the hook. I had a stack of books, an umbrella to shade me from the sun, a small keg of beer, and a younger cousin who told me in frankess while we were trading stories of stupid things we'd done as teenagers that he had once tried to have sex with what he called a "consenting stump."

His voice was a deadpan drawl. "I don't recommend it," he said. "It wasn't nearly as great as I thought it would be, going in. Stumps are not what you would call vigorous lovers. Completely unresponsive, in fact. Except for the splinters."

I laughed so hard I threw up on him, and that seemed perfect. Probably the best vacation I've ever had, just relaxing, thinking slow thoughts, and not moving. Because my job is to be on the move all the time, otherwise. At the end of that bliss, my aunt cooked up a hangover cure and kissed my forehead before I got dressed in my leathers and strapped on my goggles for the run around the lake to the capital.

"Run safe, Tuala. Come stay again whenever you can."

I promised I would and savored the memories on the road. The lapping of the waters on the shore; the silent, skinny stalking of herons in the shallows; the gurgle of ale pouring into my cup and then down my throat. My hangover dissipated by the time I showed up at Triune Council Hall for my next assignment.

They essentially told me to report to Temblor Priyit and take orders from her, and they gave me an address in the eastern hills of the city, where the folks with chests of money tend to live.

I'd met the temblor before, a Nentian immigrant who'd been blessed by the triple goddess. She'd walked out of the Granite Tunnel with Meara, the only other survivor of the collapse, but I hadn't seen her since then. I'd only heard of her behavior in more detail from Meara during our run to Göfyrd.

She answered my knock at the door, dressed in a white bathrobe.

"Temblor. I'm Tuala, master courier of the Huntress Raena."

"I remember you." She folded her arms across her chest and leaned on the doorjamb. "What's your message?"

"I've been sent to you for assignment by the Triune."

"Ah. I see. My R&R is at an end. Time to issue marching orders and march myself."

A man dressed in nothing but a towel moved in the background. The nature of her R&R was clear.

"Did you get some time off, Tuala, or have you been running all this time?"

"I got some rest, Temblor. Just returned from a week of doing nothing."

"Where's home for you?"

"Wherever I decide to sleep. I have no permanent residence." At her frown, I added the standard excuse. "No use for a home when I'd hardly ever be there. I never know where I'm going or how long I'll be away."

"So you have no possessions?"

"I own what I'm wearing."

"Do you just stay with friends wherever you're at, then?"

"Yes. Or in Raelech embassies. Often in one of Raena's temples. They get most of my pay."

"Ah. You're one of the devout ascetics." She smiled a tiny smile of condescension I've seen before. She'd decided that I was simple because I had the means to live as she did and chose not to. "No time spent with a significant other?"

"Don't have one," I said.

"Why not? You can have it all."

I shrugged in reply and then asked for my orders. There was no requirement for me to share the details of my personal relationships with a commanding officer.

She stared at me for a few moments, deciding whether to be offended by my change of subject. She chose to ignore it and stood up straight.

"Very well. Orders: We've been given leave by the pelenaut of Brynlön to march a force into Möllerud and destroy the Bone Giant army occupying that city. A vital part of that force must be a juggernaut named Tarrech, who's been given some downtime, as we have. He lives in Randulet. I can get you his exact location—"

"I'm familiar with it, Temblor. We are old acquaintances."

"Good. Bring him with all speed to Mell to meet our forces there. We will muster and march as soon as possible, and my understanding is that you'll be accompanying us."

"Aye, Temblor."

"Dismissed."

I took off a bit faster than I needed too, blowing her robe open in the wake of my passage. She'd said I should use "all speed," after all. Perhaps she would get the hint that I didn't appreciate her prying.

I let the annoyance sluice away from me in the wind of my passage and directed my thoughts to the road ahead instead of the road behind: It would be good to see Tarrech again. He and I had gone to the Colaiste together and had been blessed on the same day. And I loved visiting Randulet, nestled in the southwestern mountains. It's Rael's most isolated town, not being located on a trade route or boasting any special tourist attractions. The folks there worked hard, worshipped the triple goddess, and voted. They sent their kids to the Colaiste at age nine and most of them came back, because that's how charming the place was. They were good people. And way too far for me to reach in a day, especially after I'd already run to Killae from Bechlan, only to be told to turn around.

I directed my feet to the temple of the huntress on the west side of the city. It's on the outskirts, really, where population density ceases to be a thing and we're firmly in pastoral country, where livestock outnumber humans. It was built on a small rise in elevation that's more the idea of a hill than an actual one. If there was anything like a permanent residence for me anywhere, it was this particular temple. I spent more nights there than anywhere else, and it's where I got my post, though I corresponded with few people. They had a cot reserved for my use, and I kept a small chest of personal items underneath it: a set of winter clothes; a stick of sealing wax and a seal for my letters; and a stuffed goat toy, often patched and stitched, that I've owned since childhood. It was a gift from my parents and it's all I have left of them; my memories of my early years are as fallible and fading as anyone else's. The perfect recall didn't begin until I was blessed.

The best part of visiting temples of the huntress is the food. It's always fresh game and harvested greens, simple fare well made. No baked goods—those are at the temples to the goddesses who have a more agricultural bent. Raena states rather forcefully in her scrolls that she's provided plenty on the land; one just has to go get it.

Once I stepped across the threshold, Hunter Bran waved and welcomed me to the closest thing I had to a home. He was shorter than me and had some gray in his beard—a "lone stripe of dignity," he called it—and crinkles of amusement around his mouth and eyes.

"Staying the night, Tuala?" he asked.

"Yes, if I may."

He waved my politness away. "You know you're always welcome. We have fresh venison for this evening but could use some greens."

"I'm on it. Can I take a basket?" A stack of gathering baskets waited by the door.

"Absolutely. See you soon."

I dashed out with one of the broad baskets cradled under my arm and ran to one of the northern meadows, where spicy greens grew wild. I spent some time picking these and then had to run even farther north, to get some milder lettuces to counter the spice, and made my last stop at a humble farm that had a lovely greenhouse. One of the owners was confined to a wheelchair, and the greenhouse suited her well. She grew the most lovely herbs and tomatoes but rarely took them to market. People came to her instead. I purchased some of each—which was not technically the sort of gathering Raena favored, but neither was it baking—and made it back to the temple before sundown. The promised haunch of venison was already turning over the fire, and the hunters were happy to see me. The tomatoes and herbs were especially welcome, and a huntress took the basket from me while Hunter Bran gave me a glass of cider.

There was a young couple visiting from out of town, and I had to endure the awkward moment when they saw my Jereh band and realized I was a courier. Since it's the rarest of the blessings—only twenty-seven of us exist at any time—people who meet me for the first time often make the mistake of thinking that there must be something special about me, that I must possess some admirable quality or ability that made the Huntress Raena choose me. If I do, I'm unaware of it.

The couple was moving to the hills near Lochlaen to keep bees, grow grains, and raise goats. Their Jereh bands indicated that the man was the farmer and the woman was the apiarist.

They already held glasses of cider, so I couldn't get them one to put them at their ease and let them know I did not consider myself better than them. I fell back to my other gambit: I squatted by the fire, intentionally lowering my stature, and flashed a friendly smile at them.

"Feel like swapping stories? I'll trade you a story of me for a story of you. How'd you two meet?"

They were so cute. His father had bought some honey from her mother at market and wondered if any of her hives were mobile and available for pollinating a cornfield or two. They were indeed, and, next season, they met when her mother brought the hives to his father's farm.

"And where was this?" I asked.

"Fandlin."

"Oh! So why are you moving to Lochlaen?"

"Less likelihood of invasion from the sea," the woman said. "We want to start a family and we want them to be safe. If an army's going to come after us, we want some warning before it happens."

Everyone around the fire grunted and nodded at that. It was an entirely understandable and valid reason to move. The Bone Giants had ended many lives with their invasion, but they'd changed the course of many more. And then it was my turn.

"I was once sent to Forn to deliver a message to the Black Jaguars at the First Tree," I said, "but, of course, the Fornish don't allow you to visit their capital at all. To get a message to the First Tree, you must instead deliver it to a greensleeve stationed at their border with Rael down by Aelinmech, and they use those little shoots in their silverbark to communicate via root and stem to their leaders, leagues away. A bit spooky, but it does keep me from having to run as far."

They laughed somewhat nervously, not knowing where I was going with this. "I had to wait for a reply, so it was the greensleeve and me at this border station, and we got to talking about drinks. I made her a cocktail of spirits and herbs that was taught to me by an herbalist up in Jeremech, and she declared it the most delicious drink in the world, apart from a silverbark mushroom sour."

The couple from Fandlin and all the hunters and huntresses, feeling mellow and in sync somehow, all said, "Whaaaaaat?" at the same time. A few of them considered their glasses full of cider, privately noting, perhaps, that it might not be the most delicious drink in the world but it was quite agreeable nonetheless.

"Yes. The Fornish are quite famous for their teas and beers, but they also make a mushroom whiskey, and it is a friendly, savory, smoky roundhouse punch to the throat."

"Why have I never heard of this?" Hunter Bran asked.

"They don't export it. They only make limited quantities and they selfishly keep it to themselves."

"And you got to try some."

"I did. The greensleeve measured out mushroom whiskey, fresh lemon juice, bitters, and an egg white, shook it all up, and poured it over ice. But that's not the kicker. She had the drinks all poured, one for each of us, but held up a finger, telling me to wait. She bent down to her shin, where there were mushrooms growing on her silverbark, and she plucked off two caps and plopped one into each drink."

The chorus of surprise and disbelief was music to my ears.

"She didn't wash them or anything first?"

"Nope. That was a point of pride for her—she made sure I knew she would never do me the disservice of washing it. Told me natural flavors were the best."

"Goddess save me," the apiarist said. "And you drank it?"

"I not only drank it, I dunked that mushroom cap down in the drink like she told me to so that it would soak up the alcohol and everything, and then I ate it last."

Another round of shocked *noooos* and wincing, and then the farmer asked, "What was it like?"

"She was right: It was the best drink I've ever had. Rich with a luxury suite of flavors, textures, and aromas. Probably won't ever get another one either. How often are you going to find a greensleeve mixologist willing to share her own private stash of ingredients? But," I added, pointing to my temple, "I remember it well."

The couple was relaxed after that and the awkwardness was gone. We enjoyed our venison and field greens and I slept like the dead on my cot. I was on the road at dawn, with the wind in my hair and bugs splattering my goggles as I traveled south at top speed. I took a break every hour to recover my wind, drink some water, and take in some calories, and I made it to Randulet by sundown. I had to deliver my message before I slept again, because messages always seemed more important to the recipient when I looked my absolute worst.

But, also, Tarrech needed his time to get used to the idea and say a proper goodbye. Being ripped away from one's family on short notice was the worst. I couldn't give him much time, but I could give him this night, because I wasn't going to run any more that day.

That thing he'd been always meaning to say to his wife, or to his kids, he could say it. That one last experience. That one final meal.

The run had been pleasant up to the point where I came to the border of his property and spied his front door. All the dread I had kept resolutely shut in the back of my mind stepped right up to the fore at that point and rudely demanded a drink and some snacks.

"I don't want to do this," I said, coming to a halt and taking a moment to catch my breath. There was no one around to hear. Tarrech lived on a large parcel of land, and his nearest neighbors were a half league away on either side. "He's going to hate me. I'm the person he never wants to see."

Goddess, it hurt so much. I didn't want to be that person for anyone, but especially not for him. He and I had been best friends before seeking our kennings. After that we went our separate ways, meeting on only a few occasions. Because of that, I'd forgotten some of the old days, and maybe my memory had polished some others to a glossy shine that it shouldn't have. It didn't matter. Now I was going to knock on that door and ruin his day.

It was a winsome place. Blue-gray stone facing, a white jamb, and a red door with three small square windows in it. Dark hardwood deck in the front with a covered porch, some outdoor furniture, some bright pots of flowers with hummingbirds hovering over them, slurping up nectar. Neat rows of a garden bloomed off to one side beside a greenhouse, because his wife, Aevyn, was a master herbalist. Charming as anything I've seen.

Would he even recognize me? Only one way to find out. There was no benefit to me putting this off any longer. I walked the remaining distance to his door, recovering my wind. I knocked three times, paused, and knocked thrice more.

"Who is that?" a woman's voice called. A murmured reply, unintelligible, answered her, and then boots stomped toward the door.

He opened it and I said, "Hello, Tarrech." My throat constricted with a lump as he frowned at me at first, but once I tried a shy smile he recognized me, grinned, and the lump dissolved.

"Tuala!" he cried. "My old friend!" He crushed me in his arms and I closed my eyes, just wanting to remember the feel of it, nothing else. He smelled of cedar and vanilla.

Then he let me go and asked, "What are you—" He stopped, looking down at my Jereh band and taking in my stained leathers and goggles and my windblown hair.

"Oh, no. It's time, isn't it. This isn't a social call. You're here because they sent you."

The lump came back. His Jereh band was the gold of a married man; the last time I'd seen him it was bronze. The stones were the ruby, amethyst, and ruby of one of Raena's juggernauts. Staring at it instead of meeting his eyes, I nodded.

"No. Not yet. Please don't say it."

"I'm sorry, Tarrech. I have to. It's my sworn duty."

His breath came out of him as if I'd just stomped on his diaphragm. He closed his eyes for a while, and when he opened them they were sad, wobbling at the edges with tears, like mine were. "You and I have such power, you know?" he said. "We can do anything we want, and no one could stop us except ourselves. Except our sense of duty. And the judgment of our neighbors and friends."

Too choked up to reply, I only nodded again, but a tear ran down my right cheek and I let it stay there. A tear escaped from his left, mirroring mine, but he wiped it away. He sighed and said, "Very well. I can't close this door and be at peace. So what is your message, Master Courier?"

"Temblor Priyit, at behest of the Triune Council, summons you to muster with Raelech forces at Mell, there to march against the Bone Giants occupying Möllerud. We are to liberate the city for Brynlön but also to protect Rael from further threat."

He nodded solemnly and shrank a little bit, the weight of it settling upon his shoulders. It was me doing that to him, and I wanted to take it back, but I couldn't.

"I'm glad they sent you, at least, and not someone else," he finally said, his voice quiet. "Can I have this night, please? We'll leave in the morning?"

"Of course," I said. "After breakfast. Midmorning."

"Thank you."

I gave him the three-fingered salute and backed away, turning once he nodded his acknowledgment. I hurried off his property, since I didn't want to hear anything once he told his wife that he'd been summoned to war and, as juggernaut, he'd be the proverbial tip of the spear.

The Randulet temple of the huntress had never seen me before but had played host to other travelers and couriers in the past. Once I showed up and asked for hospitality, one look at my Jereh band was all it took for them to invite me to their cook fire. They had a straw tick in their basement for me to sleep on and it served, though I tossed and turned for at least an hour, worried at how Tarrech would behave in the morning when I came for him. If he didn't want to go, I couldn't make him. Nobody could force a juggernaut to do anything. They *were* force.

And if he did come with me and changed his mind along the way? Same thing. I couldn't do anything about it. He had to choose this himself. But the Triune Council and pretty much everyone he knew expected him to make one particular choice.

In the morning, after a leisurely breakfast and a ritualistic cleaning of my leathers, I returned to his home and knocked thrice. I zipped away to the border of his property and waved at him when he answered the door. He deserved all the privacy he could get in saying his farewells. Besides, I didn't want to hear.

The door remained open for a while, and then he stepped out, alone, with a small pack slung over his shoulders. They were still hunched, as I'd seen them last night, his head drooping like that of a doomed man.

He hadn't taken twenty steps before his wife cried out his name and ran after him. He turned and they embraced for a long while, and then they pulled apart and he kept his hands on her shoulders and spoke to her. I couldn't hear them, but I could imagine their conversation well enough.

Yes, he could stay. He could tell me to eat dirt, have me tell the Triune Council the same, and I'd never be back. No one would come after him. He could stay and grow old with her in the slow march of time.

But no one would meet his eyes after that, and he wouldn't be able to meet theirs. He'd be judged a coward and a traitor. All the respect and esteem he had as a juggernaut would be forfeit. Guilt would settle over him in great shovelfuls whenever he went to town, and it would bury whatever happiness he had in remaining home. He would be miserable. *They* would be miserable.

Not that going through with it was a prospect filled with joy. Once he used the full potential of his kenning, he'd be significantly older no matter what. There might be plenty of regrets down that path—doubtless there would—but there would be no guilt. Instead, there would be pride and honor and the country's gratitude for his service.

Aevyn didn't like hearing any of that and was vocal about it. She even pounded him on the chest a couple of times, and I didn't blame her a bit. The reality was that she was losing the man she loved *right now* and she knew it, and if she had been able to be cool about it, then I would have wondered if she really loved him at all.

Maybe Aevyn and Tarrech had managed to have everything good for a while. I supposed it could happen, for a brief time. But something or someone like me will always come along and wreck a perfect thing, because the world cannot seem to turn without struggle.

His kids came out then, cute little tykes about four or five. He hugged them, and hugged his wife again, and told them all, no doubt, that he would love them forever and hoped to be back as soon as possible.

And then he said he must go. He backed away, and blew kisses, and waved, and Aevyn held the kids back as they cried and tried to cling to him. They probably didn't understand exactly what was going on, but they knew something huge was happening, because their mother was crying too.

Reluctantly, he turned and walked to where I waited. Neither of us had dry eyes when he greeted me.

"Good morning, Master Courier."

"Good morning, Master Juggernaut. Ready and willing to muster?"

"I'm ready and willing. But not wanting."

"I understand."

He spun around to see if his wife and kids were still there, and they were. He waved to them and they waved back, a final farewell.

"Ah, well," he said, wiping tears from his cheeks as he turned his back on his home and his family, perhaps never to see them again. "We all know that blessings have a curse waiting on the other side of them. There's always a dark shadow behind the pedestal in the shrine, right? You and I have known each other too long and seen too much to pretend otherwise. It is a stone cold truth that you can't have it all. Can you, Tuala?"

I smiled at him fondly and shook my head. "No, you can't."

He visibly straightened and stood tall. "But we have our loves and duties."

"Yes. Yes, we do. We have those always."

Fintan promised more of Tuala later and then said it was time to catch up with Abhi and Olet from a slightly different perspective. He transformed into the version of himself we'd seen earlier on the trail in Ghurana Nent, in his own set of red leathers.

The master bard who taught me was a kind old woman named Aerin. To look at her when I first met her—frail and stooped with the weight of her years, a soft smile usually playing about her wrinkled lips—one would think she had never done anything more violent than wrestle a batch of cookie dough into shape. Her fingers were gnarled with arthritis and she could barely play her harp anymore. But she knew so very much, had a wealth of experience that her kenning would not let her forget, and she taught me well. More than just music or languages, though she taught me all of that too.

As part of my journeyman training, we traveled to Jereh to visit the mines in the Poet's Range, where they very gently extract the gaseous spheres of brittle rock that I use to take on my seemings and dispel them. We were staying in a visitors' cabin then, and Master Aerin was in a room next to mine. The walls were thin and sound carried easily. That's when I heard her moaning and crying out in her sleep, and I hurried to wake her.

She gasped and blinked in the candlelight until she focused on me, propping herself up on her elbows.

"Here's a lesson for you, Fintan. A hard one you won't know the truth of until later," she said. "At some point in your life, the nightmares are going to begin. If you think you've had one already, well, congratulations. But those were like celery compared to the nightmares you're going to have, which are like a rich swamp duck basted with a piquant orange glaze. By which I don't mean to say they're delicious and nourishing. They're just heavy, thick, and intense. And once they begin, they don't really ever stop."

"Master Aerin, forgive me, but I don't know what you mean."

"I know you don't. I'm just giving you a warning so that when they come, you won't be able to get mad at me for never saying anything. You're going to have horrible nightmares, Fintan. Nothing you can do about it. I'm sorry."

"But why?"

"Because something terrible is going to happen."

"What?"

"Oh, I don't know. It's different for everybody. But terrible things happen. Somebody kills their wife or husband. Someone abuses an animal. Maybe there will be a war, and you'll see more horrors than you could ever imagine. Regardless, once you're a master and something terrible happens, the Triune is going to send you out to take a good look so you can note every detail, tell them all about it, and maybe write a ballad or two. They'll get a song and maybe a lurid story they can tell their friends. They'll forget about it the next day, in most cases. But you won't. You'll have that terrible thing in your head forever."

"Oh. I guess I see. What was your terrible thing?"

She gave me a sad, patient smile. "Oh, Fintan. You're going to have your own soon enough. Why would I give you mine? That would be unkind of me."

"Right, right. Thank you for that. Is there nothing we can do, then?"

"Persist. Persevere. Bring some beauty into the world and remember that not everyone has to suffer the same way. Were we not blessed, we'd have defenses against those terrible things. Our brains would find ways to forget them or, failing that, cope somehow. But we bards are not allowed to forget. Which means our brains have to wrestle with those terrible things, over and over, to try to make sense of them, to try to change things and make them right. But sometimes what you see can never be made right. You'll just see it again and again."

I fumbled for something to say or do in response and wound up asking her if she'd like some tea.

"Sure," she said. "I'm not going back to sleep now."

So I made us tea and Master Aerin taught me some Brynt Drowning Songs there in the mountains, in the quietest hours of the night.

Master Aerin passed away some years ago, but I never forgot our conversation, of course. I was reminded of it forcefully the night after we made our escape from Talala Fouz. I was sleeping on the boat and was seized by the most powerful nightmare featuring Hathrim. It wasn't Winthir Kanek or his fury Pinter Stuken, though, at least not that first night. No, it was Gorin and Sefir Mogen. All the people that I'd seen them kill by fire, axe, or sword, or in the jaws of one of their monstrous hounds—I dreamt that they were all me. I saw the original event in its accurate form, but then the face of the victim became my face, and I felt their pain and terror.

Until someone woke me up, telling me that I was screaming in different voices and made everyone think we were under attack. It was Abhi, and he looked worried.

"You're sweating," he said.

"Well, I thought I was on fire," I said between gasps, "so that makes sense. Never seen a fire get put out by sweat, but I figure a body needs to try."

I spent much of the remaining trip upriver preparing reports for the Triune Council in conjunction with the ambassador, so that they would be informed of the upheaval in Ghurana Nent and of my best guess that the void would be filled by Viceroy Melishev Lohmet, since the king had no heir.

It kept me busy and exhausted me into a dreamless sleep, which I have since preferred to all other kinds of sleep.

Ghuli Rakhan still displayed large wealth disparities, like other Nentian cities, but they seemed less severe than elsewhere, perhaps owing to its position as a trading hub with Rael. Viceroy Naren Khusharas did not make us wait long before he gave us an audience; having a Raelech ambassador with us, as well as a letter from King Kalaad, probably did much to smooth the way. That, or the large number of Hathrim we brought in on glass boats might have made him a tiny bit curious.

Abhi came with Olet and me to see the viceroy but left his bloodcat and stalk hawk on the Raelech boat. He wasn't going to let them know he was a plaguebringer at all, since the letter Olet had from the king predated that information. Khusharas knew who I was by reputation—he'd met my lifebond, Numa, on multiple occasions in her role as a courier for the Triune. He gave me a tight smile; he was a wiry man with a narrow, angular face that he'd tried to make look fuller by growing a mustache and giving his hair as much body as possible. His voice was a high tenor and he spoke rapidly from his throne, as if he'd had five to ten more cups of tea than anybody else. After reading Olet's letter, he laughed nervously and smiled, shaking it at us.

"Wow. I mean. Really. This is. I mean, holy Kalaad's sky-blue *balls,* you know? This is *wild.* You want food for the winter for, like, *all* the people *ever,* and I just have to produce that now because you're in a hurry and the king must think I'm sitting on vast stores of grain and salt and an actual ton of dried meat. He wrote it down, did you see? It says, 'Dried meat: one *fucking* ton!' I added the 'fucking' because it seemed like an appropriate time to curse, because there are so few times when someone tells you to give away a ton of food to a stranger, and you know why? Because it's *inappropriate!*"

"He did seem confident you had sufficient supply, Viceroy," Olet said.

"Oh. That's lovely to hear! I'm *glad* he seemed confident. That's *perfect.* Do I have sufficient supplies for you? Yes. I do. I probably even have a ton of dried meat, because you can't ever have enough of it, as my father always used to say. The problem is, if I give you everything listed here, I won't have sufficient supply for *me*. For *my* city. And winter's already knocking on the door. You can tell because everyone's nipples are puckered up and they smile at each other in the street and notice how *bloody* nippy it is outside. So I know how you're going to survive the winter as long as the animals don't eat you. You'll be surviving on my supplies. How are *my* people supposed to survive the winter? Hmm? Didn't see that detail in the letter. Kind of important detail to leave out, don't you think? You have a plan for that?"

The Raelech amabassador saved us from answering by saying that Rael could easily bolster any shortfalls that the city might experience due to outfitting the expedition.

"Ah, that's great! And I'm sure that won't be free, will it? No. So first I'm out food, then to make up the difference I'm out money. One way or another, this deal cuts out my liver and feeds it to the blackwings."

"You might have fewer mouths to feed after we recruit some people in the town to come with us," Abhi pointed out.

"Oh, yeah, pretty boy? Who are you, anyway?"

"Abhinava Khose, sir. A hunter."

"Khose? I know all the hunting families here and that's not one of them."

"No, sir. I'm from the south, and I'm going along to help protect the colony in the Gravewood."

"Where in the south are you from, Abhi? Can I call you Abhi?"

"That's fine, sir. I'm from Khul Bashab."

"No kidding? I hear they have some wild stuff going on down there. Kids talking to animals or something like that. You heard anything along those lines?"

"I've heard some rumors, sir, but I haven't been down there in quite some time."

That was a sharp answer, and it was so difficult not to smile. Abhi hadn't lied, because of course he'd heard rumors. But he didn't volunteer the fact that he was the one who'd been talking to animals either. Olet wasn't going to let the viceroy probe any further on that point, proving that she was quick on her feet too.

"I'd like to point out, sir, that the boats we are giving you in this deal are worth thousands each. It may not completely wipe out the expense of replenishing your supplies, but it should lessen the sting a little bit, and I will also happily enchant some items for you while we wait for the supplies to be loaded and recruit some colonists."

"Ah. There! There, you see? That's a nice gesture right there from a daughter of the First Kenning. I got all this stuff lying around and I wish it was on fire *all the time*. Can't tell you how often I've been wanting to see some shit go up in flames. Praise Kalaad for my wish fulfillment! All right, all right, I've complained enough. That's all it is, because I got my orders here from the boss and I have to follow through. Thanks for listening, okay, and I wish you luck, because you're going to need it. Get some nipple warmers because, *damn*, I would not want to be you when winter hits up there. All right, Chamberlain? Do all this work for me, okay? Give them the food and sell their boats, then buy more food for us from Rael, and give that red-headed giant lady a bunch of shit to enchant for us. Thanks, you're a good guy. We'll have a beer later, yeah? Okay, kids, that's it. Move along. I have like ten more meetings and people are waiting. Thanks. Bye now."

News spread throughout the city soon after our strange audience that the king was dead and Talala Fouz had been burned down by a couple of Hathrim. The gaze of the city folk toward the Hathrim of our party noticeably turned from slightly awed but generally friendly to suspicious at the least and edging toward murderous. There were mutterings and the beginnings of some clustering, the early stages of a mob, and Olet quickly ordered all her people outside the walls and across the West Gravewater River to a hunting camp.

"We should be staging from there anyway. Let's set up crews to start dropping trees."

"Recruiting is going to be a bit tougher now, I think," La Mastik said. And no sooner had she said it than one of the viceroy's pages pushed forward with a summons to return to the skylight room.

"The viceroy needs to see you immediately."

She asked La Mastik to stay with the folks and get things organized and set a watch, but she brought Abhi and me along to emphasize that this was not exclusively a Hathrim enterprise.

The viceroy appeared to have drunk five more cups of tea in the short time we'd been away. He was now pacing in front of his throne and flailing his hands as he talked, in constant motion.

"Hi again, yeah, thanks for coming," he began. "Let me make sure of the facts first, Olet: You're the daughter of Winthir Kanek, hearthfire of Narvik and Tharsif?"

"The late hearthfire, yes."

"So you know he's dead."

"Yes, I've heard."

"I'm sorry for the loss."

"I'm not. He was cruel to everyone, including me. My entire reason for wishing to do this was to live a life outside his influence."

"Right, good, glad we got that cleared up. But there's still a problem. See, your cruel ol' dad killed our king. So I'm in a bit of a bind here, politically speaking. I have this city here, right, and they're watching their proverbial pecks of pickled peppers getting loaded onto carts for an expedition into the Gravewood, maybe never to return, and if you never returned I think everyone would be *fine* with that, just *spiffing*. But I've got this tactician whispering in my ear, saying, 'Hey, Naren, what if'—and this is wild, but hear me out, okay?—'what if Olet Kanek has a plan to *sucker* us? We give her a bunch of our food stores—the majority of them, to be honest—and then, instead of taking off, she lays siege to the city, and her thousands of Hathrim who look like peasants are actually soldiers and lavaborn in disguise? Talala Fouz is already toast, and our garrison is pretty small here because we sent a bunch of lads off to fight Gorin Mogen, so we're easy pickings right now. What if this is just part of a grand strategy to take Ghurana Nent down? Who knows what forces might already be striking elsewhere? Pretty clever, eh? What do you think?'"

"I think you should get a new tactician. It would be strategically stupid for me, or anyone, to try that here."

"Stupid? Why?"

"If there was some grand plan on the part of Hathrir to take down Ghurana Nent—which there isn't—it would make far more sense to try the sort of gambit you describe at Ar Balesh, so that we could cut off resupply from Rael by closing the tunnel through the Huntress Range. Then we would cut off river trade at either end, at Talala Fouz and Ar Balesh, isolating you and the other river cities in the middle, effectively beginning a siege without coming in range of the walls. Only when either end was secure would we move against the cities in the middle, and by the time we did so, you'd be weak and cut off with no hope of reinforcement."

"Holy balls, that's scary," the viceroy said in a tiny voice.

"But we've given you our boats, and I am the only person in our party who owns a decent set of armor. We are not fighters. Our desire to found a new city with people of all nations and kennings is genuine."

"If it helps, Viceroy," I interjected, "I can vouch for Olet's desire to live far from her father's sphere of influence. She hatched this plan with Jerin Mogen well before the Battle of the Godsteeth. I was there."

"Oh, that's *super* comforting. She had a conversation once with the son of another hearthfire who actually invaded us and killed thousands of Nentians. Thanks, bardy bard! How about you, hunter boy? You got any vouching to do for Olet here?"

"Well," the plaguebringer said, startled to be addressed and clearing his throat. "She has not asked me to take part in any attack on Ghuli Rakhan. All our conversations have been about establishing a city in the north."

"Oh, so she couldn't possibly be using you, then? *Lying* to you? You're not a prop she's brought along to bolster her case?"

"If I am, then I'm unaware of it. I just want to go north."

"Yeah, hey, why is that? Huh? Handsome guy like you with fancy khernhide boots, you ought to be ass deep in melons at the market, know what I'm saying? Khul Bashab wasn't good enough for you?"

"I've already seen all the animals down there," Abhi replied with a shrug. "I'm excited to explore and see something new."

"Plenty of something new in the Gravewood, for sure, yeah, no doubt. But you know something new might eat you, right?"

"I do. So far, though, everything that's tried to eat me has failed."

"Aha ha ha! Yeah. Good answer, kid. Okay, so look, Olet. I still have to do the ten things I said earlier, but now I have a hundred more because your father killed the king. I want to trust you, and, hey, I do, all right? But the situation is that I have some people who need *proof* you're not here to kill us all, and I need to *shut them up*. So here's what we're going to do. I'm going to send some guys to inspect your people, and they're going to be looking for war material." He finally stopped moving and met her eyes. "You got any of that on you?"

Olet nodded once. "We have axes for cutting timber and a few war axes like the houndsmen use, because we have some of Gorin Mogen's former houndsmen with us. We have some bows and arrows for hunting. I have a sword, and I expect most everyone has a dagger or belt knife of some kind. But we have no shields and no serious armor apart from mine—the houndsmen all surrendered theirs at Baghra Khek—and we have no hounds. I am the only lavaborn of any skill. My priestess of the flame is only a sparker. What your men will largely find among my people are plenty of personal effects and lots of tired eyes."

Viceroy Khusharas sprang into action again, pacing and gesticulating as he spoke. "Fantastic. Okay, so I'll send a couple dozen guys, and your Raelech bard can watch them as they search, to make sure they behave and don't steal or pick fights. You watch your folks to make sure they don't start anything either. As long as I get a good report and none of my guys gets set on fire, we can proceed as before and I'll be able to tell my tactician he owes me a beer or ten. Sound good? I really hope it does, because if you say no it's going to make this bad day even worse."

"Sounds good, Viceroy."

"Good. That's great. Thanks, Olet. Thing is, for all my complaining, I *want* to do this, and I want you to make it, you know? Because my king—he was an actual buddy of mine, you know? No, you didn't know, of course you didn't— Anyway, I was looking forward to writing my buddy a letter and telling him what a jerk he was for making me give you a fucking *ton* of meat. I mean, I'm pretty sure he wrote that in there just because he knew it would chap my ass and it made him laugh. And now I can't write my buddy the king a letter, and if I slow down here that's going to catch up to me and I won't be able to function. The thing is, Olet, the thing is, he *wanted* you to succeed in this venture and your absolutely huge ass of a father didn't. That's reason enough for me to support you right there. So between you and me, let's hope this all works out. I don't want my buddy's last act to turn out to be a con job, you know? I'd rather he be remembered as a visionary who placed a bet on you and won."

"I understand, Viceroy. I'm very sorry to bring such grief to your door. I hope to give you only good news from now on."

"Fantastic. That was a perfect thing, that thing you just said. So get out of here and give me only good news from now on. My guys will meet you at the bridge."

He had already turned to his chamberlain to ask what was next before we had a chance to move, but we exited as quickly as dignity would allow.

Abhi spoke to me in low tones as we made our way to the bridge. "Have you ever heard of the lizards in Forn that can change the color of their skin to match their surroundings? They're called chameleons."

"Yes, I've heard of them. I'd love to actually see one someday."

"After witnessing that performance, I think grief can be thought of as a chameleon. It can change its color or pattern, but underneath it all it's still an ugly lizard on a branch, waiting patiently for the right time to strike."

"You realize that every time I'm sad from now on I'm going to think of chameleons?"

"You are? Kalaad, I didn't mean that—"

"It's all right, Abhi. Because then I'll think of you and that will cheer me up. You're hilarious, you know."

"I am?"

"When you said, 'Everything that's tried to eat me has failed,' I almost died trying not to laugh out loud. He still has no idea you found the Sixth Kenning."

"Yeah." Abhi's eyes dropped to the ground. "I feel a bit guilty about that now. He seems like a nicer fellow than the other viceroys I've met. I mean, he's still weird, but not in a malevolent way."

"There was no way to know ahead of time. Cheer up. You can write him a letter when we get where we're going and tell him everything from a very safe distance."

The plaguebringer chuckled. "As in 'By the way, Viceroy, I forgot to mention . . . '? Yeah, okay. That's a good idea."

Fintan dispelled his old self and said, "It's time to check in on Koesha Gansu, whom we last saw in search of the northern passage and her sister, Maesi. We pick up a day or two later, after she's started to survey the northwestern coast of our continent."

*K*oesha

We round a peninsula and find a large bay shining in the sun, its shores barely visible but populated with stands of timber, deciduous species mixed in with the evergreens, and some talkative seabirds calling overhead, occasionally plunging into waters and coming up with silver spinefish in their beaks. The lookout spies a break in the wood and we draw closer, confirming that, yes, indeed, we have found fresh water, and we are all happy again. There will be baths, by the goddess. I keep myself busy charting the bay's contours while I talk to Haesha and Leisuen Korsu, my bosun, about work details.

"I want wood collected and the cook's cauldron boiling all the water before we store it. We cannot trust the purity of anything here. I know it'll take time, but we'll be safe that way."

"Aye, Zephyr."

"I want an armed watch for the water detail and also for the bathers—we'll do that in shifts. We don't know about the local animals here."

We're giddy as we step off the rowboat, booted feet crunching on a soft carpet of needles and old leaves, feathered ferns nodding at us as a gentle breeze filters through the forest. Scouts armed with bows precede us upriver, looking for a likely place to bathe and, farther upstream, a place to fill the barrels and boil the water.

One of the scouts, Baejan Moesien, returns all too soon, the happy smile vanished from her features. "Zephyr, there's a boulder up ahead you should see."

"Lead the way."

I don't question her for details, because I'll find out soon enough when I see it. But my senses sharpen, searching for danger. Is there a scent of blood or decay in the air? No, only freshness. Are there rustlings in the trees, growls of some predator nearby? We hear some birdcalls and some chittering of small forest creatures but nothing large enough to threaten us.

But when we step past the trunk of a particularly robust evergreen on the bank and I see a large gray boulder sunk in a sandy bend in the river, a perfect place for bathing, I know immediately why the scout fetched me. The rest of the scouts are there, facing out, looking into the trees nearby, not only alert but on edge.

The boulder has been carved, or chiseled, and the carvings painted. Not in some foreign language but in our own.

FETCH WATER QUICKLY AND RETURN TO SHIP, it reads. DO NOT SLEEP ON-
SHORE. DANGEROUS ANIMALS HERE. EATERS OF PEOPLE. WATCH THE TREES.
That explains why the scouts are skittish.

Below that is a list of names and dates under the heading of ZEPHYRS.
Some of the dates are from long before I was born—even before my
parents were born. How is that possible, I wonder? I've never heard of
this place before; there are no tales told of it. What horrors lie in wait
for us ahead if this clear evidence of Joabeian discovery is here but not
a single one of these zephyrs ever returned home to report it? Or did
they try to return but weren't able to make the crossing safely? Did
they remain too long? Is my best course, then, to return to safety now,
report this find, and wait yet another year for the seas to clear to make
a similar short trip? Will continuing be a mere repetition of the errors
of those before me?

I did not expect to be confronted with such a grim monument.

"Have you seen any burial markers?"

"No, Zephyr."

That doesn't mean there aren't any. Or it might mean there were
never enough left alive to do the burying. Or enough time to raise a
marker. I feel the hairs rise on the back of my neck.

The paint is still somewhat fresh; someone had renewed it, probably just last year. I should do the same to make sure it remains visible.
I skip to the most recent entries, where I begin to recognize the names
of some zephyrs who left when I was a child. And there, near the end,
is Maesi's name. Two years ago to the day. We had left Joabei two years
apart and landed on this alien shore two years apart. What happened
to her next? She obviously didn't die here; even though the figures are
chiseled, I still recognize her hand. Am I to meet the exact same fate? I
can't suppress a shiver at the thought that Maesi stood in this same
spot and had to make the same decision I must: Go on or go home.

The name beneath Maesi's is not one I recognize. That zephyr must
have come here from our other island and had taken time to refresh
the paint.

"Bathing is canceled." The scouts' shoulders droop a little, but they say nothing. "We are getting water only and returning to the ship. I don't want to lose anyone. Form up on me. Archers with eyes on the treetops. We're going to return to the boat and rethink the day's agenda."

"Aye, Zephyr," Baejan says.

I spin on my heel, drawing both the Bora and the Buran, the straight and serrated daggers Shoawei used when fighting the fire demons, subduing them to her will. Together we advance in the half-crouched spring step, ready to attack or defend, eyes darting into the forest that no longer seems so welcoming.

Stepping around the broad trunk of the ancient evergreen we'd passed on our way in, I see that Haesha and Leisuen are approaching us without concern, some thirty lengths along the path. Movement in the trees above them makes my heart fill my throat.

"Knives out!" I call to them. "Look up!"

There's a shadow shifting in the branches of the pines—not a single animal, but a churning cloud of birds. We'd heard them chirping but hadn't realized there were so many. As Haesha and Leisuen draw their weapons, the swarm shrieks in a frenzied pitch and dives at them. I break into a run to help them, the scouts following me, but the birds get there first.

They're the size of songbirds, but they're not settling for a worm here or a grasshopper there. They've realized at some point that they can go after larger prey if they work together.

Swarming behavior in birds, fish, and insects is supposed to be a defensive mechanism against larger predators, to protect individuals and reduce the number of victims. But these birds have learned that it can work as an offensive strategy as well. They lead not with their talons but their beaks.

Haesha and Leisuen slash at them with their daggers, knocking some out of the air, but others pass by unscathed and do some scathing to my most important crew. The women disappear in a screaming cloud of feathers and steel, and I belt out a battle cry as I approach, waving my daggers in an attempt to distract and terrify the birds. The scouts join in and it appears to work—that, and the efficient slaying that Haesha and Leisuen conduct even as they're getting attacked. The cloud of feathers dissipates as the birds retreat to the trees, leaving two bloodied sailors and a lot of avian corpses behind.

Haesha has lost part of her left ear, has chunks missing from her arms, and has divots in her shoulders and back. Leisuen has lost the top of her right ear and bears similar wounds. Their defensive actions kept their faces and vitals unharmed, but the birds were all after mouthfuls of meat, and many of them got it.

The archers form up around us and take some shots at the surviving birds, which have not entirely fled but remain in the upper branches of the pines, watching us.

Haesha kicks angrily at the bloody corpse of a bird. "What kind of flying devils are those?" she says. "Why are they even allowed?"

"I don't know. I'm so sorry." Belatedly, I realize I should have used my kenning to blow the birds away in a gust of wind. It simply hadn't occurred to me in the pressure of the moment, and I feel as though I've failed them. "Look, we have to get you back to the ship to stop the bleeding. We're leaving this place, getting water only."

"Good call," she says.

I sheathe my daggers and turn to Baejan. "Watch everything. Shoot anything that moves that isn't us. We're headed back."

The scout relays these orders to the others as I bend down to pick up a couple of the dead birds. Examining them up close, I see that their plumage is black, white, and gray, with black heads and beaks that are hooked cruelly at the tip. Not exactly ideal for camouflage against the pines right now, but probably excellent in the snows.

"These look like shrikes," I say, "but obviously different from the ones back home. Shrikes are normally solitary birds."

"Call them pine shrikes," Leisuen says, pointing with the tip of her Buran to a tree nearby with a few of the birds in the branches. "See how they're perched only in the pines? None of the other trees."

We hurry back to the ship, not only because Haesha and Leisuen need attention but because there are some new howls and grunts coming from the forest, and they sound hungry. I've already taken casualties, but I don't want any dead. If the birds on this continent are so aggressive compared to what we're used to seeing, then we might be in for much worse.

My mind strays into language questions as we march downstream, eyes roving for danger. What would I call those birds in my log? A *flock* seems so inadequate. They need a collective noun that fits their nature. A butchery? No: An abattoir. An abattoir of pine shrikes. Had Haesha and Leisuen not been able to defend themselves, or had we not been nearby to give them a warning, the birds might well have been able to tear into something vital—an artery in the neck, for example. As it is, both women will be permanently disfigured.

And the responsibility for that is mine.

It's an easy decision to leave without chiseling my name into that rock. All those zephyrs never returned. I want to make it home.

But I also need to know more. I can't simply return and report that my journey yielded nothing more than a monument to our country's failure. It is a central tenet of our faith that Shoawei encourages exploration and rewards it with great bounty.

Except, of course, she had clearly not rewarded any of the ships that came this way before us, including Maesi's. I am quite sure Haesha and Leisuen do not feel rewarded right now.

I send them back to the boat immediately and stay behind with a few others to get the water barrels filled. We get attacked twice while that's happening, once by some strange weasel-like creatures and once by some hopping, fanged monstrosities that are nevertheless vulnerable to arrows. The hoots and calls of forest creatures intensify. The scent of blood among the pine needles has roused the locals.

As we get the barrels loaded into the landing craft and push off, there's a crescendo of crashing in the brush and some screams of small creatures suddenly cut off. Something huge and armored lumbers out of the cover onto the beach, obviously eyeing us. It opens its mouth full of jagged teeth and roars, and I am pretty sure we all scream in response, for it is a thing of nightmares.

Baejan mutters a stream of curses, nocks an arrow, and lets fly as it rumbles down toward the water. She's on target, but the arrow pings off the creature's armor as if it were stone. It looks heavy, and the creature can't possibly be a good swimmer—everything about its dense musculature suggests that it would sink like a lead weight. This is a land-based predator, perhaps the deadliest we've ever seen, but not a creature of the seas. I'm thinking we have to be safe until it opens its mouth wide once more, but not to vocalize this time. An obscenely long tongue erupts from the cavern of its maw and extends, and extends, and keeps extending, until its tip wraps around the prow of our skiff and holds on. And then . . . pulls.

That earns a fresh chorus of screams, for against the strength of our rowing, this creature is using its tongue to pull us back to shore and into its giant mouth. If it had the strength to pull a boatload of us in, it could handle any single one of us easily.

I draw my Buran and attack the tongue, hoping it's not as invulnerable as its exterior seems to be. The serrated edges manage to cut into it, but it's much tougher than normal flesh and it's not severed, nor even cut particularly deeply. Still, it's enough to make the creature let go. The tongue unwinds and flops into the surf as some internal retraction reels it back into the mouth. The creature roars again as we surge away, frustrated that its lunch is so uncooperative.

"Thank the goddess," Baejan says, a sentiment echoed by the others. "I was disappointed we weren't staying to bathe, Zephyr, but leaving quickly was definitely the right call. If that thing had caught us on land . . ."

She doesn't have to finish. We'd all rather be dirty and alive than freshly washed immediately prior to being digested.

Once on board, I order the anchor brought up and sails unfurled. I summon winds to push us north. Haesha and Leisuen waste little time coming to see me in my cabin, bleeding through their new bandages.

"Zephyr, where are we going?" Haesha asks.

"North, as planned. We agreed to fifteen days of exploration. We still have thirteen to go."

"Don't you think we've seen enough? There's no one living here. They can't possibly survive with all those creatures prowling about."

"No, I don't think we have seen enough. We have more questions than answers. We need to see more and return with as much information as possible. Because as dangerous as this land is, it didn't destroy a single ship that came here or chisel those names in that rock."

"I'm sure krakens were responsible," Leisuen says. "There's no question about what destroys ships, so let's not pretend it's a mystery. And this extra time you're taking only increases our risk of being destroyed. If we return now, we'll be coming back with more information than any other ship before us. We'll earn our reward, our futures secure."

"That will also be the case if we continue. I'd like to know more. Shoawei exhorts us to explore."

"Then at least explore to the south," Haesha pleads. "Because we can be sure everyone went north just like you're doing, searching for the northern passage. And that way is death."

"I disagree. We don't know that everyone went north or that the south is any safer. We know only the span of days that krakens retreat from the seas. We have thirteen days. We're going to use them. And then we'll turn around."

They both scowl at me and I hope my face is projecting utter confidence, despite my own doubts. If they push me further, there's not much room for me to maneuver. So I try to stifle any wind they have building in their lungs to object.

"You have my word. We push for thirteen days and then head home."

Their lips tighten and then Haesha gives me a curt nod. "Thirteen days. Your word."

I exhale slowly once they leave. *If you are out there, Maesi, I have only thirteen days to find you.*

———

"And now, as promised, our favorite Kaurian scholar, Gondel Vedd!" Fintan threw down a seeming sphere and became the disheveled older gentleman with mustard stains on his tunic.

Gondel

I know all the modern languages, and the ancient one too, but there's no word in any of them for a mixture of euphoria and dread. A good measure of relief as well, but the euphoria and dread mean I'm not getting enough sleep.

I'm relieved that I don't need to continue to witness the aftermath of the Eculan invasion. I'm euphoric that I get to see my husband, Maron, and be amongst my familiar things and walk in the land where Reinei breathes peace. But I dread the same, since I'll doubtless need to spend time in a windless dungeon with Saviič again and face Maron, who will almost certainly be incensed at my absence and the letter I sent not five days before, saying I'd be staying in Pelemyn awhile longer.

I had thought that circumstance demanded I stay in Brynlön to help them decipher the intelligence they were collecting from the Eculans. But two days after I posted my letter on a southbound ship, a letter arrived from the mistral, ordering Ponder Tann and me back to Linlauen. I was to take the next ship home. I had to make my farewells and apologies.

Thus it is that I'm crammed in a tiny cabin, made smaller by the overwhelming number of gift baskets from grateful Brynts. They seem to have heard that I enjoy mustard, so I now have more than I could possibly consume in a year.

Though I think I'll have a go at it. I find the challenge attractive. And I do adore the Brynts and their customs.

Perhaps I can have cheese parties and say to my guests, *This is the hot whiskey mustard the pelenaut gave me, and this honey and tarragon number is from his lung, and that saucy whole-grain job is from the Könstad du Lalland, and, oh, that delightful red wine and garlic mustard? Why, that is from Second Könstad Tallynd du Böll, the tidal mariner who saved Pelemyn.*

My, my, wouldn't that be fancy. We'd all wear bibs and I would manage to stain my tunic anyway because I am highly skilled at acquiring food stains; I believe it rivals my skill with languages. It would be perfection to be chided by Maron once again for an unsightly blotch upon my person, for then I would be at home, where I am loved.

Apart from sending me home with a gift basket, the second könstad has provided me with momentous news: I've been entrusted to share the intelligence that the Brynts have found the Seven-Year Ship in the Mistmaiden Isles, though they have yet to discover its secrets. But its mere discovery is a relief for Kauria—it means the Eculans will have no cause to invade us, since what they seek is elsewhere.

Ponder is very happy also to be returning without stressing his abilities as a tempest to their fullest. He does help speed us along our way, filling our sails, but it is still a journey of weeks, during which I will be completely useless on board. I have no seamanship whatsoever. But I am determined not to let the time go idly by. There is still work to be done on *Zanata Sedam,* and for this brief while, at least, I can look forward to no interruptions.

Carving out space to work was an exercise in moving gift baskets from the desk to my bunk. I needed to reexamine the text after taking some weeks off from it; sometimes a gust of understanding can follow a calm. It would be nice to understand something here, since the mistral's letter raised more questions than anything.

It said my presence was required to address some things that Saviič had said to my replacements in Linlauen. These unnamed scholars she'd brought in were making claims that she wanted confirmed or denied. What claims? All I could assume is that they were serious enough to warrant sending for my return but not serious enough to warrant asking Ponder to bring me back immediately on the wind.

That would have to wait until my arrival, and there was no use letting it weather my peace now. The Eculan holy text awaited. I laid it open to a random page on the left and placed my translation on the right, open to the same page. I looked at them superficially to note differences and recalled my early decision to use upper and lowercase letters for my translation. The Eculan text was in a single stylized case.

I still thought it was the proper move, but now I worried that I might have capitalized proper nouns that were never intended to be such. The Seven-Year Ship, for example. By the same token, I might have missed something that should have been capitalized.

The only variation in the text that the Eculan copyist employed was the occasional underscoring of words. I assumed that these were for emphasis, especially since the most-often-underscored words were numbers, and that fit with the Eculan obsession with numerology. But perhaps an analysis of underscored words as a set would yield some pattern heretofore unseen.

I set about recording every word underscored in the Eculan text, putting hash marks next to them for each time they were repeated. The most-oft-repeated words were indeed numbers, and seven was most prominent among these, as expected. But the kennings were underscored as well, as were directions like east and west. That would suggest that the underscoring might serve in lieu of capitalization, except for several oddities, and one in particular: The noun *žalost*— a word in the old language that was often translated as *grief, sorrow, mourning,* even *regret* or *chagrin*—was often (but not always) underscored in the text. There were some other anomalous nouns like that, but *žalost* was by far the most frequent.

My next task was to examine the use of that word, combing through the text to find every instance of it and writing down the entire sentence for syntactical analysis. What leapt to my attention in this process was that in every case where the word had been underscored, it had also been placed in the syntactical slot where it might function as a proper noun. I'd been translating it as a common noun in every case, but it had resulted in some strange-sounding passages—primarily a preoccupation with grim and contradictory feelings for a religious text, such as "Only through grief may one experience the fullness of life," or "Grief is the answer to all questions." If I reevaluated it as a name, however, it made better sense.

"Reinei bring us peace," I said into a cabin full of gift baskets. "That is the answer: Žalost is their god."

THE INCONVENIENT AUTHORITY OF ARMOR

The talk in the town after that was the Eculan belief in a deity named something close to Grief, and lots of conclusions got leapt to about their society and what kind of people they must be. I refused to join in such speculation. Their invasion already told us plenty about what kind of people they were, and I wasn't interested in hearing how they might justify or rationalize their actions.

I was, however, interested in learning more about the pine shrikes Koesha described, as they sounded remarkably horrifying. And I was much more interested in knowing how Fintan had heard of Gondel's story if he'd sailed to Kauria, as he and the pelenaut said.

After a night of blissful sleep in my own bed and a morning of proper toast and relaxation, I met Fintan earlier than usual to catch up on the tales. When we reached Gondel's, I asked Fintan how he knew of the story.

"I mean, he was sailing to Kauria while you were in Ghurana Nent. So was that all fabricated?"

"Oh, no, I talked to Gondel later."

"Where?"

"Don't you want to wait and find out? It'll be in the tales."

"No. I definitely do not want to wait. This is something I need to know now, for my own ease of mind."

"All right. He did go home to Kauria, but now he's back in Brynlön, doing something up in Fornyd."

"He's in Fornyd right now?"

"So far as I know. As of a few weeks ago." I couldn't tell him the real reason—that we needed Gondel's skills to translate the Wraith's letter—but this was precisely the sort of thing that Rölly needed to know in order to protect us. Whoever the Wraith had been writing to was still out there, after all. I'd have to wait to tell him, though, and be sneaky about it. Which meant, damn it all, that I was doing spy shit.

"Why is he in Fornyd?"

"Ah, now, that is something I'll need you to wait to hear. Can't go spoiling things, can we?"

I wanted to say yes, we could and damn well should spoil things, but I choked it back and said instead, "I guess not."

Fintan smiled. "You seem in better spirits, Dervan. Everything all right with your toast this morning?"

"It was lovely. Did you sleep well?"

The bard's grin faded. "No. The nightmares have been getting worse."

"Oh, I'm sorry to hear. Hasn't it been a few days since you've seen Hollit and Orden? Maybe practicing presence in their restaurant was helping a little."

Fintan cocked his head to one side, thinking about it. "Maybe it was."

"Shall we decamp and move our business there? You said you wanted to try the sunchuck, right?"

"Do they have any?"

"Yeah. No shortage of sunchucks yet, I don't think. Their populations weren't hit by the invasion. Hunters keep bringing them in from about ten huge colonies inland that can afford to lose a few."

"Are there really so many out there?"

"Well, there are enough for this one restaurant. They're practically the only one to offer it."

"Why is that?"

"Well, have you ever seen a sunchuck?"

"No."

"They're like extra-large groundhogs with a ray of yellow quills around the neck, making them look a bit like a rising sun when they flare them out. The tips are poisoned. So it is delicious but infamously difficult to prepare. Most people don't want to go to the trouble."

"And these two Hathrim did?"

"Well, I think that's what they're used to. Hathrir is full of animals that aren't easy to prepare. Sand badgers, lava dragons, glass scorpions, you name it."

"What makes sunchucks so difficult compared to a glass scorpion?"

"Besides the poisoned quills, you have the venom sacs and the scent glands. If you don't remove them properly, the whole carcass is ruined."

"Yeah, glands will get you every time."

When we got to the Roasted Sunchuck, the place was hopping. There was a line out the door. Fintan's endorsement had done wonders for business, apparently. Still, once we got a table, Hollit and Orden came out to see us—Fintan, really—welcomed us personally, and wondered if we'd like the bladefin steak and a craft cocktail.

"I'd like to try the sunchuck if you have it," Fintan said. I noticed that he had gripped the edge of the table and his smile was somewhat forced. "And the cocktail for sure. What makes the sunchuck your specialty, if I may ask?"

Hollit beamed. "They have a wholesome vegetarian diet and it makes the natural flavor of the meat delicious. We get up early in the morning to brine the sunchucks for three hours, and then we roast them in a dry rub of herbs and spices at an even temperature for another three hours. The meat falls apart with a fork, and we serve it with flatbread, sprouts, and apples and a rich mushroom sauce for dipping."

Fintan's fingers relaxed and his shoulders visibly dropped. "That sounds amazing."

"We hope you enjoy," Orden said. "And thank you for singing that smoke meditation a few days ago and mentioning us. It's made our week."

Once they'd left, I said, "I saw you tense up and then relax. What allowed you to let go?"

"The words *mushroom sauce* did it."

I just blinked at him.

"Look, if I could explain how my system works, I probably wouldn't need help managing it, would I? I just find mushroom sauces deeply comforting, and now I've associated that with a couple of Hathrim. That's a good thing. Coming here was a great idea. And I'm glad to see them so busy."

"Me too."

"But you do know they're spies, right?"

"What?"

"Even if they're not active agents, they're spies. Come on, they're the only two Hathrim in the capital city of the kenning that cancels theirs. Even if they weren't sent here to be spies originally, they've certainly been recruited in the years since they arrived."

"Recruited to do what?"

"Nothing serious. But certainly reporting everything to someone. There's not a Hathrim embassy here—that's down in Setyrön. So most likely they report things to the ambassador there."

I shrugged my indifference, but I was beginning to wonder who wasn't a spy in Pelemyn. And then I realized that most people weren't. It was just that I was trapped in a nest of them somehow, despite my best efforts.

The roasted sunchuck was delicious and Fintan made happy moaning noises at the mushroom sauce, and we got all caught up on the tales.

And then, once we went to the wall and while he performed an instrumental song to warm up the crowd, I found a mariner and relayed an urgent message for the pelenaut: Gondel Vedd was in Fornyd. Relaying information like that didn't seem so bad. But I still felt like I'd need to take a bath afterward and scrub myself twice. I hated being a dirty spy.

The bard began his tales for the day by returning us to Khul Bashab.

Hanima

There is time enough for honey. That makes my heart full, and sometimes I think the way that feels is better than a full stomach. My bees will be able to survive the winter.

The ants of the city will likewise be okay, unless someone poisons them. Same with the wasps.

But Adithi, Sudhi, and I are far from safe. Tamhan posted those broadsides he promised and the city watch swarmed the streets, tearing them down as soon as they could and demanding to know who put them up, who printed them, and how did someone so stupid as to post such dung manage not to misspell anything? They got super shouty in people's faces and slapped them around to scare them into giving us up—or, failing that, giving them something else. It was the same old shakedown but with the kind of intensity that nearly made you ruin your pants, like waking up with a flesh eel burrowing into your rib cage. So people talked: They knew a guy who knew a guy who did a bad thing once, something real bad, and they could find him at this sour suckhole on the other side of the River District most every day.

Nobody tells the city watch where to find us, though. They can't. Adithi and I trust no one, talking only to Khamen Chorous and being careful even with him. But even if he's turned against us, he can't give us away, because he doesn't know where we're staying either. We stay somewhere new every night, now that I have my many thousands of eyes looking for unoccupied spaces, and we're telling Khamen where he can crash safely too as long as he touches nothing but the bed. My plan is to help everyone sleeping in alleys and riverbank mudflats to find a soft place to spend the night, when I can get the hang of processing all this information. I see so much and can't keep up; I'm scared of making a mistake and putting someone's life in danger.

"Somebody's going to find out," Adithi warns me. "Someone won't be careful. They'll steal something, wreck something, leave a clue, and then the swells in their fancy boots will be after us. And eventually someone will talk and say you told them where to break in and sleep."

"That doesn't matter if they don't know where *we* sleep."

"I'm just saying it's going to make things more dangerous for us. For everybody."

"The city watch can squeeze Khul Bashab all it wants, but we will slip through their grasp, Adithi. You know what we are like? We're like a fart you try to strangle into silence in polite company but it makes a defiant, triumphant squeak as it escapes the tyranny of your ass."

My friend cocked her head. "Okay, Hanima? No. I appreciate what you're trying to say, but that's not a very heroic comparison. I don't want to be a cloud of smelly gases."

"I thought it was appropriate, as the authority we're thwarting in that scenario is literally an asshole. Or metaphorically an asshole. Whatever, it was clever assplay."

"Yes, all right, I'll admit that part was good, but you made us into a poot. And not a particularly strong or robust one either."

"How can you say that? It was determined and won its freedom despite intense pressure."

Adithi struggles to keep a straight face and ultimately loses the battle. She chuckles a couple of times before continuing. "Look, I'm just saying you could have picked a nobler metaphor. Like a baby stalk hawk hatching from its shell—or maybe a fledgling taking its first flight, fighting gravity."

"Yeah, that's noble and makes *us* sound good, but that's not how the viceroy or the city watch thinks of us. I'm not saying they want to strangle baby birds—I hope they don't—but they also don't treat us like a protective eggshell would, and they definitely don't treat us equally, the way the steady pressure of gravity does. To them, we're something that needs suppression."

"Kalaad," she mutters, shaking her head. "I'm glad Tamhan is writing the broadsides, because you'd be telling people to rise up like a belch."

"That wouldn't be bad. People pay attention to belches."

"Let's move to wherever we're staying tonight," she says, changing the subject. "While the swells are out to lunch and talking about us and the watch is too busy protecting them from beggars to be looking for us."

Hoods pulled down over our features, we move through alleys until we find an empty house near the river that some ants told me about— food left out in the kitchen and nobody caring if they ate it all. It smells a bit ripe, but the rest of the place is in good condition. The bedrooms are pristine. Whoever owns it will be back, but it should be safe for a night or two.

We crash through the afternoon and wake up after dark, our new custom, and I reconnect with the hives while Adithi checks in with the horses.

The hives see plenty, but they haven't seen Sudhi yet. Wherever he's hiding, it's not where bees, wasps, and ants roam. I wonder if he's doing that on purpose. Nobody else thinks to hide from passing insects. They wear masks of civility so long as they feel human eyes upon them, but when they think there aren't any witnesses . . . well. I've heard stories. Back when I couldn't talk, I learned to listen real well. I heard that the city watch made people disappear sometimes. Almost always poor people, but occasionally someone more prosperous who'd managed to draw the ire of the viceroy. But I'd never *seen* the black tar pits of their souls until recently. It is . . . unpretty.

After sundown, most of the hives that talk to me during the day are quiet, but there is a single nocturnal species of bee that thrives on night-blooming flowers, competing only with moths and the occasional bat for nectar. And there are burrow wasps galore outside the walls that hunt along the river and stray a short distance onto city shores while they're at it. They're the ones that tell me something's up. Them and Adithi.

"The horses aren't in the stable. I mean, most of them aren't," she says. "They're down by the river for some reason."

"So the watch is at the docks?"

"No. The west-side mudflats. Where the water's dirtiest, where . . ."

"Where I used to live."

"I wasn't much better off. I was in a shack near one of the gates. Noisy and liable to be robbed as not."

"Are they in the shantytown where you were?"

"No. On the shore."

Only the poorest of the poor live there. If they don't get out when the floodwaters come each year, they just get swept away. I'm pretty sure the viceroy counts on it as a way to control the population of the poor. That's why Tamhan had no trouble finding seekers like me. When he came, we had a lean winter and a flood to look forward to, nothing more, so why not take a chance? But I still know plenty of the folks living there. It's a strange and filthy place, where everyone wears an exquisite veneer of kindness and manners over a core of desperation.

The docks are on the east side, boardwalks and some guarded warehouses reaching out to where the river flows year-round, all safely out of the squelching mudflats that teem with insects and the homeless who don't even have an alley's worth of shelter. There is a deep wall sunk at either end of the city's boundary to protect against flesh eels, but that is the only courtesy the city extends to the unfortunate. The flats lead up to the many arched gates guarded with portcullises; the east-side gates are always open, always monitored by the watch, and we aren't always welcome to travel through there. Of the four west-side arches, only one remains open regularly for our use, and passing through is always an opportunity for harassment, since it is never used by the moneyed people.

"Do the horses know what's going on?"

"Lots of angry humans. Trampling some things. They don't like it." Adithi has more of an emotional connection with the horses than a visual or auditory one. Hives aren't into emotions, so I get more sensory information.

"Okay, let me see if I have any eyes there. . . ."

The burrow wasps show me what's going on. The city watch is rifling through the few possessions the river folk have and beating them because they can. No one will fight back. No one will ever get their revenge. Maybe this is a response to the broadsides; I don't know. I can't tell what anyone is saying, if anything. The burrow wasps can share what they see, but language is just a mess of noise to them and they don't process sound well, so I can't pick anything out. I tell Adithi all this and say, "We have to help."

"We can't go down there and deliver ourselves to them."

"No, but you can make the horses ride away, right?"

"Yes, but that will give us away too, won't it?"

"How? We'll be right here."

"It'll tell them we're nearby and watching. It'll teach them that this is how they get us to respond, and they'll do it more. And it will confirm the rumor that I have the ability to control horses, when Tamhan wants people to be uncertain about that. If I do anything, it'll just make them come back on foot and push those poor people harder."

"What, so we do nothing?"

"No, we get back at the watch on their behalf. But we make it seem like it's in response to something else."

"When? I can't just sit here and not help."

"We can't help anyone if we're caught. Look, tomorrow we'll get a message to Tamhan. We'll pick a target on the watch—or he will—and we'll blame what we do on some rich guy, for an extra helping of justice."

"Let's at least go down there and help when they're done. Find out what started this."

Adithi agrees to that, and we make our way down to the flats by going out the western gate, leaving our new hooded tunics behind. We look like we're headed to our patch for the night, since we're dressed in the torn and bloodstained clothing we had from the seeking. It's easy to keep our eyes lowered, and the watchmen, having fun recounting the whupping they doled out earlier, aren't interested in harassing us.

I realize I haven't been back here since I left for the seeking. I recognize some of the faces in passing, but I don't make eye contact and I don't say anything; when they last saw me, I was mute.

"You should do the talking," I tell Adithi.

"Okay, fine, but who do we talk to?" she says. The flats are a chaotic churn of people in the aftermath, some trying to take advantage of the chaos and some trying to reestablish order.

In the middle of the worst damage there's a boy I know—or a young man, I suppose. He's kneeling in the ruin, staring despondently at a bedroll that's been trampled and torn, some personal effects scattered around it. One eye is swollen shut, and blood from a scalp wound is caking up in his hair. His clothes are the same rags I've seen him wear for the past couple of years.

I wouldn't say we are friends, exactly. We've never even shared our names with each other. But he's never tried to steal from me, and he gave me a heads-up a few times about dangers coming my way. Whenever I scored more food than I could eat in a sitting, I sought him out and gave him some. That's about as close to an alliance as you could find down by the river without joining an actual crew. We were, I suppose, a psuedo-crew of two, but we had no desire to join a crew otherwise. They indulge in the same petty cruelties that the swells do.

Adithi and I squat next to him and wave. It takes him a moment to register that we are there and another few beats to recognize me.

"Oh, hey. You didn't get hurt, did you?"

Asking after my safety first. That's a sweet guy. I shake my head and point at his with a concerned grimace.

"Yeah. They got me pretty good. And my bedroll is now just so much stuffing."

I frown but then clap Adithi on the shoulder, smile, and give two thumbs up, establishing her bona fides.

"Hi, I'm Adithi," she says.

"Hello. I'm Jahi."

"Good to meet you. We were in the city and so we missed what happened. What was the watch after?"

"They're after these kids that they say have powers over animals. Three of them. If we rat them out, we get paid. If we don't, they'll be back to run over us again."

"Is that what happened to you?"

"Yes. Knocked down by a man on a horse."

I want to talk to him but don't feel like we have privacy here. There are people nearby who can hear us, and I don't want to start talking and have to explain that I'm one of the people the watch is looking for. That would be unwise. I don't think Jahi would ever give us up, but I can't count on the rest of these people to keep our secret. With some gestures and expressions, I indicate that Jahi should come with us into the city. I want to help people, so I might as well start with him.

At the gate, we get questioned on why we're coming into the city so late, and Adithi explains it's to help Jahi get cleaned up and bandaged.

"You have a place to do that, do you?"

"Yes."

They search us "for weapons" and are disappointed that we're not carrying anything they can confiscate.

Once we're through and I confirm with a few of those nocturnal bees that we aren't being followed, I speak.

"Hi, Jahi. I can talk now."

He blinks his one unswollen eye rapidly. "What? Since when?"

"Since I got blessed."

"You? You mean you're—"

"Yes. I'm Hanima, the hivemistress. One of the beast callers they're looking for."

"Kalaad's sky-blue balls!"

"I'm sorry we couldn't help while they were doing this to you. We couldn't give ourselves away."

"Well, no, I should think not!"

"We can help you now, though. We can find a place for you to sleep each night in the city, if you're not above breaking and entering but then leaving everything alone."

"I'm not above much at the moment. I'm barely above the grave."

"Good. I'm working with Khamen Chorous to get everyone inside. It'll work as long as people don't steal stuff. Do you know him?"

"Sure. Three brown teeth, horrendous digestive issues."

"That's him. He's a good guy, though."

"How are you getting people indoors?"

"Ants have been finding vacant spaces for me. We coordinate through Khamen. You can help him if you want. We need to scale up and get more people to safety. The goal is to make it so the city watch can't do what they did to you tonight. We don't want anybody sleeping on the riverbank."

We take him to see Khamen and introduce him, explaining that Jahi will help out as needed and he'll be staying with Khamen in a new place.

Then we escort them both to a little two-bedroom house I've just learned about, which has been vacant for a couple of months at least. I was going to move there myself next with Adithi, because it would probably mean we didn't have to relocate for a while, but it's going to be better for Khamen and Jahi.

It's a wee place but pretty clean and still inside the River District; the ants took care of whatever food was there days ago. Jahi lights a candle, looks around, then looks up at the ceiling.

"A roof," he says. "I'm going to sleep under a roof."

"Roofs are the best, am I right?"

"They are," he agrees, and when he looks at me he has tears on his cheeks. "Thank you, Hanima. When you found me there staring at the shreds of my bedroll, I was thinking I wouldn't be around much longer. I think you saved my life."

"I owe you. You saved me a few times."

"Well, we have to look out for each other, don't we?"

"Yes, we do."

"Hey, look out," Khamen says, and rips a brutal beast of a fart before giggling at our cries of dismay. Adithi and I are quick to wish them a good night.

"Heading farther west," Fintan said as he prepared to take his next seeming, "let's check in with Fornish ambassador Mai Bet Ken."

I wasn't in a dungeon this time, so I finally got to see what she looked like. She was petite, like all the Fornish were, pale skinned and dark haired, and she had done something flippity and twirly with her hair so that it rose on top of her head. I know there are proper terms for such styles and some of them contain cultural significance, but I am not sophisticated in such matters. But I noticed that she had pinned flowers in her hair and it was quite pretty. And unlike many of the Fornish, who prefer vests on top of shirts, she had a full long-sleeved silk robe on, very formal-looking, with leaf and vine patterns in varying shades of green. It was beautiful work, and I must remember to ask which clans concern themselves with silk production.

Mai's brow was furrowed in concentration as she tried to grapple with new challenges.

During the night, in some loathsome unwashed warren where alcohol and other vices are sold, one of Hennedigha's so-called officers killed a Fornish citizen, right before the viceroy and the army are to depart for Talala Fouz. He strode out of there unmolested, despite multiple eyewitness reports that the Fornish man was unarmed and had tried to apologize for accidentally bumping into the officer. That news greets me with my morning tea. And then the mail arrives and it wilts all my hopes.

My request, sent weeks ago, was duly considered in the sway, and while some clans backed it, the Black Jaguars and Blue Moths denied my motion to increase our diplomatic corps in Ghurana Nent. They think our current staffing is sufficient and Forn can't afford the expenditure when the Hathrim are so unruly and there's a possible threat building on the east coast, as well as massive aid flowing to Brynlön and Rael in the wake of the Bone Giant invasion.

I am instead instructed to get what concessions I can for the Fornish contribution to defending Ghurana Nent from Gorin Mogen. The clans want the right to send settlers and merchants to Baghra Khek, since Fornish blood helped secure it. So I must request an emergency meeting with the viceroy on two counts.

While waiting, I renew my pleas to my clan to expand the tea business into all Nentian cities that can double as intelligence outposts, outlining a plan that should allow us to profit on multiple fronts.

I'm ushered in near the end of the business day. The viceroy looks tired and irritable and he wrinkles his nose at my customary cloud of floral spritzes. Tactician Hennedigha is still standing behind him, indefatigable, ready to grunt at the viceroy's command.

"What is the emergency?" Lohmet demands, without preamble or politeness.

"Last night a lieutenant in Tactician Hennedigha's army murdered an unarmed Fornish citizen in front of multiple eyewitnesses. We want him cashiered and imprisoned for his crime. It is only justice."

The viceroy turns his head to regard the tactician. "Have you heard of this?" Hennedigha gives a tiny shake of his head and the viceroy swings his sneer back to me. "What's the lieutenant's name?"

"Ranoush Mukhab." In response to this, Hennedigha grunts to get

Lohmet's attention and then shakes his head strongly. "I'm sorry, Tactician, I can't interpret your body language. Are you denying that is his name, or are you trying to communicate something else? Perhaps you could use words."

Both men glare at me in silence for daring to suggest the tactician speak clearly. But Hennedigha eventually complies. "Lieutenant Mukhab is guiltless."

"How can you know that unless you were there? People who were there state unequivocally he was at fault. He was the aggressor, not the defender. He attacked an unarmed man with a knife."

"He will not be cashiered or imprisoned."

"So Fornish citizens can be casually murdered by Lieutenant Mukhab, Viceroy? Is that what I'm hearing? Our best and blessed fought and died on your behalf at the Godsteeth, making it unnecessary for the lieutenant to put himself in harm's way and quite probably saving his life, and now he can kill us at his whim?"

The viceroy winced and pinched the bridge of his nose. "Let's step back for a moment."

"The Fornish handed you that grand victory that's allowing you to march into Talala Fouz to claim the throne with a full-strength army! We did that to protect the Canopy, and I will remind you now that every Fornish citizen is a part of the Canopy. An officer in your military has attacked and killed an unarmed citizen of the Canopy. Someone has to face the consequences. It should be the lieutenant."

"No," Hennedigha said, which I had expected, and I fired back immediately.

"Are you trying to start a war with Forn, Tactician?"

"What? No, no, he isn't," says Lohmet, shooting a quelling look at his military leader. I wonder how much control he really has over Hennedigha. "Look, we just now heard of this, and thank you, Ambassador, for bringing it to our attention. Allow us time to investigate the matter."

"How much time? Because the lieutenant is due to set sail with you tomorrow, isn't that right? Away from witnesses, away from punishment, under the protective wing of your tactician? I assure you we will not drop this or forget about it, and any delay in justice will erode our relationship."

"I understand. We will move as swiftly as possible to resolve this, and I hope to contact you later this evening."

"I'll look forward to hearing from you. There is one other matter."

"What is it?"

"The Black Jaguars, speaking on behalf of all the clans in the sway, wish to know what plans you have for that city site so recently liberated by our forces, and if those plans include settlement, they ask for permission to send settlers and merchants there to help develop it into a proper port, which would benefit both our nations greatly."

"Of course, of course," the viceroy says. This costs him nothing, so it's easily granted, and he thinks he's done me a favor now. "We will allow it to be settled, but it will not be called by the name the Hathrim gave it. It will have its own viceroy and we will keep you informed. Is that all?"

"That is all. We simply require swift justice for our murdered citizen."

The tactician swells as if taking breath to grunt again, but Lohmet cuts him off. "Hennedigha—everyone—please give us the room for a while. I have something else to discuss with the ambassador, in private."

Everyone visible shuffles out, Hennedigha departing with a sullen glare, but I know that there are others watching, bodyguards hidden behind doors in the walls.

When we are supposedly alone, Lohmet beckons me even closer and speaks in low tones to thwart those who might be listening.

"Get me a Brynt hygienist and I'll throw that lieutenant in jail," he says. "Maybe Hennedigha too, if that'll make you happy."

"What will make me happy is you upholding the law and punishing the lieutenant without trying to extort additional favors from me. Forn has already done you a favor that's paved your way to the throne, so you owe us. And, besides, Viceroy, you know that producing a hygienist is not in my power. You must make your appeal to the pelenaut of Brynlön."

"I will, of course. But your appeal added to it might carry some extra weight."

"Very well. I'll make the appeal," I tell him, "but I'd better see justice today. Your man has wronged us, and we've done nothing but help you. If you find some excuse to let the lieutenant get away with murder, our relationship will no longer be so friendly."

"You haven't had time to discuss this with the clans, Ambassador Ken. You're speaking very boldly on your own, throwing around words like *war.*"

Ah, so that is what the private meeting is really about. He wants to see if I'll wilt when he accuses me of going rogue. He never does the right thing for others, only what's right for him, and what's right for him at the moment is to keep his tactician happy in advance of his trip to the capital. If he can find a way to weasel out of this, he will, and he thinks I'm acting out of character and that might be cause to dismiss the matter. It is true he's never seen me so assertive, but until now I've had no cause to behave this way. I let my voice drop and turn cold as nightshade.

"I'm confident that I'm in the right and that the clans will see it the same way I do. My report of the incident is already on its way home, together with the remedy I'm demanding. I don't know why Hennedigha wants to protect the lieutenant so badly, but make no mistake, Viceroy: You have a serious incident on your hands. I'd like my next report to say that the matter is resolved to our satisfaction and Ghurana Nent is a nation of laws. Because if it is a nation of warlords, we can resolve it a different way. You saw what our greensleeve did to the warlord Gorin Mogen."

His eye twitches and the sweats have begun to drip down his forehead, but he's watching me closely for signs that I'm bluffing. I'm not. If he gets away with this, what kind of future will there be in this country? How many more such deaths will be waved away, while the corrupt protect one another and apply laws only to those who threaten them?

"I should add that the eyewitnesses, including the business owner, are safe at my embassy," I say. "In case Hennedigha is thinking he can make them disappear."

That part *is* a bluff, but unlike everything else I've said, it convinces Lohmet that I'm serious.

He leans back and nods once. "Thank you, Ambassador. You'll hear from me soon."

I return the curt nod and spin on my heel. It is indeed a dangerous game I'm playing, but I don't see much of an option except to play it out. I need to get the eyewitnesses protected and keep everyone on high alert through the night. We can't really stop them if they want to come for us, but they can't do it without starting a war. I'm fairly certain that I've got them. And I'm absolutely certain that I won't lift a finger to help the viceroy get a hygienist.

I was grinning when the bard dispelled the seeming of the Fornish ambassador. The viceroy was a clever man, but he clearly did not have the true measure of his opposition.

"We'll turn to Olet Kanek next, who has a hard road ahead of her— especially since the road does not actually exist yet."

After we left Ghuli Rakhan behind, I kind of missed Viceroy Naren Khusharas. He was manic and under tremendous pressure, but he was still loyal to his word and kept a wry sense of humor about things. When the final carts arrived and we were cleared to leave, a soldier sought me out and led me to the rearmost carts, pulled by wart oxen—a duty, I was told, he must perform before we departed.

"I'm sorry about the inconvenience, but I'm under strict orders from the viceroy."

"Understood. What am I to do?"

"Stand there while I pull back this tarp." The soldier untied the ropes locking down the tarp of the last wagon and pulled it off, to reveal some unmarked crates. He then produced an envelope from his cloak, with my name scrawled on it. The wax seal on the back proclaimed it to be from the viceroy.

"Can you open this for me, please?" I asked him. "My fingers are too big, and I'd just mangle it." Tiny human letters were cute but somewhat diffcult for me to handle.

"Oh. Certainly." He slit it open expertly, unfolded the note inside without looking at it, and handed it over.

It wasn't a formal letter at all. It was as informal as could be, in fact. It read:

> Behold: *a fucking ton of dried meat, as ordered by the late King Kalaad.*
>
> *Be safe, Olet, and send me good news as soon as you can.*
>
> *Do let me know what the new city is to be called. I leave that up to you, but remember that you owe me a ton.*
>
> *—Naren*

I chuckled and grinned at the soldier. "Message received. Please tell the viceroy I will do as he asks, and give him my thanks."

And then we needed to begin the long, hard work of blazing a trail without actually setting anything ablaze.

We did have experienced lumberjacks among our people; they had already done such work on the slopes of the Godsteeth under Gorin Mogen. These crews felled trees so that they would fall forward, pointing the way, and then we had road crews preparing a rough trail for the many carts to follow, removing stumps and boulders as necessary. Behind these we had fire crews chopping off branches and boughs that we'd use for firewood in that evening's camp. These were mostly composed of Nentian recruits, and La Mastik and I worked among them, making sure everything was prepared for the vanguard of the carts.

Abhi and Fintan roamed far ahead, scouting the trail and marking trees to be felled. They also had some Nentian hunters with them, who killed and gutted whatever was nearby and left the carcasses behind on the trail for the train to find and prep for that evening's dinner, allowing us to leave our stores alone and subsist on the bounty of the Gravewood. The plaguebringer assured us that the entire train would be protected from predators, and while I heard them from time to time scurrying in the trees, rustling in the undergrowth, or chirping above us, I never saw anything, much less witnessed an attack. He was as good as his word.

But I was disheartened in one regard: Everyone kept looking to me to lead. And that was not what I wanted at all.

Maybe it was just because I was the tallest damn thing in the forest apart from the trees. But I suspected it was because I was a firelord and the daughter of Winthir Kanek, and that didn't appeal to me at all. It meant that all the people of Gorin Mogen regarded me as their unofficial hearthfire, even though I'd explicitly told them I was no such thing. And it meant the Nentians were too scared of me and the other Hathrim to offer up their ideas. I made them feel powerless with my kenning and my stature.

I made the same offer to our new Nentians as I had to the Hathrim earlier: If they wanted to lead, all they had to do was ask to be heard and the Raelech bard would use his kenning to spread their voices to the entire assembly. But no one took me up on the offer. Which meant, in such a void, that people kept looking to me to make decisions.

After a week of us traveling north with no one stepping up, I broached the subject with La Mastik, whose counsel I treasure and whose character I admire. Since we had taken on new people of differing faiths, she had taken to conducting nightly prayers of various denominations, all cast widely by the bard so that everyone could hear. She first conducted Thurik's rites for the Hathrim once the night's fires were lit, and then she led the Nentians in rites for Kalaad, and then she deferred to the bard to conduct rites for the triple goddess, though he never did so since a quick poll revealed he was the only follower of that faith. I did not expect La Mastik to step outside the hearth of Thurik's Flame and work with others like that, but it was perfectly in tune with what I wished for our future: a community of different people and backgrounds living in harmony together.

"Mirana," I said, "why doesn't anyone want to lead us?"

"Including yourself?"

"Yes, including me."

"I think it is simply that we are walking into the unknown and no one wishes to be the person who makes the first misstep."

I grunted and chewed on that mentally for a while before responding. "We are in such an alien place. In Hathrir, power equaled prestige, so everyone sought it. And now we are in a different land, and because of that it seems our old culture is already gone. I am offering power, and nobody wants a slice of it."

La Mastik laughed at me. "It is not because we are in a different land. It is because the kind of people willing to stride into the unknown are of a certain character. They are focused on a vision of security for themselves and their families and living without friction with their neighbors. They are not the sort of people who want to run any business but their own."

That so perfectly encapsulated what I was feeling that I broke into a smile. "Ha! So leading is the one job they don't want?"

"That's right. In all likelihood they'd rather dig a latrine than be put in a position of responsibility."

"I would so love to dig a latrine right now."

"I know, Olet. I know. Perhaps you can push them into seeking leadership by offering positions other than the main one."

"What do you mean?"

"Something besides the equivalent of a hearthfire. Something that involves responsibility, but not *all* of it. Give them cover, in other words, so they do not feel that they are stepping naked into a den of sand badgers."

"You mean like a committee?"

"That is a dirty, dirty word, my friend. I think you should call it a council. It has more dignity."

"Like the Triune Council of Rael?"

"Yes, but not a Triune. More would be better. Spread the responsibility. Everyone has more cover that way."

That gave me much to think on, and that evening, once the fires had been lit and Mirana had performed the evening rites and prayers with her scalp lit on fire in the traditional way, I asked the Raelech bard to let me address the train.

"Good evening, everyone," I said. "I know you're all anxious to eat. But before you do, please allow me to give you something to discuss. It's something we should figure out together before we reach our destination. We are not going to have either a viceroy or a hearthfire, so we need to agree on some other method of governance. I'd like to propose one, in hopes of sparking discussion and perhaps concord." I paused to take a swallow of mead before continuing.

"It seems to me that a single leader can be efficient on the one hand, but dangerous on the other if that leader has a head full of shrieking bats. And it seems to me that elected councils can be slow and unwieldy on the one hand, but more easily replaced and accountable to the populace than single rulers. I'd like to propose a system in which we have a single leader checked by a council, and that council can also make laws checked by the single leader. The idea is that each would act as a foil against excesses. I think such foils are necessary because of my lived experience. I hope you will bear with me while I share this and that you will think of your own experience living under various rulers."

I paused for a moment and saw encouragement from the faces around my campfire. I heard calls and whoops from other fires as well.

"My father, Winthir Kanek, and Gorin Mogen were both remarkable hearthfires. They accomplished much and brought prosperity to Narvik, Tharsif, and Harthrad. They were strong leaders who more often than not led their people well. But they also had no check on their worst impulses. They both thought more of their own desires and pride than of the well-being and prosperity of their people—and if any of you Hathrim wish to disagree with me on that point, please seek me out and we will have a polite but spirited argument. I state flatly to you now that I am not my father or Gorin Mogen, nor do I wish to be. My only thought is that I want us all to prosper. And I do not think that I can make that happen on my own. I do not think any single person can.

"Our future city—a city to be named by our Nentian citizens, since it will be within the borders of Ghurana Nent—should be ruled by a steward and a council both. All should be elected by the general populace for terms to be decided." I spoke for a while about how the steward and council would check each other but emphasized that my ideas were merely a starting point.

"This is not my decree. It is the opening of discussion. Let us think on it tonight and on the trail tomorrow and come back tomorrow night to either approve it, make adjustments, or propose other methods of governance. If you would like to be heard tomorrow evening and speak on this matter, please see either me, La Mastik, or the Raelech bard. Thank you and good evening."

I made a throat-slashing motion to the bard and he nodded at me, ceasing to project my voice. I exhaled and let my shoulders slump. I squatted by the fire and shook my head. "Why would anyone want to do that every day?" I asked rhetorically. It was more exhausting than battle in one sense. I felt like I might understand why hearthfires would rather operate on the principle that the strongest shall lead; it was simple and eliminated questions. My questions began with *Did I do that right?* and proceeded to *What if I didn't?* and continued on to *What should I do next?* If my father was ever afflicted with such self-doubt, I never saw it.

But soon after that—an hour or so after dinner—people started appearing at our fire, wishing to talk to me, La Mastik, or the Raelech bard. They all had ideas to build off mine, and I learned that all one has to do to get people involved is not ask for their ideas but put one out there and ask them to respond to it.

"Okay, that was instructive," I said, after everyone had cleared off to call it a night. "Ask people to come up with something and you get nothing. Come up with something and they can't wait to tear it up."

"Welcome to leadership," La Mastik said.

"I don't want to be in leadership."

"Neither does anyone else who's sane. They'll let you do it, Olet. They just want to yell at you while you do it."

"Why doesn't someone else do it and let me yell at them?"

La Mastik raised an eyebrow at me. "Do you want a genuine answer to that?"

"Of course I do."

The priestess passed a hand over her scalp and snuffed the flames there. "Then let's step aside and talk softly."

The Raelech bard waved up at us from below and did one of those loud whispers. "Can I listen in?" he asked. "I promise not to say anything. I'm just really interested in this."

We both shrugged and the bard trailed after us as we stepped a few paces away from the fire into the darkness.

"My suggestion boils down to one thing," La Mastik said. "Stow the armor."

"What? Why?"

"As long as you wear it, you look like a military leader. You look like you have a plan and you know what you're doing. And, not incidentally, you look like you will slay anyone who disagrees with you."

"Those aren't all good things?"

La Mastik snorted. "Not when you want someone else to step up into a leadership role. We're not at war anymore, Olet. We're not invaders. We're not defending anyone except ourselves. Let that armor rest awhile."

"Okay, I hear you and I totally agree," I said. "That's very perceptive and I should do it."

"Except?"

"Except I don't have much else to wear. I mean, if I take off the armor, I'm pretty much in my undies."

"Are you kidding me right now?"

"No, I'm not. Have you seen me without my armor since Mount Thayil erupted?"

". . . I guess I haven't."

"That's because the eruption of a volcano leaves you very little time to pack your wardrobe. And have you noticed how many merchants in Ghurana Nent stock clothing in Hathrim sizes?"

"I haven't seen any."

"There you go. You're all caught up on my situation."

"Shit."

"Nentians don't make tunics in my size."

"No, no, I get it now."

I smiled. "Fortunately, we have a Nentian seamstress among our group and she's making me something. So I will do as you suggest."

"Ah. I knew you had to be lighting my candle."

Debate the next night was spirited, and we heard from people, both Hathrim and Nentian, that would almost certainly be part of the new government. Halsten Durik, the former houndmaster of Gorin Mogen, spoke rousingly about the potential for greatness in a forest like this. He had silver threads in his beard and mustache, and together with a surplus of muscle he cut an impressive figure. But his words were largely aimed at Hathrim ears, and I overheard one Nentian say to another, "He knows we're here, right?"

A Nentian man from Ar Balesh offered some very smart suggestions about sanitation and infrastructure and the sorts of incredibly boring things that save people's lives—or imperil them if they're ignored. If he didn't get elected, I'd seek him out for advice.

And at the end of that night's discussions, all I had to do was say, "That was great! Precisely the sort of thing I was hoping for. Let's continue to talk and be excited about governing ourselves."

Despite how tiring it was, I vastly preferred this to running everything myself. But I heard about it the next evening from many Hathrim who didn't prefer it at all—or, rather, from one Hathrim, who claimed he spoke for many others. They wanted me to end this "interminable discussion" and just make a decision. His name was Lanner Burgan. He had been a houndsman at the Battle of the Godsteeth, serving under Halsten, and the only reason he was still alive was because Abhi had driven the hounds to the sea and Lanner's company had been surrounded by Fornish thornhands.

He had red hair a bit darker than mine, and his beard fell down to his chest with a single braid in the middle, bound with a gold bangle at the bottom. He had shaven the right side of his head to allow someone to tattoo a stylized depiction of Mount Thayil erupting. I had seen several such tattoos appear recently, including on the side of Halsten's head; it seemed like it was something of a fad among the men, and I wondered if it was confined to former houndsmen. He was shorter than me by at least a foot, but he was much broader, his body put together in huge beefy slabs.

"How was it interminable?" I asked him. "It lasted a couple of hours, and you could tune out anytime if I understand the bard correctly. His kenning doesn't work without your consent. You only hear the discussion if you want to."

"I simply mean I'd rather hear what we're going to do and then do it."

"So you want to be reliably informed of governmental decisions."

"Yes. As long as they're your decisions." His lip curled. "Not some nebbishy Nentian."

"Oh," I said, and his words reminded me that I had heard of Lanner from somewhere else. La Mastik had reported a disturbing event she'd witnessed back in Baghra Khek. Early in the occupation, a party of Nentians sent by the viceroy of Hashan Khek arrived and Gorin Mogen invited them to his hearth, which would normally be a sign of good-will and safe passage, but then he killed them all. Lanner Burgan had participated in that slaughter. "You want me to be hearthfire."

"Yes."

"That is never going to happen, Lanner. That's a title I'm actively shunning, and you've heard me say that on multiple occasions. But I will promise you this much: Whatever is decided regarding the govern-ment's structure, I will run for office in it, to be elected or not as the people see fit."

"But what if the Nentians run everything?"

I blinked at him. "Is that a concern?"

"Yes!"

"Okay. Are you worried that Nentians would make bad decisions regarding our survival?"

"No, though they probably would. I'm worried that they'll make laws that favor them and put Hathrim at a disadvantage."

"I see. But if I was hearthfire, then might not the Nentians have the same fear regarding me? That I would make laws that favor Hathrim?"

"You wouldn't."

"I'd hope not. But I could. And if I did, would you be okay with that? If I was being unfair to Nentians, would you speak up and point that out to me?"

He looked uncomfortable. "I'm not sure."

"Would you even *notice* if laws disadvantaged others?"

"I don't know. That's impossible to know."

"I'm trying to understand the nature of your worry here. Are you worried about equality for all, or are you worried that Hathrim will be disadvantaged?"

Lanner's lip curled again, and he pointed a thick finger at me. "I can tell by the way you asked me that you think the right answer's equality for all, but it isn't. Looking after your own is always the right answer.

This system you're proposing is going to put the Nentians in charge of us, and that's not why I followed you."

"That's a good question: Why *did* you follow me?"

"I thought you'd be tough. Daughter of Winthir Kanek and marrying into the Mogens? Thought you'd have some sand."

"Sand melts at high temperatures. I don't."

Lanner's teeth flashed dull red in the firelight. "Ah, see there? That's more like it. We're a strong people. We won't allow ourselves to be led by weakness."

"Trying to find a better way to live is not weakness. It's bold. If I were clinging to old ideas and not trying to improve on what came before me, *that* would be weakness."

"The way we've always done things in Hathrir has worked out just fine."

"Maybe it worked in Hathrir for some people. But I think recent evidence suggests what worked in Hathrir does not work in Ghurana Nent. And we're in Ghurana Nent."

"Are you slagging Gorin Mogen right now? Because Gorin Mogen was the kind of bold you were just talking about. He was trying something new."

"Trying to steal something from people who are smaller and weaker than you isn't new, Lanner. It's probably one of the oldest ideas there is. But you have options. First, you can leave anytime. Barring that, you can vote for someone else when it comes time for us to hold an election. And, of course, you can run for office yourself."

"You don't run for office. You take it."

"In Hathrir, that is absolutely what you do. Not here."

"Because you say so?"

"Yes, because I say so."

"I think our people will have something else to say."

"Everyone will. That's what an election is. But maybe you and your friends can help the Hathrim come out on top."

"I'm listening."

"Pretend that the election goes the way you think it will and we are ruled entirely by Nentians. What laws or policies should be in effect to prevent them from discriminating against Hathrim or any other group of people? What policies or structures would need to be in place, in other words, to make you feel comfortable with Nentians running things?"

"I'll never be comfortable with that."

"Maybe *comfortable* isn't the right word. But regardless of who's in charge, what can we do to make sure they can't discriminate against the Hathrim?"

"It wouldn't be an issue if you'd just stand up and do what's right."

I almost rolled my eyes.

"That's precisely what I am doing, so I guess we don't have an issue. Thanks for bringing this up. Please come find me before tomorrow night's fire and share your ideas to prevent discrimination."

"Maybe I'll come up with someone else who's willing to rule the Hathrim properly."

"Maybe," I agreed, and then pointedly turned to a Nentian waiting behind Lanner to speak with me. I said hello, and Lanner got the hint that our discussion was over.

I had many more conversations with people who were by turns excited and scared, and I fell asleep utterly exhausted. Being a citizen was harder work, in some ways, than hammering at the forge. And I was sure I hadn't heard the last of Lanner Burgan. I'd been thinking that the Hathrim were going along with this much too easily and wondering when fear of the new and different would blaze up. Apparently, it was as soon as I stated concretely that doing things like we'd always done was no longer an option.

I'd have to be careful. I was fairly certain that the primary method of problem solving in Lanner's arsenal was the use of violence.

Day 25

THE GRYNEK HUNTERS

Gerstad Nara du Fesset fetched me before dawn and grinned at me as I answered the door, bleary-eyed, with a candle wavering in my hand.

"Hi, Dervan! Get dressed. Breakfast at the palace this morning. Then maybe you and I will get to cuss at somebody who deserves it." She waggled her eyebrows at me.

My jaw dropped. "The Wraith?" I whispered, though I couldn't imagine who else would be awake at this hour to overhear.

"Uh-huh. Come on."

I pivoted and tried to hurry, forgot my knee didn't like that, and fell down. That happens sometimes. I cussed plenty as I tracked down the candle and snuffed it before it could ignite my house.

"Sorry," I said.

"Oh, don't worry. Take your time, you know. But hurry up."

I did my best, and the sun was peeking over the horizon as we entered the palace. Mariners led us to the pelenaut's dining room, where Rölly and Föstyr were waiting. A plate piled high with toast and a selection of preserves made me smile, and there was a pot of tea as well.

"Sorry about the hour," Rölly said, "but I doubt my duties in the Wellspring will let me get away later. This is the best time to do this."

I assured him it was no trouble and reached for the strawberry preserves.

"I also wanted to thank you for letting me know about Gondel Vedd, Dervan. Gerstad, I'm sending you to Fornyd after this to seek him out and bring him back if you can. Otherwise, I'll ask you to have him translate something for us on the spot. I'd send Tallynd to do it, but you'll understand shortly why I need to keep her here. Let's cram in some fuel and we'll get going."

I will always remember the four of us crunching toast together before departing to confront evil. I mean, it's what I did every morning, but now I was doing it with friends. This, I thought, is how it should be.

On the way to the special holding cell underneath the palace, Rölly explained that an actual conversation would be impossible. We'd have to write a bunch of questions down and hope that the Wraith chose to answer them. There was no way to force compliance, though they were giving him the very worst food and promising better fare if he cooperated.

The cell was as described—a double wall of glass all around, filled with water and even a few fish, and in the middle of it, an air pocket with two occupants. We entered an observation area off to one side; the entrance to the cell was to our right. The residents were a little distorted because of the water, but they didn't look like nightmares. Approval Smile was not smiling, but she remained the efficient-looking professional, her skin tone edging toward the dark-brown Kaurian range. She had no smile for me now. When she saw me, she lowered her chin and snarled or hissed or something. A proper glower, it was. I returned it as best I could but probably wasn't that intimidating.

The Wraith had no malevolent glare to send my way. If anything, he looked faintly amused. Which I absolutely hated, and which was probably why he looked that way. It was difficult for me to feel triumphant when he looked so pleased with himself.

His appearance surprised me. I'd only spoken with him in darkness as he wheezed and coughed moistly, and I'd erroneously assumed he was overweight to the point of near immobility. But no, he was stick-boned, his face a long cylinder, his muscles atrophied, and he sagged in a chair with wheels on it. But I saw him move both his arms and legs, so he wasn't paralyzed; something else was wrong. His eyes, however, were focused, sharp, and laughing at me. He chucked his chin in my direction and grinned. The teeth were not in good shape.

"Föstyr, in those records you found: Did he come to Pelemyn from Festwyf this way?"

"Yes," the lung replied. "At least, we think so. The wheelchair got a mention."

"But the Brynt man who went to the Mistmaiden Isles one hundred twenty-seven years ago couldn't have been in such poor shape."

"No."

"He would have been strong and powerful when he set out. And then the Wraith possessed him."

"Yes, but the possession didn't damage the body. Look at the woman you call Approval Smile: Ysabel du Köpen. Her host body is perfectly healthy. Ursen du Mylseböck's body, on the other hand, is suffering from irreversible lung damage. The kind you take on when you nearly drown. He can't get as much oxygen per breath as the rest of us, so he stays nearly immobile by choice to make sure he doesn't damage the brain. We figure that Ursen tried to fight his possession on the Mist-maiden Isles by jumping into the sea—or perhaps he preferred death to being possessed, or it was accidental. However he wound up in the water, he didn't quite finish the job. We figure that Ysabel, whether she was possessed or not at the time, was able to swim out and rescue him, thereby saving Ursen's body and the wraith inside him. We are fairly certain that this is what happened."

"Only fairly? They haven't confirmed it?"

"More or less. We've inferred that the possession isn't an instant pro-cess and that the wraith and the human fight for control for a while. That's why they were raving when they got back to Festwyf. But it's been a long time now. The wraiths are in full control, and if Ursen and Ysabel are still in there, they're shadows of their former selves."

"Can't you simply ask them about it?"

"They're not answering many questions. Maybe they'll answer yours."

"What have they been doing the past couple of days?"

"Trying to escape, mostly. They've given up for the moment. Biding their time."

"I'd like to send them both to the abyss," Nara said, in a tone so low I almost missed it. Rölly caught it and looked at her.

"If that is truly your wish, I might let you," the pelenaut said. "When the time comes."

"What do we do now?"

"Follow me."

The pelenaut led us around the cell to the entrance, which was a gap in the glass filled with a suspended curtain of water, floor to ceiling, held there by the Fourth Kenning.

"Either Second Könstad du Böll or I must maintain this door at all times. It's extremely effective so long as we're around but dangerous otherwise. Ultimately unsustainable, and they know it. So they've decided to wait us out."

"What did they try to do?"

"Ysabel du Köpen tried to walk through it. But she found that the water followed her. Her host body would drown and then her wraith form would follow. Only when she went back into the cell did the water leave her alone. Once she understood that, there was some spirited cursing." He stopped in front of a small writing desk placed near the entrance. It held paper, quill, inkpot, and a silver tray. The cell, I noted, had a similar setup inside. "Write your questions and place them on the tray and I'll send it through."

We took turns. Nara went first and wrote only a single question, then folded the note and placed it on the tray. I wrote a two-parter: "Did Clodagh order my wife's death, and if not, who did?" I placed it on the tray next to Nara's.

I already knew the answer to the first one, because Rölly had read the journal and said there was nothing of the sort in there. But I wanted to see if the Wraith had lied about it and if he'd lie again.

Rölly took the tray and brought it to the shimmering door of water. It rippled at hip height and a slot appeared, the water flowing according to his wishes. He placed the tray in the slot; the water supported the tray's weight, pushed it through, and then closed behind it. This continued until the tray passed through the wall and Ysabel du Köpen could take it. She did, with distaste, and walked it over to the Wraith. She picked up my note first, unfolded it, and held it in front of his eyes. They scanned the question quickly and his face broke into a grin. He barked out a "Ha!" And then he shook his head, that horrible smile remaining. He either did not know who killed Sarena or he wouldn't say.

He likewise gave Nara little satisfaction, only chuckling and shaking his head again. Ysabel du Köpen tossed aside the tray with a loud clang and then made a rude gesture to us that suggested we perform biological impossibilities. Our reaction to that only caused the Wraith to laugh louder.

What an evil creature. I mourned for the good Brynt man that he had possessed long ago.

If Clodagh hadn't ordered Sarena's death, then who had? I was back to knowing nothing. And the pain of that amused him. All of our pain did.

"Why don't you just kill them now, Rölly?" I asked.

"Because we still don't know who he was writing to or who was supposed to pick up the dead drop. The site might be compromised now, but no one has come to check for a letter. We want to know who's on the other end of this traitorous correspondence. And who's their courier."

"It could be someone different every time," Föstyr said. "Someone who owes a favor who's told to do this one thing this one time, like you, Dervan. Or—this is what really worries me—these two weren't the only possessed Brynts who came back from the Mistmaiden Isles."

I frowned at the lung. "Didn't you say only those two returned from the expedition, raving in another language?"

"Those were the records we found, yes. Two of the ten returned. But there could have been other incidents over the years. These two could have arranged many such incidents themselves, considering the place of power they were in. We don't know, except that it's a possibility we never considered before. Now we need to consider it. Who knows how many of them walk among us?"

"Rölly. This narrative the bard's following about events up north—what if he knows something about the Bone Giants there?"

The pelenaut nodded. "I'm sure he does. I've been getting reports from the quartermaster at Fornyd, but there's probably more happening than she knows. Still, I asked Fintan if he had anything important to share a few days ago, and he said he didn't. Why don't you ask him, Dervan? You got this Gondel Vedd information from him. Speaking of which, Gerstad, since the questioning did not go well, you'd better be on your way to fetch him. Föstyr will give you the letter we need translated."

"Aye, Pelenaut." She saluted and departed with the lung, leaving Rölly and me behind in front of a rippling wall of water. It reminded me of standing in front of his water wall in the Wellspring, when he first asked me to work with the bard.

"I still don't want to be a spy," I told him.

"I didn't want to be the pelenaut on the verge of tumbling into the abyss with all his people. I had plans for a golden age, you know, when I took the throne. A great flowering of Brynt culture and commerce. Now I'm just trying to make sure we don't starve to death. So here we are, in a position to do something for our fellows. Our country needs our help. The only question that remains is whether or not we will give it."

"Chum and shit!" I said, clenching my fists. "Why do you have to be so good at moral clarity?"

"I know. It's annoying," he replied, and clapped me on the shoulder.

"We both have work to do. If you find out anything, please let me know."

"I will." We walked away from the prisoners without giving them a farewell glance. They were a problem solved for the moment; we had others to address.

Though I couldn't think of any way to broach the subject cleverly with Fintan once I met him for our scribe session. Bringing up the remaining Bone Giant army would just be so completely obvious that we were worried about the north and knew something he didn't. I had to protect my knowledge of the Wraith's betrayal until the pelenaut made it public. I resolved to let the matter rest for a day, hoping it wasn't a crucial day lost that would turn things one way or another.

When the bard got on top of the wall, he told everyone that his song for the day was popular in the river cities of both Brynlön and Ghurana Nent, since they all had small bands of rangers that would go into the Gravewood for a few miles on hunting and foraging expeditions. It was high-risk employment but very lucrative.

"Soon you'll know why I remembered this song and thought it would be a good day to share it."

> *I got a band of rangers and bellies to feed*
> *And the forest has food, whatever you need*
> *Fruits and meats and veggies and nuts*
> *But danger too, let me tell you what*
>
> *There's teeth and beaks and thorns and spines*
> *And everything is hungry all of the time*
> *But my rangers and I know how to survive*
> *And more than that, we know how to thrive*
>
> *(Chorus)*
> *We're just kickin' around in the Gravewood*
> *Stickin' around in the Gravewood*

Playin' around in the Gravewood
Stayin' alive in the Gravewood

I'll sell you furs and I'll sell you game
I'll tell you lies to increase my fame
I'll show you my scars and my chewed-up ear
'Cause I'm a ranger and I have no fear

If you wanna join my band there's always room
'Cause every trip out, someone meets their doom
I'm not sure if this is gonna be my time
But regardless I think I'll have more wine

(Chorus x 2)

"Today we'll hop around a bit," Fintan said after the break. "First, a return to Khul Bashab and the beleaguered viceroy, Bhamet Senesh."

This was my first look at him. As suggested by Hanima and others, he was carrying some extra pounds and they appeared in the jowls and neck, though he dressed to hide the rest of it as best he could. He had small, hard eyes and a bulbous nose, and a chin that sort of got lost in the surrounding flesh. His hair, of course, was long and impeccably kept.

B hamet

"The key to succesfully ruling people," my father explained when I reached my majority, "is to find an intelligent asshole who enjoys hurting people for money. That asshole will in turn find other, dumber assholes with a similar avarice for gold and pain, and together they will form your city watch. They get to tell people—and themselves—that they are upholding the law and protecting the population."

He waggled a finger at me in admonition. "You need to tell them too, Bhamet. This is an important fiction to reinforce with medals for their service, publicizing the punishment of the occasional criminal or the slaying of some dangerous animal near the city. The people must be shown, repeatedly, that they are being protected by your city watch. But the true purpose of a paid squad of assholes is to secure your power and protect the city's business interests. Don't skimp on assholes, is what I'm saying. There are always plenty around."

Father was full of good advice like that. At least regarding matters of statecraft, which is essentially manipulation of funds and perceptions. He hasn't been wrong yet in that field, so I follow his advice faithfully. But he lacked judgment in matters of the heart, since he died unexpectedly one morning when Mother poisoned him. Surprise! He managed to stab her in the throat for her treachery before he perished, and they died together, facedown in their scrambled eggs. It remains the most spectacular argument against marriage I've ever heard, and I tend to favor oatmeal now.

Sambhav Khatagar is my well-paid captain of the watch. He's been a good one, ruthlessly efficient and effective, until now. He even looks the part of an intelligent asshole, with a high forehead, dark glittering eyes under a thick brow, and a perpetual sneer on his face. But his inability to find these beast caller kids is trying my patience.

"You know what I'm hearing, Sambhav?" I call him that in private, and we are in private at the top of my tower, looking out a window at the city sprawling beneath us.

"No, Viceroy."

"There are dissidents gathering to discuss alternatives to our regency."

"Where are you hearing that?"

"I have some spies in my own purse. You know, barkeepers hear all sorts of things in passing. Not names—they never seem to catch their customers' names—but they hear snippets of conversation."

"There are traitors talking treason in pubs?"

"No, they're talking in the pubs about meeting somewhere else to discuss treason. And I take exception to that."

"I imagine you would."

"We can't have people thinking there are alternatives to the king and his viceroys. They might start demanding such alternatives at some point. And what's driving all this is those kids. Tell me why you haven't found them yet."

"My spies haven't heard anything about them."

"Nothing? Not a whisper?"

"Nothing at all. And our searches so far have yielded nothing. You said you wanted to keep those low-key, not let people know what we're looking for."

"Yes, and that needs to continue. I don't want to legitimize them by publicly saying what we're after. We need to make them go away as quietly as possible. Focus on your spies. They are either terrible at their jobs or they're lying to you. Because people are talking about them in the pubs and markets and everything."

"They're talking about them, sure, but not their whereabouts. Nothing specific about *them,* if you get my meaning. The talk is more about the kenning and what it could mean."

I spit out the window, frustrated. "And the Khatri kid hasn't led you to Hanima or the others? You're still following him, right?"

"Right. Nothing so far. We thought he might be contacting them through beggars in the market, but he gives to different ones every day, nothing but the same coins, and there's no pattern."

"So how do we make a breakthrough? What do you need? More muscle?"

"No. More spies like yours. The ones in pubs who can infiltrate these meetings you're hearing about."

"So: more money."

"Yes."

"Very well. See the bookkeeper. Plus I'll give you a bonus personally when you get these kids. A full year's salary."

"Thank you, Viceroy."

"Stay on the Khatri boy. He's part of this and he'll slip up eventually."

Captain Khatagar promises to do so. He leaves and I take a more practiced spit out the window. There's a balding beggar to the northeast who sets himself up near a fruit stand, and when the wind is right, my carefully launched payload of phlegm can score a direct hit on his crown. If he ever gets a hat, I'll be supremely disappointed.

I'm not worried too much about Tamhan Khatri's father when we finally do find evidence to pin treasonous charges on the boy. He'll weep over his poor misguided son and beg me not to hurt him, but ultimately he will agree that Tamhan deserves whatever he gets. His fortunes are too tied up with mine to do anything else but wail.

Gold can sometimes imprison a man more effectively than iron. Father taught me that one as well. I have most of the wealthy citizens of Khul Bashab imprisoned that way, and once I get rid of this threat, I'll be able to replenish my coffers at their expense.

"I have a new Brynt character to introduce today," Fintan said after dismissing the viceroy's seeming. "He was a mercenary gerstad in Grynek who contracted with the quartermaster there for years. And once, about twelve years ago, he published a small chapbook of bawdy poetry. You may have heard of him if your tastes run that way. And if you haven't, meet him now: Gerstad Daryck du Löngren."

The man who emerged was a clean-shaven, well-muscled Brynt man in middle age, wearing ranger armor—by which I mean he wore a helmet with a curtain of chain mail falling down the back and sides to protect his neck from predators. His nose had been broken multiple times, if the shape of it was telling any tales, but otherwise he was handsome, with laugh lines around his eyes and mouth.

When he spoke, it was a wry tenor with briars and thorns in it, the result perhaps of inhaling the smoke of too many campfires.

Daryck

You would think the sound of a city dying—dying fast in blood, not slow with discontent and dilapidation—would be so terrible that it could not fall on deaf ears. It would insist on being heard, a terror to harrow the soul, like the joke you once told to people you wanted to impress but no one laughed at the punch line, and it haunts you, the ghost of a terrible moment, long after its sound has faded.

But we never heard Grynek fall.

We were so deep in the Gravewood, seeking predators, that we never heard a single scream as some army of predators fell upon our families and friends and neighbors while we were gone.

When we were nearly home after two weeks in the forest, drawing close to the bridge over the Gravewater, the cook was the first to notice something was wrong. Gyrsön du Neddell had a nose the size of a rock pigeon roosting on his face; an upside-down carpet of hairs protruded from his nostrils like the baleen of a whale, filtering scents out of the air with every breath. He could smell better than anyone I've ever met, identify hints of berries in the breeze and lead us right to the bushes, name the variety of hops used in Fornish ales, even tell us what the squirrels had been eating by simply breathing near a pile of their pellets on the trail.

"Hey, Gerstad," he called from the back of the train, his brow furrowed and his nose scrunched up. "Might want to hold up and have a look and listen. Something's dead."

I held up a fist to bring the train to a halt, the clop of hooves and the rolling crackle of wagon wheels on gravel trailing away into a silence so profound the hairs on my neck rose. There was the soft gurgle of the Gravewater River ahead and nothing else. We should have heard noises from the city, the low bustle and hum of community, of farm animals and children's voices and people dickering in the market. I took a deep breath, trying to smell what Gyrsön smelled, but since my nose has been broken so many times and suffered some damage, it's about as useful as a plantar wart. Not that I doubted Gyrsön for a second. If he smelled something dead, then it was so. It was certainly silent as the grave, an awful silence like the kind that falls when you've disappointed your parents and they take time to stare at you with hooded eyes, consciously reminding themselves that you're their spawn and they are supposed to love you.

We couldn't see the river yet, for it was still obscured by trees, but it would be in view soon and the city walls with it. I turned around in the saddle to my corps, my dangerous dozen, and drew my lance out of its holster. They did likewise, angling points to either side for defense. There could be a gravemaw nearby. They tended to smell like death and quiet the forest around them. But no gravemaw would have rendered the city across the river silent.

The raspy call of blackwings sent a chill down my spine. I liked to keep things light, and normally I'd be joking before we headed into blood and guts, but this time not a single quip came to mind.

Using hand signals, I told my rapid and four mariners to follow me, leaving Mynstad Luren, Brön the hygienist, and three others to guard Gyrsön and the wagon in defensive formation. Once my split squad pulled away, I signaled that the two mariners immediately behind me and the rapid should ready bows while the others kept their lances out.

We moved slowly forward, casting a wary eye to either side and keeping watch on the branches above as well. It could be a scurry of meat squirrels up there that had everything spooked.

We were all spooked. Having the forest go quiet and still like this was expected deep in the trees. It was often a response to our presence, but the sounds of birds and other creatures always returned once they realized we were just passing through. This was not one of those quiets that fell into the spaces between trees and then returned. It was persistent.

I caught my rapid's nostrils flaring as my eyes darted to the left. He turned to catch my gaze and hold it. "I smell it now," he whispered, and he gave a nod to confirm what Gyrsön had already told us, a curl of disgust rippling one side of his mouth. "It's bad."

Sören du Hyller had been my rapid for ten years, and I had never seen that expression on his face before. He was a deep-running sort, the currents of his emotions flowing unseen beneath the surface. But they were no less powerful for being invisible. On the few occasions I'd made him crack a smile, I knew I'd told a pretty good joke. If he was openly showing his revulsion, then this mystery smell must be profoundly disturbing. Once we cleared the last curve of the trail and saw the bridge and the walls of Grynek over the river, I finally smelled it: rot and shit and the clammy sense of disease like wet wool in the nose.

Blackwings circled over the city and perched on the walls. No watchers stood on them or in the towers. No, the watchers were all dead, their corpses draped over the battlements or lying in broken heaps at the base of the wall. A wide trail of blood smeared the side of the watchtower, the mariner who left it behind crumpled at the base. I recognized him even from a distance: That was Ewan du Wyndyl, who'd grown up with me and been my friend for forty years.

Our breathing grew heavy as the horrible truth registered: The city had been sacked while we were away. That explained the silence and the smell.

"Check the banks," I said. "Look for scouts. Whoever did this might still be around."

But, of course, they were not. Once we confirmed that we were the only ones walking in the area, we crossed the bridge and I checked on Ewan du Wyndyl. He'd not been pierced with arrows or a spear but hacked open from above his shoulder—a cause of death that was highly improbable for a man alone in a watchtower. He'd been dead for some while, a few days at least, perhaps as much as a week or more. And the fact that he'd just been left where he fell all this time did not bode well. A week ago, we'd been in camp at the base of the Poet's

Range, skinning a den of striped murder weasels and using the guts to lure in something bigger. We got it: A hinge-mouthed bearcat came after us and got itself got. And its death in turn attracted still more hungry things, until we had ourselves a pile.

And while we made that pile, someone was doing the same thing in Grynek. Our people were sprawled all over, their bodies being gnawed on by blackwings, cats, and dogs, and always slashed rather than stabbed or punctured. There was no evidence of who had done this or why. But we scattered and searched anyway, searched the city for the perpetrators and also survivors, and found the people we loved dead with all the rest but no clues about who was responsible. We may as well have been looking for summer moths in the snow.

My parents were already gone, eternally disappointed that their firstborn had written an embarrassing collection of poems and become a sword for hire. But I found my brother and his family cut down in their home. My aunt and cousins. My friends. My lovers, both old and new. My favorite bartender, whom I'd never seen exist anywhere except behind his bar, died as he had lived, in that space.

The tap still worked. They had left the beer.

The Wellspring was littered with bodies, including those of the quartermaster and his rapids, but its treasures were left unspoiled. There was some blood and brains in there that did not belong to any Brynts, and some smeared puddles through which bodies had been dragged, which told me at least that the killers could be killed in turn and that they had dragged their dead away.

They had not come for riches; perhaps they had come because they were hungry. Though they'd left the beer alone, food stores had been raided, sheep and pigs butchered. Otherwise, they had swept through and moved on.

"Was it Raelechs?" Sören asked me when we reconvened in the public square. His mouth was carved in a straight line above his dimpled chin, whereas my face couldn't seem to rest or find an expression that was appropriate to such horror.

I shook my head. "It doesn't make sense. Raelechs use blunt weapons or spears, and everyone here was killed with a sword. And the Raelechs have plenty of food; they wouldn't need to come through here and take ours."

"But who else would come through?"

"I don't know yet," I said, "but we're going to find out."

The other members of the band trickled back. We were known—or used to be known—as the Rapid Woodsmen, a double entendre that I thought funny for the first couple of days after we registered it but which grew embarrassing as soon as some women rotated into the band, and even more so as we got older and we found that we couldn't shake it. The quartermaster had tasked us with keeping the wood across the river free of gravemaws and other large predators, to make sure they didn't get ideas about crossing and snacking on the farmers' livestock, with an eye to eventually making that side of the river habitable. In return for this we kept any furs, meat, horns, or hides we brought back for sale, and it sure beat standing watch on the wall. Besides me, the core team was Gyrsön, the cook; Mynstad Luren, the master of horse; Brön du Massyf, the hygienist; and our rapid, Sören du Hyller, who pulled water out of the brain tissue of anything that got too close to our throats. We filled out the team with a rotating stock of seven mariners for each trip, to spread the wealth around a little bit. On this particular rotation, four of the seven mariners were women. Most of us were still in the shock stages of grief, the foyer to a mansion of pain in which I knew we'd dwell for many years. Just beyond, however, a red room beckoned, a spacious expanse for rage, and I had little doubt the entire band would step in there with me for an extended period.

"All dead," Brön muttered when he returned, not really addressing me or anyone in particular. His eyes kept darting around at the buildings and bodies nearby, adding sums in his head and arriving at the same conclusion: "All of them."

Gyrsön staggered up to us, weeping, his nose and eyes red and puffy, snot dribbling down his mustache. "We should've been here. If we'd been here, we could have—"

"We'd be dead like everyone else," I told him, and swept my gaze around at the others to make sure they received the message. "The rapids and the mariners who were here did everything they could, and still they fell. They were obviously overwhelmed. And we would have been overwhelmed too, no question. As it is, we can still do something."

Mynstad Luren snorted, the old pale scar lining the left side of his face almost glowing as the rest of his face flushed in anger. "What? You think we can balance the scales?"

"No. I don't think there's a scale left for this. The scale's been melted into slag at this point and there is no way, no way, we will ever be able to measure out what's due. But we can survive, mourn, and remember, and tell whoever will listen what happened. Because whoever did this wanted no one saying a word."

Sören nodded, his face impassive. If he had wept or punched a wall or done anything to express his grief at the slaughter, I could not see it. All I could perceive was a tightening of his features, a tautness of every muscle, perhaps the deepening of a few lines on his face. His voice, too, was tight and controlled, as if he were speaking past a sob he had gulped down. "Is that all?"

"No. That was me speaking to you all as a friend. And I have one more thing to say along those lines before I speak as a gerstad: Cry when you feel like it and as long as you wish. There will be no judgment from me. But don't let it impair your duty or the need to act. Because as your gerstad I will require you to act. We should be on leave now, but obviously the situation's changed. In a moment I will give orders. Before I do, does anyone wish to say anything amongst friends?"

Gyrsön raised a shaking hand, his great nose trembling. "I just want to say to you all that I feel your grief as my own right now. And I will always love you. That is all."

We grunted assent and wept in silence after that, having nothing to add but the occasional sob. Eventually, I cleared my throat and said we should get down to business.

"First: For many reasons, which I hope are obvious but I will explain if you wish, I do not think we should be called the Rapid Woodsmen any longer. I do not wish to change it, however, without your thoughts. Are there any objections to discarding that name?"

There were none. There were some sniffles and glazed eyes and some shakes of the head but no objections.

"Good. From now on we will call ourselves the Grynek Hunters. For that is what we will do: Hunt for answers first. Who did this, and where did they go, and how many of them can we kill?"

Fire blazed in the band's eyes at those words, and fingers curled into fists. We were all going to step together into that red room of anger inside the mansion of grief.

"Yes. We will hunt them down. And we must report what happened so that the pelenaut can respond; the entire country may be unaware for all we know. We will need to move fast. So: Gyrsön, Brön, and you two," I said, pointing to the two largest mariners, "I need you to find provisions for us and load up a couple of boats down at the docks. We'll leave as soon as possible. Let the horses go. Find some crossbows and plenty of bolts but also lots of arrows for the conventional bows. And see if you can find a boat that will serve as a funeral barge. Everyone who would like to see their loved ones buried properly at sea, we will take them downriver with us."

Fresh tears sprang at the mention of that, but Brön nodded and said, "Aye, Gerstad."

"The rest of you are going to come with me to the Granite Tunnel, and we'll see if we can find any clues there. Everyone with bows ready and eyes sharp for watchers. If they left anyone behind, they'll be stationed near the tunnel entrance."

We moved out and headed for the western gates, which were thrown open. The ground was churned by large footprints and wagon ruts heading west. The invading army had exited this way. There were a few farms nestled between the city walls and the great tunnel that passed underneath the Poet's Range, and off to the south a fume of blackwings circled over a charred patch in a bean field. Sören wrinkled his nose again.

"Cooked meat," he said. "They burned their dead over there. Should we have a look?"

"No. That looks like a mess of ash and bone. I'm glad we got some of them, but it clearly wasn't enough. I'm more interested in where the living ones went."

We saw no one on the way to the tunnel. When we got there, we found that the entrance wasn't guarded because there was, quite simply, nothing left to guard.

"Aw, well, here's a crooked swamp duck dick," Luren said, one of his favorite idioms to indicate he'd just been surprised by something unpleasant, but he hadn't said it until now, even though the entire day was filled with such surprises. "What happened?"

The entrance to the Granite Tunnel, created generations ago by Raelech stonelords and connecting Rael to Brynlön's river cities, was completely caved in. The mountain had settled down into it, not merely covered the entrance—a line of trees above it had tumbled or sunk up to their lower branches, and the first of many ventilation chimneys was missing completely. It meant that our trade with Rael would now be limited to the sea, since very little, if anything, passed over the Poet's Range. Wolves, meat squirrels, and murder weasels made it too dangerous without heavy protection, and by the time one paid for mercenaries like us, the profits were all gone.

"The Raelechs must have got them," I said.

"What? Got who?" Luren asked.

"The blasted crab cakes we're hunting! Whoever they were, they swept through Grynek and right into the tunnel, headed for Baseld. Not too hard to figure the Raelechs wanted no part of an army that could wipe out a city. So they dropped the mountain on top of them."

"I hope they did," Sören said, and something like the shadow of a snarl passed across his face. "Much as I would like to personally pull their brains out of their ears, I'm glad it's done." He spat a glob of phlegm and then used his kenning to push the water in it toward the cave-in, so it splattered on the army's tomb. "But it does make me wonder who they were and how they got here without us hearing about it ahead of time."

We were out of Grynek by sundown, because we had no wish to stay there during the night. I doubted any of us would ever return in the flesh. We'd visit it often in nightmares, no doubt.

Finding a funeral barge was easy, since the actual funeral barges used by the city's undertaker were tied up at the docks. We needed all three of them for our loved ones. I tied up in burlap bags my brother and his family, my aunt and cousins, my old friend Ewan du Wyndyl, and my bartender. I figured he'd spent enough time behind that bar and he'd like to go home to the sea. We also took the keg of beer. Didn't seem right to leave it behind, unappreciated. And we had many sorrows to drown.

Sören helped me haul my people to the docks, and I helped him with his family. I let my tears flow freely, and a good bit of snot besides, and fought to breathe past the lump in my throat, which choked me as if I'd tried to swallow a sea scallop whole. Sören remained silent throughout, even while we were wrapping up his wife and children. But he did look up once and catch me staring at him. The dimple in his chin looked different somehow. Normally it resembled a relaxed if bony ass, but now it looked like the cheeks had clenched.

"I don't grieve openly, Daryck," he said. "But I assure you that I am grieving."

"Oh, of course," I replied, nodding, but that wasn't sufficient for him.

"As you said you would judge no one for their tears, I hope you will not judge me for my lack of them."

"No. I wouldn't. I don't."

"Thank you."

We wound up taking five boats from the docks, two each of our company on the barges and three each on the light cargo craft that Brön's crew had prepared. We could have all fit on one of them, for they were decent-sized boats that had bunks for twelve, but Brön quite sensibly thought it would be prudent to allow room for rescues we might find along the way.

Normally we would have sung songs or told stories or played cards—something! But we wrapped ourselves in silence like blankets and felt no urge to crawl out from under them for the days it took us to pole down the river to Sturföd. There was a dawn of hope as we neared it and saw the walls in the distance, all of us anxious to see other people and not feel like we were the only Brynts left in the world. We'd seen no one on the Merchant Trail on the way down, no campfires or wagons.

And then, drawing closer, we saw that Sturföd had suffered the same fate as Grynek. Everyone had been put to the sword. But it had happened earlier, and the bodies had lain there longer. The smell was powerful, and a cloud of blackwings rose up at our appearance, startled that something was living nearby.

We stopped only to confirm that there was no one alive in the Wellspring, and then we moved on downriver, stunned. I took my turn on one of the funeral barges with Sören du Hyller.

"All right, Gerstad, let me think something through out loud," he said as he poled us away.

"Go ahead."

"People in Grynek had been dead about a week when we got there. Presumably the people here in Sturföd died a few days earlier than that. And if it holds true downriver—Bryn preserve us, I hope it doesn't, but if it does—then they would have died well before we left on our trip and in time for someone to come on up and warn us. But you didn't hear anything about raiders or armies or anything on their way, am I right?"

"Right."

"And the quartermaster wasn't acting weird or anything?"

"No. He was perfectly fine with us leaving the city. He was hoping we'd find a good batch of murder weasels, in fact. Said he'd buy the furs."

"So either he didn't know the attack was coming, or . . ." Sören faltered, his brow furrowing.

"Or what?"

"Or . . . I don't know. I didn't know the quartermaster well. I don't know how he'd behave in a crisis."

"I don't either. Biggest crisis I ever saw him face was a lack of cake one night. That seemed like it chapped his ass pretty hard, but I don't think it really tested his mettle."

The rapid snorted, as close as he could get to a laugh. And then, almost too quietly to hear over the soft gurgle of the river, he said, "We had it good for a while, Daryck."

I matched his tone, not wishing our conversation to carry to another boat. "Yes, we did. We surely did, and we should remember that. We may never have it so good again. But we need to remember that good is possible, without letting those memories drive us mad."

He quirked an eyebrow. "You run pretty deep for a gerstad whose chief claim to glory is a collection of penis poems and fighting with goats."

"That was one time, and it was just an argument! Everybody keeps making more out of it than there was."

"Well. They won't anymore."

"No," I said soberly. "I'd much rather have them here getting the story wrong. Or telling me my poems are terrible."

"I won't tell you your cock sonnets are terrible. If anything, you should be proud. I think they stand tall."

I whipped my head around. Sören's face was blank, as if he'd done nothing but comment on the weather.

"Stand tall? Did you just make a terrible pun?"

"I don't think my puns are terrible either."

I laughed for the first time since the day before. Sören remained expressionless, but I think his butt chin relaxed a tiny bit.

When we got to Fornyd, we feared at first that it had suffered the same fate as the other cities, but longshoremen emerged on the docks and waved at us, and we pulled in. One of them, an earnest young lad, took me directly to the Wellspring to see the quartermaster. The city seemed very quiet, half empty.

"Were you attacked?" I asked him. He shook his head.

"We evacuated ahead of the invasion. The Bone Giants passed through, taking some food but leaving the rest of the city alone. Most of the city is still down at Tömerhil, but more and more are coming back every day."

"The Bone Giants? That's who did this?"

"That's what they're calling them."

"What do they want?"

The longshoreman shrugged. "They're killing machines, like blade-fins. That's all we know right now."

I saved the rest of my questions for Quartermaster Farlen du Cannym. She stared at me, unblinking, her mouth pressed into a thin line, as I reported that Sturföd and Grynek were total losses, that I had confirmed the deaths of their quartermasters myself, and that the Granite Tunnel was collapsed, with no sign of the invading army.

She closed her eyes for a few seconds and then let out a long sigh of exhaustion and took a seat. When she spoke, however, a hand curled into a fist and her voice trembled with rage.

"So they ignored my warnings."

"I beg your pardon? What warnings?"

"Gerstad, I sent a rapid upriver to warn both Sturföd and Grynek that the Bone Giants were coming and that they should evacuate their cities and let them pass through. That rapid returned to me and confirmed that the messages were delivered. But obviously neither quartermaster chose to act to save their people."

"That was the only choice? Evacuate?"

"Yes. They were unstoppable, clearly. You know that Festwyf is also lost? And Gönerled, Göfyrd, Möllerud, and Hillegöm? The Raelech city of Bennelin?"

I was gobsmacked. ". . . No."

"The tidal mariners saved Pelemyn and Setyrön; Tömerhil was never attacked, and we survived by taking the tidal mariners' advice and getting out of the way. But that's all that's left of our nation."

I felt dizzy, light-headed. ". . . Why?"

"Why what? Why did they attack?"

"No—well, yes, that too, but why didn't the quartermaster do anything? He could have saved everyone."

Farlen du Cannym shrugged. "It's not an easy thing to convince people they need to run from an invisible threat. Plenty of people fought me on the evacuation order. Some refused to evacuate, and they died. They chose to die rather than sacrifice a moment of comfortable routine. The danger wasn't real to them until it arrived in their faces, and then it was too late."

That sounded like the quartermaster of Grynek. He'd been so comfortable for so long that danger was something abstract, something the Rapid Woodsmen dealt with for him, out of sight, across the river. I liked that this quartermaster was smarter about it. I liked that she had saved her city and was first back, trying to patch things together.

"Quartermaster, I find myself without a city or a contract. Might the Grynek Hunters and I work for you but remain a unit under my command?"

She tilted her head. "You have a rapid, correct?"

"Yes. And a hygienist. A mynstad specialist in weapons and horse, a cook, and seven mariners proficient in horse archery."

"A fine company. But if you're looking for revenge, I haven't any to give you. There are no Bone Giants around. The work I have is repairing damage and making trips to clean up the other cities. That's the pelenaut's priority: burial of the dead and resettlement."

"I could not agree more with those priorities. We brought three funeral barges down from Grynek, carrying our friends and family, and would like to see them home to the sea."

"I'll have someone else see them home. I'd like your company to rest for a few days, and when the barges return, you can take them and many more back to Grynek; your company can lead cleanup efforts there for me."

"Thank you, Quartermaster."

I did not relish the duty but saw the necessity of it and felt it was the least I could do. We did rest, then we made a trip up to Grynek to make sure the Gravewater was not getting any more polluted and loaded all the bodies we could on the barges to take them to the ocean.

But upon our return to Fornyd—expecting another run for more, since there was so much more to do—Quartermaster du Cannym summoned me to the Wellspring and surprised me with new orders.

"Pelenaut Röllend believes for some reason that there might be a large force of Bone Giants somewhere on the northern coast. He's requested that we try to find out somehow if this is true, and it occurred to me that the Grynek Hunters might be uniquely suited to the mission. Naturally, I'm anxious to confirm this. If the Bone Giants are indeed to the north of us and capable of attacking, I'd prefer to know sooner rather than later."

I frowned at her. "Is there a trail leading from here to the northern coast?"

"No. We had no company such as yours here. You would be blazing the trail. Alone in uncharted stretches of the Gravewood."

I nodded, understanding her. She did not want to order me to do this, for it sounded like a death sentence to her. She wanted me to volunteer but did not think I ever, as a sane individual, would volunteer for such duty. It would be better to distract her from the question.

"What does the pelenaut wish us to do, specifically?"

"Strike north until you reach the Northern Yawn. Search for a force of Bone Giants—they may have a fleet. You are to scout only. The pelenaut wants numbers. How many of them are there? Where are they headed? How are they armed? Simple facts. He does not want you to engage them. He does not want you to do anything that may prevent an accurate report returning to me, and thereby him. It is reconaissance, nothing more. Is that clear?"

"Clear as a freshwater lake. But how do we know that there are Bone Giants up there?"

"The pelenaut managed to get hold of some of their internal communications, and a Kaurian scholar was able to translate their language. There may be a force up there somewhere as large as the one that destroyed the river cities. Based simply on timing, we believe they would be west of us now, but we don't know, and we *need* to know. Is this a force that could threaten us again, or are they intent on invading Rael, or crossing the Northern Yawn, or what?"

Without a solid trail we couldn't take a wagon of provender, which annoyed Gyrsön no end, but once we got going, we had no trouble finding enough meat to fill our bellies. We moved north without trying to establish a trail of any sort; we did not want to be tracked in turn and lead anyone back to Fornyd.

We got attacked, of course, by gravemaws and the usual sorts of hungry things that wound up feeding us, but we also ran into a small pack of meat-eating simians that we'd only heard tell of in legends: fir apes, with reddish-brown pelts and arms like tree boughs. We hated to kill them, since we suspected there were few of them left, but they were rather intent on killing us; they took out one of the rearguard mariners, roaring and backhanding him with such power that he flew bodily through the air and burst his skull open on a tree. Three of them reconsidered and retreated after Sören dropped four others, pulling water out of their brains.

Having no choice, we built a cairn for the dead mariner and promised to take him home to the sea later.

Once we reached the northern shore, still a bit chilly even in the warm months, we turned west. At a freshwater stream that emptied into the ocean, we found large footprints churning up the mud.

The Bone Giants had been there, refilling water barrels for their fleet. There was evidence of a massive camp too, the ashes of many fires indicating the army had taken advantage of the freshwater source and had rested for a day or so.

"Good," Mynstad Luren ground out between his teeth. The pale scar glowed again with his anger. He was the biggest of us, and his granite jaw tended to break knuckles rather than the other way around. "They're careless and we're going to find them. These won't be swallowed up by a mountain."

The immediate demand from the crowd was to know when we'd hear more of the Grynek Hunters. They were already heroes in my mind, and I wanted to give them all a gift basket. Something aromatic for Gyrsön, the cook. But what about the others? Fintan needed to help us out with their tastes, because we desperately needed to make plans for our baskets. And more regarding this Bone Giant army: Did we have anything to fear? Were they already crushed somehow? Or were they still out there?

It was so precisely the sort of thing that Rölly had tasked me to learn that I congratulated myself on waiting a day to ask Fintan anything. Now that the bard had brought up Daryck himself, I had an opening to ask him about the north tomorrow without it seeming suspicious.

"I promise to reveal all," Fintan reassured everyone. "But let's switch now to Abhinava Khose, who was also in the Gravewood, albeit on the Nentian side."

Abhinava

There are unseen wonders beneath our feet. In the trees and in the grasses, in the brambles and marshes, wherever we tread, there are creatures hiding or ignoring us completely, consumed by their struggle for food and shelter and the urge to mate. Once we crossed north of the Gravewater River, these creatures were almost entirely new to me. The Gravewood was a vastly different environment from the plains, and I spent most of my time agog at the wonder of it, identifying new insects, spiders, carnivores, and herbivores of a startling variety, and airborne citizens of a different variety as well. There were no cheek raptors in the Gravewood. No blackwings either. Other creatures performed the carrion duties.

I could quite happily—and profitably, I imagine—spend my life doing little else than cataloging the creatures of the world. The journal I was keeping would no doubt be prized material at any university interested in forest animals. Perhaps I could write volumes broken down into beetles, spiders, things that will eat you, and so on: *The Khose Catalog of Creatures*. That would be a much better legacy than a paragraph in a history book that ended with "He tragically died young as his kenning burned away his life."

Running away from my problems feels good right now. I know they'll still be there when I return, but maybe I'll be in a better position to face them after some time to myself. Maybe I'll be able to maintain my independence from the government and live to a proper old age. Maybe I'll forgive myself for the deaths of my family. Maybe I'll tell Tamhan how I feel, even though it carries a risk of failure even greater than seeking a kenning.

Or maybe none of that will happen. I'm probably trading one set of problems for another. Regardless, I'm going to enjoy the run. And worry about Eep and Murr.

"Look, I know that in the plains you two were at the top of the food chain, but here in the Gravewood, that's not necessarily true."

They just blinked at me.

"Do you know what a food chain is?"

They both shook their heads.

"When you're at the top of a food chain, you eat animals lower on the chain and nothing eats you. When you're at the bottom of a food chain, pretty much everything eats you. Now, I'm not saying you're at the bottom here, but neither are you necessarily at the top. There are some critters out there that would eat you if they could. So I want you to let me know when you're hungry and let me scan for danger before you go hunting, okay?"

"Murr," the bloodcat said, and the stalk hawk followed up with "Eep." That could mean "okay" or it could be them telling me to buzz off. The communication doesn't work so well in my direction, but at least they understood me. They knew that I was their friend.

One other thing worried me: I was discovering animals that my kenning didn't warn me about. There was this ten-legged hairy lizard living under a bush that Eep found and showed me. She might have just wanted me to see this weird thing, but I think maybe she was asking me if it would be okay to eat.

The legs were short and the body was quite long, and upon closer examination the hair was actually feathers. They would be well camouflaged against the trunks of the pines and blend in with needles on the forest floor as well. Fintan said he'd never seen anything like it, and neither had anyone else in the group, so I named it a pine-feathered mega skink, because I could. And after that, I was able to sense them around me. But I'd never sensed them prior to that, and I thought that was quite disturbing. It suggested that my kenning had blind spots. What else wasn't I seeing?

It happened again a couple of days later, with these bounding creatures that jumped out of the forest and attacked a wart ox at the front of the train. Once I saw them, I could tell them to cut that out and hunt something else, but they did take a nibble out of the ox and it had to be calmed down.

There was a pack of nine, and they waited patiently while Olet, Fintan, and I examined them.

"Do you know what these are?" I asked Olet.

"No. They look like these things called roos, but those are not pack hunters. And they're marsupials."

I asked the tawny animals, after teaching them body language for yes and no, "Do you use pouches for your young ones?"

They shook their heads.

"Are they born live?"

Again, no.

Half joking, I asked, "Do you lay eggs?"

They nodded.

"What strange creatures," Fintan said.

"Yeah. Hey, open up your mouths, will you? I just want to get a good look at your teeth."

They complied, and Olet made a tiny sound of surprise. "Okay, that's a lot. I thought they were cute until they did that, and now that's going to haunt me."

"They're like meat squirrels," Fintan observed. "They look harmless, but watch out."

"We'll call them toothy roos," I declared. And then I searched for more of them with my kenning and discovered there was another pack not far ahead, coming in our direction because they smelled blood. I had to send them away disappointed as well, and we got that ox patched up as best we could. I walked alongside her to make sure nothing finished her off and apologized for not stopping the toothy roos sooner.

It worried me, though, and I think Olet as well, because she asked me about it.

"How we doing here, plaguebringer? We have the animal situation under control?"

"Yes. I think. At least I'm sure I can protect against everything I know about."

"Everything you know about?"

"Right. I mean, I know what insects are and I know what mammals and reptiles are and so on. I can protect against all of those, even if I haven't personally seen the species before. I already have! There were some murder weasels stalking the rear, but I shooed them away."

"Murder weasels?"

"Yeah. They're like weasels but bigger and with more teeth, like these toothy roos and like most everything in this forest. I'd heard of them before. There was a huge bear too—not sure what kind, but it doesn't matter, because I know what bears are—and I protected some goats from a flock of bloodsucking bats. Those animals are all at least somewhat familiar. But a carnivorous roo that lays eggs? A pine-feathered mega skink? I have no frame of reference for those!"

"But you do now."

"Yes. They won't bother us down the road."

"Okay, good."

Except it wasn't good. There were still strange things out there I couldn't see coming. Not just through my kenning, but through my fire-blind eyes after listening to Fintan tell a story about a delicious but exceptionally dangerous variety of wild poultry in Hathrir called razor chickens. Apparently, they were larger than turkeys, and the roosters were anxious to mate with just about anything they thought they could fertilize. We were camped in a line for the night and our fire was in the middle of the pack. Fintan was using his kenning so that every-one in the camp could hear his stories, and we heard laughter to the north and south of us until, up to the north where Olet and La Mastik were camped, we heard a roar and a scream.

Curses flew in the night and everyone leapt up, searching for the danger but seeing nothing in the darkness. Olet called my name.

"Damn it, Abhi, get up here and stop this thing!"

Fintan and I ran north until we found her looming in the ruddy glow of her campfire, facing out. She pointed into the darkness as Murr caught up, growling by my side, and Eep landed on my shoulder. "It ate one of your people already, and I don't think it's finished."

"What did? I can't see anything."

"A gravemaw!"

"A gravemaw? Where?" I blinked, trying to will my pupils to dilate, but I saw nothing but black out there. I did hear some rather gross slobbery crunching noises.

La Mastik sighed in exasperation and crouched to her pack, yanking out an enchanted firebowl about the size of her huge palm and tossing it into the dark. She used her kenning to spark it up once its weighted bottom landed on the forest floor, and the glow from that showed me the barest outline of an armor-plated leg.

"You see it now?"

"A tiny bit of it. Can you maybe set it on fire?"

Olet fetched her sword out of its sheath, ignited the blade, and then sent a gout of flame into the darkness. It landed on something, but it didn't exactly catch. The subject roared in anger at the heat, but it didn't have hair or skin or much else combustible. That armor plating was resistant to fire as well as impervious to weapons. Still, Olet's efforts illuminated enough of the creature for me to finally see it.

I'd heard of gravemaws, of course—they're legendary eating machines—but the true nightmarish character of them can't be appreciated until you see a flash of one at night, blood on its knife-like teeth and its long, obscene tongue pulling a booted leg from one corner of its mouth into the cavern of its throat to be finished off and swallowed.

"Okay, I see it," I said. "Stop trying to set it on fire, please."

"Are you kidding?"

"No. It's not going to listen to me if you're trying to burn it alive." It was growling, its muscles bunching to spring in our direction as soon as it finished chewing.

"All right."

Using my eyesight to target, I reached out with my kenning to acknowledge it, recognize it, and then speak to it, just as Olet quit shooting fire at its armored hide. The flames burning in the firebowl on the ground she left alone.

"Hello," I said to the creature. "Stop for a minute and let's talk."

A defiant roar replied, and I had no idea what it meant, but I could guess.

"I know. The fire is out now, and it won't come back. We won't hurt you as long as you don't try to hurt any of us. I know you can understand me. Let's talk."

The growl that came was different now, but it was still just noise to my ears.

"I can't understand your meaning. But I can ask yes-or-no questions and you can reply." Once I covered what was to be done, I stepped out into the darkness, but Olet laid a restraining hand on my shoulder, the one without Eep on it.

"Are you insane? Don't go any closer."

"It'll be fine. No animals will harm me, just like fire won't harm you."

She removed her hand and I strode forward with a nervous stalk hawk and bloodcat. "These are my friends," I said. "We'll be yours as well. Can you step next to that small fire to your left, please, so I can see you better? My night vision isn't as good as yours. I'll stay on the other side of it and we can talk."

The gravemaw complied, shifting its massive bulk to one side. It was still making slurping and smacking noises, and some kind of violent digestive activity was happening in its guts. It smelled of coppery blood and rot and foul sulfuric gases, and I fought to keep my gorge from rising. Eep and Murr weren't happy about being so close either, but they stuck with me.

Once we were only a few paces apart, with only the small firebowl between us, the gravemaw wasn't so bad—with its mouth closed.

"It's an honor to meet you. My name is Abhi. This is Eep and Murr. Do you have a name?"

"Rrurrgh."

"Hi, Rrurrgh! Usually I can tell if someone is male or female, but I can't with you. Are you male or female?"

Rrurrgh shook their head no.

"You're not either one?"

No again.

"Do you participate in the birth of baby gravemaws somehow?"

Yes.

I struggled to figure out the puzzle and took a wild guess. "And you do that with males and females as a third, nonbinary gender?"

Yes.

I turned to Olet and La Mastik, who were silhouetted by the fire, along with many others who had gathered to gawk. "A third gender, can you believe it? This is even wilder than egg-laying roos! No wonder I couldn't sense them with my kenning."

"No wonder, kid," Olet said, her voice flat. I got the impression that she didn't think I was asking very important questions but only trying to be polite to Rrurrgh. I turned back to them and decided not to probe any further into gravemaw reproductive practices. It would be extremely awkward as a yes-or-no exercise anyway.

"Rrurrgh, I think all of my friends are wondering if you're still hungry. Are you full now?"

Rrurrgh nodded and then belched, the stench of which made both Murr and me flinch and gag.

"That's good," I managed. "Really good. Everyone can relax now. But we'd appreciate it if you didn't hunt anyone in our party after this. Will you promise not to eat any more of us, please?"

Rrurrgh nodded again, and I turned to see if Olet caught that, and she did.

"So that's it?" the giant asked. "No more gravemaw trouble after this?"

"No more. That doesn't mean I can't be surprised by something else, but at least you won't have to worry about them."

"One less thing," she said, and walked around to the other side of the campfire, putting it between her and us. I got the feeling that I'd failed somehow, but I didn't know how I could have done any better when gravemaws were something so different from what anyone ever thought.

"Say, Rrurrgh," I said, "are you mated with a male and female now, in a kind of family?"

Yes.

"Are they nearby?"

Yes. I confirmed that by reaching out with my kenning and locating two other gravemaws within a league. Looking that far didn't hurt, since I was looking for only one type of creature. That was valuable information right there: Wherever you found one gravemaw, there were likely two others somewhat nearby.

Rrurrgh's belly made some disgusting noises, and a new question popped into my head.

"Do you completely digest all the bones?"

No.

That made me stop and blink for a bit. "So what do you do—spit them out later?"

Yes.

"Wow. You're like a three-gendered, armor-plated owl. Do you sleep all day?"

No.

"That's cool. You probably want to sleep now that you've eaten. Is that right?"

Yes.

"Okay, I'll let you go do that, then. But if you feel like it, when you wake up, would you mind finding us tomorrow? I'd like to see you in the daylight if that's okay." I wanted to make a good sketch for my journal. The world needed to know more about gravemaws.

Rrurrgh nodded one more time and made another growling noise, then lumbered off into the black. I blinked, staring into the space they had occupied, the enormity of what I had done finally registering.

"I just had a conversation with a gravemaw, and they were kind of nice."

"Murr," my bloodcat friend said, before audibly gagging again.

I gazed down at the firebowl that La Mastik had tossed and sparked up, still burning even though there was no visible fuel in it.

"Hey . . . La Mastik?"

"Yes?"

"This thing you lavaborn do with firebowls and lanterns and stuff to keep them burning with almost no fuel. You call that enchantment, right?"

"Right."

"Can you teach me how that's done?"

"No, I'm just a sparker. I can't enchant anything. But Olet can."

"Cool. Olet, can you teach me how to enchant something so it will repel animals?"

"No. I can only enchant metals and glass to burn for a long time."

"But the process of enchantment. You can teach me that, right?"

She shrugged. "Maybe. I don't know."

"It's worth a try, don't you think? If I can enchant a wooden stake, for example, to repel animals, then cities wouldn't need to build walls anymore. I wouldn't need to be physically present to protect an area. We could plant enchanted stakes along this road we're making and keep it safe for travelers. I could protect farms from pest species. It would change everything."

Silence fell around the fire. Olet was staring at me, her eyes wide, and everyone else was staring at her.

"You're right, kid," she said. "It's definitely worth a try. Get over here."

Day 26

THE JUGGERNAUT

The idea of enchanted stakes was attractive to those who had lived near the Gravewood in the past or were thinking of moving back to one of the river cities, but many, I think, shrugged—or perhaps it was only me. Most of Brynlön was relatively safe from predators. There were bog lynxes in the marshes that occasionally attacked hunters when they thought the hunters were taking swamp ducks they'd been saving for dinner, but otherwise the dangerous animals (like sunchucks) tended to avoid humans if at all possible.

Humans, alas, were sometimes unavoidable. As were duties. I needed to make an attempt at coaxing information from Fintan without arousing suspicion or fracturing the relationship we had. Sarena had told me curiosity was natural. Spending time asking about other, inconsequential things would make the important questions seem casual, if I could pull off the light tone. I wondered if I had spent enough time asking Fintan about inconsequential things. And then I realized it didn't matter. I had to do it whether I'd prepared sufficiently or not.

We met at a dockside fishblade restaurant where they brought in fish every morning and served it raw, often with rice and some sprig of this vegetable or that. They had wooden benches outside the kitchen wagon and a bar set up serving a few brews, and all of it was under some umbrellas and netting to keep the seagulls out. The menu was different every day; it depended on what the boat brought in. The beers rotated every so often, but it was a simple place. You got fresh fish, rice, and beer. We ordered some and I threw myself into the dreaded task.

"I really enjoyed the story of Daryck du Löngren yesterday," I said. "Can you satisfy my curiosity about something?"

"Maybe," Fintan said, nodding. He took a sip of the Fornish ale he'd ordered and smacked his lips. "That's good."

"We heard Gondel's story about this traitor Vjeko—"

"Which your pelenaut fed to me."

"—Right. But you now have these two different narratives—several, really—about events in the north. And that's where the last Bone Giant army is. Maybe there was some contact with Vjeko. So . . . might you know anything about that?"

Fintan laughed through his nose, breathy exhalations more than chuckles, but the smirk on his face was plain. "Asking for spoilers again? Can't just enjoy?"

"Well . . . no. Not if you know something that can help us."

"I know things." He waggled his eyebrows. "Many things. But nothing that can help you now." His playful grin melted as he saw me frown. "Dervan, I solemnly swear: If I knew anything that could help your country at this moment, I would share it. But simply spilling what I know, out of order, does not help anyone process it. The world has changed tremendously, and we are all trying to forge new trails since the old ones have been obliterated. To do that wisely—with empathy and love for our fellow human beings—we need to see these tumultuous events through more than a single pair of eyes. We need to hear voices that aren't our own and let them all speak. And we need to see and hear them together, in order. By the time the Raelech, Fornish, and Kaurian reinforcements get here and decisions need to be made, I promise you'll be fully informed and ready to proceed."

"All right. Fine. But why do you get to decide what's in our best interest? Why don't we get to decide?"

The bard's expression blanked and he leaned away from me. "Because I am a storyteller, not your military intelligence resource. I don't like it when my government treats me like one. Even less so when other governments treat me that way. Couriers provide intelligence with perfect recall. Bards tell stories with perfect recall. They are entirely different disciplines, watched over by entirely different goddesses."

"Yet the story you're telling is informed by a couple of couriers, isn't it? Numa and Tuala, at least?"

"It is. And the tale I will tell today happens to be Tuala's. But I'm telling it at the right time to the right audience. To tell tales out of season would be a betrayal of the poet goddess, and I will not do that."

"Okay, I understand. You have my apologies for trespassing, and my thanks for explaining."

There may have been a way to push for more, but I don't think it could have been done gracefully. If I pressed him any more, there would be damage done, and I wasn't willing to do it.

But I was struck by a wave of sadness and ducked my head, pretending to search for a new quill in my bag. So often we feel unequal to the tasks that life sets before us and it is a struggle to even begin them, much less complete them, because we cannot see a way forward. All we see are obstacles—an insurmountable summit towering above us, rather than the easy step we can take to get a tiny bit closer. Perspectives can and do change, but only if we move ourselves. We must change our stance and witness the obstacles change in their turn and so learn with every step how we will overcome. At that moment I needed to remind myself that soon I would be in a different place and time, when and where I didn't have to be such a miserable spy.

We wrote down the previous day's tales and enjoyed our fish and beer. Then we walked to the wall and Fintan shared a Raelech soldier's song.

> Farewell my family and my many friends;
> All good times must have their ends
> And I am packed and leaving today.

All that I am and will become is because of
Your undying and unwavering love;
I cherish it more than I can say.

When I return I'll greet you with a smile
But until then there'll be a long lonesome while;
I will think of you often on my way.

"There will be only one tale today, for it is a long one. It's the tale of what happened when a Raelech army went to liberate the Brynt city of Möllerud, but it is more than that. It is a tale of unrequited love, eternal longing, and regret. We return to Master Courier Tuala and Master Juggernaut Tarrech now."

uala

On the road to Mell, Tarrech occasionally joked and laughed with me. We reminisced about our days together in the Colaiste, when we had stolen offal from the tanning shed and put it in the bunk of a bully who'd been mean to some younger kids. And then the fight with that bully a couple of days later when he saw us laughing about it: We kicked the snot out of him and told him he could fight kids like us, kids his own size, whenever he wanted to blow off steam. But beating up little kids was shitty, so we thought he should sleep in the shitty bunk he'd made for himself.

He didn't give anyone any trouble after that and somewhat ironically went on to become a master tanner.

"I'm glad we found him and made it right between us," Tarrech said over our campfire. We'd decided to sleep outdoors that night to honor the Huntress Raena.

"Me too."

We'd become masters some weeks before the bully had, and we visited him in Killae shortly after the ceremony where he got the master's amethyst set in his Jereh band.

"What do you two want?" he said, scowling at us. His eyes flicked to our Jereh bands and he snorted. "You became a courier and a juggernaut? There's no justice."

"I respectfully disagree," Tarrech said. "Back in the Colaiste, we were justice for the kids you were bullying. But now look at you. A master tanner! Well on your way to being a valued and respected citizen. We'd like to congratulate you, first of all—"

"Yes, congratulations!" I interrupted.

"—but also ask if you'd allow us to give you a gift."

He eyed us suspiciously. "Thanks," he said, though he didn't sound particularly grateful. "What kind of gift did you have in mind?"

"We'd like to help you start your business. Where were you planning on setting up your trade?"

"A little river village below Jeremech?" He said it like a question, as if we were testing him. But we weren't. "There's a master there who's agreed to sell to me when I'm ready."

"Why aren't you ready?" I asked.

"His tannery needs upgrades. The filter beds are old and need a thorough sifting, and the salt beds need work too. That work is expensive."

He wasn't lying about that. By law, Raelech tanning didn't allow environmental pollution of the earth or waterways, so tanners had to regularly employ one of the blessed to filter all the metals, salts, and chemicals out of their soils. The weekly work wasn't costly, because they could recycle a lot of their materials, but every twenty years or upon sale of a tannery, a thorough job had to be done or the tannery had to shut down. That fact had been drilled into all of our brains at the Colaiste. Most master tanners sold their businesses before the second major cleaning was due. This one had received its cleaning at twenty years as required, but that was nineteen years ago. Much of the equipment was thirty-nine years old and needed to be replaced.

"I think you'll find the cleaning more affordable than you thought," Tarrech said. "For you, it'll cost nothing."

He thought we were bluffing and said, "All right, let's do it." And so we did. I ran us up there super fast and Tarrech did all the expensive filter work for free—the kind of work that would take a stonecutter days, but a juggernaut could do it in hours with no ill effects.

The ex-bully had himself a pristine tannery and a bright future at the end of it, and he was weeping in disbelief and joy. He forgave us and we forgave him and wished him well. That was all Tarrech's idea. He was always more thoughtful than me. So completely easy to fall in love with.

We shared much more reminiscing before we slept that evening under a starlit, half-moon sky, and it will forever be golden in my memory. But once we got to Mell and reported for duty, Tarrech never laughed again.

The soldiers mustering at Mell were equipped with strange tall shields I'd never seen before, and they didn't carry their customary cudgels lined with stone. They had long spears instead. These, I was told, were a tactical adjustment to deal with the Bone Giants. Since they just barreled forward in huge numbers and hacked down their enemies with their long reach and powerful swords, we'd give them shields reinforced at the top to hack instead and poke them in the guts. There were plenty of archers in the army too, more than I'd ever seen mustered.

In addition to Temblor Priyit, there were two other temblors geared up in the same fashion as the soldiers, with tall shields and spears. Priyit was still commander for the operation, however, and almost as soon I arrived with Tarrech, she assigned me to scout the enemy. A run to Möllerud would take a full day, if not more, and then I'd need to sleep in hostile territory before running back.

"I'll do that in the morning, Temblor."

Both Tarrech and the temblor blinked. She said, "I need you to do it now."

"I've already run all day to get here, so I require rest."

"I require a scouting report as soon as possible."

That was all I needed to hear. My suspicions about her were confirmed.

"Tomorrow is as soon as possible if you want me to do it. If you have another courier on site, you might consider assigning them this duty."

Through gritted teeth she said, "Your insubordination is noted."

"Very well. Your willingness to exhaust couriers when we are weeks away from engagement is also noted."

"Holy shit," Tarrech said in a tense whisper. I would have laughed at him if I hadn't seen the temblor clench her fists.

"Where is this hostility coming from, Tuala?"

"That's 'Master Courier' to you, Temblor. We are not friends."

Her knuckles went white as she glared at me. She was thinking about how if she applied that fist to my head, it would be like taking a hammer to a watermelon. The strength of temblors was truly awe-inspiring. But she'd never be able to touch me and she knew it. "Understood. Answer the question."

"I escorted the stonecutter Meara to her exile in Brynlön. I heard what you did in the Granite Tunnel."

"I destroyed the invading army."

"No, Meara did that. Because you gave her terrible orders and then shouted at her for not being able to carry out those orders safely by herself. You got your entire command killed, refused to accept responsibility for your role in it, refused to sing the Dirge for the Fallen for those poor soldiers, and then took credit for the whole thing like you're brilliant."

"I didn't sing the dirge because I'm Nentian and don't follow the triple goddess," she said, responding to only one of my accusations.

"I don't care. You showed no remorse and painted our loss as a victory."

"It *was* a victory!"

"One that could and should have resulted in zero Raelech casualties from a competent commander!"

Her eyes flew wide open and she pointed to the exit. "Out. You're dismissed. Return to Killae for reassignment."

"If you send me back to the Triune Council, I'll tell them what you did and that you're unfit for command. And they're going to believe me. They know I'm devout."

"Ha! If you were going to do that, you would have already done it."

"No, I wanted to see for myself if your judgment was really as bad as Meara reported. And it is. First thing you did was order me to run a dangerous scout with no rest. I'll report that too."

"Go ahead. The Triune already knows what happened at the Granite Tunnel. Both Meara and I were fully debriefed."

"I don't think they got the proper perspective somehow. Meara was in shock and blaming herself during the debriefing, and I'm certain you blamed her too."

The temblor cocked her head to one side. "I don't understand what you're after here. You want to stay and do what? Disobey my orders?"

"I want to take orders from one of the other temblors. Give your command to either of them."

"Ridiculous."

"And put yourself on the front line. Your eagerness for battle will be your excuse for giving up command. It will be a path to redemption, like the one Meara is following in Brynlön. Otherwise, you'll get no cooperation from me."

"I don't need your cooperation, Master Courier."

"You need mine, though," Tarrech said. "And you don't have it. Not after hearing this. Choose the path of redemption, Temblor Priyit. We will fight side by side, the three of us. We will avenge our fallen and protect Rael."

I flashed a small smile of gratitude at Tarrech, but he didn't see it. His eyes were fixed on the temblor, his expression cold and implacable. It was like we were taking on bullies again.

During my travels as a courier, I've come to learn how strange other people think Rael is for our customs regarding the Colaiste. But when I left my home at age nine, I didn't think it was unusual, because everybody else was doing it. It's just the way things were done in Rael, and it was viewed as logical: If you wanted your kids to be apprenticed in a profession they'd enjoy, they needed to experience each of them to make an informed decision. And if they wanted to seek the Third Kenning, they needed to know what the risks were and what the blessed of Rael could and could not do. Since not every town could be expected to provide an adequate experience—the resources were simply not available everywhere—it made sense to nationalize the effort to ensure that every child had the same opportunity to seek their own path, regardless of background. Plus, every one of the scrolls of the triple goddess decreed that the faithful should send their kids to the Colaiste, so that tended to end arguments.

I was the daughter of hunters in Kintael, and Tarrech the son of a mason and a tailor in Randulet. We met by accident on our first day, and each liked the way the other one talked. Both of us were from small towns in the hills but our accents and idioms were very different, so we talked a lot to entertain ourselves. But we also felt drawn together as kids from a rural background as opposed to the kids from the big city, whose manners we found lacking and who did not laugh at our accents in a kind way.

Month by month, we cycled through training in different professions so that we could discover if we liked it, and if not, we could at least respect the work of those who practiced the craft. We got daily training in military exercise too, and years slipped past without either of us expressing enthusiasm for any craft beyond a polite wag of the head and an admission that it was "kind of nice, I guess."

Tarrech and I perked up near the end, once we got to meet the blessed and they spoke of what their lives were like. We spent a day with each. A courier took us for a run, which was exhilarating. But she warned us afterward that the life had its drawbacks. More time away from home than in it, for one thing. Long hours alone on the road. Not being able to discuss the work. Not being able to forget any of it.

A stonecutter built a beautiful statue before our eyes and then said they mostly had to work on walls. Walls were about as interesting to build and repair as they were to look at, which was not interesting at all. And buildings? They were made of walls.

A juggernaut briefly took on his battle form and then said it was tremendously draining to maintain. "You'll be invincible as long as the battle lasts, but afterward you'll be years older and perhaps near death. You will win most any battle but sacrifice your life in the process."

And, of course, there was the very real possibility that we'd not survive the seeking.

After that, on day one of our training by a master clerk, we exchanged a glance that said this was going to be a long month for both of us. There was nothing that sounded as good to us as being one of the blessed.

"I don't even have a preference," Tarrech said. "Any blessing sounds better than any of the professions we've tried so far. Well, except maybe for a bard. I'm not a good singer and an even worse dancer."

"Anything but a bard," I agreed. I never wanted to perform.

I don't know how I ever summoned the courage to seek a kenning when I could never find the strength to tell Tarrech how much I loved him. As the day of our graduation inched closer and we had to decide whether to seek a kenning or not, I realized I felt much more than friendship after spending years by his side. Hitting puberty probably had something to do with it, but that didn't make it any less real.

But he didn't feel the same. I was his friend, and he spoke openly to me about liking other girls. Saying "What about me?" would not have ended well. I wanted to keep what we had, at least, which was no small thing; friendship and trust are the rarest of gems, as the poet goddess Kaelin says.

And then graduation arrived during the month of our fourteenth birthday, and I was scared witless. If I became a seeker I might die—or, even worse, become a bard—but nothing else appealed. Even then I was devout, though it was to the triple goddess in general rather than Raena specifically. Being blessed by any of them would be an honor.

But I was simultaneously scared for Tarrech. He was going to be a seeker too, so he might also die or become a bard. And if he did emerge blessed, then he'd return to Randulet to join Aevyn, the girl he liked, who'd apprenticed to an herbalist the month before.

I thought that if we were both blessed, following him there instead of returning to my hometown, as many kids did, would be a pretty obvious indication that I had more than a Colaiste friendship in mind. Which meant that graduation was the end of our time together no matter what happened. I went to my seeking with puffy, watery eyes from weeping all night and morning. Everyone thought I was worried about dying.

Tarrech gave me a hug and a kiss on the forehead right before the seeking. I didn't have a courier's memory yet, but I still remember that perfectly.

Temblor Connagh, an affable sort with a full oiled beard that he'd somehow styled into little waves—he must spend a ridiculous amount of time grooming it—took over command at Temblor Priyit's request, since she wanted to fight on the front line. With that settled, I ran to Möllerud to make sure the Bone Giants were still in residence and that the route was clear. They were, and it was.

The march to liberate Möllerud began the day after my return. Tarrech was exhausted by a steady stream of soldiers who wished to meet him and say a few words about how honored they were to march with him. He replied that the honor was his and smiled back at them all, unfailingly gracious, but I saw the tension building in his shoulders, the hunching underneath the weight of their adulation.

"Why don't you let me shoo them away politely?" I asked him.

"No, it's important to them. A thing they have to do. A thing I'm obliged to accept."

"Nonsense. You're not obliged."

"I feel that I am."

"Why?"

"Put yourself in their position. If someone saved your life, would you not want to thank them?"

"Well, of course. But you haven't saved their lives."

"Not yet. But they suspect that I will. And if not them, then some of their comrades. And perhaps their families, who might be next on the Bone Giants' list of massacres. They must thank me now because they might not get to later. So I must in turn allow myself to be thanked. They might not be saying those words, Tuala, but that's what they're doing. Thanking me in advance."

I merely nodded in reply, mulling it over. After another pair of soldiers came up to speak of how honored they were, I saw the truth of what Tarrech said. It was in their faces: They were honored, as they said, but not so much as grateful, which they didn't say.

"Did you ever expect our lives would come to this, Tarrech, on the day we went to seek a kenning?"

"Not this specifically, no," he replied. "But something like this, yes. They did their duty and warned us at the Colaiste. I walked into it anyway, just like you did."

The source of the Third Kenning is an unusually deep and wide patch of quicksand near Goddess Lake. Seekings are held once a month, when each new cohort of students graduates from the Colaiste either chooses a master or says they'd like to be a seeker. The kids who want a master are sent to one in their hometown, if at all possible, so that they can easily reunite with their parents and resume or rebuild that relationship. The seekers are sent to a building on the west side of the quicksand at dawn, pointed toward a building on the east side, and told to walk there through the quicksand. If they make it, they're blessed.

Normally, crossing quicksand isn't something a body can manage. It's a colloid that basically sucks you in up to the waist and then you're just stuck, because your body density is lower than that of the colloid. At the same time, the sand or silt has formed super-dense areas around your body, and to move through it you have to apply enough pressure to reintroduce water into it and break it up, which becomes close to impossible after a while. Sinking and drowning, a fear that many people have, isn't really a danger. The danger is simply never getting out. People die of exposure or thirst.

The quicksand around Goddess Lake was different.

It would let you walk and keep walking while the depth increased, sand squishing between your toes. It was like thick water more than a resistant medium, until you got to about four feet deep. For shorter folks, that was pretty much up to the neck. Things got interesting right around there. The going got tougher, and the depth increased. You had to walk in until you were completely submerged, then one of two things happened: You'd be able to continue to walk forward with the bottom supporting you, propping you up, with only a short time spent holding your breath before you emerged, spluttering, or you'd be trapped underneath, the colloid suddenly solid, and nothing you did would ever get you to the surface again.

Seekers of the Third Kenning enjoyed a success rate higher than any other: 60 to 65 percent made it to the other side. The rest provided outstanding fertilizer for the plant life resting on top of the quicksand.

Obviously, I made it across, but I didn't know that I would when I was walking into it. They had us sort into different dressing rooms, which were really undressing rooms, because we were asked to disrobe and then walk out one at a time when they called us. We were not supposed to ask if anybody we knew had made it across or if the person before us had made it or not. When I stepped out of the dressing room, I was alone, except for the elderly woman who escorted me out and gave me a chance to change my mind. She'd watch me walk into the Goddess Sand, as it was called, and either live or die before she brought the next seeker out.

"So, uh, I just go now?" I asked her.

"Yes, sweetie."

"Is there anyone watching on the other side?"

"No. There are no windows there, nor over here. That's by design. You just walk into the dressing room. They'll be waiting for you."

It was a disorienting moment, to think that my last human contact might be with this stranger or that my last words might be about whether someone could see me naked, so I said something else.

"Goddess keep you safe."

"And you, sweetie."

And then I did it. I made it all the way across the Goddess Sand, which was super cold and gross. And when I got to the other side, I felt less elated that I had made it than worried that Tarrech may not have.

A woman who could have been the other one's twin was waiting in the dressing room. She directed me to a shower to wash off the sand and slime, and then she asked me to remove my Jereh band. Once that was gone I felt really naked, self-consciously rubbing at the skin where it had been, a slightly lighter brown than the rest of me.

"We're going to replace the stones and return it to you," she assured me. "We just need to figure out which blessing you've been given first." She gave me some baggy pants and a tunic with a basic drawstring along with a pair of really terrible boots and sent me on my way to the next room, where a tailor waited to take my measurements for a new outfit courtesy of the Triune Council. Then I was handed off to a bard, who grinned at me and ushered me outside to a straight road lined with evergreens.

"Run that way as fast as you can. If the trees start to blur, stop right away."

"Why?"

"Because it means you're a courier, and you don't want to run without protection. Most likely it's just going to be some nice exercise to burn off all the nervousness of the seeking and some of your elation at surviving it."

"How far do I go?"

"Go to the end of the trees where there's an intersection and back. Then we'll test for something else."

Halfway to the turning point, I realized I wouldn't be testing for anything else. The trees started moving way too fast, which of course was me moving way too fast, and I splattered my first grasshopper against my left cheek. It hurt a lot, because hitting anything at speed hurts a lot, and exoskeleton is tough stuff. Some of the guts got into my eye, and I still remember how that felt. I became a huge fan of goggles right then.

"Wow! A new courier!" the bard called. "I thought we might get one this time."

"Aren't there only twenty-seven?"

"Yes, except when there isn't. We had one retire three months ago. Two cohorts came through since then and no replacement. I guess Raena was waiting for you."

I walked back to him so we didn't have to shout, wiping horrible guts off my face and blinking furiously to wash out my eye with tears. I'd wasted no time in discovering a downside to my blessing. I hoped I'd get to experience an upside soon.

"How does a courier retire? They never mentioned that in the Colaiste. Doesn't the blessing last until death?"

"Not for couriers. Usually around their mid-forties, when they start to slow down, the blessing leaves them. So you have about thirty years."

"Then what do I do?"

"Most couriers wind up working for the Triune somehow. Many run for office and become members of a council somewhere. You'll be around the world's leaders and carry a lot of information in your head, so you'll get quite the education in government without even trying."

"That sounds stupendously boring."

"Maybe you'll feel differently in thirty years. And if not, there are always other professions."

I found out at dinner who'd lived and who'd died. It was a sumptuous affair in a lavish hall of that eastern building, dominated by a long table that must represent most of a full-grown tree. Tarrech was there, much to my relief, and I got a second hug from him, but not another kiss. We celebrated with a fantastic meal courtesy of the Triune Council, all of whom were in attendance, and one of them remarked that they couldn't remember when, if ever, a single cohort had produced both a courier and a juggernaut.

"Never before," the bard said, who had a history of seekings in his head.

And then we went outside and sang the Dirge for the Fallen for our schoolmates who never walked out of the Goddess Sand.

Brynt walls were not built to keep juggernauts out, because no walls were truly capable of that. They were there to slow the juggernaut down long enough for the city's rapids or tidal mariners to locate them and rip the water out of their brains. The land was always salted underneath the walls and city, so the Third Kenning could not work on them from below, but nothing prevented a juggernaut from using the land outside the city to advantage.

We wanted to keep the city as intact as possible so that the Brynts could live there again. Temblor Connagh worked out a plan with Tarrech that would keep most of the structures unbruised, they thought. If we took too many casualties, we'd pull back and rain some fire arrows in there.

Our force of four thousand soldiers and one thousand archers was probably half that of the Bone Giants, but Tarrech was worth another ten thousand all by himself. We'd camped in sight of the city the night before, daring the invaders to leave their walls and attack us, but they had no reason to abandon what they thought was a distinct advantage. At dawn they were waiting for us. The tops of the walls were lined with inexperienced archers. The bows and arrows they were using were all taken from the city armory and not built to Bone Giant size. Still, they could do some damage with those, so we lined up outside their range, directly opposite the northern gate. Our formations were cubes nine wide and deep that would fit through the gate.

Temblor Priyit was in the center of the vanguard. I stood off to one side and would operate freely with a cudgel and hunting knife. Tarrech and Temblor Connagh stood perhaps twelve paces in front, conferring one last time. They nodded and clasped arms, then the temblor left to take up his command position, somewhere in the middle of the column. Tarrech removed his boots and tossed them aside, then he looked behind him. He spotted me and waved at me to join him. I zipped over there.

"What do you need?" I asked him.

He gave me a sad smile and extended his hand. I put mine in his and he gripped it gently. "The Huntress Raena blessed us on the same day all those years ago. Maybe it was because she knew this day would come and that we would be here together. Or maybe it's a surprise to her as much as anyone. Regardless, I thought it would be appropriate to say a prayer before we begin."

"Of course. And we shouldn't hurry it either. The battle will happen when we say."

We bowed our heads and took turns thanking the huntress for our blessings and asking for her strength and favor in the battle to come. We each named the other's friendship as one of our many blessings.

"I've had many people come to me on the march here and say they would be honored to fight beside me today," he said. "And I am honored to fight beside them. But I am most honored to fight beside Tuala. Because I know she actually will be by my side."

That ended any chance I had of getting through the prayer without tears.

"Yes," I said past a lump in my throat. "I will."

When we were finished, he nodded to me, face somber. We had bloody business to do. I stepped away as he sank up to his calves in the earth. The Bone Giants were about to face the full strength of the Third Kenning.

It began with a bombardment of the gates from the earth itself; a juggernaut can turn any patch of land into a siege engine. The turf in front of Tarrech rippled and quaked before it spat boulders toward the city. The first couple missed, falling short or wide and doing some sur-face damage to the walls, but once Tarrech got a feel for it, they started hitting the gate dead-on. The first few weren't traveling fast, being more of a targeting and range-finding volley, but after that he sent three at high speed, and they splintered the gate to kindling. He sent more through to clear out the sides and to crush a cluster of giants waiting on the other side. The breach was clear for the army to enter the city, and he grunted and winced, a hand reaching up to the ribs on his left side. Moving the earth around like that did not come without a cost. But now he had to take on a juggernaut's battle form, and it would drain him severely for every minute he spent in it. He took a deep breath and growled, clenching his fists.

Solid rock flowed up from the ground underneath him, popping and crackling and reshaping itself as it sheathed his body in an impen-etrable armor. No spear or arrow would punch through it. No sword would slash through it. No hammer blow would be strong enough to shatter it, unless wielded by a temblor—and they were on our side. He became the equivalent of a sentient landslide, unstoppable and deadly yet fully capable of changing direction.

Two narrow slits remained for vision and breathing when he was finished, and he turned to the vanguard and roared, "Begin your count now!" before charging the city gate alone.

"One hundred eighty!" Temblor Priyit shouted, and the rest of her cube joined in with "One hundred seventy-nine!" the moment after-ward, and they continued to count down. We were to give Tarrech three minutes' head start before following.

The temblor began to bang the shaft of her spear against the side of her shield with each number called out, and that was quickly picked up by the rest of the soldiers. And all the while, Tarrech ate up the distance between us and the city, taking great leaps with every stride, for he was now using the strength of earth as well, the strength of a temblor combined with his own power to shape rock, propelling him forward in a suit of stone that must weigh close to a ton.

We saw panicked flights of arrows launched at him from the walls, most of which missed, but the few that hit caromed off his armor harmlessly. By the time he reached the gate, we were in the final seconds of our countdown. A hastily assembled force of Bone Giants had crowded into the gateway to confront him and he simply plowed through them, trampling them into a mess of shattered bones and crushed organs.

Then he was through and he disappeared, and we began our double-time march toward the gate. I kept pace next to them until I saw Tarrech appear on the top of the walls, tossing off the side archers who could take a toll on us—perhaps on me—before we reached the gate. Once I saw the bodies falling and all their attention was on him, I poured on the speed and reached the gate seconds later. The Bone Giants were trying to regroup and present an organized defense, after Tarrech had mowed down their first corps.

They were too tall for me to deliver fatal blows to vital organs, but their hips shattered nicely underneath my cudgel, and their femoral arteries bled just fine when I sliced into their unprotected legs.

When another of these Bone Giant armies attacked Bennelin, they did so by surprise, at a time when there were very few of the blessed present and almost none that could be effective in a fight. They met a different juggernaut a few days later, while they were marching on Fandlin. He'd caught them in the open and buried them all.

This army had wiped out the populations of two Brynt cities, including the one they now occupied. They had to have suffered some casualties, but they were still near full strength, because Möllerud and Hillegöm had likewise been protected by a few of the blessed. It was not so easy for them now.

Still, after my initial strikes made them recoil, more of them surged after me in a wave and I had to give ground. My speed offered me little advantage when I lacked room to maneuver. I still lunged forward here and there, and it slowed them, made them wary, but I kept moving back toward the gate, which needed to stay clear if Temblor Connagh's plan was to work. A quick glance over my shoulder to gauge my distance to the gate and how close the vanguard was showed me that they weren't going to make it in time.

We needed Tarrech here. I darted to the left, where the stairs to the wall were littered with bodies. I mounted them quickly and chased after Tarrech, who had moved down a bit farther than he really needed to.

"That's enough! We need you at the gate!" I called, and after a couple of repetitions he heard me and turned. "I'll take over up here!"

Tarrech nodded and rumbled down the stairs, his weight pulverizing some of them but not rendering them impassable. He essentially rolled over the Bone Giants nearest the gate like the huge boulder he was, moving back and forth and keeping the way clear until the vanguard could get through.

The Bone Giants were sending reinforcements along the walls, but they had to come one at a time and they couldn't rush me, so it was an ideal place for me to work. I didn't let any of the archers get set.

Once the vanguard came through, Temblor Priyit wasted no time using her incredible strength. That huge shield became an impressive weapon in her arms; she used it to send giants flying backward and bowling over their comrades, creating space for an advance. She had to stay in formation, however, since she was as vulnerable as anyone, temblors being granted tremendous strength but no ability to move earth or armor themselves in rock. The rest locked shields, held them high, and waited for the Bone Giants to get in range of their spears. I heard it when they did: The sound of men being punctured and the clanging of swords on shields was different from Tarrech crunching them to death. Soldiers split off to the right and left as they came in behind, extending the line and protecting the flank, creating a safe path for the archers, when they arrived, to take the stairs up to the wall.

They came in behind me soon enough, along with a couple of soldiers to keep pushing clockwise, and the archers began pouring arrows down into the city almost immediately. The Bone Giants were so clustered together in places that they couldn't miss. I checked to see if we were advancing counterclockwise along the wall as well, and we were, though a bit more slowly, since I had not worked in that direction and the Bone Giants had taken some of it back once Tarrech went down; still, Temblor Connagh's plan to turn the walls against them was going to work. Which meant it was time for Tarrech to get out. He'd done his job by taking their one advantage away from them; we were now better armed and strategically placed than the enemy was. He didn't need to spend himself to any further degree. But no one would or could tell him that except me. Temblor Priyit was on the front line and fighting very well but in no position to get Tarrech's attention, even if she could sense somehow that we had gained the upper hand; the other two temblors might not even be in the city yet, since we were still streaming in and advancing.

Tarrech was on the right flank, dealing death with every step and swing of his arms, but he was also on salted earth and had been ever since he stepped through the gate. Which meant that he wasn't drawing his power from the source of his kenning anymore but rather was spending his own life to power that suit of stone. He would have spent it anyway, even outside the walls, but it was doubtless taking a much greater toll on him this way, and I was tearing up thinking of what had happened to tidal mariner Culland du Raffert at the cleansing of Göfyrd. I wanted Tarrech to make it home.

I stepped in behind him and kept shouting until he heard me.

"Tarrech! We've won! Come on out! We can take it from here!"

He turned, saw me, and began to back up, swinging at enemies who got too close. I asked the soldiers behind us to let us pass through the shields and cover our retreat, and they flowed around us. Then we were able to turn and get Tarrech out of the city and onto fresh land, where he could shed the juggernaut's armor, retire from battle, and simply retire. The Triune would ask no more of him.

I craned my neck upward and checked the walls to make sure there were no Bone Giant archers nearby and saw that we still had that firmly in hand.

"It's safe here," I said. "Let it go."

He sighed, sank a bit into the earth, and banished his stone armor.

The man revealed as the rock fell away was not the handsome, fit, twenty-five-year-old Tarrech that had entered Möllerud. He was old and bent and in obvious agony, wobbling on weak knees.

"Auggh! Goddess, it hurts!" He gasped and clutched at my hand so that he wouldn't fall over. I took his and he squeezed as pain shuddered throughout his body, his bones and muscles shifting, his organs failing. "When you're in there and the temblor's strength is thrumming in your muscles and bones," he wheezed, "it feels so good. You feel—nngh!—invincible, and you have no idea how much it's going to cost, no idea that when the bill comes due, you simply won't be able to pay."

"No, it's okay, Tarrech. You'll be fine. You still have years left. You can spend them with your family and retire in peace."

"Not like this," he said, looking at his wrinkled hands, at the flesh sagging off his arms, at the gaps in his leather armor now that he'd shrunk and wasted away. "No, no, no. I can't go home like this. They can't see me." His eyes found mine and pleaded, a bit cloudy and unfocused, tears streaming out of the corners. "I want them to remember me the way I was before. You'll tell them, won't you, Tuala? My old friend? You'll explain. I told them before I left that I loved them. But you'll go back and tell them for me again. That I was thinking of them at the end."

"I swear to you that I will," I said, because in that moment I couldn't possibly have said anything beyond what he wanted and needed to hear.

"Thank you, Tuala. You and I will meet again. We will all meet again in the earth."

And then he groaned as he clothed himself in rock one last time, an unstoppable engine of death running on the last steam of his life, and charged back into the city, roaring at our soldiers to make way. I followed in his wake until he had pushed through to the front and launched himself at a knot of Bone Giants. Mercilessly, he smashed them into paste and cleared some room for me to work behind him, crippling those who tried to flank and surround us until, a few short minutes later, the kenning took him and he crumbled into dust, mixing with the blood of his fallen foes.

Moving at full speed and screaming incoherently, I kneecapped all the giants near him with my cudgel so that they would fall to the point where I could slash their throats, dashing in and out of their guard before they could react and getting splashed by their arterial spray. I didn't stop until I'd dislocated both my shoulders from the speed of the impacts. My wrists were also sprained, in spite of my bracers, but none of it hurt as much as my heart.

The spearmen pushed past me, enveloping me in their shield wall, and I retrieved Tarrech's Jereh band before it could be trampled and lost. That would go to Aevyn when I kept my sworn oath to him.

The army pressed forward while I sought a medic to shove my arms back in their sockets.

Once that was done, I returned to the spot where Tarrech had died, searching for pieces of him that were large enough for us to bury. I found some clods of dirt that kept together well enough to be carried out; he shouldn't rest on salted earth, and I filled my courier's satchel with his remains.

We did suffer other casualties. The Bone Giants found occasional gaps between shields and exploited them or took advantage when a soldier got their spear stuck in a body and couldn't yank it out in time to strike at the next one. Once we pushed them back from the open area near the gates, progress was slower, as we had to clear streets and buildings. They pulled off a few successful ambushes, but they were not ideally suited to urban warfare when the buildings weren't scaled to their size. I ran messages between temblors and small scouting missions to find pockets of them hiding out, while the rest of the army hauled our dead to a field where they could be buried and a memorial erected later by a stonecutter. Temblor Priyit was among those who sought out the stragglers, continuing to put herself at risk even though she was covered in blood, some of it probably hers.

Some of the Eculans escaped to the harbor and sailed a few boats to the east, which displeased the temblors, but the work was finished by midday: Möllerud was liberated and Rael safe from attack.

We had to dig a mass grave by hand since we had no other blessed among us, but there were plenty of shovels and plenty of us to do the work. The Bone Giants, however, would not rest in the earth with us. Temblor Connagh had already ordered that their bodies would be rowed out to sea, using their own boats, and dumped into the ocean far enough away that they wouldn't wash up onshore, an operation that would take days.

When it was time, I emptied my satchel into the grave so that Tarrech could rest with the men and women who fought with him. He didn't save them all, but he did wind up saving most. Not having to attack a wall or face archers and getting free access to the city made all the difference. I considered keeping a small piece of him but then thought that was selfish and unnecessary; I had perfect recall, after all, and required no reminders.

Temblor Priyit didn't join us at sunset in singing the Dirge for the Fallen, but that was easy to forgive. She spread her arms wide and looked up, mouthing some Nentian words to Kalaad in the sky as she wept for the dead, tears creating pink streaks through the blood on her face, and I appreciated it. My face looked the same, no doubt.

I thought about what Tarrech would have done in such a situation and approached her afterward. I saw her tense when she spotted me, the tight nod of greeting, the lips pressed thin.

"Temblor. You fought well today and you honored the fallen in your own fashion. Thank you. I just wanted to let you know that my grudge is buried in this field also."

She blinked a few times in surprise before replying, "Thank you, Master Courier."

"You can call me Tuala if you want."

The next morning, I ran to Killae to tell the Triune Council what had happened. And then I returned to Randulet to keep my oath and tell Tarrech's family he wouldn't be coming home.

Aevyn's eyes filled but she kept it together as I handed over his Jereh band, having known when I came to get him that he might never be back.

"Rael has its victory, Tarrech has his honor, and everyone gets to return to their cozy lives," she said. "Except for my kids and me."

"I'm sorry."

She looked down at the band and a tear escaped from her eye. "For seven years I had it all, you know? I mentioned it to him once. But he told me all we had was a single beautiful season that would eventually pass."

"Seven years is a goodly length for a season," I ventured.

"It is," she agreed. "But it wasn't enough. I wanted more."

Day 27

MUSTARD AND CHOWDER

I was morose in the morning, and after a quiet and meditative break-fast, I realized it was because I identified so strongly with Aevyn. Like her, I'd had it all for a little while. It was more than seven years, but still a little while, too little by far. It was better than many people ever enjoyed and I should be grateful. But I wished it had kept going, that Sarena was still with me. Just as so many other widows and widowers wished. Because it had not ended by natural causes, by getting old or falling sick or growing sick of each other. It had ended because someone chose to be violent, to kill for religion or patriotism or some other abstraction, and thereby rob someone else of their love.

I toyed with the idea of sending Aevyn a gift basket but recalled that I didn't appreciate such things when I was in mourning. They were just reminders of the enormity of my loss.

I could offer her some vague wisdom on how to carry on afterward, but I didn't think I was especially an expert on the subject. Apart from avoiding self-destructive behavior, I hadn't accomplished anything of note and certainly hadn't fallen in love again.

Fintan picked up on my mood when we met. "What's on your mind?" he asked.

"Aevyn. Is she all right?"

The bard shrugged. "I doubt it. She's alone with a couple of kids and emotionally devastated. But if you mean does she have enough to eat and are her basic needs met, then yes. The families of juggernauts are always taken care of in that regard."

"Did you get that story from Tuala herself?"

"Yes. I had occasion to speak with her before coming here."

"Will she be joining our forces heading to Ecula?"

"Maybe. I have no idea where she is currently, but couriers can get here fast." And then the bard ambushed me. "Tell me, Dervan, have you any news on that mysterious item of Clodagh's that Brynlön supposedly has in its possession?"

"No," I said, perhaps too quickly. "I mean, we still don't even know what we're talking about. Unless you've since been informed what the mysterious item is?"

"I haven't." He grinned at me. "So you never passed on the message?"

I shook my head and shrugged, hoping these might distract from my expression, which I was sure was practically screaming, *I'm lying right now!* "There was nothing to pass on."

"Mmm, I see. Well, I'm fairly certain I'll have to ask again next time a courier shows up. Clodagh is going to want an answer."

"She can get it from the pelenaut. I know nothing."

I felt hot and flushed for the rest of the session and actually began sweating. Why Rölly ever thought I'd be a good spy is beyond me.

Later, Fintan told his audience that the day's song would be a Kaurian homecoming hymn.

> *I'm finally tacking into port*
> *Where all my treasures wait,*
> *No longer wishing to roam;*
> *My tunic's flecked with salt spray and foam*
> *And I hope it's not too late*
> *To take my ease at home.*

There's a lady I wish to court
And in fact we have a date,
Going to dig out an old comb
And run it over my dome,
Try to calm my heart rate
Before I see my bride at home.

"When we last left Gondel Vedd, he'd just made a discovery during his journey home that the Eculan god is named Žalost. Let's pick up with him as he returns to port in Linlauen."

Gondel Vedd

Ponder Tann did me a great disservice by flying away early from the ship to inform Mistral Kira of my imminent arrival. As a result, Chamberlain Teela Parr was waiting for me as I debarked, together with an escort of liveried palace staff.

"Scholar Vedd," she greeted me, and then her eyes traveled down and back up to my face. "You look . . . as you normally do."

"What?" I looked down at my tunic. It was perhaps a bit rumpled, but it wasn't soiled with anything new, just a few old spots I could never get out. "I should allow you a bath and a change of clothes first, but the mistral wants you immediately."

"Immediately? But I have a cabin full of gift baskets with very important mus—"

"It'll be seen to carefully, you have my word," she said, and nodded once to the man on her left, who nodded back, understanding that this was now his responsibility. "Now, come along."

I really did not want to go with her. I wanted to see my husband first. But I didn't see much choice before me, so I sighed in resignation and followed her on wobbly knees. She went too fast at first and I made no effort to keep up, allowing her to remember that my top speed was slow. There was a carriage waiting at the end of the docks, but there were teahouses and restaurants and souvenir shops in between, the sorts of establishments designed to separate tourists from their money, and therein awaited my opportunity.

"Chamberlain . . ." I clutched my gut as we approached Mugg's Chowder House. "I must ask that we stop here momentarily. I must avail myself of their facilities."

"We can do that at Windsong."

"I really must insist. I won't last the carriage ride." Still cradling my gut, I waddled toward the entrance without waiting for her permission. This was the "old man's bladder trick," which Maron had taught me a couple of years ago, except I was doing a slight variation of it called "whoops, I'm incontinent!" Teela Parr growled her frustration behind me but grudgingly commanded me to make haste, and I stifled a grin. She sent her other lackey after me to "make sure I didn't get lost."

Still, losing him was easy enough.

Mugg's Chowder House was designed to serve a lot of people, because its appeal was universal to both locals and visitors. Locals loved the proprietor—whose actual name was Fuller Mugg—for his stories about visitors. And visitors loved that the chowder was always served in a Mugg's mug instead of a bowl, a spectacularly inconvenient length to go for a pun, because it made as much sense as eating a sandwich out of a champagne flute to me. But, of course, Mugg had put his mug on his mugs, a very clever illustration in which he was holding one of the self-same mugs as in a toast to the patron; it was all very meta, and he sold as many Mugg's Mug mugs as he did sides of soda bread. He served an extraordinary number of people, so he required extraordinary facilities. I was counting on Teela's picked man not to know this. People who worked at Windsong Palace tended to frequent the fancier places up on the cliffside, where the wind could be felt more strongly and they could feel in turn as if Reinei was blessing them and so on. Mugg's Chowder House was a place for the common man, like me.

We brushed past the hostess stand and headed straight for the washrooms. I paused briefly in front of the door and turned to scowl at the youngster, who looked like he was ready to follow me in. "I'll be quick as I can," I said, my disapproval clear, and his face fell as he realized he'd been about to invade my privacy.

"Right. I'll wait here," the young man said. I entered alone, walked the length of the expansive washroom, and exited out the other side, for there was a whole other wing of Mugg's over there, together with a door leading outside. I used it and turned left, heading up a different aisle of the docks but ultimately leading right past the carriage that Teela Parr had waiting for me. Beyond it there were rickshaws for hire, and I grabbed the first one in the queue and gave the driver my address. Teela had no doubt figured out by then that I'd ditched her, and I'd never be able to pull that trick on her again, but if I got to see Maron before work consumed me, it'd be worth it.

I paid the driver and burst into our humble cottage, all excited, shouting, "Maron! I'm home!" But I could tell instantly he wasn't there. We had a very small place together and the air was still, even though the windows were open.

It was disappointing but not completely unexpected. I used the opportunity to change into a clean tunic, look into a glass, and think briefly about how much I could do to make myself look presentable if only I had ever bothered to learn the procedures. To compensate I had learned to say, "Sorry, I'm a mess," in seven languages.

I almost left *Zanata Sedam* behind but couldn't bring myself to do it. I picked it up and held it underneath an arm as I left our cottage to seek out Maron at his favorite haunt, a café not two blocks away with a patio open to the breeze and a view of the ocean. I thought the seagulls could be annoying there, but he enjoyed defending his meal from airborne thieves. "I wouldn't punch anything in the world but a seagull," he told me once. "They are supremely punchable creatures. I'm at peace with that particular violence, and I like to think Reinei understands."

He was, as I expected, sitting on the patio. However, he was not alone, and I did not recognize the man sitting across from him. I was about to call out and wave, but something made me pause, uncertain. It was their expressions, the way they were smiling at each other—but especially Maron. That expression on his face was rarely shared with anyone but me.

A cold swirl of fear circled in my gut. Was Maron . . . having an affair? Considering how often I'd been absent, I supposed I couldn't blame him if he was. I could feel devastated, though.

But they weren't touching in any way. Perhaps I shouldn't jump to conclusions.

I needed to tell him I'd returned, if nothing else, so I gulped down a ball of worry and uncertainty and stepped forward into his view.

"Hello, Maron. I'm home."

When his eyes locked on mine, his mouth dropped open in surprise, then his face transformed into joy. "What! Gondel!" He leapt out of his chair to crush me in his arms, and that cold knot of fear loosened somewhat. It dissolved completely when he spoke in my ear, "Welcome back, my love."

I was home indeed.

A quick kiss, and he introduced the man sitting across from him. "Gondel, you've heard me speak of him but never met before: This is my cousin Nevel Tibb, from Teibell."

I shook his hand with shuddering relief and wished him peace.

"Come, please, sit," Maron said, gesturing to an empty chair. "Put down whatever you have there. I'd just received your letter that you'd be staying in Brynlön, and Nevel was trying to cheer me up."

"Ah! Two days after I sent the letter, I was summoned back by the mistral," I told him, "and I'm supposed to be at Windsong already. But I ditched the chamberlain at the docks to see you first."

"What?" He grinned at me, assuming I was joking. "You did not!"

Before I could sit, two priests of the gale appeared at the patio entrance and clapped their hands four times before shouting my name. They had the mistral's osprey embroidered on their shoulders. There would be no ditching them.

"Okay," Maron said, "I guess you did."

"They really want to see me about something," I explained. "I don't know when I'll get home, Maron, but it will be as soon as I can. I just wanted you to know I am back, I am safe, and I'm thinking of you."

"You are wonderful. Thank you." Maron kissed me longer this time, a farewell and a promise. "Go and be brilliant, Gondel. I'll be waiting."

Yes, ditching Teela Parr had definitely been worth it.

I presented myself to the priests and they wished me peace but said I must accompany them to the Calm, where the mistral awaited my arrival. I gave them no grief, for I had my peace now. Since I'd had no time to sit down and eat, I would even be able to appear in a tunic that only carried the ghosts of old stains instead of fresh ones.

As soon as I entered the Calm and the mistral spotted me, she ordered the room cleared for a private audience with the two priests and me. Teela Parr was there, and her hooded glare as she exited was enough to tell me I'd lost her good opinion.

"Welcome back, Scholar. You were ordered to report here immediately upon arrival, but you chose to go home first, embarrassing my chamberlain in the process." She stated these facts plainly, without anger or hurt.

"Yes, Mistral. I have no regrets."

"Do you believe, Scholar Vedd, that your personal desires supersede the needs of the state?"

"I wouldn't wish to make a blanket judgment, but in this case, yes, I do believe they did."

"Interesting. How so?"

"I did not know what you wanted of me, but I did know it would have been cruel and inconsiderate of me to return home from a war zone and not let my husband know I was safe and thinking of him. I could not have worked for the state in peace with that burden on my conscience. I can now devote my time to your problem in serenity, because I have shown my husband how devoted I am to him. And I would add that while some people are capable of fighting for abstractions, many are not."

"Abstractions such as?"

"Such as nations. Or words like *freedom* or *peace*. But everyone is capable of fighting or working for the benefit of someone they love and is motivated far more strongly by them than by an abstraction. I want to help forge a peace with the Eculans, for sure, for the sake of everyone, but especially for Maron. His safety is foremost in my mind as I work. Allowing me the time to reconnect with him was not a waste, for now I am content to focus on what you will. We have not lost a full hour. How may I help?"

The mistral ignored my question and shifted her gaze to the priests. "What say you?"

The first priest smiled serenely. "The scholar's breath blows true, Mistral. Love is the rock of peace that stands against stormy seas. He did not have enough information to weigh your needs against his, and even if he had, his still may have borne more weight. I believe he behaved morally."

Mistral Kira nodded once and shifted her gaze to the other priest, who merely said he agreed. Then the mistral dropped her eyes and nodded some more.

"You teach me well, Scholar."

"I do?"

She looked up at me and smiled shyly. "You may have noticed I am younger than you."

A difference of four decades was difficult to miss. "I did notice that, yes."

"Owing to my youth, from time to time I've found my orders disobeyed. Whenever it happens, I seek to know why. Sometimes it is because they simply thought they could get away with it—that I would not notice or wish to make an issue out of it, to keep the peace. Sometimes there is genuine ill will behind it. And sometimes, as in this case, it is because I have given orders I shouldn't have. I should not have demanded that you come here first before seeing your husband." She placed a hand over her heart. "Please accept my apology, Scholar Vedd."

"Of course, Mistral Kira."

"I do not have a lover, you see, or anyone whose care supersedes that of Kauria. I forgot that almost everyone else does. It would be good to remember that going forward, and I will attempt to incorporate policies in our forces that take that into account as we move to what may be a war footing. Gentlemen, will you consider family issues next and how the military might aid those left behind, how we might allow families to keep contact with our forces abroad, and so on?"

The two priests agreed, and she asked them to excuse us. "Please inform Teela Parr to wait five minutes, then bring in the other scholar." Once they left, it was only the two of us in the Calm. Her posture slumped a bit and her smile was more radiant. She flicked a finger at my tunic.

"You put on something that approaches cleanliness this time."

"Well, like you, I am trying to improve myself."

"You don't have to do that for me, Gondel. May I call you Gondel when we're alone?"

"Of course."

"Thanks. Call me Kira. No, see, I love it when you come in here in front of all the fancy pants looking like you got attacked by condiments and barely survived. In hindsight, I realize you may not have been aware of how much I enjoy your audiences—I teased you a little the first time, and I apologize for that too. It's priceless, the look on the courtiers' faces when I take you completely seriously. It reminds them that they don't know everything."

"Who are the fancy pants again?"

"Everybody is fancy pants here but you. That's not an insult, Gondel; I like you far more than I like them. Now, listen, we have just a few minutes before we have to be formal again, so I'm going to lay it out for you quick: I'm under a lot of pressure to launch a preemptive strike against Ecula."

"A strike? So . . . that means, then, that you've found their islands?"

"No."

"No? But how can you strike if you don't know where?"

"It's being sold as a seek-and-destroy package. And before you say that Kaurians going to war sounds like a breach of Reinei's principles, believe me, that's been discussed up and down. The priests of the gale have a bit of a schism brewing, in fact. The argument in favor says that limited, preemptive action will preserve peace in Kauria and doing nothing will bring war to our shores. Therefore, the peaceful solution is to go to war."

"Have they also claimed that up is down and the Tempest of Reinei is a light breeze?"

Her eyes widened. "I know, right? Thank you!"

"On what intelligence are they basing the assumption that war will come here?"

"The scholar we brought in during your absence claims, after extensive conversation with Saviič, that Kauria is Ecula's next target and the invasion could come anytime. Before making any decisions, I wish to make sure that we're hearing Saviič properly."

"Who is this new scholar?"

"You'll meet him in a moment. I need you to be my second opinion, Gondel. Watch what you say and who you say it to. Report your findings only to me. That means, explicitly, do not report anything to Teela or entrust anything in writing to any of the palace staff. Request audiences with me instead. If anyone—Teela or anyone—says I can't see you, do not give them any message except that you need to see me. Understood?"

One of the doors to the Calm opened and the chamberlain stalked in, followed by someone I couldn't make out. I bowed, returning to formality. "Yes, Mistral Kira." I had no idea what kind of intrigue I had stepped into, but I didn't like it. Leave town for a couple of months and a nation of peace is talking about starting a war with Ecula, with whom we've had no official contact? Madness.

The scholar soon revealed himself, and then much of the source of the madness resolved in my mind: It must be his fault. The supercilious sneer of Elten Maff the Impossibly Tidy slithered across my eyes, and I struggled to keep my face still.

I should have known it would be him. Fifteen years my junior, he'd ascended to dean of languages at the University of Bauer, where he waited for me to publish something and then criticized it. Occasionally, he published something of his own and I congratulated him for figuring out something I'd realized ten years before. I never trusted him, because he was too neat and impeccably groomed. Evilly handsome, down to the villain's mustache and dimples, he dressed in clothing that could not possibly be bought on a dean's salary. Fancy pants indeed. He even had one of those little shoulder capes on one side that served no purpose but to look fabulous. Maintaining that sort of appearance took time away from scholarship. There were at least two other scholars of the old language who I thought would do a better job than he, but I understood why Elten got the nod. He made more noise.

"Mistral, I've brought the scholar as you requested," Teela Parr said.

"Yes, thank you. Scholar Elten Maff, you know of Scholar Gondel Vedd."

"I do."

"Please confer with him regarding all you have learned in your conversations and allow him to see your notes."

"My notes?"

"Yes. You must have kept records of your conversations with the Eculan prisoner."

"Of course," he replied, but I knew from the strangled sound of his voice that he had next to nothing.

"Teela, Scholar Vedd is to have whatever he needs, no questions. And if he wishes to see me, he is to be brought here without delay, regardless of what else I'm involved in. Inform the windguard."

"Yes, Mistral."

"Thank you all. I trust you'll be able to begin straightaway, since the zephyr is waiting to hear."

That was our dismissal, and Teela led us from the Calm to the dungeons without saying a word to me. After giving her the slip at the docks, I would be privy to no more comfortable chats in the parlor with teas and orange cakes. She left instructions with the windguard at the dungeon that I was to be given whatever I wished and allowed free rein in the Calm and departed without farewell. I had truly burned a bridge there.

That left me alone with Elten Maff, who'd held his tongue to this point, enjoying, perhaps, the awkward silence.

"Your notes, please," I said.

Maff snorted. "Hello to you too, Scholar Vedd."

"Yes, Elten, my personal faults are legion, and I'm sure you'd love to list them all for me. But I've been brought back here at great urgency and the mistral said the zephyr is waiting for some reason, so can we skip all that and move along? Your notes."

"Well, ah. I don't have them with me."

"Please fetch them. I'd like to begin there."

"I could simply tell you what Saviič said."

"Simply? Please do."

"He said Kauria is Ecula's next target."

"He flatly stated that Kauria is Ecula's next target, or was this your inference?"

"It was . . . inferred."

I had inferred the possibility earlier but had never phrased it as anything but a possibility, never a certainty. "Do go on, Scholar Maff. Tell me precisely what Saviič said, in Uzstašanas, that allowed you to infer that Kauria is next."

"Well. Ahem. *Ova zemlja bi mogla biti sljedeća.*"

His pronunciation and syntax were atrocious, and I was a little surprised at first but realized what had been happening: In his written criticisms of my work, he had plenty of time to consult texts—or maybe even have someone else consult them on his behalf. He'd never spoken aloud in front of me before. I didn't consider myself fully fluent, but I was a stone's throw away and could make myself understood easily by Eculans. Elten Maff's proximity to fluency was more like several weeks' hard ride.

"He did not say that. What you just uttered was nonsense."

Maff's face purpled. "I translate the written word better than the spoken. But in essence, if they don't find what they're looking for in the north—some sacred ship that missed its last rendezvous—then they'll look here in the south. And the way they look, as we've seen, is by killing everyone."

"And did you present the information that way to the mistral, or did you tell her that he said Kauria is Ecula's next target?"

"I . . . don't recall."

I'm sure he did recall but realized that he was about to admit to a rather egregrious error. "Hence the need for notes. If you will fetch those for me, please, I'll be waiting."

Elten Maff blinked a few times before pointing a finger at the ground. "You'll wait here?"

"I'll be in the dungeon with Saviič."

"By yourself?"

"Yes, by myself. I survived such times before you got here, and I daresay you managed it in my absence, didn't you?"

"Well, yes, but . . ."

"But what?"

He broke eye contact, looking down and away, obviously disturbed by something and wishing to object but unsure how to do so plausibly. Eventually he decided to say nothing. "Never mind," he muttered. "I'll return as soon as I can."

"I'll be sure to take excellent notes of my discussion for your review," I said. He didn't like that, and he scowled at me before taking the stairs up. I nodded at the guard, who nodded back, and he unlocked the door for me that led down a hallway to Saviič's cell.

The Eculan prisoner had filled out somewhat in my absence and his sunburn had fully healed, and he now had his copy of *Zanata Sedam,* which he was reading when I stopped in front of his cell. He raised an eyebrow in surprise at my appearance.

"Hello, Saviič," I said to him in his language, taking a seat at the table outside his cell. The paper, quill, and inkpot I'd left behind were still there, but now they were dusty, having been untouched all this time. "You are well?"

"Yes." He did not inquire after my well-being. "Where is the other man?"

"I sent him to fetch his notes of your . . . talkings."

"Talkings?" He taught me the Eculan word for *conversation,* then said, "He took no notes of our conversation."

"I thought so."

"He told me you were coming. Told me not to talk to you."

"That's interesting. Did he say why?"

"Said you lie."

Audacious of him. "I have not lied to you, Saviič. I kept every promise I made to you. You hold it in your hand."

"I know. That is why I talk."

"Did you tell Elten Maff that Ecula will attack here next?"

He frowned. "No. I say maybe. I say it is possible."

"Is that because you must find the Seven-Year Ship?"

"Yes." Well, I had an answer for that, and I realized I had yet to tell the mistral or anyone about it.

"Thank you. I'm just going to make a note of that."

Saviič chuckled ghoulishly as I dipped my pen into the inkpot and carefully wrote out my two questions and Saviič's answers in both Eculan and Kaurian. That would be written proof that this was all a misunderstanding, and if Elten Maff wished to dispute my translation he could have at it.

Unless it wasn't a misunderstanding at all. What if there was something willful behind it? This pressure to turn a peaceful nation to war— that couldn't be coming from Elten Maff.

I am slow when it comes to politics but realized that it could only be

Zephyr Bernaud Goss behind it all. He had waved the faintest puff of pressure Elten's way, and Maff had bent right over. And, most likely, Elten had gone to fetch the zephyr rather than his nonexistent notes, which meant that I too would shortly be subject to such pressure.

I was alone down there. Guards would do whatever the zephyr told them to do.

"Please excuse me," I said to Saviič as I finished up the lines, replacing the quill. "I will return to talk more later. It is good to see you again."

The Eculan grunted and returned his attention to his holy text. I rose from the table with my copy of *Zanata Sedam* in one hand and and waggled the paper in the other a little, to speed the drying of the ink. Nodding my thanks to the guard outside the dungeon, I took the steps up to the ground floor and heard booted feet clapping the stone, coming in my direction. There was a low voice and then the nasal tones of Elten Maff, indistinct but recognizable. I did not want to see them. I hurried into a privy, shutting the door behind me as quietly as I could, and listened at the door. Soon they passed and Maff was saying, "She told him he could have an audience with her whenever he wanted."

"So he'll ask for one right away as soon as he feels threatened," a bass voice rumbled, and I knew it was Zephyr Bernaud Goss.

I felt threatened already. Once I heard their boots descending the stairs, I snuck out of the privy and hurried to the Calm. They would discover my absence in a minute, perhaps less. I wished I had the knees I had thirty years ago and could achieve a speed greater than that of a dyspeptic tortoise. Not that I had ever been cut out for feats of athleticism, such as running for my life.

Raised voices floated to my ears from behind. Someone was very unhappy not to find me.

Was it too late, I wondered, to begin a new career in sprinting? I applied myself to a feasibility study.

What I managed was something akin to a jerky waddle, undignified even for a penguin, and it required no outside panel of jurists to determine I should not attempt to make a career of it.

I heard boots stamping back up the stairs. By Reinei's wind, they were *chasing* me! They really did not want me talking to the mistral. Which only made me wish to do so more urgently. I turned the corner that led to the Calm and waved at the guard standing by the door. He shifted slightly upon seeing me, distributing his weight evenly. Guards tended not to look favorably at anyone rushing in their direction, even the elderly.

"Hold there," the guard called.

"Scholar Gondel Vedd to see the mistral," I wheezed as I approached, slowing somewhat. "The chamberlain must have told you I'm to be given audience?"

"Scholar Vedd? Yes, I was just told." The windguard stepped aside and hauled open the door for me. Beyond, I could see the Calm and the raised dais of the mistral, though I could not see her since we were behind the throne. Just as I passed the threshold, Zephyr Bernaud Goss rounded the corner behind, shouting for me to be stopped.

"Mistral, I have urgent news!" I shouted. "The Eculans will not attaggggh!" The windguard's hand hooked the back of my tunic at the neck and yanked. Hearing my distress, Mistral Kira whirled around, peering back at us, and saw me being detained. She flew from her dais to me on a gust of summoned wind, her blue-and-white dress billowing around her.

"Unhand him at once!" she commanded, and the windguard obeyed. Zephyr Bernaud Goss barreled into the room, Elten Maff behind him.

"Mistral, this man should not disturb you, he's wasting your time—"

"It took only two questions to determine that we are safe," I said, extending my notes to her. "I came here to tell you immediately."

"That's preposterous," the zephyr spluttered. "Safety cannot be determined by—"

The mistral held up a hand to silence him, her eyes scanning the paper. When she finished, she looked up at me. "I see that invasion is not so imminent as I was led to believe." Her eyes cut to Elten Maff, but she continued before he could interject. "Am I to understand it's still possible, though?"

"Only in the sense that anything is possible. It is unlikely in the extreme, Mistral. For I have intelligence to share regarding the Seven-
Year Ship, which I did not have time to share before." Her haste in
getting me to the dungeon made perfect sense now. She hadn't wanted
the zephyr to have time to interfere. "The Brynts have found it."

"Where?"

"It's in the Mistmaiden Isles. They found it just before I boarded the
ship home, and they entrusted me with the intelligence. So, you see, if
Ecula knows where it is—which is far, far away from here—they have
no reason to attack us."

The mistral sighed in relief. "Zephyr. I can give you a definitive answer now. You are hereby ordered to cancel all plans to attack Ecula.
Reinei is the wind, and we may all breathe his peace. Defense of Kauria
remains your sole responsibility."

"But—"

"Contact with Ecula will be made via diplomatic, not military, channels, so you won't be needed."

"This is—"

"You look upset, Zephyr. Perhaps you would benefit from talking
with a priest of the gale."

"No, I—"

"I insist." She turned to the same two priests who had been with her
before. "Gentlemen, please escort the zephyr outside and counsel him
until you're satisfied that he breathes Reinei's peace again."

When he was gone in the company of the priests, she beamed at
me. "My gratitude is boundless, Scholar Vedd. You have done your
country a great service. Please go home and enjoy a well-earned rest,
but return tomorrow morning after breakfast. For now, I have some
words to speak to Scholar Maff."

Elten Maff was sweating as I made my exit, and I smiled all the way
home. Maron was going to be so surprised and thrilled to see me again
so quickly. But when I entered, my husband pounced.

"Ah, excellent, perhaps you can tell me!" he said, gesturing to the gift baskets lining every available surface of our tiny dwelling. There must have been more than what was in my cabin stored in the cargo hold, and Teela Parr's man had made sure they delivered it all. "What are we going to do with all this mustard?"

Survivor Field laughed as the bard dispelled his seeming.

"It's true! You did that!" Fintan said, grinning at them. "Poor Maron! What are they going to do with all that mustard? Goddess help him." He let them laugh a little bit more, and then he teased them, holding up a new sphere. "Are you ready to find out what happened with Second Könstad Tallynd du Böll and that piece of the Seven-Year Ship hull?"

The roar of approval was enthusiastic.

"All right, then. Let's do it." He threw down the hollow stone, and our national heroine emerged from the gases.

Tallynd

I knocked upon the door of the given address, a piece of Eculan flat-boat hull cradled under my arm, and an elderly woman answered the door. She had a light-blue shawl draped over her shoulders—closer to white than blue, in fact—and her head had gone all gray, as mine had at the temples. Her skin sagged a bit on her bones, its color a touch sallow, perhaps, but her eyes were still bright. She saw my uniform and smiled, waving thin hands at me to enter.

"Your friend is in my liquid library," she said, leading me with a rocking waddle down a hallway. "Hasn't been this excited since the first time she had some hot sauce on her, heh, ha ha. Anyway, I'm Lamira du Öndsen."

"Nice to meet you, Lamira."

"I'm a hygienist too, but I don't practice much anymore," she said over her shoulder. "Knees are bad, back is bent, and sometimes when I sneeze I shit myself by accident. If you're planning on getting old, I don't recommend it."

"Sneezing?"

"Getting old. The one upside is that you can say whatever you want and get away with it. Well, mostly. It is kind of strange to be told by your kids that you're being rude at family gatherings, but my nephew's lips really *are* puckered all the time just like the anus of a sea cucumber, and I won't apologize for stating a fact. Can I get you some tea?"

She said this last as we rounded the corner into her liquid library, and my breath caught for a moment before I remembered to respond. "Yes, please."

Feryn was there, waiting, but she saw that I was scanning the room and gave me a moment to take in the wonder. I'd seen liquid libraries before—almost all hygienists have one, and of course the University of Pelemyn has the world's largest—but I'd never seen a private one on the scale or glamour of Lamira du Öndsen's. I imagined it must be a national treasure, and she had done very well for herself in her long career as a hygienist. Her study was full of Fornish hardwood furniture, from the silverbark desk to a beautiful butcher-block table with a silver sample bowl in the center of it. Behind her desk there was a bookcase, but the rest of the room's walls were covered in shelves populated with clear stoppered bottles of labeled fluids. These were divided into sections: WATERS, TEAS, POISONS, and EFFLUVIA, and then arranged by color. Some liquid libraries specialized in beers or wines or other potables, but Lamira had clearly chosen to focus on that which could be most salubrious and most deadly when ingested.

"This . . ." I began, and trailed off.

"It's wonderful, isn't it?" Feryn said. She stepped forward to me with a bottle in one hand and the piece of Seven-Year Ship hull in the other. The bottle was half filled with a dark liquid. "Lamira will let me sample this to confirm my suspicion, but she'd like your promise that you'll use your kenning to return every drop of it to the bottle. No wastage. This is the only sample we know of, and it's been handed down for generations."

"Generations? What is it? I mean, of course, you have my promise."

"Thank you. Will you put your piece of hull over here next to the bowl?" Feryn turned and strode to the silver sample bowl, placing her hunk next to it on the butcher block. I put mine down on the opposite side and she nodded in satisfaction. She uncorked the bottle, sniffed the rim, grimaced, and poured it into the silver basin. She looked up at Lamira. "Will you confirm this with me, Lamira?"

"I'd be delighted, because I wouldn't believe it otherwise." Waddling over so that she stood across from Feryn and me, the old woman placed a couple of fingers in the small puddle of dark liquid, next to Feryn's own fingers, and then spread the palm of her other hand across the stained piece I'd brought from the flatboat. Feryn mirrored her, with her other hand on the Seven-Year Ship piece. They closed their eyes, no doubt running a comparison of the tiny structures in that liquid to the structures in the hull varnish.

"Believe what?" I asked. "Will one of you finally tell me what's going on?"

"Read the label," Lamira said without opening her eyes, so I picked up the bottle and examined the fine script, written in a dark blue-gray ink. KRAKEN BLOOD, PELES OCEAN, it said.

"Clams and tentacles," I said. "How in Bryn's name did you get hold of this?"

"Tell you in a minute, Tallynd. Let me do this."

It was a full minute of me waiting in tense silence as the two hygienists quivered and squeezed their eyes and lips in concentration, occasionally grunting and muttering about protein chains. It gave me the chance to think about supply: If we'd managed to secure only a half bottle of the stuff over generations and the Eculans had enough to paint fleets of ships with it, then they had figured out a way to kill a whole lot of krakens. I remembered those barrels of goo that Nara had mentioned being in the hold of the Seven-Year Ship: That might have been the varnish.

"Confirmed," Feryn said, and Lamira nodded in agreement.

"Mine too," the old woman said.

Feryn turned to me and pointed at the hull. "The sealant used on these boards is made with kraken blood. Generous amounts of it too. Kraken blood all over the hulls means that, to grown krakens, those ships near the surface would look like baby krakens. Or smell like them, anyway. We know from survivor tales that they often attack in packs and work together, so they'd never attack their own. That's how the Bone Giants safely crossed the ocean: kraken-blood sealant on the hulls."

"Hold on, that's way too much. You're saying a fully grown kraken would sense a fleet of a hundred ships passing overhead and think, *Oh, never mind, that's just a hundred baby krakens,* and never investigate?"

"Yes."

"Do krakens even have that many babies?"

"We are fairly certain they do. It's a popular theory, anyway. We believe they have many children and only a few survive to adulthood, as with most sea creatures. The young would be preyed upon by full-grown specimens of bladefins, lion whales, that sort of thing. You've never heard that?"

"I've heard the theory but never put stock in it. I've never even seen a juvenile kraken, much less a baby one, and certainly not hundreds of them. I've never heard of any tidal mariner seeing a baby kraken."

"Well, you don't spend a lot of time in the deeps either. Most of your time is spent in coastal waters, right? And the babies have to exist, or else how'd we get the full-grown ones?"

I recalled from Gondel Vedd's briefing that the Eculans were supposedly looking for something in the north called "the Krakens' Nest," and I supposed that a spawning ground far out of our normal sea-lanes was plausible. And hunting a baby kraken might be little different from hunting a whale. Dangerous and cumbersome, but doable.

"Still, I don't buy that the adults would never swim up to investigate. If they smell a lot of other krakens around and they like to work together, why not join the party?"

Feryn shrugged. "I don't have these answers," she said, but it occurred to me that maybe some adults *did* investigate one of the fleets. There were only thirty-five boats in the Mistmaiden Isles, after all. A pair or trio could have surfaced for a look and discovered that those boats that smelled like babies from a distance really weren't krakens at all. "I know two things: Those fleets crossed the ocean, and the hulls are sealed with a kraken-blood mixture," Feryn concluded.

"Which means we can do the same thing," Lamira said, and cackled.

"Clams and tentacles, you're right! I think we actually found some of the stain on one of their ships. We just need to make more—a lot more. I have to tell the pelenaut."

"Return the blood to the bottle first, if you please?" the old woman reminded me, and I quickly used my kenning to pull the gunk off their fingers and out of the bowl and guided every drop back into the bottle.

"You were going to tell me how you got this," I reminded them.

I was looking at Feryn but Lamira answered. "I didn't get it myself. My grandfather did. He was a tidal mariner like you, five pelenauts ago or something like that. Fishing boat went out too far and he was sent to try to save them but didn't get there in time. Kraken took it apart, all hands lost, but on a piece of the foredeck, someone had chopped off the tip of a tentacle. He had the wits to bring it back with him in a waterproof sack for analysis, and that's all that's left."

"Not a word of this to anyone until the pelenaut sees fit to make it public," I said, and remembered to thank them before I left.

As I made my way to the palace, with questions swirling in my head—*how did the Eculans figure out how to do this,* and so on—I kept coming back to that brief story of Lamira's grandfather, the tidal mariner. He'd gotten old and he'd passed on. But he obviously had left some family behind. And on one particular day of his life, when he thought he'd failed—when he *had* failed, in fact, to save people—he'd done something vital that helped us, years and years in the future.

I wish we could see the ripples of good we do in the future. It would make us sure of our purpose and value in the wider world. But all we are allowed is to do good now and trust that some ripples of it will go forward, expanding.

"Well!" Fintan said. "Obviously the pelenaut has seen fit to make the news about kraken blood public, so discuss amongst yourselves! Tomorrow we will hear from Mai Bet Ken, Bhamet Senesh, and Hanima Bhandury. Until then, friends."

It took me a few minutes to realize that Fintan had made a huge error. He hadn't said anything about Feryn or Lamira receiving gift baskets from the pelenaut. That meant they were free to be thanked. They were about to be inundated.

Day 28

CANOPY FIRST

I stayed in bed for a while the next morning, thinking. Tallynd du Böll's words were on my mind—the ones about the ripples of good we do spreading into the future. It made me wonder if I was doing any good or perhaps if I wasn't doing enough. Surely providing the time and space for Elynea to get herself on track again was a ripple that would pay off in her children, Tamöd and Pyrella. But what else could I do? My knee kept me from doing most hard labor, but perhaps I could return to help at the refugee kitchen. It would be better for my spirit than seeking revenge for Sarena.

Resolved, I got dressed and ate a hurried breakfast before heading outside the walls and presenting myself to the kitchen as a regular volunteer. "I only have a few hours in the morning," I said to the chef, "but surely there's a potato that needs peeling or something."

The chef, a thickset woman named Höna du Rödal, who was armed with a spotless knife and a stained apron, gave me a wry smile. She used to own and run a restaurant in Festwyf but had lost everything in the invasion. Rölly had hired her to run this operation for the government in hopes that, after the crisis passed, she'd be able to use her pay to open a new place, perhaps with another investor joining in. Perhaps that investor would be Rölly.

"Okay, honey," she said. I am not remotely like honey, so I wondered if she was one of those people who call everybody *honey* so they don't have to remember names.

There was a potato that needed peeling. More than one, actually. And onions to be chopped. Carrots too. Plenty of vegetables that kept well, all going into a soup. Though I wouldn't say they were the pick of the harvest. They were lumps about which one might say, *Well, I guess that's a tater,* awarding it only reluctant status as a starch. We were scraping the bottom of someone's barrel here. I didn't see any protein being prepared, but maybe that would be coming later.

I didn't know that volunteering for a few hours made a huge difference or whether it would tomorrow. I'm sure nobody knew I was doing it except the head of the kitchen, so I couldn't imagine what ripples I was creating. But the Chef du Rödal knew I cared and wanted to help, at least, and her burden had been eased a tiny bit. Maybe that was enough, proving to someone with small acts of kindness that the world isn't entirely awful.

And maybe it wasn't enough after all. But I was going to keep doing it until I got a better idea.

My hands ached from gripping a knife by the time I had to leave to meet Fintan, but I felt that it was a good use of my morning and promised to return the next day.

"Do you know how they did it?" I asked Fintan when I saw him. "Got all that kraken blood?"

"No idea," he said. "I heard plenty of theories last night about how it could be done. Didn't think any of them presented a decent chance of surviving."

We stayed safely away from awkward topics as we worked, for which I was grateful. Not every day had to be a situation that gave me a case of stress sweats.

Since the day's tales would all take place in Ghurana Nent, Fintan shared a Nentian song with his audience.

Across the dark wide river croaked a randy muddy frog,
That was answered in a chatter of a young and sleek wheat dog,
Which spurred a word or two from an angry prairie hog,
Who muttered darkly to a bluetip sitting on a log.

The frog, well, he was single and he croaked with hopeful lust,
He yearned and burned with love and hope for a woman he could
     trust
He'd called for weeks with no luck and he figured he was bust
But he kept on croaking through the nights because he felt he must.

The wheat dog, she was pregnant and her pups were coming soon,
She stayed awake at nights in conversation with the moon
She said, I know my litter will be a blessing and a boon,
But till they're born I'll have to sing this lonesome sadsome tune.

The bluetip thought the prairie hog was like most bitter men,
Who groused and made pronouncements on things far beyond their
     ken,
She said, You'd understand more if you ventured from your den,
He said he would be et before he listened to a hen.

And then the hog got et and the pups got born,
The frog found a woman he could trust one morn,
The hen flew away, don't know where she went
It was life and death and love in Ghurana Nent.

Mai Bet Ken was the first narrator for the day, dressed in the same formal green robes but her hair adorned with different flower blossoms—reds and yellows this time.

Mai

That murderous lieutenant sailed away with Tactician Hennedigha and Viceroy Lohmet, safe for now under the aegis of powerful men. But I will not give up; I need to turn up the pressure somehow. There are many steps to war, and they have just taken a big one. They can still step back, and it is my job to convince them to do so.

In the meantime, I am in such a flutter that I can feel petals dropping from my bloom, and I'm losing sleep as I try to do the thousand tasks that must be done before I can move. I am to be Forn's ambassador to the new Nentian king; the current ambassador in Talala Fouz survived the burning of the city, but the embassy itself did not. He will move upriver, acquiring land in the other cities on behalf the Red Pheasant Clan, and someone will come to replace me, a net gain of a single diplomat when we need so much more. But my clan, at least, has agreed to send a greensleeve to establish our presence in every Nentian city and thereby ensure a close relationship with the newly blessed people of the Sixth Kenning. The Red Pheasants will serve the Canopy's interests and our own at the same time, and I am so pleased the elders have approved this. I even got a note from one who'd thought a former field worker wasn't qualified to hold such an important post despite my education, saying he was wrong about me and apologizing. Well, maybe I was wrong about him too.

My replacement knocks smartly on the door when I'm in the middle of packing up documents for the journey. He enters at my call, a young dark-haired man in the mustard robes of the Yellow Bats instead of the green I've adopted to represent all of Forn. This is most likely his first post outside the Canopy. He's had a week or so on the ship from Pont to grow a beard but somehow hasn't managed it.

"Ambassador Ken? I'm Ambassador Kav Mit Par, your relief."

I promptly drop everything and walk over to him. "Ambassador Par. Welcome to Ghurana Nent! I didn't realize your ship had come in, or I would have prepared a better reception. My apologies."

"None necessary. Your staff is excellent, and we've already been shown to our rooms and been made comfortable."

"How was your journey?"

"Plagued by a profound lack of trees, I'm afraid, but otherwise fine."

"You must have a forest full of questions for me. Please, won't you take your ease and I will answer what I can?"

"Oh, no, you and I can talk later. I understand from your clan that there are more pressing matters than my ease, and since they've sent a greensleeve, I can hardly argue the matter."

I blink a couple of times. "The greensleeve came with you? I didn't expect him to arrive for some time."

"It's true he had a good distance to travel and he nearly missed the ship, but he ran through the night, forgoing sleep, and he just made it. Our rooms are right next to each other and he told me he'd be along shortly; he just wanted to shave." Kav Mit Par takes a step back into the hallway and looks to his left, instantly spying the subject of our conversation approaching. "Ah, yes, here we are." He smiles, shifts to the edge of the doorway to make room, and says, "Ambassador Mai Bet Ken, I present Mak Fin ben Fos."

A greensleeve walks into the room, his gaze following the gesture of Kav's berobed arm. His blue eyes lock on mine, and both of us freeze, suddenly rooted.

We do not speak. There is silence: a golden time in which each of us grows in the light of the other's eyes. He is, quite simply, a beautiful man. He cannot be unaware of it, just as I am aware that sometimes I am thought beautiful too. But we have stunned each other and recognized it, and rather than ruin it with speech, we linger in tense, delicious awkwardness, savoring each second of this bright precious time when we cannot make a mistake, cannot be foolish or vain or indeed even human—just an ideal, long dreamt of, made suddenly flesh, scions of generations who lived to bear a legacy and now, finally, we are joined.

The moment stretches, neither of us willing to break it, and though I think Ambassador Par takes a ridiculously long while to recognize that his introduction has sufficed, he does eventually realize that he should make a smooth, graceful exit.

"Please excuse me," he says, and clears his throat. "I have something to do now . . . elsewhere."

Well, the ambassador is young, and I am sure he will work on his smoothness and grace.

His departure only makes the silence between us more exquisite. The air seems to shimmer, I am so gripped by emotion—a phenomenon I have noticed only twice before in my life: once when my younger brother was born, and the other when I bade farewell to my family to leave the Canopy behind, perhaps forever. How has ben Fos done this to me in mere seconds?

I direct my hand toward a silverbark settee, indicating he should sit. There is a round tea table set off to one side in front of it, made of the same sacred wood, and he gives the barest nod of acknowledgment before moving. I move at the same time to the hearth, where there is always a kettle to be boiled, and shift it over the flame to heat up.

Once done, I glance over my shoulder at him as he folds himself behind the table. *Please,* I implore him with my eyes, *do not feel you need to talk. Just sit there and be pretty.* Perhaps he is silently pleading with me to hold my tongue as well. The execution of tea service in traditional fashion, no steps spared, can be a comfort like no other to one who has never left the Canopy before. It is a ritual to which people cling, a comforting touch of home when confronted with this alien landscape bereft of trees, and I have brought visitors to tears with it in my time. I wonder if he will weep too.

I hope he does, and yet I hope he does not.

I suppose that means he can do no wrong in my eyes, and I feel how dangerous that is professionally. My judgment is already suborned regarding this man. That means I'm in danger of doing something profoundly stupid, sooner or later.

I hope it's later.

The tea service—made entirely of Fornish hardwoods, right down to the tray and spoons—waits for me on the counter. The interiors of the pot and the cups are coated with a resin that can handle the heat of the boiling water.

I present his cup and saucer to him on the palm of my hand. It's a small cup without any handle, an upside-down bell of polished inlaid wood; the beautiful panels are of different hardwoods, which a greensleeve would recognize instantly but that would stupefy almost any foreigner. While the interiors are smooth, the exteriors are finely carved with clan patterns, creating an interesting sensation on the fingertips. Back home these are called "ambassador tea sets": They are what we use to show off to people outside Forn, but they're rarely seen inside our own borders since they're too expensive. At present there are only two living crafters who can produce them. It is traditional to do honor to the crafter and thereby show the guest in what esteem he is held. This can be done verbally, but more often, as in this case, there is no need: There is a linen card on the tray with the information printed on it in plant-based inks, because this too shows off the bounty and craft of Forn. Handing him one is both part of the ceremony and a convenient excuse to remain silent, and I do that once I set down the tray on the table in front of him.

Mak Fin ben Fos reads it, holding it in both his hands, and then, instead of returning it to the tray as expected, he smiles at me and puts the card in the pocket of his waistcoat. Why? Is it because I gave it to him?

My innards feel molten, and I hope I'm not visibly sweating.

The kettle is just about ready. I spoon some of our clan's proprietary tea blend into the pot. There is no cream or sugar on the tray: It simply is not done in ceremony, and in fact it's rare in everyday use too, at least in Forn. The people of other nations seem to like their tea altered from its original taste, but we have suited our tastes to what the Canopy provides.

I bring the bubbling kettle over from the fire, gather up the sleeve of my robe, and pour water into the pot. It's flawless, not a drop spilled, and I smother a grin, because that's supposed to be what I do naturally.

Once the lid is on the pot and the kettle returned to the hearth, there is nothing to do but wait for the tea to steep. It would be acceptable to speak at this point, but I don't want to accept that from him. I want more of this mutual silent admiration. Because I can tell that he likes what he sees—which is, apart from all subjective judgments, a woman who likes what *she* sees. That shining regard in the eyes: That is the sweetest honey.

There is an upholstered silverbark chair next to the settee, angled for conversation, and I sit on the edge of it, back straight, and fold my hands in my lap, beaming at him. And thank the Canopy, he keeps his mouth shut and answers my pleased expression with his own. The silence continues.

After a slow count to sixty, I rise and present to him a strainer to place over the cup.

When he reaches out to take it from me, there is the smallest contact of skin on skin, a shivery frisson that becomes embers inside me. He holds the cup still while I carefully pour tea through the strainer. With that done, I pour tea into my own cup. He waits until I've returned to my seat and then, looking at each other over the rims, we sip once, twice, then shoot the rest, as custom dictates. It scalds the roof of my mouth, but I don't care.

He sighs in contentment, then puts his cup and saucer down with a muted but audible thud on the table. It breaks the spell, and he finally speaks, in a rich baritone that quietly steps into my mind and wraps it in a comfortable blanket. "Ambassador Ken, that was a perfect welcome. Thank you."

"You are indeed most welcome, ben Fos. I cannot express how glad I am that you are here. You have taken on a duty that will prove draining, I fear, but in service to Canopy and clan alike."

"It's that service that made me volunteer. This plan of yours will

yield bountiful harvests for years to come. And it has certainly motivated the clan like nothing I've seen."

"How so?"

"Well, we have so many young people leaving the Canopy to work
in these tea treehouses I'm going to be growing. If nothing else, you've
made a name for yourself among the parents of the clan for inspiring
their children to leave home."

I winced. "Oh, no. What is the staffing like?"

"Mostly young adults, with a few older ones to manage them. There
will be two ships leaving Pont full of staff—one is no doubt en route
and will arrive in the next couple of days, I expect. It's supposed to
have enough staff for here, Batana Mar Din, and Khul Bashab. We're
going to hop on that one to head north. The second ship will have staff
for the northern cities."

"So the clan council agreed that the Red Pheasants should staff them
all? It's truly a clan affair?"

"Everything has been done according to the request in your report.
It was masterfully written, if you don't mind me saying so."

"That's very kind." By the blossoms of the First Tree, he's shining
his sun at the perfect angle for me. At present I can only admire his jaw
and frame and demeanor, but these are impossible subjects to mention
aloud. I confine myself to saying, "I expect I'll have cause to compli-
ment your work very soon."

"I hope so. I'll get to work in the morning after a full night's sleep. I
assume you have much to do to prepare for our departure north, so I'll
not take up any more of your time."

He rises and I do the same, telling him he's been no burden at all and
my door is always open to him. He gives a nod of acknowledgment to
this, opens his mouth to speak, and then his eyes travel up to the ceiling and he pauses, choosing his words carefully.

"As an ambassador to Ghurana Nent, I expect your profession will
require you to stay away from the Canopy for many years."

"It will. And as a greensleeve, I expect, you can't wait to return to
the Canopy."

"I'm going to enjoy this time for what it is: new growth for every-one. But, yes, I'm sure I'll be grateful to be home again, whensoever that day comes."

I nearly laugh aloud at my own folly. I had felt such hope, such soar-ing exhilaration, like a fledgling taking her first flight, but this attrac-tion is an impossible one. Mak and I can be nothing to each other but a fantasy, a ghost of an impossible future that will haunt us in the dark of lonely nights. Well, I can only speak for myself. Regardless of what he feels or doesn't feel, our lives will be forever lived apart after this brief time of twining.

And that is all assuming that he's free in the first place. I can't imag-ine he's available, even though he's not wearing a wedding band. Per-haps that's on purpose, though: Maybe he's thinking that since he's out of the Canopy he might as well pretend he's free. But apart from returning the same intense regard I'm giving him, he's done nothing to suggest he's seeking a liaison.

This attraction is astoundingly inconvenient. I wish he would do something rude or gross so I could clear him out of my head. Perhaps the best way forward is to get down to business.

"May I ask if you know how long it will take to grow the treehouse?"

"I can do it in a day if the soil is cooperative. We can leave almost as soon as the ship arrives from Pont."

I wish him a good evening, in response to which he places a hand over his heart and bows, his moss-covered forearm so gorgeous against the red of the waistcoat, and wishes me an untroubled and restful night. He is so perfect I am seized by the impulse to just grab his face and gnaw on him. Only years of training to mask my thoughts and desires save us both.

When he leaves, I go to the liquor cabinet and pour myself a drink much stronger than tea: Raelech rye whiskey from Aelinmech, which, I am told, is known throughout Rael as "the Good Shit."

I wind up pouring three before retiring for the night.

I don't see Mak Fin ben Fos again until it's time to board the ship to Batana Mar Din. By that time he's grown the tea treehouse, Kav Mit

Par and I have spoken extensively about his priorities and duties going forward, and I've packed up everything and managed to convince a couple of my experienced staff members to come with me.

During the journey, ben Fos and I do get a brief time to talk again, and I am proud of myself for keeping it entirely professional.

"Your most important growth will be in Khul Bashab," I tell him, "because that is where these children of the Sixth Kenning are located. If there is anything you can do beyond what you normally do to make that tree especially grand and attract them, please do it. One of the beast callers is linked to bees, so perhaps some attractive flowering vines would not go amiss—if that's possible?"

"It's possible, certainly. You may count on me to see it done."

"Thank you. The ambassador there, Jes Dan Kuf, is not of our clan but he's of our mind. He sees the Sixth Kenning as a vital component of Forn's future flourishing. You may rely on him as you would me."

"Indeed? That's a comfort. There is no higher recommendation."

Oh, rot and ruin. Whether he knows it or not, he's an expert in pollinating my pistil. I need to leave before I nibble on his ear, but I can't without saying something oblique to let him know in what high regard I hold him.

"Thank you, ben Fos. I will anxiously await your arrival in Talala Fouz, and I hope there we might have more time to talk. Forgive me for now, but I must compose a letter to the viceroy of Batana Mar Din for you to deliver."

"Of course."

I am so smooth and graceful. Kav Mit Par should have seen that exit; the boy could stand to learn a thing or three from me.

Every day that I don't wantonly mash my face against Mak's is a victory. I would rather nurture my impossible longing than act on it and be crushed like autumn leaves underfoot.

At Batana Mar Din, I give ben Fos letters for the viceroys on the Banighel River and another for Jes Dan Kuf.

"Hurry if you can, but leave nothing undone. I would like to hear news of the beast callers as soon as you can manage."

He performs that bow again, hand over his heart, and mine practically melts. Leaving him hurts; the ship is quite lonely with him and all the treehouse staff gone. It is only my staffers and me continuing on to Talala Fouz, together with a cargo of building supplies being shipped up from Pont. Some of it is for our own use, to reestablish our embassy there, but the rest will be sold to the city for their own rebuilding efforts.

It is a cold, withering truth I must confront, that my days ahead will be filled far more with Melishev Lohmet than with Mak Fin ben Fos. Such is the patch of garden in which I must grow.

I'll see ben Fos for a brief time when he gets there, then he'll have to leave once more, sailing up the West Gravewater, building tea treehouses in all the river cities. He will make one last visit in Talala Fouz before he returns to Forn, and after that, I'll likely never see him again.

Canopy first, I remind myself; clan second; and myself last.

"And while that was going on," Fintan said in transition, "matters escalated in Khul Bashab . . ."

He took the seeming of Viceroy Bhamet Senesh.

Bhamet

The shitsnake of Hashan Khek, Melishev Lohmet, is now my king. King Kalaad the Unwell, they're calling him. I'm more surprised at the sudden vacancy, however, than at his ability to slither onto the throne. Winthir Kanek losing his blasted mind and setting his fury loose in

Talala Fouz was not a scenario I had anticipated. This is the year of unpleasant surprises, apparently.

According to the Raelechs, who had a bard in the room when it happened, the meltdown was all over his daughter and his desire to see her married to his political advantage. I will call that Exhibit B in my ever-expanding file of Why Marriage Is a Bad Idea, my parents retaining their place at the top as Exhibit A.

I already know from Melishev's responses to my requests for help that he holds no love or respect for me. If I don't wipe out these beast callers soon with my meager resources, I can expect to be replaced. Melishev didn't appear to be concerned by the threat these kids posed to the throne when he wasn't sitting on it, but I suspect that will change, if it hasn't already. The only chance I have of holding on here is to take care of the problem myself.

Captain Khatagar has made himself scarce around the tower lately, since he's hyperaware that if I see his face, I'll ask him about the elusive beast callers. When he finally does show up, he interrupts a fervid and rather humid report from Patriarch Dhanush Bursenan that attendance in the church has dropped every week since rumors of the beast callers began. The priest finishes with the indignant air of someone who expects me to do something.

"Like I told you before, Dhanush, it's past time for the church to make up some new shit," I say.

"What if it makes more people leave?"

"And what if it makes them come back? From what you're telling me, they're leaving anyway."

"It would be more helpful if the Sixth Kenning were not real," he says. "Then we wouldn't need to come up with some alternative to long-held beliefs."

"Again, Patriarch, you're complaining to the wrong guy. Denying reality is the church's business."

His sweat glands practically ejaculate in anger as he trembles and takes a breath to respond, but I cut him off with a grin.

"You see what I did there? I turned that back around on you. You were trying to be critical and I shoved it down your soup hole. I'm quicker on my feet than you and I'm sitting on my ass right now."

That's when Captain Khatagar appears, saving the patriarch from having to reply. It's just as well.

"We found one of them," he says as soon as he bursts into the room, confident that I'll know who he means—and I do, since there's nothing else on my mind except those kids. "Would you like to be present for the interrogation?"

"I would." I heave my bulk out of the throne and nod at good ol' Threat Sweat as I descend the stairs. "Pardon me, Patriarch. Urgent business. Ask for a towel on the way out, though. Looks like you're about to drown in your robes there."

He gurgles impotently at me as I pass. Everything about the man is wet somehow. His socks must be practically weaponized by the end of the day. I'll have to give him something plush and dry to make up for abusing him, though. Maybe a curly high-plains alpaca he can rub up against every few minutes. Or maybe send him a case or two of those marinated eels he likes. I do need the church on my side, and I don't need to eat any more of those things. My waistband's tight enough as it is.

I match strides with Captain Khatagar as we follow the labyrinthine twists and turns of the palace that lead to the dungeon entrance.

"Wait until we get in there to talk," I tell him. "Words are fair game around here."

"Understood."

I'm grinning as the captain opens the entrance to the dungeon and waves me in. Dungeons are such happy places. They're dark, dank, sepulchral, and full of secrets. Like what I do to prisoners before I have their bodies dumped on the plains and the things they tell me before they scream and whimper their last.

The air is thick with fear and mold and the lingering aromas of various excretions of the body. Normally I don't want to smell such things, but if they weren't present in a dungeon, I'd be disappointed. A pine-fresh scent in a subterranean space designed for terror, punishment, and death would be highly inappropriate. Once the door is properly barred behind us and we descend to the bottom of the stairs, where the guard station is, I tell the guards to go check on something far away and give them some time to get out of range before I nod at Khatagar.

"Tell me, quietly."

"We got a tip from a regular informant who frequents the slaughterhouse district. Took some work, but a team followed up and brought him in."

"Casualties?"

"One dead."

"Give every member of that team a hazard bonus, and double for the dead man's family."

"Done."

"What have you found out so far?"

"Nothing except that he shaved his head."

I winced and shivered in disgust. In a society that prized long hair, shorn skulls were horrors, and I wasn't immune to the prejudice. "Where's he at?"

"Cell five."

"Come on." I set out for the cell, fumbling for keys at my belt.

"Wait, Viceroy. There's more."

"Can't I just find out as we go along? I want to see what a beast caller looks like."

I open the door to cell five to find a filthy urchin staring back at me. He's shirtless and starving, his ribs clearly defined, dark circles of exhaustion under his eyes. His arms and legs are tied to a chair. The shaved head is a patchy job done inexpertly with a knife, since chunks of it are longer than others. His skin is smeared with splotches of brown and black, and his personal odor is an instant winner for Worst of the Dungeon.

"Tits on toast, man, why does he smell like that?" I say, gagging as Khatagar enters behind me. "Did he shit himself?"

"In a manner of speaking, I guess he did. They found him in the sewer, and he had gone down there of his own free will. It was no wonder we couldn't find him."

"How did you find him and not the others?"

"Informant saw him ducking down a hole last night. He was sleeping not far up the tunnel from there. The others might be still down there somewhere."

"I presume you have people looking?"

"Yes."

The boy's eyes flicker at that, but I see no changes around his mouth. It is just a flash of something, a hint of a reaction, but I'm not sure what it signifies.

"Good. So which one is this?"

"This is the one who has an affinity for serpents."

"Oh, the one who had the stripe of yellow hair? So that's why he shaved it. I see. And is this room, uh . . . snakeproof?"

"I think so. No vents. Door seal is tight. The drain in the floor," he says, as he points to it in the center, "is grated with small circles. You might get roaches and other bugs coming up, but nothing bigger than that."

"Very well. What's your name, boy?"

His voice is conversational, even confident, like we're sharing drinks and a nice cheese plate near the market instead of beginning an interrogation in the dungeon. No trace of fear or even nervousness. "Sudhi. What's yours?"

"Viceroy Bhamet Senesh."

"Oh, yeah? So maybe you can tell me why I'm here. I didn't do anything wrong."

"You killed a guard."

"No, I didn't."

"Yes, you did. Witnesses say one of your snakes bit his face and he died."

"That much is true, but it's also true that it's not my fault. You come up all threatening to a viper and it's going to defend itself. I didn't tell the viper to do it. Guard brought it on himself. More like he committed suicide."

"And the guard who got stung to death by bees committed suicide too?"

"I didn't see that happen until it was over. But, look, that wasn't me either. I've not done anything to you, and I haven't broken any laws. And if I'm living in the sewer, you can't exactly call me a drain on city resources, heh heh. Little plumbing joke there. You like it? I got lots of those."

"You think this is amusing?"

"Jokes are amusing to most people. Being tied up and beaten isn't so much, if that's what you mean. Those are different things, though."

"Why were you in the sewers, Sudhi, if you did nothing wrong?"

"Well, I expected to be tied up and beaten at some point, you know? Have my word questioned. And, wow, here we are."

Khatagar growls at him, "Look, boy, if you thought you were in deep shit in the sewer, you have no idea what you're in now."

"Oh, I think I have a very good idea, Captain. I'm not ever going to see the sun again. Never going to be free. Going to die down here, sooner or later. I'm thinking sooner since you need to show people there's no saving them from you, not ever. That's really why I'm here. Not because you care about your guards at the gate. You only care that we made you look weak without even trying."

Khatagar punches him in the gut and then follows up with a right hook to the jaw. I shake my head at the captain before he does any more. I wouldn't have ordered that; the words didn't bother me. For one thing, the kid was right about all of it. He's a sharp one. But I guess Khatagar doesn't like being called weak. Good to know.

The kid wheezes and spits blood, and I wait until he's recovered enough to answer more questions.

"So let me get this straight. You're probably going to die down here—your words, not mine—and you don't care?"

"I do not."

"Why?"

"I was ready to die when I went for the seeking, Viceroy. Everybody who went was ready for the same thing. They *sought it out,* hence the term *seeking,* right? Because that's the kind of city you're running here. You have hundreds, maybe thousands, in the streets, living without joy or even hope of joy, backs bent under the bootheels of rich folks, waiting for that extra ounce of pressure that will finally crush them and end it. That's the way the system's built. And when I got blessed, I saw right away that there's still no room for me in that system. I still have to live under your fancy boot. Well, I'm not playing that game. None of us will. So you either change the game and play with us, or we'll change it for you and you'll be out."

I laugh at him. "You can't change anything tied to a chair in a dungeon."

"I don't mean me personally. I know I'm done. Congratulations, you got the weakest and the dumbest of us. And I don't think I'm really all that dumb."

"No, you're not," I admit. "You're seeing things pretty clearly. Perhaps you can help me with my vision."

Bloody drool dangles from one corner of his lips as he twists them to one side. "How delightful. Do tell me. How may I aid your metaphorical sight, Viceroy?"

"Where is the source of the Sixth Kenning?"

"The source changes both location and the animals that deliver it every few weeks. When we went to our seeking, it was bloodcats in a grove of nughobes south of here. Right now it's giant fish spiders upriver from Hashan Khek. Tomorrow it moves to a troop of golden baboons in the north."

"How do you know this?"

"Once you're blessed, you sense the location of the next source."

"So this boy who found it first found it accidentally. There was no way he could have known that the Sixth Kenning was there at that time and place."

"That's right. And now he's safely out of your reach. He can organize seekings until there are too many of the blessed to eliminate. Just in case you were thinking you could make this all go away."

He might be out of my reach, but if Melishev got hold of him he wouldn't be safe at all. "What was he doing in a nughobe grove?"

"He didn't share that with me."

"Did he share with you his confrontation with my cavalry?"

"He didn't have to. I was there. Your guys threatened to shoot him because he didn't want to come back—which was stupid, because your city watch has no legal standing in the plains—and the lieutenant or whatever he was let fly. A kid stepped in front of the bolt and died. Then the lieutenant says to the rest of them that they should just kill us all to cover up his murder. Abhi got mad."

"He got mad?"

"Yeah. And then the animals reacted. Wasps and flying ants and everything. Killed them all, and they deserved it. They were your guys. Murderers."

The captain sucks at his teeth and draws his fist back. "You little—"

"Khatagar, please. He's being cooperative."

"Yeah, Khatagar, please. Thanks for reminding him of the rules of engagement, Viceroy. You leave poor folks alone as long as they cooperate in their own slow deaths or don't annoy your rich friends. But your men jump to violence at the slightest disagreement." His gaze drops from mine and he glares at the captain. "Wait until I stop cooperating, murderer. Then you can bravely beat up a malnourished boy who can't defend himself."

Khatagar's eyes sparkle with hatred. "I'm going to enjoy it. Stop cooperating anytime."

"Tell me about your friends," I say. "Tamhan Khatri. And the one they call Hanima."

He laughs and grins. "There you go, Captain. You didn't have to wait long, eh? That was quick. You evil bastards can go fuck yourselves."

Khatagar doesn't wait for my order. His fist hammers into the kid's body and face. Teeth fly. Blood splatters on the floor and walls. The captain's knuckles are quickly sheathed in red. I have to remind the captain that we still need answers out of the boy.

When he finally pauses, both of them are short of breath, though Sudhi is much worse for the wear. He has to have cracked ribs, shattered cheekbones, and most definitely a broken nose and perhaps a broken jaw.

The kid peers at the captain through an eye that's half swollen shut, and a coughing, bloody chuckle escapes his lips. "That was it? You weak, pathetic piece of shit." Contempt curdles in his tone, and Khatagar loses it.

We roar together in concert, he in his rage and me trying to stop him, but he's too fast, and I realize too late that the kid is even smarter than I thought and he saw Khatagar's soft spot at the same time I did. Khatagar snaps his neck with a twist and dull pop, and that abruptly ends my chances to extract any more information from him.

"Captain!"

"What?"

"We still don't know the other girl's name. We were going to find that out from him later, along with anything else we wanted to know, after a pleasant afternoon of slow torture."

"Oh." His dark, brooding glare changes as it sinks in that he has ruined everything. "I'm sorry, Viceroy."

"I didn't even have time to get my pincers out. The ceremonial unveiling of the instruments, that exquisite hitch in the breath as they gaze upon the steel and think of what I'm going to do to them, the sweet, sweet begging—we're not going to get any of that."

"I'm sorry," he says again, and there's a note of fear in it this time. Most viceroys are too squeamish to do their own torturing and they hire it out, though they say that it's because they're too busy to waste time on it or that they have more important things to do. But exerting pressure, finding leverage, squeezing what you need out of people—that's what leadership is all about. And there's nothing more important, in my view, than improving one's leadership.

"He manipulated you into killing him. Easily. Do you see that?"

"I do now, yes."

"Good. I want you to think on it and what you can do to prevent that from happening in the future. But in the future, regarding these kids, if you find any more of them, you will fetch me and let me handle everything, is that understood?"

"Yes, Viceroy."

"The person who tipped you off about his whereabouts: Did you pay them?"

"Yes."

"Pay them again. Triple. And relay my personal thanks."

"I will."

"And this is your mess. You clean it up. Don't delegate it either. Do it personally."

"I will. I apologize for my lack of control. It won't happen again."

"Good. And call off the search of the sewers."

"All right. But just so you're aware, we've only searched a fraction of them."

"The girls won't be down there. This kid was smart. He wanted us walking around in shit for weeks, searching for the others. I bet he even allowed himself to be seen so he'd get caught and we'd be convinced they were down there too."

"Why?"

"That I don't know, except that he wanted us to waste our time. Perhaps to give them time for something else."

"Like what?"

"We need to find that out. But we did find out that the Sixth Kenning isn't firmly established yet. We can't do anything about the hunter boy who got away. That's the king's problem now. But we can do something about the other two. And that Khatri boy. Listen carefully, Sambhav."

"Yes?"

"I'm going to let Khatri's father know that Sudhi is dead. He will tell Tamhan."

"And then Tamhan will run to tell the others and we'll have them."

"Precisely. So double your watch on him after you're finished here."

"Yes, Viceroy."

The swell of boos and jeers that came from the crowd was not for Fintan but for the viceroy. How, I wondered, did Fintan become privy to that scene in the dungeon? He moved on before anyone could ask him.

"Meanwhile, not far away, Hanima and Adithi were about to meet some important allies. . . ."

Hanima was better dressed this time. It was still simple clothing, but it was clean and everything looked to be her size.

Something has grown near the middle of the city amid news that Talala Fouz got burned down by a giant and that there's a new king, who used to be a viceroy in Hashan Khek. That news is far away, but this tree is, like, *kapoom!* In my face. In everyone's face. It's a truly enormous thing that wasn't there yesterday. One of the Fornish clans has sent a greensleeve and a bunch of their people to create a teahouse in a treehouse, and accelerating the growth of this tree was an astounding demonstration of the Fifth Kenning.

Adithi and I don't care about the risk: We have to go check it out.

We raid the closet of the house we're in, promising each other that we are only borrowing these clothes for a disguise. We even find boots that fit, and when we step out, hair all shining and combed, we look

like we have money. We do have a few coins passed from Tamhan onto
us through Khamen Chorous, so we can buy tea if we want.

That proves to be handy. There are some wee Fornish people in
maroon waistcoats at the base of the tree who welcome paying customers to be the first to experience the Red Pheasant Teahouse, but
they want to make sure people are intending to buy something before
they ascend the tree. There's a large throng of people gawking up at
the huge thing, and I don't blame them, but the line of people actually
willing to pay is rather small.

Once we jingle our purses at the barkers, they grin at us and hand us
off to another Fornish person in a waistcoat, who gives us a quick orientation. She has blond hair cropped super short—mine is considered
short, but she's one step up from scalp stubble. I wonder what it must
be like to just wake up and have nothing to do to your hair. I often hear
that people from other cultures envy us our long locks; that is a point
of pride, no doubt, but I think sometimes, on very rare occasions, we
secretly envy them for not having any to speak of.

"Hi. I'm Val Tan Vol. Is this your first time at one of our tea treehouses?"

We nod at her and this makes her happy, because she burbles,
"You're in for a treat! We have ten tea landings for the public that you
can reach by following the steps made out of living branches. They're
completely safe and will hold your weight, but of course watch your
step. Just look for someone in a maroon waistcoat at any of the landings and they'll get you seated. We ask that you don't try to go into any
of the roped-off areas up higher. Our clan also lives in this tree, and
those are our private residences. Any questions?"

"Yes. What if we need to, uh, you know, go?"

"We have facilities on every landing."

"Wow. Great."

"Enjoy!" Val gestures ahead and leaves us to go greet someone else.

We climb the steps and marvel at how it smells, how it looks, the
flowering vines draped around the trunk, and the birds already enjoying the shelter and chirping about it. We circle the trunk a couple of

times on our way up to the first landing, and it already has us far above everyone's heads below. We can see the underside of several landings above us, and we're told at the first three landings that they're already full and we'll have to keep climbing. We see small knots of people on these landings, enjoying cakes and sandwiches and tea, and I wonder where the kitchen is and where the water's being boiled. Presumably starting a fire in a tree would not be a good idea.

Halfway up to the fourth landing, we see a greensleeve. Or, rather, I do—Adithi's looking at the landing we're headed to. This fellow is standing elsewhere in the canopy, higher up to our right. He's a handsome white man with dark hair and a few days' whiskers on his jaw. Superb waistcoat, and dark pants that end at the knees because below that he has mushrooms growing on the bark of his shins. And similar bark grows on his forearms, except there I see moss and the red and yellow blossoms of tiny little iceplants. He is damn beautiful, and I guess the imagery leaks through to my hive along with some sense of my opinion, because I get this overwhelming response from them and I vocalize it without thinking.

"I want to pollinate him," I announce.

"What? Who?"

"Nectar! I mean nothing."

"Hanima? Whoooo? Oh. I see. Oh, my, yes. Good call."

"He's like. Wow. I, uh. Eeeeee!"

Adithi pats me on the shoulder a couple of times. "It's okay. You don't have to put it into words. I understand. But, hey, greensleeves are kind of important. People in Forn listen to them. We should talk to him about the Sixth Kenning."

"What do you mean?"

"Maybe he can get the clans to put pressure on the viceroy to accept us. You know. Diplomatic shit."

"Ohhh. I think you're right. Look at the older guy next to him."

"Which guy?"

"The one in the full-on fancy green robe with swirlies and stuff on it."

"Oh! I think those are vines. He kind of blended in. What about him?"

"I bet he's important. You can tell because he's wearing fancy clothes next to a greensleeve."

Some people behind us loudly clear their throats to let us know we are blocking traffic. We get moving.

"So let's do it," Adithi whispers. "Let's go talk to them."

"Fine. But how? They're like three levels up, and these stairs and bridges aren't heading that way."

"We ask someone Fornish."

Adithi hails the next Fornish person wearing a maroon waistcoat when we make it to the next landing.

"Hello," she says, smiling at us. "We have one table left on this landing. Did you want to be seated or continue on up?"

"We'd like to see the greensleeve who's up a few levels," Adithi says, trying to keep her voice low. "It's about the Sixth Kenning." The Fornish woman's smile melts like cheese on a sandwich. I think that might mean I'm hungry. The food they're serving with the tea smells wonderful, and it's difficult to think of anything else.

"I beg your pardon? You mean the Fifth Kenning?"

"No, I mean the Sixth Kenning."

The woman gives a tiny shake of her head, her eyes blinking rapidly. "There is no Sixth Kenning."

We blink back at her and then Adithi says, "Forgive me for asking, but might you be new in town?"

"Yes. I just arrived from Forn."

"Okay. That explains it. The Sixth Kenning is real, and I am positive the greensleeve will want to hear what we have to say." The woman looks like she's about to call security when Adithi adds, "This is for the good of the Canopy and your clan. I swear to Kalaad." That widens her eyes and changes her mind.

"Wait here, please. I'll make inquiries on your behalf."

She springs away from us and takes a running jump at the trunk, leaping right over the safety ropes that confine us and make us feel like we're not going to topple to our doom. She moves quickly and surely among the boughs, making leaps to handholds and branches that would kill me if I tried it, until she's out of sight a few seconds later, high above our heads.

People nearby gasp at her exit and then look at us as if we did something terrible, and we smile reassuringly and pretend that was all totally normal.

"There's one table on this landing," I tell them. "Enjoy."

They don't look like they enjoy hearing me talk, so I decide to stop there.

"This is going to be fine," Adithi whispers to me, "but just in case it isn't, get ready to run."

"Where?"

"Away. Or down first, and then away."

But the Fornish woman returns after a few minutes and asks us to follow her. She doesn't expect us to leap around the trees the way she did, thankfully, but leads us on a serpentine path upward, using some paths among boughs that were blocked off to the general public. Soon we're in the presence of the greensleeve and the man in the green robe, on a landing that's lush with flowers and birds, and they look a bit confused.

"Hello," the robed man says. He's got sandy hair that curls a bit away from his brow and he's tried to grow it long like a Nentian, but I don't think it's working out for him very well. But he has rather startling blue eyes, kind and patient, and I guess I could talk to those and pretend he's bald. "I'm Jes Dan Kuf, ambassador to Khul Bashab, and this is Mak Fin ben Fos of the Red Pheasant clan. Who might you be?"

"We're here to talk about the Sixth Kenning," Adithi replies, leaving out our names.

"Right, I understand. But you're not who we were expecting."

Adithi and I exchange a look of confusion.

"Who were you expecting?" I ask.

"They were expecting me," a voice says behind us. I turn and see it's our friend.

"Tamhan!" I cry, and not caring a bit, I run to him and crush him in my arms. He grunts in surprise or maybe I hurt him a little bit, but I don't care. "This is the best! How lucky that you're here!" My smile falters a bit as I pull back from the hug and get a better look at his face. He's tired, with half circles like upside-down mushroom caps floating underneath his eyes.

"Luck has nothing to do with it. I had an appointment," he replies. "But glad as I am to see you, I can't say that it's lucky. I'm followed everywhere now. We won't have much time before someone from the city watch interrupts us. You shouldn't be here."

"Is this . . . ?" Jes asks, his eyebrows climbing up his face, waggling a finger at us.

"Yes," Tamhan replies. "This is Hanima and Adithi, blessed with the Sixth Kenning."

A lot of smiling and bowing happens after that, and then the ambassador assures us that we won't need to worry about being seen or interrupted without warning by the city watch.

"How can you guarantee that?" Adithi says.

Jes looks to the greensleeve, who has spoken very little to this point except to exchange greetings. "Mak will make sure of it." The greensleeve nods, then tendrils or shoots or something come out of his silverbark shins and pierce or kiss the platform of tree boughs underneath it. And shortly thereafter, the foliage and branches of the massive tree move and grow to completely surround us. No one can see us from any angle when he's finished, but while it's happening we stand there slackjawed. The ambassador explains, "We're on Fornish embassy soil here. The city watch can't just barge in. My staff will stall and delay, and when they can't reasonably do so any longer, they'll warn us and we'll get the two of you hidden. Tamhan happens to be here on legitimate business, so don't worry."

I swing around with a question in my face, and Tamhan grins back at me. "I'm here to negotiate the sale of some choice chaktu meat on behalf my father."

That relaxes me somewhat. Soon enough the Fornish have us seated at a table and chairs made of living wood that grows right in front of us, and we're brought tea and cakes. I can't believe how cool it all is. And Mak is even better-looking up close than he was from afar. I feel a buzz humming inside me and I don't know how much of it is the hives and how much of it is my own silly body. I know he must have someone who loves him already, and I am way too young for him anyway, but looking at him makes me happy, so I am going to enjoy it.

We spend a little bit of time proving that we are the real deal—or, rather, I do. Adithi can't reasonably be expected to summon horses up a tree. But I name the insects within my reach that I can call to my hand, and in a few minutes they all arrive and patiently line up on my arm: honeybees, hornets, and wasps of several different kinds.

"Impressive," Jes Dan Kuf says. "Would you be able, in theory, to travel with a hive or many hives, pollinating fields as needed?"

"Easily," I answer. "I traveled with a feral hive all the way here."

"Extraordinary," Mak says, and I feel myself flushing underneath his gaze. "Think of how our countries could prosper together with the combined power of the Fifth and Sixth Kennings."

"I've been thinking quite a bit about it," Tamhan replies. "But, unfortunately, the leadership of Ghurana Nent seems opposed to the Sixth Kenning taking hold."

"I see. Could you inform me of their position as you see it?"

"Viceroy Bhamet Senesh either wants them dead or in a dungeon. I don't know how the other viceroys or this new king is going to feel about it."

The two Fornish men exchange a look and the ambassador replies, "Probably the same, alas."

"So we need a new government," I say, thinking it's the obvious thing, but the silence that falls afterward lets me know that I might have said something halfway to fully stupid. The ambassador's fingers twitch, realizing he has to say something.

"Ah. Yes, well. The Fornish government cannot directly support a rebellion. You understand we cannot get involved in your internal politics. If we support a rebellion and it fails, then our country will suffer retribution from this current government. We can't take that risk."

"Why are we here, then?"

"Well, it's a safe place to meet," Tamhan points out.

"Oh, yeah."

"And we can talk, theoretically, about ideas in the abstract," Jes says, and Mak looks visibly surprised. The ambassador presses on. "The question is, if you don't think your current government is working satisfactorily to serve your people's needs, what do you think a new government should be for? Ours is to protect the Canopy's resources, then the rights and prosperity of clans, and then the individual. The Kaurians emphasize education and trade and promote peace. The Raelechs, like us, are also protective of their resources and focused on the security of their borders. The Brynts prioritize public health above all—the withdrawal of their hygienists from every other nation proves that."

"Right now the government is supposedly protecting us from the animals of the plains," Tamhan says. "But the Sixth Kenning would make that obsolete."

"A government should help and support its most vulnerable people," I declare. "Not merely protect them from outside violence with a wall. The poverty we see down by the river should not be possible."

Tamhan nods.

"Some basic housing and income, then?" Jes says. "Admirable. Have you thought of how you will pay for that?"

His question is so predictable and frustrating that I clench my fists. "Why is it that people always question how we'll pay for doing good things for our people but never question how we'll pay for war? No, that's rhetorical, Ambassador. The attitude is that war is a necessity but helping people is not, and I cannot disagree more. The purpose of our government is to help people. We simply *must* do it, so we will find the funds to make it happen, magically if necessary, the way money for war is always magically found. Let that satisfy you."

Before the ambassador can answer, someone calls through the dense wall of leaves, "Ambassador Kuf, the captain of the city watch is here and insists that we have a surveillance subject in our custody. He's demanding to see him."

Tamhan shoots me an apologetic look. "Sorry."

"All right, bring him up, but take these extra dishes with you. It must look like only ben Fos and I have been here." The ambassador gestures to Adithi and me to rise. "Quickly. Mak will hide you behind some leaves and you can listen in, but obviously you must make no sound no matter what you hear."

The greensleeve uses the shoots on his legs again to communicate with the tree, and the branches that made our woven seats untangle and flatten back into the floor of the platform. We're ushered toward the trunk, and a screen of branches and leaves moves in front of us.

Once it's all settled, we hear some movement from the other wall of foliage, and a strange voice speaks. It sounds like a bubble of snot is trying to pop in his throat but it's too tough to die and thus he sounds perpetually half strangled and pissed off about it.

"Ah, there you are. What are you doing here?"

The ambassador replies, "Welcome, Captain Khatagar. This young man was just taking our order for chaktu meat. How can we help you?"

"Here on business, eh?" the snot-choked voice says, presumably the captain.

"Yes, sir."

"Well, go on back to your father and get to it, then."

"Of course. Ambassador, Khatri Meats thanks you very much for your order. You'll hear from us shortly."

They make farewell noises and Tamhan's footsteps retreat, but the captain's do not.

"Was there anything else?" Ambassador Kuf asks.

"You'd be well advised not to consort with that boy," the captain replies. "He's a troublemaker, you know?"

"No, I wasn't aware. It was our understanding that Khatri Meats supplies the viceroy himself, the very sustenance that your watch consumes. Was I misinformed?"

"No, the father is fine. But that boy is not to be trusted. You'd best steer clear of him from now on. You wouldn't want the viceroy to think that you're not to be trusted either."

"I'm not sure I understand. Why is he untrustworthy?"

"He's a known associate of some kids who killed some of my men."

"Oh, sun and stars! Kids, you say?"

"Vicious kids. Two girls and a boy. We got the boy and won't have to worry about him anymore." Adithi and I both clasp our hands over our mouths to keep from crying out. The captain could only be referring to Sudhi, because Abhi isn't here. No wonder we haven't heard from Sudhi! The captain continues, "But the girls are still out there, and we think he might be communicating with them somehow."

"I see. Thank you for explaining."

When the captain takes his leave and the screen of branches moves aside, I see that Adithi is silently weeping like I am.

"They got Sudhi," she says.

"I know." I sniffle and catch the ambassador's blue eyes with mine. "We are not vicious kids. We don't want to hurt anybody. We want to help."

"I know. I believe you," Ambassador Kuf says, and I believe him too. "Come back and sit. Let's have some tea. Consort with us all you want. Let's talk about Sudhi and how we can keep you safe. Or we can talk about how we can use our power to help people."

It is so strange to hear someone with any sort of power say that.

I'd like to change things so that it's not strange at all.

Hanima got applause for that ending, and Fintan promised everyone a momentous meeting in the north tomorrow.

It was a vast comfort to me—and to all Brynts—that Rölly used his power to help people. And I don't believe I am just saying that as his friend. It's been abundantly clear that his government has been doing all it can to ease the suffering of the refugees and survivors of the invasion. Recalling all the hygienists, for example, to keep this vast collection of people—inside and outside the walls—from falling prey to disease. The Fornish ambassador was correct in saying that we do focus on health above all, for nothing else is possible without that. But Hanima was also correct in saying that it shouldn't be strange for a person in power to help people.

THE NORTHERN

YAWN

When I showed up to the refugee kitchen to help in the morning, Chef du Rödal turned me away.

"Sweet of you to come back, honey, but there's no food."

"No food?" I repeated dumbly.

She shrugged. "I'm baking bread and that's it. We used up the last of the vegetables yesterday, so that's it until we get another shipment in."

"What about proteins? I know the pelenaut was going to try to do something about that."

"Oh, the pelenaut, eh? Know him personally, do you?"

"Yes."

The chef blinked. She'd been joking and hadn't expected that reply. "Well, he did do something. He mandated that a percentage of every fishing boat's catch must be sold at a steep discount to us. That doesn't make boat captains or restaurant owners in the city happy. It worked great for a few days—we got a little bit of everything and people wept because their kids got some protein—but, curiously, it hasn't worked for the past two. It's like the ocean's out of fish! Or someone's ignoring the pelenaut's decree. Or someone is hijacking it before it gets to us. If you want to help, honey, maybe go talk to your buddy the pelenaut and let him know what's going on. He might not know, and I don't have time."

"I will. Thank you."

We had made it through the winter by raiding everything we could—it wasn't quite enough, because the Eculans had raided food stores too. Imports covered some of the shortfall. But the winter crops that were normally sowed in the south of the country were never sowed, and the greenhouse operations we had in the city were never meant to feed such numbers. Planting time was coming, and I knew that Rölly was offering incentives to people to become farmers, and because of that we should be okay come harvest. But in the meantime there would be a long, lean spring and summer, and we'd be dependent on imports. The strain of losing so many cities and their supporting agriculture had finally caught up with us, despite Rölly's best efforts to anticipate and mitigate them. There were simply too many mouths to feed in this location. We didn't have enough to go around, and the people who could readily pay for the food in the city were obviously getting prioritized by producers.

I realized I didn't truly understand how food got distributed. My understanding of food was that somebody grew it or caught it or raised it and then magic happened and I was able to buy it.

Clearly something was wrong in the magic stages.

Since Rölly was busy in the Wellspring, I composed a note to be delivered to him and Föstyr, saying that something untoward was happening and the refugee kitchen wasn't getting any food. He had probably heard through other channels, but in case he hadn't, I couldn't let it slide.

I went down to the docks to see if I could learn anything, but all I really saw was that fishing boats were in or coming in and they had fish. But I didn't know if I was looking at normal, elevated, or substandard levels. I also didn't know who to talk to about the issue.

I met Fintan at the chowder house and saw immediately that there was something wrong there too: The chowder was extremely thin, mostly clam-flavored broth with a few nubbins of vegetables and very little actual meat. Here, at least, I could ask someone: my server. In the politest possible fashion, since it was not his fault.

"Sorry—I want to ask about your food supply, since the chowder seems a bit thin. Not being critical, because you have to work with what you got. Is what you're getting . . . normal?"

The server shook his head. "No, we're way down in most everything. We're good on salt and pepper and those little crackers and that's about it."

"What happened?"

Fintan and I were treated to an elaborate shrug and roll of the eyes. "What didn't happen? The pelenaut mandated a certain portion of every catch had to go to the refugees, so that reduced every restaurant's available supply right away. The fishermen had to up their prices to make up for the losses they were taking on the refugee sales. Then restaurants ordered less because they couldn't afford to pay more—or else they passed that cost on to customers. And then last night, some fishermen decided to just leave."

"Leave?"

"Yep. To Festwyf, which is being resettled, or to Setyrön, or even to Göfyrd, believe it or not, because that Raelech stonecutter the bard told us about is basically building free houses for everyone, so why not move there?"

"Why indeed? They're guaranteed to sell everything they catch here."

"But they don't want to sell part of it at a discount."

"Ugh. Okay, thanks. That makes sense." When the server left, I shook my head at Fintan. "Money." I told him how the refugee kitchen had not received anything in the past couple of days.

"If it's not getting anything, then it's not the fishermen who are the problem. It's money, like you said."

"What do you mean?"

"I don't know if this is exactly what's happening, but I bet it's something similar: Somebody's figured out that they can sell fish once to the government for refugees, steal it, then sell it again to restaurants and grocers at an even higher price because they can blame the refugee situation."

"Bryn save us. We're already in the abyss."

"You're a student of history, though, right? You know that whenever terrible decisions get made at the expense of a large group of people, it's because a smaller group of people stand to profit."

"Yes, I know. You're right." I felt so sad for Rölly at that moment. He'd tried to help and it sort of worked, but then people sabotaged his efforts. He hadn't taken greed into proper account. And he had so many decisions to make like that every day.

When, I wondered, would we get out of our own way?

With protein on our minds, Fintan's song was dedicated to fishmongers, though it was a lighthearted look at an occupational hazard. It was an up-tempo strum of a lute, which he'd stop before the last line of each verse and state, a cappella:

> *After spending all day*
> *In the sun and spray*
> *With the stink of fish*
> *I have just one wish,*
> *I have just one hope:*
> *A bath and a bar of soap.*

> *Fish guts everywhere*
> *Chunks of it in my hair*
> *What do I need, ya think*
> *To get rid of this stink?*
> *Only one way I can cope:*
> *A bath and a bar of soap.*

> *A fishblade's knife*
> *Is a part of my life*

So my friends know well
I've got a powerful smell
And I wouldn't ever say nope
To a bath and a bar of soap.

It was with some amusement that I observed some people during the applause tilt their noses down to their armpits to check the status of their personal funk. When the bard was ready to continue after the break, he said, "I've been waiting to share today's tales for a long time. It was a day that should rightly be recorded in the world's histories. Because of Olet Kanek, Koesha Gansu, and Abhinava Khose, the world is much bigger for all of us. What we learned that day—and what we still stand to learn—was made possible by them. Let's begin with Abhi."

We followed a river for a good while, every day seeming to get a bit chillier as we moved north, felling trees in a line that anyone could follow. I didn't know how rich the land was for farming, but it seemed to support a wide variety of plants and it was certainly abundant with wildlife. The resources would be fantastic if it weren't for the fact that many of the resources considered humans to be delicious.

Was this what it's like, I wondered, to be a chicken? It's not paranoia if everything really does want to eat you.

And then one day, as Fintan was telling me that some people in Rael actually like borchatta soup and there were little borchatta huts in a couple of Raelech cities peddling the world's stinkiest fish, shouts of joy and laughter ahead made us hurry to catch up to the front of the line.

The trees thinned, the river's mouth revealed itself, and there it was: the Northern Yawn, miles and miles of cold blue sea that would soon ice over—or so we imagined, anyway. Facts about the Northern Yawn were scarce, apart from the fact that it was there.

"We made it, kid!" Olet said, beaming an enthusiastic smile down at me. I think it might have been the first time I'd seen her truly happy, and it was infectious.

"We sure did."

We stood on a berm perhaps four or five lengths above a rocky beach; the river had fallen down somewhat steeply to the sea about a hundred lengths upstream before lazing the rest of the way, leaving us on something that wasn't exactly a cliff but wasn't a gentle slope either.

"I'm thinking this might be a pretty good spot—we have fresh water and we should be able to sail upriver to those falls, make a sheltered harbor there. Plenty of timber to work with. But I don't know. What do you think? Plenty of fish in the sea and critters around for us to eat?"

"I'd have to go down to the sea and put my feet in the surf to tell you about fish," I replied, "but as far as wildlife, yes, it's teeming around here, like everywhere else we've been."

"Would you mind dipping your tiny little toesies in there and doing that? I imagine everyone would like to know what we might find out there, since so little is known about the Northern Yawn."

"Only if you promise to never utter the phrase 'tiny little toesies' again."

"It's a deal, kid. I'm going to scout upriver by the falls a bit more closely and get your countrymen excited about building a city here. And naming it!"

I wondered when she'd decide I wasn't a kid anymore. Fintan said he'd head down to the shore with me, and a couple of the Hathrim wanted to come along. They had been fisherfolk back in Harthrad, before Mount Thayil erupted, and then again at Baghra Khek. They'd be fisherfolk here as well, they figured, as soon as they got a boat built. Their names were Karlef and Suris Burik, yellow-haired and blue-eyed folk with their pale skin tanned and wrinkled from spending years in the sun. They were perhaps a foot shorter than Olet, but that was still five feet taller than me. To them I guess my toesies really were tiny.

It took us a decent while to pick our way downhill and cross the beach, with Karlef making plans out loud to carve some steps into the hillside and fortify them with beams of wood so everyone could get to the beach easier.

The tide was out, revealing a large oyster bed and some tidal pools full of little creatures either trapped there or happy to remain even when high tide rolled in. Some nice-sized green-shelled crabs I'd never seen before skittered sideways away from us. They were probably super tasty. Suris commented on them and added them to a list of things she'd like to try. The oyster bed was a welcome discovery and would no doubt be visited soon. We finally got to some sand and surf and I pulled off my boots to wade in. Murr and Eep declined an invitation to join me, neither of them wanting to get wet. They remained safely outside the range of the surf.

"Ah, Kalaad!" I cried out as the first wave washed up on my legs.

"What is it?" Fintan said.

"Cold!"

The bard and the Hathrim laughed at me, but I ignored them and shivered, working my toes into the sand. Not wanting to get overwhelmed, I reached out with my kenning to just a few lengths, inquiring about what fish might be present. There were only a few, because my range was still in the shallows. I asked a bigger fish to jump out of the water just so we could see it, and it did, a shining silver wiggle that the Hathrim appreciated.

"Did you do that?" Karlef asked.

"Yeah."

"Are there more of them?"

"Probably. I need to look around some more."

Careful to limit my search to only fish and not other kinds of marine life, I tripled the area and discovered that there were plenty of fish in this cold sea. It dropped off a shelf and deepened quite quickly, in fact, where there were some huge species that a Hathrim would find difficult to wrestle aboard.

Crustaceans, check. Bladefins, check—several kinds.

Karlef interrupted me to say that there was a blur on the horizon to the right, which could be land.

"That might be an island over there," he said. "Could be a great place to build a fishing village. Might have an inlet or something for a proper harbor."

I turned to Eep, who looked so very out of place on the rocky beach. "Eep, feel like scouting a little bit? There might be an island over to the right. The northeast. Whatever. We'd like to know more about it. I'll ask you questions when you get back, like if you see any animals there."

She chirped an affirmative and took off. That let me return my attention to surveying this chunk of ocean. Next on my list: longarms.

There were a good number of them, yes indeed. Nothing remarkable there, until suddenly there was. Something ridiculously huge and sort of but not exactly like a longarm was moving to the west and rising from the depths at the same time.

"That's not normal," I thought, but apparently I said it out loud.

"What's that?" Fintan asked.

"This can't be real. Longarms don't get that big . . . unless. Unless it's a kraken. Could it be a kraken?"

"A kraken? There's a kraken out there?"

The Hathrim spat some kind of curse in their own language and I made a note to ask them what that meant later, because it sounded exactly like what I was feeling.

"I think so. It's in a hurry. Moving to the west and surfacing. And wait—there's another one coming!"

"You said it's surfacing? Krakens only surface for one thing, don't they?"

"I don't know, Fintan, I'm a hunter from the plains!"

"Well, I'm a bard from the mountains, but even I know what brings krakens to the surface!"

"A ship!" Karlef cried, pointing to the west. "See the sail just off the coast? It's headed for the ship!"

"Oh, Kalaad."

"You've got to stop it, Abhi! It's going to kill those sailors!"

"Who in the world is sailing up here?" I said. That ship hadn't been there when we first looked around from the top of the hill. It must have just sailed into view while we were making our way down to the beach.

"Save their lives and then you can ask them!"

"Right, right."

I shut my eyes to concentrate and tried to latch on to the mind of the huge thing that was similar to a longarm. It slipped through my efforts and kept moving toward the ship, because it wasn't exactly a longarm. It was the same trouble I'd had with gravemaws and toothy roos: Until I actually saw it and could attach some mental descriptors to it beyond "something like a huge longarm," my kenning was powerless. I was dealing with something unknown, and only its distant relationship to longarms had allowed me to sense its presence at all.

"I can't."

"What do you mean you can't? You have to! Those people are going to die!"

"I mean I can't! I've never seen a kraken before. But once I do see it, maybe then I can do something."

"By the time you see it they're going to be dead!"

"Maybe." I took off running through the surf, trying to keep my footing and my eyes on the sail. "Maybe not."

Murr kept pace with me; he probably didn't know what was going on, but if I was running somewhere, he was going to come along.

Fintan chased after us, and then Karlef and Suris followed. Suris said, "Can we help? Our stride is longer, and we might be able to carry you."

"Thanks, no," I called. "I need to keep my feet in the water to have a chance at making this work."

Though I could not have said what *this* was, exactly, except for a creeping sense of dread that I was about to watch a whole lot of people die in terror.

And judging by their ship, those people weren't from around here. That wasn't a Nentian craft, and it wasn't a Hathrim or a Fornish one either. I wasn't really used to seeing ships from the eastern lands on the river, so maybe it was Raelech.

"Is that a Raelech ship, Fintan?"

"That's no ship I've ever seen or heard of before," he said.

Something was bothering me about it—besides the fact that a huge creature was heading directly for it—and eventually I figured it out: The wind was at my back, but the ship's sails, coming at me from the opposite direction, were full to bursting. How was that possible, unless they had one of the Kaurian blessed on board?

It was a large craft, oceangoing for sure, and the hull was what gave it away as entirely foreign. It was painted or stained black—or perhaps the wood was naturally that color?—and swirling designs in red and white flowed back from the bowsprit on either side. It suggested that these people considered their watercraft to be works of art, not merely utilitarian transport.

I couldn't really see the people, however. Between the distance and the railings of the ship, I couldn't see a single sailor, except for one high up in the crow's nest. They wore clothing in dark blues and reds, but I couldn't tell much else. I had the merest hint of what they must be like, an incomplete picture not unlike the one I had of the kraken.

The beast introduced itself by shooting three incredibly long and slick black arms out of the water, smooth on the top and packed with purple round suckers on the bottom. I saw those arms for only an instant, as did the sailors on the boat, before they slammed down across the deck.

The effect was immediately devastating. Anyone under those tentacles had to be instantly crushed, since the actual lumber of the ship splintered. The vessel was effectively quartered and then torn up further as the tentacles withdrew; they didn't pass completely through the hull, but it was no longer a functioning watercraft.

And I was no longer playing with a blindfold of water. Those tentacles gave me an idea of the scale of the thing, a solid mental image, and my kenning finally recognized it as a kraken and not a sort-of long-arm.

"No! Stop!" I shouted, and even though my words couldn't possibly be heard by the creature, the sentiment nevertheless carried through the water, as my commands to creatures of the land carried through the air. The tentacles writhed above the ship, ready to slam down again, but instead they paused and then curled silently back into the deep. "Do not hurt any of the humans in the water!" I didn't see any but knew there had to be some—the person in the crow's nest, if no one else; they had been thrown out and fallen into the freezing ocean. "In fact, help them!" I said. "Get them to the surface, where they can breathe!"

Fintan and the Hathrim were saying things, and maybe some of them were to me, but I think most of it was curses of surprise and awe, the same sorts of words that were circling around in the back of my own mind.

"Help the people. Get them to the surface," I kept saying, and the tentacles emerged again, even as the remnants of the ship sank. This time, however, the arms were wrapped around flailing human forms, who were lifted out of the water and then dropped back into it, except that now they were closer to shore and they had a chance to take a deep breath of air. This process repeated itself as we kept running toward them, and I made sure to tell bladefins in the area not to eat any of the humans either. The second kraken arrived, and I recruited its help as well, so there were even more arms plucking people out of the sea and then dropping them closer to shore.

I hoped they could swim. Even those that could, I realized, might not make it. They still had to fight the tide and the cold and the shock of being attacked by a kraken, followed by the shock of being saved by one.

Something Fintan said finally got through to me as we ran. "Kaelin save me, but it was so *fast*," he breathed. "Those arms just rose up and—*wham!*"

I understood his surprise. I'd always thought krakens wrapped their arms around a ship and pulled it under the surface in a sort of deadly, watery hug, but instead what they did was just slap them down, creating a nearly instant shipwreck. And once the sailors were in the water, the kraken obviously had little trouble finding them. In the normal course of events, they would have been gathered up and fed to a cavernous beak.

We kept running to close the distance and help whoever made it to shore. Two sodden figures crawled out of the surf as we approached. They staggered to their feet and cast their eyes back at where their ship had been. They looked for other crew members fighting against the surf. And then they turned and saw us coming and they screamed, their voices indicating that they were women. I'm not sure if their reaction was because of the giants or because of Murr running alongside me. Each of them had two daggers tied to their belt and they pulled both of them out, adopting a stance that was quite clearly defensive and something they'd been trained to do. One of the daggers was straight-edged, and one was serrated.

"Hold up," I said, halting my advance and raising my hands. "We're freaking them out a bit. Murr, please sit here next to me so they don't think you're hungry."

"Yeah," Fintan agreed. "Let's look friendly." He called up to the Hathrim. "Karlef and Suris, try to seem tiny and nonthreatening."

"Are you joking?" Suris said. Then to Karlef, "Is he joking?"

Karlef and Suris were armed. We all were, with daggers at least. But they remained in their sheaths as we tried to communicate that we meant the women no harm and in fact we wanted to help. We said as much, but the women didn't seem to understand us. The few words they spoke sounded like nothing I'd ever heard either.

"Fintan, do you know what they're saying?"

"I have no idea. That's not a language from this continent. *They're* not from this continent. I mean, look at them."

I was looking. Their skin was similar to mine, except that where mine was a warm coppery hue, theirs had cool undertones to it. High cheekbones. Hair jet-black like that of Nentians, though they had theirs braided and pinned underneath maroon mesh caps hemmed in gold thread. The fact that they were still on top of their heads after that ordeal meant they must take extraordinary measures to secure them with pins and twine or something. They wore dark-blue jackets with gold buttons, and the lapels were edged in maroon that matched their hats. Their pants had a maroon stripe down the outside of the leg, and they wore knee-high leather boots tanned to a reddish brown.

They were disciplined. As more sailors crawled out of the Northern Yawn, exhausted and dripping, they immediately saw their crew confronting us and rushed over to back them up. We were soon outnumbered, facing a phalanx of desperate sailors with knives that they very clearly knew how to use.

Fintan observed aloud something about the crew that was unusual—apart from the fact that they weren't like any people we'd ever heard of before. "They're all women," he noted. "An all-woman crew of sailors from an undiscovered country, each wearing two long daggers. This is turning out to be a spectacularly interesting day."

They were having their own conversation as we had ours. It became clear that they were deferring to one in particular, who had a design of wavy lines embroidered in gold thread on her hat but was otherwise dressed identically to the others. This one sheathed her knives and stepped forward, looking at me. I don't know why she thought I was the leader. Maybe it was because of Murr.

She nodded once, then tapped her chest twice, just below the collarbone. "Koesha," she said.

I repeated the gesture and said, "Abhi," hoping that she was telling me her name and not demanding that I give her all my worldly goods or something.

The bard picked up on this and did the same, introducing himself as Fintan. The Hathrim were quick studies and followed suit.

Koesha pointed at each of us in turn and repeated the names, getting them a little wrong but close enough. We nodded and smiled and then she pointed at the bloodcat, raising an eyebrow in question.

"Murr." I knelt next to my friend and pointed at the woman. "Murr, this is Koesha. Will you please nod your head at her, or maybe raise a paw to say hello? That will show her you are friendly."

He did both, and a hushed whisper of awe and surprise trilled through the sailors. A couple of them visibly shivered.

I stood again and hugged myself, pantomiming a shiver. "Cold, yes? You should get warm. Will you come with us to camp?" I pointed toward the river mouth and the others quickly did the same, making various gestures to encourage them. Koesha watched us for a moment, taking in our expressions and body language, and then turned her back on us to face the others. She gave an order and the daggers disappeared.

Spinning around, she said my name and some other things after it and projected her right arm forward, palm up. It was the equivalent of "lead the way."

There were about thirty of them, all told, shivering there on the beach and dripping with salt water. They had lost who knew how many of their crew in the attack but had yet to show any grief.

That would come to them later, I knew. Grief could be delayed, but it always demanded its time.

Karlef ran ahead to inform Olet that we were coming with some unexpected guests.

I smiled at Koesha and tried to include everyone in my welcome. "Come on, Murr. Let's head back," I said. As I turned with the bloodcat toward what would be first a camp and later a city, I realized that

Eep had missed all the excitement with her scouting mission to the island. Perhaps she'd found something intriguing there too.

The Raelech bard switched his seeming directly to Koesha Gansu without comment.

Koesha

I pushed it too far. A week of sailing madly along the northern coast, always searching the shore for wreckage—Maesi's or anyone else's— and not a clue. Over another glass of wine, this time at midday, Haesha reminded me that it was time to turn back, using the timeline I'd set myself. My face must have revealed my thoughts.

"Look, I know you want to find your sister or a northern passage," she said. "But we're in dangerous territory here. Consider that returning home when no one else has is going to be a victory in itself. We can tell everyone that this continent exists and that something in the north has obviously taken our ships. But what might lie to the south? I bet no one has even gone that way, since we've all been looking for a northern passage."

I snorted. "I bet you're right."

"Let's come back next year and go south. You'll have no shortage of women volunteering to go once you demonstrate that you'll bring them home again and they'll be rewarded. Everyone wins."

"That's wisdom," I said, defeated. "Very well. So be it."

But then Leisuen knocked on the door and reported that an island had been spotted from the crow's nest. I immediately lobbied for a quick look at that, and Haesha sighed and agreed.

"I'll tell the crew we're looking at the island and then turning around."

"Fair enough."

And minutes later, three enormous tentacles shot up from the sea and clobbered my beautiful ship to flotsam. I immediately lost two-thirds of my crew—friends, classmates, many of them—and would have been lost myself if I'd been in the cabin. I was at the prow, how-ever, trying to get a peek at this rumored island, so I was shortly in the coldest waters I've ever felt and doubting my ability to survive it.

When a tentacle wrapped around my torso, I thought the end had come, but then it didn't. It lifted me to the surface, dangled me briefly over the sea, and dropped me back in, letting me swim to land.

And then, on this alien shore, we few survivors met the strangest group of people I've ever seen. Two giants with yellow hair and blue eyes, pale skin weathered by the sun; a brown-skinned man with a huge beak of a nose, some kind of jeweled band circling his right arm, and a stringed musical instrument strapped to his back; and an as-toundingly pretty young man who looks the most like us, with long dark hair and skin a warmer tone than ours, accompanied by a huge but apparently trained cat with disturbing red eyes.

We now trudge after them to some unknown location, shivering with cold in our wet clothes. I don't see a city or anything like it on the shore ahead, but they appear confident that they're leading us to some-place better.

"Do you trust these people?" Haesha asks me.

"No. But we have absolutely nothing except what's on our backs and belts. Our choices are to hope for their generosity or, failing that, take what we need."

"What do we need, Zephyr?"

I search her face for a challenge and find one there, but not the mu-tinous kind. It's the sort that a friend gives to clarify your thinking.

"We need to get warm and then secure food and shelter. We need to mourn the lost. And then we need to get home somehow. We can do that by making friends or by fighting. I'd prefer to make friends."

Haesha nods. "Aye, Zephyr."

We trudge a few steps in silence and then I mutter, "Go ahead and say it."

"You think I'm going to say we should have turned around?"

"Yes."

"No. You were right. Look at what we've found."

"What do you mean?"

"Krakens guard the northern passage. This place—*this* is where they go every summer. That's why no one has ever made it around the world."

I recognize the truth of it. "So the krakens took Maesi."

"Yes. And every ship before hers. And us too, though somehow we're not dead yet."

"And there are giants here."

"And red-eyed mega-kittens."

"And so much more. Joabei knows nothing of these things. We must get home."

"Yes. Somehow."

After another few moments and an involuntary chattering of my teeth, I add, "One step at a time. We will get there."

I've been trying not to think about the lost crew. It's almost easy right now, since we still have our own skins and these strange people to worry about. But there will be a quiet time ahead, a space in between our gasping breaths of just trying to survive, and then the grief, waiting its turn, will step in and spread itself out.

We will build a grand mourning tunnel for the lost, on the shore where we crashed. If we can fashion one, that is. Perhaps a hollowed-out bough will serve in lieu of fired clay, so that the wind can howl through it and keen for their lives. And inscribed on the base will be the individual names of our crew, as well as the names of Maesi and the captains of all the other ships we found carved into that rock in the west.

"Not everyone is going to agree that you made the right decision," Haesha added, interrupting my thoughts.

"I'd be surprised if they did," I replied. "I'll try to make it right. And make sure that they all get home."

The handsome lad with the huge cat turns out to have another friend: A raptor of some kind, feathers the color of sand, spirals in from the north and lands on his forearm before leaping nimbly to his shoulder. It's a gorgeous creature, with longer legs than most birds of prey I've seen, and while its feathers and wing shape don't look built for speed, it does appear to have the silent flight adaptations of an owl.

Falconry in the traditional sense is not all that surprising. But when the boy starts talking to the bird and it seems to reply via shakes or nods of its head, just as the cat did, I realize I'm not looking at a mere animal trainer here. There's something more going on. What was his name again?

"Obbeet?" I say, hoping that I'm getting it right.

He turns around, face expectant. I ask him if he's talking to the bird, pointing at it with one hand and making gabbling motions with the other.

He nods and says a word that might mean yes in his tongue. Then he introduces me in a roundabout way. He points first to himself and says, "Abhi," which means I'd gotten it wrong but was close. He points at me next and says my name correctly, increasing my embarrassment, then points at the bird and says, "Eep."

I raise my fist in greeting and bow my head, hoping I'm not making a fool of myself. "Hello, Eep." Abhi says something in his language— which I rather like the sound of, honestly, unlike some other languages from our part of the world—and the bird cocks its head at me, blinks, bobs its head a couple of times, and makes a noise that sounds remarkably like "Eep," its name. The boy turns and smiles at me, and it's kind and welcoming, not malicious or making fun. So I have done the right thing. And this boy, Abhi, can apparently talk to birds and cats.

"Zephyr, is that kid talking to animals?" Haesha says. "I'm only asking to make sure I'm not hallucinating."

"I think he is." A sudden thought makes my jaw drop, and I am left desperate to figure out how to ask him this question. He sees I want to communicate something and frowns. We both look down at the ground at the same time. There's no wood at all on the shore, but there are plenty of rocks. I bend to pick one up and kneel in the sand, gesturing to him to join me. He says something to Eep and the bird hops off his shoulder to stand on the ground, on the opposite side of the cat. Once the boy is kneeling next to me, with Haesha looking over my shoulder and the brown-skinned musician looking over his, I draw a wavy horizontal line in the sand with the rock's edge and then do my best to sketch some kraken tentacles emerging from it. I drop the rock, point to the tentacles, and make the same gabbling motion with my other hand.

"Did you talk to the kraken? Did you tell it to stop killing us?"

"Good question," Haesha says. "But he also might have told it to kill us in the first place."

"Maybe," I say, but keep my eyes on the boy. He makes clear through his gestures, nodding and pointing and pressing his palm out, which I think means stop, that he indeed communicated with the kraken— intervened, I suppose. Picking up my rock, he draws a tentacle wrapped around a stick-figure human and indicates that he told the kraken to lift us out of the sea.

"Sweet goddess," Haesha says. She had seen the same gestures and interpreted them as I had. "He saved us? This absurdly pretty man who wears his beautiful hair down can talk to krakens and make them leave us alone?"

"I think so."

"I would like to point out for the record that I saw him first."

Without thinking, I look up at her and laugh, because Haesha has been seeing men first as long as I've known her. But then I realize that our benefactors might think we're having a joke at their expense. I turn back to Abhi, horror-struck, and feel the heat rise in my cheeks as I struggle to explain, even though I know he doesn't understand a word I'm saying.

"I wasn't laughing at you," I tell him, pointing at Haesha and shaking my head, hoping he'll understand somehow.

"Oh, shit!" Haesha cries, realizing we've spit into the wind. "Diplomatic fuckup!" She plops to her knees next to me and prostrates herself in apology, and I do the same. I hear the rest of our crew drop down and follow our lead, because when the zephyr and first mate do something, you damn well better do the same.

Thank Shoawei and the twelve winds, I think they understand that we did not mean to insult them. Both Abhi and the brown-skinned man make noises, and when I peek up they're encouraging us to stand, and they're smiling. Even the giant man, way up near the sun, is smiling at us. He doesn't look hungry, so that's good. What was his name again? Karl-off? I am terrible at names. I think the brown fellow is Fintum.

I nod at Abhi and shiver involuntarily as I get to my feet. It's not warm up here in this northern air, and my wet clothes aren't helping. They motion at us that we should continue on. They point ahead and say some words. It looks like they want us to go inland.

We nod agreeably and follow. Haesha waits a few steps before saying anything.

"Zephyr," she whispers as the bird flies back up to roost on Abhi's shoulder. "That man must be blessed with the fabled Sixth Kenning."

"It would appear so."

"A person who can talk to krakens can go anywhere they want. Sail any ocean at any time of year."

"True. Which makes me wonder why he's here, of all places."

"Huh. That's a good point. This is the most extraordinary day. The sort you'll remember for the rest of your life, however long it lasts."

"Yes."

Haesha's teeth chatter. "I am really fucking cold."

"That's the name of our new club. Remember that."

We reach the mouth of a river that's cut through some rather steep soft stone, and it looks like a rough climb to the top. You could call it a steep hillside or even a cliff and either one would be correct. Abhi points out that we're going to scale it, and that's when I have doubts that we're being led to any kind of civilization.

Baejan, the scout leader, says aloud what I'm thinking: "If these people live here," she calls out, "why haven't they carved some blasted steps into the side of this stupid cliff face?"

Abhi and Karloof and Fin-tum or whatever they are called look both apologetic and encouraging when we get to the top. Their gestures and words seem to indicate that it's not far now, and it's not.

We arrive in the midst of a mob of people that are either copper-skinned humans like Abhi or pale giants like Karleft—none are like the brown-skinned man Fin-tum. He's the strange one, apparently. And all of them are setting up a camp, as evidenced by the tents and the new fire pits being laid. This is not a permanent settlement. They are as newly arrived to this place as we are.

But we are led to a couple of giant women who are apparently in charge and presented to them. One of them is especially tall, red-haired and blue-eyed, dressed in remarkable steel-plated armor and carrying a huge sword. The other, while noticeably shorter, is absolutely terrifying to behold. She's bald, for one thing, and also appears to have no lips. She wears the skin of some gray scaly creature, which bizarrely seems to reflect shades of red and blue. And she is pierced in many places on her face but most noticeably by a multicolored chain leading from her right earlobe to her right nostril. She carries no weapon, but I think I'm going to have nightmares about her anyway.

The red-haired one is called Olet Kanek, and I get the idea that she is the leader. The scary one is called La Mastik.

I like Olet. She squats on her haunches so that she's maybe only a foot taller than me and I don't have to crane my neck to look up at her. She gazes into my eyes and says something earnestly, and I signal with my fist that I appreciate whatever it is. Then she says something else to La Mastik, and the scary one moves away to shout something; soon after that, people who look like Abhi are bringing us blankets and dry clothes. They're women but somehow not as pretty as Abhi is. Do they ever wake up, I wonder, and wish they could be that beautiful? Which one of them is his mate? I don't see any of them paying him special attention. He appears to have only his animal companions.

The women give us the clothing and then hold up blankets, forming a screen so that we can change in privacy—or we could if the giants weren't able to look over the top of the screens so easily. Once Olet understands this problem, she shouts at the other giants to move far enough away upriver that it's no longer possible for us to be seen. It's a kindness we all appreciate, and many of my crew weep as they change out of their wet clothing, because it's tangible proof that we are going to be cared for and we have found safety.

But just as I think that all might be well—I mean, apart from the fact that we very nearly all died and we're entirely dependent on strangers for our food and shelter in an alien land with no way to get home— Olet leads the pack of us, now dry and only somewhat cold, in strange clothes bound with our wet dagger belts, to a large fire pit that some- one has laid with dry wood. Some of it had clearly been chopped up with axes; many of the giants appeared to be handy with them, and we heard the dull thunks of them all around us.

Olet smiles at us, squats next to me, and snaps the huge fingers of her right hand. The wood immediately ignites to full flame, and in the next second, every single one of us has drawn the Bora and the Buran. It's not even an order I need to give: It's an instinctive reaction born from the stories we were told as children. Olet reacts on instinct as well. She erupts from her squat, leaping backward, drawing that huge sword of hers at the same time. She sets herself in a defensive crouch, just as we have, and the length of her blade blossoms with flame.

"Fire demon!" Leisuen shouts.

"Hold!" I cry. "Wait until she makes her intentions clear!"

"Snuff that flame, Zephyr!" Baejan says.

That is something I could do. I could snuff her flaming sword by depriving it of air. But it would still be a damn huge sword and danger- ous in its own right without the fire along its length. And if I did any- thing like that now, it would give away my abilities when she didn't know I had any. Plus, we were ridiculously outnumbered. Thirty sailors against uncounted humans and giants, some of them blessed. One of them could talk to animals and had saved our lives. I wouldn't want to face him and the force he could bring to bear. Especially since he had been so friendly thus far.

"Wait! They have not been hostile to this point. If they actually attack, you have my permission to respond. But hold yourselves until they prove to be the aggressors. Do *not* strike first! Acknowledge!"

I get a chorus of grunts in reply.

The brown-skinned man—Fin-tum—steps between us and Olet. His hands are spread out, unarmed, and he waves them at us, clearly asking us to stand down. But behind Olet, more giants are gathering. They take in Olet with her sword on fire and our knives out and come to reinforce her. Some of them have long-handled axes and extraordinary beards with gold and silver threads among the braids.

I point at Olet's sword with the tip of my Buran. "Tell her to snuff that flame and maybe then we can talk about peace. Even if it's in different languages."

Remarkably, Fin-tum seems to understand this and says something to Olet. She responds and then her sword's flames extinguish, followed by the flames in the fire pit. She lowers her sword and looks at me expectantly.

"There. You see?" I call to my crew. "No harm intended. Sheathe your daggers now, all of you." I go first, and much to my relief, I hear the crew follow my lead.

Fin-tum nearly wilts in answer. Olet remains alert and so do I and all my crew, but the brown-skinned man moves forward and kneels, brushing aside some evergreen needles on the ground to get to the dirt. He gestures to my crew and then points to his eyes before pointing to Olet. They should watch her. Then he points to me, his eyes, and then at the ground. I should confer with him.

"First Mate Haesha."

"Aye, Zephyr?"

"Watch the fire demon. If she attacks, respond with fury. Hold until then."

"Aye, Zephyr."

The entire crew hears that, of course, but Haesha repeats the orders while I move to stare at the ground with Fin-tum. He scrawls with his finger in the dirt. He makes a hash mark, then two next to it, then three, and four. Underneath these numbers he draws images, and I soon recognize them. Fire, wind, earth, water. These were the kennings. Shoawei was the Second Kenning, and he appeared to know this. Fire was the First Kenning and, yes, that was the kenning of the demons. He was merely confirming that Olet was a fire demon. But then, by gestures, he indicated that his is the Third Kenning. He doesn't look like the people of the Third Kenning to me. Their islands are south of ours and close enough to trade with in the summer months. I shake my head at him, but even as I do this, I realize that we might be on a continent full of different people who have the same kennings as those I already know. And maybe more, as this beautiful Abhi lad seems to represent. Who knows how large this strange land across the ocean might be?

It's a risk, but I take it. I circle his sketch of the Second Kenning with my finger and then point to myself. His eyebrows climb up his face. He holds up two fingers and then points at me in question. I nod, and then his face looks so much like what I'm feeling that I break into a smile, and he mirrors it a moment afterward. We have both realized that the world is far larger than our elders ever knew.

He points at himself. "Fintan."

Oh, goddess. I got his name wrong too. Which meant I probably had Korleft or Karloof wrong too. "Fintan," I repeat, trying to burn it into my memory. "Koesha," I remind him, pointing at myself.

"Koesha," he repeats, nodding. Then he points at all my crew and shrugs at me.

"Are you serious? Okay." I get to my feet, checking on Olet. She's standing still, watching me. The scary giant, La Mastik, lurks in the background, but she doesn't move any closer. The men with the axes and beards shuffle forward, though, and start talking urgently to Olet.

They have one side of their head shaved clean and there's a tattoo of some kind there, a triangle with a cloud above it. Or maybe it's an erupting volcano? I've seen that body language and heard that tone of voice before. They're asking Olet why she doesn't just kill or imprison us right now, and I'm glad they're not the ones in charge. Though we have been fortunate so far, this could turn violent at any moment. Olet cuts them off with a short word that's either a negative or a promise to talk later. I recognize that tone too, because I use it myself.

I point at Haesha and say her name to Fintan. He repeats it. I keep going until I've named every member of my surviving crew and he's said it back to me, and all the while I keep an eye on the giant men. They are still distrustful at the least and murderous at the worst, held in check only by Olet.

Once through my roster, Fintan returns to Haesha, and from there he says the name of every member of my crew flawlessly. We clap twice and bow our heads to him afterward, delighted at the honor he has done us. Memory is supposed to be a blessing of the Third Kenning, and our traders have remarked upon it in their dealings with our neighbors to the south, but we have never seen it demonstrated personally until now.

We stand there smiling at one another for a time, not sure how to proceed and all of us wary of making a mistake that might end in violence. I am especially suspicious of the tattooed giants. Fintan eventually kneels before me again and starts circling kennings.

He circles fire and points at Olet. He circles wind and points at me. He circles earth and points at himself. Then he draws two more kennings, five and six. He circles six and points at Abhi, and that's our confirmation of his abilities.

I nod at Fintan and clutch my hands in front of my heart in thanks. I understand now.

I rise to my feet before the giant Olet and slowly draw my Bora and Buran, dropping them immediately to the ground, keeping my hands wide and far away from my sides. I approach her thus, in full view of my crew, smiling up at her. She frowns but sheathes her enormous sword. I keep coming, which causes the giants behind her to growl and bark at me, gripping their axes. I stop.

Olet turns on them and says something through clenched teeth, and they argue with her, which makes me question how much control she really has. Was I mistaken? Is she the actual leader?

That is cast into further doubt when the scary giant begins to scold the giant men and they back off in response. Perhaps the bald woman with no hair and no lips is the true leader, her status marked by her different appearance, and Olet the fire demon is something like her honor guard or a chamberlain? I remain frozen in place, arms wide, while this goes on. When it's settled and the men have subsided, Olet—not the bald woman—smiles and beckons me forward. I close the distance between us and embrace her awkwardly around her hips, because that's pretty much all I can reach. She goes very still and I hear nervous gasps all around us, but then her huge left hand falls gently to my right shoulder, followed shortly thereafter by her right hand on my left shoulder. It is the only way I could think to demonstrate our desire for peace without words and without kneeling and begging for our lives. And it is the right thing to do. I hear a rising chorus of cheers from all around us, more from Olet's people than from mine, because they are, in fact, far more numerous than us. It makes me quake and weep as I hold on to this enormous being, because I know I've just acted to save some lives. Despite Haesha's reassurances, I feel I should have done so earlier.

Two-thirds of my crew died because I wanted nothing more than to find my sister. Now they will be sisters and daughters no more, nor mothers either. But that, I vow to myself, is done. Maesi is found or, rather, permanently and definitively lost. Now I will not let a single member of my crew die before I die first. Let the fire demon strike me down if she wishes. Or let her prove not to be a demon at all. I embrace it either way. I am a leaf on the wind of Shoawei, and I will rest wherever and whenever she finds it fit.

Fintan switched from Koesha to the armored version of himself that he used whenever he was going to tell his own tale.

The very nature of my kenning means that every single day of my life is a historical event. I'm incapable of forgetting my personal history even if I desperately want to. All too often I want to, very much. But I have no qualms about remembering that particular day in every detail, for it was one of the few days that should live on forever. It was the day that the people of Joabei met the six nations of Teldwen, even if we were not all present at the meeting.

It was a bit scary at first, because they reacted badly to Olet's use of the First Kenning, and I was nearly caught between their long knives—not quite long enough to be called swords but longer than your typical daggers—and the Hathrim axes and Olet's flaming sword.

Koesha had indicated to me that she possessed the Second Kenning, but I didn't know if she was a tempest or something lesser, like a cyclone. If she was either of those, she might have given Olet a challenge, using her mastery of air to snuff out the flames and perhaps even bring Olet to her knees by robbing her of breath. Luckily, neither she nor Olet wanted a fight, and Koesha did exactly what she needed to do to de-escalate the situation.

The same could not be said for Halsten Durik or Lanner Burgan, the two former houndsmen of Gorin Mogen who had tattoos of Mount

Thayil on their heads. While I was smiling and learning the names of the Joabeian crew, they were insisting that the shipwrecked crew be told to move on, because they were not welcome. They thought they had the authority to determine that, since during the journey here they'd managed to get elected to the nine-member city council, along with one other of their ilk with the same tattoo. I was beginning to think of them as Thayilists, not just because of the tattoos but because their politics were tied to a way of life that had exploded. They represented a mindset among a block of Mogen's people that was forged elsewhere in wildly different circumstances, and they were not adapting to the new situation well. In Harthrad—as elsewhere in Hathrir—resources were scarce and rationed, and the population was strictly controlled because giants required a lot of resources to keep going. That meant that every new mouth to feed was taking food from the rest of the population, and it's why Mogen's people knew they wouldn't be welcome in other Hathrim cities. And we were in a situation where we probably had a severe winter ahead of us, with limited resources and no way to trade until the summer.

I understood where they were coming from, but I was disappointed that they didn't have more empathy for the shipwrecked sailors. The Joabeian situation, after all, was little different from the eruption of Mount Thayil—worse, in fact, since Koesha and company were cast ashore without any resources at all apart from their knives. Plus, they didn't choose to come here, unlike the Hathrim, who chose to invade Ghurana Nent.

Yet the Thayilists behaved as if the Joabeians had come here expressly to steal their food and their rights and that, furthermore, we were here first—by, like, a half hour, perhaps—and so the shipwrecked people didn't have the right to be here, and I nearly tore my hair out listening to that. After the Joabeians were settled with fires and spare tents and some food for the night, the council discussed—or, rather, argued—what to do, since it was rather unexpected and our resources were limited. Abhi, thankfully, spoke up in response to Halsten Durik's motion that the Joabeians be given a week's provisions and told to move on. It would be best for everyone, Halsten said, because a week's food for thirty extra people we could absorb, but not a winter's worth. Abhi wasn't on the council and hadn't deigned to speak before, but no one objected to the plaguebringer making a comment.

"Thanks," he said, nodding to the council members seated nearby. "Very quickly: I find it remarkable that the same people who purposely came to Ghurana Nent to take advantage of its resources in a supposed life-or-death situation are now objecting to someone else accidentally coming to Ghurana Nent in a truly life-or-death situation. I think it's unkind and would urge those people to discard the hypocrisy they're wearing and cover themselves with a scrap of generosity and goodwill instead. That is all."

Not a single Nentian could have been persuaded to vote against the Joabeians after that, and the Hathrim on the council knew it. They howled a bit about how that was an unfair characterization and he'd misrepresented their position, but when it came time for them to vote, they didn't want to go on record voting against basic decency. The council voted to do the obvious thing and welcome the crew to join us, and Olet, the elected steward, heartily approved.

But I could tell the Thayilists weren't done. They weren't chastened by Abhi's speech or the vote so much as aware that they had made a tactical error. They still wanted to hoard everything and share nothing but realized they'd have to achieve their goals some other way. I asked Olet if I might have a word.

"Is this council business?" she asked, her voice tired. It had been an exhausting day and it seemed like everyone wanted a word.

"It's about security," I replied, which was more Olet's purview as steward. She sighed.

"All right, come on to my tent, but let's be quick. La Mastik, will you stand outside and handle what you can?"

"Of course."

Olet's tent was a huge thing, like all the Hathrim tents were. She had to duck to get inside, but for me it had a high ceiling and I could walk in upright.

"What is it?" she asked, once she'd crashed to the ground, folded her long legs in front of her, and taken a swig from a drinking horn.

"If the Thayilist faction is still determined to get the shipwrecked crew out of here, they'll try picking a fight next. Regardless of how it plays out, they'll paint the newcomers as violent and dangerous and unable to live among civilized people. They'll do it over and over and try to sway public opinion over time if they can't do it all at once. So I just wanted to mention that, in case you hadn't already thought of it."

Olet grinned at me in relief and wiped imaginary sweat from her brow.

"Whew! So I'm not paranoid! Somebody else thought the same thing. Thanks, Fintan. Was there anything else?"

"Uh. No?" I felt embarrassed, because I should have assumed she'd already thought of it. She had grown up surrounded by such thinking.

"Well, I'm counting on you to learn their language or teach them Nentian quickly. Best way to avoid miscommunication is to communicate. Thanks again."

That was a dismissal, and I gave her a quick smile before spinning on my heel and exiting, deciding to crash for the evening before I said or did anything else to embarrass myself. I was hopeful that the day's events would be so exhausting that I'd sleep soundly and not be plagued by nightmares of the lavaborn.

I woke up to fire anyway, startled before dawn by shouts and screams. Scrambling out of my tent and grabbing my stone baton, I emerged to see a pillar of flame in the darkness near where the Joabeians were camped. It was Olet, alight from head to toe, but facing away from the Joabeians and pointing at some other Hathrim squared off against her—I couldn't tell who, since I only saw a sliver of them limned in her own firelight in the darkness. Picking my way carefully in that direction, I realized that there was a standoff with four sides and a whole lot of shouting. I needed to pick a side.

Nearest me, Olet faced off against some unknown number of Hathrim—and then La Mastik joined her, lighting up her shorn scalp as a reminder that she was a priestess of the flame. Behind Olet and La

Mastik, Koesha and Haesha were turned toward their own crew, who had once again drawn weapons in response to Olet lighting herself on fire. No longer cold and wet and terrified, they looked much more ready to attack. As I approached, it seemed they understood that Olet and La Mastik had not come for them, since the giant women were facing away and blocking the advance of other giants armed with axes. Koesha shouted a command and they shifted into ranks, just in case any of the giants got through. It was impressive discipline, and I would not want to confront those knives.

By the time I got to the center of it, I saw that the giants challenging Olet and La Mastik were none other than the Thayilists—Lanner Burgan and Halsten Durik and a few others. Though Halsten Durik had been the leader of Mogen's houndsmen, Lanner Burgan was doing all the shouting now. I didn't know if that was because Lanner was leading the faction or if Halsten was letting him take point in this conflict.

"You're taking their word over ours?" Lanner roared.

"I literally cannot take their word for anything, because they don't speak our fucking language!" Olet replied. "They haven't said anything to me. This is just me calling you on your nasty little scheme."

Arriving late as I did, I had no clue what scheme Olet might be referring to. But then I wondered if it might not have something to do with the long Hathrim houndsmen axes on the ground behind both Olet and Koesha; their backs were to each other, and four or five of the battle-axes lay between them. Given the lines drawn, I had little trouble making a decision: I would stand with Olet and La Mastik, because I could not imagine a world in which I would stand with Lanner Burgan against anyone.

"My only scheme was to protect us from their sick murder plot! Look at them! They have their knives out for us!"

"They find us threatening, Lanner. You think maybe it's because you're standing there with an axe? And trying to frame them? The idea that they got shipwrecked and then immediately plotted to murder us with weapons that weigh more than they do is just stupid."

"What?"

"I said stupid. You. Are. Stupid. I *saw* you plant those axes, Lanner."

"I did not! They stole them to disarm us."

"Oh, changing your story, eh? Fine. It's still ridiculous, because they can't pick them up. Have you ever seen the little people try to move them? It's both funny and sad. Kind of like your plan to paint them as the bad guys."

"You're completely ignoring the danger they represent—"

"Once they prove dangerous, I'll deal with it. Right now you're dangerous, so I'm dealing with you. Back off."

"What about them? Are you going to tell them to back off?"

"No. Once again, I don't speak their language. And I want your resignation from the council."

That stunned Lanner. His mouth dropped open and Halsten jumped into the silence. "Hey, that's not a decision you can make!"

"It's his decision whether to resign or not. But it's my decision to ask him to resign. Bard," she said, turning her fiery gaze down to me. "Broadcast me, please."

"Right." It only took a moment and then I nodded at her, and she spoke to the entire camp, no doubt waking up what few people had managed to sleep through the ruckus so far.

"Good morning, everyone. Steward Kanek here. Sorry to disturb your sleep, but we've got a problem. I just witnessed Lanner Burgan, a Hathrim member of the council, plant battle-axes in the camp of our new shipwrecked friends. He claims he didn't do what I saw him do and that the exhausted shipwrecked women stole these huge Hathrim battle-axes. First he said it was to murder us, then it was to disarm us. Neither is true. The truth is he was trying to frame them and sow distrust after his faction lost the council vote last night. I am asking for his resignation from the council, and I think his seat should go to one of the new women, so that they are represented in our government."

Lanner and Halsten had been seething up to that point, but at the idea of losing a seat to the newcomers they roared and charged, raising their axes high. Olet blasted them in the face with fire, and both she and La Mastik spun out of the way. Unfortunately, La Mastik spun right into me, and we both went down with startled cries. But Lanner and Halsten went down too, intentionally face-planting to the forest floor to snuff out the flames on their faces and beards.

"Do you yield?" Olet asked them, but kept a wary eye on the other Thayilists, who were wondering if they could get to her before she roasted them all. She wasn't broadcasting anymore, because I'd lost my concentration and may have bruised my spleen. But both Lanner and Halsten heard her and yielded. Their entire bodies were flammable, after all.

"Fine." With a gesture and exertion of her will, the fires went out on their faces. "I used my lowest intensity. I hope you won't be permanently damaged." She snuffed out the flames on her body too, as well as the small ground fires that had sparked up in response to La Mastik's head contacting the pine needles of the forest floor. We groaned and got to our feet, but when Lanner and Halsten began to rise, Olet told them to stay down there for a few more minutes.

"Fintan, are you all right? Can you broadcast me again?"

"Yes. Go ahead."

"An important update: Lanner Burgan and Halsten Durik just attacked me. If they will not resign, I hope the council will see fit to dismiss them for cause and hold a new election to replace them. And let me remind everyone that it is my responsibility as steward to protect this settlement from within as well as without. You are all under my protection, but most especially the newcomers right now, as they clearly have more to fear from us than we do from them. Let's all be better people."

She made a cutoff motion with her hand and I stopped broadcasting. Halsten Durik rose to his knees.

"Tell me, Steward Kanek, if you are going to dismiss councillors whenever you wish and enforce your will with fire, how are you any different from a hearthfire? Is it just the name?"

"A hearthfire would have killed you already," La Mastik said before Olet could speak. "So that's different, isn't it?"

"If you're smart you'll resign, go back to your people, and pick someone that you can influence to run for your spots," Olet said. "If you make the council act against you, what you did here will be broadcast again and the election might not go the way you'd prefer."

Olet kept the axes and asked everyone to disperse and let the newcomers relax. Once they did—Halsten and Lanner trying to look like they'd won somehow, though their beards were still smoking—I noted that Koesha ordered her crew to sheathe their knives and stand down. I didn't know how I would explain to them what had happened; it would be weeks before we had enough words to talk about such things as xenophobia and prejudice. But at least Koesha realized that Olet had prevented an actual attack on her people.

It was not a day of perfect harmony, but I hoped that the first day of our civilizations' meeting would set the tone for all the days to come, where leaders who desired peace prevailed against those who sought violence. Maybe, after enough such days, I would dream of smiling faces in accord rather than the screams of burning men.

Day 30

THE RIFT

Pelemyn was a city of sardine breath on the thirtieth day of the bard's tales. Not one but two ships had found a shoal to harvest, so practically everyone was eating them, but especially on Survivor Field, where the kitchen served them up along with flatbread to the folks who'd had nothing but bread the previous day.

"They arrived under guard, can you believe it?" the chef told me when I showed up to volunteer.

"I can."

She peered at me through narrowed eyes and folded her arms across her chest. "You did something?"

"I left a note for the pelenaut and I presume he did something."

The chef snorted. "That he did. He removed the discount from pricing, so there's no motivation not to sell to us, and then he had mariners escort the government's portion here every step of the way."

"I heard some fishermen left because of the discount."

She laughed. "Wouldn't be surprised if that was his plan all along. He wanted to get rid of the profiteers."

I laughed with her, realizing it was probably true. Rölly and his flow

studies—he'd probably seen it coming. And whoever had been hijacking the shipments was probably in a dungeon by now.

The chef set me to packing sardines in individual servings, bathed in
salt and oil and wrapped in waxed paper, while she made flatbread. I
had to leave before noon, but it was good to know that people would
be eating, regardless of the damage to their breath.

I was all ready to discuss the meeting of the Joabeians with Fintan
and enjoy the day, but my hopes were dashed when I met him at the
dockside fishblade joint. For he had someone sitting next to him on
the bench, and that someone was his wife, Numa, master courier of
the Raelech Triune.

"Shall I return later?" I asked Dervan after greeting Numa. "I can let
you have some time together."

"Nonsense," Numa said, beaming a smile at me that was stunningly
bright. "I'm here to see you, Master Dervan."

"Oh."

I gingerly sat down across the table from them, dreading what was
to come next. Because Numa would not wish to see me for social reasons. I am not one of the cool kids.

The fishblade himself, Gellart du Tyllen, came over with orders for
each of us, plus a beer for me.

"We took the liberty of ordering for you," Fintan said, "since there
was one thing on the menu—'fishblade's choice'—and we figured
you'd want to eat."

"Thanks," I said, digging into the meal right away so I wouldn't
have to think of anything to say. If I'd been clever—or petty—I would
have started asking questions and wasting time. But I didn't think of
myself as the former and hoped I wasn't the latter. I ceded the conversational high ground and waited for the attack.

She waited until I swallowed, at least.

"Any word from the pelenaut regarding the matter Fintan discussed
with you? A certain missing item?"

"Ask him yourself."

"I'm asking if you've had any word from him."

"No. Because, as I told Fintan, I am not a channel to the pelenaut."

"You're something, though."

"I'm an old ex-mariner and ex-professor who is currently a glorified scribe with a bum knee."

"Who goes way back with the pelenaut."

"Yes, we grew up together."

She pounced. "So you *are* a back channel!"

"Not for your messages. You can deliver them yourself."

"Come on. You know how this works."

"I do not."

"May I explain, then?"

"Sure."

"Okay. You can't say things in court sometimes because they're sensitive. Saying them aloud means somebody's got to own them and there's official embarrassment and official efforts to save face, and none of it is discreet or fun. Use a back channel, though, an unofficial communication, and everyone gets to save face and deal with things on the sly."

"That's fascinating, Master Courier, but I'm not one of those back channels. Even if I were, I wouldn't know what to say. This mystery object is still a mystery."

"Is it?"

"Are you implying that you know what it is? If you do, please inform me and perhaps I can make an inquiry on your behalf."

Numa paused to take a swig of beer and I flicked my eyes at Fintan. He dropped his gaze immediately, embarrassed or ashamed or something of the kind at having ambushed me like this. Or perhaps he wasn't feeling any of that and this was merely a show to allow *him* to save face. His lifebond was here to apply pressure, and he could plausibly claim that's not what he wanted or would have done. Regardless, it was distasteful business.

"I don't know what it is," she said, shaking her head. "Only that Clodagh thinks it's important."

It occurred to me that we were in a kind of negotiation. They might be willing to share something with me to get more information about what was important.

"Tell me, Numa. Have your duties ever taken you to Aelinmech?"

She blinked, surprised at the change of subject. "Yes, they have."

"Are there poison manufacturers or distillers in Aelinmech?"

She scrunched up her nose and one side of her face, unsure why I was asking. "There are distillers, to be sure. Some people consider whiskey to be a poison, and I suppose technically it is, but those are the only distillers I know of there. No distillers of poisons like I'm-gonna-murder-you poison."

"No government houses of experimentation? No brewers of potables that might not be potable?"

"What? No. Only distillers I know about are the ones that make the Good Shit, if you'll pardon my language. It's Aelinmech rye. Dare I ask why?"

"Just because you haven't heard of them doesn't mean they're not there. That is, of course, the problem with conspiracy thinking. As soon as you've decided there's a conspiracy, even plain facts come into question, because they're all part of the conspiracy."

"Let me ask you this: Do *you* know what was stolen, Dervan?"

It was a direct question, and since I knew they would know if I lied, I didn't, precisely. "I'm not sure I can say, since there's no way to verify what it is from the victim." I nodded as I said that to make sure they knew I *did* know what it was, and I kept nodding as I continued, "Whatever this mysterious thing is or isn't, the pelenaut has no plans to use it against his Raelech allies."

The two Raelechs exchanged glances after I'd stopped.

"So, just to clarify," Numa said, "we can unofficially tell someone that the thing they are worried about is nothing to worry about?"

I nodded again. "You can. This whole conversation has been about nothing."

Numa slapped the table, then pumped her fist once before spreading her fingers and holding up her palm to me for a high five. "Yeah! Yeah, Dervan! Come on, don't leave me hanging."

I tapped her palm quickly, tentatively, unsure what was happening. She looked briefly disappointed at the lack of a satisfying clapping noise, but then she smiled again. "That's how you back-channel, man! That's how! That was perfect! You're great at this! Pardon me for a second."

Numa turned to Fintan, grabbed his face, and kissed him deeply. The bard's eyes widened in surprise and rolled in my direction. I looked down at my fish and beer in an act of mercy.

"Gotta go, sweetie. I'll see you later at the embassy," Numa said, after a slurpy pop of disengagement from their lip-lock. "Thank you again, Dervan," she added, and that was my cue to look up. She was extricating her legs from the bench. "I'm off to the Wellspring to open official lines of communication, and it will be entirely pleasant because of this very important back channel."

"Oh. Okay," I managed, which was spectacularly not smooth at all. I couldn't figure out whether I had done a competent job or had just done something profoundly unwise. Numa put on her goggles, waggled her fingers at us, and then sped away as only couriers can, creating a gust of wind in her passage.

"What in the abyss was that?" I demanded.

"The word *awkward* comes to mind," Fintan said. "Sorry you had to see that."

"I don't mean your make-out session. Good for you and your entwined tongues. I mean this back-channel business. I want no more of that, you hear? Tell her when you see her later. I am out of the loop."

"All right, I will tell her. But you don't know how important that was."

"You're right, I don't."

"Well, if you hadn't reassured us it was nothing, it was going to be something. Official nastiness, leading to a deterioration of our countries' alliance. And trade."

"Oh."

That could have been something indeed. We were dependent on

Rael, Forn, and Kauria for large portions of our food supply at the moment. Any interruption in that would be felt in grumbling bellies.

But I wasn't authorized to talk about such things. Maybe Rölly had been counting on an official to-do. Maybe he was going to negotiate for something important. Far from doing anything significant, I might have set the country back and given the Raelechs what they wanted for essentially nothing in return.

"Who *does* make poisons in Rael, Fintan?" I asked.

The bard froze with a piece of fish halfway to his mouth. "You know it's kind of nerve-wracking that you keep bringing up poison while we're eating, right?"

"Just tell me."

"I don't know the answer to that. I suppose someone must be doing it, just from a statistical probability standpoint, but it would be pointless. Everyone knows the Fornish are best at it."

"The Fornish?"

"Yep. The Red Pheasant Clan in particular."

I remembered he'd mentioned that in passing before in one of his tales. "Wait—the clan of Mai Bet Ken? The tea people?"

"That's the one."

"If everyone knows they're making poison, then why aren't they being blamed for every single suspicious murder?"

"They don't administer it. They just sell it."

"But it's an instrument of death."

"So is a sword. Do you blame blacksmiths for people getting hacked to pieces?"

"No, because swords have other uses. Nonlethal ones, like ceremonies and decorating walls above the hearth and so on. Poisons have no other purpose than murder. I think we can blame them for that."

"Okay," Fintan said. "Go ahead. The same place also creates lifesaving medicines. They are in the business of researching plants and making money from them. Some of them have poisonous qualities."

"I imagine it would be difficult to find out what kind of poisons they make and who is buying them."

"The latter would be impossible. The former would be merely challenging."

"How so?"

"Well, you'd have to go to the Red Pheasant Clan and tell them you want to buy some poison. And then you'd have to convince them that you're serious and that you really want to hear about their poisons' effects before you buy."

"Clams and tentacles. Okay."

"Should I be worried? Start checking my food before I eat it?"

"No, no. Never mind. Sorry."

I was a really terrible spy.

When we reached the wall later, Fintan began with a very old song about the children of Teldwen and Kalaad, which was taught to him but rarely performed. "This will be relevant later today, I promise," he said cryptically.

> Kalaad and Teldwen gave us all their blessings
> And gave birth to the scions of four kennings:
> Thurik came first, and like his sire
> He blazed with the passion of undying fire;
> His brother Reinei aimed to please,
> His presence calming like a soothing breeze;
> The triple goddess of the earth bloomed forth
> And protected her people in the north:
> And Bryn was last, Lord of the Deep
> With all the secrets of the oceans to keep.
> Together they watched over all our shores
> To nurture life and prevent wars.

"Yesterday's tales were of a historic meeting," he said after the break. "Today includes a tale of revelations that should make us all reconsider—not change our minds necessarily, but just consider again—the stories we've been told since we were children. That will be Gondel Vedd's tale a bit later. But first, as I promised you earlier, more from Gerstad Daryck du Löngren and the Grynek Hunters."

The crowd roared as the gerstad's seeming appeared out of the smoke.

We've been prowling the northern coast for a week, moving fast in an attempt to catch up to the army we're tracking. We found evidence of another camp and watering mission at the site of a river emptying into the ocean. Brön noted that these streams were not poisoned like the Gravewater and were safe to drink without him using his kenning; settlement up here would therefore be possible without hygienists.

"Yeah, but in winter your balls would freeze, drop off, and shatter," I said.

"That will never be a problem with my balls, Gerstad, but thank you."

"So what *is* the problem, Brön? Are you chafing again?" Luren said, his tone solicitous.

"I am not chafing."

"You should put some ointment on that. Or at least some grease. Gyrsön, you got some grease our hygienist can use?"

"Sure, I can rustle up some weasel grease," the cook said.

"I am *not* using grease of any kind. If you could see the stuff living in grease, like I can, you would not apply it anywhere on your body. Trust me."

"Aha! So you *are* chafing!" Luren crowed.

Gyrsön's extraordinary nose smelled the ambush before we heard or saw the ambushers. "Uh, Gerstad, there's someone up ahead who needs a bath," he said.

"I'm perfectly sanitary!" Brön protested. "I would know." But one look at Gyrsön and I knew he wasn't teasing Brön.

"Incoming! Ready bows!" I called, and so we had arrows nocked when they attacked. If we hadn't been prepared and they'd caught us unawares, I'm not sure we would have made it.

The Bone Giants were certainly tall but not quite so tall as Hathrim. White-skinned, with stick-like anatomy and faces painted like skulls, black paint around the eyes and over the nose. The armor that gave them their name was evident. No battle cries, just the clacking of bones as they ran. And they ran right toward us; clearly, they must have heard us coming up behind them, for we'd made no effort to be quiet while dunking on Brön.

They seemed to have no sense of self-preservation; they just came at us fast with long, ground-eating strides, raised those weird crested swords of theirs, and brought the blades down with tremendous force. There were seven: Arrows brought down four of the Bone Giants, and Sören exploded the brains of the other three, but they still got two of the mariners, one man and one woman.

We weren't wearing helmets, and the swords just obliterated their heads. I'm not sure a helmet would have saved them anyway; the force would have cracked their skulls or concussed them to the point where they wouldn't be fighting back.

"I get it now," I said, looking down at the pale bodies sprawled in the pine needles where the forest gave way to the beach.

"Get what?" Gyrsön asked.

"How they beat us. They don't announce themselves with battle cries. They don't care if you take them out, because they know some- one else will get you. And they're fast and ruthless. We got off one volley before they were in close quarters. Think if we didn't have Sören with us. Think if Gyrsön didn't warn us they were coming. Think if they had more than seven, which they certainly did when they came after the cities. We had advantage of numbers, ranged weapons, early warning, and a kenning, and they *still* got two of us. We're lucky to be standing here."

"I was thinking much the same," Luren said, all traces of bonhomie gone. He was every inch a mynstad now, a professional soldier reviewing the battle. "Something for me to think on tactically." He picked up one of the giants' swords to examine it, judging the heft in his hand and giving it a few experimental swings.

The invaders all had satchels of cloth strung across their torsos, and I ordered them searched. I went over to one giant in particular, who looked different from the others. He had grown out a beard and tied it into thin braids that radiated from his jaw like the bottom half of a sunburst. The braids were stiffened somehow—with egg whites, perhaps. His satchel contained some strips of dried salted meat, a bulb of fresh water, and some wafers of terrible flatbread. But it also contained some documents in a language I couldn't read. I kept those, since the quartermaster had said the pelenaut knew a Kaurian who could translate them. There was also a bound book in there—in the satchels of all of them, in fact—that said *Zanata Sedam* on the cover.

"Why are they all reading the same thing?" Gyrsön wondered aloud. "Are they in a book club or something? Go around murdering people by day, discuss themes of angst and alienation among tall white guys at night?"

"It's probably a religious text," Sören said.

Brön spat upon one of the corpses. He considered this the ultimate insult a hygienist could deliver, and I'd seen him do it only once, to a fish head in Grynek who'd tried to pick his pocket. "Whatever book gives them permission to commit genocide can be thrown in a fire, as far as I'm concerned."

We kept one copy but left the others in the satchels. We dragged all the bodies to the shore, including our fallen mariners, and Sören pulled them out one at a time to deep water and gave them to the sea.

We stood watch during that process—or, rather, most of us did. While the majority of the band was turned away, I watched Gyrsön as he stared at the bodies. His great mustache wiggled and twitched underneath his nose, his eyes began streaming, his lips curled back from his teeth, and then, with an inarticulate cry, he charged forward and kicked one of the bodies, giving it a good cursing. Then he apologized for his outburst, because everyone had turned around.

Mynstad Luren blinked and said, "Nonsense. That is the perfect response right now. These are the people who killed our families for no reason. I'd appreciate it if you'd give them a few extra kicks for me."

"Really?"

"Yes." Luren turned back to scan the horizon but said over his shoulder, "You'd be doing me a favor."

"Me too, Gyrsön," Brön said. "Thanks."

The mariners and I all chimed in, and then we politely turned away as Gyrsön got it out of his system. We'd all taken our shots at the Bone Giants and drunk the tiniest sip of vengeance from a river we wished to drink dry, but Gyrsön hadn't yet. We protected him and the chow as a rule when we were afield, and anything that got through to him was either wounded already or off-balance enough that he could finish it with a cleaver. But he'd not had his chance at these skeletal monsters, and he had his own grief to work out, as we all did. Judging by the cursing and the repeated dull thuds of his boot against ribs, he was working it out hard.

I wondered when I'd figure out how to let my own grief go. Our teasing of Brön aside, I realized that I hadn't told a single joke since we found Grynek sacked, unless making fun of the quartermaster's lack of cake one time counted. What were jokes, anyway, and why did I used to think they were funny? Maybe I should try writing a cock sonnet, just to prove to myself that I could still do it. What if I'd been changed forever? And then I thought it would be more troubling if I *hadn't* changed after losing most everyone I knew in the world.

The really strange thing was that while of course I missed my family and friends, I was missing my bartender the most. Thinking of him made my throat close tight and tears well up. And it's not because I knew him all that well or just missed the way he poured a drink— I didn't even know his real name. Everyone used to call him Nudge. And thinking of Nudge hit me hard because he'd always been behind that bar, a steady presence in good fortune and bad, and now he wasn't. Our tiny minds latch on to one thing sometimes because we can't handle the enormity of everything, and somehow Nudge had come to represent everything I'd lost.

One night at his place, I'd been nursing a beer as someone two seats down was sobbing into their whiskey and mourning a family member they'd recently lost to illness. And Nudge leaned over the bar, put a hand on the man's arm, and said this so I barely caught it: "Remember that the dead are at peace, and never resent that they have it; you'll have it soon enough yourself. What you're feeling now is despair at all the damage you'll have to repair or endure. Their damage, yours, everyone they knew—I know it can be overwhelming. But your comfort is this: You *can* repair and endure. And you can build too. So when it's your time to rest, those who remain will gather and celebrate a life well lived."

Those words haunt me now. Can I repair, endure, and build? Can any of us? When I go home to rest forever, will anyone celebrate what I did with my life? I don't know that hunting is a thing to be celebrated. It's simply a necessity sometimes.

When Sören and Gyrsön were finished, we spent some time covering up the battle scene, kicking sand over the blood on the beach and sweeping pine needles around under the trees. It probably wouldn't be enough to fool an experienced tracker, but we hoped the disappearance of this group would be chalked up to animals in the Gravewood rather than a band of Brynt mercenaries.

We moved more cautiously after that, realizing that we must be getting close to the main army and also half-expecting some scavengers to come sniffing around at the scent of slaughter. I wondered how long it would be until this scouting party was missed and what they were doing behind the main army. Did they know they were being followed? Were they a rear guard? Or did they have some other mission—maybe somebody left something behind at their last camp and they were coming back for it?

Regardless, we had a very clear mission. The pelenaut wanted the location of the enemy and their numbers, and I considered that a first step toward vengeance.

I doubt that Nudge would consider the seeking of revenge a life well lived. It would certainly not build anything or repair a lick of the damage done. But maybe this would be how we endured.

My breath hitched in my throat at Daryck's last words, and tears practically leapt out of my eyes, for I felt his coping mechanisms—or those of his late bartender—were so close to my own. I had chosen very consciously not to seek revenge for Sarena's murder, but I understood that impulse keenly and felt how it might be an effective way to endure, if nothing else.

Looking around, I saw that several others on the wall were having feelings of their own, remembering whom they'd lost and why, and a quick glance over the edge of the wall at the wooden bleachers revealed that many in the audience at Survivor Field were dealing with the same issues. The tales of the Nentians and Hathrim and so on were affecting, to be sure, but they were different, somehow, from hearing one of our own go through what we had. Those other tales were like mere flesh wounds compared to Daryck's story, which was a knife to the heart.

"How we deal with loss varies greatly from culture to culture and from person to person, but dealing with it is something we must all do at some point," the bard said after a respectful silence. "Let's catch up with Olet Kanek, who abruptly discovered she had losses of her own to process."

Olet

People like to complain sometimes about the strain and exhaustion of labor, but rarely do they praise its meditative and restorative qualities. Since physical work requires little mental activity, it can be restful for the mind, and one can arrive at solutions to problems almost by magic instead of strain. Like a pot roast left to cook slowly throughout the day over glowing coals, solutions to problems can be reached sometimes while the brain is nominally occupied with something else.

While most in the budding city were occupied erecting shelters of one kind or another, La Mastik and I were in the crude shed, building a glass furnace that would eventually become a respectable smithing operation. We needed the furnace before building an actual forge, because we had a more urgent need for glass than for iron and steel for our new buildings. We'd brought plenty of finished products like nails with us, but we'd had no illusions about finished glass surviving a cart ride over leagues of untamed wilderness. So we'd packed lots of soda and lime instead, and the beach provided all the silica we required.

Since we'd elected two new council members to replace Halsten Durik and Lanner Burgan, I thought we were operating pretty well. The bard had come up with the idea of pairing off the Joabeian crew with various citizens to help them learn Nentian and make everyone feel more comfortable—though the Thayilists, as the Raelech called them, were still suspicious and might not ever get over their baseless prejudice.

Leisuen and Baejan were coupled with us; they helped to mix the mortar and spread it around while Mirana and I did the heavy lifting of the boulders for the furnace. I thought they were picking up Nentian pretty well from us, but I hoped we weren't giving them noticeable Hathrim accents.

Of all the problems my mind could be stewing over in the background as we worked, the one that wouldn't go away was Abhi's report that there was a man living on the island to the northeast of us. Just one man, apparently. An extremely puzzling man.

I'd asked Abhi to send his stalk hawk, Eep, on additional flyovers to get some answers.

The man she'd seen was the same one each time, as far as she could tell. There were many buildings on the western side of the island, but he stayed near one in particular, which was bigger than most of the others. Eep didn't know—most likely couldn't know—what kind of buildings they were.

There were some additional buildings on the eastern side plus some watercraft of varying sizes next to a dock, but she never saw any humans near there. She also saw nothing she could eat, which is a question Abhi asked that I thought was clever. It meant the man wasn't hunting or trapping his food. Most likely he was fishing. Or he'd brought in a huge boatload of supplies at some point.

But questions abounded. Who was he and why was he there? Why was he there alone? What had happened to all the people who'd presumably occupied the other buildings at some point? And unless he was also blessed by the Sixth Kenning like Abhi was, how did he get around in his boat without the krakens smashing it to flotsam? And where did he sail here from?

Koesha was hopeful that the stranger might turn out to be a survivor from her culture, because apparently they had been trying to navigate their way across the Northern Yawn for a good while now. She knew that many other ships had come this way, and perhaps one of them had made it to the island.

"But he's a man," I pointed out.

"Yes." She shrugged, not understanding.

"Your crew is all women, though."

"Yes. But men sail. Men sail also."

"But not with you."

"No."

"Why no men?"

She shrugged again, helplessly, not having the vocabulary to explain. She said, "Talk later."

"Okay." We had plenty to talk about later, but I was willing to be patient, since the Joabeians were friendly and happy to pitch in with building the city. Koesha and some of her crew had joined Karlef and Suris in the construction of docks down by the river as well as our first fishing boat. I knew she had plans to build a larger boat to sail home eventually, but that would have to wait, and she'd need Abhi's help to enchant the hull.

That kid's abilities were incredible, I thought, as I took one end of a boulder and La Mastik took the other and we lifted, using our legs. I could burn stuff or not burn it, and I never had to worry about burning myself: That was my whole deal. But what Abhi could potentially do with his blessing boggled my mind. Talking to animals. Telling krakens and gravemaws to just relax because they didn't need to eat us today. Telling—

I very nearly dropped my end of the boulder as the thought hit me, one of those unexpected solutions to a problem I hadn't even known my mind was working on. La Mastik gave a tiny scream of surprise.

"Aah! What? Olet, are you okay?"

"Oh! Sorry! Yeah. I just. Uh." I carefully placed the boulder with her and then sighed.

"What happened there?" La Mastik demanded.

"I just had a thought. I need to find Abhi. Do you know where he is?"

"No."

"We need to find him."

"We both do?"

"Yes."

"What about the furnace?"

"That can wait. Come on."

We made apologies to Leisuen and Baejan and left the smithing shed in search of the plaguebringer. That title took on new significance to me as we asked around. Someone had seen him near the beach, trying to install steps down the hillside.

"Olet, will you tell me what the matter is?" Mirana asked. "You're doing that thing with your jaw."

"What thing?"

"That thing where you kind of grind your teeth and the muscles ripple and you look really threatening because you're going to kill someone."

"I didn't know they did that."

"Well, they do. I've seen it before. So I'm a bit worried that you're doing it while you're looking for Abhi. What is it?"

"Maybe nothing. Maybe everything."

"Tell me."

"I don't want to say it out loud yet. But when I do, I might need to be restrained. That's your job."

"You can't be serious. I can't restrain you."

"Think up some scripture about the judicious use of force. Something about measured responses."

"There aren't a lot of those. Thurik usually advocates setting everything on fire."

"Are there any bits about not setting things on fire? I need to hear those."

"Well, there's this one really strange taboo against burning frogs."

"What? I've never heard of that."

"I know, right? We spent a whole day talking about the frog taboo in seminary. We were advised not to talk about it with our congregations, because we can't explain it. There's no reason given for it but also no punishment listed, so the advice was just to keep quiet about it unless someone asked. Thurik was just a frog guy."

"What else? That doesn't help."

"Well, you shouldn't burn your family most of the time—there are exceptions—and you should think long and hard before burning your infrastructure."

"The scriptures use the word *infrastructure?*"

"No, they list every damn thing you shouldn't burn for pages and pages, but it comes down to infrastructure. So that might be helpful."

"How?"

"If you're mad at Abhi, it might be useful to remember that he's the only reason we haven't suffered many losses in the Gravewood. And he's the only hope you have of sending out a fishing boat that won't get destroyed by krakens. Or getting the Joabeians home. Or trading those nifty animal-repelling stakes of his for all kinds of supplies. He's a vital part of our infrastructure."

"Okay. That helps. But, still, keep an eye on me."

"I will."

We found Abhi halfway down the hill with a shovel, carving out steps with none other than Lanner Burgan. The Thayilist frowned at me but said nothing. He'd trimmed a lot of his beard to make the burn damage disappear, and he was self-conscious of the fact that the outline of his jaw could actually be seen now. Abhi's bloodcat was sprawled a short distance away, napping, and his stalk hawk was down on the beach, eating something she'd slain.

"Abhinava Khose. Plaguebringer," I called. I felt my fists clench at my sides but didn't feel them ignite.

La Mastik gasped, "Olet, what the shit! Calm down right now!"

I looked down and saw that my hands were on fire. I snuffed them with a thought. But not before Abhi saw them—and my face, which I guess does a little jaw-clenching thing when I'm mad.

"Hello, Olet. You look upset and you're not calling me 'kid.' Is this about your father, finally?"

"No, it is not. I told you I didn't mind you killing him much, and that was the truth. I'm here to talk about someone else."

He dropped his shovel and slapped the dust off his hands against his legs. "All right. Shall I come up there?"

"No, let's head down to the beach." If I lost control, I wouldn't accidentally burn down the forest there. "Please excuse us, Lanner."

The redheaded giant bowed his head. "Of course."

La Mastik and I followed the Nentian boy down to the beach. His bloodcat woke up and paced by his side, casting suspicious looks up at me with those red eyes. I hadn't heard him summon the creature, but it might not have been sleeping as deeply as it had first seemed.

Once on the beach and assured of privacy, I asked him straight out through gritted teeth, "At the Battle of the Godsteeth. Did you. Kill. Jerin Mogen?"

"Oh, shit," La Mastik said. She put a hand on my arm. "Your fists are on fire again, Olet."

I ignored her, because my eyes were locked on Abhi. He didn't flinch, didn't look guilty. If anything, he looked perplexed.

"I don't know who that is. Unless you mean Gorin Mogen? He was killed by Nel—"

"I know who killed Gorin Mogen. I'm not talking about him. I'm talking about his son. Jerin Mogen."

"I'm sorry," he said with a shrug and a regretful twist of the lips. "I don't know. Maybe? I was sent there by that viceroy of Hashan Khek, you know—"

"Melishev Lohmet."

"Right. Not what you would call a savory individual. The assignment he gave me was to kill all the lavaborn I could before his army got there. I'm pretty sure he was hoping I'd die in the attempt. But I got a boil of kherns to stampede, and they trampled a lot of giants. If Jerin was among them, then—"

"No. The day before the battle. A lumber crew, not unlike the ones we used to make the road here, was clearing some trees in the foothills. And then, according to the reports we received, two hounds on patrol went wild and bucked off their riders before charging the lumber crew. The hounds stopped and returned to their riders just as strangely as they began. But then a hive of moss hornets attacked Jerin

Mogen and stung only him, and only his face. Their venom paralyzed and killed him. Was that you? Did you do that?"

His eyes fell, and the flush of guilt I hadn't seen before blazed up. He *had* killed Jerin. My entire body erupted in flames, my rage unable to be contained.

Abhi leapt back and his bloodcat did too, and he edged toward the sea, I noticed, while his bloodcat hissed and spit at me. Yeah, kid, good idea to have some water to dive into. He clasped his hands together high up underneath his chin—some Nentian pose of penitence, I guess—as he kept moving.

"Olet, I'm sorry. Melishev used me to fight off Gorin Mogen's invasion, and I went along. I let him do it for reasons that made sense to me at the time. But the whole reason I wanted to join your party here was so I couldn't be used like that again. I obviously didn't know who Jerin was."

"So you're saying it's not your fault? Did Melishev tell you to kill my father too?"

"No, I accept full responsibility for that. I watched him murder my king, though, in response to telling your father he couldn't come after you. I felt I was in the right to retaliate."

Mirana stepped in front of me, blocking my view of him as I was about to retort.

"Olet—"

I craned my neck to the side to reestablish eye contact, but Mirana put herself in my way again.

"Olet, listen to me. You're edging toward a flameout here."

"No, I'm not, I'm just upset—"

"No kidding."

"Don't I have a right to be?"

"Sure. Be upset. But also listen to my words: He has never lied to you, even now. He has done everything he said he would. And infrastructure."

"What?"

"That thing we were talking about. I'm just reminding you."

"Blast it, Mirana, let me talk to him!"

"Okay. Just talk. Maybe snuff out the flames here, okay? You're scaring his kitty cat."

The bloodcat did look pretty out of sorts. Giant women on fire were not his favorite thing. And the stalk hawk had flown over from her meal and perched on Abhi's shoulder. She'd spread her wings in front of his face in a protective manner. It was sweet and kind of funny because Abhi was trying to see over her wings the same way I was trying to see past Mirana.

La Mastik added in low tones that only I could hear, "Think of what your father would do in this situation, and then do the opposite."

That worked, but just barely. With a supreme effort, I ruthlessly snuffed out the flames and tried to reduce the rolling boil of my anger to a gentle simmer.

"If you'd like me to leave, I will," Abhi offered. "But I'll also do most anything else to make things right between us if I can."

"Oh, you want to make this right?"

"Yes."

"Then you're going to have a smoke with me for Jerin. I never got to smoke for him properly, because his parents were assholes." I wasn't sure a smoke would actually solve anything, but sometimes ritual can save someone who's drowning in seas of rage or despair. Ritual is a life preserver made from ceremony.

"Yeah, all right. But . . . I don't smoke."

"You will this one time. If you want to make it right."

"Okay. I'm not sure I'll do it correctly, but I'll try."

I grabbed for the tobacco pouch at my belt and it crumbled to ash in my hands. All my tobacco—as well as the new clothing that Nentian seamstress made for me—had been burned up in my fit of temper. The pleated strips of lava dragon hide hanging from my belt preserved a bit of my modesty, at least, and my boots were fine because they were lava dragon too, but I was beginning to feel a bit of a draft.

"Shit." I crossed my hands over my chest as the ashes of my tunic blew away.

"It's fine, Olet," La Mastik said. "It's perfect, in fact. You go get some fresh clothes and tobacco out of our quarters and calm down, and I'll stay here with Abhi. We'll have that smoke when you get back."

I spun on my heel and stalked back to camp, burnt pieces of my pants flaking off and trailing in my wake as they crumbled away.

"Don't look at me," I told Lanner Burgan, and he dropped his eyes as I stormed past, wisely keeping his mouth shut. A few others were not so wise, and I snapped, "Not now!" at them as I kept going. When I got to our lodge, I locked the door behind me and headed to my foot-locker, slapping the last shreds and ashes of incinerated clothing off me as I went and releasing the flood of tears I'd kept back until now. I figured it was half grief for Jerin and half embarrassment at losing control. At least I had another couple sets of clothes waiting for me, thanks to the seamstress. I'd need to order some more from her if I was going to treat them this way.

Cleaning myself of ash and getting dressed in fresh clothes was a meditative practice that calmed me. I buckled on all the lava dragon stuff again, including a chest piece, just in case I had another flare-up, but I resolved not to let that happen.

"You're going to have a smoke for Jerin with the guy who killed him," I told myself, speaking aloud but softly. "And you'll get past this, Olet, because your father never would have, and you're not going to be like him."

Freshly garbed and needing to prove to myself that I was back in control, I let only my cheeks erupt in flame and took pleasure in hearing the tears sizzle away. It left behind a dry crust of salt, but I brushed that away. I snuffed the fires, grabbed a fresh pouch of to-bacco and an extra pipe, and returned to the beach. No one tried to hail me this time. And Lanner Burgan, I noticed, had quite sensibly disappeared.

But Abhi and La Mastik were sitting on the beach, facing the North-ern Yawn. They'd built a small campfire, and the boy's bloodcat was stretched out in front of it. The stalk hawk was nowhere to be seen. Knowing what Mirana would probably demand, I sat down next to her so that she was between us. The bloodcat raised his head and watched me carefully but didn't growl or anything. I stuffed some tobacco into the extra pipe and handed it over to Mirana, who passed it to Abhi. It was comically huge in his hands.

"Kalaad," he said. "I've got to smoke all of this?"

"The quantity isn't important," I told him. "It's more about the ritual and the intent. We are here to speak of Jerin. The smoke carries our words to his spirit and makes sure that Thurik hears them as well. You do not have to be of our faith to participate."

"All right, but what if I cough and hack while I'm trying to say stuff? Because I'm pretty sure I will."

"They'll hear that too."

"Great. This is going to be embarrassing."

I tamped more leaves into my own pipe and ignited them both at the same time. "Suck in a breath," I told him. "Get it going." I demonstrated, taking a draw and exhaling a fine stream of smoke.

Abhi squinted and took a puff and immediately began to cough and wheeze. His bloodcat looked alarmed.

"Gack! Thppt! Auggh, that's revolting! How do you stand that?"

"The lavaborn can't burn on the outside. We like to feel the burn where we can. That pretty much means the throat and lungs."

"Hurggh. Uhh. Do I really have to do this?"

"Yes."

"I might throw up."

"I don't care."

"Is this your way of getting revenge?"

"No. Revenge is not an enterprise that leads to personal growth. I am after understanding. Reconciliation. In my culture, this is how it's done. Now, watch and listen and repeat after me."

"Khaaak! Ack. Okay."

I took a deep draw and let the smoke exit as I spoke. "We are here to smoke and remember Jerin Mogen."

Abhi drew from the pipe and coughed as he tried to speak. "Kah! Kuh. We—kaff! Kuff! Are—kak! What she said."

"Good enough. Now, just listen." I puffed and exhaled. "Jerin and I were betrothed by our parents, and we hated it. Our lives and happiness were things to be traded away for our fathers' political advantage. It was easy to despise him. Then I learned that he didn't want to turn into his dad any more than I wanted to be like mine. This place we're at—this dream come true—it was a dream we shared. I never told him that I wanted to run away with him for real. I never got the chance. I was trying to figure out some way to exit where my father wouldn't do what he did—burn things down to find me. We would maybe take off to Rael, catch a boat down to Kauria, where they have that peace thing mostly figured out, disappear into the interior somewhere. Dad wouldn't find us for years, if ever. I didn't think he could leave his cities alone long enough to fetch us."

I took another drag and blew it out slowly. "I miss Jerin and wish he were still here. His death is a huge hole in my future that I won't ever fill, and the coals of my anger about this great void in my life will never be extinguished. I'm incensed that he was lumped in with all the rest as lavaborn. Because he wasn't like the rest of them at all." I peered over at Abhi, feeling those coals flare up inside me but keeping my skin, at least, from bursting into flame. "Now you."

"Now me? What?"

"Now you smoke and respond."

"What do I say?"

"Whatever you feel. Whatever you're holding in that you want to breathe out."

"Okay." He puffed at the pipe, turned a bit green, but kept the coughing to a minimum this time. "I already regretted my actions that day, but I regret them even more now that I've heard about Jerin. I'm glad he was the sort to share a dream with. I'm glad the dream has been realized here and glad I could help in some small way to make it happen. But I'm very sorry I'm the reason he's not living the dream here with you."

Tears streamed down his cheeks and, unprompted, he took another pull and blew out a strong cloud. "If you can hear me through this,

Jerin, I'm sorry." Then he dropped the pipe, turned to the side, and retched on the beach.

When he subsided, he wiped his mouth and said, "That was strangely fulfilling. I feel much better. I mean, not about vomiting, and not about what I did. I mean it was good to say it, to breathe it out, as you said. We Nentians send our words to the sky too, just without smoke. So thanks."

"You did well," La Mastik assured him, then shot an apologetic look at me for interjecting. I gave her a small shake of the head and a smile to tell her not to worry about it. She does not know her own worth, how steadying her presence is. She kept me from burning down my infrastructure and reminded me of the giant I want to be: the one that forges instead of destroys.

But even if Abhi walked in contrition, I did not know if I could walk in forgiveness. The coals of anger still burned within me, red and waiting to blossom into flame.

Rituals may indeed be life preservers, yet still the seas rage on.

"If this next tale doesn't give you something to talk about, I don't know what will," Fintan said, then cast the seeming of scholar Gondel Vedd.

ondel

I had spent a very pleasant evening playing mustard games with Maron and figuring out how to store or otherwise regift all the generous baskets given to me by the good people of Brynlön, which far exceeded my capacity to enjoy. After a delightful breakfast, during which we mostly giggled at each other over how life can send one happiness in the most unexpected ways—no one I knew ever dreamt of a surfeit of gift baskets—I returned to the Calm, fortified with peace. Even the scowling visage of Elten Maff could not ruin my good mood. Especially when the mistral told us how it was going to be.

"You will work together from now on," she said. "I'd like you to pursue the religious angle with Saviič, since he is happy to talk about it and it has yielded us much more intelligence than direct questions. Do not, under any circumstances, share your insights with the military. You are to report to me only."

She must have said more to Scholar Elten Maff along those lines, for as we descended to the dungeon together, he was apologetic. I could tell it hurt him.

"I hope you'll forgive my lapse," he said, though he did not specify what precisely he had lapsed in. Judgment? Scholarship? The best interests of his country? "But rest assured that I am ready and willing to render what aid I can in translating the text and ensuring that Kauria remains at peace."

"I welcome your aid, Scholar Maff," I said. "What do you think about the use of the word *žalost* in *Zanata Sedam?*"

He did not answer for a while, and when he did, it was nothing of substance. "I cannot say I've thought about it at all."

"I have a theory that it might be rather important," I told him, "and I intend to test that theory today."

"Ah. Very well."

That answer satisfied me. If Scholar Maff could not help, at least he would not hinder me overmuch.

Saviič was reading his holy book when we arrived. He closed it and chuckled when he saw us together. He spoke to Scholar Maff first but pointed at me.

"Am I allowed to talk to him now?"

"Yes," he replied. "Speak freely."

Though he didn't say that correctly in Eculan. He said the equivalent of *Speak free,* which gave me a clue that he wasn't nearly at my level, and I didn't consider myself fluent yet.

"I am hoping you can help me, Saviič. I don't understand the importance of Žalost. Can you help me understand?"

The Eculan man smiled his horrible smile, but it appeared genuine this time rather than laced with malice or contempt.

"Yes. I hope so. What do you wish to know?"

"I am fairly certain that Žalost is important in your faith. So who, exactly, is Žalost?"

"He is the god of the Seventh Kenning, of course."

"What?" Scholar Maff blinked, taken entirely by surprise. "Žalost is your god?"

"Yes." He chucked his chin at me. "Gondel finally understood."

It was deeply satisfying to learn that I'd been correct but also supremely annoying to realize that Saviič had been waiting for me to figure it out on my own. He'd never answered my queries about his god before. Elten Maff's jaw dropped and he turned to me. I spoke rapidly in Kaurian.

"In the text, certain nouns are underlined, *žalost* more than any others, and the sentences made little sense if they were common nouns. I realized they might be using the underscore to denote proper nouns, and he's just confirmed it."

Maff blinked again and shook his head. "But that would mean there are other proper nouns that we've been treating incorrectly."

"Yes." I pulled out the list of underscored words I'd made on the ship. "I've written them all down. See, most of them are numbers and directions. But *žalost* is used with great frequency, and so are these others, which must stand for something else."

"That . . . that is brilliant, Scholar Vedd. Well spotted."

"Thank you. Let's ask about these others, shall we?"

I consulted my list of words and spoke again to Saviič. "If Žalost is your god, then who is, ah . . ." I picked a word that had the second-highest number of mentions in the text. "*Jarost?*" I would translate that as *fury* or *rage,* so I had a suspicion, but did not want to hint at it and give him an opportunity to deceive me.

"That is the god of the First Kenning," he said without hesitation.

Maff turned to me. "The First Kenning? He means Thurik?"

"Most likely. Their order of the kennings seems to match ours. Let's find out." I switched to Eculan and asked Saviič, "Jarost is the god of fire, yes?"

"Yes. Fire."

"Mind-blowing," Maff said.

"Scholar Maff, would you mind writing some of this down while I speak to him about these nouns?"

"Yes, of course, of course!"

"We will publish our findings together. But my name will be first."

He grinned at me. "Agreed." He moved around the desk and picked up the quill and a piece of paper. Saviič found this amusing, and he pointed.

"Ha! Now he wants to write it down!"

"Yes. We are learning so much and do not want to forget. This is great. So if Jarost and Žalost are gods of two kennings, what about these others?" I proceeded through my list and it was like turning a key in a lock, the secrets tumbling open for us.

Mir was peace, their word for Reinei. Perfect.

Talas was their word for tides, or Bryn, god of the waves. It became very interesting after that, because they had only one goddess of the Third Kenning instead of the triple goddess of the Raelechs. The word for her was *Kamen,* or stone.

I had two words left. *Razvoj,* which could be translated as growth or development, and then . . . *meso.* Meat.

"Razvoj is the goddess of the Fifth Kenning," he said. Okay, she was associated with plants. That made sense and I fed him the next word, and he smiled. "Meso is the goddess of the Sixth Kenning." That took me a minute to parse and I confirmed with him that he thought the Sixth Kenning had to do with animals.

"Well, all animals are meat," Scholar Maff mused. "At least they are to whatever winds up eating them."

"Ugh. You're right, but I just . . . ugh. This is fascinating and gross at the same time."

"So there's no triple goddess," Maff said, "but there are still three goddesses, right?"

"Yes, I think that's right. And . . . it makes a bit of sense, I think. There's a logical overlap between the triple goddess and these Eculan ones."

"How so?"

"Kamen obviously corresponds to Dinae, the Raelech earth goddess. And I think Meso aligns very well with Raena, since the huntress has a clear interest in the meat of animals. But this Razvoj matching up with the poet Kaelin—it's a little less clear."

"It works for me," Maff said. "The poet goddess is a goddess of craft, of developing one's skills, correct? I'm no scholar of the Raelech faith, but that's how I understand it. Razvoj literally means *development,* and look at the Fornish, who practice the Fifth Kenning. They develop their skills to the utmost, whatever they be. Their woodwork is the envy of the world, and they're amazing brewers and farmers and so on. Or if you wanted to translate the word as *growth,* it still works, since Forn is all about the growth of the Canopy."

"Yes. Yes, I see your point. And when one considers that plants and animals of course rely on the earth to grow, it makes sense that the Raelechs would have bunched these goddesses all together, perhaps, in the early days."

Maff laughed low in his throat. "This is amazing. You know, the Raelechs are going to shit their shorts when they hear about this."

"Ha! Yes, I think some of them might."

Fintan abruptly dispelled his seeming of Gondel Vedd and grinned out at his audience through a wispy cloud of green smoke. "Sorry to interrupt myself," he said, "but I would just like to state for the record that I am still a Raelech bard of the poet goddess Kaelin, and my shorts are super clean. Fantastically clean, in fact."

Laughter rippled across Survivor Field, and he chuckled with them for a moment.

"Okay," he said, taking out a fresh black sphere. "Back to Gondel." He tossed it down, and the seeming of the venerable scholar reappeared.

Once we understood that these nouns were names for gods of the kennings and that they roughly matched the names for the gods we already knew, apart from Žalost, we explained to Saviič that we had analogues in our culture for his gods, except for the last one.

"In Ecula, do you think of these gods and goddesses as siblings, as we do?" I asked.

"Yes. They are all one family."

"Who are their parents?"

"We have names only. We do not know anything else about them."

That was disappointing. I had hoped to hear some stories of Teldwen and Kalaad. "But in Ecula, you know that there were seven siblings and seven kennings."

"Yes. And they did not trust one another."

"They didn't?" That was quite a bit different from the stories of glorious elder days I'd heard.

"No. That was the reason for the *odvajanje*."

I blinked. "The *odvajanje*?" I looked back at Maff. "Do you know that word?"

He shook his head. "No idea."

"What is *odvajanje*? Is there a different word for it that we might know?"

He grimaced in frustration. "The fight," he said, bringing his two fists together and smacking them repeatedly. "The brothers and sisters fight. And that caused the *odvajanje*." He accompanied the last strange word by extending his long arms in front of him, palms rotated out, and then spreading them apart, as if he were performing a breaststroke. "They fight and then the *odvajanje* of the earth happened."

"Oh, gods, Elten," I said, "what if he's talking about the Rift?"

"If he is, then never mind the Raelechs, *I'm* going to shit my shorts."

"This *odvajanje*. Did it cause land to split? Create oceans? Volcanoes?"

"Yes," Saviič said, nodding to emphasize his point.

"He *is* talking about the Rift."

"Indeed he is," Maff said. "And I'll need fresh undergarments later. This is incredible."

Ignoring his commentary, I asked Saviič to explain. "So who was fighting against whom?"

"Everyone fights Žalost. The *odvajanje* was all their fault."

"Six older siblings against the youngest? Why?"

"They were afraid. Afraid of his power."

"What power?"

"His kenning."

"And so we have come full circle. Saviič, what is the Seventh Kenning?"

He shrugged. "I don't know. I was supposed to find out. On the Seven-Year Ship."

That was an unproductive avenue of interrogation. But perhaps he could furnish some additional information about the Rift. I hadn't seen many details about it in *Zanata Sedam*, but I hadn't been fully aware of what I was looking at either. Saviič might know something from other sources anyway.

"So, the *odvajanje*. In your stories, did it include volcanoes in the west? A huge area turned to glass?"

"Yes. Jarost did that."

Yes, that matched with what we thought. Thurik created the Glass Desert with the eruption of the Hearthfire Range. Not wishing to lead him to anything else specific, in case he was guessing what I wanted to hear and merely agreeing, I confined myself to asking, "And what else?"

"A huge storm, wind going in circles near an island somewhere. Still going today. That was Mir."

"He's talking about the Tempest of Reinei," Maff whispered.

"Yes, Elten, I figured that out for myself. Let him talk," I whispered back. "What else?"

"Kamen raised mountains to keep Žalost out and protect her people."

"Kamen raised mountains? Like one or two?"

"No, many mountains in a line. A string of mountains."

"How many strings?"

"Two strings. Because one was there already. It is said her people live in a triangle of mountains today."

"Does he mean Rael?" Maff said.

"I think he does. The one string he said was already there: That must be the Godsteeth. That's the range that Raelechs say was created by plates of earth crushing up against each other. But the Huntress and Poet's Ranges, those are the strange ones that no one can explain. They're not volcanic, and there's no naturally occurring reason for them to be there."

"But now we have an explanation."

"Yes. Kamen—or Dinae, whatever name you wish to call her—was trying to protect the Raelechs from Žalost."

"Or all three of the goddesses were in on that, maybe," Maff said. "The ancient Raelechs must have had some reason to group them together."

I shrugged. "Sure, that's possible. But he's saying it was Kamen alone who raised the mountains."

"Regardless of the details, it's clear from this story that the Eculans believe our continent's very strange topography was created by a family feud."

"Yes. Six elder siblings all ganging up on their baby brother." The idea that the gods had created the Rift was not a new one, but I had always been searching for some external cause or threat that made them react. I'd never thought it might be a family squabble and that the Rift might refer to their damaged relationship as much as to the physical cataclysm that split Hathrir and Kauria off from the main continent.

"That kid must have been a huge jerk," Maff said.

"Or maybe the elder six were."

"Come on, Gondel, his name means *grief* in their own language. That's a pretty big clue to his essential character."

"I'm sure the Eculans don't think they're worshipping a jerk. Maybe he feels grief over the way his siblings treated him. They certainly seem to have disowned him and written him out of history, because this is the first we're hearing about him."

"Are you thinking this might all be true?"

"I can't say. Not for me to judge, except to say that I'm sure both sides of the squabble are presenting themselves in the best possible light. But the Eculan language is very close to the old tongue and has undergone the least linguistic drift. The parallels with our own history are undeniably there. Except for the fact of the Eculans' very existence."

"Yes, that does seem odd."

I apologized to Saviič for all the cross talk in Kaurian. "We are just very surprised and excited about this information."

"I understand. This is fine."

"Thank you. Can you tell me, was Ecula—the land itself—part of the *odvajanje*? Was it split off from the continent?"

"No. The people of Žalost moved there. Žalost led us to Ecula but promised us that one day we would return to the land of bounty."

"He led you across the ocean of krakens?"

"No. Just the ocean. Krakens were not there in the old days. After we got to Ecula, Meso made them."

"The goddess Meso made the krakens. You mean she made them to keep you there?"

"Yes."

"But you've figured out how to get past the krakens now."

Saviič smiled his nasty smile. "Obviously."

Day 31

SMITTEN

The revelations about the Eculan gods were indeed all anyone could talk about until it was time for a new tale. Whether they were actually the same gods as ours under different names, or different gods with similar powers, or whether the Raelechs had it wrong all this time, and who in the abyss was this Žalost character and why didn't our faiths ever mention a seventh child of Teldwen and Kalaad?

Koesha, I remembered, had a different set of names for deities, starting with Shoawei, goddess of the winds. I placed myself in the camp of people who thought we were dealing with the same set of deities under different names. But the origin of the Rift was certainly interesting and difficult to discount, since it potentially fit so many of the facts we had. The Huntress and Poet's Ranges were oddly placed, geologically speaking, and difficult to cross. Krakens in the oceans made travel across them next to impossible—or they had until recently. The only way to attack Rael was from the sea—or risk attacking through one of the tunnels the Raelechs had made through the ranges, which they'd demonstrated they could collapse. The voracious animals of Ghurana Nent seemed to fit well with the concept of a goddess of flesh or meat. What puzzled everyone was figuring out how the Eculan goddess of the Fifth Kenning, Razvoj, could turn out to be either manifesting as the First Tree in Forn or the poet goddess Kaelin in Rael. And, of course, no one knew what the Seventh Kenning was, if it existed at all. If it did, why did the other six children of Teldwen work so hard to hide it?

It made me wonder if Rölly had asked the Wraith about the Seventh Kenning or the Seven-Year Ship. If Saviič was so willing to talk about his faith, then perhaps the Wraith would as well?

And I also wondered if Nara du Fesset had found Gondel Vedd in Fornyd yet.

Fintan looked exhausted when we met, and I soon discovered why: People kept asking him questions about last night's tales. The sorts of questions I had myself, for which he did not seem to have any answers.

After the third interruption in as many minutes at the chowder house, Fintan looked at me, pleading in his eyes. "Is there somewhere we can hide?"

I took him back to the Fornish restaurant we'd visited weeks ago, because they had some private tables screened by hedges and such, and it was also one of the few places that still had a reliable source of vegetables, since they ran their own greenhouses.

We both needed a quiet day, and so we spoke little of outside matters while we worked. But Fintan had a surprise for everyone when he took his stage on the wall that afternoon. "I am going to sing you a love song today," he declared. "For reasons. But I'm pretty sure they're not the kind you're expecting. This is a piece that proves everyone is perfectly beautiful as they are."

> Sometimes I meet a person who's neat
> Who's got everything in its proper place
> And nothing is wild, their hair's nicely styled,
> No blemishes on their face.
>
> But frankly I'm scared of people who care
> 'Bout everything being just so,

Cause what works for me is asymmetry,
Therefore, honey, you should really know:

(Chorus)
I love the mole on your upper lip
The three hairs on it you'll never clip
I love how every time we kiss
I get a bit of moley hairy bliss

I know in the past you thought love wouldn't last
Because you never got a second date
It makes me feel bad that they made you sad
And honestly I cannot relate

Because you are my type and, no, that's not hype
Or some sugary smoke I'm just blowing
The thing is, my dear, your lip's without peer
And I hope your three moley hairs keep growing.

(Chorus)

Just give me moley hairy bliss,
Yeah, just give me moley hairy bliss.

There was a lot of shuddering and shrugs and people saying, "To each his own," after that, and more than a few chuckles. But after the break Fintan said, "Only one tale for you all today: another long one from Tuala, master courier of the Huntress Raena."

*T*uala

The Triune Council granted me light duty at my request after the battle of Möllerud. I was expecting short runs in-country to deliver messages to local councils, but they gave me something else that was potentially more interesting—or more boring, or more deadly: escorting a stonecutter through the Gravewood in Ghurana Nent.

I met him by prearrangment in Dunrae in an establishment called the Queen's Meadery, with a sign outside featuring a magnificent bee on a bed of honeycomb. The master brewer was married to a master apiarist, and they knew their business. Comparing their product to all the other meadhouses I'd been to, I judged it the very best. It was cool and sweet and tart at the same time. I felt refreshed and pleasantly buzzed after only a couple of swallows.

"Powerful stuff, eh?" the stonecutter said.

"Powerful good," I agreed, and he smiled, which did not annoy me at all.

He was a lean, fit man in white linens, a choice of dress I found spectacularly optimistic. His jaw was outlined with a thin beard that he let grow to fullness on his chin, but he kept his upper lip shaved clean and his hair neatly cropped.

"I am Curragh, master stonecutter of Dinae," he told me when we met. His Jereh band, like mine, was bronze, and I saw his eyes note that. "So what did you do, Tuala, to deserve this assignment?" The corner of his mouth quirked up on one end.

"I asked for light duty. I've seen some rough stuff recently."

"Fair enough. I'm surprised they considered this light, though. Rumor has it the Gravewood is unkind to travelers." Again with the small smile. He liked his understatements. I liked his eyes. Wit and kindness danced behind them. Perhaps not a solid grasp of fashion, however.

"It's unkind to white clothing for sure." It looked fine on him in the meadery, but it would be ruined within five minutes on the trail. "You wearing that tomorrow?"

"Oh, no, I wouldn't dream of it. This is only for special occasions."

"Drinking in Dunrae is a special occasion?"

"On the eve of a job like this it is. We're following a virgin trail to a new city with one—just one!—Raelech citizen. You've been briefed, right?"

"I have. There's a lunatic bard who's hooked up with this band of Nentians and Hathrim, and he wants us to build him a nice road to get home someday."

"I can't believe the Triune is sending us to do his bidding."

"Apparently he's seen some shit and they want to hear about it. And they also want in on the ground floor of what could be a vastly profitable enterprise. Who knows what riches are hidden up there?"

"Well, there you go. This is special. I've only ever worked on roads that were already carved out by others before this. Filling in ruts and shoring up shoulders, you know. Important work that saves many a blown axle, no doubt. But those gigs are over well-worn trails and almost always boring until someone tells a good joke. This job, though, is going to be dangerous. Maybe even deadly. Because gravemaws and murder weasels don't care what meat they're eating as long as it's hot and fresh. This could be my last drink right here, you know? So I gotta wear the good linens for that."

"I see. So you have a different, more practical set of clothing to wear on the trail tomorrow?"

"I do. Had it made specially, in fact. It is the color of dust." This time his tiny smile gets me to laugh.

"Good call, sir. It sounds like you've been repairing roads often. I've probably traveled them at one time or another. Which ones should I thank you for?"

His list of credits was impressive, and I had indeed literally run across his work on many occasions. I hadn't realized that some stone-cutters specialized in roadwork.

"And you did this with other couriers, I assume, or did you work at normal speeds?"

"Often with couriers on light duty," he admitted, "though occasionally at the much slower pace. Those jobs take forever."

"I imagine so. Which couriers have you worked with?"

His list included Numa, and at her name I perked up and interrupted. "It's Numa's husband we have to blame for this. He's the lunatic bard who made the request for this project through diplomats."

Curragh raised his glass. "To Numa's husband, then."

I clinked his glass with mine. "To Numa's husband." We drank, and before we turned in, we promised to meet at dawn.

Curragh really did have a set of leathers and underclothes the color of dust, and when he showed up the next morning wearing it, I laughed.

"What? You thought I was joking about this? There's no use fighting the earth on this point. Wear any other color and it will be this one by the end of the day. I figure if I start out this way, I win at the end because I meant to be covered in dust from the start."

We slid through the tunnel to Ghurana Nent quickly, using the lane to one side reserved for couriers. We passed plenty of traders, and they had their goods tied down as they should to guard against the wind of our passage, but we could never prevent them or their animals from being startled by us. Wart oxen bugled and shat in our wake, and traders cursed and maybe shat also, for all I knew.

I made a courtesy call on the viceroy of Ghuli Rakhan and at the Raelech embassy before we began in earnest, just to make sure there were no messages that needed to be delivered. I was given a satchel full of mail for many of the Nentians and a request for a status report from the viceroy. He also gave Curragh a list of names that should be inscribed somewhere on the waypoint bunkers he would build—memorial sorts of things, or else a weird payoff to political allies and cronies who thought there was prestige in having a bunker in the woods named after them. And then Curragh and I began our work.

A laden cart on a good road could manage about five leagues a day. I didn't know if the group ahead of us had been able to make that pace, since they were clearing trees as they went, but Curragh quickly informed me that we wouldn't be able to make the typical ten leagues a day a courier and stonecutter covered on duty like this.

"There are stumps and boulders all over the place to be submerged. If we don't take it a bit slower, I won't be able to catch them all and get the surface smooth and packed. And after that first downhill slope, I can tell I'm going to need to move around quite a bit of earth to ease the grades."

We wound up moving at my kenning's slowest possible speed and only made seven leagues the first day, but we were both exhausted at the end of it. That was because, in addition to the work, we'd been attacked on three separate occasions by denizens of the Gravewood, and only my speedy application of a club to the head saved us. We each bore nothing more than some scratches to our leathers, but that sort of thing takes an outsize toll on a person's stamina. If we saw a gravemaw, we were going to simply run as fast as I could manage, road be damned.

The first bunker Curragh built was, by the viceroy's request, far larger and more luxurious than any other he would erect along the way. It was to be named after King Kalaad the Unaware, whose final order before his murder had been to provision the colony we were traveling to.

While Curragh slowly drew up the stone from the surrounding earth to construct it, I circled the site, hyperaware that something could be stalking us. I took care to watch the trees as well. There were meat squirrels and other arboreal predators to worry about.

But I will share this: For all its ridiculous danger, the Gravewood was beautiful. The leaves of scattered deciduous trees were beginning to change, and the evergreen needles of the pines delivered a sharp fresh sting in the nose, welcome and friendly.

Nothing more attacked us, and we were able to retire into the bunker to build a fire in the hearth. The chimney worked well, and I complimented him on the quick and competent build. I envied stonecutters their blessing sometimes.

"Thanks," he said. "That was a fine saving of my life you did there on multiple occasions today. I envy couriers their blessing sometimes."

It was so nearly what I had been thinking that I cocked my head at him.

"May I ask your age, Curragh, or would you think me rude?"

"I wouldn't. I will tell you without expectation of reciprocity: I am thirty."

"I'm twenty-five."

"Oh? We must have just missed each other at the Colaiste, then."

"Only just. So to pry a bit further, why the bronze Jereh band? Handsome stonecutter and all that?"

He snorted and grinned at me. "I don't mind. You're not the first to ask. Like you, I live a life on the road. Not ideal for the nurturing of relationships and tiny Raelech babies."

"Did someone shove you into this role as a one-man road crew?"

"No, quite the opposite. I sought it. I prefer the road to the cities. In between the cities you see Rael as the triple goddess made it. There's the smell of grass and wildflowers. Not so much the stench of tanneries and butcher shops and other markers of human existence."

"You're edging toward the romantic there. You should have been a bard."

"Nah. They need audiences, and for that you usually need cities. I think I merely prefer the idyllic life to the urban. And look, Tuala: Consider me curious in general about you, but please don't share anything you'd rather not. I won't ask anything specific, because . . . well, we are practically strangers and you have no reason to trust me. And couriers are asked to do so much for us. But I enjoy stories by the fire."

I dug a candle and my steel flask out of my pack and tossed it to him. "Okay. Take a pull on that while I get changed. The leathers need attention."

"Eh? What's this?"

"Aelinmech rye."

"The Good Shit? For real?"

"Yes, the Good Shit."

"Holy shit."

I lit my candle in the fire and left him in the hearth hall unscrewing the cap of the flask, while I went in search of a private room. There were plenty of them, and it dawned on me that I'd never seen a bunker built this way before. It was designed for large parties of people; multiple rooms had sleeping slabs racked along the walls. The privies—two of them with multiple stalls—were of a much more modern design than other bunkers I'd seen, incorporating the latest advice from Brynt hygienists for waterless operation.

Choosing a slab in the last bunkroom, I unzipped my pack and took off my armor. The front was dusty and bug-splattered and even required a few stitches, where some hungry creature's claws had tried to take off my leg before lunch.

I unpacked my cloths and polish and emergency sewing kit and returned to the hearth hall, sitting on one of the stone stools Curragh had made. He held out the flask to me and I took a nice, burning swallow.

"Thanks for the drink," he said, then pointed at my supplies. "Goddess, that's a lot of stuff you have there. It must take up half your pack."

"It does." I began with wiping away surface dirt and cleansing the bug guts.

"I like beautiful armor as much as the next person," he said, "but it's just going to look the same way tomorrow. Why not wait until we reach our destination?"

Quirking an eyebrow at him, I said, "I thought this bunker was a destination now."

He chuckled. "You honor me."

"Good. It is what I do."

"Honor stonecutters?"

"Not specifically, but yes. I meant in more general terms."

"Unsure I'm following you."

The pressure of my cloth revealed the rich red color of the thigh piece, and I dug into the deep grooves of claw marks to remove dirt and maybe a little bit of my dried blood before I got out my needle and thread. The claws had penetrated enough that they managed to scratch me, albeit shallowly. I needed to sew up the rent in my pants too. I shuddered to think of how shredded my leg would have been without the armor. Keeping my eyes on the work, I explained.

"At the risk of earning your contempt, I am quite devout in my worship of the triple goddess, but Raena especially. I keep the words of her scrolls close to my heart, and she teaches us that there is honor in service and duty and craft when it is pursued with a pure mind."

"A pure mind? I'm not familiar with that phrase. And no contempt here, by the way, though I know why you might expect it. I am devout to Dinae and occasionally receive some scorn for it."

"Would you mind if I quoted you the passage?" I asked, replying only to his inquiry. People often said they were devout but did not back up their breath with deeds; they were the wind on the mountain instead of the mountain itself.

"No, please do," Curragh said. "I know it occasionally has its downsides, but a perfect memory is a wondrous blessing at times."

"Even so," I replied, nodding. "Raena says: 'One may perform service and duty and craft for selfish ends and be rewarded. One should always be rewarded, in fact, for service and duty and craft. But there is no honor in selfishness. Honor comes from selflessly performing service and duty and craft. Thus, pure work from a pure mind will not only be rewarded, but you will honor yourself and the work of your fellows.' It goes on from there about the nature of honor, but that is where the 'pure mind' phrase comes from."

"Ah, thank you. But shoot the marbles for me here, since I don't want to misunderstand: You are honoring people with your duty and service?"

"Precisely. The Triune rewards me with a salary, but I give most of that to the temple. Keeping my leathers in their best condition is not only my duty but honors the craft of the armorer who made it. I try to live and work with a pure mind so that all are honored."

"Who did make your armor, by the way? It's beautiful work."

"Master Simeagh in Aelinmech."

"Oh, yes, I've heard of him."

"He does some work for the Fornish, and in return they supply him a special plant-based grease for leather maintenance. I have no idea what's in it, but it's miraculous stuff. I use it often and it keeps my leathers looking new. Probably nobody cares but me. I think—no, I'm certain—that some believe I've had too many stones hit my head. But it's important to me."

I looked up from my work to see that Curragh had leaned forward on his stool, elbows on his knees and hands clasped before him.

"I find that . . . extraordinary. In a positive way. I joked about it earlier, but my armor and my clothing are the color of dirt because to me there is nothing more holy than to be clothed in the earth. I don't clean it because it would be brushing off the goddess."

I gasped in alarm, realizing how my ritual cleaning could look to him. "Curragh, I mean no disrespect to Dinae—"

"No, no, no, I understand. I see that what you do comes from a pure mind, and I'm glad you taught me that. I try to act from the same place in my heart—or the bosom, as Dinae might put it. She voices similar sentiments to the huntress in her texts, but the phrasing is different."

I smiled. "I know."

"Ha! Of course you do. You know the scrolls better than I do. But it's good to meet someone else who tries to live a devout life. I donate most of my salary to the temple as well. I sleep there, in fact, when I'm not out on jobs. I have no permanent residence."

My eyes narrowed and lips pressed together in suspicion. "Are you making fun of me?"

"What? No, no! I don't understand."

"Did someone tell you how I live?"

"No. I never heard of you until we met last night. Do you mean to say you spend nights in temples also?"

"Yes. Every night I'm not in a bunker like this or a Raelech embassy somewhere."

"Rock me," he said, shaking his head in wonder. "The other couriers I've met don't do that."

"Nor do the other stonecutters I've met."

We laughed at the coincidence, and then, much to my embarrassment, a tear practically leapt out of my eye and ran down my cheek.

"Oh, no!" Curragh said. "What's the matter?"

I wiped the traitorous tear away with the heel of my palm. "Nothing. It's just nice to finally meet someone else who lives the way I do. I mean, there are plenty of devout Raelechs, thank the goddess, but you don't meet many of the blessed who choose the ascetic path. So I'm happy to learn that you have. It means I'm not alone."

"Oh, good. I was worried I'd offended somehow."

"Not at all." I sniffled and dropped my eyes to my leathers. Before it could get any more awkward than I had already made it, I changed the subject. "I've never seen a bunker like this one before. Who designed it?"

"I did. This is my very first build." That jerked my gaze back up.

"Really? I wouldn't have thought it was your first. It's impressive."

"Thanks. I've been waiting a long time to do something like this. The old roads already have their bunkers, you know, and it's not polite to tear down some other stonecutter's work. Not to mention disrespectful of the history of architecture. But here we have a new trade route, and I'll get to build all these designs I've had bouncing around my head for years."

"Yeah?" I grinned at him, suspecting that I had just spied the first glint of a vein that ran deep into his core. "Tell me what you have planned."

He did, at length, while I worked on my polishing chores. We finished off the contents of my flask, partly to celebrate his accomplishment and partly to celebrate finding someone else of a similar mindset. He did crush my stones about it, though.

"That whiskey is pretty fancy for an ascetic, don't you think?" He had the same tiny half smirk on one side of his mouth that I had seen yesterday, which I was coming to recognize as an indication he was having fun.

"I forgo many luxuries, Curragh, but I don't settle for shitty whiskey, and neither should you."

"You upbraid me sternly, and I take your scolding to heart." He said that with the same teasing expression.

"It's only proper. I'm honoring the distiller's craft."

"Consider me well schooled."

"Hope you enjoyed it, because that's all I have."

"I did. Thank you." He flashed a full smile at me, and I felt flutters in my stomach.

My leathers were in fine condition for the morning, so I rose and said, "We have a long day ahead, and many more after that. I'm going to get some sleep."

"Goddess give you good rest. I'm going to put a few more finishing touches on this place and turn in after that. I'll make sure to sleep in a different room so you'll have privacy. Which one are you in?"

"Last one down the hall."

"Noted. See you in the morning."

"Good rest."

And halfway out of the hall, I felt a tug on my heart to stay a bit longer. I ruthlessly ignored it and kept going, paying attention instead to the other tug on my heart, which told me to flee. Because if I stayed I would inevitably do or say something I would forever replay in my mind in a carousel of embarrassment.

I spread my bedroll out on the chosen slab near the floor and blew out the candle. In the darkness, I admitted to myself that I liked Curragh. A lot. After knowing him for one whole day.

It was probably just a reaction to Tarrech's death. *You're feeling desperate and lonely*, I told myself. *And maybe a bit drunk.* The one thing I'd held on to for so long was gone, and what was it anyway? A feeling. A ball of yearning and self-denial I'd nurtured since my Colaiste days and placed on a pedestal. I supposed it kept me safe in some ways, but it also left a void.

You can't have it all, Tuala. You can have something, though. I mean, something besides the Good Shit from Aelinmech.

Tears spilled out of my eyes again, and this time I let them run where they would.

I will remember every endearing thing Tarrech ever said or did. And I will also regret never telling him how I felt. We could have been . . . well. I don't know if we ever could have been. I don't know if Curragh and I can ever be either. He might not be so charming on day two as he was on day one.

But it is time, I thought, *that I make some different unforgettable memories. Embarrassing ones, perhaps. But not more memories of shrinking back and doing nothing. I have had enough of those. My mind overflows with nothing.*

In the morning, I voiced my hope to Curragh that we'd reach the river we were supposed to find sooner rather than later.

"My canteen is a bit low," I said.

"No need to worry about it. After you went to bed last night, I made a well in the kitchen."

"What kitchen?"

"I made that too. Not sure how clear the water's going to be. It might not have had time enough to settle."

"Never mind that. How are you going to get it out of there? I didn't see you bring a bucket."

"But I did bring a good length of rope in my pack. I made a small bucket out of very thin stone. Made a pitcher and basin for each of the privies. Didn't do much else, though. Absolutely nothing decorative. I was too tired."

"I should imagine so."

"Help me out with it?"

I nodded and he led me back to the kitchen, which he'd added on to the hearth hall. It had another hearth and chimney and, as promised, a sheltered well with a stone crossbar over it. The bucket of thin stone was sitting on the edge of the well, a gorgeous polished thing of browns, tans, and reds.

"Nothing decorative? This is beautiful."

"Thanks. But the rest of the kitchen is pretty basic."

That was true, at least. There was a stone prep table and some bench storage lockers to cache supplies and keep them safe from little critters. Future visitors would have to make improvements as they wished, but Curragh had provided the foundation for a fantastic refuge along this trail.

The rope he'd mentioned was coiled on the prep table. He tossed one end over the crossbar to me and I tied it to the handle of the bucket, which had a pour spout. Once the knot was secure, I guided the bucket gently over the center of the well and Curragh lowered it until he heard a splash. It wasn't that far down, since we were already underground.

The water we pulled up was cloudy, as he'd suspected, but the silt would settle down soon enough.

"We need to get a hygienist out here to test it," I said.

"Some other trip for sure. Looks like we'll need to find that river soon after all."

We dumped it back in and Curragh tied off the rope on the side of the well, leaving the bucket hanging. We shared a shy breakfast of jerky and dried fruit, and then we packed up, Curragh put on his dusty armor, and we emerged to begin the second day of roadwork.

I still liked him at the end of it.

And at the end of the third, and fourth, and so on.

We found the river and replenished our canteens, after boiling the water out of an excess of caution. Not a day passed in which we were not attacked several times by animals, but thankfully not by a grave-maw. Still, anyone coming this way would need to be heavily guarded.

I was usually able to track down a couple of snowshoe hares or a wild turkey or something for our evening meal, but we subsisted on dry rations otherwise.

Each bunker Curragh made was a bit different, but he made no more wells, since we were right next to the river. He did create smooth landings down to it, however, so that horses and oxen could reach it easily and water could be hauled up to the bunkers by humans.

He spent some time making fine polished-stone nameplates for each bunker, according to Viceroy Khusharas's wishes, and he always created a beautiful pitcher and basin for the privies. Otherwise, his designs were simple, utilitarian, and—most important out here—safe from predators.

During my nightly ritual cleansing and polishing of my armor, we would trade stories of beautiful places we'd visited. I told him about other countries, mostly Brynlön's unexpected bucolic river lands and Ghurana Nent's vast dry plains, the land stretching away in golds and tans like a warm, sunbaked blanket. He told me of roads off the main trails I traveled in Rael that led to small villages rarely marked on maps—a collection of services and a market, really, to serve a number of ranches and farms spread out along a vast area all along the roots of the Godsteeth. He told me of grassy green hills dotted with sheep, quilted patches of corn and beans and cabbage. And in one valley of the Huntress Range, a vast herd of wild horses roamed undisturbed, and when they moved, the thrumming of their hooves could be felt in the soles of your own feet. I vowed to visit it someday.

Each night we slept in different rooms, and each night I wished I knew how to signal my willingness to change that without embarrassing either one of us.

He clearly enjoyed my company, but I couldn't tell if he wished for anything more than friendship. He gave me no clues; he remained utterly professional and polite, which may have meant he was hiding his true feelings or it may have meant he truly wasn't interested.

It occurred to me that I was behaving in precisely the same way to him: polite and professional but never hinting that I wanted anything else. He might be wishing for more but was too afraid of giving offense and perhaps souring what was otherwise a delightful and interesting job.

We might both be denying ourselves bliss out of respect. Which was sad and sweet at the same time. Or I might be imagining everything, except my inability to flirt. That was very real, unfortunately.

When we arrived, a bald Hathrim woman named La Mastik welcomed us to the Nentian city of Malath Ashmali. And then we were hit by one surprise after another.

They had suffered only a single casualty from an animal on their way north and nothing since arriving, because they had a young man among them who'd found the Sixth Kenning.

He'd used that Sixth Kenning to save some foreign sailors from a kraken attack.

He could also prevent future kraken attacks. The people of our continent could safely cross the oceans. With his help, Rael could strike back against the Bone Giants.

That meant the world was going to change. More than it already had. And my light duty of unimportant work was suddenly the most important assignment I'd ever been given.

I spent a lot of time over the next few days with Fintan and Koesha, the leader of the Joabeian crew, getting caught up on what had happened so that I could report both to the viceroy and the Triune Council. The young man they called the plaguebringer, Abhinava Khose, gave me a letter for the viceroy, which he said should be read before I talked about him or his abilities. Then I was to give the viceroy a collection of enchanted wooden stakes that would repel animals and free the citizens of Ghuli Rakhan from living surrounded by walls.

There was no viceroy here but rather a steward and a council, both recently elected. It looked like there was tension on the council between some Hathrim members and the Nentians, but the Nentians didn't have any problems with Olet Kanek being the steward. Curragh spent his time with Steward Kanek and her council discussing infrastructure projects that he could help them with, such as building a forge and a kiln and a Brynt-style sewer system.

"Let's build a Raelech embassy here," Curragh said at the end of our third day. We were a block away from the city hall, near the edge of the drop-off that led to the beach but was not completely exposed. We could see the Northern Yawn through a screen of tree trunks. "We'll make that our quarters, and Fintan will have a room as well. And when you return to Killae, you can tell them they need to assign a diplomat here as soon as possible."

"When I return? You're not coming back with me?"

Curragh shook his head. "I don't think so. There is plenty of work for me here. A chance to do things I've never done before. A chance to put a lasting design imprint on a new city, you know? I can be founding builder and do much to establish goodwill for Rael here. It's not an opportunity that comes along all that often. It's a once-in-a-lifetime thing, honestly."

Something wrenched inside my chest at that, a crushing of a hope I didn't know I'd been harboring. I supposed I'd thought maybe we'd be able to continue our sort-of kind-of unspoken relationship in Rael, where I'd be able to ask someone for advice on how to flirt properly. But even if we did that, I mused, trying to spin the change positively, Curragh would often be on the road somewhere and I'd be on a different road somewhere else. If he remained in one place, I could see him more often, by requesting all jobs going to Malath Ashmali. And maybe it was for the best. Maybe with some time away I'd discover that I wasn't really all that enamored of him and I was still reeling from Tarrech's death.

"I understand. That would be great for you. Maybe when they assign a diplomat, they'll let me escort her back here."

"That would be my wish," he said, nodding.

I caught his eye, a shy smile forming. "Would it, now?"

He looked down, suddenly interested in his clasped hands. "Yes."

I didn't reply, just kept smiling at him and savoring the moment. I'd relive it later. Because there was so much to relive in moments like that. Flutters of hope and a swelling of euphoria, a whorl of giddiness and an internal scream of sheer terror because you're hurtling down a dark tunnel and there might be either treasure or a gravemaw at the end of it.

"Of course," he said, "you should inform all the ambassadors in Killae that if their countries wish to build an embassy here, I'll happily do so for standard rates. Olet and the council have already approved and set aside sites for each country. Basically, it's all along this street."

"What street?"

"This one right here. If you can't see it, that's because I haven't made it yet."

"Ah. I understand now. Would you want me to escort those ambassadors here too?"

"Yes." He finally looked up and met my gaze. Whatever he saw must have encouraged him, because he cleared his throat, rather unnecessarily, and said, "I'd prefer it if you never left, actually. Though I know that's impossible."

"And why would you prefer that, exactly?"

"Well, um." He looked away again and visibly gulped. "I don't want to say anything that would make you uncomfortable, so please stop me if I leap over a wall."

"I'm not stopping you. Do go on."

"Ah. Yes. Well. Tuala . . . I've never met someone so blessed with more than a blessing. Your devotion to the huntress is inspiring. You're a formidable warrior, an impeccable courier, unfailingly polite, and a stunning beauty. So I'm helplessly smitten."

"Okay, Curragh, stop right there. Not because you jumped a wall, but because that was perfect. Except you need to kiss me now." I gasped and my eyes flew wide, I was so surprised at my own brazenness. Had I really said that out loud?

That amused quirk to his lips appeared briefly, and then he kissed me, soft and warm and . . . okay, maybe it was just a tiny bit too soft. I grabbed the back of his head and pressed him more firmly against me, so thirsty for something more tangible than wishes in a lonely bunk, and then he responded. He felt that way too. When we finally broke apart, gasping, a small ovation greeted us. Some Nentians and Hathrim had gathered to watch, which I thought was strange, but I supposed we hadn't sought privacy either, so I couldn't be mad, especially since they had clapped. We gave them a smile and a wave and proceeded to ignore them.

"I'm going to sleep early because I need to leave at dawn," I told Curragh, "but I'll return as soon as I can. I don't know that I can promise more than that. But I can say I wouldn't mind some more perfect memories of moments like this. All right?"

He nodded and then pressed his forehead against mine. "Good rest. Goddess grant you a safe and speedy journey. I'll be waiting."

"Build us a beautiful embassy. I'll look forward to staying there when I get back."

Going to sleep was such a peace and I slept so well. And that run back to Rael was along a brand-new road in more than one sense. I spent a night in the first bunker Curragh built—the one with the well—and pulled up the bucket. The water had settled and cleared, and I found some other clarity as well: I missed him and his dusty clothes.

I missed Tarrech too, and always would. But holding on to him would be a poor foundation on which to build my future. At the same time, questions weren't a great foundation either, but they were all I had other than a nascent hope for something beyond wishful thinking. Was it possible for a pair of lonely ascetics to have a slice of happiness in the middle of a war? Would I be able to let my guard down enough to speak freely to him as he had to me? Or: Was he playing me? What if he was my best shot at a blissful relationship and I ruined it because of my dithering? What if, like Tarrech and Aevyn, I could have it all for just a single season? Would it be worth the pain that followed when it was over?

I have kept my heart safely cocooned for so long because I don't know what the world will be like if I tear free of it. My kenning protects my body from most danger, so I run into it unafraid. But I have no protection for my heart except to keep it to myself. There I am vulnerable, so there I am most guarded.

I am going to run down this new road because I promised myself I would. But I cannot do so without an excess of caution, and I hope Curragh will recognize that and be patient and turn out to be all I ever want to have.

Day 32

REVOLUTION

When I showed up to the refugee kitchen in the morning, Chef du Rödal set me on sardine duty again, though there was some variety in the catch that day. The bulk of the daily offering would be shrimp pasta. But still no shipments of vegetables. At least none that had reached her.

"Heard there was a scuffle at the docks last night. Fornish ship came in with a load of produce, and some fish heads swarmed it once a few pallets were unloaded. You'll notice nothing got here. But somebody's going to be serving produce in town today or selling it at the market. Whoever has it either was in on the heist of that cargo or paid whoever did it."

"A vegetable heist? Clams and tentacles."

Fintan wanted to meet at the Roasted Sunchuck again, and it was crowded as before, but there was very little on the menu—and no vegetables.

They had the same sardines as everyone else, but they weren't packed raw in oil and salt; rather, they were grilled by Hollit and served with garlic aioli and toasted baguettes with some onion jam she had lying around. They had some pasta dishes and a limited number of

sunchucks, but that was it. There was, however, plenty of beer and liquor available, because those ships kept coming in.

Hollit and Orden admitted to us that they wouldn't be able to stay
open much longer without resupply, and they'd heard several restaurants had closed already. Our favorite chowder house was closed
until further notice, as was the Kaurian restaurant. The Fornish place
was closing at end of business, Hollit said, and the Roasted Sunchuck
would in a couple of days if something didn't come in.

The meal was as delicious as everything was in their place, but we
ate with a certain measure of anxiety on the side, like when floodwaters are ankle height and rising but you're not quite panicked yet
because the water hasn't reached your nipples.

When we got to the wall later, an assortment of drummers was
waiting for Fintan. They'd been practicing a song from Joabei—the
only one he'd been able to learn from Koesha. She and several other
crew members had played the parts by slapping sticks against trunks or
buckets or crates.

"I have something fun for you today," he said as the musicians set
up. "A song from Joabei. Should get your blood pumping. The entire
point of Joabeian music is to get you dancing and out of breath. They
want you having fun and also appreciating the great privilege of
breathing right now, and I think we can all get behind those ideas.
When Koesha and a few of her crew performed this, the rest of the
crew danced and sang at the appropriate times. I can't teach you the
dance, so just do what you want there, but the song is only four lines,
and you're supposed to stop dancing and shout it in unison, one line at
a time. There's a bar of music between each line, during which you
flail around a bit, and then an extended time of dancing to the music
before shouting the same four lines again. I think you'll get the hang of
it. So get on your feet, dance as you like, and shout along when you
pick it up."

The drummers began with some pounding, grooving rhythms that
were unlike any I had heard before, and everyone was instantly de-

lighted. I did my upper-body shimmy routine, since my knee wouldn't allow actual dancing, got the words half right the second time through, and shouted them perfectly the third and fourth times.

> *The secret of the wind is passing you by!*
> *The mystery of breath hides in every sigh!*
> *The miracle of life flowing in the sky!*
> *Listen to the song of Shoawei!*

When that was finished, we did need a break, but people were smiling and laughing. Joabeian music was great.

"Three tales for you today," Fintan said after we'd rested. "Koesha Gansu first, then Hanima Bhandury, and finally Viceroy Bhamet Senesh." His first seeming revealed the ship captain from Joabei, looking pensive.

The giant woman Olet does not appear to be a fire demon. Not in the sense that we think of them, anyway. She has the horrifying powers of one but not the heart. She has a heart for peace and a mind and body willing to build it with others. She has welcomed us to this place, and I think she intends to give us a voice in its government once we learn the language of Abhi, the young man who saved us from the kraken.

That is why I have assigned most of the crew to team up with Nentians to help them with their work building the city and to learn their words, though Haesha and Leisuen are paired with the two giants who can use fire. Olet may seem benign, but the Cantos of Shoawei warn of complacency around fire. It must be diligently watched and guarded. The demon Keishun built slowly in darkness until he exploded with his horde, and Shoawei nearly perished in his ambush. We cannot afford to be taken by surprise.

And I must worry that I'm making another mistake. Is my decision to trust in Olet really the best for my crew, or am I once again barreling forward without fully considering the consequences? Sixty women are dead because I wanted to go forward instead of back.

But going back at this point is impossible. The only way home is to keep going.

We decide to learn Nentian once Fintan draws us a rough map of the huge continent we are on and it becomes clear that Ghurana Nent is closest to Joabei; its cities would become our primary ports for trade, even if we make only one trip a year. Perhaps we will do more if krakens can finally be controlled. That we are still breathing and have hope to see Joabei again is a miracle.

"But we won't get home," I tell my crew, "unless we survive this winter and get along with these people who saved our lives. They won't help us build a boat unless we first help them build this place and show them that we are a culture worth knowing."

Baejan asks what no doubt is on many minds: "If you want us to get along for the winter, how far are we allowed to take that?"

There are some giggles at that, and I smile.

"Each of you can make your own decision, of course," I reply. "There is no doubt that you have earned it. But keep in mind that these people may not have the same attitudes toward sex and reproduction that we do. It is practically guaranteed that they don't. So it may be wiser for us to wait a little while, learn some basic language, then have one volunteer try and see how everyone else reacts to the news. Can we agree on that?"

"I volunteer!" Baejan immediately says, and we all share a laugh at her eagerness.

"Okay. If their reaction is positive or at least permissive, then we can all proceed, or not, as we wish. For the short term, we should help them work and learn their language as quickly as possible. But I would like to give two orders in that regard."

The few titters and whispered conversations about possible relationships with Nentians die down immediately.

"I have already told them that our people are of the Second Kenning. But I have not told them that I am blessed, and I do not want to reveal that until it's absolutely necessary. At some point you may be asked if any of us are blessed or what the source of our kenning is, and if that happens, you should either say you don't understand the question or don't know the answer. Is that first order clear?"

Leisuen asks, "Zephyr, is it okay to say *none* of us is blessed?"

"I'd rather you did not. You can plausibly say you didn't understand the question, but if you say something that directly contradicts what may later be revealed, that could cause a problem. My hope is that I don't have cause to use my kenning again until we have built a ship and I'm filling the sails to get us home."

Some of the women clap at that prospect.

"Second order: Do not discuss the makeup of our crew or our laws. Change the subject or play dumb. Don't explain. We will wait for diplomats to handle such things much later. Our goal is to get out of here as soon as possible with as little conflict as possible."

No one has a question about that, and then I suggest we share what we learn each night over the evening fire.

"Fintan told me today that there is a country in the southern hemisphere called Kauria that also has the Second Kenning. They worship a god named Reinei, who preaches peace. Those who seek a kenning throw themselves into a whirlwind off the coast of an island. They call the whirlwhind 'the Tempest of Reinei.' So, in addition to getting home someday, I'd like to visit Kauria and see what another culture has made of the Second Kenning."

Leisuen shares that the Hathrim also came from the south and call their blessed "lavaborn." They leapt into a particular lake of lava to gain their kenning. The scary-looking bald giant with no hair or lips is a priestess of the flame named Mirana La Mastik, and she wears the fireproof hide of a lava dragon.

There is a country called Forn, where short pale people live in the trees. Another called Brynlön, where they have mastered the Fourth Kenning, thanks to a god of the sea they call Bryn. There is so much to learn.

One of the Nentians is supervising the construction of docks down by the river as well as a fishing boat, which has a couple of the Hathrim excited. They are willing to help but are not very skilled woodworkers; I get the idea from Fintan that they most often work in steel and glass and think of wood as fuel rather than construction material.

I attach myself to the dock detail and the bard attaches himself to me; he's decided apparently that I have much to teach him, and I think he might be picking up our tongue faster than we are picking up Nentian, thanks to his perfect memory.

The tools they've brought with them are different from what I'm used to, but they get the job done. The nails are thinner than ours and have broader heads. The saws are of remarkable quality, and I ask Fintan clumsily about where the mining is done.

He says much of it is done in his country, which is ringed by mountains rich in ores and stones.

It is good to have the distractions of physical labor and language acquisition almost constantly. Otherwise, I would blow apart in a shearing whirl of guilt and self-doubt. I distract myself from our loss and my decisions only for small slivers of time, and then my thoughts circle back to it.

I am not the only one who's conscious of the fact that we should all be dead right now, like every other crew who sailed east and west from Joabei, looking for the northern passage. Had I turned back when Leisuen urged me to, we'd all have made it home. But we wouldn't have found these cultures here, this information about the continent that will prove profitable beyond measure in the future, that will make us famous—or infamous—in the history of Joabei.

Perhaps history will look back and say the deaths of sixty women were worth it to gain such bounty for the rest of the country. It's easy to look at numbers on paper and make such a calculation. But that is not what I feel. I'd rather be sailing home with all of them now, still ignorant of Nentians and Hathrim and all the rest.

That is the gift of hindsight, of course. If I had chosen to sail home, I'd be stewing over the decision and wishing I had pressed on to find Maesi.

It's impossible to tell which weight would have sat heavier on my shoulders, but I am pretty sure that these certain deaths have a greater weight than simply not knowing about Maesi. I know what it was like to not know about Maesi's fate. This is worse.

We will have a ceremony for our lost crew members soon; I feel a storm coming. We will howl with the wind and wish their spirits calm. I don't think mine will ever be at rest.

"Meanwhile, in Khul Bashab . . ." Fintan said, before taking on the seeming of Hanima.

I have made some actual money with my kenning! The Red Pheasant Clan paid me on a short-term contract to bring bees and other pollinators to their grounds, but especially to the new tea treehouse, to help the plant life do its thing and thrive. They did it secretly, though, because we are still on the viceroy's Grand High Shitte Liste and about to make things worse. But I have decent clothes of my own now and I don't have to borrow from other folks' wardrobes to look presentable. It's the best.

Since I didn't really need my share of Tamhan's funding, I gave it to Adithi, and now she has decent clothes too. We still don't have a legit place to live, since we're wanted figures and sleeping in empty houses, but at least we aren't dressed in rags and half-starving anymore. It feels amazing. It feels like anything is possible. Like overthrowing a government.

After talking for long hours with Jes Dan Kuf and privately lamenting the departure of the dreamy greensleeve—he had to go grow more treehouses—we came up with a plan. It was like throwing a rock into a nughobe grove and then waiting for all the creatures hiding in there to come after you in the plains, where you could see them and deal with them. We were going to post another broadside, which would go much further than the first one, saying that the beast callers were real.

The Sixth Kenning is HERE!

We can live in harmony with animals!

Now is the time for a

NEW NENTIAN GOVERNMENT!

A Clave Republic guaranteeing

basic dignity & prosperity for ALL

Freedom from WALLS

Freedom from CORRUPT OFFICIALS

Freedom from LABOR EXPLOITATION

The Beast Callers Clave invites

Viceroy Senesh to peaceful talks

on neutral ground

to forge a new path into a new era

We wrangled over the wording a lot. I said we should include THROW BEES AT THE VICEROY'S FACE, because I thought that sentiment was one the entire city would support, but Tamhan talked me out of it during one of our secret meetings in the Fornish teahouse.

"Broadsides can only accomplish so much," he told me. "The first one announced the existence of the Sixth Kenning. This one aims to get people thinking of alternatives to our current system and plant the phrase 'clave republic' in their minds. And we can't be antagonists yet. We want people to listen to our ideas. If we begin with threats, then our ideas don't matter, you see? What matters is only defeating the threat."

"Okay, but just between us: You do want to throw bees at his face, right?"

"So much, yes. We can't say that, though."

"But we're calling for a new government," Adithi argued. "We're committing treason from the beginning. They're going to say we're traitors no matter how nicely we ask to discuss things."

"Yes. We are traitors," Tamhan admitted. "When they use the word, we're going to pour a lot of sugar on that and call ourselves 'patriots' instead. To begin with, though, we have to position ourselves as the reasonable ones. Let the viceroy overreact—because he most certainly will. Then we have the moral high ground. We get the populace on our side. Only then do we become the antagonists."

"Fine. How do we get the populace on our side if we have to hide?"

"The viceroy and the rich are going to do that for us. You saw what they did after the first broadside, when their power wasn't directly threatened. They will not react calmly to this."

We fully expect a swarm of hostility in response to our sedition. But I have literal swarms of my own, and this time I have a plan to mesh with Tamhan's.

I don't know how he's getting these broadsides printed and posted in secret when he's under near-constant surveillance, but he must have a really good network of friends.

I have a growing network too. Using reports from the hives and Khamen Chorous to distribute berths each night, we have been able to get lots of people into shelter, squatting in empty buildings and houses. I haven't been able to get everyone to safety yet, but I hope to soon.

On the morning the broadsides are posted, we are ready. It takes a few hours for them to be discovered and torn down, because Tamhan put them in different places this time. Some are exceedingly obvious, and that's to get the viceroy and the rich folks stirred up. But most of them are in low-rent areas and alleys where only the workers walk— avenues and niches where the city watch would rarely tread but plenty of other eyes would see.

But the viceroy—on his own behalf, but also on behalf of his rich cronies—moves just like Tamhan predicted. Soon after breakfast, the watch explodes into the city, tearing down broadsides and demanding to know of anyone nearby who posted them. I see this through the eyes of my honeybees, plus various hornets and wasps, as I sit on a rooftop in the Embassy District near the Red Pheasant Teahouse. And every time some muscle-y dude tears down a broadside, I reward them with a hornet sting to the face. If they back off, that's all they get. But if they start shouting at people, start anything aggressive at all, the hornets hit them again.

They'll know that I'm behind it, and that's fine.

Adithi, sitting next to me on the rooftop, is playing a different game with the horses. She and Tamhan have decided to reveal her power for the first time. She waits for them to be saddled and taken out, and then, when all seems calm, without any warning to their riders, the horses buck every single one of them into the dirt and run back to the stables.

One soldier thinks he can beat his horse into submission. It's a terrible decision. Adithi doesn't hesitate: She has another horse trot over, turn around, and kick him in the ribs. He doesn't die, but he won't be abusing any more horses anytime soon.

I watch a different scene develop: Most of the cavalry take their un-horsing and stings with expected grace—"woe is me," basically. Wherever it happens, people titter and move along. But when two get dumped near the South Side Market, a kid, maybe eight or nine years old, laughs pretty loud and points. The soldiers don't like it, and one of them shoves the kid into the dirt.

Except that kid is a member of a hunting family taking their hides to market, and they aren't going to ignore that. They step up, berating the soldier. I can't hear anything, but what I see is clear enough.

The soldier's partner comes to his side and they're telling the adults to back down. But it's a family like Abhi's, with their wagon full of weapons, and when that first soldier stupidly draws his sword, the spears and knives come out, and those two soldiers might as well be stew meat. The hunters are used to taking down much bigger and more dangerous game than a couple of dudes, and they're not scared.

The soldiers realize they've made a mistake a split second before they're pierced from multiple directions. And then they're down in the dust with wide eyes and spears in their guts, and the leader of the family points to them and then to his kid as he shouts at the shocked faces of bystanders. He was just protecting his child. The city watch was to blame. They started it. Something along those lines.

Nobody argues with them. In fact, a couple of guys walk up, looking like they want to help. The spears are yanked out, the watchmen die, and their bodies are soon loaded into the wagon, and a small crowd of people follow, half amazed and half giddy. I bring some more hornets in to keep multiple eyes on things, and I don't get the sense that anyone's run away to squeal. That in itself is remarkable.

We may have greatly overestimated the citizens' support of the city watch.

"We need to get to the South Side Market," I tell Adithi, who hasn't seen any of this like I have since there were no horses involved. "Things are going to blow up there. Two members of the watch are dead."

"From your hornets?"

"No, from some hunters. They're moving the bodies in plain view, and it seems like people are on their side. When the watch comes after them, it's going to be a fight. The leader of the hunters is making speeches, and I want to hear what he's saying."

"Do you think he's one of Tamhan's crew?"

"I have no idea. But the city watch is going to hear about it, and they can't just let this slide. They'll come after those hunters, and there's no way they're going to go quietly to the dungeon."

"Well, I'll keep them from using horses."

It takes us a quarter hour to get to the market, with Adithi guiding me. My eyes are open, but I don't see much in front of me; I'm looking instead through the eyes of multiple hornets at the goings-on ahead of us. Together with their helpers, the hunters unload the bodies and disappear into a stall featuring riverbed yams, swamp onions, and cranberries; they are muck farmers, wading up to their knees in icky water somewhere upriver in the alluvial tater beds every city depends on for basic calories. My guess is that they probably have their own wagon behind the stall, and plan to dump the bodies on the plains next time they head up to their fields. Scavengers will make sure they disappear.

The leader of the hunting family is up on his now-clear wagon bed, shouting at the crowd, and he has a piece of paper in his hand—it's our broadside!

"He has to be one of Tamhan's friends," I say to Adithi. "I'll bet you five wheels of fancy cheese that he's talking revolution."

"I can't wait to hear it," she replies. "The riders have come back to the stables and they're having trouble mounting. That's going to be their problem all day."

As we draw near enough to hear I slip out of the hornets' vision and tell them to do as they wish but ask that they remain nearby. The hunter is projecting his voice from the cart, and we edge closer to hear him.

"When has the city watch ever protected us? They literally push us around! They don't serve us; they bully us! And so it is time for us to consider a new government that does serve our interests instead of the interests of the viceroy's rich cronies!"

That's an applause line, and he gets it. Adithi and I join in.

"I have not met these beast callers yet, but I have heard that they are no friends of the rich! They were poor, living down by the river—all the seekers were!"

"Definitely one of Tamhan's," Adithi agreed. "He wouldn't know that otherwise."

"And you know what they want? The same thing you do! A government that supports them and doesn't oppress them!"

A roar of approval greets him. "A government that improves our lives instead of filling the treasuries of the viceroy's friends!"

Another roar. "A government where you get to vote for leaders who will answer to you and not to some king we'll never meet, who has no idea of what we need! That's a republic!"

That gets a loud response indeed, and I start to wonder if these are all Tamhan's friends or if the sentiment against the government is really that strong.

He points to something on the far side of the crowd, where I can't see. "Here comes the city watch to shut me up. To punish me for protecting my child! To throw me in a dungeon for speaking out against their injustice! Are we going to let them?"

The crowd roars "no," and I clutch at Adithi. "Watch over me," I say, as I leave my own sight and call out to the hornets. I send them at the city watch—a big group this time, twenty or more men led by an officer of some sort, maybe the captain—to distract the watch from the mob. They soon discover how difficult it is to follow orders with a hornet or three in the face. I make sure the captain gets special attention, not only because that will deprive them of leadership but because he could be the one who was responsible for Sudhi's death.

The hornets dive in and the watch lashes out, angry, and the mob responds in kind. I don't know what to do except keep the hornets focused on the watch, and it's remarkable how quickly they're disarmed or brought down.

I recognize that captain from his strangled-sounding voice. We heard him in the teahouse, bragging about Sudhi's death. He fights well and hurts some people, so they hurt him back. He and one other are killed, and the rest surrender after that. I come out of the hornets' heads a bit dizzy, listening to an exultant mob.

"This is wild. What's happening with the horses?" I ask Adithi.

"They're safe. One of the riders got the bright idea that if they didn't want to go out, maybe they'd go in. The rider opened the gates and stood back and the horses trotted right to their stables. I think they got the message."

"That's good, but now what do we do? We didn't expect this. I mean, Tamhan didn't plan for it to go this far."

Adithi pointed. "That man is clever." The hunter was shouting from the cart again, and people were quieting to listen. "He knows that when you have a mob, you use it or lose it."

"Friends! Hear me! Hear me! We need law. We do need a city watch. But we need a city watch that protects us rather than the viceroy. We need a new government—but we need the time and space to talk that out and make it happen. The viceroy doesn't want to grant us that. So let's make him. Let's find all the city watch and make them the same offer that I make right now to those men over there: Join us and keep the actual peace—prevent looting and property damage—or stay with a failing government and be cast out. And we'll have the protection of the beast callers! Yes, we will!"

"Pretty cheeky of him to assume that," Adithi says.

"He's right, though."

The man responds to imagined doubters. "Did you notice the hornets stinging the city watch? That was the hivemistress aiding us! And have you noticed how no cavalry has come to trample us? The horsemistress is keeping them stabled!"

Adithi's jaw drops. "Well, I guess my secret's out now for sure."

"Like you said, he's using what he's got before he loses it."

"So let us go!" the hunter shouts. "We will circle the city and secure it from the viceroy's forces! Let him stay in his tower or let him come down and talk with us! And then we will discuss our new government, right here, in the South Side Market! This will forever be the place where a new Nentian government began!"

The mob shouts their agreement, and he gestures to the west. The crowd surges in that direction. We're going to move clockwise, apparently.

"I don't know who that man is, but I bet he'll be part of the new republic," Adithi says.

"I just hope we can do this without killing anyone else," I reply. "I'm glad he's saying we should give the watch an option."

A mob is not the best, though. It's strange to be in one, to realize that, *Hey, I'm part of a mob right now,* and mobs are pretty famous for not doing anything nice to other people. No one sees a mob tearing down the street and thinks, *Oh, neat! I wonder what kindness they will bestow upon our neighbors!* No one wishes a mob would form outside their house and improve the neighborhood.

But perhaps this one can allow improvements to unfold in the future. That's what I tell myself as people get worked up and confront pairs of watchmen roaming the city. The watch is out looking for broadsides and for us, so even though there are more than three hundred of them in the garrison, they're all spread out and caught in pairs or small groups. I have a little swarm of hornets buzzing above the leaders—a couple dozen, nothing huge, but it's enough to make the watchmen understand who they're up against. Most of them surrender and pledge to join the new republic, as long as they're paid. To my great relief, the mob just takes their weapons and moves on. There is one pair of watchmen near the church, however, that have crossbows, and they fire into the crowd, thinking that's going to make them back off. Instead, the mob tears them apart. We don't have any more trouble until we get back to the stables.

The watch is in there, probably near fifty of them, and they have a defensible position—at least for a little while. But they also know it's not a castle. It can be set on fire, for example, though that would put the horses at risk. The hunter who's been leading everything tells the mob to chill out and surround the place but to let him talk. There's space cleared, and when he stands alone, he tells the soldiers to send someone out to negotiate. Adithi and I have moved closer to him but have yet to identify ourselves. I think that would instantly make us a target and that being unknown is our best defense right now. But it's good to be able to hear. The hornets are buzzing over his head and he points up to them.

"The hivemistress is watching," the hunter calls out to the stables. "And the horsemistress too."

"Yeah? So?" a voice responds.

"So it's time for a new government!"

The mob cheers. A skeptical voice rings out from the stables.

"With a couple kids running things?"

"No. With elected leaders. A republic that will still need a city watch. Most of the watch has already agreed to join us."

"What about the captain?"

"He's dead. But come on out and let's talk. You have my word you won't be hurt if you talk, even if you disagree!"

Once they send someone out, it's a done deal inside of five minutes. No one dies and it's the best. I like the not dying a whole lot.

After the muscle is firmly under our control, we go to Khul Bashab's Tower of Kalaad and issue an invitation to the viceroy to attend talks in the South Side Market about a new government. He declines and stays inside his walled compound with his bodyguards and such, which is fine with everyone.

"Good! We'll make more progress without him!" the hunter says. The city is essentially ours as long as we can keep it. I figure we'll have a week at the least before the viceroy's cousin hears about it downriver, and then another week before he can send any forces of significance up here.

That might mean we'll have a chance. Two weeks to prepare.

"Adithi. Have you seen where the next source of the Sixth Kenning is going to be?"

"It's with those baboons in the north right now."

"Yes, but where will it be next? Reach out and feel it."

She takes a moment and closes her eyes. Then they fly open and her jaw drops. "Holy hanging horse nuts!"

"Yes." A hive of burrow wasps right outside the city walls is going to be the next source of the Sixth Kenning. We'll be able to have people seek the Sixth Kenning nearby, and we'll have more beast callers on our side. I cannot help it: I do a little dance and make a high-pitched squealing noise. "You know what this is?"

Adithi laughs. "It's the best!"

"Yes! It's the best!"

Maybe it's a coincidence, but I don't think it is. The timing is too perfect. I think there's something behind this. Maybe it's Kalaad, maybe some other deity, moving silently to our benefit. I just get the feeling that we're not alone in wanting the world to change.

"Come on," I tell her, dispelling the hornets to do as they please. "Let's go to the market and see if Tamhan shows up. Maybe he'll try to explain what a clave republic is."

Hanima's words about some other deity made many of us wonder: Was it Raena—or possibly Meso—who was manipulating events in Ghurana Nent and bringing the Sixth Kenning to light since the krakens had been outmaneuvered somehow by the Eculans?

On another level, it made me wonder personally if this story of revolution and governments oppressing people made Pelenaut Röllend nervous. Or if anyone on Survivor Field felt oppressed by the pelenaut's efforts to keep them fed and healthy and their children going to school.

I am sure that someone out there thought of their situation and cast about, looking for someone to blame. But in our case, unlike the Nentians, we had a very clear enemy from outside: the Bone Giants.

Fintan grinned at the audience. "We should probably check in with Viceroy Bhamet Senesh about now, shouldn't we?"

hamet

There is a profound difference between cowardice in battle and standing up to be mowed down at harvest time when you can come back and win later. The first is a lack of courage; the second is also not courage, but rather a stupid refusal to acknowledge that the field is not yours to take on a particular day. When there's a man coming with a sickle in your direction and your choices are to bend or to stand there and be cut down, I'm going to fucking bend and come back in another season when it's my turn to be the reaper, not stand there and die.

That sounds good. I'll use that, or something like it, when someone demands that I explain how I lost Khul Bashab to a bunch of kids.

How was I supposed to keep order when I have perhaps the smallest garrison in the country and my calls for aid went ignored? How was I supposed to emerge victorious when we could never confirm that one of the Sixth Kenning kids could control horses and thereby suborn the power of my cavalry to quash civil unrest? That's the sort of vital information you want to know ahead of time, like how long your cock is and whether or not you might be about to step on it.

And you also want a kenning to counter a kenning. Pretty much a basic rule of engagement. Like, if one side has a bloodcat and the other side has a pillow, but the pillow guys are going into the fight thinking it's just pillows all around, it's not going to end well for them.

Like it didn't end well for us. Our defense was about as robust as a pillow's too. Once Captain Khatagar was taken out, the watch essentially folded.

So now I'm stuck in my tower and the compound. They don't seem intent on placing my head on a spike, which is a relief to me but very foolish of them. Because I'm going to get a message out. Eventually. After I endure a lecture from Threat Sweat himself.

He's perspiring in a self-satisfied, I-told-you-so way as he tilts up one of his chins and looks down his nose at me. "I tried to warn you," he says. "I said that if you didn't deal with this threat, it would deal with you."

"You are correct, Dhanush. You warned me. And I did my best to act on those warnings. It is not as if I have been doing nothing but casually inserting whole vegetables into my anus these past weeks. I've been dealing with their broadsides. I've set spies on them and tried to find their whereabouts. We even found one of them and removed him from the board. But the game has swung in their favor nevertheless, because we simply cannot see what they are doing."

"They are using the river people against you."

"The river people?"

"The poor, Viceroy."

"Oh, yes, I know. They are the eyes and ears and cloak of their rebellion. But listen, Patriarch. I need you to get a message to my cousin downriver. I need multiple copies sent via multiple couriers to make sure it arrives."

The priest shakes his head, throwing droplets from the tip of his nose and the tops of his ears. "I do not have multiple couriers."

"Their services are easily bought, and I can give you coin. A courier per boat on the next five boats out of town." I toss him a purse and it lands in his palm with a sort of damp squelch.

"What do these messages say?"

"Something along the lines of 'Dear Cousin, I'm trapped in this tower and I fear I may be violated. Please save me.' And then there's a bit about maybe asking the king to help retake one of his cities, since it's essentially been lost."

"The king will remove you, you know. For losing the city."

"I do. I do know that, Patriarch, but thank you kindly for taking the trouble to point out that I am doomed. But I defy anyone to do better playing the hand I was dealt. I have been constantly surprised rather than reliably informed. Your spies, I note, have delivered nothing of worth in all this time. Are they that incompetent, or have you instructed them not to work very hard?"

The patriarch practically turns into a fountain as he splutters, adding his spittle to the sweat spraying from him in his apoplexy.

"Never mind, Dhanush, never mind. It doesn't matter at this point, does it? What matters is taking back control. Because these kids don't seem like the especially devout type, do they? We haven't seen a lot of praise for Kalaad in these broadsides and these riots they've been throwing. A healthy relationship with the church is probably not very high on their agenda, if it's on there at all."

"They have an agenda?"

"Neutralizing me was one item on it, no doubt, and they've ticked off that box. What if neutralizing the church is next?"

"Well, they can't do that."

"They can't?"

"The church is an idea!"

"True, but they have plenty of other ideas, don't they? The kinds of ideas a large number of people seem to be listening to right now."

"Kalaad, you're right. We have to stop them."

"Glad we're on the same page. So you'll get these messages to my cousin safely, then?" I hand him a sheaf of sealed envelopes, all copies of the same letter.

"I will."

When he leaves, I summon the new captain of my guard up to my room and order him to bring all the incendiary arrows from the armory and leave them with me, along with a bow. I can hit every neighborhood from my windows atop this tower, and, by Kalaad, I will.

They've surprised me at every turn and I never responded in kind. Well, that ends now. They won't be expecting me to take any direct action. They expect me to give orders and work my will through my remaining men, except they're all trapped like I am. They think they have me secured and neutralized. But I'll burn this city down before I let those kids take it from me.

DUNGEON DOUBLE CROSS

I heard news that could be good or bad when I reported to the refugee kitchen in the morning. Rumors were sweeping through the city and Survivor Field that the Raelech army and supply train were less than two weeks away. That meant food! Those metaphorical floodwaters I was trying to ignore might not ever make it up to my chest and start a panic. It meant that soon we would strike back at the Eculans. That is, if the Raelechs were really coming to help.

What if, some whispered, the Raelechs wanted to take control of the Fourth Kenning? They could mount a siege, cut off our trade, and we wouldn't be able to last for any length of time. Already there was practically nothing to eat. Restaurants were closing, the markets picked clean.

I couldn't help anyone climb out of a dark conspiracy well once they'd fallen in. They'd have to do that work for themselves. Could the Raelechs betray us? Yes. But they'd have to betray their national character to do so. They had been attacked as well and had already liberated Möllerud for us. If people wanted to believe that they were coming here with the Fornish and the Kaurians to take over after that, well, I didn't know what to say to them.

The news of food was quite welcome. Chef du Rödal was on the last of her flour, and we'd have nothing but what the sea could provide until some new boats came in. Word in the markets was that there'd be some new fish soon, since the pelenaut had sent some boats to the Mistmaiden Isle called Bean.

So while the chef put me to work gutting some striped red-tail perch, we distracted ourselves from the prospect of a hungry couple of weeks ahead with speculation about what was going on in Ghurana Nent. What was going on in Khul Bashab now? Did the rebellion against the viceroy succeed? Why had we received so little news from Ghurana Nent in general? Were they essentially locked in a civil war now? Or had Hanima and Tamhan and the rest been crushed by some response from the throne?

Fintan and I met at the fishblade's benches again, since fish would be all we would have been able to find elsewhere anyway, and it was a good place to work. He played an instrumental tune for his song that day, and after the break, he addressed what most everyone had been talking about when they weren't worrying about food shortages.

"Yesterday we heard of momentous events in Khul Bashab, and I promise we'll get back to them tomorrow. Melishev Lohmet, if you recall, was not especially worried about the beast callers there when he was viceroy of Hashan Khek, but once he was king he became more concerned. Let's check in with Mai Bet Ken."

It is easy to say a city has burned down. Less so to grasp the enormity of it, the sheer scale of the damage, the ever-present char in the nostrils, the stink of ashes and burnt garbage, burnt everything.

By the time I arrive in Talala Fouz with my small staff, Melishev Lohmet and his pet army have utterly crushed any resistance—I'm not sure there was much—and the former viceroy of Hashan Khek has crowned himself the forty-fifth King Kalaad, with almost none of the infrastructure the previous forty-four kings had enjoyed.

Rumor has it he already has an epithet before he has a palace— indeed, he resides in a fancy tent in front of a construction site—and if it is true, I could not hope for a better or more accurate name than "the Unwell."

I don't think there is any need to present myself to him, so I send a message that I've arrived, I can be found on the former grounds of the Fornish embassy pitching in with the rebuilding, and, incidentally, no Brynt hygienists could be found to aid him. I was sorry about that, but I hoped he was feeling better. Though, of course, I am not sorry at all and I have no such hopes.

For a couple of weeks, that is enough. We make significant progress on the embassy building and make sure to leave a proper area for the eventual tea treehouse that ben Fos will grow when he gets here.

Thinking of him drives me to distraction, however. I managed to paint over my own hand one afternoon. I had to spend the rest of the day scrubbing it off to avoid awkward questions.

But Melishev Lohmet—now King Kalaad—summons me eventually to his royal tent. Tactician Hennedigha is not there this time, I note immediately. The king himself is dressed elaborately in what is considered high Nentian fashion, but it cannot hide that he is still very ill. I expect him to implore me again to magically secure a hygienist from Brynlön, but that's not what he wants at all. He dives into it without any inquiries into my journey or my embassy's situation or anything.

"You've heard of these kids who say they've found the Sixth Kenning?"

"Yes, you discussed it with me briefly before you left Hashan Khek."

"Well. It's real," he says, though I had not disputed its reality.

"That's wonderful news."

"No, Ambassador, it's shit. They are causing unrest in Khul Bahsab.

Stirring up the people against the viceroy and the crown. And they're killing members of the city watch. They're murderers."

I almost leap in at that point, but I wait instead. Let him ask first. "I see," I reply, forcing him to continue.

"I want Forn to help me root out these rebels, so to speak." He gives a tiny laugh. "You see, I made a pun there. It is the preferred humor of all civilized leaders, though I cannot explain why or how this came to be so."

Ignoring the king's inept attempt to be funny, I repeat to him what I believe is his point: "You are upset that they have disrupted order in one of your cities, and you want order restored."

"Yes. Obviously."

"I empathize. Can you empathize with me, perhaps, in the same way? I want a certain lieutenant brought to justice for the murder of a Fornish citizen, thereby restoring the rule of law."

"Kalaad, Ambassador, not now—"

"Yes, now. Now before anything else. You will not get the position of the sun in the sky from me until I see that lieutenant dishonorably discharged and thrown in a dungeon. And note that I said *see*, as in *with my own eyes*. I will accept no assurances. Ghurana Nent has breached trust with Forn, and so the evidence must be clear. Only when I see that lieutenant in a dungeon for murder will I be concerned with the murderers you want to see in a dungeon."

"Be careful how you speak to me."

"Be careful how you speak to the spokesperson of Forn. We have been your ally in the past—in the very recent past, I apparently need to remind you—but your refusal to enforce the law in this matter may cause the clans to reevaluate our relationship."

"The law is whatever I say it is."

Astounding. Did he think I'd have no reply to that? "Arbitrary law is no law at all and destroys people's trust in their government," I point out. "Not to mention Forn's trust in your government. Perhaps that is why you are facing unrest in Khul Bashab—is your viceroy making similarly arbitrary decisions?"

"If he is, I'm sure he's neglected to inform me," the king spits. "Look. In the confusion of the succession and my haste to get up here, this is a matter that's slipped my attention. Thank you for reminding me. But when I have this lieutenant in the dungeon, and you're satisfied, can—or rather, will—Forn send a greensleeve to take care of these rebels?"

That surprises me and I blink a few times. "Why a greensleeve?"

"Because they'll be able to handle whatever the rebels are dishing out. If Viceroy Senesh was capable of handling them, they would have been handled by now."

"Leaving aside the rather important detail of what you mean by *take care of* or *handling them*, greensleeves are not typically anxious to leave the Canopy and even less likely to agree to act on a mercenary basis. But when you have that lieutenant in the dungeon and I'm satisfied, then I will make inquiries. I wouldn't want to give you any undue hopes, however. Since Gorin Mogen and Winthir Kanek have left a power vacuum, there is plenty of jockeying among would-be hearthfires in Hathrir at the moment. One of the things they like to brag about to their people is how successful they've been at raiding the Fornish, so most all our resources are occupied fighting off timber pirates in the southwest."

"I understand. Whatever aid you can give will be welcome. My army is currently engaged in rebuilding this city, and I have these thousands of mouths out there waiting to be fed, you see, as if I have a harvest hiding up my ass and I can just pull it out anytime. I swear they act like this tent is just one huge tit for them to suck."

Is he expecting me to laugh at that? "I'm aware of the hungry people, sir."

"Right. Good. Yes. Well, that's all. I'll send for you when this lieutenant business is concluded."

As I leave I think that it will be days, but it's mere hours, right after dinner, when Melishev himself arrives with two soldiers to escort me to my proof. Wary of his intentions, I ask if I can bring a couple of my staff with me.

"I don't care," he says. "I just want this over with so we can move on."

I bring two of my staff, and Melishev hands me a scroll to read on the way: It's the cashiering of Lieutenant Mukhab's military commission and an order to imprison him for the murder of a Fornish citizen in Hashan Khek. The king babbles as we walk.

"The dungeon survived the fire, since it's underground. It's a pretty nice one too. By which I mean it's awful. Dank and plagued by creeping mold. Bad lighting. Full of rats and the bones of prisoners they've gnawed on. Also lots of things that eat rats. Rumor has it there's a face jumper prowling around there somewhere. It's a bloody bonanza."

He continues on about how you can't build a dungeon that way, you have to wait and let it grow into such a horror with years of cruelty and neglect, so his predecessors had known how to do at least one thing right. Once we descend into the dungeon, all of this turns out to be true, apart from the unverified rumor, but Melishev had neglected to mention the smell. It's much, much worse than the burnt city above; it's nearly enough to gag me. My eyes water and I must, of necessity, become a mouth breather, though I do it through a handkerchief held up to my face.

"Mmm, rot, am I right?" the king says. "Part of the terror of being chained down here is knowing that your body will be contributing to the smell sooner or later, that you, too, will offend someone's delicate senses."

"Where is he?" I prompt him.

"Ah. Just ahead, where we've placed a couple of extra firebowls."

"Please take me there."

"After you."

"No, please, you lead. I'd rather not have anyone between the exit and me."

The king chuckles at that. "Of course. I must reestablish trust and so on."

"Yes."

I'm expecting someone other than Lieutenant Mukhab to be in the cell. We had the eyewitnesses to the murder describe him to an artist, and we took written notes as well. I have studied the drawings and notes carefully. If I find someone in the cell who doesn't match them and call the king on it, I might need to make a hasty exit.

The cell in question is not lit from within, so the prisoner looms out of the darkness, his face pressed up to and framed by a couple of vertical bars, the light lurid on his features. He's a long-nosed fellow with a dimpled chin and a scar slashing through his left eyebrow, very distinguishing characteristics that would be difficult to find duplicated elsewhere and, I imagine, impossible to create on an impostor in the scant few hours since I made my ultimatum. Perhaps Melishev is experimenting with acting in good faith. But I still don't trust it.

"What is your name?" I ask the prisoner.

"Are you the reason I'm in here?" he says. His voice is a low growl, resentful and contemptuous.

"Answer my questions and I'll answer yours. Your name?"

"Lieutenant Ranoush Mukhab."

"Thank you. You are the reason you're in here. You murdered a Fornish man in Hashan Khek."

"I defended myself. He attacked me."

"Multiple eyewitnesses say you were the attacker. Regardless, he's dead because you killed him, and that was not necessary. You belong here."

He spits at my face and hisses a few Nentian insults that mean nothing to me. The spittle lands on the back of my hand holding the handkerchief over my nose and mouth.

"Rumor has it there's a face jumper down here," I tell him. "Maybe that will end your time early. Otherwise, this dank cell is the entire sum of your future."

His angry expression morphs into confusion. "What? I'm just going to be left down here forever?" Apparently no one had informed him of his actual sentence.

"I thought it would be more merciful than the alternative. You can opt at any time to be executed according to Nentian custom. I believe that entails being tied to a post outside the walls and beheaded, your body left to be eaten by the creatures of the plains. Is that correct, King Kalaad?"

"That is correct. You have only to let one of the guards know and we will end your misery," he says to the lieutenant.

"If he does opt for execution, I wish to bear witness," I say. "Not because I relish it, but because I must see that justice is done on behalf of my murdered countryman."

"I will leave instructions to that effect with all the guards," Melishev says.

"I also wish to be given leave to visit Lieutenant Mukhab at any time to verify he's still actually in here."

The king lifts a sardonic eyebrow. "Still no trust, Ambassador?"

"You have kept your word thus far and I thank you. But since Tactician Hennedigha objected so strenuously to the lieutenant's imprisonment, I worry that this is a ploy he's orchestrated to make the problem go away."

"Hey, now, listen," the lieutenant tries to interject, but I ignore him and continue talking to the king.

"Should the lieutenant escape or otherwise disappear, or if I am fed a story that he was 'accidentally' executed without my witness and his body just carried away by various creatures, I will treat that news as confirmation that I've been deceived and the Nentian government has acted in bad faith."

King Kalaad chuckles again, grinning at me and somehow sweating in this cold moist air. He shakes his head and turns to the lieutenant. "I told you she was sharp and this could happen. Sorry, Lieutenant, but this is the end. It shall be as she says."

"Wait, what? You're really going to leave me here?" His voice breaks as he confirms that they did conspire to deceive me.

"To preserve our country's good relationship with Forn? Absolutely. Ghurana Nent thanks you for your service, Lieutenant, but since you are so profoundly stupid as to commit your crimes in front of many witnesses, that will be all." He gestures toward the exit. "Ambassador, if you please? I think our work is done here."

"Hey, no, it's not!" the lieutenant shouts as I turn to walk briskly to the exit. My staffers and Melishev's follow, with the king laughing uproariously at the lieutenant's increasingly strident protests. "This is khern shit! We had a deal with Hennedigha! He's gonna hear about this. You can't leave me in this place! I didn't do anything!"

The rest of his shouting involves his dearest wish that we be violated by amorous oxen.

After the dungeon and its foul miasma, the burnt air of Talala Fouz is almost a relief. I lower the handkerchief and confront the king.

"How soon until your dungeon staff are informed of my visiting privileges?"

"I'll remain here to make sure of it now," he replies.

"Thank you. And Hennedigha? How will you handle him?"

Melishev Lohmet shrugs. "He knew going into this that you might not be fooled, and I'm delighted you weren't. There won't be any trouble from him."

"Good. Allow me time to confirm, but I can offer you this now: A greensleeve will arrive here in the next few days to help us with a project on embassy grounds. He's of my clan, so he will be more agreeable than others might be to consider your offer. When he's finished with his work, I'll bring him to you to discuss the matter. I can't speak for him or guarantee his cooperation, but I can guarantee you the opportunity to make your case."

"That suits me well. Good evening, Ambassador Ken."

My new office has bare floors and walls and has yet to be stained. It's raw, but the sawdust smells refreshing compared to the ruin outdoors. There are a couple of chairs in there, upholstered silverbark brought along on the ship, and I have a basic tea set, nothing like the fancy one I left behind as a gift to Ambassador Par. The hearth is finished, at least, the stone a lovely Raelech granite, and there's a kettle boiling water. I grin foolishly at ben Fos as I light candles.

"This is going to be a splendid room someday. For now we'll have to content ourselves with imagining its future splendor."

"I am a fan of future splendor," he says. "Bare winter branches become spring's buds, summer's fullness, and autumn's spectacular celebration."

Once we have our tea and have seated ourselves happily, I ask him about what he discovered in Khul Bashab, confident that the room is soundproof if unadorned.

"I got to meet the beast callers—two of them, anyway. The third had been captured and tortured to death by the viceroy there."

"Oh, no."

"The girls are wonderful, though. I don't know how they're being portrayed among the Nentians, but they're kind souls who want a new government to care for their people."

"So the rebellion thing is true?"

Mak nods. "They're trying to stir it up for sure."

"What do they want in its place?"

"When I left, it was still early days, and it might have evolved since then, but they're going to call it a clave republic. They vote for leadership, like the Raelechs do, but they don't have the same hierarchy of councils. There's a district council that represents citizens, a clave council that represents business, and then an executive they want to call the city minister. This would be repeated at the national level if they succeed, with a citizen council, a clave council, and a national minister."

"How many people are on these councils?"

"Five on each for two-year terms, and they are limited to serving no more than five terms."

"Interesting. And the city minister?"

"A single five-year term."

"What's the focus on the claves?"

"A young man named Tamhan Khatri is the thinker behind all this. He argues that behind every rich person is a group of exploited labor and pillaged resources. He wants to radically change the way businesses are owned and operated. No business can be owned by a single person unless it really is a single person. Ownership is always equally shared among the employees, with the original owner able to have a double share and management earning one and a half shares."

"That sounds similar to our clan business structures."

"Yes."

"But that's going to kill foreign investment."

"That's the idea, yes. They profit from a distance while people in the city are starving, and that is morally indefensible in Khatri's view. And he points right back at us and says we're doing just fine with our insular economics. He says the land of the Sixth Kenning can manage its resources as well as the Fifth does. And with all employees getting an equal share, they're going to be rewarded for their work instead of trapped in poverty."

"The rich and powerful are going to hate this."

"They already do. But it's amazing, Mai. They're ideologically aligned with us. Jes says if we can throw in with them and make it work, we'll have a powerful ally and quite probably a huge new market for our clans to move into."

"I need you to go back there," I tell him.

"What? I just got here, and I'm supposed to go upriver."

"You can go upriver later. The clan staff can be kept busy doing something until you get back. I'm under some political pressure here and also want things to go well for us—and the kids—in Khul Bashab. I . . . wait. Hold on a moment, please. I need to think through something."

"Of course." He sips at his tea and waits, and I'm grateful. What I worry about is that I'm moving too rashly and perhaps with some selfish bias. Is what I'm about to suggest truly what's best for the Canopy, or is it merely best for me, to prolong Mak's time in Ghurana Nent? Am I putting myself first here?

But no. The kids need to win, and the Sixth Kenning must grow to its full potential if we of the Fifth Kenning are to reach ours. That it benefits me by keeping ben Fos in-country a bit longer is ancillary. I smile at him and continue.

"We need to make the king think we're on his side but tell those kids we are really, really on their side. So after you grow the treehouse for us here, I'm going to take you to the king and say you'll do a lot of things you won't actually do and send you back down there with a reply for Jes Dan Kuf."

"Right now?"

"No. Right now . . ." I pause, take a deep breath, and exhale. There is nothing in this for the Canopy or the clan. For once, this is all about me. Mak waits. "Right now I feel the need to discuss personal matters. We are here for such a short season, and the sun is not long for this sky. I would eternally regret it if I did not inform you while it shines on us that, if it be to your liking, I would like to bask in its light . . . together. And if you have any reservation, then of course I shall not question or—"

Mak is suddenly no longer in his seat and his lips are a mere inch from mine.

"Yes," he says, and then again, as a question. "Yes?"

"Yes." Our mouths crush together, and I try so hard not to just chew him up. I think it's the same for him: We are both so hungry.

"I'll stop there, since kids are listening," Fintan said with a chuckle.

I made a mental note to ask someone with a firmer grasp of trade than I had about Tamhan Khatri's insular economic system. At first glance I thought it would be wrong for us to adopt such laws; we were desperate for foreign investment at the moment, to help us recover from our national disaster. It would be fine to protect workers from exploitation, however; surely we could do something along those lines.

The bard drew out another seeming sphere and imprinted it, holding up his fist, calling out to Survivor Field and the city of Pelemyn. "Are you ready for more Daryck du Löngren?"

The response was a very loud affirmative.

Daryck

We found the bony bastards after another week. Far more of them than we wanted.

We were about to make camp for the night ourselves when we crested a rise and beheld a vast sprawling field of raggedy tents spread out among the small trees and scrub of the coast. Their boats were anchored offshore, bobbing in the Northern Yawn. We saw their camp-fires and the silhouettes of their fleet by the light of a full moon. As before, they'd made camp next to a river emptying into the sea.

"There will be sentries," I said, huddled up with the crew, only nine of us now. "Maybe hunting parties too, so watch out for bones gleaming in moonlight, and don't let your eyes get drawn to those flames."

"What are we doing?" Mynstad Luren asked.

"We are scouting only. We're not attacking."

"No picking off the outliers? Getting back some of our own?"

This needed to be addressed. "There's nothing I'd like more. But look: We're the only ones who can confirm that this army is here, and the pelenaut needs to know it exists. We have to walk out of here alive. If we start picking off sentries or send some arrows in to the edges, they're going to know we're here. You've seen how long their damn legs are; they will catch up. That risks the mission. Because the mission is to confirm this army is here and its size and where they're going. That's it."

"We don't know where they're going, though," Luren pointed out.

"We know enough. They're following the coast west, stopping to camp at rivers," I said. "They could be headed for Rael or even Ghurana Nent. Maybe they're looking for a nice place to build a settlement. Maybe they're even going to stay here for the winter. But I think we can safely say they're not intent on coming down through the Grave-wood after us. We're a couple weeks west of Fornyd now, so they're not coming down for another go, unless we give them reason to. We definitely don't want to do that."

"I hear you, Gerstad, but it sure does deflate my dingus to think about leaving them alive."

The others grunted assent with the mynstad, and I saw that it would be wiser to expound rather than simply give orders. I needed them to be on board. And Mynstad Luren was being a clever bog lynx here, let-ting the band listen in to our conversation and the thinking behind the orders before I gave them.

"Look. Somebody down south found papers like the ones we found on that sunburst-bearded guy, and the pelenaut got them translated by a Kaurian scholar. It was from those papers that we learned this army might be up here. We just confirmed that intelligence was correct, be-cause, hey"—I waved at the camp—"there they fucking are. That's in-credibly valuable info by itself. It means if we can find more written intelligence, it's well worth picking up. We have a guy who can read it because they're not using a code. They're just using a language they think we can't read. So the stuff we picked up could be gold. The infor-mation in those documents might tell us all we need to know, and we can trust that it's true. The last thing we want them to think is that we survived the invasion down south. Because these guys left at the same time as the other invasion forces but with a different mission. They don't know that their armies weren't entirely successful in wiping us out. Or at least I hope they don't. We don't want to be the ones that give them a clue about that."

"So we're not going to kill *any* of them?" Luren said.

"No. It risks our safety and the mission. This information is far more important to Brynlön than killing a few giants, Mynstad. And not giv-ing them any information is just as important. Right now we know plenty and they know nothing. I know we've lost some people, but in terms of gathering intelligence it's been a good reconnaissance mis-sion so far, and I'm proud of you all. But if we go down there and kill some of them, get them stirred up and get killed ourselves, then it's all been for nothing. We fuck ourselves and our people with a kraken cock. Is that clear?"

"Aye, Gerstad."

"Good. I want it understood that we *will* get our revenge. Think of this recon as setting the table for the feast to come. Sören, I want you to slip out into the sea and get a better look at what's in the boats. Are there provisions, equipment, weapons, what? But be as quick and stealthy about it as you can. We might need to run at any moment."

The rapid nodded. "Want me to scuttle any of them?"

"You can do that? Silently?"

"Yes. Gently invite the ocean overboard to fill those flat bottoms. They sink."

I considered the risk. There was little chance they'd catch him in the act. They wouldn't discover that they were missing ships until they decided to set out again. That would seriously hamper their efforts to move west, and that was good. But it might also tell them that we were out here, and that would be bad.

"Scuttle exactly one. One they can write off as an accident. More than that and they'll suspect sabotage and someone's out here doing it. But before you scuttle it, look for any documents you can steal and keep dry. If they have navigation charts, maps, anything, I'd like to see them."

"Aye, Gerstad."

He crept down to the ocean and I turned to Mynstad Luren. "Pick three mariners and carefully scout the far edge of this camp. How far does it go? Because I think we're only seeing a portion of it from here. A good portion, but probably not the whole thing. Be silent and invisible and watch for sentries. Our victory lies in being undiscovered. Return here as soon as possible. We will depart on your return or at dawn if you're not back."

Luren took three mariners with him and they crept off into the scrub, leaving me with Brön, Gyrsön, and the last mariner. We didn't move but rather took our time counting campfires and estimating numbers based on what we saw. Sören returned within an hour.

"Nothing of note on the ships, just rope and barrels of salted meat. No documents on the ones I searched. One on the periphery's been scuttled."

I wanted to send him back out there to scuttle more, because Luren wouldn't be back for another hour or two at the least. But they'd be looking for us if we did. And they might sweep south, figuring that job needed to be done; I could bring them back to threaten our cities by going beyond my orders.

I had him wait with us for Luren's return, and when Luren got back with some numbers to report, we struck south immediately, trying to put plenty of distance between us before dawn. Hopefully the Bone Giants weren't very good trackers or would not even realize there was someone to track. And hopefully we'd be allowed to do more than simply scout the next time we encountered them.

I'm still thinking of Nudge and chewing over his words. We will repair our civilization over time. We will endure this invasion and wipe out the invaders. And we will build new defenses to make sure this can never happen again.

Day 34

THE MORAL USE
OF POWER

After my shift at the kitchen—it was all fish stew, and it would be fish stew for the foreseeable future, just to make sure what we had went as far as possible—I swung by the Roasted Sunchuck to see if it was still open, and it wasn't. The sign on the door said to check back tomorrow.

WE WILL OPEN ON DAYS WE CAN OFFER SOMETHING BESIDES FISH.

So it was back to the dockside fishblade again, and it was busier than I'd ever seen. It was one of the few places still open, and what they had was fresher than what was at the market, so everyone was there. Fintan and I had to take our food to go and work elsewhere.

While we stood in line, people chatted Fintan up. There was a lot of nervousness at the thought of the Bone Giants in the north. More than one person demanded to know what happened there, because it had been months since Daryck du Löngren had found them. If they were camped for the winter and now it was spring, did that mean they were on the move again? If so, where were they headed? Were they moving down toward the river cities? Should Fornyd be warned?

Fintan was able to put them off by promising that Second Könstad Tallynd du Böll would make an announcement about it when the tales began that day, and it wasn't his place to say anything until then.

And when we got to the wall, the second könstad was waiting. She was going to speak before Fintan's song. I nodded a greeting at her, wanting to ask if the Wraith or Approval Smile had talked yet, but I knew that I couldn't.

Fintan activated his kenning and signaled to the Second Könstad that she could begin. If he started, people might decide to tune him out before they heard the important stuff, so she needed to speak first.

"My friends and fellow citizens, this is Second Könstad Tallynd du Böll. Please listen to a few important announcements from your government."

Everybody stopped what they were doing on Survivor Field and looked up. I imagine it was the same within the city walls. She had saved the lives of practically everyone there; lending an ear was the least we could do.

"The pelenaut and I remain vigilant in defense of Pelemyn, as do all our military. I know there is some concern about the Eculan forces to the north discovered by Gerstad Daryck du Löngren and the Grynek Hunters. While there have been some developments over the winter— developments the bard will no doubt share with you in due course— there is nothing to fear from them at this time, and the quartermaster of Fornyd is staying on top of the situation. If that changes, please trust us to let you know."

She paused to clear her throat. "In the meantime, all should know that there are opportunities for settlement elsewhere, should you wish it. Göfyrd is being built anew by the Raelech stonecutter Meara, and we are sending a new quartermaster there now along with seed. We would love to see that land farmed again and that city to flourish once more. We need farmers, period, in every city, and the incentives to become one remain in place.

"Other cities that are either now open for resettlement or remain open for relocation include Möllerud, Festwyf, Fornyd, Tömerhil, and Setyrön. We will be sending a new quartermaster to Möllerud via ship with seed and supplies very soon. If you would like to be on that ship or get more information on anything regarding resettlement, please go to the new resettlement ministry, opening as we speak next to the city gate. You will see a wide booth and a banner with four lines, where you can make inquiries regarding moving to certain cities and the incentives for each. I probably do not need to tell you that the overpopulation of this city is putting pressure on our ability to feed everyone, so resettlement, now that it's available, would be best for us all. Rest assured that if you relocate to one of the coastal cities, you'll have the same access to the bounty of the sea you have here, and in all likelihood much better, since there will be fewer overall bellies to fill.

"And as for the rumors that the Raelech and Fornish armies are approaching to reinforce us, as well as a Kaurian fleet: Yes, that is true. A little less than two weeks. And while they are bringing plenty of food with them, we can frankly use all available space to house them. So, if you are on Survivor Field now or struggling in the city and thinking that you might fare better elsewhere—that may be! Now that the weather has turned, it is the perfect time to go."

She paused and smiled at everyone. "Regardless: Remember that I love you all, and the pelenaut sends his love as well. Remember to love one another. May Bryn's blessings be upon you. Thank you."

An extended wave of cheers and applause rolled out from the field and the city both, and I saw a stream of people heading toward the gate to find this new resettlement ministry. That was a very pleasant surprise, and I knew that wasn't the sort of thing one cooked up overnight. Rölly had been planning this for a while, and launching it now, when people could see that the city's resources were strained to their limits, was much more effective than it would have been even a few days ago, when people were still somewhat comfortable and could tell themselves that everything would be fine.

Tallynd left, and I didn't get a chance to ask her anything. Fintan strummed a chord and said, "While many of you check out the new ministry, I'll sing today's song and take the customary break before starting the day's tale. This one's a Fornish tune."

After forty-odd years of hard living I find
There is no freedom like peace of mind:
It is a space free of guilt and regret
And if you haven't found your way there yet
I hope you will get there someday soon.

It's a process of shedding the past,
Old memories that weren't meant to last;
Embarrassments that you've classified as crime
Don't deserve another second of your time
This morning, night, or noon.

So be free, my friends, be free,
Lay down that burden you have beside me,
Step forward and away and then we'll see
What new branches grow on your tree.

"I promised you I'd return to events in Khul Bashab," Fintan said. "This is what happened after the people's uprising confined the viceroy to his tower."

Hanima Bhandury appeared out of the oily smoke of his seeming sphere, but she had on a new outfit, a jade-green vest over a white shirt and pants tucked into some cheap but new boots.

Hanima

It is a heady thing to walk around free. And by "heady," I mean my head kind of spins sometimes with the wonder of it, this feeling that Adithi says is exhilaration.

I don't know if that's really what it is. Except that it's the best.

We can walk around in daylight! We can meet with Tamhan at the Red Pheasant Teahouse without fear of being discovered or interrupted. Because the viceroy is neutralized and for this short, sweet while we don't have to worry about the physical threat of state violence.

"The challenge," Tamhan says, "is to remain this free a month from now."

Tamhan's living at the treehouse as a guest of Jes Dan Kuf, since he finally fell out with his father on basically everything—big, shouty domestic squabble in which he may have mentioned at high volume that he's using his father's business practices as an example of what *not* to do, of what *not* to allow in a new government.

Tamhan still looks tired but so cool. Maybe it's because he's holding a steaming cup of tea painted with Fornish vinework, or maybe it's because he's braided his hair and it looks stunning on the yellow vest he's wearing, but I think it's because he has a plan and he knows some people who can make it work. That hunter who led the riot—Khenish Dhawan—has become the acting captain of the city watch and is in charge of keeping order, which means something entirely different now that we are not so interested in persecuting the poor. In fact, he's working with Adithi and me to form a new relationship with the river folk: By tonight, no one will be out in the streets. Everyone will have a bed, or at least a safe place to sleep, because a nice, polite man on a horse told them to see Khamen Chorous, who has really blossomed into a happy person who loves to help others feel safe. I figure he will make a fine minister of human dignity, which will be an actual thing if we succeed.

Khenish Dhawan is also working with Tamhan to spread word of meetings and post new broadsides around town.

"We have such a small window of time in which to work and get the populace on our side," Tamhan says over his teacup. "I'm going to need one of you to go public. Be visible. Show people that the Sixth Kenning is real and tell them the risks and benefits to the seeking."

All of this would be easier to do if there were a Raelech bard in town to broadcast things for us, but since we lack one, we have to organize and repeat ourselves in many places. I'm the one who's going public, because Adithi says my personality is better suited. That means I have to appear at most every meeting with at least a portion of my hive. Adithi does her part by having a roan mare named Sugarmane transport me around the city with Tamhan and a mounted escort, but we never use any reins. We just wave at people and otherwise keep our hands on the saddlehorns, because Adithi tells the horses where to take us.

The first place we go to is the city bank and place it firmly under our control. We seize the assets of the royal treasury, the city treasury, the viceroy's personal hoard, and those of a list of obscenely rich merchants, including Tamhan's father.

The second place we go to is the Church of Kalaad, where we meet a very sweaty man called Patriarch Dhanush Bursenan. Tamhan bows to him and announces that we just took all the viceroy's stuff.

"I'd like to leave church assets alone," Tamhan tells him, "but that's up to you, Patriarch."

I'm not sure he's listening. The few bees I've brought in with me are pretty interested in the priest, because they've identified him as a water source. I tell them to back off and none of them land on him, but he's super nervous about their buzzing around.

"Patriarch?" Tamhan prods him.

"Hmm? Yes?"

"Will the church promise not to preach against a new government or against seeking the Sixth Kenning? Or shall we seize your assets and send every church official down the river?"

His eyes narrow as he regards Tamhan, the words finally sinking in. "You'll let us stay and keep everything if we simply shrug at your treason?"

"It won't be treason if we win," Tamhan replies. "And look, from the church's standpoint, what's changed? We're all still meat moving around under the sky. How we govern ourselves doesn't really matter to Kalaad, so why should it matter to the church?"

He doesn't answer Tamhan but instead turns his moist eyes to me. "And how does the hivemistress feel about the church?"

"It's never done a single thing to help me," I reply. "But it's never done a single thing to harm me either. So I am neutral. Mostly I want not to fight with you, and I hope you want that also."

"You have no new faith to spread, no religious agenda?"

"I just told you my agenda. Not fighting. That's it."

"So how about it, Patriarch?" Tamhan presses him. "Shall we leave each other alone? We let you collect your tithes and give you time to change your doctrine to accommodate the Sixth Kenning. In the meantime, if anyone asks, Kalaad doesn't have much of an opinion about government."

He sweats harder as he thinks about it. Maybe thinking gets him overheated. Maybe he's unwell. I hope he's not going to keel over and die before he answers. Finally he purses his lips and gives a tiny nod.

"I cannot promise that the patriarchs of other cities will agree, and you may receive some resistance from them in the future. But for my part, you have my word that none of my people will preach against you, and I will report that you have been respectful to the church."

"You have my thanks."

We leave him to quietly melt, and I'm glad that it didn't come to a fight. Because I know we have plenty of fighting ahead of us.

We're doing a district a day for five days, visiting some public place in each district's five wards, and these meetings are announced via pamphlet well ahead of time. This is an organizational detail, because people are going to elect councillors to represent and govern them at the ward and district levels, plus a city minister and some other offices. The claves are going to have a five-person council that represents them collectively, and those councillors will be elected from within the claves. But the big thing, the best thing, is that we won't have the city watch acting as the fist of the city minister. They get paid by the city and their loyalty will be to the law, and the watch commander will be elected separately. Khenish Dhawan is running for that office.

Tamhan is super smart about how to run a meeting. He tells people right off the bat that they will get to see me. Then they're caught like borchatta in nets, resigned to listening to his very important but kind of boring government stuff.

While he's doing that, I'm mostly in charge of my own security. I have hornets and wasps looking at the crowd for folks with weapons and quietly let Khenish know about them if I see any, because he's sure that at some point, someone is going to take a shot at me. Or at Tamhan.

That would totally ruin my day, but I'm not afraid. And the reason why I'm not afraid is a story I tell everyone when Tamhan introduces me and I get up on whatever makeshift stage we've set up in each ward; I have all the little women buzz about me and over my head in a tight little knot, then have them dissipate. It's an easy demonstration of my power. And when the applause dies down, I begin.

"Hi." I wave to the people gathered in the first ward of the River District. "I'm Hanima. A couple of years ago, a building fell on my head and I lost my family, my ability to speak, and pretty much my ability to support myself. I lived down by the river and begged for food. The viceroy and the city watch never tried to help me, or anyone like me. Just the opposite. And there are plenty of desperate people living in this district. But then Tamhan told me I could go with some others and seek the Sixth Kenning. I went to this grove of nughobe trees, and a nest of bloodcats ate one of my nipples. I got blessed. It fixed my brain and I regained my ability to speak. I'm stronger and faster than I used to be. No animal will ever try to eat me on the plains, not even a flesh eel. I can also communicate with bees, wasps, and termites. And you know what? It's the best!"

I kind of laugh one of those exultant laughs when you are intensely aware of your good fortune. And people clap for some reason. When that subsides, I get serious on them.

"Things are easy by comparison now for me, but it's not easy for most everyone else in this city. They haven't seen the bottom of the riverbed like I have, and most of them still have a full set of nipples, you know? But I don't want them—and I don't want you—to ever suffer like I have. I want to work with the creatures of the plains and a new government to allow all people to prosper. The beast callers clave will be part of the new clave republic. And if you would like to become a beast caller yourself, then your chance is coming: The source of the Sixth Kenning will be right outside our city walls next week!"

That is another place where I have to pause, because people need to gasp and be astonished. I hold up my hands for their attention, and when they simmer down, I tell them the downside.

"The source of the Sixth Kenning moves about the country to different groups of animals, and it confers great benefits to the blessed. But I have to warn you that the success rate of seekers, if it holds true, is incredibly low in comparison to the other kennings. It's only twelve percent. So that's an eighty-eight percent chance that you'll die if you become a seeker. Though it might help if you're a vegetarian—I think we all were, and remain so. The first person to be blessed, Abhinava Khose, was a hunter and forswore taking the lives of animals before he found the source.

"But you should also consider these things before making a decision: As a beast caller, you will play a vital role in the development of our new nation. That means you will also be an enemy of the current nation. I have had to live in hiding until now because the viceroy sees us as a threat to the country. He killed Sudhi—a nice boy who got blessed with me—in his dungeon. And I hear that it's no different with the new king. He wants us all dead. That's not a joke. So even if you are blessed, you will still be in danger. There will be potential for great good. But there will be the shadow of violence around you too, until we make the country safe. So think about it, and meet me at the docks at noon six days from now if you want to be a seeker.

"That's it. Thank you for listening, and make sure you vote for wise councillors next week. Love and honey from me and my hive to you and your family. Let us work together so that we may all thrive."

On the second day of ward meetings, held in the Tanner District—

full of butchers and tanners, bootmakers and the like—Tamhan gets a lot of questions about how this government will work and how he can justify the illegal seizure of the assets of business owners. His father is in the crowd.

"How can you justify the criminal exploitation of your workers' labor, lining your homes with luxuries while depriving those who create wealth their fair share of the proceeds?" Tamhan retorts, and it goes back and forth a little bit, but Tamhan is ready for it and the crowd is on his side, because he explains that the clave republic has no problem with businesses prospering. "We just mandate that profits be shared among the employees."

And on the third day of meetings, in the Embassy District, just as Khenish Dhawan predicted, someone tries to kill me. Khul Bashab only has embassies from Rael and now Forn—we aren't big enough or important enough to warrant embassies from the other countries. We're gathered in the stone plaza of the Raelech grounds, underneath a huge statue of King Kalaad the Moist, one of the old ones whose efforts to work on the Banighel River basically made Khul Bashab's existence possible. Two men on the periphery of the crowd are wearing cloaks drawn closed around their bodies, with hats pulled low on their brows. There's one to my left and one to my right as I take the stage, and I see them both through my eyes and through the eyes of my airborne friends. I look straight at the one on my right while also keeping the left one in sight via the eyes of some hornets.

The man I'm staring at realizes he may have been spotted, and his eyes shift from side to side, looking for members of the city watch closing in. I haven't alerted Khenish of his presence yet, so the man is clear. But I smile at him from the stage and he doesn't smile back.

The man on the left brings up his arms, splitting the cloak and revealing the crossbow he'd been hiding under there.

I don't have to tell my lovelies to do anything. Once they sense a threat to me, they react as they would in defense of their queen.

But they do not reach him before he levels the bow and takes a shot at me. I turn my head in that direction, and I can tell by the way that everything slows down that I have sped up. I spy the bolt coming and it's moving fast, but not so fast that I cannot twist and pluck it out of the air. I spin with it and point at the man on the right, even as hornets descend on the man on the left and begin to sting him relentlessly.

"Khenish, that cloaked man there has a crossbow too!"

The man's eyes widen in panic and he tries to flee. I ask the hornets watching him to just keep him in sight and fly above his head. Khenish and his men surge that direction in pursuit, and he'll be caught. There's no way to outrun my lovelies.

The crowd is just piecing together what happened as the man on the left screams and drops his crossbow. There's a surge of angry shouts and I raise my hands, one with the bolt still clutched in it.

"Friends! I am safe! And you are safe too! There is no need to worry or be afraid. It is under control, as you can see."

There is no helping the man on the left. His screams cease eventually, as he dies like the guard at the gate who threatened me upon returning to the city. When that's done, I ask Tamhan to get someone over there to remove him while I continue my story and tell them of the seeking. I warn them of the risks, but now they've seen a very practical demonstration of the rewards, and I know that word of it will spread.

Khenish's men catch the second man, and he's recognized immediately as a lesser brother of the church.

Tamhan is furious when he finds out. "We offered them a truce. The patriarch took it, then violated it. We have to address this now."

"Don't go back to him," I say. "Just take all his stuff and make him come to you. Promise to give it back if he abides by the truce from now on."

"Give it back when?"

"When we truly have our government in place. And tell him we need him at the seeking. We need to give the dead to Kalaad in the sky, like Abhi did. That makes him part of this. That will make him feel like the church has a stake in the republic."

"That's good advice. Thanks."

"I think it's good that you listen to people."

Three days later, there are two hundred forty seekers at the docks, which is far more than I thought we'd have. I know the precise number because the newly cowed but still sweaty patriarch is there, and he writes down the names before they conduct their seeking. I give them all another dire warning of their probable failure and reveal only at this time that the source is a hive of burrow wasps. I'd kept the source a secret to ensure that no one tried to eliminate it before we could conduct the seeking.

"So you will either be blessed or—more likely, and I can't emphasize this enough—stung to death," I tell them. "Either way, it's not going to be painless. You can change your mind anytime from now until I escort you to the hive. And we won't be able to have everyone go today. There are simply too many of you. This will take a while, so I urge you to be patient and to think well on this."

I expect to lose some at that point, but only three change their minds. And then, in subsequent days, we add five more.

But the success rate holds true. Twelve percent. Out of two hundred forty-two eventual seekers, two hundred thirteen are sent to Kalaad in the sky. But twenty-nine are blessed with the Sixth Kenning.

A middle-aged woman becomes a friend to sedge pumas, and her knees feel a lot better.

A young woman I've seen before begging in the River District discovers that she has an affinity for khek foxes.

And Jahi, who has been homeless for so long and has survived because he was willing to be a scavenger, is now a herald of blackwings. He's a little bit disappointed, I can tell, though I can't imagine why. Once the seeking is finished and I have the chance, I take him to the Red Pheasant Teahouse for lunch. My hive is going to move into the tree permanently, at the invitation of Jes Dan Kuf and Mak Fin ben Fos. My queen will be safe there and help the tree and the surrounding Fornish vegetation.

"What is your problem?" I ask him. "And don't tell me it's nothing. Your face is drooping like a melting scoop of ice cream."

Jahi looks a lot better than he did a few weeks ago. The bruising is mostly gone, and he's gained a tiny bit of weight from having somewhat regular meals. But he grimaces and takes a sip of his tea. When he sets down his cup with a porcelain clink, he confesses. "The problem is nobody likes blackwings. Nobody's going to want me around."

"I want you around, Jahi. And blackwings may have a bad reputation, but they're actually wonderful."

"They're . . . what are you talking about?"

"I like them."

"Stop it."

"No, listen. Without blackwings and other scavengers, the dead would pose a major health problem to us. Lots of diseases could take hold. We don't have any hygienists in town anymore, you know. Blackwings are literally saving us from disease. Most people don't appreciate that, because it's easier to appreciate defeating an evil rather than to recognize and applaud the absence of it, but I do. I get it. Blackwings are important. Important like bees."

"What?"

"Without bees we don't have food. Without blackwings we don't have our health."

"But . . . okay, sure, good for the blackwings, but how can I be useful, Hanima? I'm not going to eat the dead."

"Oh! I see where your head's at now. Well, you can identify where there's a problem. If lots of animals die in a certain spot and it's not from predators, it's probably something we should be concerned about. And I think you'll find other ways to be useful as you start figuring out what they know and what they can do for us. They're smart birds. Regardless: You are a beast caller, Jahi. You are in the clave and will be paid for what you do, whatever that turns out to be. And you are my friend."

He sniffs, picks up his teacup, and I can tell he's welling up. He gives me a strangled "Thanks," and I smile at him.

"I am nothing now but love and honey, Jahi. You and I know how hard it is to live. We have slept in the mud while the viceroy ate rich food with his rich friends and laughed richly at their rich jokes. So we are going to show our city the compassion for people that our leaders never did. Compassion is the only moral use of power."

"The only moral use?"

"We can argue gently about it if you want. It is a fine day for an argument, and we have fancy cake on the table, and this lovely Fornish tea, and we are friends."

"No, I don't mean to argue. I just wonder where you heard that. From Tamhan?"

"From myself. That is a thing I just said. A thing I believe."

Jahi's jaw drops, and then he shuts it with an audible click and leans forward. "Hanima, let's have that gentle argument. But only as a sauce to your fine main dish of an idea. Because I think it is the key to understanding the heart of the Sixth Kenning and whatever deity is behind it all. It is the answer to Kalaad in the sky, who cares nothing for the meat moving underneath the sun. It is the foundation of a new faith."

"What?"

"Hanima, I think you may be a prophet."

"I—no. What? Jahi, no. I am not the religious type."

"And no wonder, when Kalaad has done nothing for you or anyone you love! Someone else has blessed you; I think that's undeniable. And it should be clear that we need—or at least the people need—a new identity. Because it is not only here that Kalaad has failed us: Think of the people of Hashan Khek, who died fighting Gorin Mogen at the Godsteeth. Think of the burning of Talala Fouz. Think of all the wretched people living in every Nentian city under this system that benefits only a few. Our country is *ready* for this. And you are the perfect person to deliver this message."

"Whose message, though, Jahi, if not mine? I'm not a goddess, so far as I know. Nobody is going to worship Hanima of the Single Boob."

"Don't be cute about this. You've been blessed by something divine. And so have I."

"Fine. I'll grant you that. But who's responsible? Kind of falls apart without a god's hook to hang our hats on."

Tamhan appears at that point, beaming at us and indicating an empty chair at our table. "May I join you?" He's looking spiffy today, though he kind of does all the time. He dresses simply with understated class, usually just two colors, and I like that his boots and belt are scuffed. They're high quality—I'd never be able to afford them—but at least he wears them out. He's not a super pretty boy like Abhi, but he's pleasant to look at, confident, and clever. And I think he finally got some sleep. He's running to be the city minister, against some rich guy who keeps calling him a dumb kid. That argument falls apart as soon as Tamhan opens his mouth, so I'm not worried that the rich guy will win. Tamhan might be young, but he is anything but dumb.

"Please," Jahi says, and before Tamhan can even fully plant himself in the chair, he asks, "What do you think of the idea that compassion is the only moral use of power?"

"Well, I . . . I rather like that. I mean, I have to think about it, because *only* is a pretty restrictive word, but it sounds like it's a quote from some religion. Which faith is that from?"

Jahi points at me. "Hers. She just made it up."

Tamhan lights up. "Hey, yeah?"

His expression tells me right away that if I don't do this, he's going to make someone else do it. "Oh, balls. This is never going to work, you guys."

"Why not?"

"Because we are very shortly going to have to kill people or be killed ourselves. There's absolutely no way we win our freedom here without violence. As we speak, there have to be troops on the way from Batana Mar Din or perhaps from farther away. They might even be here in the next few days. I can't preach compassion for everyone except in cases of people who disagree with me."

"Defending yourself and your city from oppression is a compassionate use of power."

"Oh, no. And where does that stop, Tamhan? Will we then go to war in city after city in the name of compassion? Killing people for what we deem to be their own good? Because that would hurt my heart."

"No. The key word in what I said is *defending*. We must have a strong defense as a deterrent. But we will never project our power."

"You promise?"

"I promise. We will not conquer through war. We will conquer by living so well that everyone wants what we're having. But first we must prove that we can keep Khul Bashab safe from outside threats."

"Look, Tamhan, you say that, and I trust you. But I don't trust who comes after you. They'll find a way to twist it. To corrupt it until they're stomping on other people in the name of compassion."

"That is a valid concern. The faith of Kalaad has certainly been used to justify the heinous policies of the current regime. Only one way to avoid it."

I wince and steal a wistful glance at the stairs leading to the exit. "This is a trap, isn't it? You've outflanked me."

"We need a prophet to demonstrate and spell out precisely how power is to be used compassionately."

"Balls. I knew it. You're shits, the pair of you. I love you forever, you understand. But you're shits."

"Behold the inspired words of a prophet!" Jahi says.

I throw up my hands in exasperation. "A prophet of whom?"

"Well, it's kind of your job to tell us, isn't it?" he replies.

"I'm sure divine inspiration will visit you soon," Tamhan adds.

"I take it back. I hate you both."

They laugh at me, but I hear the compassion in it. They love me too.

Hanima's conversation with Jahi was immediately exciting to me because her words rang true to my ears. I wanted to grab Fintan by the tunic before he departed the wall and shout in his face, "Tell me she's still alive!" Because I needed her to be.

And even if she didn't have answers to the question of divine inspiration, thanks to Gondel Vedd's tales we could take some educated guesses. Raena, or the Eculan deity Meso, might have had something to do with the discovery of the Sixth Kenning.

"Fintan—" I began.

"No, I'm not going to tell you what happened next," he said, flashing a grin at me. "Not now, anyway."

"I wasn't going to ask that. I have a Raelech religion question for you."

His eyebrows shot up. "Oh, yeah? Okay. Want to go have a pint at Master Yöndyr's?"

"Sure."

He was considerate and took the steps down slowly with me as I favored my knee.

"What I'd like to know is if Hanima's idea about compassion being the only moral use of power fits in with the teachings of Raena."

"That is an excellent question! Raena's scrolls never say that—nor do the texts of any other faiths I know—but I do believe it is in keeping with her teachings. There is no hunting for sport allowed, for example. If we are to take a creature's life, then we must make use of all of it and waste nothing. She condemns all trophy hunting or trapping merely for fur and so on. If we can't use the entire thing, Raena says, we shouldn't kill it."

"Okay, good enough. But what—oh. I'll wait."

We had reached the bottom of the stairs and Fintan had to respond to people calling to him and wanting a quick word, all the way to the Siren's Call.

It was still open, serving mostly fish like everyplace else, but Master Yöndyr still had some charcuterie and cheese on hand and loaves of bread for dipping in olive oil. He confessed that this was going to be the last of it, though. He'd outlasted his competitors by a few days with his stores, but even he would be serving nothing but fish and beer after this.

"So what I wanted to know," I said, attempting to pick up where I'd left off, "is how Raena's edicts about war match up with the idea that compassion is the only moral use of power."

"Ah, that's trickier. But still compatible, I think. First there's her edict that our armed forces be used primarily for defense, with very few exceptions."

"That's the rough part, isn't it? Because there are exceptions. Recent ones, like Möllerud. That was a Raelech army attacking outside the borders of Rael."

"Yes. And the allowed exception is an existential threat to our nation. The Triune Council agreed that the Eculans were such a threat, since they had wiped out one of our cities and many more of yours, and there is no indication that they won't try again."

"What other exceptions are there?"

"Soldiers may fight as mercenaries. There are plenty of codes and laws and things about becoming a mercenary or hiring them, but of course people find ways to twist those. That is not in keeping with Hanima's idea, I freely admit. While I suppose mercenaries could be hired and directed to behave for compassionate ends, that is not the typical way in which they are employed."

I had to bid Fintan farewell soon after that; the place was getting crowded, and many others were vying for his attention.

Day 35

FORTY-NINE GIANTS

I used up the last of my bread and upon inspecting my food stores realized I had a few days' worth of victuals left, nothing more. And that was counting on eating out with Fintan—a prospect that itself was threatened now. While perhaps better off by a few days, I was essentially in the same boat as everyone else.

One of the things I realized I'd been missing in my hours at the refugee kitchen was how people were coping. I arrived after breakfast was served and departed before lunch, so I never really saw the lines, how people behaved in them, or how hollow their cheeks were. I thought I knew what hunger was—I had the picture of it in my head—but I hadn't truly felt it yet. I could feel sympathy but hadn't arrived at empathy yet.

"What was breakfast today?" I asked the chef.

"Hard-boiled eggs for children. Fish stew for the adults."

She had me gutting more fish for the afternoon's stew.

"Do they complain a lot?"

"Naw. They know it won't do them any good. I'm serving up what's available, and they understand that. But they look haunted. And lots of them are talking about leaving now. I think relocating would be a good idea."

"Do you ever run out of food before you get to the end of the line?"

"I did most every day, except for this morning. I think a number of people have left already. Caught a boat headed up to Festwyf."

That still did not prepare me for what happened when I met Fintan for lunch at the dockside fishblade. It was busy as before, but as we got into line, we could see that there was a Raelech ship in port that looked like it had some significant cargo. It wasn't a fishing boat. I wondered aloud what it might be, hopeful that it would be some much-needed food for the city, and I was not the only one who was thinking such thoughts. As our queue crept forward, we could see a crowd of people forming around that ship, and soon it started to move and undulate—or, rather, the bodies did, the heads bobbing and weaving like they were enjoying a concert at first. But then it became clear that the people on the outskirts of the crowd were trying to see what was happening nearer the ship, and what was happening was the beginning of a riot.

That was a ship full of food. And there were a lot of hungry people—people who hadn't been so fortunate as I, who might have missed some meals already—who were determined to eat some of it before it got distributed, out of their reach.

On the one hand I disapproved of the violence. It is incredibly easy to disapprove of violence when one has eaten and expects to eat again soon. But I imagined I'd be down there too, participating with gusto, if I hadn't eaten in a few days and couldn't afford to stand in line to buy food, like I was doing right that second.

Still, it wasn't excusable or permissible; some mariners needed to get down there quickly, and we did see a few running toward the disturbance. They probably wouldn't be enough.

Fintan turned to me. "Have you ever seen something like this happen before?"

"No. It's pretty bad."

"Should we . . ."

"What? Get in the way?"

"Well, no. But . . ."

"I'm up for doing whatever I can to help," I explained. "I'm just not sure what we can do."

"I might be able to demand that they stop or something. Broadcast the instructions of the authorities."

"Oh, yes, that's good."

"Shall we?"

"Yes."

We left the queue, forgoing lunch, and strode with purpose toward the expanding riot—others were streaming in, like us—looking for someone in Brynt military uniform who might be able to establish some control.

As we neared the edge of the crowd, it parted before us; a group of armed men were shoving and knocking people aside. There were six of them, all Raelechs in leather armor, and they had bags of rice and flour under one arm while they swung their stone-lined staves with the other or kicked knees to make people get out of the way. I winced at that—knee pain is something I know all too well.

"What kind of shit is this?" Fintan muttered. His eyes were focused on their Jereh bands. "Master soldiers. What are they— Oh. They're mercenaries."

"Mercenaries?" I said. "As in someone's paid them to steal supplies off that ship?"

"Yes." The group had won free of the crowd and were now approaching us. Fintan called out to them, perhaps using a bit of his kenning to ensure that he was heard.

"Master Soldiers, I am Fintan, master bard of the poet goddess Kaelin. Tell me who has employed you."

Their eyes flicked in our direction, landed on Fintan, and six visages scowled at us, and a couple of them shook their heads.

"Raelech law mandates that you reveal your employer upon request.

I have seen your faces and will not forget them. Tell me now, and truly, or be banned from Raena's hall."

That made them stop. This must be one of the many codes and laws about mercenary behavior that Fintan had alluded to earlier. I hadn't known that revealing their employer was a requirement and realized immediately afterward that they had been counting on Brynts not to know that.

"Our employer is Pern du Skölyn," one said, and I gasped.

"I know that name," I said to Fintan in a low voice. "He's a merchant. Well connected."

"And he sent you to take food from that ship?" he asked the mercenary.

"Yes."

"I would seek a better class of employer, gentlemen."

"Will that be all, Master Bard?" the soldier asked with a sneer.

Fintan nodded and they went on their way, because we could not prevent them from completing their task. I wondered if they had caused the commotion or if they were only a part of a larger problem. The crowd still seemed unruly, even dangerous, but not completely out of control yet. The few mariners who'd arrived before us were pushing their way to the ship, and once they got there they could level their halberds and create some space and prevent full-scale looting. It could still turn out okay, with no real damage done except for some bruises and contusions.

There's a moment in such fraught situations, a cusp, a precipice on which we dangle or weave or sway over the abyss, in which we might fall and also might not. And then, whether because of the wind, a poor sense of balance, or an actual push, someone falls in. And then everyone dives after them. That is a mob.

Something happened near the front to push everyone into the abyss. It rippled out in our direction, a wave of rage that turned an anxious jostling into a frenzied free-for-all, and I wasn't armed. I hadn't worn my rapier since the Nentian ambassador, Jasindur Torghala, was kicked out of Pelemyn.

Fintan and I were still outside the press, and wading into it didn't seem advisable, since it was now a churn of fists, elbows, and booted feet.

The clank of armor turned my head. A phalanx of Brynt soldiers armed with swords and shields approached, lines tight, well drilled, with Mynstad du Möcher trotting beside them. I tugged on Fintan's sleeve, pulling him back. "We do not want to be in their path. And there's somebody who might be able to use your talents."

"Mynstad!" I called as she approached. "Mynstad, I have the bard here. He can broadcast your voice."

She turned her head, saw that I indeed had the bard, and gestured with a shrug of her shield. "Follow me."

Fintan and I fell in behind her as the phalanx spread itself on the periphery, putting the mob between them and the edge of the dock.

Once the soldiers had set themselves into a wall of shields, she raised her sword, shouted, *"Push!"* and then told Fintan to broadcast. The wall of shields surged forward, slamming into the rioters as she spoke. "This is the mynstad of the garrison. Disperse immediately or get dunked into the sea."

I realized that was precisely the plan. The pressure of the shields was pushing the rioters off the dock into the ocean shallows. It didn't hurt them—much—and took them out of the fight. After a few of them fell off and splashed into the ocean, and many more realized they'd be next and they had no real ability to win against that wall of shields, the mob lost interest in fighting for whatever reason got them started.

We stayed next to the mynstad as the shield wall pushed forward and people escaped to either side, the mynstad content to let them go. The real prize, if there was one to be had, would be closer to the ship's gangplank or wherever they were off-loading cargo. And the prize, such as it was, turned out to be more Raelech mercenaries with bags of food. But these hadn't managed to fight past the rioters, and now they faced the garrison.

"Lay down your arms and those stolen goods and disperse," Mynstad du Möcher said.

"Get out of our way," the leader of the mercenaries said.

The mynstad snorted, and her voice rang out for everyone to hear at the docks, thanks to Fintan. "I have a rapid in my ranks, sir. He'll pull the water from your brain on my command. This is not a fight you can win. Your choices are to walk away or be dropped where you stand. You might be hungry, but I hope you're not that hungry."

The mercenary gripped his stave and pressed his lips together, frustrated. He looked like he wanted a way out but for some reason couldn't see one. "We can't do that."

"Mynstad, if I may speak to him as a Raelech?" Fintan said. "They're not viewing this situation through the same glass as you."

"Be my guest. But if they endanger my troops, they're going to die."

"Understood."

Fintan stepped through the shield wall with permission and greeted the mercenaries. While he was away, I whispered quickly to the mynstad, "How's Nara?"

She flicked her eyes to me. "Out of town at the moment."

That was all I had time for or could plausibly ask without revealing that I knew where she was and why—though I didn't know why she hadn't returned yet with Gondel Vedd. What was going on in Fornyd?

". . . tell me your employer, as mandated by law," Fintan said as I paid attention to him. The reply was unintelligible, but I heard Fintan respond, "You may or may not be aware of further laws regarding the resigning of your commission and how you may do so without penalty. If your employer has given you an unlawful order—a fact to which the mynstad and I will attest—you can not only resign immediately but be entitled to any pay you are owed for the rest of the month."

"If we do that we'll never work again!" the mercenary shouted.

"If you die now, you will also never work again," Fintan pointed out. "And as I said, the mynstad and I will attest that you resigned for just cause."

The mercenaries took time to discuss their options, and the mynstad let them have it. She kept her eyes moving, spotting rioters climbing out of the ocean and running away, drenched and salty, and also
keeping an eye on anyone who looked like they might want to come
forward. The rioters had all cleared away, so she shouted, "Flanks!"
and the soldiers on either end moved to close them off and prevent
anyone else from approaching the ship.

Seeing this, the mercenaries announced that they resigned their
commission for moral objections and laid down their weapons and
food. And then the investigation began: How did their employer—
another well-connected rich merchant—know about this ship coming
in and what it carried? By the time we had to go to the wall for the afternoon's tales, the mynstad was accompanying constables with a
rapid to arrest not only the named merchants but some others as well.

The first one, Pern du Skölyn, had been in the Wellspring when the
shipment was mentioned. It was supposed to supply the resettlement
efforts in Möllerud and Göfyrd, with some left over for the city. It had
been prepaid by the government, and the merchants probably thought
that the government could afford to let some of it go. But I was fairly
certain the pelenaut would not see it that way.

Föstyr showed up at the wall to confirm that and asked the bard to
broadcast him. The lung named the two rich men who'd attempted to
pull off a little heist and who probably would have gotten away with it
if, ironically, the rioters hadn't also wanted a piece of the pie. In fact,
they had been getting away with it for a while; the mercenaries for
both men confirmed that this was not the first such skimming operation that they'd run. Föstyr assured everyone the two rich men would
be living on bread and water for the foreseeable future, but for everyone's information: "All incoming ships will be guarded by garrison
troops from now on, their cargoes distributed to markets and restau-
rateurs and the refugee kitchen. It will be under guard at all times to
make sure we get everyone fed during this lean time. We are expecting
the first catch from the new fishing operation we have set up off the

coast of Bean to arrive soon. And I will add that the resettlement ships to Möllerud and Göfyrd will be sailing fully stocked; if you wish to leave with them, see the resettlement ministry."

That, I thought, was the compassionate use of power. The rich men who'd been using their wealth to steal from the rest of us were punished; the rioters were pushed into the ocean shallows but not pursued beyond that. There was an understanding that people were hungry and Rölly was going to use his forces to make sure people got fed.

After the lung departed, Fintan sang a hungry song. "A bit of bother down at the docks today. Lots of folks might be feeling some pangs. This song's for everyone with a growling stomach." A speedy strum coupled with percussive slaps on the side of his lute distinguished this one.

> *Gimme something yummy*
> *For my chummy rummy tummy*
> *Gimme something really yummy for my tum*
>
> *If I don't get a cow like now*
> *Then I will steal your mama's chow*
> *Hey, is that grilled squid and crackers? I want some!*
>
> *Oh, ho, I probably gotta go*
> *Meet this old fish head I know*
> *He's not too bright but I can't say he's dumb*
>
> *'Cause he's got a side of bacon*
> *And it's yummy sounds I'm makin'*
> *For stealing it would be the best outcome*

"We begin today with a problem Brynlön faced that you may not have been aware of." Fintan took the seeming of Second Könstad Tallynd du Böll.

Tallynd

Sometimes when I am floating in the Peles Ocean, I feel weightless, both literally and figuratively. There is a relaxation to be found there that can't be found on land, an easing of the shoulders, tension floating away with the currents.

And sometimes I feel like something out there is sizing me up for dinner—which is only proper. We only eat until we ourselves are eaten someday. Water is both life and death for humans: It is the fullness of our experience, embodied by the lord Bryn.

Though I couldn't remember precisely when I started, except that it was after the invasion, I'd been praying underwater by the pelenaut's coral beds. There, amongst the myriad life, the colorful fish and the anemones, the nudibranchs and crustaceans, the rays and eels and longarms, I bore witness to the bounty of the lord Bryn and had the temerity to ask for more.

My words rose to the surface in little bubbles of air: "Please, Lord Bryn, give us another tidal mariner." For we'd had none since Culland du Raffert. No rapids either. Only hygienists had emerged from Bryn's Lung—which we did need very much, to deal with the toxins given off by the dead in the river cities and to keep disease under control in Pelemyn and Survivor Field, since we were filled beyond capacity—but not a single member of the blessed that could help defend against further attacks.

Could that mean there would *be* no further attacks? That thought comforted me somewhat—that we were getting what we needed and we didn't need any power right now, we just needed to recover.

But I worried that Culland du Raffert had angered Bryn with his decision to cleanse Göfyrd with a single, massive act of dry direction, pulling in most of the bay's water and drowning a city all at once.

Perhaps—well, almost certainly—the resultant backwash had done enormous damage to the bay. Not to mention all the dead bodies that were no doubt floating around there. I hadn't been down to investigate; it was quite likely dangerous to visit, not unlike the feeding frenzy underneath the Seven-Year Ship when we'd found it.

I conferred with Könstad du Lallend on the problem—which was a thing that I did regularly now. He came over to help me work through the charcuterie and cheese in my gift baskets. I'd never get through it all, and I thought it would be best to donate their contents to the people on Survivor Field soon.

"Have you heard about the blessed in other countries?" I asked him. "Are their seekings continuing as before, or have they changed?"

"I haven't heard from everyone, of course, and what information I have is out of date, but I am fairly certain that the Raelechs haven't had their juggernauts replaced."

"They lost them all?"

"No, they technically still have one—the fellow who buried the army that took down Bennelin in one massive turning of the earth. But the act aged him so much that he requires a cane and plenty of help going to the bathroom. He won't be much help anymore. And the one who attacked Möllerud wasn't in much better shape, I hear, when he came out of the rock, and he chose to fight on until the end instead of live that way."

"Nothing since then?"

"I don't think so. But I'll ask at the embassy tomorrow. If the kennings are fading on us, that won't be good."

"Do you think they'll tell us? Wouldn't they keep that information to themselves rather than admit that they have a weakness?"

The könstad snorted. "They don't have to fear a massive invasion from us, now, do they?"

That turned my mood black. "No, I suppose they don't."

"Sorry," du Lallend said. "I tend not to worry about the kenning, since it's entirely out of my control. I can't requisition more rapids or tidal mariners any more than you can. I plan with what I have and what I can control. We need that help from Kauria—a cyclone or two at least, to help us set up watches out to sea, and that scholar fellow who can speak the enemy's language. Intelligence gathering is more important now than having an extra rapid on the walls."

"The Kaurians will probably want to hold on to everything for their own defense."

"Probably," the könstad said around a mouthful of cheese.

"So you know nothing about Fornish greensleeves or Hathrim firelords?"

"We should ask at their embassies also."

We did follow up on that but received the diplomatic equivalent of shrugs and a polite "Was there anything else?"

The pelenaut, of course, was a tidal mariner also, and he would fight as necessary, except that we rather needed him for his leadership. That meant the burden of the fighting was on my shoulders and those of the other tidal mariner, at Setyrön, and we had both aged significantly because of the invasion already. I would, of course, bear that burden, but I wished I could get a sense of what else was swimming toward me in the dark.

Three days after that conversation, Gerstad Nara du Fesset came to fetch me in the Wellspring.

"Second Könstad, you need to come out to the lung. Something extraordinary is happening."

"What is it?"

"We have two new tidal mariners and four new rapids already."

"You mean today?"

"Yes. And there may be more coming."

I glanced at the pelenaut and he nodded to excuse me. "Go. Keep me informed," he said.

We exited via the Lung's Locks, and I sleeved out to the kenning site to meet the new blessed and help train them. Mynstad du Möcher was going to be hard taxed to house and supply them all, for they indeed kept coming.

We wound up greeting four new tidal mariners and twelve new rapids that day. It gave me such hope. And it also scared me like a bladefin frenzy. Was this embarrassment of riches intended to help us rebuild or to prepare for what was coming? I was very much afraid it was the latter. Because if it was for rebuilding, we could and should have received that help earlier.

I made sure to return to the pelenaut's coral reefs and thank Lord Bryn for the help. Though I didn't know if it was my prayers he answered or our country's need, I was grateful regardless and prayed that we would have the strength to meet whatever waves the ocean sent to our shores.

"I've been asked to inform you," Fintan said, "that the four new tidal mariners have been deployed to protect Festwyf, Göfyrd, and Möllerud from further attack. The last is here, to aid the second könstad in her duties." Fintan held aloft a sphere and said, "Next!" before dropping it and taking the seeming of Daryck du Löngren. Survivor Field cheered his appearance. It was a day of homegrown tales.

We ran south well past dawn, until the sun was at its zenith and the trees had almost no shadows, their darker selves hidden for a wee while. I judged we were far enough away to make camp, and Gyrsön had little trouble convincing me to let him build a cookfire to roast up slices of a boar that Sören took down without fuss. We left the carcass a hundred lengths behind us so that any scavengers interested in luncheon could enjoy it away from our camp.

Still, we set a watch, because this was the Gravewood, where not watching often turned into not breathing anymore.

We'd just eaten and were licking the grease from our fingers when the mariner guarding the north, Galen du Pöllan, called out. "Gerstad, we have incoming! I hear clacking bones."

I'd just been about to give the order to break camp and move on for a few hours before settling in for the night, but I ordered bows out instead and asked Galen how many were coming.

"I don't know," she responded. "Hard to see through the trees. But more than we had last time!"

That made sense. If she heard them before she saw them, that might mean quite a few incoming.

"They tracked us somehow," I muttered, and wondered who had left a clue for them to follow. It might have been something that Mynstad Luren's detail had done, but it didn't matter now. We were gonna be shucked and slurped if we didn't do something.

"Mynstad, make sure someone's watching our flanks. Everyone else, get your bows facing north—you too, Gyrsön, to the abyss with your damn pots and pans now! Galen, get back here!"

We moved to the south side of the fire and formed up, quivers slung and bows ready. We could all hear the bones now, and flashes of white could be seen between the trunks of trees.

"Fire at will. We have plenty of arrows and we don't want them in close quarters."

Luren took the left flank, and he assigned Galen to the right. She was excellent with the spear but was our least accurate archer.

Sören didn't need to be told he could start pulling water out of giant heads as soon as he could target them. Using his kenning that way was faster, more accurate, and 100 percent more deadly than archery.

Brön let fly first, and a grunt from the northern woods told me he'd hit someone. I saw a washboard of rib bones flash between the trees, and I let fly. It flickered and went down, revealing another behind it. I let fly twice more, and the others were likewise shooting as fast as possible. I had no idea if we were getting close to dropping them all, but I saw plenty in my field of vision and doubted I'd get another shot. They were close enough that I could see the dark-painted hollows around their eyes, and those swords would hack us down. I was about to shout that we switch to spears when Galen erupted from the right flank.

"Gravemaw inbound!" she said, and I whirled to locate it but saw that Galen was pointing to the northeast, not directly east. I followed the direction just in time to see the gravemaw leap into the Bone Giants' left flank and startle some actual screams from them. The beast wrapped its obscene muscular tongue around the midsection of one of the giants and yanked it toward its open mouth of scissor teeth. It crunched down into the giant and his blood gouted like juices from a ripe cherry tomato, his legs severed on one end and dropping to the forest floor like firewood and his head and shoulders falling to the other. The middle of him simply disappeared into that mouth, and he was chewed a few times before being swallowed, except the gravemaw didn't stop moving. It plowed through the giants, trampling a couple and savoring their cries of terror as it did so. They swung at the gravemaw, but their swords did no damage to the impenetrable armor of the beast. It may have even smiled, knowing that they couldn't hurt it and that it could eat another of them as soon as it felt ready for a second course.

"Keep shooting at the giants!" I ordered, realizing that this was a pearl of a chance to reduce their numbers even more. We got off two more flights, and Mynstad Luren might have taken three before one of the Bone Giants shouted some kind of order and the giants disengaged from the gravemaw to refocus on us. The giant was one of those starburst-bearded ones, obviously an officer.

The gravemaw ate him next, the tongue snaking out and whipping him around to bash his skull against a tree trunk before drawing him into those yawning jaws, but the giants followed his last order and came for us.

"Spears!" I said. "Spread to arm's length. Don't let them take a swing at you!"

That was all I had time for before they were on us, and we were too tightly bunched. Close formation was ideal when we had shields, but in this case we needed room to dodge and had little room to maneuver. So those tactics I'd worried about before—disregard for their personal safety and willingness to take a spear so the next giant behind them could take a swing—worked their terrible effect on us. Galen's spear got mired in the guts of one giant and she couldn't disengage before another cut her down, but I speared him through the throat and sidestepped the swing of another. I lashed out with my foot and kicked him over while he was off-balance and plunged my spear down into his chest.

It was nearly over then, and I saw that two other mariners had fallen. Sören was pulling water as fast as he could out of giant brains and having a devastating effect, but he was clearly looking at two coming in his direction while two others came after Brön.

Luren and Gyrsön saw his danger at the same time as I did, and we all moved to help, but muscles never move quite so fast as thoughts. Brön successfully skewered the lead giant but could not avoid the blade of the second arcing down from on high, and our spears arrived a split second too late to save him. It was quick for him, because the strike split his skull, but I knew we'd replay his death in our minds so long as we lived, wishing each time we had moved a tiny bit faster. Brön was not merely our hygienist; he was our longtime friend. The last giant fell with three spears in him, and only five Brynts and a gravemaw were left standing. The gravemaw looked at us with eyes half-lidded in postprandial bliss, speculating on whether we slightly smaller animals might represent an after-luncheon dessert course but apparently deciding against it. The beast belched like thunder before skulking away to the east, belly distended with the flesh of two giants and a significant digestive challenge ahead.

"Let the gravemaw go, Sören," I said. "It's the only reason we're still standing. They would have overwhelmed us otherwise."

There was indeed a litter of bodies around where the gravemaw had attacked, most of the dead sporting arrow shafts. That extra time to let loose arrows was no doubt the difference in the battle.

"Stay alert. Finish them all. And I want a tally."

Our dead were definitely dead; the Bone Giants did not deal blows from which one could recover. But a few of the fallen giants were still alive, until we delivered spear thrusts to their throats.

We counted forty-seven whole giants; the remains of the two the gravemaw had eaten made forty-nine. Unfortunately, it had also eaten the officer's satchel, so I'd not have the opportunity to take any additional intelligence.

I set Sören and Luren to watch and defend us from any further scavengers while I built a cairn for our dead, with Gyrsön and our last remaining mariner. The scavengers did come, but they went after the Bone Giants, mostly, and left us alone, since we represented work and the dead did not.

"We'll come back for them," I vowed. "We'll get them buried properly at sea. I want this area marked. Carve the trees. Tie strips of cloth on the branches. But then we must move directly south until we reach the Gravewater. We have to get this intelligence back to the quartermaster."

The band was silent as we worked, apart from the occasional sniffle. I felt an ache and a release in my chest, fresh sorrow at losing Brön and Galen and the others mixed with relief at our victory and a spoonful of satisfaction that we'd denied them victories twice now. And then we moved quick, new urgency underneath our feet. They wouldn't send any more after us until this band failed to report. The more distance we could put between us now, the better chances we had at staying ahead of them. Getting our report in would be a true taste of victory against an enemy who'd so far enjoyed little opposition from us, apart from tidal mariners.

We stumbled into our first camp, exhausted, but I took the first watch, because my mind was too wound up for sleep. I was second-guessing myself and missing Brön yet thrilled that we beat them and burning with the desire to fight more. I'd never get any rest that way. I needed something to focus on, some structure, and some peace. So I dug around in the papers we'd stolen, flipped over a sheet of what might be priceless intelligence, and found a clear space. I pricked my fingertip with my dagger and dipped a twig in the blood. Then I composed a cock sonnet in the dim light of our campfire while Gyrsön and Luren snored away.

It was uplifting.

I still had the knack, and when it was time to wake up the others, I went to sleep smiling.

We reached the banks of the Gravewater six days of hard marching later and marked up the spot so we'd be able to find it easily when we returned. From that spot, the bodies of our friends lay due north, and it also represented the last known position of the Bone Giant camp on the northern shore.

Sören ferried us one at a time across the Gravewater so that we could move quickly along the Merchant Trail. We had to actually drink from it and ingest some of its poison, since we no longer had a hygienist. It wouldn't kill us right away, and once we met another hygienist, some of its effects could be reversed.

We turned out to be only a couple of hours away from Sturföd, and once there we went to the docks and took a boat. There was still no clean water to be had—the wells were all fouled—so Sören used his kenning to move us very quickly downstream to rest and recovery at Fornyd.

I ordered each of them to report to a hygienist first and to drink some clean water, while I went to report to the quartermaster.

"The pelenaut's intelligence was correct," I told Farlen du Cannym. "As of seven days ago, the Bone Giants had a force of nearly ten thousand almost due north of Sturföd, heading west. And I have more such intelligence," I said, handing over the papers I took from the first officer, "at least if they're not copies of the documents he's already acquired."

They couldn't be exact copies, of course, because whatever the pelenaut had, he didn't have a poem written in blood on the back of one sheet. I neglected to tell the quartermaster it was in there. I didn't feel there was an appropriate way to explain it.

Quartermaster du Cannym was very sorry to hear we'd lost seven on the mission but was overall very pleased. We'd slain fifty-six, after all, counting that assist from the gravemaw, and brought her intelligence besides. She gave the Grynek Hunters commendations and permission to recruit a force to bury our fallen properly. "And of course you must have a new hygienist with you. You may take your pick of those I have at my command. Is there anything else I can do for you?"

It was an unexpected question; no quartermaster had ever volunteered to do anything for me before. She must have been really grateful for our service—or, I realized, she might be different from Grynek's quartermaster. Maybe she always recognized service and sacrifice, rather than expecting it, and did what she could to show her appreciation.

I pondered a moment and then said, "I don't know if it's in your power, Quartermaster, but I'd like a proper reckoning with the Bone Giants, where we do more than scout. If the pelenaut is planning one and the Grynek Hunters can be a part of it, we'd sure like to be included."

She nodded. "We all want a reckoning, I assure you. And I do believe one is coming. Rest for now, then bury your comrades properly. After that we'll see what we can do to provide that reckoning. It might not come here, but if you're willing to travel . . . ?" She raised her eyebrows in a question as she trailed off.

"Aye, we're very willing."

"Then I promise you that chance, Gerstad du Löngren. And when the time comes, I hope you'll strike a blow for me."

Day 36

KING KALAAD THE
UNWELL

It was a busy day at the docks and at the kitchen as well. Chef du Rödal was in a fine mood, and so was I. There were some staples now, thanks to that Raelech boat—cornmeal and flour and even some vegetables for me to chop again for the stews. Since the ships to Möllerud and Göfyrd had sailed with the morning tide, there was enough left over at breakfast for people to come through for seconds.

More ships came in, this time with cargoes for general sale, and true to Rölly's word, the garrison oversaw everything and guarded all transfers. His flow studies and his plans could not avoid some hunger, but it looked like we had pushed starvation back for at least a little while longer.

"It won't go so well tomorrow," Fintan predicted. We were eating at the Roasted Sunchuck, which had opened again in response to food arriving.

"Why is that?"

"This is the first day of new security measures. The criminals took today to scope them out and spot weaknesses. Tomorrow or the next day, you'll see something happen. If I were them, I'd hit the restaurants, because they're not as locked down. No chance of running into a rapid, right? So Hollit and Orden should make sure they lock up tight tonight. Maybe hire some guards."

"Why would they go after it so hard? We have enough now."

"For now," Fintan agreed. "But it's not going to last, and the next ship is uncertain. The Raelech army is bringing food, but we don't know how much. So for the next week or so, you have an environment where someone is going to want to hoard. To the abyss with everyone else, they want to make sure that their needs come first. You think the two men the pelenaut locked up yesterday are the only rich folks who think that way? Do you really think they'll be deterred?"

I frowned at the inescapable sense he was making. "There could be someone eating here right now who's scouting for a heist later."

The bard nodded. "Or anyplace else that's open and looks like it has a full larder."

We worked after that and gave Hollit and Orden a friendly suggestion about increased security for a couple of weeks.

When it was time to go to the wall, Fintan wanted to sing a song of safe travels for all their friends who had left that morning to resettle Göfyrd and Möllerud. There was still a sea of people out there on Survivor Field, but it was not so teeming as it had been before.

Who remained? Those who had found jobs in the city, those who were planning on joining the counterstrike when it was launched, and those who were waiting for their old home city to be opened to resettlement again. There were plenty out there from Gönerled and Sturföd, and quite a few remained from Festwyf—people like Elynea, who had fled the invasion but had found reasons to stay in Pelemyn rather than return to their city, which was populated with ghosts now as far as they were concerned.

> May the road be dry and kind to your feet
> May the road bring many new friends to meet
> May it bring you to good fortune and prosperity
> May it be full of kindness, hope, and charity

May the road be safe and free of wagon ruts
May the squirrels and bandits stay away from your nuts
May the blessings of all the gods drape around your head
May our paths cross again some lucky day ahead.

"We'll begin today in Talala Fouz, in the suddenly dangerous Fornish embassy," Fintan said, before taking on the seeming of Ambassador Ken.

Moments before the men burst into the room, their knives out, I had
allowed myself a small smile of contentment at the progress we were
making at the embassy and at the teahouse. Information was flowing
in and it appeared that the city might be on its way to recovery, thanks
to the efforts of Hennedigha's army. But matters were obviously not
so well in hand as I thought.

The men spilling into my office are Hennedigha's uniformed soldiers, and I throw up my hands in surrender, wondering if this is the
end of my life. One of them is a lieutenant, perhaps a friend of the
murderer in prison. Is this revenge, perhaps, where someone is thinking that if I go away, then so does the problem?

I say nothing, just wait for either talk or action.

They stop, seeing no one in the room but me, and the lieutenant
speaks. "Ambassador, you'll need to come with us."

"Of course, Lieutenant. May I ask where we are going?"

"To see the king."

"He didn't need to send you. I would have come at his request."

"Regardless. Let's go." He waves the tip of his knife toward the door, as if I did not know where the exit was.

"Certainly," I tell him, and begin to move while keeping my hands raised. "But you also don't need your weapons. I promise not to put up a fight."

We have no thornhands on site and Mak is en route to Khul Bashab, or else these fellows would have had a very brief fight before they died. My staff protests and demands to know where I'm being taken as we leave the embassy, but they wisely stay away from the knifepoints.

"Take care of the Canopy," I tell them, which sounds like an innocuous Fornish farewell to the Nentians, except that we'd never phrase it that way. That is instead a code phrase, and several of them nod to acknowledge that the message is received: I'm being taken against my will and might not return. They need to inform Pont and the leaders of my clan and wait for a response. It will likely be months before anything happens, but there will eventually be consequences for this—I hope.

I'm bundled into a carriage with the curtains drawn; there are no witnesses to my exit, other than my staff.

We do not go to the palace, or such as it is at the moment. That would have been a short ride. Instead, we travel to one of the city gates—I'm not sure which one, with the curtains drawn—and pass through them after a brief stop.

My slim hope that this is a mistake is crushed. Anyone leaving the city walls in the company of soldiers is unlikely to be seen again.

When the carriage stops and I'm told to get out, there's a small party waiting for me, and one of them is the king. There are no other civilians. There are, however, four posts planted in the ground, stained with blood and affixed with rusted shackles.

Melishev Lohmet—who is now widely known as King Kalaad the Unwell, the perfect sobriquet—looks very ill indeed. The color of his coppery skin has gone a bit gray, and the muscle underneath his left eye keeps twitching. He's still dressed at the peak of Nentian fashion, as if the clothes will reassure everyone that everything is fine. But he's swaying unsteadily on his feet, and that's a problem, because he's not trying to do anything but stand still and keep the cheek raptor perched on his forearm steady. He's not quite able to manage it, and the bird is squawking and flapping its wings in annoyance.

I say nothing as Hennedigha's men shackle me to a post. We all know it's for executions, so there's no reason for me to ask what he is planning. I'll be patient and learn of his grievance when he's ready. And then, I suppose, I'll be dead.

When the soldiers back away, Melishev and I stare at each other, and eventually he snorts derisively. "I know what you did, Ambassador Ken."

"I've done lots of things, King Kalaad. You'll have to be more specific."

"I should say I know what you didn't do. You never requested a hygienist for me from Pont. I checked up on it, you see. Took some time, but I found out."

"I presume you also found out there was no hygienist to be had?"

"No, you were right about that. But still, you lied to me."

"There was no point in asking for a nonexistent resource."

"Oh, I beg to differ. The point was to keep your promise to me. You said you would ask. You said!" His face darkened with rage for a moment, but then he stepped back, the effort taking something out of him.

"You're right. I apologize. I should have followed through."

"Funny how people apologize so quickly when they're tied up outside the city walls. You know what this animal is?"

"I do. That's a cheek raptor."

"Very good. You know what they do?"

"They use their talons to tear off the cheeks of larger animals, including humans, and eat them."

"Excellent. And then what?"

"And then nothing, as far as they're concerned That's all they eat. They let their prey bleed to death or, more likely, get eaten in the last moments of their lives by other animals of the plains, who are drawn to the scent of their blood and probably their screaming."

Melishev blinks rapidly. "That's . . . that's very good. Yes, very good. This one here, you see," he says, waving clumsily at the one on his arm, "is trained. You can tell because he hasn't eaten my face yet. But at a word from me, he'll eat yours."

"I understand. I hope you understand that my death will not improve your relationship with Forn."

"They're not going to know you died. You're just going to disappear."

"As many others, no doubt, have disappeared during your time as viceroy."

"Oh, my, yes. So many I've lost count." He grins nastily, a look I've seen before.

"But my staff knows it was you who sent for me," I remind him. "They're going to know that you made me disappear."

"Nonsense. Rogue elements of Hennedigha's army spirited you away! Nothing to do with me. No." He blinks, slowly this time, and shakes his head to clear it. He looks like he needs a bed more than anything else. "No, it was someone who has a serious issue with the Fornish. Maybe they were mad at you for planting a huge tree in the city and spoiling their view of majestic ash heaps. We'll have to hunt for the scoundrels for sure. Conduct a very thorough investigation, eh?" He laughs, and the soldiers take their cue and laugh along.

Shaking my head, I say, "I don't see the benefit, Your Majesty. Killing the ambassador of an ally because they failed to secure something they could not possibly secure seems counterproductive. I helped you defeat Gorin Mogen, and I can help you in the future. How does my death do anything for you?"

His cheeks redden again, and spit flies out of his mouth as he clenches a fist and shouts, "It'll fucking give me pleasure!" He takes a step forward, but he's unbalanced by the act and he tries to compensate by leaning backward. It quickly turns into a flailing attempt to stay upright, which ultimately fails. His arm waves, he lets go of the raptor's tether, and it launches itself into the sky as he falls heavily on his ass.

Curses fly after the raptor as a couple of soldiers move in to help the king. Now that he's down, he can't get up. He's angry and embarrassed but incredibly weak. I say nothing as he's pulled upright by his arms and steadied. The cheek raptor doesn't look like it's ever coming back; it's flying directly away from me, out to the plains.

"But perhaps," Melishev says, as if he hadn't just fallen over and lost his weapon of choice, a string of drool dangling from his lower lip, "I will defer my pleasure until later. Take her to the dungeon. If I must rot, then she can rot with me. Throw her in the cell next to Lieutenant Mukhab. Maybe the rats will get her. Maybe she'll get a nasty infection of the lungs. She won't smell so sweet anymore, that's for sure."

There is absolutely nothing I can say to change his mind, so I say nothing. Speaking, in fact, might serve only to provoke him to order my death by other means. Remaining mute will give him the sense that he has won. Begging for my release won't make a bit of difference but might make him feel good, and I don't want that at all. He's clearly suffering, and I'd rather not interfere with that. Especially since I'm to endure plenty according to his whim.

Back into the carriage I go, to be ushered to a pseudo–death sentence in the dungeon, a sort of euphemistic end that would allow people to say later, *She died in the dungeon,* as if it were dying of natural causes. As if it couldn't be helped.

I rely on my training to reveal nothing during the trip, knowing that anything I do or say will be reported back to Melishev later. He will want to hear that I cried. They may very well lie to him, knowing he wants to hear that, but that's out of my control. I control what I can and give them nothing to report.

The dungeon smells just as foul as it did earlier, but Lieutenant Mukhab is not so sane as he was when I first met him. That had been his first day in the cell, and he spoke robustly, lucid and hale. Now his desperation to be freed is raw and keening. His voice is a scratchy wheeze through a phlegm-coated throat, moist coughs interrupting his cries for freedom.

"Pleeease," he whines. "Let me out. I'm sorry. For the thing. I won't do it. I didn't do it. Won't do it, though. Again."

"Brought you a friend, Lieutenant," one of the soldiers said.

"A friend? To get me out?"

"To keep you company. The lady who put you in here."

"What lady? The viceroy put me in here. The king. The shitsnake."

"The lady who wanted you in here. The ambassador."

"Ambassador? The green one? Unsmiling? Not my friend. Never my friend. My friend gets me out. Hey, be my friend? Are you my friend?"

The jingle of the keys in the lock is obscenely loud, as is the groan of the hinges. A hand shoves me into the dark, and the door clangs shut behind me.

"Kalaad," one of them mutters. "Remind me not to get locked up. It's not good for your health."

Lieutenant Mukhab's cries echo off the walls for a seeming hour after they leave. I have no way of knowing how long it truly is, though. Eventually he dissolves into weeping and sniffling. I have, by that time, long since found myself a dry spot in the inky black in which to sit and brood.

I'm cut off from the sun, and I must face the prospect of never seeing it again. Even if someone were to come looking for me, all Melishev has to do is lie and claim he doesn't know where I am, and they'll have to move on. Maybe someone on my staff will look for my bones outside the city. Maybe the Canopy will send a new ambassador in a few months, and maybe they'll be clever enough to figure out where I am, but by that time I will most likely be dancing on the precipice of madness, if I haven't already fallen off it. The lieutenant's condition does not suggest the mind is capable of enduring this darkness for long. I have, in all likelihood, reached the end of my story.

At least I had that stolen season with Mak Fin ben Fos. Those memories should keep me stable for a while at least. And even if I have no hope for myself, I can nurture a hope for those kids down in Khul

Bashab. With the king distracted by rebuilding Talala Fouz and by his own failing health, they might actually have a chance at winning.

"Hello? Is there anybody there? Someone who can hear me? They said someone came in, but I've forgotten already. Forgotten who they said. They said, 'Brought you a friend,' but I don't know who. Who's my friend? Welcome to the dark. It's just like this, day and night. It's really all night, all the time! Except sometimes it's wetter and there are rats. They bite if you try to eat them. Word to the wise. Hello? Hello-ooo?"

It stinks in here and it's cold and damp and miserable, but the worst part about this is that the only company I'll have for the foreseeable future is the mad murderer next door.

Fintan dispelled his seeming and dragged a finger down from his eye, simulating a tear's track, but made no other comment. I hoped that wasn't the end of Mai Bet Ken.

"To complete today's tales in Ghurana Nent," he said, "we'll move eastward to the colony of Malath Ashmali."

I was expecting Abhi or Olet, but instead the bard took the seeming of Koesha Gansu.

Koesha

Baejan asks for our attention around the fire when it's time to share. I've come to treasure our nightly fires, when we can speak in our native tongue and relax. Before we begin, though, I always make sure that Fintan isn't around; I think he would understand quite a bit of what we're saying now, and while I don't think we're saying anything especially private, privacy is nice to have anyway.

My soldier grins widely at our faces circled around the fire.

"You may remember, sisters, that I volunteered to go first. Well, tonight I ride!"

Spontaneous cheers erupted and some hoots and ululations.

"I do this as a service to my country, of course. I won't enjoy myself at *all*." She rolls her eyes with a tiny smile on her face and we laugh. Then her eyes fly wide open at a sudden thought. "Oh, Shoawei save me, what if I don't enjoy myself at all?" That only makes us laugh louder. She beams again and waves, backing out of the circle. "Good night, sisters! I shall tell you what comes of it later! Ha ha. See what I did there?"

We send her off with a fresh round of cheers, and I hope we haven't misjudged the Nentians on this. Some cultures have prudish ideas about sex, and we haven't learned enough of their language to have a discussion about it. Faster to find out the hard way, so to speak.

But we have prepared as much as one could reasonably expect before sticking our faces into the wind. We have shelters built now—lodge houses, mostly, of human and giant sizes, and of an architecture totally foreign to us. But they're warm and keep the rain off, so I like them.

The fishing-boat design we've been working on is also strange, but I've enjoyed learning something new. And I've contributed some tweaks for efficiencies, since fishing boats are the lifeblood of Joabei and we have learned a thing or two in our centuries of fishing. I think the Nentians respect my skills and will be open to working on a Joabeian design for us next. I just have to convince Olet and the council of nine to approve the labor for it.

There is no currency here yet; there is only labor and a cooperative spirit. Olet and the council are basically setting priorities at the moment, but they do plan to issue a currency eventually or, more likely, adopt the Nentian one. They've completed their glass forge now, and they are working on a steel forge next, and a kiln will follow soon after.

That's the one I'm waiting for. I want a proper memorial erected on the beach for our crew, with a howling wind tube on top to mourn their loss forever.

The kiln would come sooner, they claim, but it's low priority since we don't have a ready source of clay nearby anyway. That might need to be something we import; the Raelech stonecutter who came here and decided to stay claims there is a source several leagues away to the southwest, but the question remains whether we want to go get it ourselves, penetrating into a portion of the Gravewood that hasn't been rendered safe by Abhi, or just put "clay" on our list of items to trade.

We have taken a few small test rides on the fishing boat to prove it seaworthy—up and down the river, and out into the shallows only. Abhi accompanied us each time to make sure no krakens attacked, and now he is in the process of enchanting the hull, so he won't need to be present going forward.

That is such a source of hope for us all. If he can successfully enchant a hull, then we can sail home regardless of the season, without fear of krakens.

We are going to test his enchantment soon. The giant woman, Olet, is intensely interested in Abhi's reports of a man living on the island to the north, since his stalk hawk reports that he is tall and pale like the Hathrim. That disappointed me at first, since I'd originally hoped that the hermit might be a shipwrecked Joabeian from some earlier exploration of the Northern Yawn. But as details about the island kept developing with successive airborne scouts, that hope was dashed.

"Is he lavaborn?" Olet asks aloud, and often. She is worried he might be a former hearthfire or might want to be the hearthfire of this community and ruin the fragile government she has built.

I hope in concert with her that he is not. He might be a fire demon, unlike Olet and La Mastik, who have proven to be mild-mannered people in defiance of all our culture's tales of the First Kenning. I'm not sure we should be going to the island at all; Olet's determination to confront this mysterious person seems to carry all the risks of poking a porcupine.

Speculation abounds regarding his presence there. "Maybe he's someone powerful who got exiled for doing something horrific," Haesha suggests. That's my favorite theory at the moment. Other ideas are more or less lurid, but no one is putting forth the idea that this is a perfectly normal, harmless fellow. His mere existence on that island is not normal and is therefore dangerous somehow.

Haesha reports to me that the man shot some arrows at the stalk hawk and the creature was understandably outraged. He missed, thankfully, but she complained loudly when she returned to Abhi's shoulder, and it took him some time to figure out what happened. When he did, Haesha saw him pass judgment.

"He didn't like his friend being in danger. First time I ever saw him look upset. I think Abhi is a good man." She sighs. "I saw him first! But he hasn't seen me yet. Maybe I'm not his type."

I laugh at that. Some of the other crew are thinking of pairing off with Nentian men now that Baejan has decided to blow that door open. But Haesha has yet to find one she likes besides Abhi.

As for the man on the island, I think that if he is dangerous, Abhi will be able to handle him. Haesha reports that his kenning has granted him some extraordinary speed and healing and that he has a background in hunting. The boy is potentially as lethal as he is pretty.

Everyone seems to have forgotten that I admitted we are a people of the Second Kenning on the day the kraken attacked. That's good. So far I haven't had to reveal my powers, and I like it that way. But I figure if this man from the island winds up coming here and causing trouble, I can do some subtle things before I do something obvious like taking his breath away.

With any luck, this encounter will be fruitful and we'll get started in earnest on our ride home. I can't wait to hear the bells chiming in the harbor of Joabei again, Shoawei reminding us that there is music and poetry in the faintest stirrings of wind.

Day 37

THE SEVENTH
KENNING

The chowder house had reopened, and their speciality was of their previous high quality, since they'd finally enjoyed a restock as well. However, when I met the bard there after my shift at the kitchen, he looked absolutely terrible, his eyes half closed and dark circles underneath them.

"Are you ill?" I asked.

"I didn't sleep more than an hour."

"Oh. Nightmares again?"

Fintan nodded. "Really bad. I thought that visiting the Roasted Sunchuck was helping. It was, I think. Just . . . last night was rough."

"The Hathrim burning people?"

"Yes. But only me. They all took turns melting me down. And something else horrible too. You'll hear about it later. Today's stories are the kind I've been waiting to tell to unburden myself, in hopes that it will give me some peace."

"I'm sorry. I know it didn't exactly work out the way you hoped the last time you told such stories. But I do hope you'll be able to get a good night's rest soon."

We sat in silence for a while because I didn't know what else to say, and he was slow to respond. In such situations it's best to be patient. Finally, after drinks arrived and he'd taken a sip, he spoke.

"I used to wonder why Master Aerin lived in relative seclusion, but I think I'm beginning to understand. She had to fill her days with peace and order to balance out whatever it was that plagued her mind at night. I think I'm going to need that too, when this is over. Like, me and a big green field and some sheep or goats or something." A small smile played on his lips as he imagined it. "Yeah."

"Maybe the Fornish have a potion to help you sleep?" I ventured.

"Maybe. You know, I should ask. Never really thought about how lack of sleep can mess you up until recently."

"Definitely ask."

"Yuhh." His eyes drooped, his head lolled, and within seconds he appeared to be unconscious in his seat. I ate quietly, not wishing to wake him. When he began to dream, I was worried at first, but then he began to mumble.

"Sheep," he said. So it was a good dream, as long as no Hathrim showed up to incinerate them. He cheered on his ovine heroines in his sleep. "Yeah. Go for it, sheep. Eat that meadow . . . eat it all. It knows what it did. No mercy."

I felt bad about waking him when it was time for him to perform, but after a few minutes of recovery he was alert and ready to go.

"You just sat here and watched me nap? That must have held all the thrills of watching a rock sit in the sun," he said. "Sorry about that."

He looked much better for the rest, and I didn't regret it.

He played an instrumental and then spoke to everyone in a loud whisper after the break. "I'm going to tell you a secret. Just between us tens of thousands."

Laughter from the field greeted him.

"Today you're going to learn something that's been a long time coming. Three tales, starting with Abhinava Khose."

Abbinava

The little wooden stakes I enchanted and drove into the ground surrounding camp appeared to be doing their job. No one had suffered an attack from the ground since I established the perimeter.

A definite limitation of the enchantment was that the warning was confined to the medium of earth. Nothing airborne was affected—though I think that's a good thing. We wouldn't want to repel birds and insects, since they're vital pollinators. It does, however, mean that people need to worry about the occasional airborne attack. The Joabeians warned us of some birds that they call pine shrikes, which were apparently responsible for Haesha and Leisuen's injuries. I hadn't seen or felt any in the area, but that didn't mean an abattoir of them, as Koesha called it, wouldn't show up later. We lost one of the Hathrim to a scurry of meat squirrels that fell on her from the trees. The trees may be rooted in the earth, but they do not conduct the warning to anything living in their branches. Olet didn't want me enchanting the trees themselves, because there was no telling how soon they might need to be cleared.

The first stake I successfully enchanted had to be destroyed, since it actively repelled Murr. I crafted all subsequent ones with an exception for bloodcats. That meant the camp was vulnerable to them, but since Murr was the only bloodcat around for many leagues, it wasn't a real danger. The greatest peril would come from other strange animals of a type I hadn't met yet and therefore could not include in the enchantment. I left birds out of the enchantment entirely so that Eep and all the other winged creatures could land on the ground without trouble.

Enchantment took a lot out of me. I could usually only do two or three stakes a day before I began to feel excessively tired. But two a day would suffice, Olet assured me. The idea was to build up a stock of them over the winter so that they'd have plenty to trade in the spring. Protection from land-based predators would be one of the camp's first and best exports. There weren't any flesh eels up this far north, but I made sure to include them in the enchantment; that alone would give people the freedom to move about south of the Gravewater. Land-based trade could begin if small caravans—no more than five wagons—took a stake with them.

That work, while tiring, did not take up an especially long chunk of my day. That left me free to pursue my other interests: Finding new creatures, drawing them in my journal, and exploring the unseen deeps of the Northern Yawn with my kenning. And thinking of Tamhan and wondering what he was doing while I shivered in the cold.

I was often accompanied by a woman from the shipwrecked crew as I meandered about. Her name was Haesha, and she would point to things and I would tell her the word for it in Nentian. She would repeat it back to me and sometimes try to use it in a very simple sentence. Almost every member of their crew was paired up like that with a Nentian as they tried to learn our language and help out as best they could. Their best was pretty good on all counts, from what I could tell. I didn't know much about them except that they were from an island nation called Joabei and they'd been trying for many years to find a northern passage around the world. Fintan was picking up a lot more of their language than I was, since he had that perfect memory, but he was also probably the only one really trying. The Joabeian crew had decided it made more sense to learn the language of their hosts rather than teach theirs to us. Plus, they didn't seem especially eager to hang out with the Hathrim or learn their language. There was still a lot of mistrust on both sides. I could tell that Haesha had many questions to ask me but understood that she would need to wait awhile before she could ask them properly.

That didn't stop her from trying, at least once a day, to draw something in the sand and talk about it.

One day was particularly embarrassing.

I heard through Fintan that one of the Joabeian crew had shared a bed with a Nentian man the night before. He looked concerned about it, but I didn't understand why. Maybe he just didn't like gossip.

"Is that a problem?" I asked.

"Not yet," he said.

"How would it be a problem? People are going to be people."

"We don't have the ability to talk about relationships yet," he said. "What if that had significance to the Joabeians beyond mere sex? What if jealousies start to develop on one side or the other or both? What if—"

"People are going to be people," I repeated. "So, yes, all of that will happen and more."

And what happened to me was that once we were down at the beach, Haesha drew simple figures of a man and a woman in the sand and correctly identified them. Then it got awkward as it became clear she wanted to learn the word for kissing.

She didn't try to kiss me, but she did make kissing noises and faces and said a phrase in her language that I knew was a request for how to say that in Nentian. She remembered the Nentian formulation for it and asked, "How you say?"

I shifted my weight and scooched away before answering, trying to be clear that I wasn't looking for a practical demonstration, and then I told her the word in a flat voice, not meeting her eyes or smiling. This was just teaching.

What followed after that was a whole lot of pantomime and me trying to guess what she wanted. She stood and spread her hands over her abdomen, palms flat. Then she pushed them forward and ran them up and down in a spherical shape. "Woman," she said, then pointed to her imaginary large belly with one hand and said, "Small woman inside."

"Pregnant," I guessed. "Or baby. I'm not sure which."

She wanted the words for both, of course, and with some additional drawing in the sand, she understood which was which.

My urgent hope that she would stop there was silly and in vain, because people were going to be people. Through additional drawings, gestures, and some rather terrifying grunts, she made it clear she'd like to know some Nentian words for making a baby.

I leapt to my feet and backed away, shaking my head. As far as I was concerned, Haesha could learn those words from her crewmate who had performed such actions the previous night.

My scramble startled Murr and Eep, who both came to my side and faced Haesha, Murr growling low in his throat and Eep spreading her wings in a threat display and screeching.

Haesha immediately prostrated herself in that body language we'd come to understand was a Joabeian apology. I calmed myself and then my friends and felt like an ass for overreacting.

"Haesha, it's okay."

She peeked up at me and I repeated myself to make sure she understood from my voice and face that I wasn't angry with her. I held up my hand and said, "Wait," which she understood. She rose to a kneel with her hands folded in her lap, a stance of patience. I found a clear stretch of sand near where I was and knelt, after asking Murr and Eep to move aside and give me some room. Normally I wouldn't bother, but if the Joabeians were thinking of pairing up with various Nentians for some reason, I needed to break that egg and poke the yolk fast.

I drew six figures in three pairs and then beckoned Haesha to approach and look at them. She came over and adopted the same posture as before in the sand, a patient kneel. I pointed to the first couple on the right, a man and a woman, then drew a heart between them. I taught her the word for that kind of relationship and that orientation, and she repeated it. Then I pointed to the next two couples: two women and two men. I drew hearts between each and taught her the single word for those relationships and orientations. Some languages have separate words for them, but Nentian used a single word: *sakhret*.

I tested her and she repeated the correct words for each relationship. I then circled the two men and pointed at myself. "I am sakhret. Abhi is sakhret."

Her eyes widened and her mouth formed a tiny *o* of surprise, and I waited for some hint of condemnation to appear there, but none did. Instead, she smiled and chuckled.

"Abhi sakhret," she said, and put curled fingers up to her eyes and made a little whimpering sound, as if she was sad. Then she smiled and chuckled again to communicate that she wasn't really sad but meant it in more of an "Aw, bad luck" sort of way. Then she spoke at length in her language, not a single word of which I understood, and she knew that, but we both realized after spending days together that much can be communicated through tone of voice and expression. In this case she was entirely friendly and bubbly, and she ended by nodding and saying, "Abhi good," so I didn't worry too much about what I missed. But I think she understood why I had been reluctant to discuss terms for intercourse with her earlier. I didn't want her to think that I was interested in it with her or any other member of her crew.

"Haesha good too," I replied. Then I very purposely rose, turned to face the water, and pointed. "Krakens," I said.

"Yes. Krakens," she replied.

We had been making a habit of traveling down to the beach every day, partially for ease of drawing in the sand, and partially so that I could conduct a census of the krakens nearby. If our theory about this being their breeding ground was correct, then at some point I should become aware of an increase in the kraken population. The number had remained stable for a couple of weeks, but even that was useful to know. We were getting a vague idea about how long their gestation or spawning or whatever it was took. And once the little krakens were born and the temperatures dropped precipitously, we should see the population decrease as they moved out of the Yawn and into warmer seas. That day there was an increase in population, and because of our earlier conversation, I could tell Haesha why. "Baby krakens," I said, and held up my hands twice, all fingers spread, to test her. She chewed her lip before guessing. She gave me the word for thirty instead of twenty, but that wasn't bad. We hadn't reviewed numbers in a week.

This area, the spawning ground, was the reason no one had ever successfully navigated the Northern Yawn. For the scant few months in which this sea was free of ice, it was simply full of krakens.

If I could come up with an enchantment to protect ships—to repel krakens, at least, if not prevent other hazards—it would have a greater effect on the world than even the enchantment of stakes to allow free movement across the Nentian plains. People could sail anywhere and trade! Or, unfortunately, invade.

The stories we'd heard about the surprise invasion of Rael and Brynlön by strange giants from across the sea made me wonder if the krakens might not have been a kind of blessing instead of a curse. Indeed, what if they were there precisely to keep the continents separate? Would it be right for me to make them obsolete? Protecting fleets against krakens might usher in a new age of war.

But it seemed that an age of war had descended upon us anyway, without my interference. Someone across the ocean had solved the riddle of krakens before me. Perhaps I would only be evening the scales. Perhaps I was supposed to do this.

The Sixth Kenning *had* been hidden for an awfully long time. Had someone found it years ago, no doubt we would have been crossing the oceans years ago. But now that one culture had already found a way to neutralize the kraken threat, ours needed an answer, and . . . I wound up being bitten by a bunch of bloodcats? That seemed like a ridiculous chain of cause and effect. It sounded like I was looking through "lenses of destiny," as my father would have put it. People put them on to convince themselves that they were special and not just meat like everyone else. It was most likely me assigning divine significance to a matter of coincidence.

Karlef and Suris had been working with Koesha and others to build a fishing boat—a project that did much to soothe tensions. It was finished now, and they had proven it seaworthy and were going to let me try to enchant it, but Olet had made clear that she wanted that island off to the northeast explored before a single spinefish got pulled out of the water. Eep's assertion and subsequent confirmation that there was a man living on that island had everyone curious. I was leaning a bit more toward furious; he'd shot a couple of arrows at Eep and missed. But his intent was clear, and it provided me a certain clarity regarding his character.

We saw him one day, observing us from a distance, in a small vessel. No doubt the smoke of our many campfires had drawn his attention. He was too far away for us to make out any features, and no doubt he had the same difficulty. But even though we stood on the shore and waved to him, he behaved as if there was nothing to see and rowed back to his island. The krakens didn't bother him, everyone noted.

Enchanting a boat, I learned, was much more difficult than enchanting a stake. There's a lot more surface to be covered and I tired after an hour of pressing my hands to the hull, infusing it with what I hoped was a ward against krakens. It would take days, and I informed Olet of the fact after the first hour.

"That's okay. We're going to get started on the next project, though."

"What's that?"

"Koesha would like to get her people home. For that, we're going to need a bigger boat."

They moved the fishing boat to one side and began prepping a major operation. Leisuen and Koesha were both competent shipwrights, and while the Hathrim weren't expert woodworkers, they were excellent at moving heavy stuff around, and once it was made clear that this project would send the Joabeians away, the Thayilist faction did all they could to speed construction.

Once I had enchanted the entire hull of the fishing boat, I informed Olet, and she got so excited that she set La Mastik's head on fire and said that's how hot she was to find out more about the man on the island. For the trip across to the island, she was sending Haesha, Fintan, Suris, and me. Eep would come with me, but Murr would stay behind and nap in my tent.

Suris rowed, while Fintan and Haesha did their best not to look nervous. I trailed my fingers in the water over the side to monitor the activity of krakens as we cruised over the top of them.

Once we cleared the river mouth, there was some time before we floated directly over the drop-off to the deep channel where most of them were nesting. My three companions took turns asking me what the krakens were doing, because they couldn't stand the suspense.

"Still nothing," I said in answer to Fintan asking, "How about now?"

But that changed once we were directly above the deep water. A whole lot of movement, a surge of bulk and tentacles toward the surface.

"Oh, shit," I said, and that was the wrong thing to say, since it instantly panicked the others.

But a second after I said it, the movement roiling in the deeps subsided and coiled back into darkness and whatever passed for kraken contentment.

"It's okay," I said, and repeated it a couple of times until the shouting stopped. "They're not coming. Keep going, Suris."

"What happened?" Fintan asked.

"They sensed the ship all at once and reacted. I don't know how they can tell we're up here, but it was a definite reaction. Four or five of them at least began to rise toward us, fast, but once they began rising the ward must have reached them and they changed their mind. I think we're going to be fine. I'm going to continue monitoring, of course, but there's no need to worry at the moment."

Suris sighed heavily in relief and pulled at the oars. "If you make me shit myself, I'm going to sit on your head."

"Ha. Okay. I'll be careful."

Suris had incredible stamina to go with her strength, and she had us rowed out to the island in an hour. The docks that Eep had scouted were on the eastern side, but it would have taken much longer to get there, so we dropped anchor in the shallows and waded up to a rocky beach on the southern coast. I asked Eep to fly around and locate where the man was, if she could.

"Right," Fintan said. "Any ideas about what we should do until we hear back from Eep?"

"Head for the buildings?" I offered, with a shrug and a gesture toward the cluster of thatched roofs we could see in the distance.

We did that. Once we gained a bit of elevation from the beach and could see the buildings better, they were uniformly unimpressive—except for one.

There was a line of long, low stone houses with sloppy masonry and poorly thatched roofs. The rock was a washed-out gray, and the mortar was cracked. A stable of similarly poor construction squatted to one side, along with some other buildings that had served various functions. My guess was that the longhouses were bunkhouses for laborers, all long gone. The focus of their labor must have been the exquisite structure that nearly preened in the sunlight, it was so pretty. I'm not an expert in architecture, but it was unlike anything I'd ever seen in Ghurana Nent. And the materials had quite obviously been imported. The roof was made of fired clay tiles infused or glazed with some sort of sparkling material so that it winked and shone in the sun. The stone of the walls was not a jumble of random rocks but rather finely cut stones plainly quarried elsewhere and shipped to this island. Which meant the docks had seen some significant cargo come in at some point.

Eep returned, and once she was situated comfortably on my shoulder, I asked her if she had found the man. She nodded.

"Is he near that shiny house?"

The answer was affirmative. Since we could see no one in front of it, I guessed.

"Is he behind it, in the back?"

Yes, he was.

"We have a destination!" Fintan crowed. "Let's go."

As we neared the place, I noticed that the island was pretty quiet. There weren't a lot of trees around and there wasn't a variety of vegetation either. It was tundra, basically, some spare and basic grasses and the dying remnants of ephemeral succulents. With so little food, it was no surprise that wildlife was lacking. But it seemed to me to be an especially barren place, which led me to wonder aloud to the others.

"Why would anyone want to spend all the resources that house represents to live *here*? I mean, why move to an island that's frozen most of the year, that no one knows about, and that's surrounded by krakens?"

"Good questions," Fintan said. "I was thinking along those lines myself. This represents extreme hermitage, except for the vast expenditure of resources. Normally hermits tend to be ascetic, don't they? But that house is pretty lush. Or plush. Something like that. And how did they get everything past the krakens, by the way, since they presumably didn't have a convenient member of the Sixth Kenning shepherding them across the Northern Yawn?"

"I don't know," Suris growled from above us, "but thinking about all that, I already don't like this man, whoever he is. I know there's four of us and Haesha has some pretty great knives, but I find myself wishing I had a squad of houndsmen at my back right now. This is all wrong."

"Good point," Fintan said. "We should not be going into this meeting unwary. But we shouldn't be rude either. Technically, we're the trespassers here."

Seen up close, the house was still beautiful but clearly not quite up to date in its maintenance. There were gardens and flower beds that had not been planted this year. The windows were filthy. There were cobwebs around the front door and along the eaves of the front porch. It appeared to be abandoned, except we knew that it was not.

Circling around to the back, we saw that the grounds were much better kept, though still not up to what anyone would consider top shape. There was a series of square garden beds, and in a distant one knelt a man wearing a kind of hat to shade his head from the sun. He was harvesting a variety of squash or gourds I couldn't quite identify, using a small knife to cut off the stems. The hat unfortunately cast his features in shadow, and he was wearing gloves and was otherwise covered completely by his clothing, so I couldn't even guess at his origins.

"I'm glad he's got something going on back here," I said. "I was about ready to conclude he must live on fish and seaweed. I can't sense much that's edible on the island in terms of animals."

"Maybe he's got a ton of dried meat in his basement," Suris speculated.

"Don't call out until we get a bit closer," Fintan said to us quietly. "I want to see his reaction. In fact, is it all right if I do the talking?"

"Sure," I said. "You're the one who speaks all the languages anyway. If he doesn't speak Nentian, I'm out of luck."

Haesha pointed. "Bad man?"

Fintan shook his head. "We don't know."

She nodded but walked differently after that, with her knees slightly bent, ready to spring to either side or perhaps charge forward, knives drawn. It was not perhaps the friendliest of approaches, but he might not be the friendliest of hermits. I tried to appear unconcerned and unthreatening.

Fintan eventually called out to the man. His head jerked up from contemplating his squash plants, and he froze except for his face. A curl of a snarl rippled along his lip until it fixed in a hateful grimace that promised he'd use the knife in his hand to harvest our organs if only we were close enough to do so.

"Uh," I said, while my mind screamed, *Run!* because that was my instinctive reaction to his expression.

Fintan kept saying things that I realized meant *hello* in every language he knew. He eventually said it in Nentian, but the man didn't react to that one. He reacted to a greeting in Brynt. Which was extremely odd, since he didn't look like any Brynt person I'd ever met or seen from afar. He was protecting his skin from the weak northern sun because his skin was as pale as milk, and Brynt folks tended to be the opposite of pale.

As if he'd just realized or remembered that we could actually see his face, his features smoothed out and his snarl flattened into something noncommittal. Then he stood and tried on a transparently fake grin as he took off his hat so we could see him better. He had a head of fine white hair and enough wrinkles on his face to indicate that he'd passed sixty years a while back, maybe even seventy. He said the Brynt word for *hello* and then exchanged some words with Fintan.

"Don't trust him," I told the bard in an undertone. Just because he hadn't spoken Nentian yet didn't mean he couldn't understand it. "Don't tell him I have the Sixth Kenning or how we got across the channel."

"I won't. But we can get closer and introduce ourselves."

"If he asks about Eep," I said, since she was now perched on my shoulder, "tell him I'm a hunter who's into falconry."

Since Fintan was the only one among us who spoke Brynt, it was an awkward meeting, and I didn't understand anything except what Fintan chose to translate.

"His name is Lorson" was the first scrap of information we received.

Lorson was a strange new thing to my eyes. He was sort of like a stunted Hathrim—that is, pale skinned and taller than most humans, but shorter than Suris, Olet, and their folks. He gave a friendly nod to Suris as if they were of a kind, but if that were the case, why didn't he speak the Hathrim tongue? And why was his jaw clean-shaven if he had any cultural kinship with the Hathrim?

"He wants to know how we got here," Fintan said.

"We should ask him the same question. He'll say the same thing we say to him, no doubt: by boat."

Fintan gabbled with him some more, and eventually Lorson's eyes dropped to consider Haesha. His brows climbed up his head and remained there as Fintan continued, and once the bard stopped talking, he responded in a short sentence, and it was Fintan's turn to look surprised.

"As you thought, he came here by boat from across the ocean, but he spent some time in Brynlön. He wants to come see our camp."

"He's not going to invite us in for tea?" Suris asked as Lorson sheathed his knife on his belt. I found the belt unusual, because it was made of cloth instead of leather, and I noticed that the rest of his clothing did not look especially Brynt or Raelech or like anything familiar.

His tunic was a long-sleeved sort, with the sleeves hugging his arms much more tightly than I've seen, and if I wasn't mistaken, it was made from undyed cotton threads. His pants were made of tougher material—hemp, I guessed—and his shoes were made of the same fabric, with no soles to speak of. These were also undyed, so far as I could tell. For a man who lived in an extremely fancy house, his clothing was very plain. Or maybe these were just the threads he wore while gardening, and he had a closet full of silk robes in the house.

"Apparently tea is not on his agenda," Fintan replied.

"We know from Eep that he has a boat, and we saw him in it the other day. You should ask him where it is," I said.

After Fintan relayed the question, Lorson spoke and pointed to the east, where Eep had reported seeing watercraft.

"Yep, east side. He says he'd be happy to follow us in his boat so that we don't have to ferry him back after the visit. He says he's delighted to have new neighbors."

He certainly looked delighted now. He was beaming at us and nodding and trying to look as pleasant as possible. I might have believed it if I hadn't seen that flash of pure hatred earlier.

Bringing him over for a visit was something we'd discussed prior to coming out, and Olet was prepared in case that happened, but something about this didn't sit well with me.

"Doesn't he want to bring along some friends?" I asked.

"Ha. Good one." Fintan spoke at length with Lorson before pausing to translate. "He's here alone for the moment but will be joined by some companions before the ice comes. He asked if we have kennings and I told him I'm a bard, since that's obvious from my Jereh band anyway. That's all, though."

"Why does he live here, of all places, with or without companions?"

Fintan's translation, when it came, caused Suris and me to snort in disbelief, and I am sure Haesha would have done the same if she had been more proficient in our tongue. "He says he's a simple man with simple tastes."

"That house does not display the simple tastes of a simple man," Suris said.

Fintan traded words again and said, "That's his master's house, and since he's gone, Lorson can't invite us in."

"So he's the gardener?"

"He says yes, he's the gardener, among other things."

I didn't believe it but said nothing. Fintan told Lorson we'd wait for him to come around to the south side of the island and we'd row across together to the budding city site. Lorson waved and immediately set off to the east, not pausing to grab any supplies from the house or to take anything with him. We had no choice but to return to our boat if we were going to remain polite, but once he was out of earshot, I voiced my doubts.

"He didn't behave like a man who has a master," I said. "That little tidbit came out later."

"And where exactly is he from?" Suris wondered aloud. "He's not Hathrim, I can tell you that for sure. We don't make them that small."

"He said it was either east or west, it didn't really matter which way we sailed. It's on the other side of the world from here. He didn't question the idea that Haesha's crew came from across the Larik Ocean, so I think he's telling the truth about that."

"Bad man? Good man?" Haesha asked, since she couldn't understand much of what we were talking about. She wanted just the essentials, and I had to shrug with one shoulder since Eep was on the other.

"We still don't know," I replied, though I was privately pretty sure of the answer.

The bard took a breath and waggled a contemplative finger in the air. "I have to say this, with the caveat that I can't be sure, but he appears to fit the descriptions I've heard about the Bone Giants who invaded Brynlön and Rael. I haven't seen one of them yet, but they're supposed to be a couple feet shorter than Hathrim and possess pale skin."

"But don't they also wear bone armor and have their faces painted like skulls?" Suris asked.

"That's what I've heard about the invaders, yeah," Fintan agreed. "But maybe Lorson is what they look like when they're at home."

"I don't like him," the Hathrim woman said.

"Me neither," I chimed in. "He snarled first and then never stopped smiling. Which one was fake, do you think?"

"He might have simply been startled," Fintan said. "We did surprise him, and maybe he doesn't like surprises."

"That is one way to look at it," Suris agreed. "Another way is to admit that he's clearly a lying creep."

Fintan stopped and threw up his hands. "What do you want me to do? Chase him down and say, 'Sorry, you can't come over because you're too creepy, so just stay here and pretend we're not over there'?"

"No. I want you to not trust him. Don't give anything away."

"Done. I've given him the absolute minimum. I'm not an idiot."

"I don't think you are, Fintan. You might be unguarded, though. Give him too much information and he can use it against us."

"How? He's unarmed and wearing cloth."

"He has that knife. And he could have weapons in his boat."

"If he brings any out, we'll tell him to leave them. But let's not be rude."

"I have no plans to be rude. I'm just going to be wary."

"Fine."

A silence descended then, the kind that often falls when someone says that something is fine when it is obviously not.

Haesha scanned our faces, then nodded once, having come to a conclusion. "Bad man," she said.

Fintan dispelled the seeming and held up another sphere. "Skipping ahead a short while into the future, here's the steward of the new colony."

Olet

I didn't want to be watching from a window when our visitor came calling, but La Mastik had insisted. The lodge we'd constructed served as sleeping quarters for many of the Hathrim at night and a community space by day. It was going to be the city hall and haven of the city we were calling North Haven, or at least the equivalent of that in the Nentian tongue: Malath Ashmali. The Nentians had voted upon the name from about ten different submitted suggestions, and I liked it. From the windows spaced along the eastern side of the lodge—more like holes in the wall, since we didn't have glass in them yet—one could see the top of the path leading down to the riverside dock. That path was going to need widening and shoring up for the transport of cargo, and that was on the ever-growing list of things to do for the Raelech stonecutter who'd come to stay with us.

"Like it or not, Olet, you're too important to risk to a stranger with unknown sympathies and abilities," Mirana said. "So you're going to stay out of sight until we're sure of him."

"But I need to hear what he says."

"I don't think you *need* to, but we'll invite him to sit at a hearth outside the window. You can see and hear him easily from there. Assuming he even speaks a language we understand."

When the stranger arrived, La Mastik had already set up a hearth in a ring of rocks and had a friendly blaze going. Stumps were arranged around it to sit on, and I thought it was a welcoming if rough setup. Koesha was watching with me from the window, and when she saw Haesha, she went outside to talk to her and get updated. Suris came in and said she didn't trust him. My eyes flicked to my sword, standing just inside the door. Hopefully I wouldn't need to use it.

La Mastik was dressed in her priestess clothing, the lava dragon hide and the glass chains and everything, but she hadn't lit her scalp on fire. She was standing so that I saw her left side in profile. The newcomer, then, came to stand at her right and was more or less facing me. He glanced at the window, but if he could see anything at all, I doubted he spied much detail; I was standing in shadow.

He was a strange old fellow, white-haired, wrinkled, and wiry, perhaps two full feet shorter than La Mastik, but two feet taller than Abhi. Though his skin was papery and bore signs of advanced age, his posture was good and he appeared to be strong. His clothes were little better than rags, though; I wondered how he'd deal with the cold.

Abhi took up a position across the fire from La Mastik, his stalk hawk perched on his shoulder, and the Raelech bard stood between him and the newcomer. Koesha and Haesha were conferring behind them. The bard made introductions in Brynt, which was annoying. I didn't know much of that language, except to recognize how it sounded. The man's name was Lorson, and the bard presented my friend as Mirana La Mastik.

"La Mastik?" the man said, then spoke in Hathrim. "Does that mean you are lavaborn? I see you wear the fireproof hide of the dragons."

"I am," she said.

"You speak Hathrim?" Fintan said, blinking in surprise.

"Yes, I picked up a little a long time ago," the man said, and though he spoke with an accent, it sounded faultless to me. He was either being modest or deceptive, and I thought it might be the latter, since Fintan was surprised he spoke it at all.

"But when I said hello to you in Hathrim on the island, you didn't respond. What other languages do you speak?" the bard asked.

"A couple from across the ocean. Nothing you would know," Lorson replied.

"So, to be clear, you don't speak Nentian, Raelech, Fornish, or Kaurian? Or Joabeian?"

"No. Just Brynt and Hathrim."

"That's an odd combination, since those countries are not even remotely close to each other."

"From my home they're almost equidistant, just opposite directions across the oceans."

"Do your people cross the oceans often?"

"No. But neither do yours, I imagine."

"No."

Lorson twirled his finger around in a circle. "So this camp is mostly Nentians and Hathrim?"

"Mostly, yes," La Mastik said. "It's called Malath Ashmali."

"You have the Third Kenning here with the bard," he noted. "And you're of the First Kenning. How many other blessed are there in Malath Ashmali—did I say that correctly?"

"Yes. I'm not actually sure how many blessed there are. We know our shipwrecked friends, for example," she said, pointing at Koesha, "are of the Second Kenning, but we don't know how many are blessed. We're still learning to speak with them."

"Ah, I see. But no Brynt water breathers, like a rapid?"

"No."

"And you're the only one blessed by the First Kenning?"

La Mastik tilted her head and paused just a moment, and because I had known her for years, I knew what that meant. She didn't trust him and she was going to lie.

"Yes," she said.

"Good," Lorson said with a pleasant smile, right before it turned into a nasty leer and his hand shot out to grasp her forearm.

"What—ow! That hurts! Let go—"

La Mastik flailed at him with her free arm and he caught it with his other hand, his face now a full-on snarl. I could see she tried to spark his hair and failed. She screamed, and while I didn't know what he was doing to cause such a reaction—he seemed only to have grabbed her forearms—I knew something terrible was happening. Lorson's hair was visibly growing and coming in dark at the roots instead of white.

His wrinkles disappeared, replaced by smooth planes, and his sagging jowls firmed up into a sharp jawline. Meanwhile, Mirana was aging before my eyes, deep grooves etching her face. First Fintan and then Abhi tried to pull him off her, and though Abhi moved much faster than I thought anyone could, Lorson kicked them away as if they were toddlers.

A knife hilt appeared in his side, thrown with deadly accuracy by Koesha and quite likely doing some damage to his intestines or maybe even a kidney, but he didn't so much as flinch. That's when I knew Lorson wasn't fully human and I needed to kill it with fire.

"I knew it," Suris ground out next to me. "You should kill him now."

I nodded and lit him up from head to toe. His clothing was nicely flammable, but once that was all ignited, I kept pouring it on to his head, turning up the heat and doing my best to melt his face.

He noticed.

"Graah! Where are you, firelord? Face me, you coward!"

He shouldn't have been able to talk or form a coherent sentence through the flames. He should be screaming and dying, but he was standing there on fire as if he were lavaborn, looking about for me.

He knew it had to be someone else sparking him up, because Mirana La Mastik had somehow died of old age in a matter of seconds. He let her go and she fell in a frail heap of bones, shrunken in her armor.

Growling in frustration, he swung his gaze to Fintan and Abhi, who were clutching their ribs and trying to get up. He took a couple of steps in their direction.

I ducked my head through the window and called out, "Don't let him touch you!" That drew his attention to me. He could see me now that I'd moved into the light.

"Ah, there you are!"

Another hilt sprouted from his torso. It was Koesha's other long knife, which pushed out his back to the right side of his spine, but it didn't rock him backward or have any visible effect. Koesha was deadly with those—or at least she would be against a human target.

"Yes, here I am, shitbird."

Lorson casually removed the blades from his body, and while there was some blood on them, it didn't seem like enough. "Can you come out and play?" he said, mocking me through the flames.

"Be right there," I said. I scooped up my sword, yanked it free of the scabbard, and lit it. I stepped outside to find Lorson already charging me. He threw the knives horribly—they sailed wide and were really no more than a distraction. He wanted to get his hands on me like he did to La Mastik, and he had no choice but to keep coming, because I kept pouring fire into his face. I stopped his charge with a straight kick to the chest and he staggered back, but then he ducked underneath the swing of my sword. I kicked him again to make sure he kept his distance, catching him in the gut as he rose to grab me, and that robbed him of momentum. I sent a fresh gout of white-hot flame to his scalp, and finally—finally!—he started to feel it. His skin crisped and bubbled.

"Augghh!" he cried. He dropped into the dirt and rolled around, trying to snuff the flames, and I took the opportunity to step forward and bring my sword down on his unprotected skull.

It split open and he stopped rolling because, unlike Koesha's blades to the torso, a busted head could not be shaken off. I let his body keep burning and hurried over to Mirana, just in case. But no: She was definitely dead. The imprints of Lorson's fingers and thumbs had left deep purple bruises on her arms, but otherwise she simply looked about sixty years older than she had been five minutes ago. And I realized that she'd seen the danger that Lorson represented when I hadn't. If she hadn't kept me in hiding, or if she'd told the truth and let him know that there was a firelord to worry about, he might have killed me first.

"You saved my life," I whispered, even as I absorbed the truth of it. "Thank you."

At that point, the sequence of events caught up with me and I whirled around to find Fintan. "Bard!" I shouted in my native tongue. "What in the name of Thurik's blistering cock just happened?"

I was not the only one saying something along those lines. People from the camp were running over to investigate the screams, and Koesha had retrieved her knives to make sure they were still actually made of steel. She was gesturing first to them and then to the burning body in disbelief, talking to Haesha in her own tongue. The bard and Abhi both were still clutching their ribs, but they looked otherwise unhurt. The plaguebringer's bloodcat was at his side now, hackles raised and growling at anyone who came too close, and the stalk hawk had flown up into a tree.

"Well," the bard gasped and replied in Nentian so that everyone could understand, "he killed La Mastik and then you killed him."

I switched languages out of courtesy. "Yeah, I was there for that part. But why did he do that?"

"I have no idea. He didn't tell us ahead of time that he planned to kill anybody."

"Except for the murderous expression on his face when we first hailed him," Abhi said.

"Yeah, I did see that too," Fintan admitted. "I just didn't think he'd follow through so brazenly. I mean, who walks alone into a huge camp like this and thinks they can take everyone?"

"Well, there's no doubt in my mind that we did the right thing. This was definitely a kill-first-and-ask-questions-later kind of deal. He targeted Mirana and murdered her in front of witnesses because he clearly thought he could get away with it. Which is scary," I said.

"I agree," Fintan said. "Did you hear him ask before he moved if there were any rapids or firelords around? That's all he was afraid of. He acted like he was invulnerable otherwise."

"He kind of was. I mean, it seemed so, anyway. He didn't even care about those knives in his guts. Look at Koesha. She still can't believe it. And it took a whole lot of fire before he felt it."

"And he was strong," Abhi added. "Far stronger than he looked."

"So are you, eh, kid?"

Abhi shrugged. "My speed and strength came with my kenning. But if you stab me, I'll feel it. And if you set me on fire, I'll burn right away."

"Were you going to use your kenning on him?"

Abhi shook his head. "Not much I could have done. My stakes are repelling creatures, so I can hardly call them into camp. And I couldn't ask any animals to attack a man on fire in any case."

"Come here," I said to the two of them. "Look at what he did to Mirana. She's old."

They squatted next to me and we examined her body. Except for the bruises, she didn't appear to be harmed; she simply looked like an old lady.

"It seemed like he was getting younger as she was getting older," Fintan said. "Did you see that too?"

Both Abhi and I nodded, and then the plaguebringer said, "He was like a leech." When I blinked at him incomprehendingly, he said, "I mean he was a parasite that requires physical contact to do his thing, or else he could have done it to any of us from a distance."

That fit with my battlefield assessment of his tactics. "Fintan, in all the stories you have in your head, all the lore you've ever read, have you ever heard of anything like that? Somebody siphoning away all the vitality of your life and somehow using that energy to fuel their own regeneration—"

"That's what he was doing, wasn't it?" Abhi interrupted. "Not just growing younger but ignoring the fire and not caring about the knives. He used everything he stole from La Mastik and kept regenerating until he couldn't anymore."

"Oh! So that's why he went after Olet!" Fintan said. "If he defeated her, he'd have been really hard to kill after that. He could have wiped us all out."

"Guys."

"Sorry, Olet." The bard looked abashed. "We're just catching up to conclusions you'd already reached. To answer your question: No, I've never heard of anything like this before."

"Was he really alone on that island?"

"He appeared to be. We saw no one else. He said his master was away."

"His master? So there could be another monster like him out there?"

"Could be."

"There's a fancy house on the island," Abhi said, "and he's not going to be back. We might be able to find some answers there. I'd like to go just to make sure he didn't have any pets. Or prisoners."

"Good idea," I said, nodding. "I'll go with you, just in case the master turns up. And if he doesn't turn up, that's fine. I'm still going to burn it all down."

I was all for leaving right that second but then realized we couldn't. The people of Malath Ashmali needed to be told what happened. Koesha needed to be reassured that her knives were fantastically deadly and would still kill most anything. A funeral smoke needed to be held for La Mastik. And we needed to make sure this thing—this lifeleech, Lorson—didn't find a way to live again. Couldn't be too careful about something like that. Plus, I really wanted to wipe every trace of this creature from the earth.

I supervised his disposal. Using someone's donated sheet, I snuffed out the flames on his still-burning body and wrapped it up so that there would be no possibility of contacting his skin. Then a crew of Hathrim bore it down to the beach, where I set it all on fire again and left it there, unhallowed and unmourned. Suris volunteered to stay and make sure it burned all the way to ash.

And then, with heavy boots and heavy heart, I returned to camp to say farewell to my oldest and best friend, Mirana La Mastik.

Who would keep my counsel now? Who could I trust to advise me from a place of love and loyalty?

She told me on more than one occasion that Thurik said all cities were born in fire and blood. It was a favorite passage of Gorin Mogen, in fact, though he had not been particularly devout. Turned out Thurik was right, both about Baghra Khek and Malath Ashmali. I never thought it would be my fire and her blood, though.

———

That tale got everyone talking, but Fintan held up a hand. "Wait! There's more. There's me, about an hour after that." He took on the seeming of his past self.

Like everyone else in Malath Ashmali, I wanted to know what exactly had happened and what kind of weird creature Lorson was. He couldn't tell us, so we had to go back to that island if we wanted any answers.

After we said farewell to La Mastik, that's precisely what we did. Olet joined us this time, along with Abhi and Koesha and the Raelech stonecutter, Curragh. He'd missed the fight with Lorson because he was working on building a Raelech embassy, but I felt better having him along with us for this trip. Olet wore her armor, and she brought one of the huge houndsmen's axes with her in addition to her sword.

Abhi asked his stalk hawk and bloodcat to keep their senses alert and warn us against anyone approaching.

Olet suggested we search the outbuildings before we tackled the main house, and that proved to be both instructive and ominous.

"These were built by hand, and rather poorly too," Curragh said. Inside the largest, we discovered that there was a well protected from the snows. A table next to it held stacks of plates and cups. There was a privy with ten stalls. A kitchen with no food or utensils in it. And then there was room after room of bunks. Olet asked me to keep a count of the beds; there were eighty-four all told. Most peculiar was that the rooms, while all open, possessed doors that could be locked only from the outside.

The smaller buildings served either a single purpose or no purpose at all that we could tell. There was a bathhouse, judging by the tubs within and the hearth for heating water, but said water would have had to be hauled over from the well in the other building. Another building was clearly a stable for absent livestock, and another was simply a large empty hall with a spacious hearth opposite the door. A recreation room, perhaps? Dancing? A space for morning exercises during the long winter months?

Whoever used to occupy the buildings, they were long gone now. A thick layer of dust coated everything, and we sneezed often.

"My theory," Olet said on our way to Lorson's master's house, "is that these buildings housed the laborers used to build this fancy thing ahead of us."

"Okay, but then why were their bunkrooms locked from the outside?" I wondered aloud.

"I bet they were deceived. He behaved friendly at first, just like he did with us, offered them pay, and once he had them on the island he was in control. They had to do what he said or he would drain their life away. We should definitely take the time to search the docks and vessels there too."

Curragh shook his head after a few more steps. "I don't know, Olet. I can tell from here that whoever built that nice house knew what they were doing, as opposed to whoever built these others. From an architectural standpoint, they were constructed by completely different sets of laborers."

"Interesting. But you do think this house was built by hand, not by Raelech stonecutters?"

"Oh, yes. That's definitely carpentry, not the Third Kenning. Even that well in the bunkhouse—that was dug by hand."

We stood before the front door, and I couldn't even tell what kind of wood it was made from. Perhaps somebody from Forn would recognize it.

Abhi asked Murr and Eep to remain outside, which I imagined they preferred in any case.

Inside the building, it became abundantly clear that all the materials were imported by ship. There did not appear to be anything native to the island here: Not even a plank of the indigenous fir was in evidence. The floors and furnishings were made of hardwoods I did recognize from Brynlön and Forn. The baths and kitchen used plenty of marble from Rael. There was a trophy room with the gruesome heads of animals from Ghurana Nent mounted on the wall, along with some javelins, spears, and a large bow. In another room there were display cases full of glass knives and sculptures from Hathrir. I thought for a while that there was curiously nothing from Kauria, until I ran across a Mugg's Mug mug from Linlauen sitting in a kitchen cupboard. I'd never been there myself, but I'd heard it described as a must-see tourist attraction.

The pantry was extremely interesting to me, as the island did not seem to host any animals beyond some insects and worms. It contained, as one might expect, plenty of dry goods and even more preserved vegetables and fruits, lined up and labeled in jars. Fresh produce had to come from the garden in season or not at all.

The cutlery was the good stuff from Hathrir, the finest steel possible. It was stamped with the Mogen family crest, in fact. I doubted Gorin Mogen himself had made the knives, but someone he'd trained certainly had. The rest of the kitchenware was likewise first-rate; it was the demesne of a modern gourmet chef who probably had only fresh fish or dried meats to work with.

In contrast to the modernity of the kitchen, the living spaces were filled with antiques. Looking at a silverbark couch and tea table with a couple of rocking chairs opposite, I shook my head.

"I've seen drawings of these before. They're museum pieces. Priceless. I'd feel like an outlaw if I sat on them."

"They look designed for taller people, though," Olet said. "I'm not shy about trying them out. If they snap under my weight, oh, well. Bastard killed Mirana, so I'm not going to cry about his furniture."

She sat down on the couch, and it groaned under her weight but didn't buckle. Olet sniffed in disdain.

"Not bad, but not great either. Mediocre. Unless someone has a compelling argument against it, I think we should take all his stuff. Especially the dining room table and chairs. Those would work for the Hathrim."

"Well, he said he had a master who'd be returning soon," I reminded her.

"If he wasn't lying, sure, we should worry about that. Here's the test—bedrooms and bathrooms: Is there more than one that looks lived-in? Are there two? Will we find different toothbrushes? If Lorson was a servant of some kind, we should find his humble room some-where else besides the master suite, right?" She pointed at the stairs leading up and down. "Which way do you figure the bedrooms are?"

"Most likely up," Curragh said. "Unless they're in the back of this main floor." We hadn't gone there yet.

"Let's split up. I'll head upstairs with Koesha. Curragh and Abhi, please check out the basement. Fintan, you can finish looking around this main floor."

As boots clomped on stairs going up and down, I drifted toward the back half of the sprawling house. I found a tea room with a bewilder-ing array of looseleaf teas from Forn and Kauria, along with antique tea sets that also belonged in a museum.

"Somebody had to know this guy was living up here," I thought aloud. "If he wasn't buying all this himself, he had to have an agent down on the continent buying it for him. And even if he did buy it all himself, someone still had to sail it up here—past the krakens—and help him move it in. You'd need a wagon . . . which we'll probably find down at the docks."

The next room was at once familiar and welcoming and strangely uncomfortable. It was a rather large library with floor-to-ceiling shelves, complete with a rolling ladder to access the top ones. The room was long and narrow, seeming to spread across the entire back half of the house. There was a single upholstered chair next to the one window on that wall, angled so that the light would shine down on whatever book he was reading. A small bistro table next to it held a saucer and teacup. There was also a beautiful varnished silverbark table with a prize open on top: an atlas of the world! And I mean the world, not just the portion of it I already knew. Joabei was there, across the ocean and in the northern latitudes, as well as some other clusters of islands and land masses that I'd never seen before. They were labeled Omesh, Ecula, Bačiiš. Presumably the Bone Giants had come from one of them.

"There could be a room full of gold downstairs," I breathed, "and it wouldn't be worth more than this. This is priceless." I committed the pages of the strange continents to memory on the spot.

Curious to see what else might be on the shelves, I peered at some spines. They were in Brynt, and while I recognized some titles, there were far more that were unfamiliar. I kept going and, when I reached a bookcase full of titles in Hathrim, realized that he had organized the library by language. Nothing in Raelech or the other continental languages, so Lorson hadn't been lying about not speaking them. But most of the shelves in the library, as I progressed, were filled with titles written in a language I didn't recognize, except that it might bear some relation to a long-dead mother tongue called Uzstašanas.

Lorson had mentioned that he'd come here from across the ocean, so I was most likely looking at his native language, but . . .

"This place doesn't make any sense," I muttered to myself.

There were two more floors of additional riches, no doubt, and not a single explanation for why anyone would want to live here in isolated luxury. People with such expensive tastes usually wanted someone else around to see how finely they were living. Traditional hermits were notorious for settling in extremely humble caves with very few possessions. About all I could conclude about Lorson was that he had been a nontraditional hermit. Unless he had been exiled here.

Something about the room itself was bothering me, nibbling away in a dark corner of my mind, dimly felt but unseen. I spun around, looking for anything that didn't belong in a library, but got nothing except a reinforcement of the observation that it was a strangely shaped room, more like a long, extra-wide hallway than a space planned to be a library.

Before I could speculate, Abhi and Curragh called out and I answered. They showed up moments later, even as I heard Olet's heavy footsteps clomping down the stairs.

"What did you find?" I asked.

"It's basically storage and plumbing and stuff like that," Curragh said. "Lots of dusty boxes, no weird smells. There might be spiders."

"There are definitely spiders," Abhi said. "Poisonous ones too. Anything interesting here?"

"Yes. An atlas! Not just of our continent, but the whole world! It tells us what, if not exactly who, is across the oceans! Can you believe it? And it proves that the northern passage exists and can be navigated, as long as one doesn't have to worry about krakens."

"What about krakens?" Olet said, entering the room with Koesha.

"They're the only thing standing in the way of the northern passage. Koesha should be able to get home if Abhi can keep the krakens away. And if it becomes safe, think of what it would mean for trade! What was upstairs?"

"Proof that Lorson was a liar. This is his house. There's nobody else coming. There are three bedrooms but only one is lived-in—and it's the fancy one. The others don't even have sheets on the beds and the closets are empty."

"Toothbrushes?"

"Ha! Just one."

"So strange. I feel like we're missing something, though."

"An explanation, yes," Olet said.

"Right, but I mean this house is missing something. It has a room full of teapots and ceramic cups but it doesn't have something it should have, and it's bothering me. I just don't know what it is. And this library. It's not right."

"What do you mean?" Abhi said. "It's full of books, like a library should be."

"Indulge me, okay? Just . . . look at this room and see if you see anything out of the ordinary, all right? I don't want to say anything to prejudice your thoughts. Give it a look."

Everyone stood in place or turned around, scanning the room. With any luck one of them would be able to identify the bothersome detail that was escaping my consciousness. If they had no luck, they would merely think I was stranger than they already did.

Before long, Koesha began to circle the room, glaring at the books as she went. She wasn't reading them, so she must be looking for something else.

Curragh was the first to notice something, however. "This room isn't right."

"How so?"

He pointed at the single window with the reading chair. "There should be more than one window. You don't build a long room like this with only one natural light source. Whole room is out of balance. And stunted."

"Stunted?"

"If this room was supposed to be built symmetrically, then there shouldn't be a wall right behind you," Curragh said. "In fact, the missing window this room should have would most likely be placed behind that wall. So there's—wait." He strode to the window, pressed his nose to the glass, and looked right. "Yes. There's another window. There's another room behind that wall."

"There can't be. There's no door. Unless the entrance is on the other side."

"I can go look," Abhi volunteered.

"This thing!" Koesha said, pointing to a book near me. She had progressed to my side of the room and stopped. She often said that exact phrase when she wanted to know the Nentian word for something.

"Book?" I guessed.

"This is book," she said, looking at me for confirmation.

"Yes."

She pointed to another and said, just to make sure, "This is book."

"Yes."

"All books," she said, sweeping her arms wide, "have dirt. But not dirt." She rubbed the tips of her fingers together and blew on them. "Small dirt. What is that thing?"

"Dust! Small dirt is dust. The books are dusty."

"Yes. All books are dusty. But not this book." She pointed to one above her head—above mine, really, and more easily reached by Olet—which shone with frequent use. The letters on the spine were gold-lined and glinted in the light so that I couldn't make them out.

"Olet, can you read the spine of that? I can't see it."

The giant woman strode over, towering over Koesha, and said, "Your pardon." Koesha scooted to the side and Olet squinted at the volume's spine. "Not sure if I'm saying this right, but it looks like *Zanata Sedam.*"

That meant nothing to me at the time. "Can you pluck it out, please?"

"Sure." There was an audible click as she did so and then a creak and groan from the bookcase as it shifted next to me.

"What the—"

Koesha clapped in delight and said something happy. Then she shouldered past me, apparently knowing exactly what to do, and hauled on the edge of the bookcase. It was a bit heavy for her, so Olet handed the book to Abhi and pitched in. The bookcase was set on a rail-and-roller system hidden from view up near the ceiling, and a por-tion of the case kicked out and slid in front of the other, revealing a room behind where Curragh said the window should be, and was.

"Aha!" I exclaimed. "That's what was missing! An office! All this stuff to read and nothing to write with."

"I have questions," Olet said.

"I think we all do," Abhi said.

"First, who builds a secret room inside a secret house on a secret is-land? Second, what kind of secrets require such a room?"

I clapped my hands and rubbed them together in anticipation. "I can't wait to find out." There was a mess of correspondence on the desk and many crates of files. He appeared to favor a sepia ink and an old-fashioned quill. "But thanks to Curragh and Koesha for figuring out it was here. I don't think we would have otherwise."

Koesha hummed happily and said, "You are welcome."

Curragh tried to answer Olet's questions. "Maybe this was a precaution against exactly what happened—him dying and no one being around to protect this place. He simply didn't want his records to be found."

I stepped inside and examined a shelf of knickknacks and goodies mounted above the writing desk. There was sealing wax, boxes of matches, pots of ink, and a mysterious pouch next to a pipe. I opened the pouch, took a whiff, and handed it to Olet. "Tobacco."

"Excellent!" Olet said. "Looting this guy is already making my day. In fact, I think I'd better get on that and let you rummage around here. You'll tell me what you find later?"

"Absolutely."

"Abhi, will you take Curragh back downstairs and inventory everything there?"

"Uh," Curragh said, obviously trying to think of an excuse he could make to get out of it.

"Don't worry, I won't let the spiders get you," Abhi reassured him. "Everyone is going to be very polite and respect boundaries."

"Good," Olet said, nodding. "I'm going to take Koesha down to the docks and see what's there. We'll be back as soon as we can and compare notes."

That left me alone to make sense of the office. I began with the desk, pulling up the comfy chair, which sat a bit high off the ground for me, but that was all right.

It quickly became clear that I'd need to sort the correspondence into Brynt and the unknown language similar to Uzstašanas. That was a shame, since there was a tantalizing journal written in the unknown language. Nothing in Hathrim, though, at least not immediately visible.

Once I had a stack of Brynt letters in front of me, I began to peruse them. After reading the one on top, I had to do so with my jaw dropped. They were a mix of Brynt and the other language, addressed to the

"Immortal Lorson," greeting him from Pelemyn and informing him that the pelenaut continued to be foolishly occupied with the well-being of his people, or unaware of their plans, or otherwise unprepared for what was to come. Once I realized that these letters were speaking of the Bone Giant invasion—and, furthermore, that they came from someone in Pelemyn who was obviously a spy—I organized them by date and then attempted to piece together what happened and see if I could figure out who was writing them. The signature, Vjeko, bore no significance to me, but I knew I had to inform the pelenaut quickly if he was not already aware of this traitor in his midst. I also needed to understand how Lorson was involved. Was he the mastermind behind the whole thing?

The letters followed a frustrating pattern. The greeting and first line about the pelenaut were in Brynt, and the closing was also in Brynt, but the bulk of the letters were in that indecipherable tongue.

But I did get to an interesting missive listing the Brynt cities attacked in the invasion, with their status written down afterward.

Festwyf: Destroyed
Fornyd: Abandoned and then repopulated in the single
    act of intelligent leadership by the Brynts, so it remains
Sturföd: Destroyed
Grynek: Destroyed, but army buried in the Granite
    Tunnel by Raelechs
Pelemyn: Remains (tidal mariner sank fleet)
Gönerled: Destroyed
Göfyrd: Destroyed, but army subsequently drowned by
    tidal mariner
Setyrön: Remains (tidal mariner sank fleet)
Möllerud: Destroyed
Hillegöm: Destroyed
Bennelin: Destroyed, but army subsequently lost to
    juggernaut

In sum, we have weakened Brynlön significantly but only destroyed one Raelech city, while losing all forces except for the one at Möllerud and the other two deployed to the north.

That "we" was damning evidence of espionage. The writer of this letter was an enemy of both Brynlön and Rael, and Lorson—who was obviously not immortal—had been one too.

This letter had been written before the army at Möllerud had been destroyed. But what forces had been deployed to the north?

I doubted this communication had been one-way. Lorson had to have written back—but if so, how were the deliveries made? I hardly expected it to be in person. Someone was acting as a courier.

My best guess, based simply on the location of the island's docks and the language involved, was that the courier was coming by boat from Brynlön rather than overland. Unless there was some other northern port about which no one knew. A possibility, considering how much we didn't know already.

Koesha's crew was working hard on a seaworthy icebreaker vessel that would leave as soon as it was finished, regardless of the weather, which Abhi was going to enchant against krakens. I knew they were going to go east to prove the feasibility of the northern passage to their people, and I thought perhaps I'd go with them if Tuala or some other courier didn't return before then. They probably wouldn't mind dropping me off at Pelemyn first. They could meet the Brynts and take on a cargo of trade goods.

Plus, as much as I was enchanted by Malath Ashmali and the potential it had, I thought I'd rather not be around firelords anymore. Olet joined my nightmares the night before along with Gorin Mogen and Winthir Kanek, and together they all set me on fire. I felt my skin melting and smelled burning hair before I woke up. I know she's not like the other two—except that she did burn someone when she got mad enough. She had legitimate cause, unlike Mogen and her father, but still. My imagination was preoccupied with what she *could* do to me rather than what she *would* do, and as a result, I got very little rest.

Perhaps, with some distance and some diverting mysteries to solve, I'd dream of something else.

I kept going through the letters. Most of it was in that unreadable script, but the last letter was signed off in Brynt in a stunning fashion:

May you thrive in the power of the Seventh Kenning,
Vjeko

I blinked and sat back in the too-big chair, flabbergasted. "So is that . . . what he did? That thing he did to La Mastik was the Seventh Kenning?"

I froze, replaying the events of Lorson's attack in my head to make sure I hadn't misinterpreted. Then, following a hunch, I went to the crates of documents stacked along the wall and started looking at the files inside. All matched the handwriting in the journal on the desk, and the numbers, at least, were readable. All I paid attention to were the dates.

It only took a couple of crates to determine that they were arranged in chronological order, about ten years to a crate. I stood back and counted.

"There are twenty crates," I breathed, a little terrified at what that meant.

Cursing in six languages, I began to move them aside to get to where the oldest one should be, on the bottom right.

The journals in there were yellowed and a bit gnawed on by bugs, the ink faded after so much time, but I could make out the date of the first journal I pulled out, written in the same crabbed hand that filled the pages of Lorson's latest journal. It was further back than I'd expected; it was more than three hundred years ago.

Lorson had lived for more than three hundred years. Perhaps here, perhaps elsewhere before moving to the island. And we saw him grow visibly younger while La Mastik grew visibly older. The Seventh Kenning, therefore—at least Lorson's particular manifestation of it—allowed one to extend their life at the expense of another's. It's not that he ever stopped aging; he could just turn back the clock every so often and enjoy unnatural strength. How strange, I thought—or, perhaps, how perfectly logical—that while every other kenning advanced the age of the user, the seventh reversed it.

Well, at least I knew one of the secrets he was keeping up here. But where was the source of this Seventh Kenning? What god would ever allow such a thing? And how many more monsters like Lorson were out there?

"That's all for now," Fintan said, throwing down a pellet and dispelling the seeming of his former self. An upswell of protests rose from Survivor Field, and the bard spoke over them. "But I'm sure you have plenty to talk about, eh? *That* was a story. And all true. More tomorrow!"

He grinned and waved as the roar of the crowd grew louder, supremely pleased with himself now that he'd delivered some revelations to which he'd obviously been building for some time. Our great enemy finally had a name—some ancient evil bastard who wished us all dead. But now he was killed instead. I could see people yelling both at Fintan and at one another as they put the pieces of the truth they had together, the grim satisfaction that Lorson was dead and charred to ash, and the utter fury that Vjeko had yet to be identified or caught. So far as they knew, anyway. I had a few more pieces than my fellow citizens, which might be, in this one peculiar instance, the slightest mark in favor of being a spy.

"Nice!" I said, and waved at the bard from the top of the stairs as he turned, triumphant, to bask in congratulations. I assumed that Rölly would like to speak to Fintan soon, because that was the very information we'd been asking for—who had Vjeko, the Wraith, been writing to all this time? I wanted to see if the Wraith and Approval Smile would be more willing to answer questions now that their co-conspirator and perhaps leader was dead, and I couldn't do that with the bard in tow, so I left him behind to enjoy others' reactions to his revelations.

Then I recalled that when we had breakfast at Tallynd's house some days ago, Fintan remarked to Rölly that he had already shared something with him in private about events in the north: Had it been Lorson's existence? I was willing to bet it had. Which meant Rölly had known all this time and had deliberately waited until now—perhaps for political reasons, perhaps for the purposes of espionage—to reveal it. I didn't know what game he was playing or why; I just knew enough to realize he was playing a game. Which really meant I shouldn't try to play. Who knew how deep the secrets ran?

When I arrived at the palace and asked to see Rölly, I was told in no uncertain terms that he was occupied for the rest of the evening and not seeing anyone until further notice. Same answer when I asked for the lung.

They were probably doing precisely what I wanted to do: asking the Wraith to talk again. I couldn't fault them for that.

Thinking back on the bard's earlier assurances, I could see how this news, while a bit late, wasn't crucial to our survival. Lorson had been dead for the winter. But I was positive that the Wraith hadn't known that any more than we had, because he wouldn't have used me to send him a letter otherwise.

Frustrated but having plenty to think on and realizing I would have to be patient, I went home to try to connect the dots.

Day 38

THE BATTLE
OF KHUL BASHAB

An early knock on my door proved to be a pair of longshoremen in Rölly's livery waiting to deliver an enormous gift basket of jams, marmalades, and preserves for my morning toast, along with a fresh loaf still hot from the oven from my favorite baker.

The note that came with it was from the pelenaut. He wrote that the reason for the basket would be made clear later in the day, but he wished to thank me on behalf of a grateful nation.

"What? What is this for?" I asked the longshoremen. But they just shrugged and bade me a good morning.

I opened a jar of Kaurian orange marmalade and slathered it on a toasty slice of the fresh bread, and it *was* a good morning.

The refugee kitchen was abuzz with talk of the bard's tale and speculation about the source of the Seventh Kenning and the possibility of destroying it, as well as the happy prospect of sailing to lands across the ocean and meeting people there like Koesha's, who weren't Eculan and intent on destroying us.

And Fintan was all smiles when I met him.

"Slept well?"

"I did. Completely exhausted. And glad to have gotten that story out of me. Plus, I got a tremendous gift basket this morning from the pelenaut."

"Me too."

"On behalf of a grateful nation?"

"Yes."

"Well, I've been informed I'm to broadcast him before the tales today, so that will be instructive, no doubt."

And it was.

When we got to the wall, Rölly was there, beaming at me, and he gave me a hug and said thank you in person.

"Did he talk?" I said in low tones, knowing he would understand the pronoun.

"Yes. A little, anyway. I'll have to fill you in a bit later, but when they heard that Lorson was dead, they suddenly wished to talk to us. This means you don't have to keep the Wraith a secret anymore."

"What about Nara?" I still hadn't heard anything since she'd been sent to Fornyd to fetch Gondel Vedd.

His smile faded somewhat. "That will definitely have to wait, I'm afraid."

"Is she all right?"

"She's alive," he said in a tone that implied we should be grateful.

"Oh, shit."

He patted me on the shoulder. "We'll talk soon. I need to do this and get back."

"Okay."

He shook hands with Fintan and said a few pleasant things while I worried about Nara, then the bard broadcast him to the city.

"This is Pelenaut Röllend. I have good news to share with you all. The traitor, Vjeko, has been caught, along with one other." He had to wait for a roar of approval to die down. "We have had them in custody for some small while, and you heard yesterday that his co-conspirator, Lorson, was destroyed in early winter by Olet Kanek.

"The architects of the Bone Giant invasion have thus been rounded up, for the most part. We still do not know how the letters from Vjeko were getting to Lorson, and we do not know why the Seven-Year Ship never sailed this time, unless it was perhaps to provoke the invasion. We will continue to search for answers, and Vjeko will pay. But we know this much: We were wronged, and targeted, for no legitimate reason but the hatred of these men. And soon we will strike back at Ecula to make sure they cannot target us again!"

He paused there for applause, and when it was finished, he named Gondel Vedd, Fintan, Gerstad Nara du Fesset, and me as instrumental in making the conspiracy plain. The pelenaut assured everyone that we'd all been thanked and given gift baskets and he was also going to ship one to Olet Kanek on the nation's behalf.

I was surprised at the reason for the gift basket; as far as I knew, Nara and I hadn't done much except get used as pawns. Yet I knew people would ask me how I'd helped expose the conspiracy. Was there a heroic way for me to say I deposited a letter underneath a garbage bin?

I noticed that Rölly neglected to mention that the Wraith was an actual wraith possessing the body of an old Brynt soldier, and he hadn't named Ysabel du Köpen at all. I'm sure he had his reasons for that, and I looked forward to learning what they were.

But he left the audience in a fine mood for Fintan to begin the day's tale. He had a gang of musicians join him for some happy dance tunes, and that had everyone feeling even better.

"I have a long tale for you today from the hivemistress. As she expected, the monarchy of Ghurana Nent would not let their rebellion stand. So here is what happened in Khul Bashab not so long ago."

Hanima

I am happy for Jahi, because he figures out pretty soon what black-wings are good for: spotting trouble. We hear about the force coming upriver about a day before they get here, thanks to him, because black-wings tend to follow large sources of food moving on the plains in hopes that some of it will die and become delicious carrion.

Like me, Jahi can see through the eyes of his animals, but he can't hear or smell much of anything, which is probably a blessing, consider-ing how often blackwings hang around dead stuff.

He counts a couple thousand soldiers coming from Batana Mar Din on a large fleet of riverboats. The viceroy's cousin has sent significant reinforcements.

"We don't have a couple thousand fighting dudes, do we?" I ask Tamhan and Khenish Dhawan over a cup of tea. Tamhan's the city minister now, having soundly defeated his opponent in the election, and Khenish is the watch commander. Tamhan called this hasty meet-ing after I informed him of what Jahi saw.

"No," the minister admits. "We have walls and thirty-one beast call-ers, counting you and Adithi. The city watch is effective at keeping the peace in the streets, but they're not what I'd call a loyal fighting force at the moment. Tough to convince them that our rebellion is really a thing to fight for. Especially since they'd be outnumbered ten to one or more."

"They're not going to open the gates for the monarchists, are they?" That is what Tamhan says we should call people loyal to the king now: monarchists. Making it clear that they are loyal to a person instead of a republic.

"No, we'll have people we trust at the gates. I think much of what the city watch will be doing is making sure we don't get defeated from within."

Khenish nods at this but makes no comment. I remind myself that I really should think of him as Commander Dhawan now.

"So, Hivemistress: What can the thirty-one members of your clave do to defend from without?"

"Well, not all of them have affinities that can help us. I mean, that one guy with the moths? Not a devastating military asset. Unless tactical moths are a thing I didn't know about."

"They might have a psychological effect, but otherwise you're right. So what can we use? Let's lay it out so we can come up with a strategy."

The short version of what we come up with is that I need to get the clave together and start calling some beasts from the Hunter Gate, while Tamhan works to get the food supplies in from the Farmer Gate right away so that these military dudes can't snack on our victuals once they find the gates closed.

It's a close thing, getting all the chaktu into the city with a ton of provender before these barges full of bad guys show up. But when they do, it's pretty obvious they were sent upriver with sketchy information. They are super surprised to find all the gates closed and people on the other side refusing to open them. They thought they were going to reinforce the city watch and go home after a few days. Instead, their demands to be admitted are rebuffed with invitations to fondle and/or provide suction to various body parts of our guards. They don't believe us when we say we're independent from Ghurana Nent now.

At least, not at first.

It takes them a while to figure out that, besides closing all the gates, we've brought in the animals from the walled-off farms and tater beds and stripped them down as much as possible. We're really, really not going to let them in, and the viceroy is not in charge. Neither is Captain Khatagar, because he's dead, see?

That's when they ask to speak to whoever is in charge now, and that's what gets Tamhan talking to them through the bars. They don't believe he's in charge, though.

"You're a kid," the captain of the force splutters.

"I'm the elected minister for the city, sir, and I speak with full authority."

"Ministers are appointed by the viceroy or the king."

"Not here. They're elected."

"Look, kid—"

"You may call me Minister Khatri."

"Whatever. You need to let me speak to the viceroy or there's going to be trouble."

"I demand that you return to Batana Mar Din and tell the viceroy there to recognize our independence. You are not welcome in Khul Bashab."

The man blinks a few times. "You're not entirely sane, are you? Look, I know your garrison is depleted and there's no way you're keeping us out. If we have to break in there, you're not going to like what happens next."

"Captain—are you a captain?"

"Tactician Varman."

"Ah. Tactician Varman, this city is protected by the Sixth Kenning. All the animals of the plains are ours to command. You are quite literally surrounded. Should you fire a single arrow or draw a sword in anger, you will find our defense is quite robust. We will respond gently at first, with some insect stings, perhaps, just as a warning. I hope you will take heed of our warning and depart before it's necessary to take a life. But should you press us, you won't like what happens next."

"All right. Have it your way, kid. I tried to warn you."

"Likewise, Tactician. Since you will not leave, please note that the rebuke you are about to receive is not an accident, nor is it the sum of what we can do."

That is my cue. I throw some hornets at the tactician's face. Figuratively, anyway. Tamhan keeps talking while they fly in.

"Please remember that you were rude and dismissive first, and I sincerely hope you won't escalate things from here."

"Shit, kid—"

That's when the hornets hit him. Five stings to the face allow us all to appreciate the tactician's surprising vocal range.

He hollers a lot and then, when he can use his words again, he promises Tamhan that he will personally flay him in the city square.

"Don't escalate, Tactician. Just walk away and let everyone live. Hornets are only the beginning. Think of what else is out there. All the animals of the plains!"

He doesn't think about it very much. He staggers away and starts shouting orders. They're going to tear up the docks and use the lumber to make ladders. Or at least that's the plan at first. Burrow wasps quickly teach them that if they pick up a hammer, they'll be stung. They don't have a lot of cavalry or archers and absolutely nothing in the way of siege equipment, because this is all a surprise to them. So the plan is to bug them with one kind of bug or another and make their lives gross, squirmy, and occasionally painful but mostly nonlethal.

I say *mostly* because there are some things we don't let slide, like scouts and hunters.

The tactician brought some horses with him upriver, and he sends several mounted pairs of scouts around to the other side of the city to see what's happening, but they haven't yet absorbed the idea that they're surrounded. It's just not real to them.

Jahi is watching them from the sky with his blackwings, so we know exactly where they are. When they get near the Hunter Gate, Adithi has their horses dump them in the grass and run for the gate to join our fine stables. And then the sedge pumas and wheat dogs we have hiding in the grasses take care of the scouts. The tactician simply never hears back from anyone he sends to scout the far side of the city.

He sends three pairs spaced out over half-hour intervals before he thinks to try a large group of twenty, which represents all his horses.

"That's nice of him," Adithi says. "Now that I have all his horses, I can go to sleep."

I don't get to join her, dang it. I'm still fulfilling my role as a harrier and making sure they don't get a ladder built out of dock planks.

The tactician sends a hundred men around on foot to check out the Hunter Gate, and we let them go. They freak out just fine all by themselves when they see the remains of the scouts, blackwings feasting on them since the sedge pumas and wheat dogs have had plenty by then. They stick together and return to report, finally, that everyone's dead and the horses are gone.

That's when the tactician realizes he's been losing this whole time and he'd better withdraw and have a good think. We assume that, anyway, since he orders everyone off the docks and upriver into the walled farm paddocks. They have the ability to make camp, since they had to do so to get here, but they don't have a lot of food left, since they assumed they'd be guests of the viceroy. They make fires and the ground's already safe from flesh eels, so they feel relatively safe and we're content to let them stay out there and pillage whatever they like from what we left behind. But hunting parties never come back. They get hunted instead.

Once they've made their fires, I let my hives rest and I leave to get some rest myself. We have other plans for the evening.

About three hours before dawn—when most everyone is asleep—the spider queen goes to work.

She targets one soldier per tent; most of them sleep four. Poisonous sickle spiders sneak in, silent as the grave, and sink their fangs into a bit of exposed leg. The soldiers don't even feel it at first, but the toxins will hurt like nothing else after about twenty minutes and they'll want to cut off their legs to make it stop. They'll be fine if they stick it out. They just won't be walking on those legs for a few days, and a good portion of the remaining force will need to take care of them.

Tactician Varman's swollen face is much more polite the next time I see him. He's at the same gate, and Tamhan makes him wait. During that time, he remembers to call Tamhan by his title.

"Minister Khatri, I have come to ask if you have taken any prisoners."

"I haven't. Anyone you're missing is not coming back."

We've taken their horses, of course, but I think he's letting Varman assume they're dead too.

"What you've done is unforgivable."

Tamhan shrugs. "I haven't asked for your forgiveness. You were warned and you're trespassing. I think you should be thanking me."

"Thanking you?"

"Think of all the many ways you could have died yesterday, Tactician, but didn't. We didn't have to send sickle spiders, you know, or have them bite only a quarter of your men. We could have sent face jumpers. We could have sent one to *your* tent, because, yes, we knew where you were sleeping. We could have wiped out every one of you as soon as you arrived, but instead we have shown you restraint and mercy."

That last phrase is another cue for me. I bring down a small cloud of hornets to buzz over Tamhan's head. The tactician flinches at the sight of them.

"So let me state again, because I am merciful, that you are not welcome here as an agent of the monarchists. You and your men need to leave by noon, without damaging our farms, where we let you sleep free of charge last night. If you do not, then my mercy will be at an end. The animals of the plains will feast, and let me be very clear that they will start with you, not your men. The choice here is yours, and if you make the wrong one, you personally will pay for it."

The tactician seethes, and I can tell he wants to get shouty and call Tamhan a stupid kid and threaten him, but he takes a few breaths, having learned a thing or two, and says instead, "You caught us by surprise. But I'll be back with an army that's prepared to deal with you. I'll be back with Tactician Hennedigha."

"You could live here in peace instead," Tamhan offers. "Join us. Bring your family or start one, and live in harmony with the animals of the plains."

The tactician sneers. "What? And be ruled by—"

"Duly elected representatives of the people? Yes. It's far better than becoming a meal for something hungry. I think the choice before you is pretty clear: You can follow this violence in your heart right now and die outside these walls either today or when you return, or you can put down your sword and live inside these walls in peace and prosperity. I want that for you. I want that for everyone. Please think about it."

The tactician scoffs and walks away, and his men are sailing down the river before noon, many of them wailing at the searing pain in their legs.

They will be back—of that we have no doubt—but it's an important visual for the city. The district council, the ward councils, and the clave council all watch them go from on top of the walls, and they're ebullient afterward. Word spreads: We defeated the monarchists without losing a single man of the watch. Plus we scored about two dozen really nice horses.

The farmers go back to their places, herding out the animals they brought in; Tamhan has a meeting with the farmer clave, where he explains that it's not over and in fact they might lose their farms when the monarchists return.

"But we'll rebuild," he tells them. "And after that I don't expect we'll have trouble again. They need to come after us with everything and be convinced they can't win. Then we'll be safe."

The handsome greensleeve Mak Fin ben Fos bids us farewell and good luck in the Red Pheasant Teahouse. He has to return to Talala Fouz to inform the head Fornish ambassador what we're up to and announce to the king that he's failed spectacularly to "take care of us." He gives me a hug before he goes, during which I realize that I'm a bit taller than he is, because the Fornish are kind of short people, and he smells like silverbark, grass, and wood mushrooms.

"I want one of those handsome menfolk when I grow up," I whisper to Adithi as I watch him depart.

She rolls her eyes at me. "We have plenty of them here. You just never bothered to look around before."

"Well, I'm looking now. How do I get one?"

"I don't know. I mean, usually it's a thing your parents work out with the boy's parents, but that's a skyboned way of doing it, if you ask me."

"It is. And parents aren't an option in my case."

"Sorry."

I shrug. "So what do I do?"

Adithi scrunches up her face, uncertain. "I think you're supposed to flirt. I've heard people use that word but I don't really know what it means. It might involve playing with your hair and giggling."

"What kind of nonsense is that? I'm not doing that."

Adithi throws up her hands, helpless. "People who have food and shelter all the time think up wild stuff to do, you know?"

Either Jahi or Tamhan asks me every day if I've been struck by divine inspiration yet, and I keep telling them no, because it's true. But they're getting nervous; rumors are spreading that Hennedigha is coming with a huge army of ten thousand, and folks are wondering aloud if maybe we've made a fatal mistake by declaring independence. These rumors are being spread, no doubt, by advance members of Hennedigha's forces, slipping into the city on this boat or that. He's clearly much better at his job than Varman is. And those same spies are most likely reporting that Viceroy Senesh is still isolated in his compound and that we are woefully unprepared to stand a siege, because in the conventional sense that's true. We have very little traditional manpower. We have instead a flexible plan that hinges on keeping most of the beast callers in hiding for now. With spies roaming about and some people loyal to monarchists, we don't want to advertise what we can do or who can do it. Let them think we're all about bugs.

But Tamhan gets tired of waiting and does something to make me mad. I wake up one morning and see broadsides of my face everywhere. It's a flattering portrait, so that part is nice. I look unusual and striking because my hair is still short, and I'm not sure if I'll grow it long now or not; I kind of like the reminder that I was once so destitute that I slept in the mud and long hair wasn't an option. But above my head it says COMPASSION IS THE ONLY MORAL USE OF POWER, and then underneath my shoulders it says HANIMA.

I stomp into Minister Khatri's council office, because he has one now in the Embassy District and so do I, though I don't use it. I spend most of my time at the teahouse, because my bees are there. "Tamhan, what are you doing? I told you, I'm not a prophet!"

"You're talking about the posters? It doesn't say you're a prophet on there. I checked."

"But men keep coming up to me to say, 'Actually, it's not the *only* moral use,' and I liked my life before that, when they had nothing to actually say to me."

He smiles at me and chuckles. "I am sorry about that. But not sorry at all at spreading your idea. It fits perfectly with what we are trying to accomplish in our claves and government, and we need the people to buy in. We need to shift away from the mindset that greed doesn't matter and that we have no responsibility for others, nor they for us. Your words move us there. Your deeds move us there. People have noticed what you've done for the poor."

"Because you've been telling them, right?"

"Right. But they've also noticed that you have put people to work—what's this business you're starting up?"

"The Hivemistress Hothouse! Vegetables year-round, thanks to my Fornish partners and my workers, who are the best— Hey, you changed the subject! I'm still mad at you!"

"I liked the new subject better. Why are your workers the best?"

"Well, they're so happy and productive. Because they have jobs and a place to sleep now and they know that they are sharing all profits equally with me."

"You're not taking the double share allowed by the new law for business owners?"

"Nope. Reward beyond need is greed."

Tamhan's face lights up and he claps, followed by a victorious fist pump. "That's it! That's the next broadside."

My head drops and I cover my eyes. "Tamhan, no, please. The men will come up to me and say, 'How do you *actually* know what someone needs?' And then they'll ask what about this, or what about that? Every minute in public will be sparring with someone over where the line is."

"Defining the line can be the next broadside after that. This series is going to do wonders for our new culture. People need to be challenged on this, Hanima, and, yes, they're going to respond. Challenges to the established order are always questioned. We have to question them all the same."

I like arguing with Tamhan, because he's not a condescending dingus but he's often right and I see things differently afterward. But since I don't like losing, I often wind up telling him in a huff that he's never getting any honey from my hive.

Jahi interrupts before I can respond, bursting into the office. "Minister! The king's army is coming. It's big."

"By river?"

"On land, south shore like us. And they're hauling siege towers."

"How far?"

"Two days."

"So if we leave now, we can catch them a day away in the night?"

The herald grins. "Indeed we can."

"Let's go, then. According to plan, Hivemistress?"

"Sure. But I plan on resuming this conversation."

"I would be disappointed if you didn't. But know before you go that I appreciate you."

Tamhan doesn't come with us, because he has other preparations to make. Adithi, Jahi, a few other new beast callers, and I ride out, performing our contracted duty to defend the city. Hennedigha, who I've heard is quite competent, is clearly coming to subdue us. Perhaps even burn us down on the orders of King Kalaad the Unwell. We need to remove his ability to do that before he reaches the city, because then our walls and the ability to snipe at them over time will give us the win.

My ass is sore and it's late when we reach the army camped for the evening, but, unlike them, we have nothing to fear from the night.

We dismount, reach out with our kennings to those creatures with whom we have an affinity, and get to work.

Talikha Ghowal, the bat girl, begins. She brings a cloud of hopper bats to fly over the army and shriek until they're all awake and feel like they have to do something. That something is, inevitably, the use of archery. As soon as the bows and crossbows come out, my burrow wasps, Jahi's blackwings, and Talikha's bats note their positions. The bats and blackwings bank away into the night, and then it's time for Vibodh and Charvi to bring the pain. The archers are clustered near the rear of the army, along with much of the supply train. The part where they thought it would be safest, in other words, against a traditional foe.

The ground underneath the army begins to quake and rumble. They're not sure what's coming—they can't see much beyond the lights of their fires, but they probably assume it's a cavalry charge.

It's just a regular charge, though. A regular, unstoppable charge of ebon-armored rhinos, called by Vibodh. The army doesn't see them in the darkness until they're trampling through their campfires, tossing men up into the air with their horns or just shattering them with brute force. The few who get off shots quickly realize the truth of the saying that the only way to knock down an armored rhino is with a bigger rhino. The archers either get out of the way or get plowed. Those who do get out of the way and mutter a prayer to Kalaad over the close call soon realize that we're not done. Because Charvi brings a herd of stampeding thunder yaks behind the rhinos and everyone gets plowed anyway. And since her affinity includes wart oxen, close relatives to the thunder yaks, all the supply-train oxen go wild and kick the carts over and stomp on the food.

The rhinos and thunder yaks turn west at the riverbank, only a small number of the yaks having fallen to retaliatory strikes. They leave the back quarter of Hennedigha's army in ruins, broken and bloody on the plains. The rest of the army is panicked, putting their backs to the river, paranoid about another stampede.

That's when the last member of our party, Manu Samman, does his thing. Out of the mud and the soft soils full of worms and such come the worst of the creepy crawlies: wheelmouths and carver centipedes. They slither up boots unnoticed, lightly scampering up the backs of pants and tunics, and only when the centipedes bite an exposed neck or the wheelmouths bore into an eyeball with their rotary mouthparts do the soldiers realize that they've been outflanked.

I feel confident in saying that more than one man loses his shit at that point. And even though it's probably only fifty or so men targeted by crawly critters, they make enough noise about it to scare the rest.

We have no idea if we've managed to hurt Hennedigha personally in our attack, since we don't know what he looks like, but we can hope. We do know that they won't sleep well after that, but neither will we. We need to get back to the city.

We switch to a fresh team of horses, and I wince against the damage my backside and legs are taking. I'm going to need a few days of lying on my stomach, I think, after this.

A couple of hours into our return, Jahi notes that the army has apparently decided to march on through the night, having their sleep and supplies ruined. They'll reach the city tomorrow afternoon and probably assault it right away, since they know now what happens if they stop to rest.

"On the one hand, this is probably good," Jahi muses, "because they're going to be exhausted by the time they get to us. But on the other hand, they'll be desperate to get to us, because they know what will happen in the night if they don't. And we did nothing to their siege towers."

That argument—whether or not to go after the siege towers—had raged for some while in our planning session. In the end, we weren't sure that the rhinos could take them down and we were positive the thunder yaks couldn't, and to try would mean greater risk to our animal friends than simply trampling a bunch of scrawny humans.

"But we got their archers, and that's what we needed, right?" Adithi says. "We didn't want them shooting fire arrows into the city."

Vibodh says, "We may have gotten the archers, but we didn't get all their bows and arrows. Someone else can still pick those up and use them."

That's a sobering thought, as is the fact that we don't have much of a plan for the siege towers. The only animals we're sure can take them down would be a boil of kherns, but the only one capable of calling them would be Abhi, and he's who-knows-where now.

Fire arrows would work, except that Commander Dhawan says we don't have any and can't easily make them, which is disappointing but perhaps not all that surprising. It's not like Khul Bashab was expecting to be under siege before we came along.

When we get back to Khul Bashab, I ask if there's a vat of ointment or salve or something I can just swim in.

"My nethers," I whimper at Adithi. "They're tender."

She grins. "Stop whining. You heal fast now, remember?"

"Oh, yeah! I forgot! Thanks, buddy! I feel better already."

I'm thinking I'll check in with Tamhan before wandering off to take a pre-battle nap. And then, abruptly, I'm thinking I won't. Because someone shoots a flaming arrow—the sort we supposedly did not have—out of the Tower of Kalaad right toward the magnificent tree that forms the Red Pheasant Teahouse.

"My bees!" I cry. "My lovelies!"

And then another arrow shoots toward the Tanner District. Another arcs toward the River District.

Bhamet Senesh is setting his former city on fire in advance of the monarchist arrival. He wants us weak and distracted, and I have to admit, fires throughout the city are going to distract us.

Commander Dhawan had wanted to storm the tower before this, and I'd argued against it because someone would wind up dying and we couldn't go on saying we used power morally if we attacked monarchists for being stupid.

But leaving him alone, I now saw, was pretty stupid of me. I thought that he would surrender if we defeated Hennedigha in the field and that would be the end of it; he couldn't hope for someone to come save him after that.

I send a message to my hive that they must evacuate immediately—even the queen. Because the smoke from the fire could put them to sleep and make evacuation impossible later.

"Jahi, can you send a few blackwings into his tower windows to mess with him? Peck his head, scratch him up, but don't kill him?"

My hornets and wasps could get there, but not as quickly, and I was afraid that they'd sense how upset I was and go too far.

"Sure, but why do we care if he lives?"

"Because we are more powerful than he is. So we have to have the morals to match."

"Oh. Right. A higher moral standard than the viceroy is a pretty low bar, but we should exceed it anyway." He closes his eyes for a few seconds, reaching out with his kenning. I see three blackwings flying toward the tower. "Done."

"Thanks. Now let's go get him out of there."

"By ourselves?"

"Yes."

There's no need to bring reinforcements, but they meet us there anyway. By the time we get to the tower's gates, Commander Dhawan is already talking through it to someone inside, with a squad of his men behind him. His demands to be let in, however, are not persuasive. Jahi and I ask to be allowed through, and the city watch parts before us until we're at the gate, standing next to the commander. He's shouting at a snarling man on the other side of the gate. The snarling man takes a breath to shout back and then he sees me and his eyes go wide, his expression turning from anger to surprise.

"Hello," I say. "It looks like you might recognize me. I'm Hanima Bhandury, the hivemistress."

"Yes," the man says. He's stout and shorter than Dhawan, with his hair stuffed underneath a hat, the way many guards do to keep it from being used against them in a fight. "I've seen the broadsides."

If those turn out to help me here, I'll have to give Tamhan some honey after all.

"What's your name?"

"Gunin."

"Nice to meet you, Gunin. So, hey, listen, the viceroy is trying to burn down the city, which is pretty rude when we've been super considerate of you all here. You understand that I could have sent my bees and hornets and wasps to sting him to death at any time, right?"

He nods and gulps, his eyes looking for hornets in the air around me. "Right."

"But I didn't do that, because I don't like to hurt people. I'm not here to hurt him now. I just need him to stop hurting the people he's supposed to be caring for. That's why we had a rebellion in the first place."

"You're disloyal—"

"Yes. You're absolutely right. We can't be loyal to someone without compassion, who would burn down his own city out of spite. But we don't want to hurt him or hurt you or anyone here. We want him to stop, and we'd like to send him down the river to his cousin, alive and well. And I'd like to give you a choice, neither of which involves punishment: You can go with the viceroy if you like, or you can stay here with us and join the city watch."

"No, he can't," Dhawan growls, and I have to round on him.

"Yes, he can. Gunin can change his mind and his heart, Commander Dhawan, and if he does, we should welcome him. Gunin, if you open this gate so we can stop the viceroy, then help the commander and the watch put out the fires he's started, you'll have a job here and all will be forgiven. Same goes for anyone in the compound who wishes to join us instead of fight. It would be such a better day for all of us if you did that. Because we don't want to hurt anyone. But we will if we must to prevent the rest of the city from being hurt, and, unfortunately, we would need to start with you. Please come work for us, okay?"

"Never been asked *please* before," he says. "I got your word and I believe it. But what about him?" He points at Dhawan. I turn my head and stare accusingly at the watch commander. He knows what he did. His jaw clenches, but he doesn't contradict me.

"Let us in, help put out the fires, and you have a job on the watch. Same pay. You have my word."

"Good enough," Gunin says. He reaches to unlock the gate and as he does so, a few other guard folk spill out of the actual tower and shout at him, calling him a traitor. Since he's gone too far to pretend he didn't mean it, Gunin follows through and lets us in. But it's also too late for him to defend himself. Gunin gets run through on the spot by some monarchist, and then there's an awful lot of swordplay between the two sides while Jahi and I dart around the knot of men and head for the tower door.

"He's out of his room," Jahi says. "He escaped to the landing and shut the door behind him, a little bloody but otherwise okay. I have my birds removing the remaining arrows, one at a time. There are quite a lot of them."

"Good," I say, and enter the tower with Jahi behind me. There's a foyer of sorts with plush carpets and tapestries and shiny stuff and things in it, and beyond that an expansive lounge bleeds red like an open wound, with a cherrywood bar and dozens of liquor bottles in front of a mirror and lots of soft cushions for important buttocks to sit on when the viceroy is having a reception. Off to the left there's a staircase that winds up into the ceiling, which means that it spirals around the outside and the rooms of the tower are in the center. We have to go up to find the viceroy, but two burly meatsacks with swords grunt at us and appear unmoved by my words of peace. I'm pretty sure I'm faster than they are, so rather than argue, I just sprint for the stairs, Jahi close behind. As we slip by, the grunting becomes aggrieved protests, then shouted accusations of incompetence as one guard blames the other for not blocking the stairs. They start clomping after us, but they won't catch up as long as we maintain speed.

We have to stop at the landing of the next floor because there's a mildly competent guard standing in our way. He's got a hand out to stop us, so I grab it and whip him behind me. Jahi gives him a helpful push down the stairs, since he's already off-balance, and he tumbles to bowl over the other two fellas, who are trying to catch up. We don't encounter any more resistance for a few more floors, noting in passing that each landing has its own decorating concept and is furnished more expensively than most entire homes.

"I want all the river people—the ones who weren't in crews, like you and me—living in here after he's gone."

"Perfect," Jahi says. "I'll see to it."

Shouting from above alerts us that we're getting close to someone. Another orbit around the tower reveals it to be a pack of royal guards attending to the viceroy on a landing.

I've never actually seen him before this. He's a bit bloodier about the face than normal, I expect, since beaks and talons have had their way with him, but apart from his fancy boots and clothes and the extra weight he's carrying due to a rich diet, he doesn't look like he ought to be in charge of anything. There's not a smidgen of kindness in his features. Deep brows cut in the middle with a frown line, jagged teeth clenched in a snarl, and dead, dark eyes devoid of empathy. Yelling at a guy trying to clean his wounds, instead of being grateful that he has anyone to look after him.

"Pardon me, Viceroy, but you'll need to come with us now," I say.

The tangle of men whirls around to see us standing there, and the guards all look at one another to see if anyone recognizes us or possibly to judge whether they can blame someone else for the fact that we are currently existing in the same space as they are.

"Who are y—oh. Oh!" A tiny hint of a smile curls the edges of the viceroy's mouth. "Are you Hanima? The hivemistress?"

"I am."

"Excellent! Welcome." He turns his attention to the four men clustered around him. "Gentlemen, listen to me very carefully. Are you listening? Good. This is important. Nothing is more important than what I need you to do right now. Forget all about me and instead simply kill her. Kill her immediately!"

They hop to it with gusto and a chorus of manly roars. Swords out, muscles flexing, boots gleaming, they leap to casual murder on the sayso of a formerly rich man whose assets we've seized. I don't have time to explain, however, that they're probably never going to get paid for this, because the viceroy has left us no room for chitchat.

I'm not an expert at combat, but I'm significantly faster than any of these fellows now, and I know that knees are pretty important to keeping people upright and also super vulnerable to pressure. I wait for the first dude to swing and I dodge it, lunge forward to hold on to his arm, and stomp hard on the side of his knee, which he's bent already in his follow-through. Something crunches and he cries out, dropping the sword as he crumples to clutch his joint. Another dude slices at my head and I duck under his swing, crouching onto all fours and spinning around, delivering a heel to the side of his knee. It buckles but he's not disarmed; once he's down at my level he tries to hack at me from the floor, but I roll away and get to my feet.

"Hey, stop that or I'll throw bees at your face."

He quite sensibly stops, and I check on Jahi, who has rendered his first attacker unconscious somehow and is busy tossing the last one down the stairwell, because the stairs have proven to be reliably helpful in making guards disappear.

We turn to confront Bhamet and he's shaking his head, disgusted at his paid muscle moaning on the floor. He's not even paying attention to us. "They're untrained kids who don't even weigh a hundred pounds. You guys are terrible."

He's not sorry for setting the city aflame or for ordering my death. He's not afraid of me either, because he knows I'm not the murdery type. He's simply a villain who's disappointed that he can't win with mercenaries anymore, and I have to quash an upswell of rage at the thought, for fear that my bees will come and end him. This man chose to make so many lives miserable when he could have chosen to make them better. He used his money to secure power and then used his power to secure more money. If he had at any point been open to working with us to help people—to truly leading instead of profiting on misery—he would not have inspired the revolution that unseated him.

I really, really want to punch him, or maybe deliver a swift kick to the groin, but he's beaten and pathetic now, utterly impotent. He's just sitting there and bleeding, and he's not making eye contact.

Commander Dhawan and his crew come up the stairs and take Senesh away to be locked up while we put out the fires he started. I'm very sorry Gunin and some others died or got wounded over this man, and I want to make sure we are cleansed of him.

Much of Tamhan's preparation for the siege involved setting up fire teams, so that helps tremendously. And since the Fornish are culturally conditioned to be paranoid about fire, they've already extinguished the fire from the first arrow by the time we get outside. I let my hive know it's safe to return.

As always, it's the poorest who are hit hardest: The shantytown where Adithi used to live is lost completely, and some people die because the buildings are so close together and built so cheaply.

I'm covered in soot and smell like smoke by the time I stagger into a bathhouse hours later. I have to get freshly scrubbed and convince myself it's a new day before Hennedigha's forces arrive.

I am not an active participant in the defense of the city, except as an observer on the western wall. I've told Commander Dhawan and Tamhan that the local hives have been depleted enough just seizing control of the city and conducting the seeking, and the few stings they can deliver won't be of much use against an army of many thousands. So I watch them come until it's time to do my one assigned task, these men marching to subdue us to the will of another man many leagues away who demands our loyalty and our taxes but gives us nothing in return but a viceroy steeped in cruelty.

It makes me sad. Especially since they are probably under the impression that they are coming to "liberate" us when we are already liberated.

Tamhan stands next to me and sees the tears on my cheeks.

"I'm sorry it's come to this too," he says softly.

"Promise me again, Minister Khatri. We are never, ever going to do what they are doing right now. March on a city and threaten their lives to make them do what we want. So many people are going to die."

"I promise. There should never be a need. I'm confident that we can be self-sufficient."

"Thank you."

There were still many thousands of men and four siege towers in Hennedigha's army, intent on returning Khul Bashab to the rule of King Kalaad the Unwell.

Each one of those men was beloved by someone far away. Someone who would wonder why they had to die at all, whether the cause they fought for was worth it, and who'd find it difficult to weigh those lives against the need of some vague national pride or even one powerful man's wounded personal pride. I could tell them already, before the bloody aftermath: No, their lives and deaths were not meant to be spent like coins to buy power for corrupt men. But neither are our lives to be sacrificed to bad ideas.

Jahi and Commander Dhawan join us. Jahi's blackwings are going to deliver a signal, flying unerringly to the person who needs to receive it.

"We should start before they get too close," Dhawan says, and Tamhan gives him the go-ahead. Jahi sends a bird to Adithi around at the Hunter Gate, where she's amassed all the horses and all of the fire arrows that the viceroy had stashed in his tower. The blackwing just flies low and caws three times at her, which is her cue. Forty horse archers ride with her out to the west side of the walls and form up right beneath them, in clusters of ten, then charge forward to get in range of the siege towers. The king's infantry pulls out pikes, expecting them to try to breach, but Adithi has no intention of that. The archers pull up in bowshot range and just pour fire arrows at the siege towers. It only takes one to catch and weaken the whole thing, if not destroy it, and Hennedigha reacts as soon as he realizes what they're trying to accomplish. He orders his front infantry to charge. And then, from somewhere, arrows start pouring back at the horse archers. Jahi's on it; he has probably fifty blackwings—a not unusual number in any situation—soaring high above the army. The birds dive right at the infantry and go for the eyes, because nothing is so delicious to them as a juicy eyeball. That slows them down.

Three horses, or the people riding them, get hit, but Adithi retreats to the Hunter Gate before any more damage can be done. The infantry doesn't get a chance to engage. Her job is finished.

The rest of the beast callers join us on the wall, ready to help however Dhawan needs.

My task is what Commander Dhawan calls a "special recon op": Find Tactician Diyoghu Hennedigha. No engagement, just observation. We know he's not dressed differently from the others, or we would have spotted him already. But still, orders have to originate from somewhere, and he's probably not at the very back or at the very front. The central authority is most likely somewhere in the actual center.

"Ready?" Dhawan asks me. I nod yes. He's going to have the rest of the beast callers act in sequence, and the theory is that Hennedigha will do something—perhaps many things—in response, and hopefully I'll spot him giving orders.

Some have already been given, because the soldiers near the riverside are mobilizing to try to save at least one siege tower, with an impromptu bucket brigade. I didn't catch where that came from, however.

"Vibodh," Commander Dhawan says. "Send in the rhinos."

As we did the previous night, we charge their rear flank with rhinos to soften them up, then follow with a stampede of Charvi's thunder yaks. These turn left at the river to circle around for another pass if necessary. But we don't stop there this time.

We tear at them with packs of wheat dogs and prides of sedge pumas. We ram them with a herd of gut goats. And then, while they're all turned toward the plains and looking at the ground, Jahi's blight of blackwings descends from the sky on the riverside and goes for their eyes. It's a much bigger flock than the one he brought before.

Between these various charges, we've trampled, chewed up, or disemboweled another quarter of the king's army, which means Hennedigha is at half strength before we even come back for another pass.

It's chaos that demands a response. And my wasps spy one man losing his mind, spittle flying from his mouth as he shouts, and nobody tells him to shut up. He's allowed to behave like that, and they clearly defer to him.

"Hennedigha is behind the first two siege towers on the right, almost directly between them," I announce.

"Are you sure?"

"No. But if he's not the king's tactician, he's somebody else important, because people do whatever he says and repeat his words. Tactician Varman is there, shouting whatever he shouts."

"Very well." Dhawan turns, spots a somewhat nebbish but also kind of cute fellow who's gathered his hair into a bun and looks distinctly uncomfortable in his own skin, and strides over to him. "Consult with the hivemistress, then proceed. Deploy the tactical moths."

I cup a hand to my ear. "Pardon me, Watch Commander, what did you say?"

"Deploy the tactical moths."

"Thank you! I don't think I'm ever going to get tired of that." I scoot down to the man and give him a quick side-hug. "This is going to be great!"

He looks uncertain. "It is?"

"Oh, yeah, it'll be the best. Because they probably won't have much heart to fight if we get rid of their leader. So, hey, I'm going to just have a small cloud of wasps hover directly over his head so you can target him, all right? I'm going to do that now, so you can . . . do your thing. What is your thing again?"

"My thing is deploying the tactical moths?" He says it like a question because he probably can't believe this is his life now.

"Yes! Yes. Do that. Is it okay if I keep my arm around your shoulders while we do this? Because it's a thing we're doing together."

"Killing a man with insects?"

"Yes. It's not something I normally like to do, like eat breakfast, but this is the guy who brought all these other guys here to kill us all. So is it okay?"

"I guess?"

"Awesome! What's your name again?"

"Lavi."

"You smell good, Lavi."

"I do?"

"You do. But I'm not flirting. Unless maybe I am. I'm not clear on what flirting is. I'm just really nervous because, you know—war zone!—so I'm talking a lot but I also want you to relax and I'm probably not doing a very good job of helping you there. I was just commenting on your pleasant smell so that's one less thing you have to worry about, you know. Be confident."

"Thanks?" he tried.

I hum with pleasure and close my eyes, determined not to say anything else. I reach out instead to the wasps in the field and ask them to circle above Hennedigha, seeing him in a collage of swirling compound viewpoints.

"Target locked," Lavi the kinda-cute moth man says. "Here we go."

Moths, he confided to me earlier in a rare series of declarative statements, are the ultimate party animal.

"All they want is a good time, and they will pursue any hint of a party to their deaths," he explained. "Despite being highly flammable, for example, they enjoy flying into fires, because the flames look so festive."

"What if you tell them there's all kinds of fun waiting for them down this one guy's soup hole?"

"They're probably not going to believe you, but they'll go investigate anyway just so they don't miss out. Plus, they like soup. Or they think they do."

And that is why a vast shudder of white moths descends upon the face of the king's tactician, Diyoghu Hennedigha, whispering their ecstasy that he has decided to throw a party in his mouth, just for them.

He puts up a decent fight. There is some spirited flailing. An attempt to cover his mouth and nose with his arms is effective for about three seconds. The thing is, moths *tickle*. And as his arms move to swat at them elsewhere about his face and neck, they land on his lips. Their wings are blocking his nose. He can't breathe that way, and he's running out of air anyway because of all the flailing, so he has to open his mouth. He breathes in a moth or two and they flutter and spread their dust around, and then he's coughing. More moths fly in and he can't get them out unless he keeps his mouth open, but more just keep coming. Hennedigha falls to his knees in a flutter of moth wings, and the men around him, most likely his lieutenants, are losing their nerve as they watch this, because it truly is a horrifying way to go. That gives me an idea.

"Maybe suggest that the guys around Hennedigha have party mouths too," I say, even as Hennedigha crumples fully, choking to death on moths.

The shudder of moths contracts and then fans out, and once the lieutenants realize they're next, they abruptly decide they don't want to be and don't need to be, because Hennedigha is dead. They turn and run, and I do believe that they recommend such action to their fellows. And many of them, having seen their comrades get trampled and bitten and their siege engines destroyed long before they ever reached the walls, heartily agree that going home would be more prudent than dying of moth mouth.

It's a general retreat of thousands. Four or five thousand, at least? I don't know, but it's lots of lives. Lots of guys who get to see their families again, maybe start their own families, and tell everyone not to mess with Khul Bashab. I squeeze the shoulder of the super-cute moth man.

"Yay! We did it! And you still smell good." Lavi freezes in my grip and I let him go. "Ohhhkay. I'm just going to back off now and be embarrassed. Sorry. I am really bad at flirting. But if you want to have tea or something later, the answer's yes."

"You mean if I ask you if you wanna party?"

"Yes."

He flinches, as if this immediate positive feedback is a hammer blow to his emotional equilibrium, but then he smiles shyly.

"Whoaaa. Maybe we could have a tea party later?"

"Yep. Uh-huh. That is a thing I would like."

There is plenty of cheering and hugging going on at the sight of the retreat. I remind everyone to have their critters back off and let them go. But then we see the carnage left behind, the blackwings and all the other scavengers dropping down to feed, and the juicy joy of winning kind of dries up real quick.

The minister orders Commander Dhawan to bring Bhamet Senesh up here. We want him to witness the battlefield from the wall before seeing him off.

"It was a complete rout of your nation's biggest and best army," Tamhan says when he arrives, sullen and caked with dried blood. Tamhan points to the blazing hulks of the siege towers and the field of dead lying behind a haze of smoke. "They never even made it to the walls. You caused more damage to the city than they did. So do us all a favor and admit it to yourself, inform your cousin and the king: We are no longer part of Ghurana Nent's monarchy, and we are going to prosper here with the Sixth Kenning. If anyone wishes to take part in that prosperity, they should send someone to negotiate."

Bhamet Senesh blinks. "You're letting me go?"

"Yes. You're being exiled. My order has the unanimous approval of the district and clave councillors. Never return, Bhamet, or it will be you feeding the blackwings."

He doesn't say anything in response, obviously waiting for us to say we are just joking before we kill him anyway, because that is what he would do. But we have firmly established our power now, so killing him would be both unnecessary and immoral. We send him down the river instead, with some food and the clothes on his back, and make sure to tell him that all the city's homeless will be living in his former home and wearing his clothes and spending his money.

He keeps waiting for the punch line, or the executioner's axe, until we untie his basic raft and push him off from the docks, waving and smiling at him and wishing him a peaceful life.

"Wait, you're really doing this?" he says as a few feet of water separate him from us.

"Bye-bye!" I call.

"But there are scavengers out there! You haven't even given me an oar!"

"You don't need one! You'll be fine! Probably. Except for the cabbage."

He looks down at the basket of food we gave him, wondering if the head of cabbage in there is going to explode. But that's not what I mean. Jahi and I hired a bunch of formerly homeless folks to gather on the riverbank with some cabbages that have gone bad, and the viceroy hasn't seen any of them, since he's been paying attention to us. That was in keeping with his tenure as viceroy: He never paid attention to the homeless, unless it was to torment them. But they take their cue and chuck all their produce at Bhamet Senesh with a combination of righteous fury and glee, and a few of them hit their target. One even thunks him upside the head and he squeals, and it is the sweetest music. There is general celebration at his dismay and humiliation. I do a little dance right there on the dock, and some of the council joins in.

I suppose that wasn't very compassionate of me. But exile and a well-deserved cabbaging are extremely mild punishments for one such as he. I had a difficult time persuading the council that we couldn't claim to be any different from the monarchists if we executed him on the posts outside the walls, and it hurt me to argue for his life when he so clearly valued no one's but his own and never did anything to help anyone unless they helped him first. It hurt most that I was giving Sudhi's murderer a chance to live unbruised. I might have a nightmare or two about that and spend more time than I should worrying about him coming back to finish me off. But I pointed out to the council that we would also be giving him a chance to die. Without the Sixth Kenning, travel in the open in Ghurana Nent is still an extremely chancy business.

But he probably will be fine. Everything for miles around already has a fallen army to eat. He might look good to a cheek raptor, but as long as he stays on the river he should be safe, and once he gets to Batana Mar Din, someone will haul him ashore.

Bhamet Senesh doesn't know that. He spews forth a stream of curses and imprecations and resorts to begging as the river current sweeps him away. We watch and listen until he's gone.

"That was *really* satisfying," Tamhan says. "He's gone in a hail of cabbage and I have no guilt. It's perfect."

"That's right, Minister Khatri. It's the best."

"Cabbage and exile instead of capital punishment. I like it."

I don't know if the rest of Ghurana Nent will follow our lead or if there will be more war, but I do know that I have plenty of work to do now, regardless. A hive to help thrive, a business to grow, a city to develop into its best self. And a date for tea with Lavi the moth man.

"So there you have it, friends," Fintan said, dispelling his seeming. "Khul Bashab is a free city and remains so, as far as I know. I have heard nothing to the contrary since I learned of these events."

Day 39

VOYAGERS

The entire city seemed to be in a fantastic mood in the morning. Or it may have been just me. I had some delicious toast and preserves and headed down to the refugee kitchen and said a bubbly hello to Chef du Rödal, who immediately set me the task of chopping onions to see if that might bring me back down to earth. It didn't, but someone else did.

The chef brought her to me just as I was grabbing onion number three, saying only, "This woman was asking for you."

"Oh, thanks. Hello. I'm Dervan du Alöbar."

The chef disappeared after casting a disapproving glance at the pile of unchopped onions, a nonverbal admonition to hurry up. The woman in question, of middle age and carrying some middle-aged weight like me, had large eyes and a beautiful head of curly hair.

"Master du Alöbar, I'm Dame Nyssa du Valas. I work at the Nentian embassy."

I thought about Rölly's explusion of the ambassador weeks ago. "We still have an embassy?"

She snorted. "We do, but there isn't much for me to do until we get a new ambassador. It's why I was free to seek you out after I heard the pelenaut mention your name yesterday. First of all, whatever you did to help uncover the conspiracy, thank you."

"Very welcome," I said, deciding to keep it at that and hoping she wasn't going to ask me what I did. She didn't.

"Forgive me for asking, but by any chance might you be related to Sarena du Söneld?"

I put down my knife and brushed off my hands on my apron, giving her my full attention. "Yes. She was my wife."

"Oh. I wondered if that might be the case, because I thought I recognized your name. I'm so sorry. It was such a shame how they got to her."

"What do you know about that—and who are *they*?"

"*They* are the Nentians. I was a colleague of Sarena's, you see."

"A spy, you mean?"

"Yes. Counterintelligence against whatever they had running here. A maid who keeps her eyes and ears open. A few weeks ago—and I reported this to the lung—I overheard the former ambassador talking to a guest about how the Red Pheasants in Forn gave them the poison they found so useful here. The guest suggested it must have been extraordinarily fast-acting if the target couldn't be saved by a hygienist. But the ambassador replied that it was a slow-acting poison that affected the liver and was incurable by hygienists. That's when I realized that they had poisoned Sarena."

I swallowed past a lump in my throat. "So the Nentians killed her?"

"Yes."

"Why?"

"She had done something to annoy the king—I don't know what, unfortunately. That wasn't discussed."

"Wait, which king? The one that got burned to cinders by Winthir Kanek? King Kalaad the Unaware?"

"No, the new one. King Kalaad the Unwell. Melishev Lohmet."

"Melishev?" Something like a cold fist clenched in my belly. "He ordered her death while he was still a viceroy?"

"Yes."

I could hear my voice heating, rising in anger while the cold inside spread. "And you told the lung this and they've done nothing?"

"No, they expelled the ambassador."

"That was for something completely unrelated! I was there!"

"That's what they had to do, Master Dervan. They couldn't expel him for murdering a spy or they would know that I was a spy."

"So the pelenaut knows as well."

"Of course."

I shook my head, trying to think of why Rölly and Föstyr would have kept this from me. They'd obviously had plenty of opportunity to tell me the truth. They could have told me while I was in the dungeon, if nothing else. Why keep it a secret? I asked Nyssa another question.

"Why did you come to tell me this?"

"Well, partially it was to introduce myself as a colleague. But also I wondered if you might have heard anything about Melishev. Whether he's still alive or not and whether Sarena has been avenged."

"I haven't." I remembered that Rölly had decided some while ago to send a hygienist to Brynlön, whose first order of business would no doubt be to return Melishev Lohmet to full health. He'd expelled the ambassador before that. Which meant he'd sent help to Melishev after knowing full well that the shitsnake had ordered my wife's death.

My friend the pelenaut had some explaining to do.

"Okay. Thank you, Nyssa. I appreciate you sharing this with me."

She nodded with a tight-lipped smile. "I hope we'll meet again in happier times."

After she had gone, I returned to chopping onions and let the fumes assail my eyes. They needed a good cry at that point, and I could weep openly without anyone asking what troubled me. Part of me wanted to run straight to the palace to confront Rölly about it, but I realized that I needed to off-load some emotion first, so wielding a sharp knife against defenseless vegetables was an ideal outlet.

All this time I had been fighting so hard to keep from swimming with the bladefins without grasping that I had no choice in the matter. Someone—or rather many someones, including Rölly, the Wraith, and even Sarena—had tossed me into the ocean, and now it was either swim or drown. Or, I supposed, it was more like seeking a blessing in Bryn's Lung: The only way out was through. If I stayed where I was, the crabs and eels would feast on my flesh.

Making my way through this world of espionage might ultimately be fatal. But staying where I was—remaining passive, trying to be the good guy—had only brought me pain and the overwhelming sense that I was a fool and a plaything. If someone had condemned me to the abyss, I was going to claw my way out or die trying.

Once I'd resolved to fight, the ice in my guts thawed somewhat but never went away.

The first thing I asked Fintan when I met him for lunch was if he'd heard whether or not Melishev was still alive.

"When Numa was last here a few days ago, she had not heard anything different. So as far as I know, he's still breathing. Why?"

Shaking my head, I replied, "Just morbid curiosity. Did you sleep well?"

"Tolerably." He nodded, then raised a couple of fingers tentatively from the table, eyeing them instead of me. "If you want to talk about anything, Dervan, I'm here for it. Goddess knows you've been here for my troubles."

"Thank you, Fintan."

We got to work after that but spoke no more of other subjects. It was kind of him to be available, but I didn't feel I could verbalize anything yet. I also did not know if I could trust him. Opening myself up would only make it easier for him to shove in a knife if he couldn't be, so it was best to keep my doubts and worries close.

Fintan's music for the day was an old Brynt Drowning Song, and quite a few of us clapped and sang along.

> When the sails are full of the winds all blowing
> And bladefins are following the chum that you're throwing

You need a fine catch to earn the money that you're owing
Or you'll wind up dead in the abyss.

You gotta do the right thing and do a friend a good turn
You gotta work and play, love and hate, make mistakes and learn
You gotta sail close to shore and avoid the kraken's churn
Or you'll wind up dead in the abyss.

My lifebond says I'm living in my prime
My body says it's smelly under all this grime
And I say I gotta make the most of my time
Before I wind up dead in the abyss.

"Today is a day of voyages," Fintan said after the break. "We'll begin with our favorite scholar in Kauria."

For some days, I got so lost in the joy of learning this fabulous new information about the origins of the Rift that I forgot people were being killed over it. But it gradually became clear in our discussions with Saviič that the Eculans harbored a vast sense of grievance against the west and felt that we deserved any atrocities they committed, somehow, because of what happened long ago. We, the various children of Žalost's siblings, had deprived them of the kennings for all these centuries. The Eculans saw themselves as the wronged party; an invasion, therefore, would just be taking back what was stolen from them.

Or, as Elten Maff put it, "They just want our stuff, and this story tells them it's okay to take it."

A summons from the mistral interrupted our work. With apologies to Saviič, we left the dungeon for the rarefied air of the Calm. There I was unexpectedly reunited with Ponder Tann, the tempest who'd traveled with me to Brynlön.

"Ponder! You look well!"

He broke into a grin. "And you look disheveled. Which means, in your case, like a happy and healthy and very distinguished scholar. It is good to see you." He exchanged greetings with Elten Maff once I introduced them, and then the mistral asked Elten to excuse us.

"My summons was only for Scholar Vedd. I have a matter to discuss with him."

"Of course. My apologies. It was a misunderstanding." He bowed and left the room.

The mistral waited until he was gone and then she said, "Not a word of this to him."

"Understood."

"Good. I have two jobs for you, Gondel. First is to find out from Saviič, as best you can, where exactly we can find Ecula and where we can find whoever's in charge once we get there."

"All right."

"Second, I need to you write two letters in the Eculan language. One is a letter of introduction for Ponder here, which will identify him and ask that he be taken to their leader as an ambassador of Kauria. The other is a letter to their leader that Ponder will deliver."

"I see. And the contents of this letter?"

She produced a couple of sheets of paper for me written in a neat hand and said, "It's all here. But basically it informs the Eculans that the Seven-Year Ship they're looking for is in the Mistmaiden Isles."

"Oh. So Ponder . . ."

". . . is to deliver that to the Eculans. Yes."

"And that will . . ."

". . . ensure the Eculans don't attack Kauria."

"That's a relief; a great peace to be sure," I said. "But won't that bring Eculans to the doorstep of Brynlön once more?"

"I wouldn't call the Mistmaiden Isles a doorstep. If you're looking for some sort of ethical conundrum in pointing a hostile nation in the general direction of an ally, let me assure you I've already considered that. I'm informing the pelenaut about this. They will have time to muster a response to any force sent in that direction. In fact, they'll have an opportunity to *ambush* any such force well away from their cities. Regardless, we—or, rather, the other nations—can't hit them back until we know where they live. But Kauria can peacefully open diplomatic channels and then share information with our allies. Do our part for the war effort without actually going to war. Ponder is going to do us—and the world—this service."

The enormity of it hit me. An extended journey in the wind would age Ponder tremendously. He might be incredibly old after this single mission. Or lost forever in the wind, like my brother.

"Hope you can get some good directions out of that guy," he said to me. "Otherwise I'll be losing a lot of time out there."

"I, uh . . . yes. How much time do I have to work on this?"

"We need it done as quickly as possible," the mistral replied. "For Kauria's safety."

"Of course." I blinked, too stunned to remember what propriety dictated I should do next.

"Do you have any other questions?" the mistral asked.

"Well, for Ponder, perhaps. Might we have a drink, Ponder? I feel like one would suit me right about now, or whenever you might be free."

"I'd be delighted," he said. "Meet you at Mugg's Chowder House for a pint at six?"

"That would be perfect."

The mistral nodded once. "Excellent. I'll expect to hear from you soon, Scholar Vedd. All other projects are suspended while you work on this one, and Scholar Maff is not to be included in any of it. If that requires you to send him away while you question Saviič, then do so. He may inquire with me if he wishes."

"And Scholar Maff is being excluded because he might still be in the employ of Zephyr Goss?"

"The zephyr or someone else. He has proven himself susceptible to pressure, so I cannot trust him."

I don't remember leaving the Calm, but I do know that I didn't go back to the dungeon to begin work as quickly as possible. Instead, I went straight to Mugg's Chowder House and ordered their largest beer, getting a good head start on Ponder's eventual arrival. The bartender recognized my traumatized expression and put out a bowl of squid crackers to take the edge off. Or increase my thirst.

"Let me know when you want something to eat, love," she said, because, by long-standing cultural tradition, no one counted squid crackers as food.

I gave her a nod of thanks and took a long pull on the beer. Then I spread out the papers Mistral Kira had given me and read them.

The letter of introduction was formal Kaurian language, and I had little hope of translating it well into Eculan. But beyond that, I doubted anyone would read it before taking a hack at Ponder. He'd need to learn how to shout something soothing and then sail the letter to them from a safe distance. Maybe if they took time to read it, they'd take him to their leader. Maybe. And then he'd hand over the second letter, which I read next:

> *Dear Leader,*
>
> *The armies you sent to the west have all been slain. To avoid further loss of life, do not send any more. We understand that you are looking for the Seven-Year Ship. We have found it and are happy to inform you that it is docked at the largest of the Mistmaiden Isles. Had you asked for our help, we would have given it. You instead sent an invasion.*
>
> *The peoples of our continent stand ready to be your trading*

*partners in the future, if you wish peace. If you wish war, we
stand ready for that too. We hope you will choose peace. Our
messenger can provide charts to the location of the Seven-Year
Ship.*

*Yours in kindness,
Kira*

"They're going to kill him," I said.

"What's that, love? You could kill for some grub?" the bartender called.

I had no appetite at all, but until I ordered food she'd keep asking every time I talked to myself. "A mug of chowder, please."

"Coming right up."

When the steaming mug arrived, I crunched a handful of squid crackers over it in the time-honored ritual and then ignored it.

Could I suggest edits to the letter? Make some edits in translation, perhaps? I wasn't sure the other nations actually desired peace with Ecula. And I also didn't think all the Eculan armies had been wiped out; that hadn't been the case when I left Brynlön, but perhaps it was true now. Regardless, the tone of the letter was martial and threatening. Almost as if it had been written to reignite a war rather than end it. I had little hope that a patient leader would respond well to it, and the Eculans had thus far not proven themselves patient in diplomacy.

And while I had returned home happy in the prospect that the Eculans wouldn't need to come to Kauria to find their precious religious artifact, I hadn't given much thought to how they would be informed of it. If there was a safe way it could be done, I was pretty sure this wasn't it.

Dread congealed in my gut like the chowder in the mug as my mind cycled through ways to avoid what I was sure would be a disaster. I was interrupted by the bartender after an indeterminate time.

"Something wrong with the food, sweetie?"

I blinked. "Hmm? No, it's beautiful." I checked on the mug—it had developed a thin skin of gelatin, and the crumbs of squid crackers lolled in it like jetsam.

She cocked her head at me. "I meant, how does it taste?"

"No idea. But thank you. It's wonderful. I'm a very satisfied customer."

"Are you sure?" Apparently, I was no more trustworthy in her eyes than Elten Maff was in the mistral's.

"Oh, yes, I'm just waiting for a friend—in fact, there he is!"

Ponder waved from near the door, took the seat next to mine, and ordered mugs of beer and chowder.

"Hope you're hungrier than your friend," the bartender said, before pulling his draught. Ponder's eyes slid over to my mug and he winced.

"Ugh. Gondel, why would you waste that?"

"You want it?"

"No, I think you should keep it."

"Okay." I waggled the mistral's letter at him. "Have you read this?"

"I have."

"And you're going to deliver it?"

"I am going to try."

"The Eculans are going to kill you."

"That is a distinct possibility."

"So why would you do this?"

"Because it's a chance for peace. It's not just the mistral that orders me to do this. It's Reinei. Riding the wind on a mission of peace is what being a tempest is all about."

The bartender delivered Ponder's beer and promised that the chowder would be right out. He lifted his full mug, clinked it against my nearly empty one, and we drank. I wiped my lips clean and sighed.

"Okay, okay, let's just, you know, step back a second, all right? A mission of peace sounds fantastic. You speak that phrase into the wind and who can say no, right?"

"I can't."

"Precisely. But there should be a way to seek that peace without a high risk of your death. If the journey of an unknown distance doesn't get you, someone in Ecula will. And if there's little to no chance of you coming home, it's not a peace mission. It's a suicide mission."

"You're going to help me figure out the journeying part."

"I'm not sure I can, though. Saviič is not trustworthy. I know he comes from the east, but that's about all I can reliably say about him, since the Eculan armies also came from that direction. We can't know if a single thing he's said about his native land is true. Are there really five islands, or are there islands at all? Are the other nations he claims are over there fictional? We have no way of knowing."

"We do have a way. I can go out there and look."

"But, Ponder," I protested, "you'll be giving up your life for this."

"I know. Most of it, anyway. I'm not thinking of my life. I'm thinking of all the ones I can save."

"Have you discussed this with your family and friends?"

"I have. They understand and honor my sacrifice."

"What if you don't need to sacrifice, though? Your kenning is powerful, but the price you have to pay isn't worth it. Let's find a way to accomplish this without you having to pay it."

"Okay. I'm listening."

"If I can get Saviič to tell the truth—he does that when it serves his religious interests—and get you a reliable heading, how far can you fly without undue aging?"

"I can cover about fifteen leagues an hour until I fall out of the sky from exhaustion or boredom, whichever comes first."

"So you could conceivably reach three hundred leagues in twenty hours."

"If I just pee into the wind, eat and drink whatever I bring with me on the fly, sure."

"That hardship would be worth it, don't you think, in exchange for decades of life?"

"Sure. I'd pee on myself anytime for that. But how do you know these islands are three hundred leagues away?"

"I don't. I was speaking hypothetically, trying to establish what's in the realm of possibility. I'm going to find out so that you don't have to spend yourself unnecessarily."

"I appreciate it. You are a good friend, Gondel."

Unaccountably, I began to weep. "Stop it, Ponder. You're doing what my brother did. You're saying goodbye. Telling people the things we should say all the time but never do, because this is your last chance to do it."

His face fell and he nodded. "I know. What I'm doing is painfully obvious. But it doesn't remove my need to say it. When you're looking ahead to eternity, you can't let the precious present slip by unremarked."

"I understand. I'm closer to mortality than you are, and it's often on my mind."

We bade each other farewell and I staggered home and hugged Maron, who understood as if by magic that the embrace was all I needed and I would speak of what troubled me when I felt like it. He handed me a message from the mistral that had arrived while I was out. It said to report to her first thing in the morning, and I only nodded in response. We crawled into bed, and my perfect husband just let me hold him all night.

In the morning I departed without breakfast or tea. The mistral was practically bouncing with the news she wished to share.

"We've had some messages from the pelenaut," she said. "A ship came in almost immediately after you left the Calm yesterday. The first bit of news is at least mildly annoying: They've moved the Seven-Year Ship from the Mistmaiden Isles, so now we have to tell them to move it back so that we're not lying to the Eculans and they can find it where we said it would be. The second bit of news is astounding: They found out how the Eculans crossed the ocean—their hulls are treated with a stain made from kraken blood."

"Blood? But their fleet had hundreds of ships," I protested.

"So?"

"So that's a lot of dead krakens, isn't it? How did they manage it?"

"I think they managed it over many, many years. But perhaps you'll discover a better answer before the rest of us. Do you remember that stolen intelligence you translated in Pelemyn, which indicated that there was another invading fleet somewhere to the north?"

"Yes."

"The Brynts have found that fleet and the army it carries."

"They have? Where?"

"Camped on the coast of the Northern Yawn."

"Did they find the Krakens' Nest?"

"No idea. The pelenaut said a company of rangers found the fleet anchored due north of a spot midway between Fornyd and Sturföd. And they retrieved this batch of files from a strangely bearded fellow. The papers you saw before were taken from just such a one in the south." She produced a leather satchel with numerous dark stains on it that might be blood. "They'd like you to translate again, and they further request that you return to Pelemyn in case any more intelligence comes in."

I frowned at the possibly bloody satchel as I took it. "I have to go back to Brynlön?"

"You don't have to. I'm not ordering it. But they've requested it. You may go or not, as your conscience dictates. But I would appreciate it if you'd translate this, at least, as a favor to the pelenaut. It may save lives."

"Of course."

"And if you won't go, I'll send Scholar Maff."

"What? He's not—"

"Very qualified? I know. But I rather like having the most qualified people here, so if you want to stay, I'm not going to fight it. Have you made any progress with Saviič yet on the precise location of Ecula?"

"No, I haven't even begun. I've been thinking of how to broach the subject in such a way as to get the truth from him. He's lied in the past about numerous things. But if we appeal to his fanaticism, then we get the truth. So I was wondering if we could get a drawing of the Seven-Year Ship?"

"Absolutely. The pelenaut sent us one."

"He did?"

Getting what I asked for immediately was terrible news. I'd been asking as a way to stall the entire project.

"Yes. It's a remarkable craft. Kind of a blend of styles." She handed me a fine rendering of a ship that looked, to me, like it would float. That is pretty much all I could tell about it, since whether a ship floats or not is, in the end, the only relevant detail.

"Excellent," I said, though it wasn't excellent at all. "I shall confer with him and see if this is indeed the ship they're looking for, and if it is, then he'll want us to inform his leadership immediately, no doubt."

The mistral frowned. "What if it isn't the right ship, though?"

"Then that would be good to know too, wouldn't it?"

"Yes. Yes, of course. Proceed."

Scholar Maff was not in the dungeon when I arrived. Saviič was asleep and I had to wake him and wait for him to eat and refresh before we spoke of serious things.

"Saviič," I said, and offered him the drawing with my fingertips. "Do you recognize this ship at all?"

He took the drawing, drew it through the bars, and I watched his face as he absorbed it. His eyes blinked rapidly at first, then widened. He looked up at me, incredulous.

"This is the Seven-Year Ship! I remember it from when I was a boy."

"Good! We know where it is."

"You do? Where?"

"Far to the north of here, on the largest of four islands in a cluster."

"Was there anyone on the ship?"

"No. From what I understand, it was sitting at a dock with no one around. No crew, no cargo."

"It was at a city, then?"

"No."

"You said there was a dock."

"Yes, a single dock in a sheltered bay. But no city. We should inform your people back in Ecula."

"Yes! They need to know! But . . . my boat is destroyed."

"We can get someone there without a boat. We are of the Second Kenning. We can send someone through the air, if we knew where to send him. We could send a message from you, in fact. Would you like that?"

"Yes! That would be good! I will need quill and paper."

"Of course. We will need to know where to go to deliver your letter and how to find the person you want."

"Yes."

I handed him several sheets of paper and the inkpot and quill from my table. He thanked me, sat on the floor, and used his bunk as a makeshift desk.

"I will need some time," he said. "There is so much to say."

"I'll be back later, then."

The mistral would never approve delivering what he wrote. Too much risk of there being a code embedded in it. All we needed were the directions, and we'd deliver whatever I wrote instead. And I needed to think of something to say that would keep Kauria safe and wouldn't get Ponder killed.

I returned to Mugg's and ordered oyster shooters: a raw oyster, an ounce of vodka, and two dashes of hot sauce in a shot glass, easily consumed in a single, slimy, spicy gulp. The barkeeper—a different one from the previous day—blinked at me.

"It's ten in the morning, sir."

"I assure you that if you were in my current position you would not care for the time of day either. You would require fortification immediately. So I beg you on humanitarian grounds to bring me four, please."

The barkeeper raised his hands in surrender. "Coming right up."

They took a while to arrive—probably because no one in the kitchen had shucked any oysters yet—but when they did I slammed them down in sequence, gasped and coughed, then set to work with some paper and ink.

I composed a letter that I hoped Mistral Kira would approve:

To the Leader of Ecula:

We have heard you are looking most urgently for the Seven-Year Ship, a vessel of some significance to your people, which is long overdue. We have found it and left it alone, as it is clearly important to you and we have no wish to disturb.

The several search parties that you sent to our lands to look for it, each composed of ten thousand armed men, were unfortunately misinterpreted as invasion forces and had to be destroyed. Please forgive our mistake. Misunderstandings happen when people do not communicate, and we hope to communicate better with you in the future to our mutual benefit.

You may find the Seven-Year Ship docked by itself in a bay of the island marked on the enclosed chart, and you are free to visit it or not, as you wish.

Should you wish to trade with us, please send merchant vessels that cannot possibly be mistaken as armed forces or colony ships and we will all happily profit.

Our messenger does not speak your language but will gladly bear any written message you wish back to us.

Wishing you peace,
The Allied Leaders of the West

There. That would let them know that their invasion had been dealt with but wouldn't level a threat that they would feel bound to answer. It should give Ponder a better-than-even chance of getting out of there with a reply. As long as the mistral didn't slay me for daring to revise her work, this might work out just fine. I paid the barkeeper and returned to Windsong Palace, perhaps taking the steps to the dungeon a bit unsteadily by the time I got there.

"Ready, Saviič?" I asked.

"Yes!" he replied. "I have a letter. And directions."

Ecula's capital was located counterintuitively on the smallest of their five islands, he explained. The *kraljic*—their word for *king*—was always available to receive the words of the faithful such as Saviič. Our courier should land on the northeastern edge of the island near an unmistakable fortress and hail any of the many guards there, shouting, "I bring word from the faithful!" in the Eculan tongue to prevent immediate execution.

"Would you mind writing and signing a short note to the effect that the bearer of our tidings should not be harmed in any way and should be brought to the *kraljic* immediately for news of the Seven-Year Ship?" I asked.

"Of course. That is a good idea," he said, and set about it. When that was done, he brought over a map that was his best attempt to represent Ecula's location in relation to Kauria.

"When he sees land, it is all one long range of islands from north to south," he explained. "They are different countries grouped in clusters. Ecula is five islands. Five! No other country is five islands. And there is much space between clusters, between countries. If your man sees three islands, that is Bačiiš; go north to find Ecula. If he sees four, that is Omesh; go south."

"Okay. I will tell him. But, Saviič, this is crucial for him to know: How many leagues must he fly across the Peles Ocean before he can expect to see these islands?"

Saviič looked pained. "Twelve hundred? Thirteen? I am not sure."

My mouth went dry. "Are you sure?"

"It was many days for me in the ship, and I took readings by the stars every night. Yes, I am sure."

That would take Ponder four twenty-hour days of flight to make the journey, at a minimum. There was no way he'd be able to sustain that. Not without places to rest.

"Are there places for my courier to rest along the way? Small islands or reefs to sleep and recharge?"

Saviič frowned. "I saw none. We know of none. It is all water between here and there. Why would he need to rest? He will fly with the wind."

"But he will age many years."

"Yes. But this is important."

I nodded, not voicing my belief that it wasn't important enough to sacrifice a man's life. I hoped my despair didn't show on my face. Ponder would have to become the wind to travel such a distance without rest. He would be middle-aged when he got there, and perhaps even older than me when he returned home. I thanked Saviič and then changed the subject.

"Saviič, I have the opportunity to travel north toward the Seven-Year Ship. There's a chance that you might be able to go see it. Would you like that, if I can secure permission for you to go?"

"Yes!" he cried, his eyes wide. "Seven thousand times I say yes!"

"Very well. I will inquire. But you understand that you will still be a prisoner during this journey? I trust you, but my government does not, because of the invasion of the north."

"I understand. That is fine. Seeing the Seven-Year Ship is all I desire."

"Good. I can make no promises. But I will request that you accompany me north."

"Thank you!" he cried. "May Žalost bless you!"

I was not sure I wanted Žalost's blessing, but I smiled at him for the kind thought behind it.

The simple solution of what I needed to do had become clear to me at some point during the dizzying euphoria of oyster-shot aftermath. I wanted to be with Maron and still help both Brynlön and Kauria by continuing my work with Saviič and the Eculan language. I must, therefore, take Maron and Saviič with me back to Brynlön.

I hoped I could convince everyone it was the best course to take.

I could not speak for anyone else, but that particular tale filled me with both hope and dread. Hope that Gondel Vedd could still help us, and dread that somehow it had all gone wrong. Because while that sequence of events had clearly set him on a path that would lead him somehow back to Fornyd rather than Pelemyn, Fintan had not had any contact with the scholar since he had left Fornyd to perform in Pelemyn. That was forty days at least. And though we had sent Gerstad Nara du Fesset up to fetch Gondel, something had obviously gone awry with that mission. Something bad was happening in Fornyd, and Rölly had yet to tell me what it was. Which I supposed was in keeping with him having yet to tell me that Melishev Lohmet had ordered Sarena's death.

The bard said, "As Scholar Gondel Vedd was deciding to sail back in hopes of helping somehow, the plaguebringer Abhinava Khose was thinking along similar lines."

He took on the seeming of the young Nentian man.

bhinava

I roared out of sleep and startled my friend awake. He growled at me in irritation, one half-lidded red eye glowing at me in the dying coals of the fire.

"Kalaad, Murr. What if I'm an agent of chaos?"

"Murr," he said, and shut his eye pointedly and turned his head. It was either too early for such considerations or he didn't care. He did shiver, though, and sigh heavily. I got up to put some more logs on the fire. It was still dark outside, and if I was lucky I'd be able to get another couple of hours of sleep.

We'd kindly been given our own dwelling in the city, since surprisingly few people wished to sleep next to a bloodcat and a stalk hawk. In that sense we were living luxuriously compared to many of the other colonists, who were bunked together in tents or the buildings that the Raelech stonecutter was raising out of the ground. But maybe those arrangements, with all that body heat, were advantageous considering that the long-expected snow had arrived and the temperature was well below freezing in the day, let alone the night.

Murr and Eep did not like the cold even a little bit, and I did not blame them. It was bracing in the morning; I went outside and sucked in a sharp lungful of air and said, "Ah, how crisp!" and then I went back inside before my nose started running. There was little for me to do except enchant stakes for the city to trade and wait for Koesha's crew to finish building their strange double-hulled boat, which I would be enchanting. I'd already enchanted the first inner hull and was waiting for them to complete the outer hull. Once that was done and we gave it a test voyage, we'd be setting sail in the dead of winter. Haesha assured me that the rounded outer hull—especially the front—was ideal for breaking through ice. It put all that weight down on the top of the ice and shattered it, instead of expecting a sharp prow or keel to break it from the side. This was something that Joabei had been doing for a long time, Haesha told me, since they had quite a bit of ice near their northern island.

Our little home was cozy enough as long as I kept feeding the fire, but I was beginning to worry about Murr and Eep, who were showing signs of depression. And I had taken to worrying—even in my sleep—that I was going to cause more harm than good with my kenning. There was no way for me to anticipate the long-term effects of enchanting these stakes. Nor did I know how long they would work before they needed to be replaced. What if they only lasted a couple of months, or a couple of seasons? I had been having nightmares in which a family had settled on the plains somewhere with one of my stakes planted in the ground, thinking they were safe, and then one day it stopped working and when they went outside after breakfast they were torn apart by wheat dogs or sedge pumas.

And, of course, if the enchantment on the ship hulls stopped working, the krakens would destroy them.

The most distressing thing about it was that someone would have to die—or a ship would have to be lost—before I knew how long the enchantments lasted.

The only solution to the problem, if we wanted to stay on top of it, was to get a whole lot more people blessed with the Sixth Kenning and to have them systematically renew the enchantments on stakes and hulls and whatever else we did. That meant the beast callers clave would need to register these things—or, rather, people would need to register their enchanted items with the clave and contract with us to keep the enchantments current. It wasn't like a Hathrim firebowl, where if the enchantment failed, you'd just be in the dark. Those enchantments did fail after a long while, so it was reasonable to assume that mine would as well.

When I voiced these concerns to Olet and the city council, they blinked at me, leaned back in their chairs, and cursed.

"Well, shit," Olet said, and the others all echoed that in some fashion or another. But they agreed that the clave would need to actively work on this and that a warning would need to be issued with the stakes we traded. I'd also need to make more-targeted enchantments in the future, because humans would want some animals around but not others; these first ones were so broadly warded that they would repel house pets as well as gravemaws.

A couple of members of the council who were logistics-minded folks volunteered to coach me on developing best practices for the clave, and that was kind of them. I wondered if anyone could coach me on how to make a graceful exit.

Malath Ashmali was going to be a prosperous city, I had no doubt. But the crushing cold meant that it wasn't an ideal place for me or my companions to settle. And . . . Olet was never going to really be at ease around me. I stepped over a line with her, and she can't truly forgive or forget it. I don't imagine anyone would. That she hasn't incinerated me for it is testament to what an extraordinary person she is. But it would be best for us both, I think, if I were elsewhere.

I told Haesha that I'd like to leave with them, if that was okay; the Raelech bard had already indicated that he was going to hop aboard. I could have just headed back down to warmer climes with Murr and Eep, because Curragh had built bunkers along the road south, but I still didn't want to place myself under the influence of a Nentian viceroy until I knew it was safe. Heading east sounded best to me, even though it took me farther away from Tamhan. For one thing, it would ease demands on my time. If I stayed in Malath Ashmali, there would always be more requests for me to do this or that; a journey would allow me to see new animals and continue to fill my journal with little-known facts about the world's creatures. That was truly my passion now. Perhaps I would catch a glimpse of the fabled fir apes or see the pine shrikes that attacked Koesha's crew. I caught myself wondering how Rrurrgh, the nonbinary gravemaw, was doing. I kind of missed them. They were as sweet as a nightmarish man-eating predator could be.

Quietly seeking out Teldwen's creatures to say hello was also probably the best way to avoid becoming a destabilizing influence in the world. I didn't want my actions, however well intentioned, to lead to any more deaths. Best to let my few enchantments work for a while in the world and see what good or ill they produced before making any more.

I would have so much to share if I ever saw Tamhan again. Doubtless he would too. We could probably spend days just catching up, and that would be so fine. Neither of us was the sort of person to respond to *What have you been doing?* with *Oh, nothing.* Might as well do some things worth telling him about later. I wanted to run to him now, but I sensed it wasn't time to circle back yet. But my road will lead me to Khul Bashab again someday.

My heart is there.

A vast collective "Awwwww" rolled out over Survivor Field, and I grinned. Who among us does not enjoy a nice hearty pining once in a while? Though it was doubtful Tamhan had a clue, I hoped that he knew he was loved.

Fintan switched his seeming next to the daughter of Winthir Kanek.

Olet

I am not a hearthfire.

I am the elected steward of Malath Ashmali, administering in conjunction with the council, but it is a tempestuous business at times. Though Halsten Durik and Lanner Burgan are off the council, the two other Thayilists who got elected in their place keep proposing ridiculous things the council must vote upon and reject, which the Thayilists then point to as proof that the other members are anti-Hathrim. They shout a lot and pound the tabletops but get little accomplished. When other council members complain to me about it, I remind them that enduring their shouting is far better than enduring their axe swings. I worry that the Thayilists want to push things that far; their words suggest that violence might be a more efficient way to govern than council meetings, and I will need to be on my guard on several fronts. They would especially like to embarrass me or figure out some way to remove me from office, but the best defense against them is competent government. People tend not to seek a fight when they are safe, warm, and fed.

I must remind people often that the council has much more sway over city matters than I do. People keep coming to me for quick decisions, though, because no one wants to face a council or to wait their turn. Better, they think, to just ask the giant redhead what she wants when you see her around and then do it.

The strange icebreaker craft that most of the city worked on in some capacity survived its test voyage down the river and successfully circled through the ice and back to the dock, much to everyone's relief. No kraken attacks, though Abhi said that there was only one left, the rest of them and their spawn having left for warmer oceans to the east and west. The remaining kraken lurked very deep, and it was very old, if he had any sense for such things.

"No one else would have a sense for such things, so I'll take your word for it," I said. It was supposed to come out as a gentle tease, but it sounded more acerbic, judging by the hurt look on his face.

Abhi illustrated the value of blissful ignorance to me; had I not known he was the killer of Jerin and my father, I'd have liked him without reservation. He's a likable kid. But knowing that he killed two people close to me outweighed the countless times he saved others and made this settlement possible. Emotional scales are unfair.

Koesha carefully inspected the craft when it returned and pronounced it fit. Then they began to load up for their journey east. Abhi and Fintan were going with them, so Curragh and I would be the only blessed remaining.

I was relieved the stonecutter would be staying on. He's made a huge difference for us; between his work and looting Lorson's stores, we'll not only survive our first winter, we'll do so fairly comfortably.

Abhi left behind a bunch of enchanted stakes for us to use and trade, though he took quite a few with him as well. I think he must be aware that he's already a historical figure, but I don't think anyone knows yet how much impact his kenning will have on the world. Will he be a footnote in scholars' works or the sort of person about whom entire books are written? I'd wager a lava dragon hide on the latter.

When the supplies were all aboard and it was finally time for the ship to sail, I held fast to a resolution I made after Koesha revealed one night that at first she and her sailors thought I was a fire demon: I gave every single Joabeian sailor a hug goodbye. I had to do it on my knees and it was as awkward as dancing with a sand badger, hugging tiny women and trying to be gentle and firm at the same time. But when they finally made it home and told their people of the Hathrim, we wouldn't be the fire demons of their cultural nightmares. We'd be very tall, very strong people who liked to cuddle.

When the sailors were all aboard, together with a few Nentian men who had decided to hook up with them, the two blessed passengers paused to say their farewells, shivering a little bit in the frigid air. Abhi, I noted with a wry smile, carefully stood back out of hugging range. I wouldn't have tried it with that stalk hawk on his shoulder anyway. And I didn't know that I had a hug for him either. Despite our smoke on the beach, those coals of resentment still smoldered in my breast.

Abhi held a hand over his heart and bowed his head before meeting my eyes. "Thank you, Olet," he said, "for letting me come along. It quite probably saved my life—or saved years of it, anyway, since I didn't have to spend them fighting off the government. I have learned so much. I'm glad I could be helpful here, and I hope Malath Ashmali will continue to be the peaceful city you and Jerin dreamt of building."

"You are welcome. Thank you for saving our lives many times over; I'm sure we would have suffered many casualties without your protection. I hope you'll come back to visit when it's warm again. There's a firebowl waiting for you and your friends in the cabin in the meantime."

He nodded, thanked me again, and boarded with his bloodcat and bird. I meant every word; he is always welcome. But if I never see him again, that will be fine too. He simply reminds me of what I lost.

The Raelech bard threw his arms wide and smiled at me. "Do I get a hug too?"

"Only if you promise not to tell anyone."

"I cannot make such a promise. The world must know of the huggable firelord of the north."

It was then that I realized what a dangerous precedent I had set. The bard would make sure that everyone who came to settle or visit here would half-expect me to hug them. I'd have to weld some spikes onto my armor to discourage it.

As I stood with the council and waved farewell to Koesha and her crew crunching through the river ice, I realized that they might be the last people to bear report of me to the outside world. I had discovered the undiscovered country, and any number of disasters could happen now that the plaguebringer was leaving. I might never be seen or heard from again.

But I think I'd be okay with that. Even if this settlement doesn't survive, or if it's only me that doesn't see the spring, at least I survived long enough for this to come to fruition: a city free of hearthfires and kings.

Jerin would have loved this place. And I know La Mastik did. Because it's home now. For me and anyone else who wishes to live outside the sphere of violent men.

There was an audible sigh from Survivor Field as Fintan returned to himself, and the bard nodded.

"Sounds great, doesn't it? I mean, apart from the cold. That is no joke. But thanks to Abhi, it should be possible for people to move up there. To the best of my knowledge, Malath Ashmali is doing well and has no doubt begun to trade with Ghuli Rakhan. I was on that ship with Abhi heading east across the Northern Yawn, thinking it would be a noisy but otherwise uneventful journey. We had no idea, of course, that a Bone Giant army had camped for the winter to the east of us and that we were heading directly for it. What happened there will unfold in the coming days, but I will leave you today with the thoughts of Koesha, who was, like Olet, enjoying a rare moment of peace now that she had set sail again."

Koesha

It's snowing on top of the ice pack and we are crunching through it, the rounded bow and hull of the newly named *Nentian Herald* cracking and crumping through the sheets in an entirely satisfactory cacophony.

We are headed east through the Northern Yawn until we can turn south and visit the Brynt city of Pelemyn. From there we will sail to the harbor of Joabei, completing our circuit of the globe, and we're confident that we can make it. Because krakens, whether here or in what these continentals call the Peles Ocean, will not destroy this ship. The smile on my face is answered by the rest of the crew and most of our guests. We have such hope of fair winds and fortunes now.

The exception to the general happiness is Abhi, unfortunately. He and his animals are rather miserable aboard a ship. The fact that they have a cabin to themselves with a firebowl in it and plenty of blankets is the only thing making the journey bearable for them. We cannot sail south to warmer seas and lands quickly enough for their taste. Unfortunately, they will have to endure the cold for a good while longer. The *Nentian Herald* is breaking through the ice very well, but it's not speedy.

But Baejan is radiant. She's pregnant and bringing her Nentian man home with her. Several other members of the crew are in the same situation. The men are going to be surprised when they reach Joabei, but I doubt it will be unpleasant for them. Just . . . surprising. I'm proud of the fact that we managed to leave Malath Ashmali without revealing why our crew is entirely composed of women. That was, and remains, excellent discipline—especially since we were asked repeatedly and more often near the end there. We still don't have the language to explain well; perhaps we will by the time we get to Joabei. And once we are there, they will understand why we made such choices.

Since we never got any clay before we left, the Raelech stonecutter was kind enough to create a stone monument for us on the beach, even crafting a mourning tube to our specifications. It's a fitting memorial, and the mourning tube howls very well with the wind blowing through it, but the location is far enough away from the village that it disturbs no one.

I still feel the loss of my crew keenly. I still miss Maesi and always will. But I am proud of what we survivors are about to accomplish, thanks in part to Abhi but thanks also to our own perseverance. And I am grateful to the goddess Shoawei for encouraging us to see the world. She pushed us, eventually, into the path of the Sixth Kenning, which will allow us to end our relative isolation as a nation. This northern passage will finally be made and Joabei will enter a new era. It may be an era of prosperity or one of war. It may turn out to be both. We are all leaves in the wind of Shoawei; may the swirls and eddies of her goodwill bring us to many new shores.

END OF VOLUME TWO

To be concluded in *A Curse of Krakens*

DUNGEON NOTES

Scholars Gondel Vedd & Elten Maff, interviewing Saviič.

We have learned that Eculan deities match continental ones! Behold:

KENNING	CONTINENTAL	ECULAN
First/Fire	Thurik	Jarost
Second/Wind	Reinei	Mir
Third/Earth	Dinae	Kamen
Fourth/Water	Bryn	Talas
Fifth/Plants	Perhaps Kaelin?	Razvoj
Sixth/Animals	Perhaps Raena?	Meso
Seventh/unknown	Unknown	Žalost

Kamen (or Dinae) raised the Poet's and Huntress Ranges to protect against Žalost!

How does the First Tree figure in this?

Meso created the krakens!

THIS SHIT IS <u>WILD</u>!

KAURIAN CALENDAR

Though Ghurana Nent insists on a different timekeeping system for their internal use, the Six Nations otherwise use the Kaurian Calendar. It begins on the day of the Spring Equinox and ends on the last day of winter. It uses eight-day weeks: ten months have four weeks, but months six and twelve have three, for a total of 368 days. A few days are usually subtracted from the last week of the year to ensure that the Spring Equinox falls on Bloom 1, which means in practical terms that Thaw is often only twenty-one to twenty-two days long. Bloodmoon 1 is usually the day after Autumn Equinox.

The Giant Wars began in the winter of 3041 with the eruption of Mount Thayil and the destruction of Harthrad, followed closely by the du Paskre Encounter and the capture of Saviič in the east.

SPRING SEASON

Bloom (32)   Rainfall (32)   Foaling (32)   (96 days)

SUMMER SEASON

Sunlight (32)   Bounty   (32)   Harvest (24)   (88 days)

AUTUMN SEASON

Bloodmoon (32)   Amber   (32)   Barebranch (32)   (96 days)

WINTER SEASON

Frost (32)   Snowfall (32)   Thaw (21)   (85 days)

DAYS OF THE WEEK

Kaurian Language

Deller, Soller, Tamiller, Keiller, Shaller, Feiller, Beiller, Reiller

Raelech Language

Delech, Solech, Tamech, Kelech, Shalech, Felech, Belech, Ranech

ACKNOWLEDGMENTS

Thanks first to everyone who read *A Plague of Giants*, reached out to me, and said they loved it. That meant so much to my super-delicate, turbo-tender writer feelings, and I appreciate you more than I can say. Thanks also to anyone who reviewed it or spoke about it with your friends and spread the word; that's all tremendously helpful, and while I probably didn't see what you did there, I am grateful nonetheless. Thank you for sharing.

I have a wonderful bunch of folks who keep me happy and sane and write with me from time to time, or else give me a break from writing. Thanks to Amal El-Mohtar and Stu West and the Ministry of Coffee; Alexandra Renwick and all the fine folk at Timber House; Brandon Crilly and Marie Bilodeau for tea, pastries, and words on Sunday mornings; and Kelly and Derek Avery for gin, nachos, and a shared loathing of mosquitoes.

For a long time I've appreciated the support of K. C. Alexander and Jason Hough; they are wonderfully encouraging friends who holler at me from the West Coast to get on my word horse and ride, and I tend to text them way too early from the east.

Thanks and many delicious tacos to Delilah S. Dawson and Chuck Wendig, who write brilliant stories and are also brilliant friends.

The Metal Editor, Tricia Narwani, was a mega-genius once again, helping me improve the story in myriad ways, and I am so lucky to work with her and all the spiffy peeps at Del Rey: David Moench, Melissa Sanford, Julie Leung, Alex Larned, Keith Clayton, and Scott Shannon. I am grateful also to Kathy Lord for the copyedits and Gene Mollica and David Stevenson for the cover.

My family remains the reason for everything, and I am blessed to have them in my life.

ABOUT THE AUTHOR

KEVIN HEARNE hugs trees, pets doggies, and rocks out to heavy metal. He also thinks tacos are a pretty nifty idea. He is the author of *A Plague of Giants*, co-author of the Tales of Pell with Delilah S. Dawson, and the *New York Times* bestselling series The Iron Druid Chronicles.

kevinhearne.com
Twitter: @KevinHearne
Instagram: @kevinhearne

ABOUT THE TYPE

This book was set in Dante, a typeface designed by Giovanni Mardersteig (1892–1977). Conceived as a private type for the Officina Bodoni in Verona, Italy, Dante was originally cut only for hand composition by Charles Malin, the famous Parisian punch cutter, between 1946 and 1952. Its first use was in an edition of Boccaccio's *Trattatello in laude di Dante* that appeared in 1954. The Monotype Corporation's version of Dante followed in 1957. Though modeled on the Aldine type used for Pietro Cardinal Bembo's treatise *De Aetna* in 1495, Dante is a thoroughly modern interpretation of that venerable face.